Ruth Rendell

Classic British crime fiction is the best in the world –
and Ruth Rendell is crime fiction at its very best.
Ingenious and meticulous plots, subtle and penetrating
characterizations, beguiling storylines and wry
observations have all combined to put her at the very
top of her craft.

Her first novel, *From Doon with Death*, appeared in
1964, and since then her readership has grown
steadily with each new book. She has now received
seven major awards for her work: three Edgars from
the Mystery Writers of America; the Crime Writers'
Gold Dagger Award for 1976's best crime novel for
A Demon in My View; the Arts Council National
Book Award for Genre Fiction in 1981 for *Lake of
Darkness*; the crime Writers' Silver Dagger Award for
1985's best crime novel for *The Tree of Hands*; and
in 1986 the Crime Writers' Gold Dagger for *Live
Flesh*.

The
RUTH
RENDELL
Mysteries

An Inspector Wexford Omnibus
featuring

THE BEST MAN TO DIE
AN UNKINDNESS OF RAVENS
THE VEILED ONE

CRESSET EDITIONS

This edition published in 1992 by Cresset Editions,
an imprint of Random House UK Ltd,
20 Vauxhall Bridge Road, London SW1V 2SA

First published in Great Britain by Arrow Books Ltd in
1990

0 7529 0452 3

Printed and bound in Great Britain by
Mackays of Chatham

THE BEST MAN TO DIE

*For George and Dora Herbert,
in gratitude for their
helpful advice*

1

Jack Pertwee was getting married in the morning and the Kingsmarkham and District Darts Club were in the Dragon to give him what George Carter called a send-off.

'I don't like the sound of that, George,' said Jack. 'I'm getting married, not buried.'

'It comes to the same thing.'

'Thanks very much. I'll buy you another drink for that.' He moved up to the bar but the darts club chairman intercepted him.

'My round, Jack. Don't you take any notice of George. Marilyn's a lovely girl and you're a lucky man. I know I speak for us all when I say there's no one here who wouldn't like to be in your shoes tomorrow.'

'His pyjamas more like,' said George. 'You ought to see them. Black nylon they are with a karate top. Cor!'

'Keep the party clean, George.'

'What's it to be then, gentlemen?' said the barman patiently. 'Same again?'

'Same again, Bill, and have one yourself. No, Jack, man is a monogamous animal and there's no partnership on earth to touch a happy marriage. Especially when you're starting off on the right foot like you and Marilyn. Bit of money in the Post Office, nice little flat and nothing to reproach yourselves with.'

'You reckon?' Jack was in a hurry to gloss over that right foot and reproaching stuff. The chairman's homily called to mind the short − but too long − talk he and Marilyn had suffered two days before in the vicar's study. He downed his beer, looking around him uncomfortably.

'The first ten years are the worst,' he heard someone say, and he turned, suddenly nettled. 'Well, damn it,' he said, 'you are a bloody cheerful mob. I notice it's the bachelors who don't have a good word to say for marriage.'

'That's right,' the chairman concurred. 'Pity there aren't a few more husbands to back me up, eh, Jack? Charlie Hatton now. There's an ux-ux-what's the word I want?'

'Don't ask me. What the hell does it matter, anyway? You and your words. This is supposed to be a stag party, not an annual general meeting. What we need is someone to liven things up.'

'Like Charlie. Where d'you reckon he's got to?'

'He said he'd be late. He's bringing the lorry down from Leeds.'

'Maybe he's gone home first.'

'He wouldn't do that. The last thing he said to me on Wednesday, "Jack", he said, "I'll get along to your rave-up on Friday even if I have to knock the guts out of her. I've told Lilian to expect me when she sees me". No, he'll come here first all right.'

'I hope nothing's happened to him, that's all.'

'Like what?'

'Well, he's had that lorry hi-jacked twice, hasn't he?'

'Bloody old woman you are, George,' said Jack, but he too had begun to feel uneasy. It was nine-thirty, only an hour to go before the Dragon closed. Charlie was going to be his best man. Marvellous wedding he'd have if they found his best man at midnight somewhere in the Midlands with his head bashed in.

'Drink up,' said the darts club wit, 'and I'll tell you the one about the girl who married the sailor.'

'I've heard it,' Jack said dolefully.

'Not this one you haven't. Same again, please, Bill. There was this girl, you see, and the night before she got married her mother said, "Now whatever you do, don't let him . . ."'

'Hold your horses, mate. Here's Charlie now.'

They were all big men, topping six feet, but Charlie Hatton was a little fellow with a brown face and very brilliant sharp eyes. They flashed quickly and calculatingly over the

8

assembled company before Charlie smiled. He showed a set of perfect white teeth which no one there but Jack knew were false. Charlie was sensitive about having false teeth at thirty – why hadn't all that wartime milk and orange juice set him up for life as it had his contemporaries? – but he didn't mind Jack knowing. He didn't mind what Jack knew about him, within reason, that is, although he had ceased to confide in him as absolutely as he had in the days when they had passed through Kingsmarkham Primary School together. They were friends. In another age and another society it might have been said that they loved each other. They were as David and Jonathan, but if anyone had hinted such Jack would have poked him on the nose, and as for Charlie ... The drinkers in the Dragon all privately and rather proudly believed that Charlie was capable of anything.

Marilyn Thompson was Charlie's wife's best friend; Charlie was going to be Jack's best man and one day he thought he would be godfather to Jack's first child. Many a time they had drunk thus together, as boys, as youths, as men, and come out under the same starlit sky to walk beside each other up the familiar High Street where every house was a landmark and every face part of a shared history. There might have been no one else in the pub tonight but the two of them. The others were but background and audience. Jack was passing through a door tonight, dying a little, and as always Charlie would die with him too.

If these emotions stirred under the stubbly balding crown, Charlie showed none of them. His grin wide, he slapped Jack on the back and peered six inches up into the bridegroom's handsome red face.

'I made it then, me old mate. My brother Jonathan, very pleasant hast thou been unto me; thy love to me was wonderful, passing the love of women ...'

'I reckoned you would,' said Jack and his heart was filled with joy. 'I'd have had it in properly for you if you hadn't. What're you going to have?'

'Not that gnat's piss, for a start. Eleven bloody hours I've driven today. You're a mean devil if you can't run to scotch, Jack.'

'Give me a chance, I . . .'

'Put it away. It's only my fun, you know me. Seven doubles, Bill, and you needn't look like that. No wonder they reckon the beer's on the turn in here. I've taken the lorry back to the depot and I'm walking home if that's what's worrying you. Happy days, Jack, and may all your troubles be little ones!'

Charlie had opened his wallet with a flourish, taking care that its contents were visible to all the patrons of the bar. His pay packet was there unopened and he didn't open it now but paid for his round from a wad of notes held together with an elastic band. It was a thick wad and although most of the notes were green, some were blue.

'How the rich live,' said George Carter.

'You want to make something of it, do you?'

'No need to get touchy with me, mate. I must want my head tested sorting mail all day when I could be picking up wads of it on the lorries.'

'You ought to know. It's your bloody head. Take it along to a trick cyclist if it bothers you.'

'Break it up,' said the club wit. 'I was just telling you about this girl and what her mother said on the night before she got married to the sailor.'

'Who got married?' said Charlie. 'Her mother? Bit late in the day for that, wasn't it? O.K., mate, it's only my fun, but Jack and me heard that one our last term at school. And the sailor said, "Have it your own way but if we don't we'll never have kids". Right? That the pay-off?'

'Thank you and good night.'

'Don't be like that,' said Jack. Charlie had a knack for rubbing people up the wrong way. Funny *he* never fell foul of him. 'My round, I think.'

'Can't have that, Jack. Seven more doubles, Bill. Jack, I said *put it away*. I can afford it. There's plenty more where that came from. I come in late, didn't I, so I've got lee-way to make up?'

'No more for me,' said the man whose joke Charlie had spoiled. He patted Jack's shoulder and said good night while the others drank their whisky in an awkward silence.

'Last orders, gentlemen, please,' said the barman.

George Carter dipped his hand into his pocket and brought out some small silver. 'One for the road then, Jack?'

Charlie looked at the little coins. 'What's that? Your missus's housekeeping?'

George flushed. He wasn't married; Charlie knew he wasn't married; knew moreover that his steady had chucked him two weeks before. George had got the deposit ready for a house and made the first down payment on a dining suite. 'You bastard,' he said.

Charlie bristled at him, a smart little fighting cock.

'Nobody calls me a bastard.'

'Gentlemen, gentlemen,' said the barman.

'Yes,' said the chairman, 'pack it in. Talk about folks being touchy, Charlie. No wonder they're touchy when you pick on them the way you do.' He smiled breezily, struck an orator's attitude. 'Now the evening's drawing to a close, and I reckon we ought to take the opportunity of conveying to Jack here the heartiest good wishes of the Kingsmarkham and District Darts Club. I for one . . .'

'We'll take it as said then, shall we?' said Charlie. 'A hearty vote of thanks for the chairman.' He put another fiver on the counter. As red as George had been, the chairman shrugged and gave Jack a nod which was meaningful and sympathetic but which Jack ignored. Then he went, taking another man with him.

The barman wiped the counter in silence. Charlie Hatton had always been cocky but in the past weeks he'd become insufferable and most of the meetings had broken up like this.

Of the stag party now only Jack, Charlie, George and one other remained. He was a lorry driver like Charlie, his name was Maurice Cullam and until now he had scarcely opened his mouth except to pour alcohol down it. Now, having witnessed the rout and ignominy of his friends, he took his last drink and said:

'Been seeing much of McCloy lately, Charlie?'

Charlie made no reply and it was Jack who said, 'Why, have you?'

'Not me, Jack. I keep my hands clean. Money's not everything. I like to sleep quiet in my bed.'

11

Instead of the expected explosion, Charlie said softly and mildly, 'Time you did. Time you slept for a change.'

Maurice had five children born in six years. Charlie's crack could be taken as a compliment and as such, to the relief of George and Jack, Maurice took it. He smiled sheepishly at this tribute to his virility. Considering Maurice's wife was an exceptionally plain woman, there were a good many ripostes Charlie could have made, ripostes which might have been transparently insulting. Instead he had chosen to flatter.

'Time, gentlemen,' said the barman. 'Here's wishing you all you wish yourself, Mr Pertwee.' The barman usually called Jack by his Christian name and Jack knew "Mr Pertwee" was a mark never to be repeated, of the respect due to a bridegroom.

'Thanks a lot,' he said, 'and for a grand evening. I'll be seeing you.'

'Let's be toddling, Jack,' said Charlie, and he tucked his fat wallet away.

The air was soft and mild and the sky scattered with many stars. Orion rode above them, his belt crossed by a wrack of midsummer cloud.

'Lovely night,' said Charlie. 'Going to be a fine day tomorrow, Jack.'

'You think?'

'Happy is the bride that the sun shines on.' Drink had made George sentimental and he turned his mouth down lugubriously as he remembered his steady and the down payment on the furniture.

'You have a good cry, mate,' said Charlie. 'Nothing like a bit of a weep to make a girl feel better.'

George led the Kingsmarkham group of Morris dancers and in the past Charlie had fripped him when he appeared in his motley suit, his cap and bells. He bit his lip, clenching his fists. Then he shrugged and turned away. 'Get stuffed,' he muttered. The others watched him cross the road and make his unsteady way down York Street. Jack raised one hand in a feeble salute.

'You shouldn't have said that, Charlie.'

'Ah, he makes me sick. Let's have a bit of a sing-song then, shall we?' He put one arm around Jack's waist and the other, after a barely discernible pause, around Maurice's.

12

'One of them old music-hall ballads of yours, Charlie.'

They meandered along under the old overhanging house fronts and Jack had to duck his head to avoid cracking it on a lamp in an iron cage. Charlie cleared his throat and sang:

'Mabel dear, listen here!
There's robbery in the park.
I sat alone in the Y.M.C.A.,
Singing just like a lark –
There's no place like ho-ome,
But I couldn't go home in the dark!'

'Yoo-hoo!' yelled Jack in Wild Western imitation, but his voice tailed away as Inspector Burden of Kingsmarkham C.I.D. emerged from Queen Street and approached them across the forecourt of the Olive and Dove. ' 'Evening, Mr Burden.'

' 'Evening.' The inspector viewed them with cool distaste. 'We wouldn't want you to do anything likely to lead to a breach of the peace, would we?' He passed on and Charlie Hatton sniggered.

'Copper,' he said. 'I reckon I've got more in this pocket than he gets in a month.'

Maurice said stiffly, 'I'll say good night then, Jack.' They had come to the Kingsbrook bridge and the beginning of the footpath to Sewingbury that followed the waters of the river. Maurice lived in Sewingbury, Charlie in one of the new council flats on the far side of the Kingsbrook Road. The footpath was a short cut home for both of them.

'Wait for Charlie. He's going your way.'

'I won't, thanks. I promised the missus I'd be home by eleven.' Charlie had turned his back, making it plain he didn't want Maurice's company. 'Powerful stuff, that,' Maurice said, his face pale in the lamplight. 'I don't reckon I should have mixed it.' He belched and Charlie sniggered. 'Cheers, Jack, see you in church.'

'Cheers, mate.'

Maurice vaulted the stile and, by a miracle, landed steadily on his feet. He passed the wooden seats, ducked under the willows, and the last they saw of him was his undulating shadow. Jack and Charlie were alone.

They had drunk a great deal and the night was warm, but

on a sudden they were both stone-cold sober. Both of them loved women and in that love as in every emotion they were inarticulate, yet in no impulse of the heart were they so tongue-tied as in this great and pure friendship of theirs.

As with the Greeks, they had found in each other an all-embracing spiritual compatibility. Their women were their pride and treasure, for bed, for hearth and home, for showing off, for their manhood. But without each other their lives would be incomplete, lacking, as it were, the essence and the fuse. They had never heard of the Greeks, unless you counted the man who kept the Acropolis restaurant in Stowerton, and neither could now understand the emotion which held each of them, preserving him in silence and a kind of despair.

If Charlie had been a different man, a cultivated man or effeminate or living in a bygone age when tongues were more freely unloosed, he might now have embraced Jack and told him from a full heart how he entered wholly into his joy and would die for his happiness. And if Jack had been such another he would have thanked Charlie for his unstinted friendship, his generous loans, his hospitality and for bringing him Marilyn Thompson. But Charlie was a sharp little lorry driver and Jack was an electrician. Love was between a man and a woman, love was for marriage, and each would have died before admitting to anything more than that they 'got on well' together. They hung over the bridge, dropping stone chippings into the water, and then Charlie said:

'I reckon you need your beauty sleep, so I'll be on my way.'

'We got your present, Charlie. I wasn't going to say nothing till the others had gone, but it's a real grand job that record-player. It quite knocked me back when I saw it. Must have set you back a bit.'

'I got it cost, mate.' Another stone dropped and splashed in the darkness beneath.

'Marilyn said she'd be writing to Lilian.'

'She has, too. A lovely letter come from her before I went up north. A real educated girl you got there, Jack. She knows how to put a letter together all right. You don't grudge the outlay when you get a letter like that. I brought you two together and don't you ever forget it.'

'Ah, you know how to pick them, Charlie. Look at Lilian.'

14

'Well, I'd better get looking at her, hadn't I?' Charlie turned to face his friend and his shadow was short and black against Jack's long one. He raised his hard little hand and brought it down on Jack's resoundingly. 'I'll be off, then.'

'I reckon you'd better, Charlie.'

'And if I don't get the chance tomorrow – well, I'm no speechmaker like Brian, but all the very best, Jack.'

'You'll get the chance all right. You'll have to make a speech.'

'Save it up till then, eh?' Charlie wrinkled his nose and winked quickly. The shadows parted, he negotiated the stile. 'Good night, me old love.'

' 'Night, Charlie.'

The willows enclosed him. His shadow appeared again as the path rose and dipped. Jack heard him whistling, 'Mabel, dear, listen here' under the stars and then as the shadow was absorbed and lost in the many tree shadows, the whistle too faded and there was no sound but the gentle chatter of the stream, the Kingsbrook that flowed everlastingly over its bed of thin round stones.

Many waters cannot quench love, nor the floods drown it.

2

Detective Chief Inspector Wexford didn't care for dogs. He had never had a dog and now that one of his daughters was married and the other a student at drama school, he saw no reason why he should ever give one house-room. Many an anti-dog man joins the ranks of dog lovers because he is too weak to resist the demands of beloved children, but in Wexford's household the demands had never been more than half-hearted, so he had passed through this snare and come out unscathed.

When therefore he arrived home late on Friday night to find the grey thing with ears like knitted dishcloths in his favourite chair he was displeased.

'Isn't she a darling?' said the drama student. 'Her name's Clytemnestra. I knew you wouldn't mind having her for just a fortnight.' And she whisked out to answer the telephone.

'Where did Sheila get it from?' Wexford said gloomily.

Mrs Wexford was a woman of few words.

'Sebastian.'

'Who in God's name is Sebastian?'

'Some boy,' said Mrs Wexford. 'He's only just gone.'

Her husband considered pushing the dog on to the floor, thought better of it, and went sulkily off to bed. His daughter's beauty had never ceased to surprise the chief inspector. Sylvia, the elder one, was well-built and healthy, but that was the best that could be said for her; Mrs Wexford had a magnificent figure and a fine profile although she had never been of the stuff that wins beauty contests. While he . . . All he needed, he sometimes thought, was a trunk to make him look exactly like an elephant. His body was huge and

16

ponderous, his skin pachydermatous, wrinkled and grey, and his three-cornered ears stuck out absurdly under the sparse fringe of colourless hair. When he went to the zoo he passed the elephant house quickly lest the irreverent onlooker should make comparisons.

Her mother and sister were fine-looking women, but the odd thing about Sheila was that her beauty was not an enlargement or an enhancement of their near-handsomeness. She looked like her father. The first time Wexford noticed this – she was then about six – he almost hooted aloud, so grotesque was the likeness between this exquisite piece of doll's flesh and her gross progenitor. And yet that high broad forehead was his, the little tilted nose was his, his the pointed – although in her case, flat – ears, and in her huge grey eyes he saw his own little ones. When he was young his hair had been that flaxen gold too, as soft and as fine. Only hope she doesn't end up looking like her dad, he thought sometimes with a rich inner guffaw.

But on the following morning his feelings towards his younger daughter were neither tender nor amused. The dog had awakened him at ten to seven with long-drawn howls and now, a quarter of an hour later, he stood on the threshold of Sheila's bedroom, glowering.

'This isn't a boarding kennels, you know,' he said. 'Can't you hear her?'

'The Acrylic Swoofle Hound, Pop? Poor darling, she only wants to be taken out.'

'What did you call her?'

'The Acrylic Swoofle Hound. She's a mongrel really, but that's what Sebastian calls her. She looks as if she's made of man-made fibres you see. Don't you think it's funny?'

'Not particularly. Why can't this Sebastian look after his own dog?'

'He's gone to Switzerland,' said Sheila. 'His plane must have gone by now.' She surfaced from under the sheets and her father saw that her hair was wound on huge electrically heated rollers. 'I felt awful letting him walk all that way to the station last night.' She added accusingly, 'But you had the car.'

'It's my car,' Wexford almost shouted. This argument he knew of old was hopeless and he listened to his own voice with a kind of horror as a note of pleading crept into it. 'If the dog wants to go out, hadn't you better get up and take her?'

'I can't. I've just set my hair.' Downstairs Clytemnestra let out a howl that ended in a series of urgent yelps. Sheila threw back the bedclothes and sat up, a vision in pink baby doll pyjamas.

'God almighty!' Wexford exploded. 'You can't take your friend's dog out but you can get up at the crack of dawn to set your hair.'

'Daddy . . .' The wheedling tone as well as the now seldom-used paternal appellation told Wexford that a monstrous request was to be made of him. He glared, drawing his brows together in the manner that made Kingsmarkham's petty offenders tremble. 'Daddy, duck, it's a gorgeous morning and you know what Dr Crocket said about your weight and I *have* just set my hair . . .'

'I am going to take a shower,' Wexford said coldly.

He took it. When he emerged from the bathroom the dog was still howling and pop music was issuing from behind Sheila's door. A degenerate male voice exhorted its hearers to give it love or let it die in peace.

'There seems to be an awful lot of noise going on, darling,' said Mrs Wexford sleepily.

'You're joking.'

He opened Sheila's door. She was applying a face pack.

'Just this once, then,' said the chief inspector. 'I'm only doing it because I want your mother to have a quiet lie-in, so you can turn that thing off for a start.'

'You are an angel, Daddy,' said Sheila, and she added dreamily, 'I expect Clytemnestra has spent a penny by now.'

Clytemnestra. Of all the stupid pretentious names for a dog . . . But what else could you expect of someone called Sebastian? She had not, however, yet "spent a penny". She flung herself on Wexford, yelping frantically, and when he pushed her away, ran round him in circles, wildly gyrating her tail and flapping her knitted ears.

Wexford found the lead, obligingly left by Sheila in a prominent position on top of the refrigerator. Undoubtedly it was going to be a beautiful day, a summer's day such as is unequalled anywhere in the world but in the South of England, a day that begins with mists, burgeons into tropical glory and dies in blue and gold and stars.

'Full many a glorious morning,' quoted Wexford to Clytemnestra, 'have I seen, flatter the mountain tops with sovereign eye.'

Clytemnestra agreed vociferously, leaping on to a stool and screeching hysterically at sight of her lead.

'Bear your body more seemly,' said Wexford coldly, switching from sonnet to comedy without varying his author. He looked out of the window. The sovereign eye was there all right, bright, molten and white-gold. Instead of mountain tops it was flattering the Kingsbrook meadows and turning the little river into a ribbon of shimmering metal. It wouldn't do him any harm to take this ungoverned creature for a short jaunt in the fields and the experience would give him a splendid ascendancy over Inspector Burden when he walked into the station at nine-thirty.

'Lovely morning, sir.'

'It was, Mike. The best of it's over now, of course. Now when I was down by the river at half seven . . .'

He chuckled. Clytemnestra whimpered. Wexford went to the door and the dog screamed for joy. He clipped on the lead and stepped forth into the sweet peace of a summer Saturday in Sussex.

It was one thing to boast afterwards of pre-breakfast hiking, quite another to be actually seen leading this freak of nature, this abortion, about the public streets. Observed in uncompromising midsummer light, Clytemnestra looked like something that, having long lain neglected at the bottom of an old woman's knitting basket, has finally been brought out to be mended.

Moreover, now that she had achieved the heart's desire for which she had turned on her shameless, neurotic display, she had become dejected, and walked along meekly, head and tail hanging. Just like a woman, Wexford thought crossly. Sheila would be just the same. Hair out of curlers, face cleaned up, she was in all probability downstairs now

19

calmly making her mother a cup of tea. When you get what you want you don't want what you get. . . . *On a fait le monde ainsi.*

He would, however, eschew the public streets.

From this side of town, the footpath led across the fields to the bank of the stream where it divided, one branch going to the new council estate and Sewingbury, the other to the centre of Kingsmarkham High Street, at the Kingsbrook bridge. Wexford certainly wasn't going to embark on a sabbath day's journey to Sewingbury, and now they had mucked up the Kingsbrook Road with those flats, there was no longer any point in going there. Instead he would walk down to the river, take the path to the bridge and pick up his *Police Review* at Braddan's on his way home. They always forgot to send it with the papers.

In agricultural districts pastureland is usually fenced. These meadows were divided by hedges and barbed wire and in them great red cattle were grazing. Mist lay in shallow patches over the hollows and where the fields were lying fallow the hay was nearly ready to be cut, but it was not yet cut. Wexford, very much a countryman at heart, marvelled that the townsman calls grass green when in reality it is as many-coloured as Joseph's coat. The grass heads hung heavy with seed, ochre, chestnut and powdery grey, and all the thick tapestry of pasture was embroidered and interlaced with the crimson thread of sorrel, the bright acid of buttercups and the creamy dairy-maid floss of meadowsweet. Over it all the fanning whispering seed and the tenuous mist cast a sheen of silver.

The oak trees had not yet lost the vivid yellow-green of their late springtime, a colour so bright, so fresh and so unparalleled elsewhere in nature or in art that no one has ever been able to emulate it and it is never seen in paint or cloth or women's dresses. In such things the colour would be crude, if it could be copied, but against this pale blue yet fixedly cloudless sky it was not crude. It was exquisite. Wexford drew in lungfuls of scented, pollen-laden air. He never had hay fever and he felt good.

The dog, who had perhaps feared a pavement perambulation, sniffed the air too and became frisky. She poked about in the brambles and wagged her tail. Wexford undid the lead clip and let her run.

With a kind of stolid tranquillity he began to reflect on the day's work ahead. That grievous bodily harm thing was coming up at a special court this morning, but that ought to be all wrapped up in half an hour. Then there was the possibility of the silver on sale at the Saturday morning market being stolen goods. Someone had better go down and have a word. . . . No doubt there'd been the usual spate of Friday night burglaries, too.

Mrs Fanshawe had regained consciousness in Stowerton Royal Infirmary after her six-week-long coma. They would have to talk to her today. But that was the uniformed branch's pigeon, not his. Thank God, it wasn't he who had to break the news to the woman that her husband and her daughter had both been killed in the car crash that had fractured her skull.

Presumably they would now resume the adjourned inquest on that unfortunate pair. Burden said Mrs Fanshawe might just recall why her husband's Jaguar had skidded and over-turned on the empty fast lane of the twin track road, but he doubted it. A merciful amnesia usually came with these comas and who could deny it was a blessing? It seemed downright immoral to torment the poor woman with questions now just for the sake of proving the Jaguar's brakes were faulty or Fanshawe was driving over the seventy limit. It wasn't as if any other vehicle had been involved. No doubt there was some question of insurance. Anyway, it wasn't his worry.

The sun shone on the rippling river and the long willow leaves just touched its bubbling golden surface. A trout jumped for a sparkling iridescent fly. Clytemnestra went down to the water and drank greedily. In this world of clean fast-running water, of inimitable oaks and meadows which made the Bayeux tapestry look like a traycloth, there was no place for somersaulted cars and carnage and broken bodies lying on the wet and bloody tarmac.

The dog paddled, then swam. In the sunshine even grey knitted Clytemnestra was beautiful. Beneath her flat furry belly the big shallow stones had the marble veining of agate. Upon the water the mist floated in a golden veil, spotted

21

with the dancing of a myriad tiny flies. And Wexford who was an agnostic, a profane man, thought, Lord, how manifold are thy works in all the earth.

There was a man on the other side of the river. He was walking slowly some fifty yards from the opposite bank and parallel to it, walking from the Sewingbury direction to Kingsmarkham. A child was with him, holding his hand, and he too had a dog, a big pugnacious-looking black dog. Wexford had an idea, drawn partly from experience in looking out of his office window, that when two dogs meet they inevitably fight. Clytemnestra would come out badly from a fight with that big black devil. Wexford couldn't bring himself to call his charge by her name. He whistled.

Clytemnestra took no notice. She had gained the opposite bank and was poking about in a great drifting mass of torn grass and brushwood. Further upstream a cache of rubbish had been washed against the bank. Wexford, who had been lyrical, felt positively pained by this evidence of man's indifference to nature's glories. He could see a bundle of checked cloth, an old blanket perhaps, an oil drum and, a little apart from the rest, a floating shoe. Clytemnestra confirmed his low opinion of everything canine by advancing on this water-logged pocket of rubbish, her tail wagging and her ears pricked. Filthy things, dogs, Wexford thought, scavengers and dustbin delvers. He whistled again. The dog stopped and he was just about to congratulate himself on his authoritative and successful method of summoning her, when she made a plunging dart forward and seized the mass of cloth in her mouth.

It moved with a heavy surge and the dog released it, her hackles rising. The slow and somehow primeval erecting of that mat of grey hairs brought a curious chill to Wexford's blood. The sun seemed to go in. He forgot the black dog, coming ever nearer, and his joy in the morning went. Clytemnestra let out an unearthly keening howl, her lips snarling back and her tail a stiff prolongation of her backbone.

The bundle she had disturbed eddied a few inches into the deeper water and as Wexford watched, a thin pale hand,

22

lifeless as the agate-veined stones, rose slowly from the
sodden cloth, its fingers hanging yet pointing towards him.

He took off his shoes and socks and rolled his trousers to
his knees. The man and the child on the other side watched
him with interest. He didn't think they had yet seen the hand.
Holding his shoes, he stepped on to the stones and crossed
the river carefully. Clytemnestra came to him quickly and
put her face against his bare leg. Wexford pushed aside the
willows that hung like a pelmet and came to the rubbish
pocket, where he knelt down. One shoe floated empty, the
other was still on a foot. The dead man lay face-downwards
and someone had smashed in the back of his head with a
heavy smooth object. One of these very stones, Wexford
guessed.

The brambles shivered behind him and a footstep crunched.

'Keep back,' Wexford said. 'Keep the child back.'

He turned, shielding what lay in the water with his own
big body. Downstream the child was playing with both dogs,
throwing stones for them into the water.

'Christ!' said the man softly.

'He's dead,' said Wexford. 'I'm a police officer and . . .'

'I know you. Chief Inspector Wexford.' The man
approached and Wexford couldn't stop him. He looked
down and gasped. 'My God, I . . .'

'Yes, it isn't a pleasant sight.' The thought came to Wexford that something very out of the way had happened. Not
so much that here on a fine June morning a man lay murdered, but that he, Wexford had found him. Policemen don't
find bodies unless they are sent to look for them or unless
someone else has found them first. 'Will you do something
for me?' he asked. The newcomer's face was green. He
looked as if he was about to be sick. 'Will you go down to
the town, to the nearest phone box and get on to the station?
Just tell them what you've seen. They'll do the rest. Come
on, man, pull yourself together.'

'O.K., it's just that . . .'

'Perhaps you'd better let me have your name.'

'Cullam, Maurice Cullam. I'll go, I'll go right away. It's

just that – well, last night I was having a drink with him at the Dragon.'

'You know who it is then? You can't see his face.'

'I don't need to. I'd know Charlie Hatton anywhere.'

3

He looked a right Charlie in those tails and striped trousers. That would be something funny to say to his best man when he came.

'You and me, we look a pair of right Charlies, Charlie Hatton.'

Quite witty really. Jack often thought he wasn't quick enough to match Charlie's easy repartee, but now he had thought of something that would make his friend smile.

Dear old Charlie, he thought sentimentally, the best friend a man ever had. Generous to a fault, and if he wasn't always strictly above-board – well, a man had to live. And Charlie knew how to live all right. The best of everything he had. Jack was ready to bet all the crisp honeymoon pound notes he had in his pocket that Charlie would be one of the few guests not wearing a hired morning coat. He had his own and not off the peg, either.

Not that he looked half bad himself, he thought, admiring his reflection. At his age boozing didn't have much visible effect and he always had a red face anyway. He looked smashing, he decided, shyly proud, as good as the Duke of Edinburgh any day. Probably the Duke used an electric shaver though. Jack put another bit of cotton wool on the nick on his chin and he wondered if Marilyn was ready yet.

Thanks to Charlie boy, they'd been able to splash a bit on the wedding and Marilyn could have the white satin and the four bridesmaids she'd set her heart on. It would have been a different story if they'd had to find the key money for the flat themselves. Trust Charlie to come up with a long-term interest-free loan. That way they'd be able to blow some of their own savings on having the flat done up nicely. How well it had all worked out! A fortnight away by the sea and when they came back, the flat all ready and waiting for them. And it was all thanks to Charlie.

Moving away from the mirror, Jack looked into the future, twenty, thirty years hence. Charlie would be a really rich man by then. Jack would be very much surprised if his friend wouldn't be living in one of those houses in Ploughman's Lane like the one where he sometimes did electrical jobs with real old French furniture and real oil paintings and the kind of china you looked at but didn't eat off. He and Charlie had had a good laugh over that particular house, but there had been something serious in Charlie's laughter and Jack had guessed he aimed high.

They'd still be mates of course, for there was no side to Charlie Hatton. It wouldn't be beer and a hand of solo then, but dinner parties and bridge games with their wives in cocktail gowns and real jewellery. Jack grew dizzy as he thought of it, seeing them sitting with tall glasses on a shady patio and, strangely, seeing them too as they were now, untouched by the hand of time.

Abruptly he came back to the present day, his wedding day. Charlie was taking a hell of a time about coming. Maybe there was some difficulty about Lilian's dress or he was waiting for her to get back from the hairdresser's. Charlie was dead keen on Lilian doing him credit and she always did, always looked as if she'd just stepped out of a bandbox. After Marilyn, she'd be the best dressed woman at the wedding, blonde, shapely, in the green dress Marilyn had got so superstitious about. Jack dabbed at his chin again and went to the window to watch for Charlie.

It was ten-thirty and the wedding was fixed for an hour's time.

She was blonde, shapely, pretty in Sheila Wexford's style but without Sheila's transcending beauty. Her face was rather blunt, the features unfinished putty dabs, and now it was swollen with crying. After they had told her Wexford and Burden sat helplessly while she flung herself face-downwards on the sofa and sobbed into the cushions.

Presently Wexford moved over to her and touched her shoulder. She reached for his hand, clutched it and dug in her long nails. Then she struggled up, burying her face in his hand and her own. The expensive velvet cushions were blotched with her tears.

Wexford glanced quickly around the smartly, even luxuriously, furnished room. Over the back of one of the chairs hung a blue and green flowered dress, a green coat, long wrist-buttoning gloves. In the middle of the long teak dining table lay Lilian Hatton's wedding hat, an elaborate confection of satin leaves and tulle as green and fresh as the real leaves he could see through the picture window in the Kingsbrook meadows.

'Mrs Hatton,' he said gently and she raised her face obediently, 'Mrs Hatton, weren't you worried when your husband didn't come home last night?'

She didn't speak. He repeated the question, and then she said in a voice choked with sobs, 'I didn't expect him home. I only half-expected him.' She dropped Wexford's hand, recoiling as if in taking it she had done something indecent.

'When he didn't come,' she said, 'I thought he hasn't made it, he hasn't made Jack's party. He's stopping off on the road, he'll be in in the morning, I . . .' The sobs were uncontrollable and she gave a long piteous cry.

'I won't trouble you any more now, Mrs Hatton. You say you mother's coming? If I could just have Mr Pertwee's address . . .'

'Jack, yes,' she said. 'Jack'll take this hard.' She drew a long breath, twisting her hands. 'They'd been pals since they were schoolkids.' Suddenly she stood up, staring wildly. 'God, Jack doesn't know! It's his wedding day and Charlie was going to be his best man. Oh, Jack, Jack, poor Jack!'

'Leave it to us, Mrs Hatton,' said Inspector Burden. 'We'll tell Mr Pertwee. Bailey Street, is it? We'll tell him. There's your front door bell now. I expect that'll be your mother.'

'Mum,' said Lilian Hatton. 'What am I going to do, Mum?' The older woman looked past her, then put her arms around the shaking shoulders. 'Marilyn said I shouldn't wear green to a wedding, she said it was unlucky.' Her voice was very low, a slurring mumble. 'I bought that green coat just the same. I never got as far as the wedding, Mum, but it was unlucky, wasn't it?' Suddenly she broke into a terrible, loud and demented scream. 'Charlie, Charlie, what am I going to do, Charlie?' She held on to her mother, clawing at the lapels of her coat. 'Oh my God, Charlie!' she screamed.

'I never get used to it, you know,' said Burden quietly.

'Do you think I do?' Wexford had amiable, sometimes distinctly fond feelings for his subordinate, but occasionally Burden made him impatient, especially when he instituted himself keeper of the chief inspector's conscience. He had a smug, parsonical face, Wexford thought unkindly, and now his thin mouth turned piously down. 'The worst is over anyway,' he said crossly. 'The bridegroom won't go into transports of grief and you don't put off your wedding because your best man's been done in.'

You callous devil, said Burden's look. Then the neat, well-modelled head was once more averted and the inspector re-entered his silent, respectful reverie.

It took only ten minutes to get from the Hatton's flat to Bailey Street where, at number ten, Jack Pertwee lived with his widowed father. The police car stopped outside a tiny terraced house with no garden to separate its front door from the pavement. Mr Pertwee senior answered their knock, looking uneasy in a too large morning coat.

'Thought you were our missing best man come at last.'

'I'm afraid Mr Hatton won't be coming, sir.' Wexford and Burden edged themselves courteously but firmly past him into the narrow hall. 'I'm very sorry to tell you we have bad news.'

'Bad news?'

'Yes, sir, Mr Hatton died last night. He was found down by the river this morning and he'd been dead since midnight or before.'

Pertwee went pale as chalk. 'By gum,' he said, 'Jack'll take this hard.' His mouth trembling, he looked at them both and then down at the knife-edge creases in his trousers. 'D'you want me to go up and tell him?' Wexford nodded. 'Well, if that's the way you want it. He's getting married at eleven-thirty. But if I've got to tell him, I suppose I've got to tell him.'

They both knew Jack Pertwee by sight. Most Kingsmarkham faces were familiar to Wexford and Burden remembered seeing him the night before arm-in-arm with the dead man, singing and disturbing decent citizens. A happily married man himself, he had the deepest sympathy for the widow, but in his heart he thought Jack Pertwee a bit of a lout. You didn't have to tread softly with such as he and he wondered scornfully why the fellow's face was lard-coloured.

Impatiently he watched him lumber blindly down the steep narrow staircase and when the bridegroom reached the bottom, Burden said curtly:

'Your father's told you? Hatton was murdered last night. We want to know the lot, where you'd been and what time you left him.'

'Here, go easy,' said the father. 'It's been a shock. They were old mates, my boy and Charlie.'

Jack pushed past him into the poky front parlour and the others followed. The wedding flowers had come. Jack had a white rose in his buttonhole and there were two more, their stems wrapped in silver foil, on the fumed oak sideboard. One was for the bridegroom's father and the other would never be worn. Jack plucked the flower out of his morning coat and closed his fist slowly over it, crushing it into a pulp.

'I'll get you a drop of whisky, son.'

'I don't want it,' Jack said with his back to them. 'We was drinking whisky last night. I never want to touch it again.' He pulled his black immaculate sleeve across his eyes. 'Who did it?' he shouted.

'We hoped you'd be able to tell us that,' said Burden.

'Me? Are you out of your bloody mind? Just show me the bastard who killed Charlie Hatton and I'll . . .' He sat down heavily, spread his arms on the table and dropped his head. 'Charlie,' he said.

Wexford didn't pursue it. He turned to the father. 'What was it last night, a stag party?' Pertwee nodded. 'D'you know who was there?'

'Jack, of course, and poor old Charlie. Then there was all the darts club lot, George Carter, fellow called Bayles, Maurice Cullam from Sewingbury and a couple of others. That right, Jack?'

Jack nodded dumbly.

'Charlie got there late, Jack said. They left at closing time, split up outside, I reckon. Charlie and Cullam'll have walked home across the fields. That right, Jack?'

This time Jack lifted his head. Burden thought him a weak womanish fool, despising his red eyes and the muscle that twitched in his cheek. But Wexford spoke gently.

'I realize this has been a blow to you, Mr Pertwee. We won't bother you much longer. Did Mr Cullam and Mr Hatton walk home together?'

'Maurice went first,' Jack muttered. 'About twenty to eleven it was. Charlie . . . Charlie stayed for a bit of a natter with me.' A sob caught his throat and he coughed to mask it. 'He said he wished me luck in case he didn't get the chance today. Christ, he didn't know he'd never get another chance.'

'Come on, son, bear up. Let me give you a little drop of scotch. You owe it to Marilyn to keep going you know. It's your wedding day, remember?'

Jack shook off his father's hand and lurched to his feet.

'There isn't going to be no wedding,' he said.

'You don't mean that, Jack, think of that girl of yours, think of all them folks coming. They'll be getting to the church in a minute. Charlie wouldn't have wished it.'

Stubbornly Jack said, 'I'm not getting married today. D'you think I don't know what's right, what's proper?' He wrenched off his tie and flung his morning coat over the back of a chair.

His father, with a working man's regard for hired finery, picked it up, smoothed it and stood draping it over his arm like an outfitter's assistant. Bewildered by the holocaust of events, by death that had suddenly changed a world, he began apologising, first to the policemen: 'I don't know what to say, his best man to die like that . . .' and then to his son: 'I'd give my right hand to have things different, Jack. What can I do for you, son? I'll do anything you say.'

Jack dropped his handful of bruised petals. A sudden dignity made him straighten his back and hold his head high. 'Then get down to that church,' he said, 'and tell them the wedding's off.' He faced Wexford. 'I'm not answering any more questions now. I've got my grief. You ought to respect my grief.' Still the old man hesitated, biting his lip. 'Go on, Dad,' Jack said fiercely. 'Tell them it's all off and tell them why.' He gasped as if suddenly, at this moment, it had come home to him. 'Tell them Charlie Hatton's dead!'

Oh, Jonathan, thou wast slain in thy high places . . . How are the mighty fallen and the weapons of war perished!

'A best man, indeed,' said Burden. 'Everyone's best man.'

You callous devil, thought Wexford. 'Naturally Pertwee'd be upset. What did you expect?'

Burden made a moue of disgust. 'That sort of grief, that's the widow's province. A man ought to have more self-control.' His pale ascetic face flushed unbecomingly. 'You don't suppose there was anything . . . ?'

'No, I don't,' said Wexford. 'And why can't you call a spade a spade? They were friends. Don't you have friends, Mike? A pretty pass we've come to if a man can't have a friend without being labelled queer.' He stared aggressively at Burden and declaimed loudly and meaningfully, 'O brave new world, that has such people in it!'

Burden gave a stiff repressive cough and maintained silence until they reached York Street. Then he said coldly, 'George Carter's place is down here, old Pertwee said.'

'He's the Morris dancer, isn't he? I've seen him cavorting about on summer nights outside the Olive and Dove.'

'Lot of affected nonsense.'

But George Carter wasn't wearing his cap and bells this morning. From the brilliantined hair and the smart lounge suit, Wexford gathered that here was a wedding guest.

He hinted at the unlikelihood of Jack Pertwee's being married that day and was inwardly amused to observe that this piece of information – the fact that Carter would be deprived of his cold chicken and champagne – distressed him more than Hatton's death. The wedding guest did not exactly beat his breast but he looked considerably crestfallen.

'All that money wasted,' he said. 'I know, I was making plans for my own wedding, but then you won't want to know about that. Pity Jack had to be told, really. I don't seem to be able to take it in. Charlie Hatton dead! He was always so full of life, if you know what I mean.'

'And very well liked, I gather.'

George Carter's eyebrows went up. 'Charlie? Oh well, mustn't speak ill of the dead.'

'You'd better speak the truth, Mr Carter,' said Burden, 'and never mind whether it's ill or not. We want to know all about this party last night. The lot, please. You can take your time.'

Like Jack Pertwee and yet utterly unlike him, Carter took off his jacket and loosened his tie. 'I don't know what you mean by the lot,' he said. 'It was just a bunch of mates having a drink.'

'What happened? What did you talk about?'

'O.K.' He gave them an incredulous glance and said sarcastically, 'Stop me if I'm boring you. Charlie come into the Dragon at about half nine, maybe a quarter to ten. We was drinking beer so, of course, Charlie has to make us all feel small by paying for whiskies all round. A crack hand at that, was Charlie Hatton. I made some comment and he bit my head off. This the sort of thing you want to know?'

'Exactly the sort of thing, Mr Carter.'

'Seems a bit mean, that's all, with the poor geezer dead. Then someone else was telling a joke and he sort of – well, humiliated him, if you know what I mean. He was like that, always had to be top dog. He drank my drink because I said something about all the money he was always flashing around and then he made a dirty crack about . . . Well, that doesn't matter. It was personal. He got at our chairman too and he left with a couple of the others. Geoff had already gone. There was me and Charlie and Maurice and Jack left and we went when they closed. And that's the lot.'

'You're sure?'

'I told you there was nothing much. I can't think of any more . . . Oh, wait a minute. But it was nothing.'

'We'll have it just the same, Mr Carter.'

George Carter shrugged impatiently. 'I don't even know what it was about. Nothing, I reckon. Maurice said – it was after the others had gone – Maurice said, "Seen much of McCloy lately, Charlie?" I think those were his words. I know the name was McCloy but it didn't mean nothing to me. Jack didn't like it and he was a bit shirty with Maurice. I reckon Charlie looked a bit sick. God, it was all so . . .

well, it was nothing. But Charlie'd always rise. I expected him to rise. I don't know why. He didn't. He just made a crack about Maurice needing to sleep quiet in his bed. Said it was time he did, meaning that Maurice had so many kids and . . . well, you can get the message.'

'Not altogether,' said Wexford. 'Had Cullam suggested that Hatton couldn't sleep quiet in *his*?'

'That's right. I forgot that bit. I wish I could remember his words. Something like "I don't have nothing to do with McCloy, I like to sleep quiet in my bed". '

Very interesting Wexford thought. Far from being popular, Hatton had evidently had a host of enemies. He had spent less than an hour in the Dragon and during that time he had succeeded in needling at least four men.

'You mentioned all the money Hatton used to flash around,' he said. 'What money?'

'He always had wads of it,' said Carter. 'I've known him three years and he was always flush. But he'd had more lately. He bought four rounds of double scotches last night and it didn't even make a hole in what he'd got.'

'How much had he got, Mr Carter?'

'I didn't count it, you know,' Carter said with asperity. He blew his nose on his clean white wedding handkerchief. 'He'd got his pay packet, but he didn't touch that. Then he had this roll of notes. I told you I didn't count them. How could I?'

'Twenty pounds, thirty, more?'

Carter wrinkled his forehead in an effort of concentration. 'He paid for the first round out of a fiver and the third with another fiver. He'd got two fivers left, then. As well as that there was a wad of oncers.' He indicated with two parted fingers a quarter of an inch. 'I reckon he was carrying a hundred quid besides his pay.'

33

4

By lunchtime Wexford and Burden had interviewed all those members of the darts club that had been present at Jack Pertwee's stag party with the exception of Maurice Cullam, but none of them had been able to do more than confirm that Hatton had been aggressive, vain and malicious and that he had been carrying a great deal of money.

They returned to the police station, passing the parish church on whose steps a June bride and her attendants were being photographed. The bridegroom moved out of the throng and Wexford felt a strange sentimental pang because it was not Jack Pertwee. Then he pulled himself together and said, as they mounted the station steps under the concrete canopy:

'Now if we were cops inside the covers of a detective story, Mike, we'd know for sure that Hatton was killed to stop Pertwee getting married today.'

Burden gave a sour smile. 'Easier to kill Pertwee, I'd have thought.'

'Ah, but that's your author's subtlety. Still, we aren't and he wasn't. The chances are he was killed for the money he was carrying. There was nothing in his wallet when I found him.'

The foyer of the police station enclosed them. Behind the long black sweep of counter Sergeant Camb sat fanning himself with a newspaper, the sweat dripping down his forehead. Wexford made for the stairs.

'Why not use the lift, sir?' said Burden.

The police station was not yet half a dozen years old, but ever since its completion the powers that be, like fussy

34

housewives, had been unable to let well alone, adding innovation after innovation, perpetually trying to improve their
handiwork. First there had been the stone tubs on the forecourt, a constant temptation to vandals who got a more than
commonly satisfying kick from ravishing these particular
flowers. Then came the consignment of houseplants for the
offices, *tradescantia* and *sanseveria* and *ficus elastica* that
were doomed from the start to dehydration and ultimately
to have their pots serve as repositories for cigarette ash.

Last year it had been glass sculpture, a strange green tree,
a very Yggdrasil, for Burden's sanctum, and for Wexford
an inky-blue, amorphous pillar that in some lights grossly
resembled the human figure. These, too, had been fated,
Wexford's broken by a pretty young woman who was helping him with his enquiries and Burden's one day inadvertently put out with the rubbish.

That should have been the end of it. And then, just as the
foyer was beginning to take on a shabby, comfortable look,
the lift arrived, an elegant black and gilt box with a sliding
door.

'It isn't working yet,' Wexford said, a shade nervously.

'That's where you're wrong. Been operating since this
morning. Shall we try it?'

'I should just like to know what's wrong with the stairs,'
Wexford exploded. 'It's a downright disgrace wasting the
ratepayers' money like this.' He stuck out his lower lip.
'Besides, Crocker says walking upstairs is the best exercise
in the world for me with my blood pressure.'

'Just as you like,' said Burden, turning his face away so
that Wexford should not see him smile.

By the time they reached the third floor they were both
out of breath. The flimsy yellow chair behind Wexford's
rosewood desk creaked as he lowered his heavy body into
it.

'For God's sake open a window, Mike.'

Burden grumbled that opening windows upset the air con-
ditioning but he complied, raising the yellow venetian blind
and letting in a powerful shaft of noonday sunshine.

'Well, sir,' he said. 'Shall we re-cap on what we know
about Charlie Hatton?'

'Thirty years old, born and bred in Kingsmarkham. Two

35

years ago he got married to a Miss Lilian Bardsley, sister of the man he's in business with. Bardsley's got his own firm, transporting small electrical goods.'

'Was Hatton a full partner?'

'We'll have to find out. Even if he was, I can't see he could get that flush driving loads of irons and heaters up to Leeds and Scotland a couple of times a week. Carter says he had a hundred quid on him, Mike. Where did he get the money from?'

'Maybe this McCloy.'

'Do we know any McCloys?'

'Not that I can recall, sir. We shall have to ask Maurice Cullam.'

Wexford wiped his brow with his handkerchief and, following Camb's example, began to fan himself with the morning paper. 'The philoprogenitive Cullam,' he said. 'He had one of his quiverful with him when I found Hatton this morning. He's a lorry driver too, Mike. I wonder . . . Hatton had his lorry hi-jacked twice this year.'

Burden opened his pale-blue eyes. 'Is that so?'

'I remembered,' said Wexford, 'as soon as Cullam told me whose the body was. Both times were on the Great North Road and no one was ever done for it. Hatton got knocked on the head the first time but the second time he wasn't hurt, only tied up.'

'Once,' said Burden thoughtfully, 'is fair enough. Occupational hazard. Twice looks fishy. I want to hear what the doctor has to say. And if I'm not mistaken that's him outside now.'

Dr Crocker and Wexford had been at school together. Like Jack Pertwee and Charlie Hatton, they were lifelong friends, but their friendship was a casual business and their manner to each other, dry, irreverent, often caustic. Crocker, some six years the chief inspector's junior, was the only man Burden knew who could get the better of Wexford and match his acid tongue. A tall lean figure with deep lines carved vertically down his brown cheeks, he came into the office looking as cool as he did on a winter's day.

'I used your lift,' said the doctor. 'Very smart. Whatever will they think of next?'

'Pictures are threatened,' said Wexford. 'The inspector here is to have a suitable flower piece and I a Constable landscape.'

'I don't know much about art,' said Crocker, sitting down and crossing one elegant lean leg over the other, 'but there's one painting I *would* like to have. Rembrandt, The Anatomy Lesson. Lovely thing it is. There's this poor devil, this corpse, you see, lying on the table with his guts laid open and all these students . . .'

'Do you mind,' said Wexford. 'I'm just going to have my lunch. You doctors bring your revolting trade into everything. We can hear your ideas on interior decoration another time. Now I want to know about Charlie Hatton.'

'Perfectly healthy bloke,' said the doctor, 'bar the fact that he's dead.' He ignored Burden's glance of reproof. 'Someone bashed him on the back of the head with a heavy smooth object. I'd say he was dead by eleven but it's impossible to be accurate about these things. What did you say he did for a living?'

'He was a lorry driver,' said Burden.

'I thought that's what you said. He'd got a marvellous set of teeth.'

'So what?' said Wexford. 'He ought to have had good teeth.' Rather ruefully he ran his tongue over the two stumps that held in place his upper plate. 'He was only thirty.'

'Sure,' said Crocker, 'he ought to have had his own being a war baby and a cog in the welfare state. The point is he didn't. What I meant was he'd got just about the finest set of *false* teeth I've ever seen. Lovely ivory castles. Very nifty grinders Charlie Hatton had, all cunningly contrived to look more real than the real thing. I'd be surprised if they cost less than two hundred quid.'

'Rich man,' said Wexford ruminatively. 'A hundred pounds in his wallet and two hundred in his mouth. I wish I could believe he'd come by it honestly, driving his lorry up and down the Great North Road.'

'That's your problem,' said the doctor. 'Well, I'm away to my lunch. Tried the lift yet?'

'In your capacity as my medical adviser, you advised me

to walk upstairs. Physician, heal thyself. About all the exercise you get is pressing the button on your automatic gear change. You want to watch your blood pressure, too.'

'I should worry,' said Crocker. He went to the door where the sunshine showed off his elegant figure and absence of paunch to best advantage. 'All a matter of metabolism,' he said airily. 'Some have it rapid.' He looked back at Wexford. 'Others slow. The luck of the draw.'

Wexford gave a snort. When the doctor had gone, he opened the top drawer of his desk and took from it the contents of Charlie Hatton's pockets. The wallet was there, but it was empty of money. It was still soaking wet and now Wexford carefully removed from its leather partitions a photograph of Lilian Hatton, a driving licence and a darts club membership card and spread them in the sun to dry.

In the pocket there had also been a clean handkerchief with a small card caught between its folds. You couldn't see the card until you unfolded the handkerchief and now Wexford looked at it for the first time. It too was wet and the ink writing on it indecipherable, but it was still recognizable as the pasteboard square dentists use to remind patients of their appointments. On the top was printed: *Jolyon Vigo, B.D.S., L.D.S., R.C.S., Eng., Dent. Surg., 19 Ploughman's Lane, Kingsmarkham, Sussex. Tel: Kingsmarkham 384.*

Wexford held it up in the bright shaft of sunlight.

'The source of the delectable dentures, d'you reckon?'

'Maybe Vigo can tell us where the money came from if Cullam can't,' said Burden. 'My wife goes to Vigo. He's a good dentist.'

'A fly one too, if you ask me, getting a sharp little customer like Charlie Hatton to part with two hundred for thirty-two teeth. No wonder he can afford to live in Ploughman's Lane. We're in the wrong job here, Mike, and no mistake. I'm going for my lunch now. Join me? And then we'll go and root Cullam out of his domestic bliss.'

'May as well use the lift,' said Burden with a trace of self-consciousness.

It was more than Wexford's life was worth to admit his craven fear of the lift. Although a notice inside clearly stated its capacity to carry three persons, he was secretly afraid that it would be inadequate to bear his vast bulk. But he hesitated for no more than a moment before stepping inside and when the door was closed he took refuge in clowning.

'Soft furnishings, table linen, cutlery,' he said facetiously, pressing the button. The lift sighed and began to sink. 'First floor for ladies' underwear, stockings . . . Why's it stopping, Mike?'

'Maybe you pressed the wrong button.'

Or it won't stand my weight, Wexford thought, alarmed. The lift came to rest at the first floor and the door slid open. Sergeant Camb hesitated apologetically on the threshold.

'Sorry, sir. I didn't know it was you. I can walk down.'

'*Three* persons are permitted, Sergeant,' Wexford said, hoping his now very real trepidation didn't show. 'Come along.'

'Thank you, sir.'

'Not bad, is it? The tribute of a grateful government.' Come on, come on, he thought, and pictured the three of them plummeting down the last thirty feet into the basement.

'You off to see Mrs Fanshawe, I suppose?' he said superfluously. The lift floated lightly, steadied and the door opened. Must be stoutly built, thought Wexford, like me. 'I heard she'd regained consciousness.'

'I'm hoping the doctors'll have broken the news about her husband and her daughter, sir,' said Camb as they crossed the black and white checkerboard foyer of the station. 'It's not a job I fancy. They were all the family she'd got. She hasn't a soul in the world barring her sister who came down and identified the bodies.'

'How old is she?'

'Mrs Fanshawe, sir? Fifty odd. The sister's a good bit older. Horrible business for her having to identify Miss Fanshawe. She was a nasty mess, I can tell you. Face all . . .'

'I'm just off for my lunch,' said Wexford firmly.

He marched through the swing doors in front of the others and Camb got into his car. The stone flowerpots on the forecourt sported bright pink bouquets of *pelargoniums*, their magenta-splashed faces turned gratefully to the noonday sun.

'What was all that about?' asked Burden.

'Mrs Fanshawe? It's not our cup of tea. She and her husband were driving home from Eastbourne in Fanshawe's

Jaguar. It overturned in the fast lane on the twin-track road on the other side of Stowerton. Their home was in London and Fanshawe must have been in a hurry. God knows how it happened, there wasn't another thing on the road, but the Jag overturned and caught fire. Mrs Fanshawe was flung clear, the other two killed outright. Badly burned too.'

'And this Mrs Fanshawe doesn't know?'

'She's been in a coma since it happened six weeks ago.'

'I remember now,' said Burden, lifting the plastic strip curtain the Carousel Café hung up in hot weather to keep out wasps. 'The inquest was adjourned.'

'Till Mrs F. regained consciousness. Presumably Camb's going to try and get her to tell him just why a seasoned driver like Fanshawe overturned his car on an empty road. Some hopes! What d'you fancy for lunch, Mike? I'm going for the salad myself.'

'Two ham salads,' said Burden to the waitress. He poured himself some water from a chilled carafe.

'Getting quite transatlantic the old Carousel,' said Wexford. 'And about time too. Not so long ago the water used to steam away like a perishing engine on these tables in hot weather. What's the betting this McCoy's running a big racket, paying Charlie Hatton to leave his lorry unattended and paying him to keep other lorry drivers occupied whenever the chance presents itself? Lorries are always getting hijacked. They leave them in these lay-bys while they have a little kip or a cup of tea. Hatton could have done a nice little distracting job there. Fifty or a hundred quid a lorry depending on the load.'

'In that case, why does McCloy kill the goose that lays the golden eggs?'

'Because Hatton gets scared or fed-up and threatens to rat on him. He may even have tried blackmail.'

'I shouldn't be a bit surprised,' said Burden, spreading butter on his roll. The butter was almost liquid. Like the rest of humanity, he reflected, the Carousel staff were disappointingly inconsistent.

5

'But my daughter wasn't in the car.'

Seldom had Sergeant Camb felt so sorry for anyone as he did for this woman who lay against the piled pillows. His heart ached for her. And yet she was in one of the nicest private rooms in the hospital; she had a telephone and a television; her nightgown was a silly frou-frou of frills and spilling lace and on her thin fingers the rings – diamonds and sapphires in platinum – rattled as she clasped and unclasped the sheet.

It's true what they say, money can't buy happiness, thought the simple sergeant. He had noticed there were no flowers in the room and only one 'get well' card on the table by the chair where the policewoman sat. From her sister, he supposed. She hadn't anyone else now, not a soul in the world. Her husband was dead and her daughter . . .

'I'm very very sorry, Mrs Fanshawe,' he said, 'but your daughter *was* in the car. She was travelling back to London with you and your husband.'

'They didn't suffer,' put in the young policewoman quickly. 'They can't have felt a thing.'

Mrs Fanshawe touched her forehead where the dyed hair showed half an inch of white at the roots. 'My head,' she said. 'My head aches. I can't remember things, not details. Everything's so vague.'

'Don't you worry,' said Camb heartily. 'You'll find you'll get your memory back in time. You're going to get quite well, you know.' For what? For widowhood, for childlessness?

'Your sister's been able to supply us with most of the details we need.'

They had been close, Mrs Fanshawe and Mrs Browne, and there wasn't much about the Fanshawes Mrs Browne hadn't known. From her they had learned that Jerome Fanshawe had a bungalow at Eastover between Eastbourne and Seaford and that he and his wife and daughter had driven down there for a week's holiday on May 17th. The daughter Nora had left her post as an English teacher in a German school before Easter. She was between jobs, at a loose end, Camb had gathered, otherwise nothing would have induced her to accompany her parents. But she had accompanied them. Mrs Browne had been at their Mayfair flat and seen them all off together.

They had left Eastover days earlier than had been expected. Mrs Browne couldn't account for that, unless it had been because of the wet weather. Perhaps no one would ever know the reason, for Jerome Fanshawe's Jaguar had skidded, crashed and caught fire five miles from the hospital where the sole survivor now lay.

'I won't bother you for long,' Camb said gently. 'Perhaps you can't remember much about the crash. Do you think you could try and tell me what you do remember?'

Dorothy Fanshawe had forgotten who these kind though tiresome people were, just as she had again forgotten where she was. Her sister had been to see her and made her very tired and various strangers had moved her and pummelled her in a familiar manner that made her angry. Then someone had told her that Jerome was dead and had waited for her to cry. Mrs Fanshawe had twisted her rings – they were a great comfort to her, those rings – and said:

'Then it's all mine now, mine and Nora's.'

They thought she was wandering and they went away. She was glad to see the back of them with their interfering ways and their lack of respect. There was only one person she wanted to see and that was why she stared so searchingly into the young pretty face of the policewoman. But she had been in a coma, she wasn't mad. She knew very well this wasn't the right face. 'Am I in London?' she asked clearly and briskly.

'No, Mrs Fanshawe,' said the sergeant, thinking how

quavering and weak her voice was. 'You're in Stowerton Royal Infirmary, Stowerton in Sussex.'

'You seem very well-informed,' said Mrs Fanshawe, pleased because she had succeeded so well in pulling herself together. 'Perhaps you can tell me why my daughter doesn't come to see me? Haven't they told her I'm here? Nora would want to know. She'd come home.'

'Oh, Mrs Fanshawe . . .' The policewoman sounded very wretched, almost distraught, and catching her eye, Sergeant Camb gave her a sharp reproving glance. Better leave it, the look said. Maybe it's more merciful this way. Let her learn about it by degrees. The mind has its own way of softening blows, he thought sententiously.

'Now back to the – er, accident,' he said. 'Just try and see if you can tell me what happened when you left Eastover. It was getting dark and there wasn't much traffic on the road, it being a Monday. It had been raining and the road was wet. Now, Mrs Fanshawe?'

'My husband was driving,' she began and she wondered why the man's face wore such a sloppy expression. Perhaps he had noticed her rings. She slid them up and down her fingers, suddenly remembering that the five of them were worth nearly twenty thousand pounds. 'Jerome was driving . . .' What a silly name it was. Like *Three Men in a Boat*. That made her giggle, although the sound came out like a harsh cackle. 'I sat beside him, of course, and I was knitting. I must have been knitting. I always do when Jerome drives. He drives so fast,' she said querulously. 'Much too fast and he never takes any notice when I tell him to go slower, so I do my knitting. To keep my mind off it, you know.'

Mean and selfish Jerome was. A man of fifty-five hadn't any business to drive like a crazy teenager. She had told him that, but he had ignored her like he ignored everything else she ever said. Still, she was used to being ignored. Nora never took any notice of what she said either. When she came to think of it, the only thing she and Jerome had ever agreed about was what a difficult, trying and utterly maddening creature Nora was. It was exactly like her to go away and not get in touch with her parents. Jerome would have something to say about that . . . Then there swam pleasantly into her muddled mind the recollection that Jerome would never have anything to say about anything again, never drive at eighty-five or pick on Nora or do those other terrible and humiliating things. Tonight, when she felt better, she would write to Nora and tell her her father was dead. With Jerome out of the way and all that money for themselves, she felt they would have a much happier relationship . . .

'I was knitting a jumper for Nora,' she said. What a marvellous constitution she must have to remember that after all she'd been through! 'Not that she deserved it, the naughty girl.' Now, why had she said that? Nora had been naughty much naughtier than ever before, but for the life of her Dorothy Fanshawe couldn't remember of what that naughtiness had consisted. She wished the policeman or whoever he was would wipe that mawkish sheeplike expression off his face. There was no need for anyone to feel sorry for her, Dorothy Fanshawe, of Astbury Mews, Upper Grosvenor Street, W.1. She was a merry widow now, rich in her own right, soon to be well again, the mother of a good-looking talented only daughter. 'I don't remember what we talked about,' she said, 'my *late* husband and I. Nothing, probably. The road was wet and I kept telling him to go slower.'

'Your daughter was in the back seat, Mrs Fanshawe?'

Oh! really, how absurd the man was! 'Nora was *not* in the car. I keep telling you. Nora went back to Germany. No doubt she is in Germany now.'

To the sergeant the jerky bumbling words sounded like the raving of a madwoman. In spite of what the doctors said, it seemed to him probable that the accident had irremediably damaged her brain. He didn't dare take it upon himself to enlighten her further. God knew what harm he might do! Sooner or later, if she ever got her reason back, she would realize that her daughter had resigned from this German job six weeks before the accident, that she hadn't breathed a word to her aunt or her friends about the possibility of her returning to Europe. The girl's body had been identified by her aunt, Mrs Browne. She was dead and buried.

'I expect she is,' he said soothingly. 'No doubt she is. What made your husband swerve, Mrs Fanshawe?'

'I was knitting.'

44

'Did you hit something, did a tyre burst?'

'I told you, I didn't look. I was knitting.'

'Did your husband cry out, say anything?'

'I think he said "My God",' said Mrs Fanshawe. She couldn't really remember anything, only that she had been knitting and then she had woken up in this bed with her nosy, bossy sister sitting beside her. But Jerome was always saying 'My God' or even 'My Christ'. He had a limited vocabulary and she had stopped telling him not to be blasphemous twenty years ago. 'I don't remember anything else,' she said. That was all they were going to get out of her. She wasn't going to waste her strength. She needed it for the letter she was going to write in a minute to Nora.

Camb looked compassionately at the quivering febrile mouth and the long unfiled nails that played with those rings. Mrs Fanshawe had told him nothing. Perhaps he ought to have realized it was too soon, or his superiors ought to have realized. They would have to go now anyway. The young lady doctor had said ten minutes, but they must have been here twenty. Here was the nurse coming now. Funny uniforms they wear these days, he thought, eyeing the girl's navy-blue nylon overall and hat like a white forage cap. Poor Mrs Fanshawe was staring at her desperately. No wonder, exhausted and broken-hearted as she was.

No, it wasn't Nora. Just for a split second Mrs Fanshawe thought it was. But Nora never wore an overall, she despised housework – and this girl was wearing an overall, not the rather smart dress for which Mrs Fanshawe had first taken it. She had a cap on her head too. Was it possible that her sister had taken on a new maid for the Fanshawes' flat and not said anything about it? More than possible, considering how interfering her sister was. Interfering but irresponsible. A responsible person would have sent for Nora by now.

'What's your name?' Mrs Fanshawe said sharply.

'Rose, Mrs Fanshawe. Nurse Rose. I've come to make you more comfy and bring you your tea. You could drink a nice cup of tea, couldn't you? I'm afraid you'll have to run along now Sergeant. I can't allow my patient any setbacks, you know.'

Very talkative, thought Mrs Fanshawe. Takes a lot upon herself. She tried to sit up.

'Rose,' she said, 'I want to write a letter to my daughter, my daughter in Germany. Will you fetch me writing paper and a pen, please?'

She doesn't know, Camb thought, she's new. Nobody's told her. Just as well. He intercepted the policewoman's glance and crushed it with a frown.

'We *are* getting better, aren't we?' said the nurse skittishly. 'Writing letters! Well, I don't know, I'm sure. I'm certain you haven't got any paper of your own. I'll tell you what I'll do, I'll just pop down the corridor and borrow some from Mrs Goodwin in number four. Then I'll post your letter when I go off duty, shall I?'

'That will be very kind of you,' said Mrs Fanshawe austerely. 'Then you can bring the tea.'

A pert girl and probably untrainable, she thought. Time would show. At any rate, Jerome wouldn't be there to upset this one, catch her in corners and smack her bottom like he had the Danish *au pair*. Jerome was dead. She'd always said he'd kill himself driving like that and now he had. Why hadn't he killed her too? What good fortune had decreed that she be saved and be sitting here in her own bed in her own flat?

But it wasn't her own bed and her own flat. Very carefully Mrs Fanshawe marshalled her thoughts and her memories. Jerome was dead, Nora was in Germany and she was in Something-or-other Royal Infirmary. A hospital. Very thoughtful of someone to have engaged a maid for her in hospital.

Unless this Rose was a nurse. Of course, she must be a nurse. What a fool I am, thought Mrs Fanshawe. I feel exactly as if I were having a very prolonged dream but every time I come out of it I'm so tired I fall back into it again.

The inaccurate information given by all these busybodies didn't help at all. People were so inefficient these days. First her sister had forgotten to inform Nora, then this policeman said Nora had been with her and Jerome in the Jaguar. They must all think she was out of her mind. As if a mother didn't know where her own daughter was! Why, she even remembered Nora's address.

Goethestrasse 14, Köln, West Germany. Mrs Fanshawe was very proud of the way she wrote Köln like that instead of Cologne. What reserves of strength and intellect she must have to remember details like that! And after all she'd been through. Presently the nurse came back with the paper.

'Thank you, Nurse,' said Mrs Fanshawe to show what a fine grasp of things she had. She tried to hold the pen, but it zig-zagged all over the paper like that Planchette thing her father had used long ago.

'Why not let me write it for you?' said Nurse Rose.

'Perhaps it would be better. I'll dictate. Shall I begin?'

Nurse Rose had to exercise all her powers of concentration to sort out from the mumblings and digressions exactly what Mrs Fanshawe wanted to say. But she was a kind-hearted girl and, besides, it always paid to be attentive to patients in the private wing. Last year when one of them had left after only a fortnight she had given Nurse Rose a travelling clock and a nearly full bottle of *Rochas' Femme*.

' "Dearest Nora", ' she read aloud, ' "I am almost well again and think you should come and see me. Poor Daddy would have wished it. I expect auntie has told you everything and you have been too busy to come, but please come now. We will let bygones be bygones. Love from Mummy". That all right, Mrs Fanshawe? I've got some stamps, enough to make up to ninepence. I think I'll pop it in the post now when I go for my tea.'

Coming back from the pillar box at the end of Charteris Road, Nurse Rose met the Private Wing sister.

'I've just been posting a letter for poor Mrs Fanshawe, Sister,' she said virtuously. 'I like to do what I can, you know. Anything to cheer them up. She was so keen to get a letter to her daughter off tonight.'

'Her daughter's dead.'

'Oh, Sister, you don't mean it! Oh God, how dreadful! I never dreamt, I never guessed . . . Ooh, Sister!'

'You'd better get back on duty, Nurse, and do try not to be so impulsive.'

6

The child who opened the door to him was the one that had been out in the fields with his father. He was a boy of about seven, big for his age, aggressive looking and with food adhering to his face in greasy red and brown streaks.

'Who is it, Dominic?' came a voice from the sleazy depths of this small and totally inadequate council house.

'A man,' said Dominic simply.

'What does he want?'

To put an end to all this pointless colloquy, Wexford stepped into the hall, then the living room. Three more children were watching athletics on television. The remains of lunch were still on the stained crumb-scattered tablecloth and a woman sat at the table feeding a baby from a bottle. She might have been any age between thirty and sixty and Wexford set the lower limit so low only because of her young children. Her hair was thin and fair and long, caught back with an elastic band, and her face was thin and long too, wizened and pinched. A weariness that was as much chronic boredom as physical tiredness seemed the most dominant thing about her. It was the sordid exhaustion of poverty, of overwork, of perpetual near-incarceration, of eternal nagging demands, and to be left alone just to sit for perhaps only five minutes in unthinking apathy was her sole remaining desire. To this end she never wasted a word or a gesture and when she saw Wexford she neither greeted him nor even lifted her head, but said to one of her little girls:

'Go and fetch your dad, Samantha.'

Samantha jerked a thick black cat off her lap and trailed listlessly via the kitchen to the back garden. A middle-class

48

woman, a woman with more money and fewer children, might have apologized for the squalor and the smell of a hundred stale meals. Mrs Cullam didn't even look at him and when he asked her at what time her husband had come home on Friday night she said laconically, 'Quarter past eleven.'

'How can you be so sure of the time?'

'It was a quarter past eleven.' Mrs Cullam put the baby on the table among the crumbs, removing its napkin which she dropped on the floor, and said in the same low economical tone, 'Get me another nappie, Georgina.' A strong smell of ammonia fought with the cabbage. The baby, which was female, began to cry. Mrs Cullam lit a cigarette and stood against the table, her hands hanging by her sides, the cigarette dangling from her mouth. Georgina came back with a grey rag, sat down and watched her brother poke his fingers in the cat's ears. 'Leave the cat alone, Barnabas,' said Mrs Cullam.

Her husband came in, drying his hands on a tea cloth, the black dog cowering at his heels. He nodded to Wexford and then he turned off the television.

'Get up, Samantha, and let the gentleman sit down.' The child took no notice and made no sound when her father slapped one arm and yanked her up by the other. He viewed the room helplessly, paying particular attention to the discarded napkin, but there was no disgust on his face, only a vaguely resentful acceptance.

Wexford didn't take the vacant seat and something in his expression must have told Cullam he wanted privacy, for he said to his wife. 'Can't you get them kids out of here?'

Mrs Cullam shrugged and the ash from her cigarette fell into a plate of congealing gravy. She hoisted the baby on to her hip and dragging a chair close up to the television set, sat down and stared at the blank screen. 'Leave the cat alone, I said,' she remarked without heat.

'What were you wanting?' Cullam asked.

'We'll go into your kitchen, if you don't mind, Mr Cullam.'

'It's in a right old mess.'

'Never mind.'

Mrs Cullam made no comment. She switched on the television without looking up. Two of the children began to

49

fight in the depths of their armchair. Wexford followed their father into the kitchen. There was nowhere to sit so, pushing aside the handles of four encrusted saucepans, he leant against the gas cooker.

'I only want to know who McCloy is,' he said mildly.

Cullam gave him a look of not altogether comfortable cunning. 'How d'you know about McCloy, anyway?'

'Come on now, you know I can't tell you that.' The children were screaming now above the sound of the racy athletics commentary. Wexford closed the door and he heard Mrs Cullam say, 'Leave the bleeding cat alone, Barnabas.' She had wasted a word. 'You know who he is,' Wexford said. 'Now you can tell me.'

'I don't know. Honest I don't.'

'You don't know who he is, but last night in the pub you asked Mr Hatton if he'd been seeing much of McCloy lately. You wouldn't touch McCloy because you like to sleep quiet in your bed.'

'I tell you, I don't know who he is and I never saw him.'

Wexford removed his elbow from its dangerous proximity to a half-full plate of cold chips. 'You didn't like Mr Hatton very much, did you? You wouldn't walk home with him, though he was going your way. So you went on ahead and maybe you hung about a bit under those trees.' Pursuing the line, he watched Cullam's big beefy face begin to lose colour. 'I reckon you must have done, Cullam. A strong young fellow like you doesn't take thirty-five minutes to get here from the Kingsbrook bridge.'

In a low, resentful voice, Cullam said, 'I was sick. I was nearly home and I come over queer. I'm not used to scotch and I went into the gents down by the station to be sick.'

'Let me congratulate you on your powers of recovery. You were fit enough to be out on a country walk at seven-thirty this morning. Or were you just popping back to see you'd left Hatton neat and tidy? I want to see the clothes you wore last night.'

'They're out on the line.'

Wexford looked at him, his eyebrows almost vanishing into the vestiges of his hair, and the implications in that look were unmistakable. Cullam fidgeted, he moved to the crock-filled sink, leaning on it compressing his lips.

50

'I washed them,' he said. 'Pullover and trousers and a shirt. They was – well, they were in a bit of a state.' He shifted his feet.

'Charming,' Wexford said unkindly. '*You* washed them? What d'you have a wife for?' For the first time he noticed the washing machine, a big gleaming automatic affair, and the only object in that kitchen that was not stained or chipped or coated with clotted food drips. He opened the back door and eyed the sagging clothesline from which the three garments Cullam had named hung between a row of napkins. 'The blessings of modern mechanisation,' he said. 'Very nice too. I often remark these days how the roles of the sexes have been reversed.' His voice became deceptively friendly and Cullam licked his thick lips. 'A man can be dead tired after a week's work but he can still give his wife a helping hand. One touch of a button and the family wash comes out whiter than white. In fact, a gadget like that turns chores into pleasure, you might say. Men are all little boys at heart, when all's said and done, and it's not only women that like to have these little playthings to make a break in the daily round. Besides, they cost so much, you might as well get some fun out of them. Don't tell me that little toy cost you less than a hundred and twenty, Cullam.'

'A hundred and twenty-five,' said Cullam with modest pride. He was quite disarmed and, advancing upon the machine, he opened the gleaming porthole. 'You set your programme . . .' A last uneasy look at the chief inspector told him his visitor was genuinely interested, paying no more than a routine call. 'Put in your powder,' he said, 'and Bob's your uncle.'

'I knew a fellow,' Wexford lied ruminatively, 'a lorry driver like yourself. Big family too and we all know what inroads a big family makes. He got in bad company, I'm sorry to say. His wife kept on at him, you see, wanting more gear about the house. He'd already turned a blind eye when a couple of his lorries got hi-jacked. Well, you can't call it a crime, can you, looking the other way in a café when somebody's nicking your vehicle from a lay-by?' Cullam, closed the porthole, keeping his head turned. 'They paid well, this bad company. Mind you, this fellow jibbed a bit when they offered him two hundred to knock off a bloke who wouldn't

51

play along with them, but not for long. He reckoned he'd a right to nice things the same as this bad company he'd got in with. And why not? We're all equal these days. Share and share alike, this fellow said. So he hung about in a lonely spot one night, just where the other fellow was due to pass by and – well, Bob's your uncle, as you so succinctly put it. He's doing twelve years, as a matter of fact.'

Cullam looked at him, truculently disillusioned.

'I saved up my overtime for that washer,' he said.

'Sure it wasn't McCloy's little dropsy for services rendered? Isn't a man's life worth a hundred and twenty nicker, Cullam? There's a sump on that machine of yours, you know. I can't help asking myself if there's blood and hair and brains in that sump, you know. Oh, you needn't look like that. We could find it. We can take that machine apart this afternoon, and your drains. They're a funny council, Sewingbury. I knew a family – six children in that case there were – they got evicted neck and crop just because they cracked a drain-pipe. Vandalism, the council called it. We'll get your drains up. Cullam, but we're busy right now. I don't reckon we could find the labour to get them put back again.'

'You bastard,' said Cullam.

'I didn't hear that. My hearing's not what it was, but I haven't got one foot in the grave. I'd like to sit down, though. You can take that rubbish off that chair and wipe it, will you?'

Cullam sat on his washing machine, his long legs dangling. Behind the closed door the programme had changed from athletics to wrestling and once more the baby had begun to cry.

'I told you,' said its father, 'I don't know who McCloy is and I don't. I just said that to Charlie to needle him. Always bragging and boasting, he got on my wick.'

Wexford didn't have to absorb any more of the squalor to see what Cullam meant. This house was the very embodiment of sleazy noisy discomfort. It was a discomfort which would have brief pause only while its inhabitants slept and it extended from the top to the lowest level. The man and his wife were weighed down by almost every burden known to the philoprogenitive, ill-paid artisan; their children were miserable, badly brought up and perhaps ill-treated; their home overcrowded, even their animals wretchedly tormented. The parents had neither the character nor the love to make coping and organization tenable. He remembered Charlie Hatton's brand-new flat, the pretty young wife with her smart clothes. These two men did the same sort of job. Or did they?

'If I tell you how it was,' Cullam said, 'you won't believe me.'

'Maybe not, try me.

Cullam put his elbows on his knees and leant forward.

'It was in a café,' he said. 'One of them places where they have rooms for drivers to kip down for the night. Up on the A.1 between Stamford and Grantham. I was coming up to my eleven hours – we're not supposed to drive for more than eleven hours – and I went in and there was Charlie Hatton. I'd seen his lorry in the lay-by. We had a bite to eat and got talking.'

'What load do you carry?'

'Tyres, rubber tyres. While we was having our meal I looked out of the window and there was a fellow there – in the lay-by – sitting in a black car. I don't know why, but I didn't much like the look of him. I said so to Charlie, but all he said was I was like an old woman. He was always saying that to folks. Then he got me and two more drivers to go into his room for a hand of pontoon. He said it was quieter in there, but I couldn't see the lay-by from his room and after a bit I went outside. The fellow in the car was still there.'

'Did you take the number? Could you describe him?'

'I don't know.' Cullam gave him a shifty look. 'I never took the number. I sat in the cab for half an hour and then this fellow went off. Charlie'd said he wanted to phone Lilian and when I come back over the road he was in a phone box. I wanted a light for my fag – I'd run out of matches – so I opened the door of the box and just asked Charlie for a light. Well, I don't reckon he'd heard me coming. "Tell Mr McCloy it's no dice", I heard him say and it was then I said had he got a match? He jumped out of his skin like he'd been stung. "What the hell are you up to", he shouts at me, "interfering with my private phone calls?" He was as white as a sheet.'

'You connected this call with the man in the car?'

'I reckon I did,' Cullam said, 'I did afterwards when I thought about it. My mind went back a couple of months to when Charlie'd asked me if I'd like to make a bit on the side. I wasn't interested and that was all there was. But I never forgot the name McCloy and when Charlie got so cocky in the pub I thought I'd needle him a bit. That's all.'

'When was the café incident, Cullam?'

'Come again?'

'When did you overhear Hatton's phone conversation?'

'Way back in the winter. January, I reckon. Not long after Charlie had his lorry pinched and got hit on the head.'

'All right. That'll do for now, but I may want to talk to you again.'

Wexford went back through the Cullams' living room. The children had disappeared. Mrs Cullam still sat in front of the television, the baby asleep now in her lap, the dog lying across her slippered feet. She moved her head as he crossed the room and for a moment he thought she was going to speak to him. Then he saw that the movement was a mere craning of the neck because for an instant he had obstructed her view of the screen.

Dominic, Barnabas, Samantha and Georgina were sitting on the kerb poking sticks through the drain cover. Wexford wasn't inclined to be sentimental over the Cullams but he couldn't help being touched that they who were poor in everything had been affluent, extravagant and imaginative in one respect. If they never gave their children another thing, they had at least endowed them with names usually reserved to the upper classes.

Dominic, whose face was still coated with food, looked up truculently as he passed and Wexford said, because he couldn't resist it:

'What's the baby called?'

'Jane,' said Dominic simply and without surprise.

When Wexford got home for his tea Clytemnestra wagged

her darning-wool tail at him but she didn't get out of his chair. Wexford scowled at her.

'Where's Sheila?' he asked his wife.

'Dentist's.'

'She never said anything about toothache.'

'You don't go to the dentist's because you've got toothache any more. You go for a check-up. She's having that molar of hers crowned.'

'So I suppose she won't feel up to taking that creature out in the morning. Well, she needn't put it on to me. I've got enough on my plate.'

But Sheila danced in gaily at six o'clock and smiled at her father to show off the triumph of orthodontics.

'There, isn't that great?' To satisfy her Wexford peered into the perfect mouth. 'That filling was getting a bit of a drag,' she said. 'Very shy-making for close-ups. An actress has to think about these things.'

'I bet Bernhardt never bothered about her teeth,' said Wexford to annoy her.

Sheila opened her eyes wide and fixed her father with a precisely constructed look of wistful adoration. 'Did you often see Bernhardt when you were a young man, Pop?' she asked.

Wexford's reply was an ill-tempered snort. He pushed a cup of tea to his daughter who rejected it in favour of cold milk. This she sipped slowly, very conscious of the picture she made in her cream linen dress, her pale hair slightly but attractively disordered, Roman sandal thongs binding her long legs to the knee. Wexford wondered what life held for her. Would she succeed and the future be a succession of triumphs, starring parts, world tours, fame, the increasing terror of growing old? Or would she marry some young idiot like this Sebastian and forget all her aspirations in the possession of two children and a semi? Because he was a father and no longer young he confessed to himself that he would prefer the latter. He wanted her to be safe. Nothing on earth would have made him tell her so.

No such thoughts troubled her, he fancied. Living in the moment, she drank her milk and began to prattle on about her visit to the dentist.

'If I ever settle down . . .' Sheila said this in much the same tone of incredulity as she might have said, 'If I ever die'. 'If I ever settle down, I wouldn't mind a house like his. Not in Kingsmarkham of course. Stratford might be nice or the Cotswolds near Stratford.'

'Within commuting distance,' Wexford put in slyly.

His daughter ignored him. 'One of those black and white houses it is. Terribly ancient and full of atmosphere. Of course, the surgery part's all modern. New copies of *Nova* and *Elle*. I thought that progressive.'

'Thoughtful too,' said Wexford, 'what with everyone in Kingsmarkham being bi-lingual.'

'Your generation just wasn't educated, Pop, but I can tell you I hardly know *anyone* who doesn't read French. Anyway, the old fuddy-duddies can look at the antiques.' Sheila put her glass down and tossed her head. 'Georgeous painting on the walls, and some marvellous glass sculpture.'

Sounds like the police station, Wexford thought. 'And where is this shrine of culture?' he said aloud.

'Ploughman's Lane.'

'He wouldn't be called Vigo would he?'

'Mm-hm, he would.' Sheila sat on the sofa and began painting shiny black lines on her eyelids. 'It's about time you and Mummy stopped going to that dreary old Richardson in the High Street and switched to Mr Vigo.' The most difficult feat of her artistry completed, she started to stroke her lashes with a mascara wand. 'Mr Vigo is an absolute dream. One of those fair-haired characters with a craggy face. Madly sexy.' Wexford winced and hoped she hadn't seen. His daughters were still little girls to him. Who the hell did this craggy fair fellow think he was, projecting his dreamy sexiness at his little girl? 'Of course he's not *young*,' said Sheila serenely.

'All of thirty-five, I daresay. One foot in the grave and the other on a bar of soap.'

'About thirty-five,' said Sheila seriously. She held her eye-lashes up with two fingers to curl them. 'He's got a baby of six months and – something rather tragic. His older child's a mongol. Ghastly, isn't it? It's eight now and Mr Vigo hasn't seen it for years. He and his wife tried and tried to have another one and they did, but it took them all those years. Of course he worships the baby.'

56

'How do you know all this?' Wexford asked. She was a detective's daughter all right. 'I thought you went to get your tooth done, not do a survey.'

'Oh, we had a long talk,' Sheila said airily. 'I don't suppose you can understand, but I'm interested in human nature. If I'm going to be a real actress I'll have to know what makes people tick. I'm getting quite good at summing people up.'

'Bully for you,' said her father sourly. 'I've been trying for forty years and the margin of error's still about eighty per cent.'

Sheila looked at herself in her handbag mirror. 'Mr Vigo's got a very smooth sophisticated manner. Cool, if you know what I mean. I sometimes think dentists have a very interesting relationship with their patients. They've got to be nice, have the right psychological approach, otherwise, you'd never go back to them again, would you? It's such an intimate thing. I mean, can you think of any other situation, Pop, when a man gets so close to a woman except when he's actually making love to her?'

'I sincerely hope nothing like that happened.'

'Oh, Pop . . . I was just saying what it was *like*. I was making a sort of comparison.' Sheila giggled and twisted a strand of hair around one finger. 'Although, when I was going he did give me a sort of squeeze and said I'd got the loveliest mouth he'd ever seen.'

'My God!' said Wexford, getting up. 'If you don't mind what you say to your father, you might remember he's also a detective chief inspector.' He paused and then said, not realizing the effect his words would have, 'I may go along and see this Vigo.'

'Oh, Pop!' Sheila wailed.

'Not because of your lovely mouth, my dear. In pursuance of an enquiry of my own.'

'Well, don't you dare . . .'

All this time Mrs Wexford had been placidly eating ginger biscuits, but now she looked up and said calmly:

'What a silly girl you are. I often think it's a blessing intelligence isn't necessary in the interpretive arts. If you've finished with your face you'd better take that dog out.'

At the word dog, Clytemnestra uncurled herself.

'All right,' said Sheila meekly.

7

They stood under the willow trees, looking at the river. Anyone who didn't know them might have taken them for a couple of businessmen out for a Sunday afternoon stroll.

But almost everyone in Kingsmarkham knew them and knew also by now that this was the spot where Charlie Hatton had been murdered.

'I said we'd have to talk to everyone in the darts club,' said Burden, stopping down at the water's edge, 'and I reckon we have. Funny, isn't it? Pertwee's the only one who could put up with Hatton for a moment, but no one's willing to come out with it. It's always the others who were daggers drawn with him. The one you're talking to is all tolerance and forbearance. The farthest he'll go is to admit a sort of resentment. Does a man do murder because a mate of his riles him in a pub or because he's got more money than he has?'

'He might if he was going to get some of the money,' said Wexford. 'A hundred pounds is a lot to a man like Cullam. We're going to have to watch Cullam, see if he does some big spending in the next few days. I'm not at all happy about the way he washed the clothes he was wearing on Friday night.'

Burden was advancing gingerly across the river, trying not to get his feet wet. He trod on the projecting stones which the water lapped without covering. Then he bent down and said, 'There's your weapon.'

From the bank Wexford followed the direction of his pointing finger. All but one of the stones were furred at their perimeters and partly on their surfaces with green weed.

Burden was pointing to the only one that looked bare, as if until very recently it had lain with its exposed area embedded in the river's gravelly floor. He squatted precariously and lifted the stone in both hands. Then he eased himself to his feet and scrambled back to Wexford.

It was a big stone, not round, but elongated and shaped rather like a mandolin. The side which had lain on the river bed was green and moss-grown and there was nothing about it except for its shape and its anomalous position in the water to show that it might have been used as a lethal weapon. Wexford grasped it in both his hands, raised it high and brought it down hard to meet the empty air. Hatton had been walking along in the dark and someone had waited for him among the willows and the brambles, the stone ready for use. Full of whisky, his thoughts fuddled and far away, Hatton had given warning of his approach. He had been whistling and probably not bothering to tread softly. The stone had been raised high just as Wexford was raising it now but brought down that time on the back of Hatton's skull. Once, twice, more than that? As many times as it took to kill. Then Hatton had rolled into the water. His killer had rifled his wallet before casting the stone into the stream.

Wexford thought all these things and he knew Burden was following his thoughts, matching them, so he didn't bother to say anything. He dropped the stone and it rolled a little before falling into the water with a soft plop.

Across the meadows he could see the flats of the council estate, the sun striking their plate-glass windows and making them blaze as if the whole place was on fire.

'Since we've come so far,' he said, 'we may as well have another chat with Mrs Hatton.'

Her mother was with her and three other people. Jack Pertwee sat on the smart-checked tweed sofa holding the hand of a girl with a monumental pile of black hair and eyelashes like shoe brushes. Mrs Hatton and her mother were both in black, smart unseasonable black relieved with a great deal of showy costume jewellery. The window's suit looked brand-new and Wexford couldn't help wondering if she had actually been out the previous afternoon to buy it. She wore

a white blouse with an ostentatious frilly jabot and a big
paste spray on one lapel. Her stockings were dark and her
shoes, though also apparently new, the outdated, stiletto-
heeled, pointed kind of gleaming black patent. She looked
as if she were about to set off for a provincial cocktail party,
an office party of female executives.

At first Wexford felt a curious distaste and then he thought
about the dead man and what he knew of him. This was the
way Charlie Hatton would have liked his widow to look,
brave, defiant, bedizened. The last thing a cocky little man
like Hatton would want was a kind of spiritual suttee.

He surveyed the rest of the company. Plainly they had
interrupted a mourning tea party. The girl on the sofa must
be the bride whose nuptials Hatton's death had deferred.
And the other man?

'My brother, Mr Bardsley,' said Mrs Hatton. 'Him and
Mum came to keep me company. This gentleman is Mr
Pertwee.'

'We've met,' said Wexford graciously.

'And Miss Thompson,' said Mrs Hatton. She spoke in a
low dutiful voice. Her eyes were swollen under the thick
green and black make-up. 'They were all very fond of Charlie. Would you like a cup of tea? You can if you want. You're
welcome.'

'We won't, thanks, Mrs Hatton.'

'Well, sit down then, there's plenty of room.' She said it
proudly, indicating the several empty chairs. They were good
chairs, upholstered and cared for, not the uncomfortable
dining seats with hard backs a less affluent hostess would be
obliged to offer latecomers. Looking at the branched hanging
lamp of teak and smoky glass, the velvet curtains and the
big colour television set, Wexford decided that Hatton had
done his wife proud. Cullam and he were both lorry drivers,
both lived in council accommodation, but that was all they
had in common. He glanced at Bardsley, the brother, a fair
rabbity man, like his sister but less well-favoured, and he
observed his suit. It was very likely his best suit – today of
all days he would surely wear his best suit – but it was a
cheap off-the-peg affair.

'Please forgive me, Mrs Hatton, if I ask a few routine
questions,' he said. She gave him a pleased earnest nod. 'You

and Mr Hatton were in business together, I understand, Mr Bardsley?'

'That's right.'

'Was it a full partnership?'

Bardsley put his teacup down and said in a melancholy voice, 'I was thinking of taking him into partnership, but business hasn't been that good lately. As it was, he just worked for me.'

'Would you mind telling me what wages you paid him?'

'Well, I don't know . . . I don't rightly like to.'

'Of course he don't,' Jack Pertwee suddenly interrupted belligerently. 'What's it got to do with what happened on Friday?'

'That's right, Jack,' murmured the girl and she squeezed his hand.

'You can see Charlie did all right for himself. You've only got to look around you.'

'Don't make trouble, Jack,' Mrs Hatton said with that peculiar intense control of hers. 'The officers are only doing what they have to.' She fingered her brooch uneasily. 'Charlie usually brought home a bit over twenty pounds a week. That's right, isn't it, Jim?'

Jim Bardsley looked unhappy about it and his voice became aggressive. 'I've been lucky to make that much myself lately,' he said. 'Charlie was one of the sort that make a little go a long way. I reckon he was careful.'

Marilyn Thompson tossed her head and a lock of hair drifted from the elaborate structure. 'He wasn't mean, anyway,' she flared, 'if that's what you mean by careful. There's not many men who aren't even relations that'd give someone a record player for a wedding present.'

'I never said he was mean, Marilyn.'

'It makes me sick. What you want to do is find who killed him.' The girl's hands trembled and she clenched them. 'Give us a cig, Jack.' Her hands enclosed Pertwee's wrist as he held the lighter and they were no more steady than his. 'You lot,' she muttered, 'you lot don't reckon nothing to a working man. If he hasn't got a nice home you call him a layabout.' She glared at Wexford, pushing back her hair. 'And if he's got things like your class take for granted you jump right on him, say he must have nicked them. Class, class, class,' she said, tears trembling on the brush-bristle lashes. 'That's all you think about.'

'Wait till the revolution comes,' said Bardsley nastily.

'Oh, shut up, the pair of you,' Mrs Hatton said shrilly. She turned to Wexford, her controlled dignity returning. 'My husband did overtime,' she said, 'and he had his side lines.'

Side lines, Wexford thought. He got a little overtime and he made it go a long way. The man had colour television, false teeth worth two hundred pounds; he gave his friend a record player for a wedding present. Wexford had seen that glass and teak lamp in a Kingsmarkham shop and noted it had been priced at twenty-five pounds, one and a quarter times Hatton's weekly wage. When he was killed he had had a hundred pounds on him.

'If he's got things like your class take for granted,' the girl had said, 'you say he must have nicked them.' Curious, really, Wexford reflected, watching her huddled now in the crook of Pertwee's arm. Of course she was very young, probably got a Communist shop steward for a father, and doubtless went about sneering at people better-educated and better-spoken than herself. It was an aggressive type that had even reached Kingsmarkham, a type that talked pacifism and the rights of man and brotherly love without the energy or courage to do anything that might bring these desirable conditions nearer.

And yet he said nothing to provoke her outburst. Neither for that matter had Bardsley beyond hinting that Hatton had been prudent. Had she risen to this intangible slight bait because she knew Hatton's wealth had been dishonestly come by? If she knew it, green and uncouth as she was, Pertwee would know it also. Everyone in this room but Burden and himself might know it. Not for the first time he reflected on the power of grief. It is the perfect unassailable defence. Pertwee had already employed it the previous morning effectively to terminate interrogation. Mrs Hatton, even more expertly, kept it under a piteous control that only a brute would have the brashness to disregard. She was moving about the room now, balancing painfully but stoically on her high heels, taking empty cups and plates from each of her guests with a gentle murmur for every one of them. Wexford took in the looks that passed to her from each of her visitors, her mother's merely solicitous, Pertwee's indicative of deep affection, Bardsley's shifty, while the thwarted bride leaned forward, stuck out her chin and nodded her utter committed partisanship.

'Did your husband have a bank account, Mrs Hatton?' Burden asked as she passed his chair.

The sun was full on her face, showing every stroke and grain of make-up, but at the same time driving expression from it. She nodded, 'At the Midland,' she said.

'I'd like to see his paying-in book.'

'What for?'

The truculent harsh voice was Pertwee's. Wexford ignored him and followed the widow to the sideboard from a drawer of which she took a long cream-coloured book. He handed it to Burden and said, apparently inconsequentially:

'When did your husband get his false teeth, Mrs Hatton?'

Pertwee's muttered 'Bloody nosey-parker' made her flinch a little and throw a desperate glance over her shoulder. 'He'd always had them. Had them since he was twenty' she said.

'This present set?'

'Oh, no. They were new. He went to Mr Vigo for them about a month back.'

Nodding, Wexford eyed the paying-in book over Burden's shoulder and what he saw astonished him far more than any of Hatton's prodigality. Some three-quarters of all the slips in the book had been torn out and with the exception of three, all the stubs had been torn too.

On the most recent remaining stub the date was April and on that occasion Hatton had paid into his bank account the modest sum of five and fourpence.

'Fourth dividend on the pools that was,' Mrs Hatton said with a miserable gulp.

The other two stubs were filled in each with amounts of two pounds.

'Mrs Hatton,' he said, beckoning her into a corner. 'The purpose of these stubs in a paying-in book is for the holder to have a record of the amount of money he had deposited in his bank. Can you suggest to me why Mr Hatton tore them out? They must have been filled in at the bank either by Mr Hatton himself or else by the cashier who was attending to him.'

'It's a mystery to me. Charlie never talked about money to me. He always said . . .' She gulped again and a tear trickled through the make-up. 'He always said, "Don't worry your head about that. When we got married I promised I'd give you everything you want and so I will. You name it, you can have it". ' She bent her head and began to sob. 'He was one in a million was Charlie. He'd have got me the moon out of the sky if I'd wanted it.' The girl Marilyn got up and put her arms around her friend. 'Oh, Charlie, Charlie . . . !'

The drawer was open, Hatton's cheque book exposed. Wexford leafed through it and saw that Hatton had paid twenty-five pounds for the lamp on May 22nd. Thirty pounds had been paid to Lucrece Ltd., High Street, Kingsmarkham (his wife's wedding outfit?), and another thirty in the same week, the last week of May, to Excelsior Electrics, Stowerton (Pertwee's record player?).

Then came three blank stubs, lastly one filled for fifty pounds cash. There was no stub for Vigo, the dentist. Hatton must have paid for his teeth in cash.

He put the books back in the drawer and stood waiting for Mrs Hatton to recover. Her mother and brother had departed to the kitchen from where Wexford could hear their muted whisperings and the funereally careful clink of cups.

The widow's eye make-up had transferred itself to Marilyn Thompson's handkerchief. 'I keep breaking down,' she said. 'I can't seem to stop myself.'

'Yeah, but just reckon what you've been through, love.'

'I don't know what I'd do without you two.'

Pertwee said nothing but his baleful pugnacious look was absurd in its intensity and Wexford was almost embarrassed. He said lightly, 'Does the name McCloy mean anything to you, Mr Pertwee?'

That it meant nothing, less than nothing, to Mrs Hatton he was sure at once. Of Pertwee and the girl he was less certain. The latter's lower lip stuck out and her eyes flickered. For an instant she was a primitive creature looking for a hole to hide in. Pertwee had reddened, possibly only with anger at Wexford's persistence.

'Sounds Irish,' was all he said.

'Doesn't it also sound familiar?'

'Not to me, I don't know any McCloy. Never heard of him.'

'Strange then that you should have discussed this Mr McCloy with your friends in the Dragon on Friday. Is he a local man?'

'I told you I'd never heard of him.' Pertwee bit his lip and looked down at his knees. Wexford watched him feel for the girl's hand, but she was occupied with Mrs Hatton, dabbing at her face and smoothing her hair. Forsaken, deserted, the hand came up to Pertwee's brow and pushed into the greasy black waves. 'Can't you leave us alone now?' he pleaded and Wexford felt impotently that once again the man was enclosing himself within the unimpregnable defence of grief. 'I never knew what went on on the lorries,' he said. 'I wasn't Charlie's only friend. He had hundreds of friends. Ask Jim Bardsley, ask Cullam.' Pertwee's eyes were glazed and dull. 'Let someone else do dirt on his memory.'

Jim Bardsley had an apron tired round his waist. He moved gingerly about the kitchen, putting away crockery, as if he were afraid his touch might damage or contaminate the pristine glory of its equipment. The Hatton flat and the Cullam house had one thing in common, an automatic washing machine. Mrs Hatton had plenty besides mixers, electric tin-openers, a steam iron as well as the huge scarlet refrigerator and the cooker with eye-level grill.

'You transport this kind of stuff, don't you, Mr Bardsley?' Burden asked. 'I suppose Mr Hatton got it wholesale.'

'I daresay,' Bardsley said cagily.

Irons, electric fires and so on, was that the load you lost when Mr Hatton's lorries were hi-jacked?' Bardsley nodded unhappily. 'Doubtless you were insured?'

'Not the second time, not in March when they knocked it off at Stamford. I had to stand the loss myself.' Bardsley untied his apron and hung up the tea cloth that appropriately enough in this flat, was a large linen facsimile of a pound note. 'Set me back, I can tell you. I reckon poor old Charlie was glad I hadn't taken him into partnership. Mind you, they found the lorry both times. It wasn't damaged, just the stuff gone, that's all. That second time Charlie'd pulled into a lay-by and gone to sleep at the wheel. The villains didn't harm him, thank God. Just tied him up and put a gag in his mouth.'

'But he was injured on the previous occasion?'

'Had a bit of concussion,' Bardsley said. 'There wasn't any mark to show, bar a bit of a bruise.'

'Ever heard of the name McCloy,' Mr Bardsley?'

'It doesn't ring a bell,' said Bardsley and Burden believed him. 'Mind you,' he added, 'I've seen my own stuff flogged of in the market here. Known it was mine but couldn't prove it. You know what them stallholders are, up to all the tricks.' He scratched his head. 'I was a bit too nosy that time and I haven't seen the stall here since.'

'If you do, Mr Bardsley, come straight to us. Don't argue about it, come straight to us.'

'O.K.' said Bardsley, but without hope. Burden left him contemplating the printed tea cloth as if, were it possible to transmute it to paper, reduce its size and multiply it manifold, he would be a happy man.

'First of all,' said Wexford, 'I'd like to know exactly how much there is in the account.'

The bank manager became pedantic and precise, 'Exactly six hundred and nine pounds, four and sevenpence.'

'I take it that's a current account? He didn't have anything on deposit, did he?'

'Unfortunately, no. When Mr Hatton began paying large sums in I did attempt to persuade him to open one, the rate of interest being so desirable, you understand. Five per cent, as you doubtless know. But Mr Hatton wouldn't. "I'm one for the ready, Mr Five Per Cent", he said to me in his amusing way.' The manager sighed. 'A very likable, amusing man, poor Mr Hatton. One of the best.'

That's a matter of opinion, Wexford thought. 'What were these large sums?'

'Really, it seems most unorthodox, but if you insist.' A large ledger was opened and horn-rimmed glasses set on the manager's nose. 'Mr Hatton opened this account in November of last year,' he began, 'with the sum of one hundred pounds.' Payment for the first lorry hi-jacking, Wexford thought, a nice little bit of compensation for his concussion. 'Nothing was added to it until January when two separate payments of fifty pounds were made.' Two more hi-jackings, set up by Hatton, who had kept the drivers occupied at pontoon in a carmen's café? Wexford felt rather pleased. All the pieces in his puzzle were falling neatly into place. 'Then in March, March 15th, a further hundred was paid in, but no more after that until May 22nd.'

The manager paused and Wexford made a mental note to find out whether any lorries had been hi-jacked on Hatton's A.1 route during the penultimate week of May. Evidently Hatton got a hundred when he was personally involved, fifty when it was someone else to be knocked on the head and left in a ditch. Such a likable, amusing man!

'How much?' he said coldly.

The manager readjusted his glasses.

'Er . . . let me see. . . . Good heavens. No, it isn't an error. Really, I wasn't aware . . . As a matter of fact, Mr Hatton paid five hundred pounds into his current account on May 22nd.'

And what in God's name, Wexford thought flabbergasted, did Hatton have in his power to do that was worth five hundred pounds? What could a lorry be carrying that its load was so valuable to a thief as to make Hatton's a feasible reward? There would have to be several men involved in the racket, McCloy himself, two or three men to commandeer the lorry and incapacitate the driver as well as Hatton. McCloy would want the lion's share of whatever the load realized and if Hatton, a mere decoy, got five hundred, the three henchmen would be worth at least five hundred apiece. Four times five and what for McCloy? A thousand, two thousand? That meant a cargo to the value of four or five thousand pounds. At least. For McCloy wouldn't get anything like the cargo's true value in his underworld market.

Well, it should be easy enough to find out. A hi-jacking of that magnitude wouldn't be likely to be quickly forgotten by the police in whose district it had occurred. He couldn't understand why he didn't recall it himself. It must have made front-page news. The last week but one in May, he repeated to himself. Presumably they'd never done anyone for the job. They certainly hadn't done Hatton.

'And after that?' he said calmly.

'Regular payments of fifty pounds a week over the past six weeks.'

Wexford checked an explosion of astonishment. 'But no more large sums?'

'No more large sums,' said the bank manager.

It was obvious what had happened. Hatton had done his jobs for McCloy and the last one had been something spectacular. So spectacular – perhaps involving great injury or death. Why the hell couldn't he *remember* it? That Hatton, finding some weak spot in McCloy's armour, had commenced to blackmail him. A lump sum down on May 22nd and then fifty pounds a week.

It must have been nice while it lasted, Wexford reflected amorally. What was more exhilarating to a poor man than a sudden influx of unearned cash, springing from a seemingly limitless fertile source? How could such a one as Hatton restrain himself from making a splash? It came into Wexford's mind that money metaphors often have to do with water, gushing, springing, and that business men talk of liquidity and cash flow.

He came to the Kingsbrook bridge and paused for a moment on the parapet, listening to the soft suck and chatter of the stream. Everlastingly the Kingsbrook rattled over its stones, hindered here and there by tree roots or a growth of weed, but ultimately unimpeded, always moving, glittering in the sun as if gold pieces gleamed beneath its ripples.

By the water's edge Hatton had met his death. Because a source less abundant and less generous than this river had dried up?

8

'There are only three McCloys in this district,' Burden said on the following morning. 'I've seen them all and they struck me as perfectly ordinary honest citizens. A couple in Pomfret are brothers. One's a teacher at the comprehensive school and the other's lab assistant. James McCloy, who lives here in town, runs a very small unsuccessful sort of decorating business.'

'Small fry?' said Wexford, still thinking of his fish and water metaphors.

'Very small. No sign of any more money than is needed to keep the wolf from the door. Still, I've been through the trade directory and come up with something a bit more hopeful. There's a firm in London, in Deptford, calling themselves McCloy & Son Ltd., and what d'you think their line of business is?'

'*Etonne-moi*,' said Wexford after the manner of Diaghilev to Cocteau. Burden looked at him suspiciously, so he said with amused impatience, 'I don't know, Mike, and I'm not in the mood for this suspense stuff.'

'They spray the laminated surfaces on to small electrical equipment.'

'Do they, indeed?'

'I've put through a call to London and I'm waiting for them to ring me up. If there's anything at all promising I'm off to Deptford.'

'While you're waiting,' said Wexford, 'you might get on to Stamford police, Stamford in Lincolnshire. I'd like to know just what did happen when Hatton's lorry was hi-jacked on the 15th of March and if they've got any McCloys in their district.'

'Stamford, sir? Isn't there a bridge there where poor old Harold won a victory before coming a cropper at Hastings?'

'Wrong one,' said Wexford. 'This is a charming little ancient town of grey stone which the A.1 now fortunately by-passes. Shakespeare mentions it. "How a good yoke of bullocks at Stamford fair?" You might also ask them if they had a big hi-jacking at the end of May. It might not have been near them, of course, but it was so big they'll likely have heard of it.'

The pretty toy of a lift had borne his weight serenely on four occasions by this time and he no longer felt much trepidation on entering it. As it sank obediently to the ground floor, he thought again about McCloy's mysterious feat of modern highwaymanship. He had checked the file of that period and found nothing. Now he too was waiting for a phone call, promised for the afternoon. Scotland Yard would enlighten him when they had consulted their records. But how could it have escaped his knowledge and the newspapers?

Sergeants Camb and Martin were gossiping in the foyer when he emerged from the lift. He gave a low cough.

'Just discussing this Fanshawe inquest, sir,' said Camb respectfully.

'I thought it had been adjourned.'

'The coroner wants to resume now, but I've told him we've nothing to go on. I'm all for waiting till Mrs Fanshawe perks up a bit.'

'In a bad way, is she?' said Martin. Like an old woman in a supermarket queue, Wexford thought derisively.

'That accident's turned her brain, I reckon. She's no more fit to appear in court than she was six weeks ago. God knows, I can sympathize. Her husband's dead and her only child. It's not funny, I can tell you, trying to tell a sick woman her daughter's dead when she keeps insisting she's alive and in Germany.'

'Maybe she is alive,' said Wexford, more from a mischievous desire to throw a spanner in the works than from conviction. He was sick and tired of the name Fanshawe. He didn't burden the uniformed branch with his problems and he didn't see why he should have to listen to Camb's maunderings. 'Maybe it was someone else in the car.'

'Oh, no, sir; the aunt identified the girl.'

'Well, it's your problem, Sergeant. You're the coroner's officer.' Wexford added annoyingly, 'We all have our troubles and we must deal with them as best we can.' He swung open the door and said over his shoulder, 'I don't know what you think you're doing, Martin, distracting the coroner's officer in the execution of his duty. If you want a job just run upstairs and say McCloy to Mr Burden. I'm away to the dentist myself.'

'Not in much pain, sir, I hope?'

'You're behind the times,' said Wexford, chuckling. 'You don't go to the dentist these days because you've got toothache, you go for a check-up.'

It was too fine a day for the car. Wexford crossed the road to Grover's newspaper shop and turned into York Street. In the display window of Joy Jewels the sun set the rhinestone ropes and little gilt collarets ablaze, and the plane tree leaves shadowed the pavement in damask tablecloth patterns. After the petrol station and the little houses, in one of which George Carter lived, were left behind, the street petered out into a country lane. Such was the incline of the hills at this point and the arrangement of the trees that, looking straight ahead, nothing that was not absolutely pastoral could be seen. A stranger to the district, coming over the brow of the hill, would have stopped astonished and perhaps a little peeved to see Ploughman's Lane lying beneath him.

Not that there was anything to dismay the aesthetic purist. Through the centuries about twenty-five houses had been built in Ploughman's Lane, first of all for the minor gentry, the widows and kinsmen, for instance, of the lord of the manor; in more recent times equally large and widely spaced dwellings had been put up for the professional class.

From where he stood Wexford could see roofs, a yellow patch of new thatch on the far left, red tiles some fifty yards from it, then the pinnacled and turreted grey slate so dear to the heart of the Victorian bourgeoisie; next, half lost among the spread arms of a black cedar, the pinned-down tarred fabric that roofed a split-level ranch bungalow.

He descended briskly, glad of the shade the thickening

71

trees afforded. A Bentley swam out from behind the ranch house's tamarisk hedge, accelerated arrogantly and, passing him, drove him back flat against the hedge.

'And if I should chance to run over a cad,'

Wexford quoted,

'I can pay for the damage if ever so bad.
So pleasant it is to have money, heigh ho . . .'

God Almighty, he was getting as bad as Maurice Cullam! He had noted the number of the Bentley. Very nice cars they all had around here. There was another Bentley outside the grey slate Gothic place with a smart yellow Cortina snuggling up against it. Married bliss, thought Wexford, grinning to himself. Even the wives' cars were sizable. No minis and no second- or third-hand jalopies. But women would never be equal, he reflected, pleased to have discovered a new profundity, until the day came when men stopped thinking it natural that their wives should always have the smaller car. And they always did, no matter how rich they were; no matter, come to that, if the wives were richer or bigger than the husbands. He tried to think of a wife who had a larger car than her husband's and he couldn't think of one. Not that he particularly wanted women to be equal. As far as that went, he was quite satisfied with the *status quo*. But to have lighted upon a new yet universal truth amused him and he went on thinking about it until he came to Jolyon Vigo's house.

The tall dark girl got off the London train and as she passed through the barrier at Stowerton station she asked the woman collecting tickets where she could get a taxi.

'There's only one. But he won't be busy at this time of day. You might be lucky. There you are! I can just see him, waiting on the rank.'

She watched the girl march briskly down the steps. Very few women as smart and cocksure as that one arrived at Stowerton station, even from London, even in the height of summer. The ticket collector, who had just had a new perm, thought the girl's geometrically cut and excessively short hair awful. It made her look like a boy, or how boys used to look in the days when men had some self-respect and went to the barber's. Flat-chested and skinny too, like a stick all the way down. You had to admit, though, that that kind made a good clothes prop. The suit she was wearing was the colour and texture of sacking, a foreign-looking suit somehow with those buttoned pockets, but the ticket collector was willing to bet it hadn't cost a penny less than forty guineas. It hardly seemed fair that a kid of – what would she be? Twenty-three? Twenty-four? – had forty quid to throw away on a bit of sacking. Money talks all right, she thought. It was money that gave that snooty lift of the chin, too, that master-ful stance and walk and that stuck-up voice.

The girl approached the taxi and said to the driver:

'Will you take me to Stowerton Royal Infirmary, please?'

When they got to the hospital she opened her brown leather bag to pay him and he noticed that, as well as the English money, she had some funny-looking foreign notes in her wallet. He half hoped she would give him one of them by mistake so that he could make a scene, but she didn't. He summed her up as a sharp little piece with a head on her shoulders. She was a stranger to the place but she knew where she was going. As he reversed, he saw her march confidently into the porter's office.

'Can you direct me to the private wing?'

'Straight down the drive, madam, and you'll see a notice with an arrow.' The porter called her madam because she had asked the way to the private wing. If she had asked for Ward Five he would have told her morning visiting in the public wards was forbidden and he might, because he was feeling benevolent, have called her love. On the other hand, he couldn't imagine anyone like this ever wanting a public ward. She was madam, all right, a proper little madam.

Nurse Rose was late with her bed-making on Tuesday morn-ing. She had seen to Mrs Goodwin by nine o'clock and stopped for a chat and a bit of buttering-up. You were half-way to being a lady's maid with these private patients and if they wanted you to paint their fingernails while they told you their life histories you couldn't choose but obey. Just the same, she would have been well ahead but for those police-men turning up again and wanting to ask poor Mrs Fan-shawe more questions. Of course she couldn't make Mrs Fanshawe's bed while they were poking about and it was nearly twelve before she managed to get the poor deluded creature into a chair and the sheets whipped off.

'It might take a letter a week to get to Germany, mightn't it?' said Mrs Fanshawe, taking her rings off and amusing herself by making them flash in the sunlight right into Nurse Rose's eyes.

'Weeks and weeks,' said Nurse Rose, blinking. 'You don't want to worry about that.'

'I should have sent a telegram. I think I'll get you to send one for me.'

Once bitten, twice shy, thought Nurse Rose. She wasn't even going to humour Mrs Fanshawe any more. Stick her neck out and her life would be a succession of errands for Mrs Fanshawe, running about the town sending crazy mess-ages to a girl who didn't exist.

'Would you like me to brush your hair?' she asked, pum-melling the pillows.

'Thank you very much, my dear. You're a good girl.'

'Back into bed then. Ooh! You're as light as a feather. Don't leave those lovely rings on the table, now.'

Nurse Rose had really been very helpful, Mrs Fanshawe thought. She didn't seem or look very intelligent, but she must be. She was the only one who didn't keep up this nonsense about Nora being dead. And how she envied her those rings! Funny little thing. . . . When Nora came she would get her to run up to the flat and root out that paste thing she'd once bought on a whim at Selfridges. It wasn't worth more than thirty shillings, but Nurse Rose wouldn't know that and she decided she would definitely give it to Nurse Rose.

She lay back comfortably while her hair was brushed.

'While you're getting my lunch,' she said, 'I'll think how I'm going to word my telegram. Oh, and you might take my sister's card away. It's getting on my nerves.'

Nurse Rose was glad to escape. She came out of the room, pulling her bag of soiled linen, and because she wasn't looking where she was going, almost cannoned into a tall dark girl.

'Can you tell me where I can find Mrs Dorothy Fanshawe?'

'She's in there,' said Nurse Rose. She had never seen anything like the shoes the girl was wearing. They were of brown calf with a copper beech leaf on the instep and their shape was so strange and outlandish that Nurse Rose decided they must be the extreme of fashion. Nothing like them had ever been seen in Stowerton, nor, for that matter, Nurse Rose believed, in London. 'Mrs Fanshawe's just going to have her lunch,' she said.

'I don't suppose it matters if that's held up for ten minutes.'

Not to you, Nurse Rose thought indignantly, whoever you may be. But she couldn't let those desirable shoes vanish without any comment and she said impulsively, 'I hope you don't mind my asking, but I do think your shoes are super. Where did you get them?'

'Nobody minds a compliment,' said the girl coldly. 'They were made in Florence but I bought them in Bonn.'

'Bonn? Bonn's in Germany, isn't it? Ooh, you can't be! You can't be Nora. You're dead!'

Earlier that morning Wexford had quoted Justice Shallow and now, as he contemplated Jolyon Vigo's house, he thought that this was just the sort of place Shallow might have lived in. It would have been a mature house already in Shakespeare's time, a 'black and white' house, timbered, solid, so perfect a place to live in that it seemed in advance to confer upon its owner grace and taste and superiority. A climbing rose with yellow satiny flowers spread across the black striped gables and nestled against the tudor roses, carved long ago by some craftsman on every square inch of oak. On either side of the front path a knot garden had been planted with low hedges and tufts of tiny blossom. It was so neat, so unnatural in a way, that Wexford had the notion the flowers had been embroidered on the earth.

A coach-house of slightly later vintage served as a double garage. It had a small belvedere and a vertical sundial under its pediment. The garage doors were open – a single untidy touch – and within Wexford saw two cars. Again it amused him to note the general application of what he was beginning to think of as Wexford's Law. A woman was in the act of opening the door of a pale blue Minor. She slammed it and, carrying a child in her arms, squeezed between the small vehicle and the huge, finned Plymouth, dragonfly blue, that stood a foot from it.

The phrase 'a woman with a child' somehow suggested a peasant and a shawled baby. Eyeing her, Wexford thought that to say a lady with an infant would be better.

'What d'you want?' she said in the sharp high-pitched voice of the local gentry. Before she could add, as she was evidently about to, that she never bought anything at the door, he announced himself hurriedly and asked for her husband.

'He's in the surgery. You go round by the pleached walk.'

Marvelling that anyone could say this without a trace of self-consciousness or humour, Wexford looked her up and down. She was a plain young woman, thin and dark with a worn face. She put the child into a pram and wheeled it down the path. The boy was big and handsome, blue-eyed and fair-headed. He looked as though by being born he had sapped his mother's strength and left her a used-up husk. Wexford was reminded of a butterfly, fresh and lusty, that has escaped from a dried chrysalis.

He was not precisely sure what a pleached walk was, but when he came upon it there was no mistaking it and, smiling to himself, he descended a flagged step and passed into a green tunnel. The trees whose branches met and interwove above his head were apples and pears and already the young green fruit hung abundantly. The walk led to some greenhouses and what had once been a stable, now converted into a surgery. Amid all this sylvan glory the notice giving the dentist's working hours struck a discordant note. Wexford opened a latched horse-box door and entered the waiting room.

A pretty girl in a white coat came out to him and he reminded her of his appointment. Then, having no inclination for *Elle* or *Nova*, he sat down and viewed the room.

It was a funny place for Charlie Hatton to have found himself in and Wexford wondered why he hadn't attended the dentist in the town. On these walls were none of the usual posters bidding young mothers to drink milk in pregnancy and bring their toddlers for a twice-yearly check-up. Nor was there any notice explaining how to get dental treatment on the National Health Service. You couldn't imagine anyone sitting here with a handkerchief pressed to a swollen jaw.

The walls were papered in a Regency stripe and the one or two pieces of upholstered furniture looked like genuine antiques. The curtains were of dark chintz patterned with medallions. A small chandelier caught the sun and made rainbow spot patterns on the ceiling. Wexford thought the place was just like the sitting room of a person of taste. There were dozens like it in Kingsmarkham. But this was just a dentist's waiting room and it made him wonder what the rest of the house would be like. He was in for a surprise. He was admiring a stylish flower arrangement, observing how cunningly a spray of jasmine had been made to tremble half in, half out of the vase and trail against the console table, when the girl came back and told him Mr Vigo would see him now.

Wexford followed her into the surgery.

There was nothing out of the ordinary here, just the usual chairs and trays of instruments and contraptions of tubes and clamps and wires. Ice-blue blinds were lowered to keep out the noonday sun.

Vigo was standing beside one of the windows, fingering some instruments in a tray, and when Wexford came in he didn't look up. Wexford smiled dryly to himself. This air of being always overworked, preoccupied by esoteric matters was, he knew, characteristic of some doctors and dentists. It was part of the mystique. In a moment Vigo would glance round, show surprise and make some swift apology for being engaged on matters beyond a policeman's comprehension.

The dentist had a fine leonine head, the hair fair and abundant. His jaw was strong and prominent, the mouth thin. One day when he was old this would be a nutcracker face but that was a long way off. He seemed to be counting and when he had finished he turned and reacted as Wexford had expected he would.

'Do forgive me, Chief Inspector. A little matter that couldn't be left. I understand you want to talk to me about the late Mr Hatton. I've no more patients until after lunch, so shall we go into the house?'

He took off his white coat. Under it he was wearing a slate-blue suit in tussore, the cut, material and colour not quite masculine enough for his height, and heavily muscled chest. He had the figure of a rugby international and he made Wexford, who was just on six feet, feel short.

Wexford followed him through the pleached walk and they entered the house by a glazed garden door. It was like stepping into a museum. Wexford hesitated, dazzled. He had heard of Chinese rooms, heard of Chinese Chippendale, but he had never seen a room furnished in the style. The brilliance of its colours turned the remembered garden outside into monochrome. His feet sank into a carpet whose blues and creams evoked a summer sky and, at Vigo's behest, he lowered himself uneasily into a chair with a yellow satin seat and legs of rearing dragons. The dentist moved with apparent carelessness between tables and cabinets loaded with china and jade and stood, a faint smile on his thin lips, under a long picture of red fish painted on silk.

'I don't know what you can have to ask me about Mr Hatton's teeth,' he said. 'He didn't have his own teeth.'

Wexford had come to talk business and yet for a moment he could not. Talk of false teeth in this setting? His eye fell on a set of chessmen ranged on a table in a far corner. They were two armies, one of ivory, one of red jade, and the pawns were on horseback, the white armed with spears, the red with arrows. One of the red knights on a panoplied charger had a contemporary Western face, a raw sharp face which called to mind absurdly that of Charlie Hatton. It grinned at Wexford, seeming to prompt him.

'We know that, Mr Vigo,' he said, wrenching his eyes away and fixing them on an eggshell thin service, made to contain jasmine tea. 'What surprises us is that a man of his means should have such superb false ones.'

Vigo had an attractive, rather boyish laugh. He checked it with a shake of his head. 'A tragedy, wasn't it? Have you any idea who could have . . . ? No, I mustn't ask that.'

'I've no objection to your asking, but no, we've no idea yet. I've come to you because I want you to tell me everything

78

you can about Mr Hatton with particular reference to anything you may know about the source of his income.'

'I only know that he drove a lorry.' Vigo was still savouring with pride and joy his caller's astonishment. 'But yes, I see what you mean. It surprised me too. I don't know much but I'll tell you what I can.' He moved to a cabinet whose door handles were the long curved tails of dragons. 'Will you join me in a pre-luncheon sherry?'

'I don't think so, thank you.'

'Pity.' Vigo didn't press him but poured a glass of Manzanilla for himself and sat down by the window. It gave on to a shadowed court whose centrepiece was an orrery on a stone plinth. 'Mr Hatton made an appointment with me at the end of May. He had never been a patient of mine before.'

The end of May. On the 22nd of May Hatton had paid five hundred pounds into his bank account, his share, no doubt, of the mysterious and elusive hi-jacking haul.

'I can tell you the precise date, if you like. I looked it up before you came. Tuesday, 21st May. He telephoned me at lunchtime on that day and by a fluke I had a cancellation, so I was able to see him almost immediately. He'd had dentures since he was twenty, very bad ill-fitting ones, by the way. They made him self-conscious and he wanted a new set. I asked him why he'd lost his own teeth and he said the cause had been pyorrhoea. Knowing a little of his circumstances by this time – at any rate, I knew what his job was – I asked him if he realized this would involve him in considerable expense. He said that money was no object – those were his actual words – and he wanted the most expensive teeth I could provide. We finally arrived at a figure of two hundred and fifty pounds and he was perfectly agreeable.'

'You must have been surprised.'

Vigo sipped his sherry reflectively. He touched one of the chessmen, a crenellated castle, caressing it with pride. 'I was astonished. And I don't mind telling you I was a little uneasy.' He didn't elaborate on this unease but Wexford thought he must have been worried lest the two hundred and fifty wasn't forthcoming. 'However, the teeth were made and fitted at the beginning of June. About a month ago it would have been.'

'How did Mr Hatton pay you?'

79

'Oh, in cash, he paid me on the same day, insisted on doing so. The money was in five-pound notes which I'm afraid I paid straight into my bank. Chief Inspector, I understand what you're getting at, but I couldn't ask the man where he got his money from, could I? Just because he came here in his working clothes and I knew he drove a lorry . . . I couldn't.'

'Did you ever see him again?'

'He came back once for a check. Oh, and a second time to tell me how pleased he was.'

Again Wexford was becoming bemused by the colours, by the seductive spectrum that caught and held his eye wherever he looked. He bent his head and concentrated on his own big ugly hands. 'On any of his visits,' he said stolidly, 'did he ever mention someone called McCloy?'

'I don't think so. He spoke about his wife and his brother-in-law that he was in business with.' Vigo paused and searched his memory. 'Oh, and he mentioned a friend of his that was getting married. I was supposed to be interested because the chap had sometimes been here doing electrical repairs. Hatton said something about buying him a record player for a wedding present. The poor fellow's dead and I don't know whether I ought to say this . . .'

'Say on, Mr Vigo.'

'Well, he did rather harp on what a lot of money he spent. I don't want to sound a snob but I thought it vulgar. He only mentioned his wife to tell me he'd just bought her something new to wear and he tried to give me the impression his brother-in-law was something of a poor fish because he couldn't make ends meet.'

'But the brother-in-law was in the same line of business.'

'I know. That struck me. Mr Hatton did say he had a good many irons in the fire and that sometimes he brought off a big deal. But frankly, if I thought about that at all, I imagined he had some side line, painting people's houses perhaps or cleaning windows.'

'Window cleaners don't speak of bringing off big deals, Mr Vigo.'

'I suppose not. The fact is I don't have many dealings with people of Mr Hatton's . . .' Vigo paused. Wexford was sure he had been about to say 'class'. 'Er, background,' said the

80

dentist. 'Of course you're suggesting the side lines weren't legitimate and this may be hindsight, but now I look back Mr Hatton did perhaps occasionally have a shady air about him when he talked of them. But really it was only the merest nuance.'

'Well, I won't trouble you any further.' Wexford got up. It must be his over-sensitive suspicious mind that made him see a relieved relaxing of those muscled shoulders. Vigo opened the carved oak door for him.

'Let me see you out, Chief Inspector.' The hall was a largish square room, its flagged floor dotted with thin soft rugs, and every inch of burnished ancient wood caught the sunlight. There were Blake prints on the walls, the Inferno scenes, Nebuchadnezzar with his eagle's talons, the naked Newton with his golden curls. Stripped of his blue tussore, Vigo himself might look rather like that, Wexford thought. 'I had the pleasure of a visit from your daughter the other day,' he heard the dentist say. 'What a very lovely girl she is.'

'I'm told she's much admired,' Wexford said dryly. The compliment slightly displeased him. He interpreted it as spurious and ingratiating. Also there had been a note of incredulity in Vigo's voice as if he marvelled at such an old goose begetting a swan.

The front door swung open and Mrs Vigo came in, holding the child. For the first time since his arrival, Wexford remembered that there was another child, a mongol, confined somewhere in an institution.

The baby which Vigo now took in his arms was perhaps six or seven months old. No one could have doubted its paternity. Already it had its father's jaw and its father's athletic limbs. Vigo lifted the boy high, laughing as he chuckled, and there came into his face an intense besotted adoration.

'Meet my son, Mr Wexford. Isn't he splendid?'

'He's very like you.'

'So they tell me. Looks more than seven months, doesn't he?'

'Going to be a big chap,' said the chief inspector. 'Now that we've each complimented the other on his handsome offspring, I'll take my leave, Mr Vigo.'

81

'A mutual admiration society, eh?' Vigo laughed heartily but his wife's face remained grave. She took the boy from him roughly as if so much exaggerated worship offended her. Again Wexford thought of the mongol whose fate no amount of money could change. Grief fills the room up of my absent child, lies in his bed, walks up and down with me . . .

Wexford went out into the sunshine and the knot garden.

9

The call from Scotland Yard came through half an hour after Wexford got back to the station. In the whole country only two lorries had been hi-jacked during the latter part of May and neither was on Hatton's regular route. One had been in Cornwall, the other in Monmouthshire, and they had been loaded with margarine and tinned peaches respectively.

Wexford looked at the memo Burden had left him before departing for Deptford:

'Stamford say no records of any thefts from lorries in their area during April or May.'

It was unlikely that Hatton could have had a hand in the Cornwall or Monmouthshire jobs. Margarine and tinned fruit! Even if there had been tons of it, a fourth or fifth share couldn't have amounted to five hundred pounds. Besides, wasn't he underestimating Hatton's haul? He had banked five hundred on May 22nd, *drawn out* twenty-five pounds for the lamp. Another sixty had gone on clothes and the record player. And all this while, Wexford guessed, Hatton had been living like a king. True, the first and perhaps the second blackmail payments had come in before he was obliged to pay for his teeth at the beginning of June, but he had blithely paid two hundred and fifty for them in cash when the demand came.

Surely that meant that although Hatton had banked only five hundred on May 22nd, he had in fact received more, perhaps even twice that sum. He carried notes about with him in his wallet, on one occasion, at any rate about a hundred pounds.

Suppose there had been no mammoth hi-jacking at the

end of May? That would mean that all Hatton's wealth had been acquired through blackmail, and blackmail entered into not as the consequence of a hi-jacking but of something else.

There was a lot more to this, Wexford thought with frustration, that met the eye.

'There seems to be a lot more to this than meets the eye,' said Sergeant Camb indignantly. 'Mrs Fanshawe's own sister identified the dead young lady as Miss Nora Fanshawe.'

'Nevertheless,' the girl said, 'I am Nora Fanshawe.' She sat down on one of the red spoon-shaped chairs in the station foyer and placed her feet neatly together on the black and white tiles, staring down at the shoes Nurse Rose had so gushingly admired. 'My aunt was probably very strung up and you say the girl was badly burned. Very disfigured, I suppose?'

'Very,' said Camb unhappily. His immediate superior and his superintendent had departed ten minutes before for a conference at Lewes and he was more than somewhat at a loss. What the coroner was going to say to all this he dreaded to think.

'Mrs Fanshawe's sister seemed quite certain.' But had she? He remembered the scene quite vividly, taking the woman into the mortuary and uncovering the faces, Jerome Fanshawe's first and then the girl's. Fanshawe had been lying on his face and the fire had scarcely touched him. Besides, the woman had recognized the silver pencil in his breast pocket, his wristwatch and the tiny knife scar, relic of some schoolboy ritual, on that wrist. Identifying the girl had been so extremely distasteful. All her hair had been burnt away but for the black roots and her features hideously charred. It made him shudder to think of it now, hardened as he was.

'Yes, that's my niece,' Mrs Browne had said, recoiling and covering her own face. Of course he had asked her if she was quite certain and she had said she was, quite certain, but now he wondered if it was mere association that had made her agree, association and horror. She had said it was her niece because the girl was young and had black hair and because who else but Nora Fanshawe could have been in

84

that car with her parents? Yet someone else had been. . . .
And what the hell was the coroner going to say?

His eyes still seeing the charred appalling face, he turned
to the young hard untouched face in front of him and said:

'Can you prove you're Nora Fanshawe, miss?'

She opened the large hide handbag she was carrying and
produced a passport, handing it to Camb without a word.
The photograph wasn't much like the girl who sat on the
other side of the desk, but passport photographs seldom are
much like their originals. Glancing up at her uneasily and
then back to the document in front of him he read that Nora
Elizabeth Fanshawe, by profession a teacher, had been born
in London in 1945, had black hair, brown eyes and was five
feet nine inches tall with no distinguishing marks. The girl
in the mortuary hadn't been anything like five feet nine, but
you couldn't expect an aunt to tell the height of a prone
corpse.

'Why didn't you come back before?' he asked.

'Why should I? I didn't know my father was dead and my
mother in hospital.'

'Didn't you write? Didn't you expect them to write to
you?'

'We were on very bad terms,' the girl said calmly. 'Besides,
my mother did write. I got her letter yesterday and I took
the first plane. Look here, my mother knows me and that
ought to be enough for you.'

'Your mother . . .' Camb corrected himself. 'Mrs Fanshawe's a very sick woman. . . .'

'She's not mad if that's what you mean. The best thing
will be for me to phone my aunt and then perhaps you'll let
me go and have something to eat. You may not know it, but
I haven't had a thing to eat since eight o'clock and it's half-
past two now.'

'Oh, I'll phone Mrs Browne,' Camb said hastily. 'It
wouldn't do for her to hear your voice just like that. Oh
dear, no.' He was half convinced.

'Why me?' said Wexford. 'Why do I have to see her? It's
nothing to do with me.'

85

'You see, sir, the super and Inspector Letts have gone to Lewes . . .'

'Did the aunt recognise her voice?'

'Seemed to. She was in a bit of a way, I can tell you. Frankly, I don't have much faith in the aunt.'

'Oh, bring her up,' Wexford said impatiently. 'Anything to make a change from lorries. And, Camb – use the lift.'

He had never seen her mother or her aunt so he couldn't look for family resemblances. But she was a rich man's daughter. He looked at the bag, the shoes, the platinum watch and, more than anything, he sensed about her an air, almost repellent, of arrogance. She wore no scent. He took from her in silence the passport, the international driver's licence and Mrs Fanshawe's letter. It occurred to him as he turned them over that Nora Fanshawe – if she was Nora Fanshawe – probably stood to inherit a vast sum of money. Jerome Fanshawe had been an affluent stockbroker. It might be that this girl was a con woman and he and Camb the first victims of a colossal deception.

'I think we had better have an explanation,' he said slowly.

'Very well. I don't quite know what you want.'

'Just a moment.' Wexford took Camb aside. 'Was there nothing but this Mrs Browne's word to identify the dead girl?' he asked rather grimly.

Camb looked downcast. 'There was a suitcase in the car with clothes in it,' he said. 'We went through the contents of two handbags we found in the road. One was Mrs Fanshawe's. The other had nothing in it but some make-up, a purse containing two pounds and some silver and a packet of cigarettes.' He added defensively, 'It was a good expensive handbag from Mappin and Webb.'

'My God,' said Wexford in disgust, 'I just hope you haven't landed us with a female Tichborne claimant.' He went back to the girl, sat down on the opposite side of the desk and gave a brisk nod. 'You went on holiday with Mr and Mrs Fanshawe to Eastover?' he asked. On what date was that?'

'May the 17th,' the girl said promptly. 'I am a teacher of English at a school in Cologne and I gave up my job at the end of March and returned to England.'

'Since when you have been living with Mr and Mrs Fanshawe?'

86

If the girl noticed that he didn't refer to them as her parents she gave no sign. She sat stiff and tense with her finely sculpted head held high. 'Not at first,' she said and he sensed a faint diffidence creep into her voice. 'My parents and I hadn't been on good terms for some time. I went back to live with them – or rather, to stay with them – in the middle of May. My mother wanted me to go down to the bungalow with them and because I wanted – I wanted our relations to improve – well, I said I would.' Wexford nodded noncomittally and she went on. 'We all drove down to Eastover on Friday, May 17th . . .' Her shoulders stiffened and she looked down at her folded hands. 'That night I had a disagreement with my parents. Is there any need for me to go into details?' Without waiting for Wexford's consent to her reticence, she swept the quarrel aside and said, 'I felt it was useless to try and patch things up. We were worlds apart, we . . . The result was that on the Saturday morning, I told my mother there was nothing for me in England and I was going back to Germany to try and get my old job back. I took one of the suitcases of clothes I had brought with me and went to Newhaven to get the boat for Dieppe.'

'And did you get your old job back?'

'Fortunately I did. There's a shortage of teachers in Germany as well as here and they were only too glad to see me. I even got my old room back in the *Goethestrasse*.'

'I see. Now I should like the name and address of the authority who employ you, the name of your landlady and that of the school in which you've been teaching.'

While the girl wrote this information down for him, Wexford said:

'Weren't you surprised to hear nothing from Mr or Mrs Fanshawe during the past six weeks?'

She looked up and raised her straight, rather heavy, black eyebrows. 'I told you we'd quarrelled. My father would have expected an abject apology from me, I assure you, before he condescended to write.' It was the first show of emotion she had made and it did more to make Wexford believe her story than all the documentary evidence she had furnished him with. 'These silences were commonplace with us,' she said. 'Especially after a set-to like the one we had that night. Six months could have gone by. Why should I imagine any harm had come to them? I'm not a clairvoyant.'

'But you came as soon as Mrs Fanshawe wrote.'

'She is my mother, after all. Now do you suppose I might go and get myself some lunch?'

'In a moment,' Wexford said. 'Where are you planning to stay?'

'I was going to ask you to recommend somewhere,' the girl said a shade sardonically.

'The Olive and Dove is the best hotel. I suggest you get in touch immediately with your late father's solicitors.'

The girl got up and not a crease marked the skirt of her suit. Her self-confidence was almost stupefying. Camb opened the door for her and with a crisp 'Good afternoon' she took her leave of them. As her footsteps died away, the sergeant burst out miserably:

'If she's Nora Fanshawe, sir, who, for God's sake, was the girl in the road?'

'That's your problem, Sergeant,' Wexford said unkindly.

'It could well be yours, sir.'

'That's what I'm afraid of. Haven't I got enough with a murder on my hands?'

Lilian Hatton was an easier nut to crack than the girl who called herself Nora Fanshawe. She broke down and wept bitterly when Wexford told her that her husband's supplementary income had come from a criminal source. He was almost sure that it was all a revelation to her and he watched her in sad silence as she covered her face and shook with sobs.

'I have been given your husband's log book by your brother, Mrs Hatton,' he said gently as she recovered herself. 'Now I also want to know if you keep any sort of diary or engagement book yourself.'

'Just a pad by the phone,' she gulped, 'where I kind of jot things down.'

'I'm going to ask you if you'll kindly let me borrow that.'

'You think,' she began, dabbing at her eyes as she came back with the pad, 'you think someone – someone killed my

Charlie because he wouldn't go on – go on doing these jobs for them?'

'Something like that.' Now was not the time to suggest to this woman that her husband had been a blackmailer as well as a thief. 'Who knew Mr Hatton would pass along the Kingsbrook path that night?'

She twisted the damp handkerchief in hands whose nails were still pitifully and bravely painted the way Charlie Hatton had liked them, red and shiny and glittering. 'All the darts club,' she said. 'And me – I knew. My mum knew and my brother, Jim. Charlie always came that way back from the pub.'

'Mrs Hatton, did your husband ever receive any callers in this flat that you didn't know? Strangers, I mean, that he wanted to talk to alone?'

'No, he never did.'

'Perhaps when you were out? Can you ever remember your husband asking you to go out and leave him alone with anyone?'

The handkerchief was torn now, sopping wet and useless as an absorbent. But she put it to her eyes and brought it away streaked black and green. 'When he was home,' she said, 'I never went out. We always went out together. We was like – like inseparable. Mr Wexford . . .' She gripped the arms of her chair and two red flame-like spots burned in her cheeks. 'Mr Wexford, I've heard all you've said and I've got to believe it. But whatever my Charlie did, he did it for me. He was a husband in a million, a good kind man, a wonderful man to his friends. You ask anyone, Jack. . . He was one in a million!'

Oh! withered is the garland of war! The soldier's poll is fallen. . . Strange, Wexford thought, that when you considered Charlie Hatton you thought of war and soldiers and battles and Hatton had waged it with unscrupulous weapons, winning rich spoils and falling as he marched home with a song on his lips?

How sentimental he was getting! The man was a blackmailer and a thief. If life was a battle and Charlie Hatton a soldier of fortune he, Wexford, stood in the position of a United Nations patrol whose job it was to prevent incursions on the territory of the defenceless.

'I don't want to ask you anything more now, Mrs Hatton,' he said to the widow as he left her weeping among the dead man's ill-gotten glories.

In the High Street he encountered Dr Crocker emerging from Grover's with a copy of the *British Medical Journal*.

'Been making any good arrests lately?' asked the doctor cheerfully. 'Now, now, mind your hyptertension. Want me to take your blood pressure? I've got my sphyg in the car.'

'You know what you can do with your sphyg,' said Wexford, proceeding to tell him in lurid detail. 'I reckon just about the whole population of Kingsmarkham knew Charlie Hatton would be taking the field path home that night.'

'No reason why it should be a local man, is there?'

'I may not be a wizard with a sphygmomanometer,' said Wexford derisively, 'but I'm not daft. Whoever killed Charlie Hatton knew the lie of the land all right.'

'How come? He'd only got to be told by Charlie that he'd be leaving the High Street by the bridge and walking along the local river.'

'You think? You reckon Hatton would also have told him the river bed was full of stones one of which would make a suitable weapon for knocking off his informant?'

'I see what you mean. There could be one or more brains behind the killing but whoever struck the blow, albeit a henchman, was Kingsmarkham born and bred.'

'That's right, Watson. You're catching on. My old mate,' Wexford remarked to no one in particular, 'albeit a sawbones, is coming on.' Suddenly his voice dropped and tapping the doctor's arm, his face hardening, he said, 'D'you see what I see? Over there by the Electricity Board?'

Crocker followed his gaze. From Tabard Road a woman wheeling a pram had emerged in Kingsmarkham High Street and stopped outside a plate-glass display window of the Southern Electricity Board. Presently two more children joined her, then a man holding a third child by the hand and another in his arms. They remained in a huddle on the pavement, staring at the dazzling array of kitchen equipment as if hypnotized.

'Mr and Mrs Cullam and their quiverful,' said Wexford.

The family were too far away for their conversation, an apparently heated and even acrimonious discussion, to be audible. But it was evident that an argument was taking place between the adults, possibly as to whether their need of a refrigerator was greater than their desire for a mammoth room heater. The children were taking sides vociferously. Cullam shook one of his daughters, cuffed his elder son on the head, and then they all plunged into the showroom.

'Will you do something for me?' Wexford asked the doctor. 'Go in there and buy a light bulb or something. I want to know what that lot are up to.'

'What, spy on them and report back, d'you mean?'

'Charming way you put it. That's what I spend my life doing. I'll sit in your car. Can I have the keys?'

'It's not locked,' Crocker said awkwardly.

'Is that so? Well, don't come screaming to me next time one of the local hippies pinches a load of your acid off you. Go on. A forty watt bulb and we'll reimburse you out of petty cash.'

The doctor went unwillingly. Wexford chuckled to himself in the car. Crocker's cautious approach to the electricity showroom, his quick sidelong glances, called to mind days long gone by when Wexford, then a sixth-form boy, had witnessed this same man as a child of ten, scuttling up to front doors playing 'Knocking Down Ginger'. In those days the infant Crocker had run up paths lightly and gleefully to bang on a knocker or ring a bell and, elated with an enormous naughtiness, hidden behind a hedge to see the angry householder erupt and curse. There was no hedge here and Crocker was fifty. But as he entered the showroom, had he too experienced a flash of memory, a stab of nostalgia?

Jesu, Jesu, thought Wexford, once more evoking Justice Shallow, the mad days that I have spent! And to see how many of my old acquaintance are dead. . . . Enough of that. On the lighter side it reminded him of Stamford and he wondered how Burden had got on. Somehow a little business in Deptford didn't quite match up with his own ideas of McCloy's origins.

Samantha Cullam scuttled out on to the pavement. Her mother came next, lugging the pram. When the whole brood were assembled their father regimented them with a series of fortunately ill-aimed blows and they all trailed off the way they had come. Then Crocker appeared, duplicity incarnate.

91

'Well?'

'Don't snap at me like that, you saucy devil,' said the doctor, immensely pleased with himself. 'I set traps, as the Psalmist says, I catch men.'

'What did Cullam buy?'

'He didn't exactly *buy* anything, but he's after a refrigerator.'

'Getting it on the H.P. is he?'

'Money wasn't mentioned. They had a bit of a ding-dong, Mr and Mrs, and one of the kids knocked a Pyrex dish off a cooker. That brute Cullam fetched him a fourpenny one, poor little devil. They're all dead keen on getting this fridge, I can tell you.'

'Well, what about these traps you laid?'

'That was just a figure of speech,' said the doctor. 'Didn't I do all right? I bought the bulb like you said. One and nine if you don't mind. I'm not in this for my health.'

10

'They call themselves McCloy Ltd.,' Burden said wearily, 'but the last member of the firm of that name died twenty years ago. It's an old established set-up, but I reckon it's on its last legs now. In this so-called affluent society of ours folks buy new stuff, they don't want this reconditioned rubbish.'

'You can say that again,' said Wexford, thinking of Cullam.

'The Yard put me on to six other McCloys all more or less in the hardware business or on its fringes. Not a smell of anything fishy about one of them. Stamford have given me a list of local McCloys and there again not a sniff as far as they know. But I'll be off to Stamford in the morning to have a scent round. The local force have promised me all the help I need.'

Wexford lounged back in his swivel chair and the dying sun played on his face. 'Mike,' he said, 'I wonder if we haven't been starting from the wrong end. We've been looking for McCloy to lead us to his hired assassin. We might do better to find the hired assassin and let him lead us to McCloy.'

'Cullam?'

'Maybe. I want Martin to be Cullam's shadow and if he goes and pays cash for that refrigerator we're really getting somewhere. Meanwhile I'm going to make Hatton's log book and Mrs Hatton's engagement book my homework for tonight. But first, how about a quick one at the Olive and Dove?'

'Not for me thanks, sir. I haven't had an evening in for a

week now. Divorce is against my wife's principles but she might get ideas as to a legal separation.'

Wexford laughed and they went down in the lift together. The evening was warm and clear, the light and the long soft shadows more flattering to this market town High Street than the noonday sun. The old houses were at their best in it, their shabbiness, the cracks in their fabric veiled, as an ageing face is veiled and smoothed by candlelight. By day the alleys that ran into a scruffy hinterland were rat-hole rubbish traps but now they seemed romantic lanes where lovers might meet under the bracket lamps and as the sun departed, watch the moon ride over a Grimms' fairy tale huddle of pinnacled rooftops.

As yet it was only eight o'clock and the sun reluctant to leave without treating its worshippers to a pyrotechnic display of rose and gold flames that burnt up the whole western sky. Wexford stood on the south side of the bridge and listened to the river chuckling. Such an innocent river, for all that it knew a secret, for all that one of its stones had put a man out of sight of the sunset!

All the street windows of the Olive and Dove were open, the curtains fanning out gently over window boxes and over fuchsias that dripped red flowers. On the forecourt a band of Morris dancers had assembled. They wore the motley coat of jesters and one of them was hopping around on a hobby horse. To his amusement Wexford picked out George Carter among the company.

'Lovely night, Mr Carter,' he said jovially. Rather shame-facedly Carter waved at him a stick with ribbons and bells on. Wexford went into the saloon bar.

At a table in the alcove on the dining-room wall sat the girl Camb had brought to him earlier in the day, an elderly woman and a man. Wexford brought his beer and as he passed them the man got up as if to take his leave.

'Good evening,' Wexford said. 'Have you decided to stay at the Olive?'

The girl was sparing with her smiles. She nodded sharply to him and said, naming his rank precisely, 'I'd like you to meet my father's solicitor, Mr Updike. Uncle John, this is Detective Chief Inspector Wexford.'

'How do you do?'

'And I don't think you've met my aunt, Mrs Browne?'

Wexford looked from one to the other. Marvellous the way he always had to do Camb's work for him! The aunt was looking pale but excited, the solicitor gratified. 'I'm quite prepared to accept that you're Miss Fanshawe now, Miss Fanshawe,' Wexford said.

'I've known Nora since she was so high,' said Updike. 'You need have no doubt that this is Nora.' And he gave Wexford a card naming a London firm, Updike, Updike and Sanger of Ava Maria Lane. The chief inspector looked at it, then again at Mrs Browne who was Nora Fanshawe grown old. 'I'm satisfied.' He passed on to an empty table.

The solicitor went to catch his train and presently Wexford heard the aunt say:

'I've had a long day, Nora. I think I'll just give the hospital a ring and then I'll go up to bed.'

Wexford sat by the window, watching the Morris dancers. The music was amateurish and the performers self-conscious, but the evening was so beautiful that if you shut your eyes to the cars and the new shop blocks you might imagine yourself briefly in Shakespeare's England. Someone carried out to the nine men a tray of bottled beer and the spell broke.

'Come into the lounge,' said a voice behind him.

Nora Fanshawe had removed the jacket of her suit and in the thin coffee-coloured blouse she looked more feminine. But she was still a creature of strong straight lines and planes and angles and she was still not smiling.

'May I get you a drink, Miss Fanshawe?' Wexford said, rising.

'Better not.' Her voice was abrupt and she didn't thank him for the offer. 'I've had too much already.' And she added with a dead laugh, 'We've been what my aunt calls celebrating. The resurrection of the dead, you see.'

They went into the lounge, sat down in deep cretonne-covered armchairs and Nora Fanshawe said:

'Mr Updike wouldn't tell me the details of the accident. He wanted to spare me.' She beckoned to the waiter and said without asking Wexford first, 'Bring two coffees.' Then she lit a king-size cigarette and slipped it into an amber holder. 'You tell me about it,' she said.

'You don't want to be spared?'

'Of course not. I'm not a child and I didn't like my father.'

Wexford gave a slight cough. 'At about ten o'clock on May 20th,' he began, 'a man driving a petrol tanker on the north to south highway of Stowerton by-pass saw a car overturned and in flames on the fast lane of the south to north track. He reported it at once and when the police and ambulance got there they found the bodies of a man and a girl lying on the road and partially burned. A woman – your mother – had been flung clear on to the soft shoulder. She had multiple injuries and a fractured skull.'

'Go on.'

'What remained of the car was examined but, as far as could be told, there was nothing wrong with the brakes or the steering and the tyres were nearly new.'

Nora Fanshawe nodded.

'The inquest was adjourned until your mother regained consciousness. The road was wet and your mother has suggested that your father may have been driving exceptionally fast.'

'He always drove too fast.' She took the coffee that the waiter had brought and handed a cup to Wexford. He sensed that she would take it black and sugarless and he was right. 'Since the dead girl wasn't I,' she said with repellently faultless grammar, 'who was she?'

'I'm hoping you'll be able to tell us that.'

She shrugged, 'How should I know?'

Wexford glanced at the curled lip, the hard direct eyes. 'Miss Fanshawe,' he said sharply, 'I've answered your questions, but you haven't even met me half-way. This afternoon you came to my office as if you were doing me a favour. Don't you think it's time you unbent a little?'

She flushed at that and muttered. 'I don't unbend much.'

'No, I can see that. You're twenty-three, aren't you? Don't you think all this upstage reserve is rather ridiculous?'

Her hand was small, but, ringless and with short nails as it was, it was like a man's. He watched it move towards the cup and saucer and for a moment he thought she was going to take her coffee, get up and leave him. She frowned a little and her mouth hardened.

'I'll tell you about my father,' she said at last. 'It might just

96

help. I first knew about his infidelities when I was twelve,' she began. 'Or, let me say, I knew he was behaving as other people's fathers didn't behave. He brought a girl home and told my mother she was going to stay with us. They had a row in my presence and when it was over my father gave my mother five hundred pounds.' She took the cigarette stub from her holder and replaced it with a fresh one. This sudden chain smoking was the only sign she gave of emotion. 'He bribed her, you understand. It was quite direct and open. "Let her stay and you can have this money". That was how it was. The girl stayed six months. Two years later he bought my mother a new car and at just the same time I caught him in his office with his secretary.' She inhaled deeply. 'On the floor,' she said coldly. 'After that it was an understood thing that when my father wanted a new mistress he paid my mother accordingly. By that I mean what he thought the girl was worth to him. He wanted my mother to stay because she was a good hostess and kept house well. When I was eighteen I went up to Oxford.

'After I got my degree I told my mother I could keep her now and she should leave my father. Her response was to deny everything and to tell my father to stop my allowance. He refused to stop it – mainly because my mother had asked him to, I suppose. I haven't drawn it for two years now, but . . .' She glanced swiftly at her bag, her watch. 'You can't always refuse to take presents,' she said tightly, 'not when it's your own mother, not when you're an only child.'

'So you took a job in Germany?' Wexford asked.

'I thought it would be as well to get away.' The flush returned, an unbecoming mottled red. 'In January,' she said hesitantly, 'I met a man, a salesman who made business trips to Cologne from this country.' Wexford waited for her to talk of love and instead heard her say with a strange sense of shock, 'I gave up my job, as I told you, and came back to London to live with him. When I told him that if we were to be married I wouldn't ask my father for a penny he . . . well, he threw me out.'

'You returned to your parents?'

Nora Fanshawe raised her head and for the first time he saw her smile, an ugly harsh smile of self-mockery. 'You're a cold fish, aren't you?' she said surprisingly.

'I was under the impression you despised sympathy, Miss Fanshawe.'

'Perhaps I do. Want some more coffee? No, nor do I. Yes, I went back to my parents. I was still sorry for my mother, you see. I thought my father was older now and I was older. I knew I could never live with them again, but I thought . . . Family quarrels are uncivilized, don't you think? My mother was rather pathetic. She said she'd always wanted a grown-up daughter to be real friends with.' Nora Fanshawe wrinkled her nose in distaste. 'Even upstage reserved characters like myself have their weak spots, Chief Inspector. I went to Eastover with them.'

'And the quarrel, Miss Fanshawe?'

'I'm coming to that. We'd been on surprisingly good terms up till then. My father called my mother darling once or twice and there was a kind of Darby and Joan air about them. They wanted to know what I was doing about getting another job and all was serene. So serene, in fact, that after we'd had a meal at the bungalow and a few drinks my mother did something she'd never done before. My father had gone off up to bed and she suddenly began to tell me what her life with him had been, the bribery and the humiliation and so on. She really talked as if I were a woman friend of her own age, her confidante. Well, we had about an hour of this and then she asked me if I had any romantic plans of my own. Those were her words. Like a fool I told her about the man I'd been living with. I say like a fool. Perhaps if I hadn't been a fool I would have been the dead girl in the road.'

'Your mother reacted unsympathetically?'

'She goggled at me,' said Nora Fanshawe, emphasizing the verb pedantically. 'Then, before I could stop her she got my father out of bed and told him the whole thing. They both raved at me. My mother was hysterical and my father called me a lot of unpleasant names. I stood it for a bit and then I'm afraid I said to him that what was sauce for the gander was sauce for the goose and at least I wasn't married.' She sighed, moving her angular shoulders. 'What do you think he said?'

'It's different for men,' said Wexford.

'How did you guess? At any rate, for once my parents

presented a united front. After my mother had obligingly betrayed all my confidences to him in my hearing, he said he would find the man – Michael, that is – and compel him to marry me. I couldn't stand any more, so I locked myself in my bedroom and in the morning I went to Newhaven and got on the boat. I parted from my mother just about on speaking terms. My father had gone out.'

'Thank you for unbending, Miss Fanshawe. Have you been suggesting that the dead girl might have been your father's mistress?'

'You think it impossible that my father would drive his wife and mistress together to London? I assure you it's not unlikely. For him it would simply have been a matter of bringing the girl along, telling my mother she was coming with them and paying her handsomely for the hardship occasioned.'

Wexford kept his eyes from Nora Fanshawe's face. She was as unlike his Sheila as could be. They had in common only their youth and health and the fact, like all women, of each being someone's daughter. The girl's father was dead. In a flash of unusual sentimentality, Wexford thought he would rather be dead than be the man about whom a daughter could say such things.

In a level voice he said, 'You gave me to understand that as far as you know there was no woman at the time but your mother. You have no idea who this girl could be?'

'That was the impression I had. I was evidently wrong.'

'Miss Fanshawe, this girl clearly could not have been a friend or neighbour at Eastover whom your parents were simply driving to London. In that case her relatives would have enquired for her, raised a hue and cry at the time of the accident.'

'Surely that would apply whoever she was?'

'Not necessarily. She could be a girl with no fixed address or someone whose landlady or friends expected her to move away about that particular weekend. She may be listed some- where among missing persons and no search have begun for her because the manner of her life showed that occasional apparent disappearances were not unusual. In other words, she could be a girl who led a somewhat itinerant life in the habit of taking jobs in various parts of the country or moving about to live with different men. Suppose, for instance, she had spent the weekend in some South Coast resort and tried to hitch a lift back to London from your father?'

'My father wouldn't have given a lift to anyone. Both he and my mother disapproved of hitch-hiking. Chief Inspector, you're talking as if everyone in that car is now dead. Aren't you forgetting that my mother is very much alive? She's well on the way to recovery and her brain isn't affected. She insists there was no one in the car but my father and herself.' Nora Fanshawe lifted her eyes and her voice lost some of its confidence. 'I suppose it's possible she could be having some sort of psychological block. She wants to believe my father was a changed man, that no girl was with them, so she's convinced herself they were alone. That could be it.'

'I'm sure it must be.' Wexford got up. 'Good night, Miss Fanshawe. Thank you for the coffee. I take it you'll be staying here a few days?'

'I'll keep in touch. Good night, Chief Inspector.'

The next step, he thought as he walked home, would be to investigate the missing persons list in the holiday towns and London too, if those proved fruitless. That was routine stuff and not for him. Why, anyway, was he following this road accident that wasn't even properly his province to distract his mind from the urgency of the Hatton affair? Because it had features so distracting and so inexplicable that no-one could simply explain them away?

Of course it would turn out that the dead girl was merely someone Jerome Fanshawe had come across that weekend and who had taken his fancy. Nothing so dramatic as Nora Fanshawe had suggested need have happened. Why shouldn't Fanshawe just have said to his wife, 'This young lady has missed her last train and since she lives in London I said we'd give her a lift'? But in that case Mrs Fanshawe would hardly deny the girl's presence.

There was more to it than that. There was the handbag. Camb had searched that handbag and found in it nothing but make-up and a little money. That wasn't natural, Wexford reflected. Where were her keys? Come to that, where were all the other things women usually stuff into bags, handkerchiefs, dress shop bills, receipts, tickets, pen, letters? The things which were there were anonymous, the things which were not there were the objects by which someone might be identified.

Wexford let himself into his own house and the dog Clytemnestra galloped to meet him.

'What would you do,' Wexford said to his wife, 'if I brought a young girl home and offered you a thousand pounds to let her stay?'

'You haven't got a thousand pounds,' said Mrs Wexford.

'True. There's always a fly in the ointment.'

'On the subject of young girls and money, Mr Vigo has sent a whacking bill for your daughter's tooth.'

Wexford looked at it and groaned. 'Pleached walks!' he said. 'Chinese Chippendale! I just hope one of my customers pinches his orrery, that's all. Is there any beer in the house?'

Suppressing a smile, his wife stepped over the now recumbent form of the knitted dog and went into the kitchen to open a can.

A pewter tankard at his elbow, Wexford spent the next couple of hours studying Hatton's log book and Mrs Hatton's engagement diary.

It was the week immediately preceding May 21st which interested him. On the 22nd Hatton had paid five hundred pounds into his bank and two days prior to that had either been in possession of a large sum of money or confident of acquiring it, for on the 21st, a Tuesday, he had ordered his new set of teeth.

Mrs Hatton's engagement diary was a calendar in the shape of a rectangular book. The left-hand pages bore a coloured photograph of some English beauty spot with an appropriate verse, both for the picture and the time of year, while the right-hand pages were each divided into seven sections. The days of the week were listed on the left side and a space of perhaps one inch by five was allowed for brief jottings.

Wexford opened it at Sunday, May 12th.

The photograph was of Kentish fruit orchards and the lines beneath it from *As You Like It:* 'Men are April when they woo, December when they wed. Maids are May while they are maids, but the sky changes when they are wives.'

Not true of the Hattons, he thought. Now to see how Mrs Hatton had occupied herself during that particular week.

Nothing for Sunday. Monday May 13th: *C. left for Leeds. Mother to tea.* Tuesday May 14th: *Rang Gas Board. C. home 3 p.m. Pictures.* And here in Hatton's log book was the Leeds trip confirmed. He had stopped twice on the way up, at Norman Cross for lunch at the Merrie England café, and at Dave's Diner near Retford for a cup of tea. His room in Leeds was with a Mrs Hubble at 21 Ladysmith Road, and on the return journey he had stopped only once and again at the Merrie England. There was nothing in the log book at this stage to make Wexford even pause. Hatton had done the journey in the shortest possible time, leaving no possible spare moment for undercover activities. He turned back to the diary.

Wednesday, May 15th: *C. off work. Rang doctor. Mem, N.H.S., not private.* Interesting. Hatton had been ill and at that time apparently not in funds. Thursday May 16th: *C. summer flu. Ring Jack and Marilyn put off dinner.* There was no entry for Friday May 17th.

Saturday, May 18th: *C. better. Doctor called again. Jim and mother came.*

That completed the week. Wexford turned the page to Sunday, May 18th: *C. left for Leeds. Mem, will ring me 8 p.m. J and M came for drinks and solo game.* Opposite was a photograph of a large country house and the lines: 'It is a truth universally acknowledged that a single man in possession of a good fortune must be in want of a wife.' Wexford smiled grimly to himself. Monday, May 20th: *C. bad again. Left Leeds late. Home 10 p.m.*

Quickly Wexford checked with the log book. Yes, here was Hatton's entry that he had been too ill to start the return journey until noon. He had driven home slowly and stopped twice on the way at the Hollybush at Newark and at the Merrie England. But had he really been ill or had he been shamming, crafty sick to give himself extra time in Leeds? For however he acquired that money he must have acquired it, Wexford was certain, during the 19th or the 20th of May.

Tuesday, May 21st *C. fit again. Day off. Saw Jack and Marilyn. Appointment 2 p.m. with dentist.*

A precise little woman, Lilian Hatton, if not exactly verbose. Impossible to tell if she knew anything. The last place to which she would have confided her secrets was this calendar diary.

It didn't look as if Hatton had been up to much on that Monday morning in Leeds, but you never knew. There was always the night between Sunday and Monday to be considered. For all Wexford knew or could remember there might have been a bank robbery in that city at that time. It would all have to be checked. He wondered why the Fanshawe business kept intruding and upsetting his concentration, and then suddenly he knew.

Fanshawe had crashed his car on Monday, May 20th; an unidentified girl had died on May 20th and also on May 20th something big had happened to Charlie Hatton.

But there couldn't be a connection. Fanshawe was a wealthy stockbroker with a flat in Mayfair and, apart from a bit of moral nastiness, not a stain on his character. Charlie Hatton was a cocky little lorry driver who had probably never set foot in Mayfair all his life.

It was just a curious coincidence that Hatton had been killed on the day following that of Mrs Fanshawe's regaining consciousness.

Wexford closed the books and emptied his tankard for the third time. He was tired and fanciful and he had drunk too much beer. Yawning ponderously, he put Clytemnestra outside the back door and while he waited for her, stood staring emptily at the cloudless, star-filled sky.

11

'Good morning, Miss Thompson,' Wexford said with a heartiness he didn't feel.

'Mrs Pertwee, if you don't mind.' She picked up one of the wire baskets that were stacked outside the supermarket and gave him a selfconscious, defiant stare. 'Jack and me got married very quietly yesterday afternoon.'

'May I be among the first to offer my congratulations?'

'Thanks very much, I'm sure. We didn't tell no one about it, just went off to church quietly by ourselves. Jack's been so cut up about poor Charlie. When are you going to catch his killer, that's what I want to know? Not putting yourselves out, I reckon, on account of him being a working fella. Been different if he was one of your upper crust. This capitalist society we live in makes me spit, just spit it does.'

Wexford backed a little, fearing she might suit the action to the word. The bride snapped her toothbrush eyelashes at him. 'You want to pull your socks up,' she said relentlessly. 'Whoever killed Charlie, hanging'd be too good for him.'

'Dear, oh dear,' said Wexford mildly, 'and I thought you progressives were dead against capital punishment.'

She banged into the supermarket and Wexford went on his way, smiling wryly. Camb eyed him warily as he entered the police station.

'Getting interested in this Fanshawe business, I gather, sir. I met Miss Fanshawe on my way in.'

'So interested,' Wexford said, 'that I'm sending Detective Constable Loring down to find out who's missing in the holiday towns and it might be worth our while to check with London too.'

Burden had left for Stamford. Stepping into the lift, Wexford decided to do the London checking himself. Young women were beginning to get on his nerves. There were so many of them about, and it seemed to him they caused as much trouble to a policeman as burglars. Now to see how many of them were missing in London. This task was for him somewhat *infra dig*, but until Burden and Sergeant Martin brought him some information he had little else to do, and this way he could, at any rate, be certain it was well done.

By lunchtime he had narrowed his search down to three out of the dozens of girls missing in the London area. The first was a Carol Pearson, of Muswell Hill, interesting to him because she had worked as a hairdresser's improver at a shop in Eastcheap. Jerome Fanshawe's office was in Eastcheap and the hairdresser's had a barber's shop attached to it. Hers was also a significant name because she had black hair and her disappearance was reported on May 17th.

The second girl, Doreen Dacres, was like Carol Pearson, black-haired and aged twenty, and his interest was aroused because she had left her room in Finchley on May 15th to take a job in Eastbourne. Nothing further had been heard of her either in Finchley or at the Eastbourne club address.

Bridget Culross was the last name with which he felt he need concern himself. She was twenty-two years old and had been a nurse at the Princess Louise Clinic in New Cavendish Street. On Saturday May 18th she had gone to spend the weekend with an unnamed boy friend in Brighton, but had not returned to the clinic. It was assumed that she had eloped with her boy friend. Her hair was also dark, her life erratic and her only relative an aunt in County Leix.

Young women! Wexford thought irritably, and he thought also of his own daughter who was making him scrape the bottom of his pocket so that at some future possible never-never time she might be able to smile without restraint before the cameras.

The long day passed slowly and it grew very hot. Clouds massed heavily, dense and fungoid in shape, over the huddled roofs of the town. But they did nothing to diminish the heat, seeming instead to enclose it and its still, threatening air under a thick muffling lid. The sun had gone, blanked out by sultry vapour.

To an observer Wexford might be thought only to be sitting, like many other inhabitants of Kingsmarkham, waiting for the storm to break. He did nothing. He lay back by the open window with his eyes closed and the warm breathless air came to him just as in another cooler season heat fanned from the grid lower down the wall. No one disturbed him and he was glad. He was thinking.

In Stamford, where it was raining, Inspector Burden went to a country house supposedly occupied by a man named McCloy and found it deserted, its doors locked and its garden overgrown. There were no neighbours and no one to tell him where McCloy had gone.

Detective Constable Loring drove along the promenades of the south coast towns, calling at police stations and paying particular attention to those clubs and cafés and amusement halls where girls come and go and pass each other. He had found a club where Doreen Dacres had been engaged but where no Doreen Dacres had arrived and this comforted him. He even telephoned Wexford to tell him about it, his elation subsiding somewhat when he heard the chief inspector had also found this out three hours before.

The storm broke at five o'clock.

For some time before this heavy clouds had increased and in the west the sky had become a dense purplish-black, a range of mountainous cumulus against which the outlines of buildings took on a curious clarity and the trees stood out livid and sickly bright. In spite of the clammy heat, shoppers began to hurry, but the rain which fell so readily when rainy days preceded it, now, after a fortnight's drought, held off as if it could only be squeezed out as a result of some acute and agonising pressure. It was as though the clouds were not themselves mere vapour but impermeable sagging sacks, purposely constructed and hung to contain water.

The first whispering breeze came like a hot breath and Wexford closed his windows. Almost imperceptibly at first the trees in the High Street pavement began to sway. Most of the merchandise outside greengrocers' and florists' had already been taken in and now it was the turn of the sun-blinds to be furled and waterproof awnings to take their place. The air seemed to press against Wexford's windows. He stood against them, watching the dark western sky and the ash-blue cumulus now edged with brilliant white.

The lightning was the forked kind and it branched suddenly like a firework and yet like the limb of a blazing tree. As its fiery twigs flashed out and cut into the inky cloud, the thunder rolled out of the west.

Wexford dearly loved a storm. He liked the forked lightning better than the zig-zag kind and now he was gratified by a second many-branched display that seemed to spring and grow from the river itself, blossoming in the sky above the Kingsbrook meadows. This time the thunder burst with a pistol-shot snap and with an equal suddenness, as if at last those swollen vessels had been punctured, the rain began to fall.

The first heavy drops spashed in coin shapes on the pavement below and in their tubs the pink flowers on the forecourt dipped and swayed. For a brief moment it seemed that the rain still hesitated, that it would only patter dispiritedly on the dust-filled gutters where its drops rolled like quicksilver. But then, urged on as it were by a series of multiple lightning flashes, it hesitated no more and, instead of increasing gradually from the first tentative shower, the water gushed forth in a vast fountain. It dashed against the windows, washing off dust in a great cleansing stream, and Wexford moved away from the glass. The sudden flood was more like a wave than rain and it blinded the window as surely as darkness.

He heard the car splash in and the doors slam. Burden, perhaps. The internal phone rang and Wexford lifted the receiver.

'I've got Cullam here, sir.' It was Martin's voice. 'Shall I bring him up? I thought you might like to talk to him.'

Maurice Cullam was afraid of the storm. That didn't displease Wexford. With some scorn he eyed the man's pale face and the bony, none-too-steady hands.

'Scared, Cullam? Not to worry, we'll all die together.'

'Big laugh,' said Cullam, and he winced as the thunder broke above their heads. 'I don't reckon it's safe being so high up. When I was a kid I was in a house that got struck.'

'But you got out unscathed, eh? Well they say the devil looks after his own. Why have you brought him here, Sergeant?'

'He's bought that refrigerator,' said Sergeant Martin. 'And a room heater *and* a load of other electrical bits and pieces. Paid cash for them, a couple of quid short of a hundred and twenty pounds.'

Wexford put the lights on and behind the streaming glass the sky looked black as on a winter's night. 'All right, Cullam, where did you get it?'

'I saved it up.'

'I see. When did you buy that washing machine of yours, the one you washed your gear in after Hatton died?'

'April.' As the storm receded and the thunder became a distant grumbling, Cullam's shoulders dropped and he lifted sullen eyes. 'April, it was.'

'So, you've saved another hundred and twenty pounds in just two months. What do you get a week? Twenty? Twenty-two? You with five kids and council house rent to pay? You've saved it in two months? Come off it, Cullam. I couldn't save it in six and my kids are grown up.'

'You can't prove I didn't save it.' Cullam gave a slight shiver as the overhead light flickered off, then on again. A rolling like the banging of many drums, distant at first, then breaking into a staccato crackling, announced the return of the storm to Kingsmarkham. He shifted in his chair, biting his lip.

Wexford smiled as a zig-zag flash changed the gentle illumination of the office into a sudden white blaze. 'A hundred pounds,' he said. 'That's pathetic payment for a man's life. What's yours worth, Sergeant?'

'I'm insured for five thousand, sir.'

'That's not quite what I meant, but we'll let it pass. You see, an assassin is paid according to his own self-valuation. Never mind what the victim's life's worth. If a road sweeper kills the king he can't expect to get the same gratuity as a general. He wouldn't expect it. His standards are low. So if you're going to employ an assassin and you're a mean skinflint you pick on the lowest of the low to do your dirty work. Mind you, it won't be so well done.'

Wexford's last words were drowned in thunder. 'What d'you mean, lowest of the low?' Cullam lifted abject yet truculent eyes.

'The cap fits, does it? They don't come much lower than you, Cullam. What, drink with a man – drink the whisky he paid for – and then lie in wait to kill him?'

'I never killed Charlie Hatton!' Cullam leapt trembling to his feet. The lightning flared into his face and, covering his eyes with one hand, he said desperately, 'For God's sake can't we go downstairs?'

'I reckon Hatton was right when he called you an old woman, Cullam,' Wexford said in disgust. 'We'll go downstairs when I'm good and ready. You talk and when you've told me where McCloy is and what he paid you, then you can go downstairs and hide your head.'

Still on his feet, Cullam leant on the desk, his head hanging. 'It's a lie,' he whispered. 'I don't know McCloy and I never touched Hatton.'

'Where did the money come from then? Oh, sit down, Cullam. What sort of man are you, anyway, scared of a bit of thunder? It's laughable, afraid of a storm but brave enough to wait in the dark down by the river and bash your friend over the head. Come on now, you may as well tell us. You'll have to sooner or later and I reckon this storm's set in for hours. Hatton had fallen foul of McCloy, hadn't he? So McCloy greased your palm a bit to walk home with Hatton and catch him unawares. The weapon and the method were left to you. Curious, you were so mean, you even grudged him a proper cosh.'

Cullam said again, 'It's all a lie.' He twisted down into the chair, holding his head and keeping it averted from the window. 'Me bash Charlie on the head with one of them stones? I wouldn't have thought of it ... I wouldn't ...'

'Then how did you know it was a river stone that killed him?' Wexford pounced triumphantly. Slowly Cullam raised his head and the sweat glistened on his skin. 'I didn't tell you.'

'Nor me, sir,' said the sergeant.

'Jesus,' Cullam said, his voice uneven and low.

The black clouds had parted to show between them shreds of summer sky turned sickly green. Against the glass the unremitting rain pounded.

Stamford police knew nothing of Alexander James McCloy. His name was on the voters' list as occupying Moat Hall, the small mansion Burden had found deserted, but plainly he had left it months before. Burden plodded through the rain from estate agent to estate agent and he at last found Moat Hall, listed in the books of a small firm on the outskirts of the town. It had been sold in December by McCloy to an American widow who, having changed her mind without ever living in the place, had returned it to the agent's hands and departed to spend the summer in Sweden.

Mr McCloy had left them no address. Why should he? His business with them had been satisfactorily completed; he had taken his money from the American lady and disappeared.

No, there had never really been anything in Mr McCloy's behaviour to make them believe he wasn't a man of integrity.

'What do you mean, "really"?' Burden asked.

'Only that the place was never kept decently as far as I could see, not the way a gentleman's house should be. It was a crying shame to see those grounds neglected. Still, he was a bachelor and he'd no staff as far as I know.'

Moat Hall lay in a fold of the hills perhaps a mile from the A.1. 'Was he always alone when you saw him at the house?' Burden asked.

'Once he had a couple of chaps with him. Not quite up to his class I thought.'

'Tell me, were you taken all over the house and grounds to make your survey or whatever you do?'

'Certainly. It was all quite above board – none too clean, but that's by the way. Mr McCloy gave me a free hand to go where I chose, bar the two big outhouses. They were used for stores he said, so there was no point in me looking. The doors were padlocked anyway and I got what I wanted for my purpose from looking at the outside.'

'No stray lorries knocking about, I daresay?'

'None that I saw.'

'But there might have been in the outhouses?'

'There might at that,' said the agent doubtfully. 'One of them's near as big as a hangar.'

'So I noticed.' And Burden thanked him grimly. He was almost certain that he had found him, that he could say, 'Our McCloy was here,' and yet what had he achieved but dredge up a tiny segment of McCloy's life? The man had been here and had gone. All they could do now was to turn Moat Hall upside down in the forlorn hope something remained in the near-derelict place to hint at its erstwhile owner's present refuge.

'Are you going to charge me with murdering him?' Cullam said hollowly.

'You and McCloy and maybe a couple of others when you've told us who they are. Conspiracy to murder, the charge'll be. Not that it makes much difference.'

'But I've got five kids!'

'Paternity never kept anyone out of jail yet, Cullam. Come now, you wouldn't want to go inside alone, would you? You wouldn't want to think of McCloy laughing, going scotfree, while you're doing fifteen years? It'll be the same sentence for him, you know. He doesn't get off any lighter just because he only told you to kill Hatton.'

'He never did,' Cullam said wildly. 'How many times do I have to tell you I don't know this McCloy?'

'A good many times before I'd believe you. Why would you kill Hatton on your own? You don't have to kill a man because he's got more money and a nicer home than you have.'

'I didn't kill him!' Cullam's voice came dangerously near a sob.

Wexford switched off the light and for a moment the room seemed very dark. Then, as his eyes grew accustomed, he saw that it was no darker than on any summer evening after heavy rain. The light had a cold bluish tinge and the air was cooler too. He opened the window and a light fresh breeze clutched at the curtains. Down below on the forecourt the tub flowers had been flattened into a sodden pink mush.

'Listen, Cullam,' he said, 'you were there. You left the

bridge ten minutes before Hatton started. It was twenty to eleven when you said goodbye to Hatton and Pertwee and even walking none too fast you should have been indoors at home by eleven. But you didn't get in till a quarter past. The following morning you washed the shirt you'd been wearing, the pullover and the trousers. You knew a river stone had been used to kill Hatton and today you, who get twenty pounds a week and never have a penny to bless yourself with, spent a hundred and twenty quid on luxury equipment. Explain it away, Cullam, explain it away. The storm's blowing over and you've nothing to worry about except fifteen years inside.'

Cullam opened his big ill-made hands, clenched them and leant forward. The sweat had dried on his face. He seemed to be having difficulty in controlling the muscles which worked in his forehead and at the corners of his mouth. Wexford waited patiently, for he guessed that for a moment the man was totally unable to speak. Terror had dried and paralysed his vocal chords. He waited patiently, but without a vestige of sympathy.

'The hundred quid and his pay packet,' Cullam said at last. His tone was hoarse and terrified. 'I . . . I took it off his body.'

112

12

'What did he want it for, Charlie-bloody-Hatton? I've been in his place, I've seen what he'd got. You ever seen his wife, have you? Got up like a tart with her new frocks and her jewellery and all that muck on her face, and not a bleeding thing to do all day long but watch that colour telly and ring up her pals. They hadn't got no kids, yelling and nagging at you the minute you get in, crawling all over you in the night because they're cutting their bloody teeth. You want to know when my missus last had a new frock? You want to know when we last had a night out? The answer's never, not since the first baby come. My missus has to buy the kids' clothes down at the jumble sale and if she wants a pair of nylons they come off the Green Shield stamps. Bloody marvellous, isn't it? Lilian Hatton's got more coats than a perishing film star but she has to go and spend thirty quid on a new outfit for Pertwee's wedding. A hundred pounds? She wouldn't even miss it. She could use it for spills to light her fags.'

The flood-gates had opened and now Cullam, the reticent, the truculent, was speaking without restraint and from a full heart. Wexford was listening with concentration, but he did not appear to be listening at all. If Cullam had been in a fit state to observe behaviour he might have thought the chief inspector bored or preoccupied. But Cullam only wanted to talk. He was indifferent to listeners. All he required was the luxury of silence and a nearly empty room.

'I could have stuck it all,' he said, 'but for the bragging. "Put it away, Maurice," he'd say. "Your need's greater than mine," and then he'd tell me about the new necklace he'd bought for his missus. "Plenty more where that came from," he'd say. Christ, and I can't find the money to buy my kids new shoes! Two kids I'd got when I'd been married as long as Hatton. Is it fair? Is it right? You tell me.'

'I've listened to the party political broadcast,' said Wexford. 'I don't give a damn for your envy. Envy like yours is a hell of a good motive for murder.'

'Yeah? What would I get for killing him? I wasn't in his will. I've told you what I did. I took the money off his body. Five kids I've got and the milkman don't come till eleven in the morning. You ever tried keeping milk for five kids without a fridge in a heatwave?' He paused and with a shifty, fidgety look, said, 'D'you know what Hatton'd have done that Saturday if he hadn't been killed? Wedding first, Pertwee's wedding, and Hatton all got up in a topper with his tarty wife. Round the shops afterwards, not to buy anything, just to fritter. Charlie told me it wasn't nothing for them to get through twenty nicker poking about in the shops. Bottle of wine here, some muck for her face there. Then they'd have some more booze at the Olive, have dinner. Off to the pictures in the evening and in the best seats. Bit of a contrast from me, isn't it? If I want to relax I go out in the garden, anywhere to get away from the kids' bawling.'

'Are you a Catholic, Cullam?'

That surprised him. He had perhaps been expecting a tougher comment and he hunched his shoulders, muttering suspiciously, 'I haven't got no religion.'

'Don't give me that stuff about children then. Nobody makes you have children. Ever heard of the pill? My God, they knew how to plan families twenty years, thirty years before you were born.' Wexford's voice grew hard as he warmed to a favourite theme. 'Having kids is a privilege, a joy, or it should be, and, by God, I'll get the County down on you if I see you strike that boy of yours on the head again! You're a bloody animal, Cullam, without an animal's . . . Oh! what's the use? What the hell are you doing anyway, cluttering up my office, wasting my time? Cut the sob stuff and tell me what happened that night. What happened when you left Hatton and Pertwee at the bridge?'

Stamford had promised to give Burden all the help they could and they were as good as their word. A sergeant and a constable went back with him to Moat Hall and the locks on the two outhouses were forced.

Inside they found oil on the concrete floor and, imprinted by that oil, a tracery of tyre marks. Apart from that there was nothing to show a suspect occupancy but two crushed cardboard cases in one corner. Both had contained canned peaches.

'No joy here,' said Burden to the sergeant. He threw the flattened cardboard down in disgust. 'I've got things like this in my own garage at home. The supermarket gives them to me to bring my wife's shopping home in on Fridays.'

He came to the doorway and started across the deserted yard. As surely as if he could see them actually arriving, see them now, he pictured the stolen lorries driven in. The big doors would open for them and close on them and McCloy and the men who were 'not quite up to his class' would unload them and store the cargoes here. Back-slapping, laughing immoderately, Charlie Hatton would go into the house for a drink and a 'bite to eat' before driving the lorry away and abandoning it.

'I'd like to go over the house,' he said, 'only breaking and entering's not in my line. We'll have to wait for permission from the expatriate lady in Sweden.'

Cullam got up and wandered to the window. He looked as if he expected Wexford to hinder him, but Wexford said nothing.

'He was flashing all this money about in the Dragon. On and on about it he was when we walked up to the bridge.' Cullam stood by the window, staring fixedly now at the road he had trodden with Hatton and Pertwee. The wet pavements cast back mirror reflections. Wexford guessed the Kingsbrook must have swollen now, its stones submerged under a mill-race. 'Pertwee told me to wait for Charlie Hatton,' Cullam said. 'I wouldn't do that. God, I was sick of him and his money.' Slowly he pushed a hand through his thin towcoloured hair. 'Anyway, I told you, I wasn't feeling too good. I just walked along the path in the dark.'

Thinking of what you were going home to, Wexford

thought, and what Hatton was. There would have been no sound down there but the sibilant trickle of water. Above Cullam, above the web of black branches, a tranquil galaxy, a net of stars. Greed and envy took from a màn's heart everything but – well, greed and envy. If Cullam had noticed anything as he walked it would have been the rubbish, the flotsam that the river sucked in and gathered on its journey through the meadows.

'Did you wait for him?'

'Wait, nothing!' Cullam said hotly. 'Why would I? I hated his guts.' Wexford wondered how long since anyone had made so many damaging admissions in this office in so short a space of time. Cullam burst out violently. 'I was sick then. I threw up under the trees. And I felt bloody, I can tell you.' He shuddered a little, but whether at the memory of this vomiting by the water's edge or of something even uglier Wexford could not tell. He watched the man narrowly, not caring for the wariness of his eyes and the way his hands had begun to twitch. 'I'm not used to whisky. A half of bitter's more my line.'

'You're not the only one,' Wexford said sharply. 'What happened then? Did you hear Hatton approach?'

'I'd heard him for a bit by then. I could hear him whistling a long way behind. He was whistling that stupid little old song of his about the man who was scared to go home in the dark.' Wexford looked up and met the shifty eyes. They slid away furtively, the pink lids blinking. Was Cullam a complete clod or did he realize how macabre his words had been? A man would have to be totally deficient in imagination to fail to be struck with a kind of horror and awe.

> 'Mabel, dear,
> Listen here,
> There's robbery in the park . . .'

Burden, who had heard them, had memorized the words and repeated them to his chief. 'Robbery in the park . . .' How did it go on? Something about there being no place like home but he couldn't go home in the dark. It was Wexford's turn to shiver now. In spite of his age, his experience, he felt a cold thrill run through him.

'Then it happened,' Cullam said suddenly. His voice trembled. 'You're not going to believe this, are you?'

Wexford only shrugged.

'It's the truth. I swear it's the truth.'

'Save your swearing for the dock, Cullam.'

'Christ . . .' The man made a sudden effort and the words tumbled out fast. 'The whistling stopped. I heard a sort of sound . . .' He had no descriptive power, few adjectives but hackneyed obscenities. 'A kind of choking, a sort of – well, God, it was horrible! I felt so bloody bad, anyway. After a bit I got up and – and I went back. I was scared stiff. It was sort of creepy down there. I couldn't see nothing and I – I stumbled over him. He was lying on the path. Could I have a drink of water?'

'Don't be a damned fool,' Wexford snapped.

'You needn't be so rough with me,' Cullam whined, 'I'm telling you, aren't I? I don't have to tell you.'

'You have to, Cullam.'

'I struck a match,' the man mumbled. 'Charlie's head was all bashed in. I turned him over and I got blood on me.' The words slurred and he gabbled. 'I don't know what come over me. I put my hand inside his coat and took hold of that wallet. There was a hundred quid it it, just on a hundred. He was all warm . . .'

Wexford stared at him aghast. 'He was dead, though?'

'I don't know. . . . I don't . . . Christ, yes, he was dead! He must have been dead. What are you trying to do to me?' The man put his head in his hands and his shoulders shook. Wexford took hold of his jacket roughly, pushing him so that his head jerked up. The tears on Cullam's cheeks awoke in him a nausea and a rage so fierce that it was all he could do to prevent himself from striking him. 'That's all, everything,' Cullam whispered, shuddering. 'The body rolled down the slope into the water. I ran home then, I ran like hell.' He put his fists into his eyes like a child. 'It's all true,' he said.

'The stone, Cullam, what about the stone?'

'It was laying by him. By his legs. I don't know why but I chucked it back in the water. There was blood on it and hair, bits of hair and – and other bits . . .'

'A bit late in the day to get squeamish, wasn't it!'

Wexford's tone was savage, its effect electric. Cullam sprang to his feet and let out a great cry, drumming his fists on the desk.

'I never killed him, I never, never . . . ! You've got to believe me.'

Burden had just come in, damp and disgruntled, when Wexford erupted bull-like from the lift.

'Where's Martin?'

'Don't ask me. I've just driven close on two hundred miles and I . . .'

'Never mind all that. I've got Cullam upstairs and he's come out with a fine tale.' Controlling his voice with an effort, he gave Burden a swift précis. 'Says he took the money off Hatton's corpse. Maybe that's all he did. I just don't know.'

'But you'll hold him? Keep him here on a charge of stealing the hundred quid and the pay packet?'

'Something like that. Martin can deal with it. I want you and Loring and anyone else going spare over in Sewingbury to turn Cullam's house upside down.'

'In case he's got McCloy's blood money hidden away?'

'Mike, I'm just beginning to wonder,' Wexford said wearily, 'if McCloy isn't a myth, a fiction. Cullam's a damned liar and all we know of McCloy rests on his word alone. Why shouldn't he have fabricated McCloy as a neat little red herring?' He sighed. 'Only he hasn't got any imagination,' he said.

'McCloy exists all right,' Burden said emphatically. 'He's an elusive sort of bird but he exists.'

It was eleven when Wexford got home. They had searched Cullam's house, grubbing through soiled unmade beds, cupboards full of clothes that smelt of food spills, drawers containing a jumble of broken rubbish. They had searched but the only money they had found was two and eightpence in Mrs Cullam's handbag, a white plastic handbag with black grease in its creases. And their only sinister discovery was bruises and contusions on the legs of one of the children. . .

118

'Give me an ounce of civet, good apothecary,' said Wexford to Clytemnestra, 'to sweeten my imagination.' In the belief that he had told her she was a good dog, Clytemnestra wagged her plumed grey tail. The door opened and Sheila came in. 'What are you doing home on a Wednesday?' said her father ungraciously.

'That thing came off my tooth. I was eating a Milky Way and it collapsed. So I had to come down and see Mr Vigo.' She gave him a disarming smile and kissed his cheek. Her hair was dressed in a pyramid of fat ringlets and she looked like a Restoration wench, maid to Millamant, scene stealer, fit to be kissed in corners.

'Well, did he fix it up?'

'Mm-hm. On the spot. He said he wouldn't charge me.'

'Charge you? Me, you mean. And I should hope not.'

Wexford grinned, sloughing off the memory of Cullam's filth like a soiled skin. 'Now you've got false teeth,' he said, 'you mustn't expect to eat toffee.'

'I haven't got false teeth. I've just got a crown. D'you want some of my coff-choc? It's Nes and drinking chocolate mixed up. Quite groovy.'

'I don't think so, lovey, thanks all the same.'

'Mr Vigo and I got quite matey,' said Sheila. She dropped on the floor and, lying on her stomach with her elbows on the carpet, looked up into his face. 'He gave me tea in that Chinese room of his. I was scared to move, he's obviously so crazy about all that stuff. His wife came in and banged the door and he was furious because it made the china rattle; he said she just didn't understand.'

'How quaint. What you might call a new one.'

'Oh, Pop, it wasn't like that. When I went the receptionist was just leaving and she walked down into the town with me. She said Mr Vigo had really married for money. She was an heiress and she had a hundred thousand pounds and Mr Vigo wanted money to collect that Chinese stuff. He only stays with his wife now because of the baby. And he goes away most weekends. Sometimes he doesn't come back till quite late on a Monday night. The receptionist thinks he's got a girlfriend in London. She seemed a bit jealous. D'you know, I got the idea he sleeps with her too.'

Wexford kept his face unmoved, but for the faintest flicker

of what he hoped looked like sophisticated amusement. He wasn't shocked by what he had been told; he was astonished that it should have been said to him by his own daughter. In a way he was proud and grateful. Nearly forty years had passed since he was Sheila's age. Could he have spoken such words to his father? He would rather have died.

Sheila stretched, got up easily. 'Since I'm home,' she said, 'I may as well do my duty. Fancy ten minutes down by the river, dog?'

Wexford said quickly, 'No, not there, sweetheart.' What, allow his child to walk alone by those dark waters? 'I'll take the dog.'

'Really?'

'Go on. Get off to bed. That hair looks as though it'll take a lot of coping with.'

Sheila giggled. 'You'd be surprised.' He stared, somewhat appalled, as she lifted the wig like a hat and dropped it over a cut-glass vase.

'My God, it's a wise father that knows his own child!' He eyed her eyelashes suspiciously, her long fingernails. How many more bits were take-off-able? Wexford, who was hardly ever shaken from his equilibrium by the devious excesses of criminals, was perpetually astonished by his own daughter. Smiling wryly, he fetched the lead and yanked Clytemnestra from the best armchair.

The night air was fresh, washed by the storm into a cool clarity. Hardly a star showed, for the sky was veiled by a lacy wrack, bleached snow-white by the moon that rose in a clear unclouded patch. The meadow grass he had compared to a tapestry had since that earlier walk been cut and the land had become a pale stubbly desert. It was cold for the time of year. When he came to the river he saw that it was much swollen. In places the stones were totally submerged under the racing water.

Wexford whistled up the dog and stepped on briskly. He could see the bridge now, its stones gleaming silver and the hart's tongue ferns between them like shivering slivers of metal. Someone was standing on the parapet, leaning over and looking down. It was some time before Wexford could decide whether it was a man or a woman and when he

120

realized it was a woman he called out a brisk, cheerful good night so that she should not be afraid.

'Good night, Chief Inspector.' The voice was low, ironic, immediately identifiable. Wexford approached Nora Fanshawe and she turned to face him.

'A fine evening after the storm,' he said. 'How's your mother?'

'She'll live,' the girl said coolly. A reserve that was part distaste blanked her features. Wexford knew that look. He had seen it hundreds of times on the faces of people who fancied that they had said too much to him, opened their hearts too wide. Presumably they imagined their confidences led him to regard them with disgust or pity or contempt. If only they knew that to him their revelations were but bricks in the house he was trying to build, rungs on the ladder of discovery, twisted curve-edged pieces in the current puzzle!

'Nothing fresh come back to her?'

'If you mean about the girl in the car, she says there was no girl. I know when she's telling the truth.'

'People never remember what happened immediately before they got hit on the head,' Wexford said cheerfully, 'especially when their skulls are fractured. It's a medical fact.'

'Is that so? I mustn't keep you, Chief Inspector. Did you know your dog's out in the road?'

Wexford retrieved Clytemnestra from the path of a solitary oncoming car. The driver wound down his window and cursed him, adding that for two pins he'd tell the police.

'Blooming thorn in my flesh, you are,' Wexford said to the dog as he clipped the lead on. 'A source of humiliation.' He watched the girl retreat into the Olive and Dove, the moonlight casting her shadow black, straight and attenuated.

13

Detective Constable Loring was delighted at the prospect of a day in London. He was mortally afraid of Wexford who, he felt, treated him with a just but unremitting harshness. Someone had told Loring of the chief inspector's almost paternal fondness for his predecessor, Mark Drayton, and of his disillusionment when Drayton had come to grief. It had been over some mess with a girl and a bribe. Drayton, they told him, had worn his hair long, had been surly and sarcastic and clever and a devil with the women. Loring, therefore had his own hair cropped eccentrically close and was as eager, as bright and cheerful as he could be. Cleverness, he felt, must come hereafter. At present he couldn't compete with Wexford and Burden who were constantly being clever all over the place. As for the women . . . Loring was healthily keen. It afforded him considerable pleasure to be going to London on a quest for three missing girls. Wistfully he thought how very gratifying it would be to find the right one and perhaps hear an appreciative Wexford call him Peter. Drayton had frequently been favoured by the use of his Christian name.

For all his dreams and his naïveté, Loring was a perfectly competent officer. He made his mistakes and he was frank about them. At twenty-one he was six feet tall, as thin as he had been at fourteen, and desperately anxious for the day to come when he had finally grown out of his acne. For all that – the spots were far less noticeable than he believed – the girls he asked out usually accepted his invitations and the older women he interviewed patted their hair and smiled when he began his questions. With luck, he sometimes thought, when he put on a bit of weight and got rid of those damned spots, he might one day look rather like John Neville. He was surprised and somewhat chagrined by his reception at the Eastcheap hairdresser's.

Carol Pearson was the girl whose disappearance he was investigating and he had already called on her mother in Muswell Hill. A skittish lady of forty with the mental age and taste in dress of eighteen, she had simpered over him and offered him gin. God knew, you were only young once – Mrs Pearson looked as if she intended to be young several times over – and if Carol chose to pop off with her boy friend for a couple of months, she wasn't one to stand in her way. The boy friend was married, so what else could poor Carol do? The fact was she was sick to death of that job of hers, threatening to leave any time. Did Loring know the miserable wages they paid, the fact that the girls practically had to live on their tips! The boy friend had money. He was a travelling salesman, Mrs Pearson said vaguely. But she couldn't recall his name, hadn't been able to tell the police when they asked before. Jack, Carol had called him. She never wrote letters. Easy come, easy go like her mother she was, and Mrs Pearson gave him an ingratiating smile. She'd turn up one of these fine days.

So Loring had taken the tube to Tower Hill, getting lost a couple of times on the way. He walked up Eastcheap and picked out the office of the late Jerome Fanshawe by the brass plate on its marble doorway. Roma, the hairdresser's where Carol Pearson had worked, was diagonally opposite. Loring went in.

Never in his life had he seen anything like that receptionist. She wasn't the sort of girl you would dare to kiss, supposing you wanted to. Her hair was an artfully and deliberately tangled mass of red curls, the face beneath a miracle of paintwork, an artist's achievement of cream and amber light and shade with sooty eyes and blanked-out mouth. She wore a near-ankle-length black skirt, backless red boots and a short red caftan embroidered in gold.

Both her white telephones rang simultaneously as Loring entered. She lifted the receivers one after the other, said into each, 'Good morning. Roma. Will you hold the line one moment?' before resting them side by side on her enormous appointments book. 'Can I help you?'

Loring said he was a police officer and produced his card. She betrayed no surprise. 'One moment, please.' The telephone conversations were consecutively resumed, appointments made in the book. Loring glanced down the salon. Nothing like it had ever been seen in Kingsmarkham where clients still sat isolated in separate cells. Here the walls were lined in what looked like huge slices of pumpernickel. The chandeliers were black and silver mobiles and the floor a seemingly frozen lake of scarlet. Most of the assistants were men, tired worn-looking young men in light-weight suits drifted all over with many-coloured hair.

'If you've come about Carol Pearson,' the receptionist said contemptuously, 'you'll want Mr Ponti. One moment, please.' The left-hand phone had rung again. 'Good morning. Roma. Will you hold the line a moment, please? He's in the gentleman's salon and he's styling so you can't . . . Just *one* moment.' She lifted the second phone. 'Good morning. Roma. Just one . . .'

'Thank you for all your help,' Loring said. He retreated into the street and entered the door to what he would have called the barber's. It was not very different from its Kingsmarkham equivalent. Things in the world of fashion evolve more slowly for men than for women.

Mr Ponti looked more like a master at a public school than a hairdresser. He was tall and thin and he wore a perfectly plain, almost ascetic dark suit. The only indication that he had in fact been 'styling' was the handle of a pair of scissors protruding from his breast pocket and which Loring, so overpowering was the pedagogic impression, had at first taken for the rims of spectacles.

The other stylists leapt aside deferentially as he wove his way along the aisle between the chairs. The daylight from the door showed suntan powder on his cheekbones and now that he was close to, Loring saw him as an actor made up to play some academic part. The stoop was there, the vague though sharp expression, the myopic eyes.

A very faint trace of an Italian accent came through as he spoke. 'Carol?' he said. 'We have had the police here before and I told them, we cannot help.' He took the black leather handbag from Loring and fingered it appreciatively. 'This is very nice quality, very good.' With a shrug, he swept shut a concertina-style folding door that partly closed off the shop. 'Listen, she would not have this. I don't like to be cruel, but she was a cheap little girl. No style, no elegance. Ha!' From the interior of the bag he took out the Woolworth compact and the lipstick in its grazed metal case. 'These she might have, this cheap rubbish.' His long thin nose quivered disdainfully.

Loring thought him an odious man. 'Have you ever had a Mr Jerome Fanshawe among your clients?'

The name was evidently familiar. 'The stockbroker from across the street? I am told he is dead in a car accident.' Loring nodded. 'He has never been here.'

'Sure of that?'

'I never forget a client's name. All my clients are personally known to me.' Ponti snapped the bag shut and leant against the counter, looking bored.

'I'm wondering if Miss Pearson knew him,' Loring said, flinching from the scent of the man's after-shave. 'Did she ever mention him or did you ever see her go into his office?'

'I know nothing.' Ponti slid the door aside an inch and snapped his fingers. 'Those shots of Carol,' he called authoritatively, adding to Loring, 'I showed them to the other policemen. You may care to look at them.' He fixed his pale brown eyes on Loring's own haircut and studied it reflectively and with faint distaste.

The photographs were pushed round the edge of the door and Loring took them. 'I used her once as a model,' said Ponti. 'She was no good, no damn' good at all.'

They looked all right to Loring. He had a simple taste in feminine beauty, demanding no more than that a girl should be pretty and fresh and smiling. For these shots Carol Pearson's hair had been dressed in fantastic pyramids of sausage curl, some of which spiralled to her shoulders. She looked ill-at-ease as if she wore instead of her own hair a Britannia helmet and she seemed to be shrinking beneath the weight, peering upwards with a nervous half-smile. Her eyes were painted ridiculously with diagonal lines radiating from the lower lids and her ear lobes dragged down by encrusted pendants. Under the *maquillage* she was a pretty girl, classically lovely, and Loring recalled sickeningly that it might be she who had come to her death, hideously disfigured, in blood and fire and water.

'No damn' good at all,' the hairdresser said again.

Doreen Dacres had turned up.

It was a curious story Loring heard from her married sister in Finchley. Doreen had gone to take up her club job in Eastbourne, arrived early and been kept waiting in a deserted lounge. There a well-informed cleaner had enlightened her as to what some of her new duties might consist of and Doreen, taking fright, had debunked into the street.

She had only five pounds in the world. Room and job in London having been abandoned, she took stock of her situation. The married sister had made it clear she wouldn't be welcome as a lodger with her and her husband, and their parents were in Glasgow, a city to which Doreen had sworn she would never return. Finally she had taken her luggage to a boarding house and, nervous that the club might catch up with her, booked herself in as Doreen Day and taken a shop assistant's job in the same name.

It was only when she wanted some clothes sent on that she had contacted her sister, six weeks later, by telephone. Thankfully, Loring crossed her off his list.

His last port of call was the Princess Louise Clinic in New Cavendish Street and he was directed by its porter to the nurses' home. This was a pleasant four-storey Regency house with white pillars flanking a bright blue front door liberally decorated with polished brass. A woman who called herself Home Sister came down to him and, before Loring could speak, she placed one pink finger against her lips.

'Quiet as a mouse, please. We mustn't forget the night staff are all getting their beauty sleep, must we?'

There was a deep silence in the hall and a sweet scent far removed from the strong antiseptic of the hospital proper. It made Loring think of young girls, bevies of girls, whose freshly bathed bodies, as they passed through this place, left behind a mingled memory of Jasmine and Russian Leather and French Fern and New Mown Hay. He tip-toed after this stout navy-blue woman, who seemed to him half wardress and half mother superior, into a little lounge where there were chintz-covered chairs and flowers and an old television set.

'The girl who had the room next to Nurse Culross will be the best one to help you,' said Home Sister. 'Her name is Nurse Lewis, but of course it's out of the question that she should be disturbed if she's still sleeping.' She fixed him with a fierce censorious eye. 'Out of the question,' she said again. 'If you were the Home Secretary himself I wouldn't do it.' Apparently she was waiting for some show of defiance, and when Loring merely returned her look meekly, she lost some of her asperity and said, 'I'll make enquiries but I can't promise anything. Meanwhile, perhaps you'd care to look at some books.'

By this she meant magazines. The Princess Louise Nurses' Home was less sophisticated then Vigo's waiting room and it offered instead of *Nova* and *Elle* the *Nursing Mirror* and two copies of *Nursery World* which Loring saw were fifteen years old. Left alone, he stared out into the street.

An annexe to the clinic was a maternity hospital, part of it but distinctly separate from the larger building. While he waited, Loring saw a Bentley draw up and a young girl emerged leaning heavily on the arm of her husband. Her body was huge and unwieldy and evidently she was already in labour. Ten minutes passed and a Jaguar appeared. A similar little tableau took place, but in this case the potential mother was older and her maternity dress even more indicative of the *couturière* from whom it had come. The Princess Louise Clinic was busily fulfilling its function of replenishing the upper classes.

It was nearly five o'clock before the door opened slowly and Nurse Lewis came to him. Her eyes were heavy and she looked as if she had just wakened. She wore no make-up and she looked spotlessly clean, her blouse stiff and crisp from the launderer, her pale, almost cream-fair hair damp and streaked where a coarse-toothed comb had just passed through it.

'I'm sorry if I've kept you. I'm on nights you see.'

'That's all right,' Loring said. 'I work nights myself sometimes. I know what it's like.'

127

Nurse Lewis sat down and her bare legs gleamed. Her pink toes were like a little girl's in a little girl's sandals.

'What did you want to know? I talked to the police before.' She smiled earnestly. 'I told them all I knew about Bridie Culross, but that wasn't much, you see. Bridie didn't make close friends with girls, she was a man's girl.'

'I'd like to hear anything you can tell me, Miss Lewis.' Just let them talk. He had learnt that from Wexford. 'About what sort of girl she was. She had a lot of boy friends?'

'Well, this isn't a teaching hospital so there aren't any medical students. She'd been here for a year since she qualified and she's been out with all the housemen.'

Loring wrote that down.

'The man she was most keen on – well, I never knew his name. She called him Jay.'

'As if it were an initial, do you mean? Like short for John or James or – Jerome?'

'I suppose so. I told the police all this before, you know. They weren't very interested.'

'You see, we don't usually bother very much about missing girls.'

'Why are you bothering now?'

'Let's leave that for a moment, shall we, Miss Lewis? Tell me more about this Jay.'

She crossed her long bare legs. 'I never saw him,' she said. 'He was married, I'm afraid. Bridie didn't worry much about that sort of thing. Oh, and I remember her saying his wife had been a patient here.'

Charming, Loring thought. He visits his sick wife and picks up one of the nurses on his way out.

'I know what you're thinking', said Nurse Lewis, 'and it wasn't very nice. He'd got lots of money and a nice car and all that, Bridie . . .' She hesitated and blushed. 'Well, Bridie lived with him actually.'

'Lived with him? In his house?'

'I didn't quite mean that.'

'Oh, I see.' Nurses, who ought to be used to the facts of life, were astonishingly prudish, he thought. 'Er – she went to spend a weekend with this man on Saturday, May 18th? In Brighton, wasn't it?'

'That's right, with Jay.' Nurse Lewis was still blushing at

128

the implications of this weekend. 'She didn't come back. I heard Matron say she wouldn't have her back this time if she came.'

'She'd done it before, you mean?'

'Well, she'd been late a good many times and sometimes she didn't bother to come in after a late night. She said she wasn't going to dress operations and cart bedpans around for the rest of her life. She was going to have it soft. That's what she said. I thought she'd gone away with Jay to live with him properly. Well, not properly, but you know what I mean.'

'Tell me, did he give her presents? Did she have a very good black handbag with a Mappin and Webb label? This one?'

'Oh, yes! He gave it to her for her birthday. She was twenty-two. Look . . .' She frowned and leant towards him. 'What is this? You've found her handbag but you haven't found her?'

'We're not sure yet,' said Loring, but he was.

Wexford would be displeased if he went back with just this and no more. Loring would have liked another day in London, but it was hardly worth facing Wexford's rage, the necessary preliminary to granting it. He went into the main hospital building and rang the bell at the enquiry desk. While he waited he looked about him, reflecting that he had never been in a hospital like this one before. His impression was that he was the first person to enter it for a long time with less than five thousand a year and he thought of Stowerton Infirmary where the outpatients sat for hours on hard chairs, where the paint was peeling off the walls and where everyone seemed to be in a hurry.

Here, instead, was an atmosphere of lazy graciousness as in a large private house. A very faint odour of disinfectant was almost entirely masked by the scent of flowers, sweet peas in copper jugs and, on the enquiry desk, a single rose in a fluted glass. The floor was carpeted in dark red Wilton.

Loring glanced up the branched staircase and watched the receptionist descend. He asked for a list of all the patients who had entered the Princess Louise Clinic in the past year and his request was received with a look of outrage.

It took him nearly half an hour, during which he was passed from one official personage to another, before he got the permission he wanted.

The list was long and imposing. Loring had never seen *Debrett* but he felt that this catalogue might have been a section of it. Nearly half the names on it were preceded by a title and among the plain Misters he recognized a distinguished industrialist, a former cabinet minister and a television personality who was a household word. Among the women was a duchess, a ballet dancer, a famous model. Loring couldn't find Dorothy Fanshawe. He searched all through the list again because he had been so certain her name would be there. It wasn't there.

J for Jerome, but J also for John, James, Jeremy, Jonathan, Joseph. Was Bridget Culross's lover the husband of the Hon. Mrs John Frazer-Bennet of Wilton Crescent or the husband of Lady James Fyne of The Boltons? Loring concluded and supposed Wexford would also conclude him to be the late husband of Dorothy Fanshawe.

14

The young Pertwees were honeymooning in Jack's father's house. Their own flat wouldn't be ready for a fortnight and Jack had cancelled the hotel booking. There was nowhere else for them to go and nothing much to do. Jack had taken his annual holiday, so here he was at home. Where else would he be? It was, after all, the only honeymoon he would ever get. Usually in his spare time he did a bit of painting or decorating or went to the dogs or down the Dragon. Marilyn made her dresses and giggled with her girl friends and went to meetings calculated to stir up social strife. These are not occupations for a honeymoon and the young Pertwees felt that to follow their old ways during this period, provided as it were for festive idleness and the indulgence of love, would be a kind of desecration. As Jack put it, you can't stay in bed all day, so they spent most of the time sitting hand in hand in the little-used parlour. Marilyn was only articulate on the subject of politics and Jack was never talkative. Neither of them ever read a book and they were abysmally bored. Each would have died rather than confess this to the other and they knew in their hearts that their silence was no threat of future discord. Everything would be fine once Jack was back at work and they were in their own flat. When there were his workmates to discuss and the furniture and having her mother to tea. Now they filled their silences with sad reflections on Charlie Hatton and although this too was no subject for a honeymoon, their shared memory of him expressed in hackneyed and sentimental phrases passed the time away and, because it was selfless and sincere, strengthened their love.

It was thus that Wexford found them.

Marilyn let him into the house, her only greeting a shrug. He, too, could be laconic and brusque and when Jack rose clumsily to his feet, Wexford said only, 'I've come to talk to you about McCloy.'

'You talk then. You tell me.'

The girl smiled at that. 'Give us a cig, Jack,' she said, and she gave her husband a fond proud look. 'Yes,' she said, coming up close to Wexford, 'you give us a lecture. We'd like to know, wouldn't we, Jack? We don't mind listening, we've nothing else to do.'

'That doesn't sound too good on your honeymoon.'

'Some honeymoon,' Jack grumbled. 'You think this is the way I'd planned it?'

Wexford sat down and faced them. 'I didn't kill Charlie Hatton,' he said. 'I didn't even know him. You did. You were supposed to be his friend. You've got a funny way of showing it.'

A spasm of pain shivered the red from Jack's face. He took his wife's hand and he sighed. 'He's dead. You can't be friends with a dead man. All you've got is his memory to hold on to.'

'Give me a piece of your memory, Mr Pertwee.'

Jack looked him full in the face and now the blood returned, beating under the skin. 'You're always playing with words, twisting, being clever . . .'

His wife cut in, 'Showing your bloody education!'

'Leave it, love, I feel the same, but it's no good. It's . . . You've made up your mind Charlie was a crook, haven't you? It wouldn't be no good telling you what he was really like, generous, good-hearted, never let you down. But it wouldn't be no good, would it?'

'I doubt if it would help me to find who killed him.'

'He found us our flat,' Jack said. 'D'you know what he did? The bloke that's got it now, he wanted key money. Two hundred he wanted and Charlie put that up. On loan, of course, but he wouldn't take no interest. May the 21st it was. I'll never forget that date as long as I live. Charlie'd been driving all the day before, driving down from the north. But he come here in the morning to say he'd found this flat for us. I was at work but Marilyn got a couple of hours off

132

from the shop and went down there with him. Promised the bloke the money, he did, more like he was her dad than – just a friend.

May the 21st. The day Hatton had ordered his teeth. Just after the robbery that never was. Here was another example of what Hatton had done with the small fortune he had somehow got out of McCloy.

'I'll let you have it whenever you want, Charlie said. Just say the word. You should have seen him when we did say the word! I reckon giving things away made him really happy.'

'This place,' said Marilyn, mildly for her, 'well, it's not the same without Charlie Hatton and that's a fact.'

Sentimental twaddle, Wexford thought harshly. 'Where did he get all his money, Mrs Pertwee?'

'I could ask him that, could I? I could just come out with it like that? I may be common working class but I was brought up right. I've got manners. So, for God's sake, leave me out of it.'

'Mr Pertwee?'

He would have to answer, Wexford thought. He had said too much and been too self-controlled to plead distress as an excuse this time. Jack put his fist up to his forehead and leant on his elbow.

'Where did he get it? Two hundred and fifty pounds for his teeth, two hundred for you . . .' How it mounted up! 'Money for his furniture, his wife's clothes, your wedding present, money going week by week into the bank. He was earning twenty pounds a week, Mr Pertwee. What do you earn?'

'Mind your own damn' business.'

'Come on now, love,' said Pertwee miserably. He looked at Wexford, biting his lip. 'Bit more than that,' he said. 'Bit more in a good week.'

'Could you lend your best friend two hundred pounds?'

'My best friend's dead!'

'Don't stall, please.' Wexford said sharply. 'You knew what Hatton's life was, Pertwee. Don't tell me you never asked yourself where all that money came from. You asked yourself and you asked him. How did Hatton get to be a rich man on May 21st?'

And now Pertwee's brow cleared. He sighed and there was

133

a tiny gleam of triumph in his eyes. 'I don't know. You could ask me from now till Doomsday. I can't tell you because I don't know.' He hesitated. 'You asked me about McCloy,' he said. 'Charlie didn't get no money from McCloy on May 21st. He couldn't have.'

Then Wexford questioned him and probed and used all the subtlety years of experience had given him. Pertwee held his wife's hand, shook his head, answered monosyllabically and at last he dried up.

At the special court held to give his case its preliminary hearing, Maurice Cullam pleaded guilty to stealing one hundred and twenty pounds from the dead body of Charlie Hatton and was remanded in custody. Further charges might be preferred against him, Burden intimated.

He didn't believe Cullam was a murderer. His house had been searched from top to bottom but no money had been found. Cullam had no bank account and no more than a few shillings in the Post Office. The only effect of the search was the incidental discovery of such savage bruises on the legs of Samantha Cullam as to necessitate her removal into the care of the county authority. Further charges would be preferred against her father, but they would not be in the nature of murder or larceny.

'What's your next step?' said Dr Crocker idly, on his way back from examining the little girl's injuries. 'A bastard who's beat up a kid like that wouldn't stop at murder, if you ask me.'

'It doesn't follow.'

'The trouble with you lot you're always looking for complications. Here's the boss now. I've just been asking Mike here if you've got a vacancy for me on your staff, seeing how I've helped you with your enquiries.'

Wexford gave him a sour look. 'Cullam's no killer.'

'Maybe not. Prefers his victims undersized and female,' and the doctor launched into a heated tirade against the arrested man.

'Oh, I'm sick of the whole bloody thing,' Wexford shouted suddenly. 'I've spent the entire morning trying to pump Pertwee. Sentimental fool! Everyone knows Hatton was a thief

134

and a twister, but Pertwee won't talk because he doesn't want to sully the fellow's memory.'

'It's not a bad principle,' said Burden.

'Any principle's bad, Mike, if putting it into practice means a murderer goes free. Hatton did jobs for McCloy and one weekend in May he started squeezing his old employer. He squeezed him pretty hard, I can tell you. Two hundred pounds for Pertwee, two hundred and fifty for Vigo. . . . Oh, I can't go into it all again.'

'So you're giving up?' said the doctor.

Burden looked deeply shocked and he clicked his tongue old-maidishly. But Wexford said calmly, 'I'm going to try another line for the present and I'm relying on you to smooth the path. You're supposed to be a doctor, after all.'

Mrs Fanshawe was alone when they got back to the Infirmary, but she was out of bed. Wrapped in a black nylon négligé – afterwards Crocker called it a *peignoir* – she was sitting in an armchair reading *Fanny Hill*.

'A chief inspector and an inspector and a doctor to see you,' said Nurse Rose. Mrs Fanshawe tucked *Fanny Hill* under her new copy of *Homes and Gardens*. She knew now that Nurse Rose was a nurse and not a maid and that she was in hospital. But that was no reason why the girl should take the attitude that her patient was honoured by this visit. Mrs Fanshawe knew what was due to her. Besides, she was glowing with the self-confidence of someone who, having been distressingly and obtusely disbelieved for days, has now proved her point. Nora was alive; Nora was here, or at least, a couple of miles away in Kingsmarkham. Probably this deputation, sent from whatever authority it was that had stupidly persisted in burying her, had been sent to apologise.

Hastily Mrs Fanshawe grabbed a handful of rings from the jewel case her sister had brought in and it was a lavishly decorated hand that she extended graciously to Wexford.

Wexford saw a discontented face with sagging chin muscles and lines pulling the mouth down at the corners. Mrs Fanshawe's eyes were hard and bright and her voice acid when she said:

'I'm not mad, you see. Everyone thought I was insane

135

when I said my daughter was alive. Now, I expect, they'd like to apologize.'

'Certainly, Mrs Fanshawe. We all apologize.' Apologies cost nothing. He smiled blandly into the petulant's face and suddenly he remembered what this woman's daughter had told him. How her father had paid her mother to let him have his women in the house. 'No one thought you were mad,' he said, 'but you'd been in a serious accident.' She nodded smugly and Wexford thought, She's no madder than she's ever been. But what did that amount to? She had never, he considered, been very bright.

Nurse Rose scampered in with two more chairs and she bridled, giggling a little, when all three men thanked her effusively.

'You can get me another cushion,' said Mrs Fanshawe. 'No, not a pillow, a proper cushion. And then you can ring my daughter.'

'In ten minutes, Mrs Fanshawe,' said Nurse Rose, tired but bright as ever.

'Just as you like.' Mrs Fanshawe waited until she was gone and then she said pettishly, 'This is supposed to be a private room, not that anyone would think so the cavalier treatment you get. Half the time you ring the bell they don't come.'

Wexford said dryly, 'You don't find it as comfortable as the Princess Louise Clinic?'

'What's that supposed to mean?'

'I understand you were in the Princess Louise Clinic in Cavendish Street in London last year.'

'You understood wrong then. The only time I've ever been in hospital was when my daughter was born.' She sighed impatiently when the door opened and Nurse Rose entered with tea for four. 'I thought you were under-staffed? These gentlemen are officials. They aren't paying a social call.'

But Dr Crocker said, 'Thank you very much, my dear,' and he ogled Nurse Rose outrageously. 'Will you be mother, Mrs Fanshawe, do the honours?'

The rings clinked as she poured the tea. She eyed him suspiciously. 'Well, my daughter's alive,' she said, 'and I've never been to the Princess Louise Clinic. What else d'you want?'

Wexford just glanced at Burden and Burden said, 'Your

136

daughter's alive but there was a dead girl lying by the wreckage of your car. Any idea who she could be? The name Bridget Culross mean anything to you?'

'Nothing at all.'

'She was a nurse.' Mrs Fanshawe's sniff told him eloquently what she thought of nurses. 'She was twenty-two and a girl who might be she was dead in the road with your husband.'

'She was never alive in the car with my husband.'

'Mrs Fanshawe,' Wexford said carefully, 'are you quite sure you gave no one a lift from Eastbourne, from Eastover?'

'I am sick of this,' said Dorothy Fanshawe. 'I don't know how many times I've told you. There was no one else in the car.'

He looked at her and he thought, *Would* you tell me? Are you ashamed that your husband flaunted these women at you, paid you? Or is it that you don't care any more, haven't cared for years, and there really was no one in the car?

Dorothy Fanshawe watched her rings winking in the sunlight. She avoided meeting the eyes of these tiresome men. They thought her stupid or a liar. She knew very well what they were getting at. Nora had been talking to them. Nora hadn't the decency and the discretion to keep silent about Jerome's nasty habits.

How stupid these men were! Their faces were all embarrassed and prudish. Did they really suppose she cared what Jerome had done? Jerome was dead and buried deep. Good riddance. All the money was hers and Nora's now, more money than all those foolish-looking men would earn between the lot of them in their lifetimes. As long as Nora didn't do anything stupid like marrying that Michael, there was nothing in the world to worry about.

Dorothy Fanshawe drank her tea and put the cup down with a sharp tap. Then she rang the bell and as the door opened, said:

'We shall want some more hot water.'

She had been going to say please, but she cut the word off and swallowed it. Suddenly Nurse Rose, so plump and pink and young, had looked just like that maid Jerome used to paw about when she was making the beds. She smiled a little, though, for Jerome was dead and there were no maids or nurses or soft young flesh where he had gone.

'Exhumation!' Burden exclaimed. 'You couldn't do it.'

'Well, I could, Mike,' said Wexford mildly. 'I dare say we could get an order. Only she's been dead so long and the face was in a mess then and . . . God, I could wring Camb's bloody neck!'

'The aunt was so sure,' Burden said.

'We'd best get that Lewis girl down from the Princess Louise Clinic, show her the clothes. But if the girl was Bridget Culross, what was she doing in Fanshawe's car with Fanshawe's wife?'

'I believe Mrs Fanshawe, sir.'

'So do I, Mike. So do I.' Wexford said it again to convince himself. 'I think Fanshawe was capable of taking the girl to his bungalow and sleeping with her while his wife was there. I believe Mrs Fanshawe would have stood it. As to the girl – well, we don't know enough about her to say. But Nora Fanshawe knew nothing of it and Nora Fanshawe was with them until the Saturday. They thought she was going to stay on. So where does Culross come in? And where was she stowed away on the Friday night?'

'It's very disgraceful,' said Burden and he made a face like someone who had been shown a disgusting mess of offal.

'Never mind that. Leave the ethics and concentrate on the circumstantial evidence. The more I hear of them the more I go back to my old idea.'

'Which is?'

'In the light of our fresh information, this: Bridget Culross never knew Fanshawe. His wife was never a patient at the Princess Louise Clinic, therefore he isn't Jay. Probably she went to Eastbourne or Brighton with Jay, rowed with him and tried to get back to London on her own. Maybe she hitch-hiked. A lorry driver put her down on the Stowerton By-pass, she thumbed a lift from Fanshawe – maybe she stepped out into the road, he couldn't stop, hit her head and crashed. How's that?'

Burden looked dubious. 'That means to thumb her lift she

would have had to be standing on the soft verge between the two carriageways.'

'And any normal hitch-hiker stands on the nearside and waits for someone coming down the slow lane?'

'Mm-hm. On the other hand we do know that Mrs Fanshawe heard her husband call out "God!" just before the crash; in fact, that was the last thing he ever did say.'

'I hope,' said Wexford, 'the cry was heard by Providence and interpreted as a plea for forgiveness.' He chuckled sourly. 'So he sees the girl standing on the road, cries out, swerves, hits her. Why did she have only a little loose change in her handbag, no keys, nothing to identify her? Why would a lorry driver put her down on the by-pass instead of in the town?'

'It's your theory, sir.'

'I know it is, damn it!' said Wexford.

But he kept thinking about that lorry driver. Charlie Hatton had passed that way a quarter of an hour before the accident. He couldn't have seen the accident. Could he have seen the girl waiting to thumb a lift? Or could he have been the driver who had left her there? The trouble was Charlie Hatton had been driving in the other direction.

It had been May 20th and on May 21st Charlie Hatton was a rich man. There must be a connection. But where did McCloy come into all this?

Every police force in England and Wales was now looking for Alexander James McCloy, light brown hair, medium height, aged 42, late of Moat Hall, near Stamford in Lincolnshire; because of Burden's recent discoveries; they were looking for him in Scotland too.

This time it was Mr Pertwee senior who admitted him into the house. Still hand-in-hand the honeymooners were watching television.

'Christ, do we have to?' Marilyn said crossly when her husband got up and switched off the party political broadcast. 'What d'you want this time?'

Wexford said, 'In November of last year your friend

139

Hatton arranged to have the lorry he drove for his employer Mr Bardsley hi-jacked. When I say arranged, I mean he did so under the instructions of his other employer, Alexander James McCloy. Hatton got a little tap on the head and they tied him up, just to make things look more realistic. Fortunately, Mr Bardsley was insured. He wasn't, though, when it happened again in March. That time he had to stand the loss himself, unaware, of course, that a good percentage of it was finding its way directly into Hatton's pocket.'

He stopped and looked into Jack Pertwee's pale face. Jack returned his stare for an instant and then dipped his face down into his hands.

'Don't you admit nothing, Jack,' said Marilyn fiercely.

'On the 19th of May,' Wexford continued, 'Hatton drove up to Leeds. He'd been ill and he took it slowly, returning on the next day, Monday, May 20th. While he was in Leeds or on the road he encountered McCloy. He encountered him or discovered something about him to McCloy's disadvantage. Enough, anyway, to put him into a position from which he was able to blackmail McCloy to the extent of several thousand pounds.'

'It's a filthy lie,' said Jack in a choking voice.

'Very well, Mr Pertwee. I'd like you to come down to the police station with me, if you please . . .'

'But he's just got married!' interrupted the father.

'Mrs Pertwee may accompany him if she chooses. The situation has arisen that information is being deliberately withheld in a murder enquiry. Are you ready, Mr Pertwee?'

Jack didn't move. Then the hands that clutched his forehead began to tremble. Marilyn put her arms around him protectively, but not gently, and her lips twisted as if she would have liked to spit in Wexford's face.

'Blackmail?' Jack stammered. 'Charlie?' He took his hands away and Wexford saw that he was weeping. 'That's crazy!'

'I don't think so, Mr Pertwee.'

'He couldn't have,' Jack said, mouthing something Wexford didn't quite catch.

'What did you say?'

'I said, he couldn't have. McCloy's inside. You're a copper, aren't you? You know what I mean. McCloy's in prison.'

15

The news from Scotland came through at almost exactly the same time as Jack Pertwee's revelation. Alexander McCloy had been sent to prison for two years on April 23rd, having been found guilty with two other men of organizing a break-in at a supermarket in Dundee on early-closing day, and stealing goods to the value of twelve hundred pounds. A caretaker had been slightly injured during the course of the robbery and McCloy would have received a heavier sentence but for his unblemished record.

'So while Hatton was in Leeds that May weekend,' said Wexford in the morning, 'McCloy had already been safely locked up in Scotland for a month.'

'It looks that way,' said Burden.

'And that not only means he wasn't available to be black-mailed, but also that Hatton's source of – well, I was nearly going to say legitimate, income was cut off. In fact, in May Hatton found himself shorter of money than probably at any time since he was married.'

'Mrs Hatton said that when he was ill during the previous week he hesitated about sending for the doctor privately. By that time he'd presumably spent whatever he'd made when they nicked Bardsley's lorry in March.'

'At his rate of expenditure,' Wexford cut in, 'he probably had. It must have given him quite a nasty feeling. Panicked him, I daresay. Can't you imagine him, Mike, looking to the future when he wouldn't be able to stand all those rounds in the Dragon or take his wife frittering on a Saturday afternoon or cut a fine open-handed figure at his friend's wedding?'

'I imagine he quickly looked round for another source of supply.'

'We'll go up to the Stowerton By-pass,' Wexford said, getting up, 'and to do some reconnoitring. Our two cases are converging, Mike, and unless I'm mistaken, they're soon going to bump.'

'There was no suitcase,' said Sergeant Martin, 'but I want you to look at the clothes she was wearing. They're in a bad way, Miss Lewis. You must try to keep calm.'

She was a nurse and trained to control herself. Martin took her into another room where the burnt torn clothes lay like rubbish heap rags on the table. Each blackened tattered garment lay separate from the others and there was something in this arrangement that suggested a parody of a draper's window.

The bodice of the coat and of the dress were charred fragments, although their skirts were almost intact and patches of orange and yellow showed between the scorch marks. The dead girl's brassière was an ellipse of wire from which every shred of cotton and lace had been burnt away. Margaret Lewis shuddered, keeping her hands behind her back. Then she touched the orange shoes, the white lace stockings as wide-meshed and fine as a hair-net, and she began to cry.

'I gave her those stockings,' she whispered, 'for her birthday.'

Their tops only were charred, but a long brown mark ran down to the knee of one of them where a flame had licked. Martin put his arm under the girl's elbow and led her away.

'I'll tell you everything I can about Bridie,' she said and she gulped the tea Loring had brought her. 'And everything she told me about Jay. She met him in October while she was nursing his wife. The wife was in a long time on account of having a threatened toxaemia and Bridie used to go out with him after he'd visited her. She'd come off duty at eight-thirty, you see, and he'd just about be leaving.

'Well, he dropped her after his wife left the clinic and I thought that was the end of it. But it wasn't. He turned up again in May and the whole thing was on again. Bridie started talking about marrying him. Oh, it was awful, really, and I didn't used to listen much. I wish I had now.'

'Did you ever see him, Miss Lewis?' Martin asked.

Margaret Lewis shook her head. The colour had come back into her cheeks and she wore no make-up to smear when she dabbed at the lids with a spotless handkerchief. 'We weren't working in the same department, you see. Lots of people must have. You'll have to ask the other girls. Bridie said he was quite old, lots older than her, and that was the one thing that made her – well, hesitate, if you know what I mean.'

'So you wouldn't know if this is him?' And Martin showed her a photograph of Jerome Fanshawe. It had been taken by flash at a company dinner and the face was hard, confident, heavily jowled, but because of its arrogance and its strength and despite its age, not unattractive to women.

She looked at it with the distaste of the very young and, not answering him, said, 'I told you they went to Brighton on the 18th of May?' Loring nodded. 'Bridie was going to be met by him at Marble Arch. I saw her go off in that yellow coat and dress. She said she'd have to amuse herself during the daytime because Jay would be at his conference. That's why he was going, you see, to be at this conference.'

Loring gave another encouraging smile. This was the sort of thing Wexford wanted. Then he remembered his search through the clinic's patient list.

'The man we had in mind,' he said carefully, 'we couldn't find his name among the clinic's patients, you know. His wife denies she was ever in there.'

The girl touched the photograph and looked up at him in bewilderment. 'How old is she, for goodness' sake?'

'The wife? Fifty, fifty-five.'

'I'm sorry,' Margaret Lewis blushed. 'I think this has been my fault. Jay's wife was in the *maternity* department. They're always separate, you know, the general and the maternity departments in hospitals. Always. Bridie had done her midwifery and she was nursing Jay's wife when she was ill before the birth and while she was having the baby.'

*

Burden was driving. With the accident plan Camb had given him on his lap, Wexford looked up and said:

'Park in the next lay-by, Mike, and we'll walk.'

An ancient milestone which had always stood on the bank since this highway was the coaching road to London, by chance pin-pointed the crash spot. From it a slow incline wound down into the valley.

The northbound and southbound sections of the by-pass, opened a year before, were separated by a strip of grass on which grew clumps of thin birch trees. Fanshawe's Jaguar had struck one of these trees, overturned and caught fire. Wexford and Burden waited for two cars and a van to pass and then they crossed the road to the centre strip.

A large area of this grass had been burnt but by now new growth had replaced it and there was nothing but a ragged black stump to show where the crash tree had been.

'First,' said Wexford, 'we'll work on the assumption that the girl was in the car with the Fanshawes, she was Jerome Fanshawe's fancy piece and he was driving her back to London. Who sits where? Mrs Fanshawe in the back and her supplanter next to Don Juan or vice versa?'

'Surely there must have been some amount of pretence, sir,' said Burden, wrinkling his fastidious nose. 'It can't have been all open and above-board. The girl would have sat in the back.'

'It's the seat on the driver's left that's called the suicide seat, Mike, and whereas the girl died, Mrs Fanshawe is still alive. If the girl was there at all, she sat in the front.' Wexford made a sweeping gesture with his right hand. 'Up comes Fanshawe, driving like a maniac he was at eighty or so. Now there's no evidence of a burst tyre and the windscreen didn't shatter. What did Fanshawe see that made him cry out "God!" and pull the wheel over?'

'Something in the road?'

'Yes, but what? A big piece of metal or a wooden box? He'd have sailed right over cardboard. Anyway, they didn't find anything in the road afterwards.'

'A dog?'

'Fanshawe wouldn't have crashed for the sake of a dog. And he didn't hit one because there was no body.'

144

'Then he saw the girl herself,' said Burden carefully, 'stepping out of the centre section to wave him down.'

'But we're assuming the girl was *in* the car. Don't you agree with me now that she can't have been?'

Burden walked a little way away from him and stopped by the black birch stump. 'If the girl stepped off here,' he said, taking a couple of paces towards the fast lane, 'and Fanshawe thought he was going to hit her, why didn't he swerve to the *left*, into the middle lane, instead of to the right? The road must have been clear as there were no witnesses to the accident. He swerved inwards, to the right, mounted this centre strip and hit the tree.'

Wexford shrugged. A car in the fast lane leapt past them at seventy. 'Feel like experimenting, Mike?' he said with a grin. 'Just pop out into the road now, wave your arms and see what happens.'

'You can, if you're so keen,' said Burden, involuntarily retreating from the edge. 'I want to stay alive.'

'Funny that girl didn't. Mike, it couldn't have been straight suicide, could it?'

Burden said thoughtfully, 'I suppose it could have at that. Assume she has no connection with Fanshawe, assume she went to the South Coast with another boy friend who ditched her so that she had to hitch a lift as far as here. The driver that brought her to this point might then have dropped her at her own request. She crosses the centre section, waits until a fast car comes and steps out suddenly in front of it. Of course, that doesn't explain why Fanshawe pulled to the right instead of to the left.'

'And it doesn't explain why everything that might have identified her was *removed* from her handbag. If she was a suicide, there's no possible reason why she should have removed it herself. Anyway, you seem to have forgotten our main reason for coming here. The crash occurred at ten to ten and Hatton passed on the other highway, going in the other direction, at approximately twenty to. Impoverished Hatton, desperate to replenish the empty coffers. Suppose he passed a little later than that and saw the girl step out? Now, if Fanshawe were still alive, if, say, he'd killed the girl without damage to his car, and had simply driven on, Hatton might have blackmailed him. But Fanshawe is dead, Mike.'

Now it was Burden's turn to shrug and look baffled. He eyed the other highway, the southbound section, the hedge that bounded it, the meadows behind that hedge. The road came to a crest some fifty yards to the north of where they stood and above this ridge nothing but the pale milky sky was visible.

'If there was some sort of foul play,' he said thoughtfully, 'if, for instance, the girl was pushed into the road . . . Oh, I know it's fantastic, but haven't you got something of the sort in mind yourself? If she was pushed and Hatton, approaching over the brow of the hill, was a witness, why didn't whoever it was doing the pushing, see him first? His lorry was an outsize very high van and anyone standing here would see the top of it appearing over the crest seconds before its driver could see him. Look, here comes a lorry now.'

Wexford turned his eyes towards the brow of the hill. The lorry's roof loomed above it and it seemed that some seconds passed before the cab came into view.

'It was dark,' he said.

'Anyone standing where we are could see its headlights at precisely the same time as its driver saw him.'

The same thought striking each man simultaneously, they walked towards the crest. Beneath them half Sussex lay spread, broad meadows, green and gold, the dense bluish shadows of woodland and in the folds between, farmhouses and the occasional pointing spire of a church. Through this pastoral landscape the road wound its twin white ribbon, hummocking here, dipping there, and sometimes entirely concealed by the green swelling land.

Not more than twenty yards beyond the crest, the southbound section widened into an arc and in this lay-by the occupants of two cars sat picnicking.

'Perhaps he parked here for a bit,' Burden said. 'Walked up this way for – well, a natural purpose or just because he needed air. He hadn't been well, after all.'

But Wexford looked at the view and said presently, 'Where every prospect pleases, and only man is vile.'

The huge American car with its splayed fins dwarfed every

146

other vehicle in the Olive's car park. Crossing the forecourt with Burden, Wexford saw on closer scrutiny that it was neither new nor well cared for. One of its headlamps was broken and the rust on its chrome rim showed that it had been broken a long time. Scratches marred the bluish-green finish on its wings. Here in this tiny car park in a small country town it was an unwieldy mass of metal that doubtless gave a poor return for the petrol it devoured. It took up an immense amount of space but its seating capacity was small.

'Reminds me of one of those prehistoric monsters,' said Wexford, 'all brawn and no brain.'

'Must have been grand once, though.'

'That's what they said about the dinosaurs.'

They sat in the saloon bar. In the far corner Nora Fanshawe sat on a leather settle beside a huge fair man with a small head. His expression was vapid, his shoulders of Mister Universe proportions. Another dinosaur, Wexford thought, and suddenly he was sure this was the owner of the car.

'We keep running into each other, Miss Fanshawe.'

'You keep running into me,' said the girl dryly. She wore another of her finely tailored, neatly stitched suits, navy blue this time and as slick and business-like as a uniform. 'This is Michael Jameson. You may remember, I mentioned him to you.'

The hand that took Wexford's had a damp palm. 'Nice little place this, if a bit off the map.'

'Depends where you make your maps.'

'Come again? Oh, I see. Ha ha!'

'We were just going,' said Nora Fanshawe. Then her strong masculine voice quavered a little as she said, 'Ready, Michael?' Suddenly she was vulnerable. Wexford knew that wistful pleading look. He had seen it before in the eyes of plain women, the pathetic terror of rejection that, because it deprives them of confidence, makes them plainer.

Jameson got up sluggishly, reluctantly; he winked at Wexford and that wink was as eloquent as words.

'Off to see your mother, Miss Fanshawe?'

The girl nodded and Jameson said, 'The old girl keeps her on her toes.'

'Let's go, Michael.' She linked her arm in his and held it

147

tight. Wexford watched them go, telling himself he was a fool to let the scene upset him. She was gruff, rude, unfeminine. She was also peculiarly honest and she lacked the talent of self-deception. Not for a moment did Wexford doubt that she knew this man was quite unworthy of her, in intelligence, in probity, in character. But he was good looking and she had money.

'A bit of an oaf,' said Burden.

Wexford lifted the curtain and between the fuchsias he saw Jameson get into the huge car and start the engine. Nora Fanshawe was not the kind of woman who looks on courtesy from men as her right. The car was already in motion before she got herself into the passenger seat. Jameson had not even opened the door for her from the inside.

16

'I want you all to concentrate,' Wexford said. 'Don't tell me it was a long time ago and you can't remember. It was only about seven weeks ago. You'll be surprised what you can remember if you try.'

They were sitting in Lilian Hatton's flat, Wexford confronting the three people on the sofa. Mrs Hatton wore a black cotton frock and all the jewellery Charlie had ever given her. Her face was white and tense, still stained by the tears she had shed when Wexford had revealed her husband's source of income. Was it a revelation or had she always known? Wexford couldn't make his mind up about that. For all her short skirt and her make-up and the equipment in her kitchen, she was essentially at heart a Victorian wife, helpless, clinging, accepting all her husband's quirks with unquestioning passivity. She would no more have asked Charlie if the brooch she wore was brought with ill-gotten money than her nineteenth-century counterpart would have asked her lord and master to admit that his presents to her were the result of cheating at cards. Hers not to reason why, hers but to accept and praise and adore. Now, as he faced her, Wexford wondered how this anachronism would fend for herself in the world Charlie called a battlefield.

'He always talked about fighting for what you wanted,' she had said wretchedly, 'about being one up on the next man. Planning his – his stra . . . His stra – something.'

'Strategy?'

'That's it. Like as if he was a general.'

A soldier of fortune, Wexford thought, a mercenary.

The other two knew all right, the young Pertwees. They

149

had finally admitted as much and now Marilyn said sullenly, 'He was getting back at the big nobs. What does losing a load mean to them? They're all robbers, anyway. Capitalism's organized robbery of the working classes. Charlie was only taking back what was due to him.'

'Having his revenge on society perhaps, Mrs Pertwee?'

'Yeah, and why not? When we've got a real people's government in this country, folks like Charlie'll get their fair shares and there won't be no crime. Or what you call crime. When we get real socialism.'

'Charlie always voted Conservative,' said Lilian Hatton. 'I don't know, Marilyn, I don't think . . .'

Wexford interrupted them. There was no room for laughter in this flat, yet he wanted to laugh. 'Let's postpone the political discussion, shall we? Mrs Hatton, you've had time to think now and I want you to tell me all you remember about your husband's departure for Leeds on Sunday, May 19th and his return on the 20th.'

She cleared her throat and glanced hesitantly at Jack Pertwee, waiting perhaps for more masculine directions and more masculine support.

'Don't you worry, Lily,' said Marilyn. 'I'm here.'

'I'm sure I don't know what I'd do without you. Well . . . Well, Charlie'd been ill and I didn't want him to go but he would insist.'

'Was he worried about money, Mrs Hatton?'

'Charlie never bothered me with things like that. Oh, wait a minute though . . . He did say the doctor would have to wait to get paid. I remember him saying that. D'you want me to go on about that Sunday?' Wexford nodded. 'Jack and Marilyn came in the evening for a three-handed solo.'

'That's right, said Marilyn, 'and Charlie rung you from Leeds while we was here.'

Mrs Hatton looked at her admiringly. 'So he did. Yes, he did.'

'What did he say to you?'

'Nothing much. It was mostly – well, asking me how I was and saying he missed me.' She sniffed and bit her lip. 'We didn't like being separated. We couldn't sleep away from each other.'

'More like sweethearts than man and wife they were,' said Jack and he put his arm around her shoulders.

'Did he say he was still feeling unwell?'

'Bit under the weather. He'd have come back that night else.'

'Did he sound pleased, excited?'

'Down in the dumps, if anything.'

'Now I want you to be very exact about this. Precisely what time did your husband come home on the following night, the Monday night?'

She didn't hesitate. 'Ten on the dot. He's said ten the night before and I'd made him a chicken casserole. Charlie'd bought me a kitchen timer back in March, but it went wrong and had to go back to the shop, and that was the first time I'd used it. I set it for ten and it just started pinging when Charlie put his key in the door.'

'How was he when he came in?'

'In himself, d'you mean? He'd had his sickness back, he said, and he'd had to stop a couple of times on the road. He'd have been back earlier if he hadn't stopped. He wanted to get back earlier, you see, to surprise me.' Emotion overcame her and she breathed quickly, fighting back the tears. 'I . . . He . . . he said it was stifling in the lorry and he'd had to get a breath of fresh air on the Stowerton By-pass. He walked in the fields a bit where it was cool.'

'Think carefully, Mrs Hatton. Did he say he had seen anything of interest while he was in those fields?'

She looked at him in bewilderment. 'No, he only said it had done him good. He felt fine, he said, and I could see he did. On top of the world he was that night, a different man. He was having his meal and we talked about Jack's wedding.' Her voice grew hoarse and she leant heavily against Jack's arm. 'Charlie wanted me to have a whole new outfit, dress, coat, hat, the lot. He said – he said I was his wife and he wanted me to be a credit to him.'

'And you always were, love. Charlie was proud of you.'

'What happened the next day?' said Wexford.

'We had a bit of a lay-in.' She bit her lip. 'Charlie got up at nine and then he phoned a fellow he knew who was leaving his flat. Charlie'd said he'd come down and look at

151

it when he'd had his breakfast and that's what he did. You tell it, Jack, it's your turn.'

Jack eased away his arm and patted the widow's hand.

'Charlie came down to the works but I couldn't get away. I was off doing the wiring in them new houses over Pomfret way. He said he reckoned he'd found us a flat and I said, take Marilyn with you. I can see him now, old Charlie, pleased as punch and grinning like he always did when he was going to do something for you. Bobbing up and down he was like a monkey on a stick.' He sighed and shook his head. 'Old Charlie,' he said.

Impatiently, Wexford turned to the wife. 'You went with him?'

'Yeah, he came down to Moran's.' Moran's was Kingsmarkham's biggest draper's. 'That old bitch, that manageress, didn't want me to go at first. Not that there's much trade to speak of on a Monday morning. I'm leaving in a month anyway, I said, and if you don't like it you can give me my cards and I'll go now. Straight out I said it. I'd made her look real small in front of Charlie and she never said another word. Well, me and Charlie we went to look at this flat and there was this geezer who was leaving, a right queer if you ask me, wanted two hundred quid key money before he'd let us have it. I could have smacked his face then and there. In a dressing gown he was. There'll be forced labour for his sort one of these fine days and I was just going to come out with it when Charlie said that was all right and we'd find the money somehow. He could see I was dead keen on the place.'

'He paid over the money?'

'Don't be so daft. He said something about consulting with Jack, though if I wanted it Jack'd want it too all right, and then we went. I was fuming. I'll put up the money, Charlie said when we was outside, and you can pay me back when you're rolling. How about that, then?'

'Yes,' said Jack, 'how about that?'

'Did Hatton take you back to the shop?'

'Of course he didn't, he wasn't my keeper. He walked up with me as far as the Olive and then he said he'd got to make a phone call. He went into that box outside the Olive and I never saw him again for a couple of days.'

'Why would he make a phone call from a box when he had his own phone at home?'

The married pair were thinking what he, under other circumstances might have thought. A married man with a phone of his own makes calls from a box to his mistress. Mrs Hatton looked innocent, subdued, armoured by her memories. Then Marilyn laughed harshly. 'You're crazy if you're thinking what I think you are! Charlie Hatton?'

'What do you mean, Marilyn?' the widow asked.

'I'm thinking nothing,' said Wexford. 'Did your husband come home for his lunch?'

'About half-past twelve. I asked him what he was going to do with himself in the afternoon and it was then he said he was going to get his teeth seen to. He kept getting bits of food under his plate, you see. He was very ashamed of having false teeth was Charlie on account of being so young and all that. And on account of me . . . He thought I minded. Me mind? I wouldn't have cared it . . . Oh, what's the use? I was telling you about getting his teeth fixed. He'd often said he'd see about getting his teeth fixed. He'd often said he'd see about getting a real good set when he could afford it and he said he thought he'd go to Mr Vigo.'

'I'd sort of recommended him, you see,' Jack put in.

'You?' Wexford said rudely.

Jack lifted his face and flushed a deep wine colour.

'I don't mean I went to him for my teeth,' he muttered. 'I'd been up at his place once or twice doing electrical work and I'd sort of described what the place was like to Charlie. Sort of about the garden and all the old things he's got up there and that room full of Chinese stuff.'

Mrs Hatton was crying now and she wiped her eyes, smiling reminiscently through her tears. 'Many's the laugh Charlie and Jack used to have over that,' she said. 'Charlie said he'd like to see it. Like to have a dekko, he said, and Jack said Mr Vigo was rolling in money. Well, he'd have to be a good dentist to make all that, wouldn't he? So Charlie thought he was the man for him and he phoned then and there. You'll never get an appointment for today, I said, but he did. Mr Vigo had a cancellation and he said he'd see him at two.'

'And then?'

153

'Charlie came back at four and said Mr Vigo was going to fix him up with a new set. Mr Vigo was as nice as pie, he said, no side to him. He'd given him a drink in this said Chinese room and Charlie said when he was rich he was going to have stuff like that, rooms full of it and vases and ornaments and – and a little army of chess men and . . . Oh God, he'll never have anything where he is!'

'Don't, Lily, don't, love.'

'When did Mr Hatton give you the key money for this flat of yours?'

'It was a loan,' said Marilyn Pertwee indignantly.

'Lend it to you, then?'

'He came round with it to Jack's dad's place on the Wednesday.'

'That would have been the 22nd?'

'I reckon. We handed it over to this bloke as had the flat the next day.' Jack Pertwee stared hard at Wexford. The dull eyes were glazed now, the face pallid yet mottled. Wexford could hardly suppress a shiver. God help the man who murdered Charlie Hatton, he thought, if Pertwee gets on to him before we do.

'Isn't it about time we got shot of that thing?'

Sheila removed Clytemnestra from her father's chair and contemplated the mass of hairs the dog had moulted on to the cushion. 'I'm getting a bit fed up with her myself,' she said. 'Sebastian's supposed to be coming for her tonight.'

'Thank God for that.'

'All right if I have the car to take him to the station?'

'What, is he scared to cross those fields alone?' Mabel, dear, listen here, there's a robbery in the park . . . 'I may want the car. He's young and healthy. Let him walk.'

'He's got a verruca,' said Sheila. 'He had to walk here and back when he brought her a fortnight ago. I'd be meeting him now' – she gave her father a disgruntled look – 'only you've always got the car.'

'It *is* my car,' said Wexford absurdly, and then, because it was a game that he and Sheila played, 'It was my turquoise. I had it of Leah when I was a bachelor. I would not have given it . . .'

'For a wilderness of verrucas! Oh, Pop, you're a honey really. There's Sebastian now.'

Mrs Wexford began calmly laying the table. 'Don't say anything about his hair,' she said to her husband. 'He's got peculiar hair and you know what you are.'

Sebastian's hair resembled Clytemnestra's, only it wasn't grey. It hung on to his shoulders in shaggy curls.

'I hope the Swoofle Hound hasn't been too much of a bore for you, Mr Wexford.'

Wexford opened his mouth to make some polite denial but Clytemnestra's transports at the sight of her owner made speech impossible for a while. She hurled herself at his long legs and plummeted her body against his jacket, a garment which Wexford incredulously identified as part of the full dress uniform of a commander in the Royal Norwegian Navy.

'You'll stay and have a meal?' said Mrs Wexford.

'If it isn't too much trouble.'

'How was Switzerland?'

'All right. Expensive.' Wexford was beginning to nourish the unkind thought that the holiday would have been even more costly had he had to pay boarding kennel fees, when Sebastian disarmed him by producing from his haversack a large box of chocolates for Mrs Wexford.

'Suchard!' said Mrs Wexford. 'How kind.'

Encouraged, Sebastian made short work of roast beef and Yorkshire pudding, occasionally reaching under the table to fondle Clytemnestra's ears.

'I'll drive you to the station,' said Sheila and she gave her father a confident smile.

'That'd be great. We might take Clytemnestra into that Olive place. She likes beer and it'd be a treat for her.'

'Not in my car, you don't,' said Wexford firmly.

'Oh, Pop!'

'Sorry, sweetheart, but you don't drink and drive.'

Sebastian's expression combined admiration for the daughter and a desire to ingratiate himself with the father. 'We'll walk down.' He shrugged. 'It's such a hell of a way to your station, though.' He eyed the banana custard. 'Yes, thanks, I will have some more. The trouble is I'll have to walk Sheila back, unless she goes home by the road,' he added unchivalrously. 'We heard about your murder even in Switzerland. Down in those fields at the back, wasn't it?'

Wexford seldom talked shop at home. Probably this young man wasn't pumping him and yet . . . He gave a non-committal nod.

'Odd,' Sebastian said. 'I went to the station that way a fortnight ago, across the fields.'

Wexford intercepted his wife's glance, deflected it, said nothing. Sheila said it for him.

'What time was it, Seb? About ten?'

'A bit after that. I didn't meet a soul and I can't say I'm sorry.' He ruffled the dog's curly coat. 'If I hadn't jumped smartly out of the way, Clytemnestra, you mightn't ever have seen your papa again. Big American car nearly ran me down.'

'They do nip into that station approach,' said Sheila.

'Station approach, nothing. This was in the fields. In that lane that leads up to the stile thing. Great green car swept in at about forty and I practically had to dive into the hedge. I took the number actually but what with all the kerfuffle about my holiday I lost the bit of paper I wrote it on.'

'A courting couple?' said Wexford lightly.

'Could have been. I was too busy taking the number to look and I was scared of losing my train.'

'Well we won't go by the fields this time, and I'll trail all the way back by the road if it makes you happy, Pop.'

'You can take my car,' said Wexford. 'Stick to bitter lemon in the Olive, eh?'

17

'Here's my theory,' said Burden, 'for what it's worth. I've been thinking about it, though, and it's the only possible solution. We've talked a lot about hired assassins but the only hired assassin in this case was Charlie Hatton, hired by Bridget Culross's boy friend.'

'Fertile,' said Wexford, 'but I'd like it amplified.'

Burden shifted his chair a little nearer those of Wexford and the doctor. The wind and the sunlight filled the office with a pattern of dancing leaves. 'Jay is a rich man. He must be if he can afford to pay for three months in that clinic of yours just because his wife's having a difficult pregnancy.'

'Money down the drain,' commented Crocker. 'Do just as well on the N.H.S.'

'He's rich enough to pay someone to do his killing for him. You can bet your life he's a one-time friend of McCloy's. He arranges for Hatton to be waiting on that by-pass at the point where he's going to drop the girl on their way back from this conference.'

'Just what conference, Mike? Have we checked on Brighton conferences that weekend?'

'The National Union of Journalists, the Blake Society and the Gibbonites all met there,' said Burden promptly.

'What are the last lot?' put in the doctor, 'a bunch of monkeys?'

'Not gibbons,' said Burden, unsmiling. 'Gibbon. *The Decline and Fall* man, the historian. I reckon they're just another collection of cranks.'

'And Jay took a girl to Brighton, but left her alone all day while he gossiped about Gibbon?' said Wexford thoughtfully. 'Well, stranger things have happened. Go on.'

'He faked a quarrel with her in the car on the way back to London and turfed her out of the car in a rage. Hatton was waiting for her, hit her over the head, emptied her handbag and made off back to his lorry. The next day Jay paid him his blood money. You can be sure that call Hatton made from a phone box was to Jay, telling him that the deed was done. And no one would have been any the wiser if Hatton hadn't been greedy and started soaking Jay.'

The doctor made a derisive face. 'Pardon me as a mere layman, but that's a load of old rubbish. I'm not saying the girl couldn't have been dead before the car hit her. She could have. But why should Hatton put her in the road? He couldn't be sure a car would come along and hit her. Besides, he could so easily have been seen. And he was a small man. He wouldn't have had the strength to carry her across the southbound highway. Why bother, anyway? If her death was supposed to look like the work of some vagrant maniac, why not kill her behind the hedge and leave her there?'

'What's your idea then?' said Burden sourly.

Crocker looked uppish. 'I don't have to have theories. I'm not paid for this kind of diagnosis.'

'Come down from your perch, Paracelsus,' said Wexford 'and put yourselves in our shoes for a moment. Have a shot at it.'

'The trouble with you lot is you believe everything you're told. I don't. I know from experience people distort the truth because they're afraid or they have a psychological block or they want to be over-helpful. They leave things out because they're ignorant and when you tell them you want to know everything, they sort out what everything is to them. It's not necessarily everything to the expert who's asking the questions.'

'I know all that,' said Wexford impatiently.

'Then, Mrs Fanshawe says the girl wasn't in the car, not because she's ashamed to admit it but because she's literally forgotten. Of course she was in the car. She hitched a lift a couple of miles before the crash and all that period is a blank to Mrs Fanshawe. Naturally she's not trying to clear the blanks. The very word "girl" is a red rag to a bull to her.

158

You're bothered because there were no keys and no other identification in that expensive handbag. She left them in her suitcase and she left that suitcase in Jay's car.'

'Why?'

'So that Jay would have to come back for her. It was on the seat and after a few miles he'd realise and come back. Or so she thought. When he didn't she knew she could get it back all right at a later date. Presumably she knew where Jay lived. *In extremis* it would be an excuse for having it out with him and confronting the wife.'

'But Jay didn't come back and she got fed-up with waiting, so she hitched a lift from Fanshawe.'

'That's the simple natural solution, isn't it?'

'What you're saying amounts to that Jay is just a more or less harmless philanderer. Why didn't he come forward when we found the girl?'

The doctor gave a sardonic and superior laugh. 'Thanks to a spot of inefficiency on someone's part, you told the Press the dead girl was Nora Fanshawe. Why should Jay stick his neck out? If he'd ditched the girl on the outskirts of Stowerton it was because he never wanted to see her again. He's not likely to pop up and help you with your enquiries.'

Wexford said quietly, 'Where does Charlie Hatton come into all this?'

'If you don't mind, I'll answer that question with a question of my own. What makes you think he didn't have a source of supply completely separate from McCloy or Fanshawe or Jay?'

Wexford looked at Burden and he saw uneasiness creep into the inspector's face. He couldn't allow for this sort of doubt. It was unthinkable. 'He was behind that hedge,' he said stoutly. 'He saw that girl pushed into the road.'

'Get away!'

'Oh, not from the central strip of grass.' Wexford paused for effect. The quivering leaf shadows played, danced and died as the sun went in. 'From a car,' he said, 'she was thrown out of a car.'

The sunlight came and went intermittently. Alone now, Wexford watched the cloud masses drift above the High Street roofs and cast their shadows now on a house front, now on the road itself. The sun blazed briefly, appearing from time to time embedded in a golden nest.

Presently he took his railway timetable from his desk drawer and looked up the afternoon trains to London. There was a fast one at two-fifteen.

The lift was waiting for him, its door invitingly open. By now Wexford had lost all his inhibitions about it. He stepped inside and pressed the ground-floor button. The door closed with a whisper and sank on a sigh.

Someone on the first floor must have summoned it, for it trembled and its floor seemed to rise a fraction. Then it shivered and stopped. Wexford waited for the door to slide but nothing happened.

It was a solid door with neither glass nor grille. Impatiently Wexford tapped his foot. He glanced at the control panel and wondered why the light marked one hadn't come on. Probably it had been summoned and whoever was waiting had got bored and used the stairs. In that case, why wasn't the light on? He stuck his thumb on the ground-floor button. Nothing happened.

Or rather, the worst, what he had always feared, had happened. The damned thing had broken. It had got stuck. Very likely it was between floors. A tremor of panic touched one corner of his brain and he dismissed it with a fierce oath. He tapped smartly on the door.

Was the thing sound-proof? Wexford had never had much faith in sound-proofing methods, having lived during the early part of his career in a series of flats highly commended by their agents for the seaweed board allegedly incorporated in their walls and ceilings. They hadn't stopped him being driven nearly mad by the piano from upstairs and the incessant drumming of children's feet. They couldn't sound-proof a dwelling house, he thought furiously. It would be just like 'them' to succeed in the utterly pointless achievement of sound-proofing a lift. He knocked on the door again and then he pressed the button market Emergency. If anything, the little black and gilt box settled into an even deeper immobility.

There was a little leather seat, like the extra seats in a taxi, folded into the wall. Wexford pulled it down. It creaked when he sat on it. Glancing about him with simulated ease, he assessed the volume of the lift. Seven by four by four. As far as he could see there was no means of letting air in or carbon dioxide out. He listened. He might have been stone deaf, the silence was so deep.

How long could anybody as big as he remain confined in a space seven by four by four? He had no idea. It was ten minutes to two. He got up and the seat snapped back into the wall. The sound made him jump. He brought both fists down against the panelling and pounded hard. The lift quivered and that disquieted him. For all he knew it was hanging by a thread.

It might be better to shout. But shout what? 'Help, let me out!' was too humiliating to consider.

'Is there anyone there?' he called, and because that sounded like a medium in a sèance, 'Hey, the lift's stuck!'

Under the circumstances, it would be wiser to save his breath. It was possible that most of the rooms were empty. Burden and Martin and Loring were all out. Camb might be sitting downstairs (downstairs!) at his desk. Someone would be sitting there. It was equally certain that his cries were unheard.

With an unpleasant sinking feeling, Wexford faced the fact that unless Burden returned two hours earlier than he had said, it was likely that no one would want to use the lift. Camb was at his post, Martin in Sewingbury. It hadn't escaped Wexford's notice that most of the uniformed branch preferred the stairs. He might be there till tea-time and if so, would he still be alive at tea-time?

Two o'clock. If he didn't get out in five minutes he would miss that train. That didn't matter too much. Without checking at the Princess Louise Clinic, he was almost sure he had the answer. Guesswork perhaps, but inspired guesswork. If he died they would never know . . .

Sick of shouting, he flapped down the seat again. Probably it was only his fancy that the air in the tiny box was growing thick. Panic would not help at all. It was outside the indulgences he allowed himself. Outside them too was the thread of terror that told him he was a rat in a hole, a fox in a stopped earth. Briefly he thought of Sheila. No more of that, that way madness lies . . .

161

Two-fifteen, Wexford took out his notebook and a pencil. At any rate, he could write it all down.

'I don't know where he gets his crazy ideas,' said the doctor indiscreetly. Burden gave him a neutral smile. 'If I was in your place I'd want to try it out. Have you got something else on this afternoon?'

'Nothing Martin and Loring can't see to without me.'

'Shall we take my car, then?'

'Don't you have a surgery?' asked Burden, who thought the whole plan unorthodox.

'My afternoon off. I rather like this dabbling in forensics.'

Burden didn't. He wondered what Crocker would say if he suggested accompanying him to a patient's bedside. 'All right,' he said reluctantly. 'But not the by-pass, for heaven's sake.'

'Cheriton airfield,' said the doctor.

The place hadn't been used for years. It lay on the far side of Cheriton forest beyond Pomfret and it was a favourite haunt of L-drivers. Teenagers below the permitted age of provisional licence holders got their parents to bring them on to the disused runways where they kangaroo-hopped in comparative safety.

Today it was deserted. The greens between the runways had been ploughed up and used for a turnip and sugar beet crop. Beyond the rows of regularly planted beet the pine forest climbed over gently undulating hills.

'You can drive,' said the doctor. 'I fancy the victim's role.'

'Rather you than I,' said Burden, who was wearing his new Gannex.

He shifted into the driving seat. The runway was as broad as the northbound highway of the Stowerton By-pass.

'Presumably she was a strong healthy girl,' said Crocker. 'You couldn't push anyone like that out of a moving vehicle if she was in full possession of her faculties. He must have hit her on the head first.'

'You're suggesting he had an unconscious girl beside him?'

'They had a row and he'd socked her,' said the doctor laconically. 'Now I'm her and I'm unconscious. The road is clear. You wouldn't do it from the fast lane, though, would

162

you? Something might just come whizzing up behind you and that'd be awkward. So it's the middle lane. Go on, move over.'

Burden eased into the centre of the runway. 'That row of beet on the right corresponds to the central strip,' he said. 'Fanshawe swerved to the right to avoid the body.'

'So *he* says.'

'What do I do? Leave the passenger door on the latch?'

'I reckon so. Trickle along and then push me out.'

Crocker rolled himself into a ball, his arms around his knees. Burden didn't dare drive at more than a snail's pace. He was doing five miles an hour. He leaned across, swung the door wide and gave the doctor a light push. Crocker rolled easily into the road, staggered and stood up. Burden stopped.

'You see?' Crocker dusted himself off with a grimace. 'I told you he was crazy. See where I landed? Right in the slow lane. And you'd hardly got the car moving. Our mystery man was going at a fair lick. The girl would have rolled right over to the left, almost on to the grass verge.'

'D'you want to try it in the fast lane, just for the record?'

'Once is enough,' said the doctor firmly. 'You can see what would happen, anyway. The girl mightn't have rolled into the slow lane, but she'd have landed in the middle of the road. You just couldn't get a body into the fast lane itself from a moving car.'

'You're right. Necessarily, having been thrown from the left, it would roll towards the left, in which case Fanshawe in the fast lane would have passed cleanly to the right of it.'

'Or if mystery man was in fact driving in the fast lane and the body landed plumb in that lane, Fanshawe would have swerved to the *left* to avoid it and never hit that tree in the central strip. There's only one possibility and we've proved that's not tenable.'

Burden was sick of being told his job. 'Exactly,' he said hastily. 'If the girl was thrown out to the right and her head was towards the middle lane with her feet towards the central strip, only then might Fanshawe have swerved to the right. He would have swerved instinctively to avoid the head.'

'But that, as we know, is impossible. If you're driving a car you can only throw someone out from the passenger seat on the left, not from one of the back seats, and that means the victim is always going to land way over to the left.'

'I'll go back and tell him,' said Burden thoughtfully, and he let the doctor take the wheel to drive them back along the runway between the lines of green leaves.

'Chief Inspector gone out?' Coming out of Wexford's office, Burden encountered Loring in the corridor.

'I don't know, sir. Isn't he in his office?'

'You imagine he's hiding under his desk, do you, or maybe he's filed himself away in the filing cabinet.'

'I'm sorry, sir.' Loring raised a yellow venetian blind. 'His car's there.'

'I know that.' Burden had come up the stairs. He went towards the lift, pressed the button to summon it. When he had waited a minute and it hadn't come, he shrugged and walked down to the ground floor. Sergeant Camb turned from the woman who had lost a Siamese cat.

'Mr Wexford? He hasn't gone out.'

'Then where the hell is he?' Burden never swore, even as mildly as that. Camb stared. 'He was going to London. I'd reckoned he'd go on the two-fifteen.'

It was half-past three. 'Maybe he went out the back way.'

'Why should he? He never does unless he's going into court.'

'Blue eyes,' said the woman plaintively, 'and a coffee coloured mark on his neck.'

The sergeant sighed. 'All Siamese cats have blue eyes and brown marks on their backs, madam.' He picked up his pen and said to Burden, 'To tell you the truth, I've been tied up all the afternoon, trying to get hold of the engineers to see to that lift. Inspector Letts said it wouldn't come when he pressed the button. I reckon it's stuck between floors.'

'And I reckon,' said Burden, 'Mr Wexford is stuck in it.'

'My God, you don't mean it, sir?'

'Give me that phone. D'you realise he's been in there nearly two hours? *Give me that phone.*'

It was afternoon visiting at Stowerton Infirmary. It was also consultants' day. That meant an exodus of hundreds of cars which the woman on traffic patrol usually controlled efficiently. Today, however, a huge bluish-green car with battered fins, parked half across the drive, blocked the exit. It was locked, keyless, immovable, and behind it a traffic jam stretched nose to tail from the car park.

In vain four ambulance men had tried to lift it and hump it against the gate of the porter's lodge. Presently Vigo, the orthodentist, got out of his own car to lend a hand. He was bigger and more powerful than any of the ambulance men, but all their combined efforts couldn't shift it.

'Probably belongs to someone visiting a private patient,' said Vigo to the consultant gynaecologist whose car had come to a standstill behind his.

'Better get a porter to ring the private wing.'

'And fast,' said Vigo. 'These people ought to be shot. I've got an appointment at four.'

And it was five to when Nurse Rose knocked on Mrs Fanshawe's door. 'Excuse me, Mr Jameson, but your car's blocking the drive. Could you move it please? It's not just visitors that want to get out.' Her voice took on an awed tone. Outrage had been committed. 'Personal request of Mr Vigo and Mr Delauney. So if you wouldn't mind . . .'

Michael Jameson got up languidly. 'I don't know these guys.' He gave Nurse Rose a long appraising look. 'But I wouldn't want you to get in bad with them, sweetheart. I'll shift it.'

Nora Fanshawe touched his sleeve. 'You'll come back for me, Michael?'

'Sure, don't fuss.' Nurse Rose opened the door for him and he walked out ahead of her. 'Dead bore, this hospital visiting,' the women in the room heard him say.

Mrs Fanshawe had painted her face for the first time since regaining consciousness. Now she touched up her thin lips with scarlet and rubbed at the eyeshadow which had settled in greasy streaks into the folds of her lids. 'Well?' she said.

'Well what, Mother?'

'I take it you're going to marry that waster?'

'I am and you'll have to get used to it.'

'Your father would never have allowed it if he were alive,' said Mrs Fanshawe, twisting her rings.

165

'If my father were alive, Michael wouldn't want to marry me. I wouldn't have any money you see. I'm being quite frank with you. I thought that's what parents wanted, frankness from their children.' She shrugged and flicked a fair hair from the shoulder of her blue suit. Her voice was ugly, stripped bald of convention and pretence. 'I wrote to him and told him my father was dead.' She laughed. 'He came down here like a shot. I've bought him,' she said. 'I tried the product and liked it and now I'm going to keep it. The principle is that of the mail order catalogue.'

Mrs Fanshawe wasn't shocked. She hadn't taken her eyes from her daughter's face and she hadn't flinched. 'All right,' she said. 'I can't stop you. I won't quarrel with you, Nora.' Her voice didn't waver. 'You're all I've got, all I've ever had.'

'Then there is no reason why we shouldn't be a happy little family, is there?'

'A happy family! Frank you may be, but you're deceiving yourself. He's got his eye on that nurse already.'

'I know.'

'And you think you've bought him!' All Mrs Fanshawe's self-control couldn't stop the bitterness breaking through. 'Buying people! You know where you get it from, don't you? Your father. You're your father all over again, Nora. God knows, I tried to keep you innocent, but he taught you, he taught you people could be bought.'

'Oh, no, Mother,' said Nora Fanshawe equably. 'You taught me. Shall we have some more tea?' And she rang the bell.

At four-fifteen the lift slid down to the ground floor. The door began to slide and Burden felt sick, his bowels turned to water. He couldn't look. The two engineers came down the stairs, running.

The foyer was full of people. Grinswold, the Chief Constable, Inspector Lewis and Letts, Martin, Loring, Camb and, nearest the lift, Dr Crocker.

The door was open. Burden had to look. He stepped forward, pushing people aside.

'Gangway!' said the doctor.

Wexford came out, grey in the face, the doctor's arm about his shoulders. He took two heavy steps.

'Bricked up,' he said, 'like a bloody nun!'

'God, sir. Are you all right?'

'It's all in the book,' Wexford gasped. 'I've got it all down in the book. Nothing . . .' he said, 'nothing like a rarefied atmosphere for making the brain work. Cheaper than going up Everest, that lift.'

And then he collapsed into the sling Crocker and Letts made with their arms.

'I'm just going off duty,' said Nurse Rose, 'and the night staff are in the kitchen, so you won't mind finding your own way, will you?' She peered at him in the dim light of the corridor. 'Didn't you come visiting Mrs Fanshawe? I thought so. You'll know where to go, then. He's in room five, next door but one to hers.'

Burden thanked her. Turning the corner, he came face to face with Mrs Wexford and Sheila.

'How is he?'

'He's fine. No after-effects. They're only keeping him in for the night to be on the safe side.'

'Thank God!'

'You really care about poor old Pop, don't you?' When she smiled, he could have kissed her, she looked so like her father. Crazy, really, that this enchanting perfect face was the copy and the essence of the heavy wrinkled face that had been haunting him all the time he had made out his arrest and read out the charge. He didn't want to seem sentimental and he managed a cheerful grin. 'He's dying to see you,' she said. 'We were just a stop-gap.'

Wexford lay in bed in a room that was just like Mrs Fanshawe's. He had an old red checked dressing gown across his shoulders and a fuzz of grey hair showed between the lapels of his pyjama jacket. A grin curled the corners of his mouth and his eyes snapped.

Tip-toeing, Burden crossed to the bed. Everyone in hospital tip-toes, except the staff, so he did too, glancing nervously about him. The cooking smell and the disinfectant smell with which the corridor was redolent were drowned in here by the carnations Mrs Wexford had brought her husband.

'How are you feeling?'

'Perfectly all right, of course,' Wexford said impatiently. 'All those damned flowers. Makes the place look like a chapel of rest. I'd come out now only that bloody Crocker and his henchmen keep getting at me, sapping my strength.' He sat up with a jerk and scowled. 'Open that beer, will you? Sheila brought those cans in for me. She's a good girl, chip off the old block.'

Burden rinsed the glass from Wexford's supper tray and from the washbasin took the toothglass for himself. 'A private room, eh? Very grand.'

Wexford chuckled. 'Not my idea, Mike. They were heading for the general ward when Crocker remembered Monkey Matthews was in, having his veins done. We came to the conclusion it might be an embarrassment for him after I did him a couple of years ago for stealing by finding. Don't worry, I'll take care to tell him what saving his face has cost me.' He looked round him complacently. 'Eight quid a day, this room. Good thing I wasn't in that lift any longer.' He drank his beer, wiped his mouth with a man-size Kleenex. 'Well, have you done the deed?'

'At five-thirty.'

'Pity I wasn't there.' Suddenly he shivered. 'The skin of my teeth . . .' Then he laughed. 'Teeth!' he said. 'That's funny.'

Footsteps that didn't tip-toe sounded outside and Crocker marched in. 'Who gave you leave to have a booze-up?'

'Sit down, not on the bed. Nurse Rose doesn't like it. We were just going to have a post-mortem. Interested?'

The doctor fetched himself a chair from the empty room next door. He flopped into it. 'I've heard who it is over the grapevine. By God, you could have knocked me down with a feather.'

'I leave that to others,' said Wexford. 'The intemperate fellows who aren't content with feathers. They use stones.' He met the doctor's eyes and saw there the astonishment and the eagerness for enlightenment he loved to see. 'Murderers aren't unknown among the medical profession,' he said. 'What about Crippen? Buck Ruxton? This time it happened to be a dentist.'

18

'It's always a problem,' said Wexford, 'to know where to begin. Where's the beginning? I often think novelists must have my trouble. Well, I know they do. I used to know a chap who wrote books. He said it was easy to end and the middle just happened naturally, but he never knew where to begin. How far do you have to go back in a man's life to find what makes him do things? To his childhood, to his parents, to Adam?'

'Let's not go back that far,' said Burden. 'We'll be here all night.'

Wexford grinned at him. He banged his pillows and pulled their corners round his shoulders. 'I think I'll begin ten years ago,' he said. 'But don't worry. You know how time flies.'

'Vigo wasn't here ten years ago.'

'He was getting married. He married a rich girl, probably not entirely for her money. But the money set him up in practice here and bought his house for him. They had a child.'

'It was mongoloid,' said the doctor. 'Been in an institution since it was six months old. Vigo took it very hard.'

'Who wouldn't?' said Wexford. 'Look at Vigo. What Hitler would have called the perfect Aryan type and clever with it. If you were stud farming humans, wouldn't you choose Vigo as your ideal stallion?' The doctor gave a grudging nod.

'And if you were Vigo, wouldn't you expect to sire splendid progeny?'

'Everyone does.'

'May be. Everyone hopes, let's say, and sometimes the

most unexpected people are lucky.' He smiled to himself and finished the last drop of beer Sheila had brought. 'I reckon Vigo blamed his wife. Don't tell me that was unfair. Life's unfair. They didn't have any more children for eight years.'

The doctor leant forward. 'They've got a son now,' he sighed. 'Poor kid.'

'If he's poor it's his father's fault,' Wexford snapped. 'Don't give me that sentimental stuff. This is the real beginning, Mrs Vigo's second pregnancy. She had high blood pressure, she got toxaemia.'

'A threatened toxaemia, surely,' the doctor corrected him pedantically.

'Whatever it was, she was admitted to the Princess Louise Clinic in New Cavendish Street two months before the birth. You can imagine Vigo's feelings, was it going to go wrong again?'

'Toxaemia doesn't lead to mongoloid babies.'

'Oh, shut up!' said Wexford irritably. 'People don't reason in cases like that. He was scared and depressed and he took up with one of the nurses he met when he was visiting his wife. Maybe he'd always been a bit of a philanderer. I've got my own reasons for thinking that.'

'In your notes,' said Burden, who had the book open on his lap, 'you said he dropped Bridget Culross after the child was born healthy and normal.'

'That's conjecture. Let's say he was too taken up with the child – he's crazy about that child – to bother about outside interests. Did you check with the clinic?'

'I did. Mrs Vigo was admitted last October and remained in the clinic until two weeks after the child was born at the end of December. Bridget Culross was on duty in the ward where her room was from November 1st until January 1st.'

Wexford leaned back. 'It had to be someone with a Christian or surname beginning with J, you see. Jerome Fanshawe, we thought at first, but that couldn't be because Mrs Fanshawe was past the age of childbearing. I seriously considered Michael Jameson. It wouldn't at all surprise me to know he's got a wife somewhere.' He lowered his voice. Mrs Fanshawe was two doors down the corridor. 'A Michael Jameson might just as well call himself Jay as Mike and he had the right kind of car. But we'll come to that later. Anyway, it wasn't

170

either of them. It was Jolyon Vigo. With a name like that you'd be glad of a convenient abbreviation sometimes.'

'You say he dropped the girl. Why did he take up with her again?'

'A man has a child,' said Wexford. 'If he worships the child it may, for a while, bring him closer to his wife. But these things wear off. Can the leopard change his spots? The girl thought she'd a chance of getting him to marry her. No doubt, he'd even considered that when he thought his wife wasn't ever going to give him a child. Now he wanted his bit of fun on the side but he wasn't going to lose his son for it. Not on your life. And that's the crux.'

The doctor crossed his legs and shifted his chair a little. 'Where does Charlie Hatton come into all this?'

Wexford didn't answer him directly. Instead he said, 'Vigo and Culross were carrying on their affair intermittently. If it wasn't all that of a regular thing, that's probably because the girl nagged him about marriage and he stalled.'

'You can't possibly know that,' Burden objected.

Wexford said loftily, 'I understand human nature. On the 18th of May Bridget Culross had a long weekend off and, by chance, the Blake Society were also having their weekend conference in Brighton over the next three days. Vigo picked Culross up at Marble Arch and drove her to Brighton in his car, a big Plymouth sedan.'

'How do you know it was the Blake Society? Why not the Gibbonites?'

'Vigo's got Blake drawings all over his hall walls. Did you check their room bookings?'

'They booked in at the Majestic in their own names. Two adjoining rooms. They vacated them on Monday afternoon, Monday May 20th.'

Wexford nodded. 'Perhaps it was their first weekend together. Bridget Culross spent it pressurising Vigo into agreeing to divorce his wife. Or trying to. I don't know what happened. How could I? I'll make a guess that she knew they'd have to pass through Kingsmarkham, or near it, on their way back to London, and she tried to persuade Vigo to take her back with him to the house in Ploughman's Lane and confront his wife together.' He cleared his throat. 'Men don't like that kind of thing,' he said. 'They had a fight.

Want to know where? I guess she put the pressure on really hard when they reached the point where the road passes nearest to Kingsmarkham. That's about three miles south of the spot where the body was found. No doubt they got out of the car and my guess is the girl said she'd make her way to Ploughman's Lane on her own if he wouldn't come with her. Vigo's a big powerful man. They struggled, she fell and hit her head. He had an unconscious, perhaps dead, girl on his hands. You see his dilemma?'

'Whatever he did next, his wife would find out, divorce him and get custody of the child,' said Burden.

'Exactly. He began some quick thinking. First remove all identification from the expensive handbag he had given her himself. No doubt, a good many people knew where she had gone, but she had assured him no one knew his name. Vigo's an intelligent man, a medical man who knows something about police methods. They wouldn't search for a girl with a reputation like Bridget Culross's and no near relatives to give a damn. Suppose she was found dead in the road, knocked down by a passing vehicle? It would be assumed she'd quarrelled with her boy-friend, hitched a lift to Stowerton and been knocked down crossing the road or trying to hitch a second lift. He put her on the passenger seat, laying her flat with her head on his lap so as not to mark the seat with blood. Probably he had a newspaper or an old rug to cover his knees, something he could burn when he got home.

'He entered the by-pass where at that time of night and during the week, the road was comparatively clear. Now he wouldn't dare drive too fast – no one could open a car door and throw a body out at any speed – so he kept to the slow lane.'

'What then?'

'Things went according to plan. He drove along at twenty or thirty miles an hour and when there were no other vehicles in sight, he shot the girl out and she landed as he had expected with her head well over into the fast lane . . .'

'Wait a minute,' said the doctor sharply. 'That's not possible. It can't be done. We tried it and . . .'

'Wait a minute by all means,' said Wexford, and in execrable French, '*Pas devant les infirmières.*'

'Tea, coffee, Ovaltine or Horlicks,' said a bright voice whose owner had tapped on the glass panel in the door.

'Ovaltine would be very wholesome,' said Wexford blandly. 'Thank you kindly.'

'A chiel's among ye, taking notes,' said Wexford. 'In other words, Charlie Hatton.' He sipped his Ovaltine with an inscrutable expression. 'He had parked his lorry in the lay-by just over the brow of the hill and was taking the air in the field on the other side of the hedge.'

'You mean he saw Vigo push a girl out of his car and did nothing about it?'

'Depends by what you mean by nothing. In my experience the Charlie Hattons of this world aren't over-anxious to get involved with the police even as indignant observers. Hatton did something. He blackmailed Vigo.'

'Can I have a couple of your grapes?' said the doctor. 'Thanks. The only grapes I ever taste are the ones I nick from my patients.' He put one in his mouth and chewed it, seeds and all. 'Did he know Vigo?'

'By sight, I daresay, or else he knew the car. You'll get appendicitis.'

'Rubbish, old wives' tale. Anyhow, I've had it. What happened next?'

Wexford took another Kleenex and wiped his mouth.

'Hatton went home to his wife. Five minutes later Jerome Fanshawe came along, driving like the clappers, spotted the girl in the road too late and shouted out, "My God!" She was lying, remember, with her body and legs in the middle lane and her head over the fast lane. Fanshawe swerved. Wouldn't it be instinctive in those circumstances to avoid the head at all costs? So he swerved to the *right*, mounted the turfed centre section and crashed into a tree. That, I think, sums up the entire intervention of the Fanshawes into this case. For once in his life, Fanshawe was the innocent victim.'

Burden nodded agreement and took up the tale. 'On the following morning,' he said, 'Hatton mulled over the whole business. He made his telephone call about the flat for Pertwee and then went down to see it with the girl Marilyn.

173

Immediately there was a call on his purse. The tenant of the flat wanted two hundred pounds key money.'

'And that clinched it,' said Wexford. 'He left Marilyn at the Olive and Dove and she saw him go into a phone box. We may be sure he was phoning Vigo, making an appointment for the afternoon.'

'I thought you said he made the appointment later from his own home?' said the doctor.

'He *phoned* again from his own home. That was just a blind for his wife. You may be sure he'd already made it clear to Vigo what he wanted and that he would phone again as if legitimately asking for an appointment. Of course it happened that way. If it hadn't, do you suppose Vigo would have agreed to an appointment that same day, only an hour afterwards? He's a busy man, booked up weeks in advance. Charlie Hatton wasn't even a patient of his. I've no doubt that in the morning Charlie told him he wanted hush money out of him and he'd have the best set of false teeth Vigo could provide. Free of charge, of course.'

'It must have been a hell of a shock to Vigo,' said Crocker thoughtfully. 'The night before he'd taken a risk and acted on the spur of the moment. The chances then of its coming out were fairly high, I'd have thought. But Fanshawe's crash was an unforeseen stroke of luck for him. Seeing it in the morning paper and seeing that the girl had been identified as Nora Fanshawe made him safe. By the time the real Nora turned up things would be so confused, the truth would very likely never come out. Who would have imagined his actions had been seen?'

'Naturally he paid up,' said Wexford. 'Paid and paid. My guess is that when he phoned the first time Hatton asked him to draw a thousand pounds immediately from his bank, a sum which he was to give to Hatton, and did give him, during his visit to Ploughman's Lane that afternoon, the afternoon of May 21st. Must have been rather bizarre, mustn't it, that consultation of Hatton's? The mind boggles, as they say. You have to picture the blackmailer lying back in his chair with his mouth open while his victim, desperate, at bay, if you like, probed about, measuring him for his new teeth.'

'On the following day, May 22nd, we know Hatton paid

five hundred pounds into his own account, keeping two hundred for the Pertwees' key money and the remaining three hundred for incidental expenses, furniture, clothes and other frivolity. The weekly payments of fifty pounds a time followed at once. I reckon Hatton got Vigo to leave the money in some prearranged hiding place down by the river on Friday nights somewhere along the route Hatton took on his way home from the darts club. And one Friday night . . .'

'Yes, why that particular Friday?'

'Who can say at what point the victim of blackmail reaches the end of his tether?'

'Mrs Fanshawe,' put in Burden unexpectedly. 'You see, that wasn't quite right, what you said about the Fanshawes' intervention having come to an end. Mrs Fanshawe regained consciousness the day before Hatton was killed. It was in the morning papers, just a paragraph, but it was there.'

'You've got something there, Mike. Nora was still missing, but once Mrs Fanshawe could talk, Vigo might believe she'd tell us the girl's body couldn't be that of her daughter. Hatton was an important witness with someone else now to back up his story. Once he'd had all he wanted out of Vigo . . .'

The doctor got up, stood for a moment staring at Wexford's flowers and then said, 'It's a good story, but it's impossible. It couldn't have happened that way.' Wexford smiled at him. Crocker said irritably, 'What are you grinning like that for? I tell you there's an obvious flaw. If anyone throws a body out of a car, even feet first, it's going to fall well over to the left. Vigo would have had to be driving right on the grass section itself for the girl's head to have been in the fast lane. And as to that theory of yours about the head being on his lap to stop bloodstains getting on the passenger seat, it's nonsense. That way her *feet* would have been in the fast lane and Fanshawe would have swerved to the *left* to avoid her head.'

He stopped and gave a defiant snort as the nurse came back with a sleeping pill.

'I don't want that,' said Wexford. He slid down in the bed and pulled up the covers. 'I'll sleep, I'm tired.' Over the top of the sheet he said, 'Nice of you two to come. Oh, and by the way, it's a foreign car. Left-hand drive. Good night.'

19

'Electrician,' said Jack Pertwee on the doorstep. 'You've got a switch that wants fixing.'

'Not me,' said the girl. 'I only work here. Wait a bit. . . . Is this it?' She fumbled among some loose sheets of paper on a table beneath the mullioned window and her face reddened with indignation. 'You was supposed to come last week.'

'I was off last week. This is my first day back. Don't work yourself up. I've been here before. I can find my own way.'

His first day back. His first job on his first day, the first return to normal routine after the earthquake. Jack didn't know why he had chosen to come here – there were a dozen names who needed him on his list. Perhaps it was because some unformed unrecognised hunger in his subconscious cried for the solace and the refreshment of looking on beautiful things; perhaps because this place was unique in his experience, alien, and remote from anywhere he had ever been with Charlie.

But as always when he found himself at the house in Ploughman's Lane, a clumsiness dragged at his feet and his deft fingers began to feel all thumbs. He was like a barbarian who, having entered a forsaken Roman villa, stood dazzled and amazed, overcome by the awe of ignorance. He crossed the hall and pretending to himself that he did not know the precise location of the switch – there was no need to, he was alone now – he opened door after door to peer in wonderment at the treasures within. A muttered 'Pardon me, lady' would have been his defence if one of them had been occupied but there was no one about and Jack looked his fill

176

undisturbed at velvet and silk, dark tables inlaid with ivory, pictures in gilt frames, flowered china holding real flowers, a bust in bronze, a pomander whose orange spicy scent was brought to him on warm sunlight.

Afterwards he was unable to say what had suddenly brought Charlie so vividly to his mind, except perhaps that the memory of his dead friend was never far from it. Maybe this flash of pain, sharper and more real than any he had yet felt, came when he opened the door of the Chinese room. It was here, just inside the door, that his task awaited him and he stepped for a moment on the threshold stunned into immobility by the strange rich colours. It was too early yet for the sun to have reached the back of the house but the reds and golds, the unearthly sea greens and citrus yellows, blazed fiercely enough in shadow. Jack put down his tool bag and gazed about him numbly. He had been here before and yet it seemed to him that he had never seen the room until this moment. It was as if his nerves had been stripped raw and, unprotected, received the impact of these glorious yet intolerable colours in a series of vibrations like electric shocks.

Half in a trance he approached the chessmen that Charlie had called an army and saw in the face of one of them, a red knight, the perfect facsimile of his dead friend's face, sharp, cunning, astute and kind. A longing to possess and preserve it seized him but he was afraid even to touch the delicate carved jade and he heard himself give a low sob.

It was his awed and perhaps childlike descriptions of this house which had, he supposed, led Charlie here. Just as he, Jack, might have gone to the grocer's, so Charlie Hatton had come here to buy the best. Jack's sorrow dissolved in admiration of that audacity. His friend had penetrated this museum too and that not as a servant or a workman but as a customer. Vigo had brought him into this room and drunk with him. Jack could imagine Charlie's cocky poise, his hard brown hands even daring to lift a cup or finger a silk picture while he commented on its quality, its desirability, with brash impudence. Had he recognised himself at the head of that scarlet army? And the Philistines slew Jonathan. . . . How are the mighty fallen and the weapons of war perished!

Jack turned away from the sharp little faces that seemed

177

to scrutinise him and, opening his bag, squatted down in front of it. He felt worn out, exhausted at ten in the morning, and the girl's voice behind him made him jump.

'Thought you might fancy a cup of tea.'

He could guess his own expression and he didn't want her to see his face. 'Mr or Mrs about?' he asked. 'I'd better see one of them.'

'Haven't you heard then? She's gone away and taken the boy. The police arrested him yesterday for killing that lorry driver.'

There had been tears in Jack's eyes and now his eyelids burned as they sometimes did after an evening with Charlie in the smoke-filled bar of the Dragon. He was staring into the heap of tools but not seeing them. His brain had become an empty red space. He got to his feet and there was a hammer in his hand, although he couldn't remember selecting it from the heap.

The red light before his eyes split into a spectrum of insane red and gold and sea green that roared as it twisted and leapt about him, as if a kaleidoscope could make sound as varied and as fantastic as its changing pictures. Behind him another, shriller noise echoed. The girl had begun to scream.

'A bull in a china shop,' said Wexford.

He picked his way through the fragments which littered the carpet, stopping occasionally to lift between finger and thumb a sliver of transparent porcelain. His expression was impassive and cold but a little heat entered it as he approached the table where the chessmen had been. Not a piece remained intact, but here and there among the red and white gravel he found a delicate spear with an amputated hand still grasping it, a fragment of ivory lace, a horse's hoof.

Burden was kneeling down, smoothing out torn remnants of the silk pictures. A big rough footprint scarred the scales of the painted fish, the print of the same foot that had ground saké cups to dust.

'Frightening, isn't it?' said Wexford. 'Barbarity is frightening. I'm glad I don't know . . .'

'What all this stuff was worth?' Burden hazarded.

'Not so much as all that. I meant I'm glad I don't know it's uniqueness, its age, its quality really; looting must be like this, I suppose, wanton, revengeful.'

'You said Charlie Hatton was a soldier of fortune.'

'Yes. Is there any point in going to talk to his comrade-in-arms? I suppose we have to.'

Jack Pertwee was in the kitchen with Sergeant Martin. He was sitting down, his arms spread and his body slumped across the table. Wexford shook him roughly and jerked his head back. Their eyes met and for a moment Wexford still held on to the electrician's coat collar, shaking it as might a man who has brought a destructive dog under control. Jack's jowls shook and his teeth chattered.

'You're a fool, Pertwee,' Wexford said scornfully. 'You'll lose your job over this. And for what? For a friend who's dead and can't thank you?'

His voice almost inaudible, Jack said, 'The best . . . The best friend a man ever had. And it was me sent him here.' He clenched his fist, drove it hard against the table.

'Oh, take him away, Sergeant.'

Jack dragged himself to his feet. His fist opened and something fell to the floor, rolled and came to rest at Wexford's feet. The chief inspector stared downwards. It was the red knight's decapitated head. The wicked sharp face, tricked into expression by a ribbon of sunlight, grinned widely and showed its teeth.

'Charlie,' Jack whispered. He tried to say it again but great agonised sobs tore away the name.

AN UNKINDNESS OF
RAVENS

To Sonia and Jeff

1

She was a neighbour. She was an acquaintance of Dora's and they spoke if they met in the street. Only this time there had been more to it than passing the time of day.

'I said I'd tell you,' Dora said. 'I said I'd mention it. She had that strange look she sometimes has and, to tell you the truth, I was awfully embarrassed.'

'What did she say?' Wexford asked.

' "Rod's missing" or "Rod's disappeared" – something like that. And then she asked me if I'd tell you. Because of who you are, of course.'

Detective chief inspectors have better things to do with their time than waste it listening to the complaints of women whose husbands have run off with other women. Wexford hadn't been in the house five minutes before he decided that was what had happened. But she was a neighbour. She lived in the next street to his. He ought to be glad really, he thought, that it hadn't the makings of a case for him to investigate.

His house and this one had been built at the same time, in the mid–1930s when Kingsmarkham was growing out of being a village. And structurally they were much the same house, three bedrooms, two receptions, kitchen, bathroom and downstairs loo. But his was a home, comfortable and full of lovingly collected things and this was – what? A shelter to keep the rain off, a place where people could eat, sleep and watch television. Joy Williams took him into the front room that she called the lounge. There were no books. The carpet was a square surrounded by mustard yellow vinyl tiles and the furniture a three-piece suite covered in grainy

183

mustard-coloured synthetic leather. The 1935 fireplace, which in his house had been replaced by one of York stone, accommodated an electric fire of complicated design, part Regency, part medieval, and with a portcullis effect at the front. Above it hung a mirror framed in segments of green and yellow frosted glass, a fine specimen of Art Deco if you liked that sort of thing. The only picture was a composition in coloured silver paper of two cats playing with a ball of wool.

'She's rather a colourless person,' Dora had said. 'Doesn't seem interested in anything and always seems depressed. I don't suppose living with Rodney Williams for twenty years has done much for her.'

Joy. Dora had said rather apologetically that it was a misnomer. She was a woman whose whole self had turned grey, not just her hair. Her features had once been good, were probably still good, only her awful complexion, lined, pitted, pinkish-grey, rough and worn, masked them. Apparently she was forty-five but she looked ten years more. Up until his arrival she had been watching television and the set was still on, though with the sound turned off. It was the biggest set Wexford had ever seen, at any rate in a domestic setting. He guessed she spent a fair proportion of her time watching it and perhaps felt uneasy when the screen was blank.

There was no seat in the room that did not face it. He sat on the end of the sofa at an angle, turning his back. Joy Williams's eyes flickered over the flashing figures of skaters taking part in some contest. She sat on the extreme edge of her chair.

'Did your wife tell you what I . . . ?'

'She said something.' He interrupted to save her the embarrassment he could see already mottling her nose and cheeks with dull red. 'Something about your husband being missing.'

Joy Williams laughed. It was a laugh he was to hear often and get to know, a harsh cackle. There was no humour in it, no gaiety, no amusement. She laughed to hide emotion or because she knew no other way of showing it. The hands in her lap stretched and clenched. She wore a very wide, heavily chased platinum or white-gold wedding ring with an even more ornate platinum or white-gold engagement ring containing amid the pits and pyramids a minuscule diamond.

'He went on a trip to Ipswich and I haven't seen him since.'

'Your husband's a sales representative, I think Dora said.'

'With Sevensmith Harding,' she said. 'The paint people.'

She need not have added that. Sevensmith Harding were probably the biggest suppliers to builders' merchants and home decorating retail stores in the south of England. Sevenstar matt and silk emulsion coated a million walls, he thought, between Dover and Land's End. He and Dora had just had their second bedroom done up in it, and if he wasn't much mistaken the paintwork in Mrs Williams's own hall was the newest shade in Sevenshine non-drip high gloss, Wholewheat.

'He covers Suffolk for them.' She began pushing the rings up and down.

'It was last Thursday he went – well, yesterday week. It's the twenty-third now, that must have been the fifteenth. He said he was going to Ipswich to stop the night and start first thing in the morning.'

'What time did he leave?'

'It was evening time. About six. He'd been home all afternoon.'

It was at this point that Wexford had his thought about the other woman. It would be a good three and a half hour run from Kingsmarkham to Ipswich even via the Dartford Tunnel. A salesman who was legitimately going to drive to Suffolk and could have started at four instead of six would surely have done so.

'Where did he stay in Ipswich? At a hotel presumably?'

'A motel. Outside Ipswich, I think.'

She spoke listlessly, as if she knew little about her husband's work and took no interest in it. The door opened and a girl came in. She stopped on the threshold and said, 'Oh, sorry.'

'Sara, what time did Dad go when he left?'

'Around six.'

Mrs Williams nodded. She said, 'This is my daughter Sara,' pronouncing the name so that the first syllable rhymed with 'car'.

'I believe you've a son too?'

'Kevin. He's twenty. He's away at university.'

The girl stood with her arms over the back of the yellow plastic armchair no one was sitting in, her eyes fixed on her mother in a more or less neutral way, though one that tended towards the hostile rather than the friendly. She was very slender, fair, with the face of a Renaissance painter's model, small-featured with a high forehead and a secretive look. Her hair was exceptionally long, reaching almost to her waist, and with the rippling appearance hair has which is usually done up in plaits. She wore jeans and a tee-shirt with a design on it of a raven and the letters ARRIA superimposed over it.

She picked up a photograph in a chrome frame off the only table in the room, a bamboo affair with a glass top almost hidden by the sofa back. Passing it to Wexford, she stuck her thumb at the head of the man sitting on a beach with a teenage boy and a girl who was herself five years before. The man was big, tall, but out of condition and running to fat around his middle. He had a huge domed forehead. His features, perhaps because they were dominated by this bare dome, looked insignificant and crowded together, the mouth a lipless slit stretched into a smile for the camera.

Wexford handed it back to her. She replaced it on the table, let her eyes linger on her mother for a moment, a curious, faintly contemptuous look, and walked out of the room. He heard her feet going upstairs.

'When did you expect your husband to come back?'

'The Sunday night, he said. I didn't think much about it when he didn't. I thought he'd stayed another night and he'd be back Monday, but he wasn't and he never phoned.'

'You didn't phone the motel yourself?'

She looked at him as if he had proposed to her some gargantuan and complex task quite beyond her capacity, writing a fifty-thousand-word thesis perhaps or devising a computer programme.

'I wouldn't do that. I mean, it's a long-distance call. I haven't got the number anyway.'

'Did you do anything?'

She laughed the dry humourless cackle. 'What could I do?

186

Kevin was home for the weekend but he went back to Keele on the Sunday.' She spoke as if action in such a matter could only be taken by a member of the male sex. 'I knew I'd have been let know if he'd had an accident. He's got his name on him, his bank card and his cheque book and ever so many things with his name on.'

'You didn't phone Sevensmith Harding, for instance?'

'What good would that have done? He never went in there for weeks on end.'

'And you haven't heard a word from him since? For – let's see – eight days, you've had no indication where he might be?'

'That's right. Well, five days. I expected him to be gone the first three.'

He would have to ask it. After all, she had called him in. As a neighbour to confide in certainly, but primarily as a policeman. Nothing he had heard so far made him feel even a preliminary inquiry into Rodney Williams's whereabouts was called for. Looking at Mrs Williams, the house, the daughter, the set-up, he could only wonder with an unkindness he would never openly have expressed even to Dora why the man had stayed so long. He had run off with another woman, or run off *to* another woman, and only cowardice was holding him back from writing the requisite letter or making the obligatory phone call.

'Forgive me, but is it possible your husband could be – ' he sought for a word and came out with a mealy-mouthed one he despised ' – friendly with some other woman? Could he have been seeing another woman?'

She gave him a long, cold, unshocked look. Whatever she might say, Wexford could tell his suggestion had already crossed her mind and done more than cross her mind. There was something in that look which told him she was the sort of woman who made a point, a principle almost, of avoiding admitting anything unpleasant. Push it away, suppress it, get out of the habit of thinking, don't wonder or think or speculate, for that will make you unhappy. Don't think, don't wonder, turn on the telly and in mindless apathy stare at the screen until's it's time for bed and the doctor's little Mogadon that comes on a permanent prescription you pick up at reception.

Of course, he might be doing her an injustice. All this was only in his imagination. 'It's just a possibility,' he said. 'I'm sorry I had to suggest it.'

'I don't know what he does when he's away days and nights on end, do I? All our married life he's been away selling as much as he's been home. I don't know what floozies he's had and I wouldn't ask.'

The old-fashioned word suited the room and Mrs Williams's grey, Crimplene-clad, scurfy respectability. For the first time he noticed the thick sprinkling of dandruff, like a fall of flour, on the shoulders of her blouse. He had given her a solution which to most women would be the least acceptable, but she, he thought, was relieved. Did she suspect her husband of having been up to something *illegal* so that something *immoral* would be seen as a happier alternative?

You suspect everyone and everything, he told himself. You policeman!

'Do you think we ought to do anything?'

'If you mean by that should you report him as a missing person and the police takes steps to find him, no, certainly not. The chances are you'll have word from him in the next few days. If you don't, I think your best course will be to see a solicitor or go to your Citizen's Advice Bureau. But don't do that before you've been on to Sevensmith Harding. The likelihood is you'll find him through them.'

She didn't thank him for coming. He hadn't even been home yet, he had called on her on his way home, but she didn't thank him or apologize for taking up his time. He looked back and saw her still standing on the doorstep holding the door, a very thin angular woman in fawn blouse and unfashionably cut dark green trousers with bell bottoms and a high waist. Her front garden was the only one in Alverbury Road with no spring bulbs out, not a narcissus to relieve the bit of lawn and the dark yew hedge.

It was a cloudy evening, bright as noonday still, April-cool. This little honeycomb of streets was like an orchard in springtime, puffs and clouds of pink and white blossom all over the gardens and drifts of petals already lying on the pavements. A great weeping cherry, pink as ice cream, had taken over his front lawn.

His wife was sitting in an armchair placed in much the

188

same position at the same angle to the fireplace as the chair Joy Williams had sat in, in a room of the same size and proportions to the one he had just left. But there the resemblance ended. A log fire was burning. It had been a cold winter and the spring was cold and protracted, frosts threatening nightly to nip that blossom. Dora was making patchwork, a bedspread in blues and reds, all shades of blues and reds in a multiplicity of patterns, and the finished part covered the long red velvet skirt of the housedress she had taken to wearing in the evenings because of the cold. Her hair was dark and plentiful. Wexford had told her she must be a gipsy to have hair still not grey at nearly sixty.

'Did you see Mike today?'

She meant Detective Inspector Burden. Wexford said no, he had been at court in Myringham.

'Jenny came in to tell me she'd had the results of the amniocentesis. The baby's all right and it's a girl.'

'What's amniocentesis?'

'They stick something through the abdominal wall into the womb and take out a sample of amniotic fluid. The fluid's got cells from the foetus in it and they grow them like a sort of culture, I think. Anyway, the cells divide and they can tell if Down's Syndrome is present and spina bifida too. And of course they can tell the sex by whether the chromosomes come out XY or XX.'

'What a lot you know! Where did you pick up all that?'

'Jenny told me.' She got up and transferred the patchwork to the seat of the chair. 'They can't do an amniocentesis till the sixteenth week of pregnancy and there's always a risk of losing the baby.'

He followed her out into the kitchen. He was more than usually aware this evening of the warmth and light in his own house. It occurred to him that Joy Williams had offered him nothing, not even a cup of tea. Dora had opened the oven door and was looking critically at a steak and kidney pie that was almost ready on the top shelf.

'Do you want a drink?'

'Why not?' she said. 'Celebrate Jenny and Mike's healthy baby.'

'I'm surprised she took any risk,' he said when she had

189

her sherry and he his Bell's and three parts water. 'She's very set on having this child. They've been trying for years.'

'She's forty-one, Reg. At that age there's also a much higher risk of having a mongoloid baby. Anyway, all's well.'

'Don't you want to hear about your Mrs Williams?'

'Poor Joy,' said Dora. 'She was rather pretty when I first knew her. Of course, that was eighteen years ago. I suppose he's gone off with some girl, has he?'

'If you knew that I don't know what you roped me in for.'

Dora laughed. She had a rich throaty giggle. Immediately she said she knew she shouldn't laugh. 'He's such an awful man. You never met him, did you? There's something so secretive and deceitful about him. I used to think no one could be so obviously like that if they really had something to hide.'

'But now you're not so sure.'

'I'll tell you something I was scared to tell you at the time. I thought you might do something violent.'

'Sure,' he said. 'I've always been so wild and free with my fists. What are you on about?'

'He made a pass at Sylvia.'

She said it defiantly. Standing there in the long red dress, holding the sherry glass, her eyes suddenly wide and wary, she looked astonishingly young.

'So?' His elder daughter was thirty, married twelve years, and the mother of two tall sons. 'She's an attractive woman. I daresay men do make passes at her and no doubt she can take care of herself.'

Dora gave him a sidelong look. 'I said I was scared to tell you. She was fifteen at the time.'

The violent feelings she had predicted were there to hand. After all those years. His fifteen-year-old daughter! He resisted the temptation to bellow. Nor did he stamp. He took a sip of his drink and spoke coolly. 'And, like a good little girl, she came to mother and told her?'

Dora said flippantly, 'Sweet of her, wasn't it? I was touched. I think the truth was, Reg, she was scared stiff.'

'Did you do anything?'

'Oh, yes. I went to him and told him what her father was. He didn't know. I don't think there was ever much communication between him and Joy. Anyway, it worked.

He made himself very scarce and Sylvia didn't baby-sit for them again. I didn't tell Joy but I think she knew and was disillusioned. Anyway, she didn't adore him any more the way she used to.'

'I was adored once,' Wexford quoted.

'And still are, darling. You know we all adore you. You haven't forfeited our respect, running after little girls. Can I have some more sherry?'

'You'll have to get it yourself,' said Wexford, opening the oven and taking out the pie. 'All this drinking and gossiping. I want my dinner.'

2

The firm of Sevensmith Harding had been founded in 1875 by Septimus Sevensmith who called himself a colourman. He sold artists' materials in a shop in the High Street in Myringham. Paints for exterior- and interior-decorating use came along later. After the First World War in fact, when Septimus's granddaughter married a Major John Harding who left a leg behind him at Passchendaele.

The first great house-building boom of the eighties and nineties were past and gone, the next due to begin. Major Harding got in on it. He began manufacturing in huge quantities the browns and greens dear to the hearts of builders creating the terraces and semidetacheds which were growing in branches and tentacles out of South London. And towards the end of the decade he brought out a daring shade of cream.

Already the company had been renamed Sevensmith Harding. It kept its offices in Myringham High Street, though the factory behind was soon to be moved to sites on distant industrial complexes. With the disappearance of its retail trade the shop as such also disappeared.

The world's paint industry enjoyed a steady growth during the 1960s and early 1970s. It is estimated that close on five hundred companies make paint in the United Kingdom but the bulk of the sales volume is handled by a few large manufacturers. Four of these manufacturers dominate the British Isles and one of them is Sevensmith Harding.

Today their paints, Sevenstar vinyl silk and Sevenstar vinyl matt emulsion, Sevenshine gloss and satin finish, are manufactured at Harlow in Essex, and their wallpapers, borders and coordinating tiles at Crawley in Sussex. The head offices in Myringham, in the centre of the High Street opposite the Old Flag Hotel, have more a look of solicitors' chambers or the establishment of a very refined antique dealer than the seat of paint makers. Indeed, there is scarcely anything to show that they are paint makers. The bow windows with their occasional pane of distorted glass that flank the front door contain, instead of cans of paint and display stands of delighted housewives with brushes in their hands, a *famille noire* vase of dried grasses on one side and a Hepplewhite chair on the other. But over the door, Georgian in style and of polished mahogany, are royal armorial bearings and the legend: 'By appointment to her Majesty Queen Elizabeth the Queen Mother, Colourists and Makers of Fine Pigments'.

The company chairman, Jeremy Harding-Grey, divided his time between his house in Monte Carlo and his house in Nassau, and the managing director, George Delahaye, though he lived in Sussex, was seldom seen in the vicinity of Myringham. But the deputy managing director was a humbler person and altogether more on the level of ordinary men. Wexford knew him. They had met at the home of Sylvia's father-in-law, an architect, and since then the Gardners had once been guests at a drinks party at the Wexfords' and the Wexfords guests at the Gardners'. But for all that Wexford would not have considered himself on the kind of terms with Miles Gardner to warrant dropping in at Sevensmith Harding when he found himself in Myringham at lunchtime to ask Miles out for a drink and a sandwich.

A fortnight had passed since his talk with Joy Williams and he had virtually forgotten about it. He had dismissed it from his mind before he went to bed that same night. And if he had thought about it at all since then it had only been to tell himself that by now Mrs Williams and her solicitor would be settling things to her satisfaction or that Williams had returned home, having found like many a man before him that domesticity is the better part of economics.

But even if Williams were still missing there was nothing to justify Wexford's making inquiries about him at Sevensmith Harding. Let Joy Williams do that. He wouldn't be missing as far as his employers were concerned. No matter how complex a man's love life he still has to go to work and earn his bread. Williams earned it on too humble a level though, Wexford reflected, for it to be likely Miles Gardner had ever heard of him.

He and Burden had both been at Myringham Crown Court, witnesses in two separate cases, and the court had adjourned for lunch. Burden would have to go back to watch his case – a rather ticklish matter concerning the receiving of stolen goods – through to the bitter end, but Wexford's day, at least as far as appearing in court went, was over. As they walked towards the hotel Burden was silent and morose. He had been like this since they came out of court. If it had been anyone else Wexford would have supposed his mood due to the dressing down, indeed the scathing tongue-lashing, meted out to him by the alleged receiver's counsel. But Burden was impervious to such things. He had taken that sort of stick too many times to care. This was something else, something closer to home, Wexford thought. And now he came to think of it, this, whatever it was, had been growing on Burden for days now, weeks even, a morose surly misery that didn't seem to affect his work but militated badly against his relations with other people.

He looked the same as ever. There was no sign of anxiety or care in his appearance. He was thin but he had always been thin. Wexford didn't know if it was a new suit he was wearing or last year's cleaned and the trousers nightly pressed in the electric press his wife had given him for Christmas. ('Like those things you get in swish hotels,' Burden had said proudly.) It was a happy marriage, Burden's second, as happy as his first. But almost any marriage Burden made would be happy, he had a gift for marriage. He was uxorious without making himself ridiculous. There couldn't be anything in his marriage that was bugging him. His wife was pregnant with a longed-for child – longed for by her at any rate. Burden had a grown-up son and daughter by his first marriage. Wexford considered an idea that came to him and then dismissed it as absurd and out of character. Burden was the last man to dread the coming child just because he was now in his mid-forties. That he would take in his stride.

'What's wrong, Mike?' he asked as the silence became oppressive.

'Nothing.'

The classic answer. One of the cases in which a statement means the precise opposite of what it says, as when a man in doubt says he's absolutely certain.

Wexford didn't press it. He walked along, looking about him at the old market town which had changed so much since he had first known it. A huge shopping complex had been built, and since then an arts centre, incorporating theatre, cinema and concert hall. The university term was three weeks old and the place was thronged with blue-jeaned students. But up at this end of the town, where preservation orders proliferated and buildings were listed, things were much the same. Things were even rather better since the local authority had woken up to the fact that Myringham was beautiful and worth conserving and had therefore cleaned and tidied and painted and planted.

He looked into the bow windows of Sevensmith Harding, first at the Hepplewhite chair, then at the vase. Beyond the dried grasses he could see a young girl receptionist talking on the phone. Wexford and Burden crossed the road and went into the Old Flag.

Wexford had been there once or twice before. It was not a place ever to be crowded in the middle of the day. The busy lunch trade went to the cheaper brighter pubs and the wine bars. In the smaller of the lounge bars where food was being served several vacant tables remained. Wexford was making for one of them when he caught sight of Miles Gardner sitting alone.

'Won't you join me?'

'You look as if you're waiting for someone,' Wexford said.

'Any congenital company that offers itself.' He had a gracious warm manner of speaking that was in no way affected. Wexford recalled that this was what he had always liked about him. 'They do a nice prawn salad,' Miles Gardner said. 'And if you can get here before one they'll send up to the butcher for a fillet steak.'

'What happens at one?'

'The butcher closes. He opens at two and then the pub closes. There's Myringham for you.'

Wexford laughed. Burden didn't laugh but sat wearing the sort of stiff polite expression that indicates to even the most insensitive that one would be happier – or less miserable –

on one's own. Wexford made up his mind to ignore him. Gardner seemed delighted with their company and, having bought a round of drinks, began to talk in the easy rather elegant way he had about the new house he had just moved into which Sylvia's father-in-law had designed. It was a valuable gift, Wexford thought, to be able to talk to people, one whom you had only just met and the other a mere acquaintance, as if they were old friends whom you conversed with regularly.

Gardner was a small, undistinguished-looking man. His style was in his voice and manner. He had a much taller wife and two or three rather noisy daughters, Wexford remembered. From the new house and the time it had taken to get itself built, Gardner had moved on to talk of work, lack of work and unemployment, eliciting mild sparks of interest from Burden, at least to the extent of extracting monosyllables from him. Sevensmith Harding had battled against laying off workers at their Harlow factory and the battle had been won – allowing for the few redundancies which Gardner insisted had been acceptable to the men and women concerned.

'Yes,' said Burden. 'I daresay.'

Always reactionary, he had until a few years back threatened to become unbearably right wing and Blimpish, but Jenny had reversed the tide. Burden was far more of a moderate now. He did not, as he once would have, launch into a tirade against unemployment benefits, Social Security payments and general idleness. Or perhaps it was only this depression of his that made him forbear.

'The whole attitude towards work and employment and keeping one's job is changing, I find,' Gardner said. He began talking about what he thought gave rise to these new patterns and made it interesting enough. Or so Wexford thought. Burden, eating prawn salad rather too rapidly, kept looking at his watch. He had to be back in court by two. Wexford thought he would be glad to be rid of him for a while.

'Isn't what you're really saying,' he said to Gardner, 'that, in spite of the threat of unemployment and the inadequacy of unemployment benefits, men seem to have lost that craven fear of losing their jobs they had in the thirties?'

'Yes, and to a great extent, any rate among the middle

196

class, lost the feeling they used to have that they had to stick in a hated job or career for the rest of their lives just because it's the one they went into at twenty.'

'Then what's brought this change about?'

'I don't know. I've thought about it but the answers I come up with don't satisfy me. But I can tell you that just as the fear has gone, and the respect for employers because they were employers, so had pride in one's job and the old loyalty to a company. My marketing manager is a case in point. Time was when you could say a man in that position would also be a responsible person, someone you could trust not to let you down. He'd have been proud – and yes, I'll say it, *grateful* – to be where he was and he'd have had a real feeling for the firm's welfare too.'

'What's he done?' said Burden. 'Decided to change his career in midstream?'

It was said acidulously but Gardner gave no sign of having noticed the edge to Burden's voice and replied pleasantly.

'Not so far as I know. He simply walked out on me. He's on three months' notice, or supposed to be. First we get a phone call from his wife saying he's sick, then not a word until a letter of resignation comes, very clipped and curt, and a note at the bottom – ' Gardner looked almost apologetic – 'quite an *insolent* sort of note, saying he'd be in touch with our accounts department about his superannuation.'

'Had he been with you long?'

'All his working life, I gather, and five years as marketing manager.'

'At least you'll have no difficulty in finding a replacement in these hard times.'

'It's going to be a case of promotion for one of our best reps. That's always been Sevensmith Harding's policy. Promote rather than take in from outside. Only usually, of course, we're given a bit more time.'

Burden got up and said he must get back to court. He shook hands with Gardner and had the grace to mutter something about its having been good to meet him.

'Let me get you another beer,' said Wexford when Burden had left and been described (very much to his surprise) by Gardner as a 'nice chap'.

'Thanks so much. I don't suppose they'll sling us out before two-thirty, will they?'

The beer came, one of the 130 varieties of 'real ale' the Old Flag claimed to stock.

'It's not by any chance my neighbour Rodney Williams you'll be promoting, is it?'

Gardner looked at him, surprised.

'Rod Williams?'

'Yes. He lives in the next street to me.'

Gardner said in a patient tone, 'Rod Williams is our former marketing manager, the one I was telling you resigned.'

'Williams?'

'Yes, I thought I explained. Perhaps I didn't say the name.'

'Somebody,' said Wexford, 'is getting hold of the wrong end of the stick here.'

'It's you,' said Gardner, smiling.

'Yes, I expect it is. Somebody has given me the wrong end of the stick. Am I to take it then that Williams wasn't one of your reps and didn't cover the Suffolk area for you?'

'He was once. He did once. Up till five years ago. We kept to our customary policy and when our former marketing manager took early retirement due to a heart condition, we promoted Rod Williams.'

'As far as his wife knows he's still a rep. That is, he's still spending half his time selling up in Suffolk.'

Gardner's eyebrows went up. He gave a twisted grin. 'His private life is no affair of mine.'

'Nor mine.'

It was Gardner who changed the subject. He began talking about his eldest daughter who was getting married in the late summer. Wexford finally parted from him with a promise to be in touch, to 'get Dora to give Pam a ring and fix something up'. Driving home to Kingsmarkham, he thought for a while about Rodney Williams. There had been no room in his own marriage for alibis. He wondered what it would be like to have a marriage in which a permanent, on-going, five-year-long alibi existed as an integral part of life. Unthinkable. Unimaginable. He stopped trying to identify and thought about it with detachment.

What had happened perhaps was that five years ago Williams had met a girl with whom he wanted to spend time without ending his marriage. Keeping his promotion a secret from his wife would have been a way of achieving this. Probably the girl lived in Myringham. While Joy Williams believed her husband was staying at a motel outside Ipswich he was in reality seeing this other girl, no doubt sharing her home and doing his nine-to-five job at Sevensmith Harding in Myringham.

It was the sort of situation some men chuckle over. Wexford wasn't one of them. And there was another aspect, one that few men would find funny. If Williams hadn't told his wife about his promotion he presumably also hadn't told her about the considerable increase in salary that went with it. Still, there was no more mystery. Williams had written to the company. Joy had phoned with excuses. Back in Alverbury Road Williams was still perhaps managing to shore up a few fragments of deceit against discovery.

It was nine at night and he was still in his office, going through for the tenth time the statements he had taken for the preparation of a case of fraud against one Francis Wingrave Adams. He still doubted whether they would constitute a watertight case and so did counsel representing the police, though both knew he was guilty. On the final stroke of nine – St Peter's clock had a dead sound too, like St Mary Woolnoth's – he put the papers away and set off to walk homewards.

Lately he had taken to walking to and from work. Dr Crocker recommended it, pointing out that it was less than half a mile.

'Hardly worth it then,' Wexford said.

'A couple of miles' walk a day could make a difference of ten years' life to you.'

'Does that mean that if I walked six miles a day I could prolong my life by thirty years?'

The doctor had refused to answer that one. Wexford, though feigning to scoff, had gone some way towards obeying him. Sometimes his walk took him down Tabard Road past Burden's bungalow, sometimes along Alverbury Road where the Williams family lived, and there was an occasional longer route along one of the meadow footpaths. Tonight he intended to drop in and see Burden for a final assessment of the Adams' business.

But now he began to feel that there was very little left to say about this man who had conned an elderly woman out of £20,000. He wouldn't talk about that. Instead he would try to get out of Burden what was happening in his life to account for his depression.

The Burdens still lived in the bungalow Burden had moved into soon after his first marriage where the garden after twenty years or more still had an immature look and the ivy which tried to climb up the house had been ruthlessly cut back with secateurs. Only the front door changed. It had been all colours – Burden was a relentless decorator – but Wexford had liked the rose pink best. Now it was a dark greenish blue – Sevenshine Oriental Peacock probably. Above the door, now dusk had come, the porch light was on, a lantern of leaded lights in the shape of a star.

Jenny came to let him in. She was halfway through her pregnancy now and 'showing', as the old wives say. Instead of a smock she wore a full-sleeved, square-necked dress with a high waist, like the one the woman is wearing in Vermeer's *The Letter*. She had let he golden-brown hair grow and it hung to her shoulders. But, for all that, Wexford was shocked by her appearance. She looked drawn and dispirited.

Burden, having years ago agreed to stop calling Wexford 'sir', now called him nothing at all. But Jenny called him Reg. She said, 'Mike's in the living room, Reg,' and added in a way quite unlike her usual self, 'I was just going to bed.'

He felt constrained to say he was sorry for calling so late, though it was only twenty past nine. She shrugged and said it didn't matter and she said it in a way which seemed to imply that nothing much mattered. He followed her into the room where Burden was.

On the middle cushion of the three-seater settee Burden sat reading *Police Review*. Wexford would have expected Jenny to have been sitting beside him but she hadn't been. Beside a chair at the far end of the room lay her book face downwards and a piece of white knitting that had a look about it of the knitter's having no enthusiasm for her task. In a glass vase on the windowsill dying wallflowers stood in three inches of water.

'Have a drink,' said Burden, laying down his magazine. 'There's beer. There is beer, isn't there, Jenny?'

'I don't know. I never touch the stuff.'

Burden said nothing. He left the room, went out to the kitchen and came back with two cans on a tray. Burden's first wife would have said, and Jenny once would have said, that they must have glasses to drink the beer out of. Jenny, languidly sitting down, picking up book and knitting but looking at neither, said, 'You can drink it out of the can, can't you?'

Wexford began to feel awkward. Some sort of powerful angry tension that existed between these two seemed to hang in the air like smoke, to get in his throat and give him a choky feeling. He snapped the top off his beer can. Jenny was holding the knitting needles in one clenched hand and staring at the wall. He had no intention of talking about Francis Wingrave Adams in her presence. On other occasions like this he and Burden would have gone into one of the other rooms. Burden sat on the settee, wearing his half-frown. He opened the beer can with a sharp, rough movement and a spurt of froth shot out across the carpet.

Three months before Wexford had seen Jenny soothing and practical when her husband had dropped, not a spoonful of beer, but a bowl of strawberry mousse on the paler newer carpet of the dining room. She had laughed and told him to leave the clearing up to her. Now she gave a cry of real distress and jumped up out of her chair.

'All right,' said Burden. 'All right. I'll do it. It's nothing anyway. I'll get a cloth.'

She burst into tears. She put one hand up to her face and ran out of the room. Burden followed her. That is, Wexford thought he had followed her but he came back almost immediately holding a floorcloth.

'Sorry about that,' he said on his hands and knees. 'Of course it's not the beer. It's just any little thing sets her off. Take no notice.' He lifted an angry face. 'I've made up my mind I'm simply not going to take any notice any more.'

'But if she's not well, Mike . . .'

'She is perfectly well.' Burden got up and dropped the cloth onto the tiled kerb of the fireplace. 'She is having an ideal trouble-free pregnancy. Why, she wasn't even sick.

201

When I remember what Jean went through . . .' Wexford could hardly believe his ears. For a husband – and such a husband as Burden – to make that comparison! Burden seemed to realize what he had said and a dull flush crept across his face. 'No, honestly, she's perfectly fit, she says so herself. It's simply neurotic behaviour.'

Wexford had sometimes thought in the past that if every instance diagnosed by Burden as neurotic were taken as sound, almost the entire population would have to be tranquillized, not to say confined in mental hospitals. He said, 'The amniocentesis was all right, wasn't it? They didn't tell her something to worry her?'

Burden hesitated. 'Well, as a matter of fact they did.' He gave an ugly humourless laugh. 'That's just what they did. They told her something to worry her. You've hit the nail bang on the head. It doesn't worry *me* and I'm the child's father. But it worries her like hell and I'm the one who has to bear the brunt of it.' He sat down and said very loudly, almost shouting, 'I don't want to talk about it anyway. I've said too much already and I've no intention of saying any more. I feel like learning a formula to explain my wife's conduct and repeating it to people when they first come in the door.'

Wexford said quietly, 'You can do it extempore for it is nothing but roaring.'

He got a glare for that. 'I came to talk about Adams. Or are you too preoccupied with your domestic fracas to care?'

'I told you, I'm simply not going to take any notice any more,' said Burden, and they talked about Adams not very profitably for the next half-hour.

Dora was in bed when he got home, sitting up reading. While he undressed he told her about the Burdens.

'They're too old to have babies,' was all she would say.

'Flying in the face of nature, would you call it?'

'You'd be surprised, my lad. I might. And by the way, Rod Williams hasn't come back. I saw Joy and she hasn't heard a word.'

'But I had the distinct impression she'd phoned Sevensmith Harding,' Wexford began.

'You told her to, you mean. You told her to phone them

and find out if they could tell her anything and she's going to.'

That wasn't what he had meant. He got into bed, sure now that he hadn't heard the last of the Williams affair.

3

For more than a couple of weeks now he had been keeping his eye on the dark blue Ford Granada parked outside his house in Arnold Road, Myringham. It had appeared there for the first time soon after Easter. Graham Gee couldn't see it from his front windows nor, because of the tall lonicera hedge, from his front garden. He saw it when he drove his own car out of the entrance to his garage each morning and when he drove it in each afternoon at 5.30.

At first (he told the police) he thought it might have something to do with the boy opposite, the teenage son of the people in the bungalow. But it was too respectable a car for that. Well, it was *then*. Dismissing that theory, he wondered if it belonged to some commuter who was using Arnold Road as a station car park. Arnold Road wasn't very near Myringham Southern Region Station, it was a good quarter of a mile away, but it was probably the nearest street to the station not clogged on both sides with commuters' cars.

Graham Gee began to see the presence of the Ford Granada outside his gate as the thin end of the wedge. Soon there would be a hundred rail travellers' cars parked in Arnold Road. He was not a commuter himself but a partner in a firm of accountants in Pomfret.

Arnold Road was known as a 'nice neighbourhood'. The houses were detached, standing in large gardens. There weren't any rough elements, there wasn't any trouble, except perhaps for the theft of dahlias from someone's front garden the previous autumn. So Graham Gee was surprised to notice one morning that the Granada's hub caps had gone. Perhaps they had always been gone though, he couldn't remember.

Still, he knew the wheels hadn't always been gone. The car hadn't always been propped up on bricks. Dirty now, streaked with rain, it sat on its brick supports, looking as if it might after all be the property of the teenager opposite.

He still did nothing about it, though he knew by now that it was there all the time. It wasn't driven there in the morning and taken away in the evening. For a week now it hadn't been drivable. It took the smashing of a rear window to get him to do something.

The rear window had been broken, the front doors opened and the interior stripped. The radio had been removed, the headrests taken off the front seats, and something dug out of the dashboard, a clock perhaps. Though the boot was open, the thieves hadn't thought it worth their while to help themselves to the snow shovel inside. Gee phoned the police.

There was no need for the police to go through the procedure of tracing the driver through the Vehicle Licensing Department in Swansea, for the vehicle registration document was in the Granada's glove compartment along with a road map of southern England, a ballpoint pen and a pair of sunglasses.

Vehicle registration documents have named on them the 'keeper' of the vehicle, not its owner, a fact which was also of assistance to the police. The one listed the keeper as Rodney John Williams of 31 Alverbury Road, Kingsmarkham.

Why had Williams dumped the car in Arnold Road when Sevensmith Harding's own car park was less than a quarter of a mile away behind the company's High Street offices? That car park was never locked. It had no gates, only an opening in the fence and on the fence a notice requesting 'unauthorized personnel' not to park there.

'I don't understand it,' Miles Gardner said. 'Frankly, we've been wondering what to do about recovering the car but we don't know where Williams is. He didn't mention the car in his letter of resignation. Apparently, wherever he was when he first left, he's no longer with his wife, otherwise we would have tackled her. He's disappeared into thin air. It's a bit much really, isn't it? I gather the car's in a state, not much more than a shell?'

'The engine's still there,' said Wexford.

Gardner made a face. They were in his rather gloomy though luxurious office, a room not so much panelled as lined with oak, the decor dating from those between-wars days when hardwood was plentiful. None of your Sevenstar matt emulsion here, Wexford thought to himself.

There were more framed photographs than in the average elderly couple's living room. On Gardner's desk, placed to catch his eye every time he looked up, was a big one of tall Mrs Gardner and her three girls, all affectionate nestling and entwined arms. The walls were reserved for various groups and gatherings of men at company functions or on sporting occasions. One was of a cricket match with a tall gangling man going in to bat. Rodney Williams. The high forehead, slight concavity of features that would no doubt show more clearly in profile, the thin mouth stretched in a grin, were unmistakable.

Gardner looked at it dolefully.

'He was a lot younger then,' he said. 'The company had a crack team in those days.' He made as if to take the photograph down, angered no doubt by the sight of the permanently grinning Williams, but seemed to change his mind. 'The whole thing's extraordinary. He was very keen on cars, you know, one of those car men. You don't think anything's happened to him, do you?'

The euphemism that always signified death . . .

'If you mean some sort of accident, I don't know but I don't think so. It's more what has he been up to, isn't it?'

Gardner looked mystified.

'It looks to me as if he may have been up to something he shouldn't have been, he's been on the fiddle. Either he decided he'd made enough out of it and was going to call it a day or else something happened to make him think discovery was imminent. Now, the most likely place for him to have been cooking the books is here. Do you have any thoughts on that one?'

'He wouldn't have had the opportunity. He never went near any books, so to speak. Do you want me to have our chief accountant up? I mean, as far as I can see, any fiddle

206

he was up to would have to be an expenses fiddle and Ken Risby would be the man to tell you about that.'

Gardner made a call on the internal phone. While they waited for Risby Wexford said, 'There is nothing small, portable but of considerable value he could have stolen? No cheque coming into his hands he could have falsified? No forgery he could have perpetrated?'

Gardner looked simply bewildered. 'I don't think so. I'm sure not. I mean, I should know by now. Good God, the man's been gone over three weeks.' He jumped up. 'Here's Ken now. He'll tell us.'

But Risby was not able to tell them much. He was a thin, fair man in his thirties, with a nervous manner, and he seemed as shocked by Wexford's suggestion as Gardner had been. You'd think the pair of them lived in a world where fraud had never been heard of, Wexford thought impatiently, and every businessman was a sea-green incorruptible.

'He was a mite heavy on his expenses sometimes but that's all, that's positively all. He never had the handling of the firm's money. What makes you think he's done something like that?'

'You think about it. Look at it for yourself. For five years the man's been lying to his wife about his position with this firm. What salary was he getting, by the way?'

'Twenty-five thousand,' said Gardner rather grudgingly.

More than Wexford had expected, £5000 more. 'And lying about that too. You can bet on it she thinks he was getting less than half that. One day he tells her he's going to Ipswich, a place he doubtless hasn't set foot in for five years, and off he goes, dumps his company car in the street, and disappears. Apart from getting the lady he's in cahoots with to phone here and say he's ill and apart from writing his resignation he's never heard from again. And you ask me why I think he's been up to something? Tell me about the man. If he's not a man who'd steal or forge, is there some other disgraceful thing he might have done?'

They looked at him. Having no imagination, they didn't know and couldn't hazard guesses. Wexford had plenty of imagination and very little knowledge of marketing.

'For instance, he couldn't have been selling this paint of

yours at prices over the odds and pocketing the difference? Something like that?'

Gardner, who had looked as if he would never smile again, burst out laughing.

'He never actually *sold* anything, Reg. It doesn't work like that. He never handled money. He never handled money in any shape or form.'

'You make him sound like royalty,' said Wexford. 'Anyway, will you, Mr Risby, have a good look at your books for me, please? Do a supplementary audit or whatever.'

'Really not necessary, I assure you, not necessary at all. I'd go into court at this moment and swear there's not a squeak of a discrepancy in my books.'

'I hope you'll never have to go into court on this matter, but don't count on it.' Risby's eyes opened wide at that one. 'And do as I ask and check the books, will you? And now,' Wexford said to Gardner, 'I'd like to see that letter of resignation Williams wrote to you.'

Gardner called his secretary in to find it. Wexford noticed he called her Susan, and what was less expected, she called him Miles. The letter was typed and by someone not accustomed to frequent use of a typewriter.

Dear Mr Gardner,
This is to give you notice of my resignation from Sevensmith Harding from today. I am afraid it is rather sudden but is due to circumstances beyond my control. I shall not be returning to the office and would prefer you not to attempt to get in touch with me.

Yours sincerely,
Rodney J. Williams
PS. I will contact the Accounts Dept. about my superannuation refund in due course.

Wexford said, 'Everyone in this office calls each other by their Christian names but Rodney Williams called you Mr Gardner? Is that right?'

'No, of course not. He called me Miles.'

'He doesn't in this letter.'

'I took that to be because he thought the occasion demanded something more formal.'

208

'It's a possibility. Don't you find it odd when a man on three months' notice gives you one day's? Wouldn't you have expected a more detailed explanation for common courtesy's sake than "circumstances beyond my control"?'

'Are you suggesting someone else might have written that letter?'

Wexford didn't answer directly. 'I'll take it with me if I may. Maybe have some experts look at that signature. Can you let me have a specimen of his signature? One we *know* is his?'

Nine separate sets of fingerprints have been found on and in the car. These would presumably include the prints of whoever had vandalized it. The others would be Williams's, Joy's, Sara's, Kevin's. Early days yet to ask these people to let him check their own prints against those in the car. A lot of hairs, fair and grey, had been on the upholstery. No blood, of course, nothing dramatic. There was one odd thing, though. On the floor of the boot, along with the shovel, were some crumbs of plaster the lab had identified as either Tetrion or Sevensmith Harding's Stopgap.

It took a few more days to get a verdict on the letter.

A manual portable machine, the Remington 315, had been used to type it. There was a chip out of the apex of the capital A on this machine, a similar flaw in the ascender of the lower-case t and a smudging of the head of the comma. As to the signature, it wasn't Wiliams's. The handwriting expert was far more categorial than such people are usually willing to be. He was almost scathing in his incredulity that anyone could for a moment have believed that the signature was made by Williams.

When Joy had told Dora of her intention to phone Sevensmith Harding she had followed this up with a request to 'send' Wexford round to her house once more. This time Dora had said in quite a sharp way that her husband wasn't a private detective and Wexford, of course, hadn't gone. But Williams's disappearance had stopped being a private matter. At any rate, he thought, he wouldn't be unwelcome at 31 Alverbury Road. The answer to a prayer, in fact. He walked round there in the evening, at about eight.

This time the girl Sara let him in. She spoke not a word but closed the front door after him, opened the living-room door, left him and went back upstairs.

Joy Williams was watching television. The programme was one of those contests in which teams of people go through ridiculous or humiliating ordeals. Men in dress suits and top hats were trying to walk a tightrope over what looked like a lake of mashed potato. Just before the door was opened he had heard her laughing. She didn't turn the set off, only the sound. He thought she looked anything but pleased to see him. Her expression had very quickly become sullen.

Yes, she admitted, they had a joint bank account. Rod was away so much they had had to. Wexford asked her if he might seen some recent bank statements.

She hunched herself, arms wrapping her thin body, right hand on left shoulder, left hand with the ugly showy rings on right. It was a habitual gesture with her which a psychiatrist might have said began as a way of protecting herself from assault. She had the green trousers on and a knitted jumper, its shoulders sprinkled with fallen hairs and dandruff.

'How often does your bank send you statements?'

'It's been once a month lately.' Her eyes strayed to the silent but tumultuous screen. A contestant had fallen into the mashed potato. 'They made a mistake over something and Rod complained, so they started sending statements once a month.'

Dr Crocker had told Wexford of a recent visit to one of his patients, a woman ill with bronchitis. The television had been on in her bedroom, all her six children sitting there watching it. When he tried to examine her she had protested angrily at his request that the set be turned off.

'I pull the plug out now without a by-your-leave,' said the doctor. 'If the TV's on or their video I don't ask any more, I pull out the plug.'

Wexford would have liked to do that. He would have done it if he had had just a fraction more evidence for disquiet over Rodney Williams. It was curious that Joy, who had come close to pestering Dora for his attention, was now making it plain she didn't want him here.

'Will you show me the statements?'

She turned her head reluctantly. 'OK, if you want.' He had put his request very politely as if she would be doing him a favour and she responded as if she was.

It didn't take her long to find the statements. She wasn't going to miss more of her programme than she had to. As he began to look at the statements she leaned across and summoned a little sound out of the television, so that shrieks, exclamations and commentary were just audible. He wondered what could possibly distract her, what real event or shock, and then he knew. The phone bell. Somewhere, elsewhere in the house, the phone began to ring.

She jumped up. 'That'll be my son. My son always phones me on Thursday nights.'

Wexford returned to the monthly bank statements. Each one showed the sum of £500 paid into the account more or less at the beginning of the month. A salary cheque apparently. Several objections to that one. Williams's salary had been £25,000 a year and there was no way £500 a month, even after all possible deductions, could amount to as much as that. Secondly, the sum would vary, not be a set round figure. Thirdly, it would be paid in on the same day of the month, give or take a day each way, not sometimes on the first and sometimes on the eighth.

It was evident what had been going on. Williams had another account somewhere into which his salary was paid. From that account he transferred £500 a month into the account he had jointly with his wife. If this was so, and it must be, it was going to be useless asking Joy, as he had intended, if her husband had drawn on their joint account since his disappearance.

Sevensmith Harding would make no bones about telling him where this other account was. The problem would be the intransigent bank manager refusing to disclose any information about a client's account. He looked at the April statement again. Five hundred pounds had been paid in on 2 April. No May statement had yet been sent to Mrs Williams as May was only half over.

She came back into the room, looking brighter and younger, her face more animated than he had ever seen it. She had been talking to her son, her favourite.

'I'd like you to give your bank a ring,' he said, 'and ask

them if the usual five hundred was paid into the account at the beginning of the month. Will you do that?'

She nodded. He asked her to tell him about the last afternoon and evening Williams had spent at home. Rod had mowed the lawn in the afternoon, she said, and then he'd taken her shopping to the Tesco discount. She couldn't drive.

'We came back and had a cup of tea. Rod had a sandwich. He didn't want more than that. He said he'd get something on his way to Ipswich. Then he went upstairs and packed a bag and left. He'd be back on Sunday, he said.' She gave one of her dull laughs. 'And that was the last of him. After twenty-two years.'

'What did you do for the rest of the evening?'

'Me?'

'Yes, what did you do? Did you stay at home? Go out? Did anyone come here?'

'I went over to my sister's. She lives in Pomfret. I went on the bus. I had something to eat and then I went to my sister's.'

'And Sara?'

'She was here. Up there.' Joy Williams pointed to the ceiling. 'Studying for her A-levels, I suppose.' She made it sound an unworthy, even slightly disgraceful thing for her daughter to have been doing.

There was something wrong with this description of how the evening had been passed, something incongruous, only Wexford couldn't put his finger on what.

'I'd like to talk to Sara,' he said.

'Do as you like.'

She twisted round in her chair and looked fully at him, the television for the moment forgotten.

'She'll be in her bedroom but you can go up. She won't object.' The awful laugh came. 'Rather the reverse if I know her.'

212

4

So young Sara, who looked like one of Botticelli's girls, a Quattrocento virgin, had been caught in bed with a boyfriend. Or not in bed, most probably. On the yellow plastic settee or in the back of a car. It was difficult with daughters. You knew what your enlightened principles were but things looked different when it was *your* daughter. Still, that hardly justified Joy's snide insinuation. Wexford, going upstairs, decided that as well as disliking what he knew of Williams, he didn't care for Mrs Williams either. Not that it mattered whether he liked them or not. It made no difference. Perhaps the woman did have some justification. She was going through a bad time; she, who was surely in the process of losing her man, would feel bitter towards a daughter gaining one. And the discovery of Sara and the boy might have been made very recently.

He knew which bedroom it was because music was coming from behind the door. Rock music of some kind, soft with a monotonous drumbeat. She must have heard his feet on the stairs by now. He had taken care to make a bit of noise, not difficult on the linoleum covered with thin haircord. He knocked on the door.

She didn't say, 'Come in!' She opened it herself. Wexford had often noted reactions to a knock at the door. They offered indications of character and motivation. The woman, for example, who calls out 'Come in!' is more open, relaxed and easy-going than she who opens the door herself. The latter will be cagey and reserved. In the thirty seconds or so before she opens the door, what has she put away in a drawer or hidden under a magazine?

213

He could see that Sara had created the room herself. What attractiveness it had had nothing to do with the furniture, carpet and curtains provided by her parents. It was the smallest bedroom. Wexford had had an extension built on to his own house when the girls were little but this house remained as it had originally been. There would be a large front bedroom for the husband and wife, a slightly smaller back room – in this case for the son – and a tiny boxroom no more than nine feet by seven for the daughter. She had put posters all over the walls, one of a red horse galloping in the snow from the Yugoslav Naive school of painting, another of a thin naked black man playing a guitar. Between them hung a tennis racket, a corn dolly and a montage of Tarot cards. Perhaps the most striking poster was the one that faced the door. A harpy-like creature with the head and breasts of a woman and the body, wings and claws of a raven, clutched at an unfurling ribbon on which was painted the name – acronym? – ARRIA. Wexford remembered the tee-shirt Sara had been wearing when first they met. The raven woman had a face like Britannia or maybe Boadicea, one of those noble, handsome, courageous, fanatical faces, that made you feel like locking up the knives and reaching for the Valium.

Bookshelves that looked as if put up by Sara herself held a paperback *Life of Freud*, Phyllis Grosskurth's *Havelock Ellis*, Fromm, Laing, Freud on the *Wolf Man* and *Leonardo*, Erin Pizzey and Jeff Shapiro on incest and child abuse, but not a single work of fiction. With her tiny radio providing background music, she had been sitting at a dressing table that doubled as a desk, swotting for an exam. It was evidently chemistry. The textbook lay open at a page of formulae.

'We're trying to find your father, Sara. I wouldn't exactly say he's disappeared but he's making himself very hard to find.'

She had fixed him with her grave contained look. He noticed her skin, creamy and smooth like velvet, with a gold dusting of freckles on her small nose. When she opened the door to him she had been holding a green felt-tipped pen in her hand. On the back of the other hand she had drawn a green snake. Teenagers had always drawn on their hands, they had done so when he was in his teens and when his daughters were in their teens, but now some sort of specific

214

fashion for it has sprung up. To have black and red and green drawings on your hands and arms and body was the 'in' thing. Sara had drawn with her green pen a spotted snake, not curled around itself but stretched out and slightly undulant, its forked tongue extended.

'Have you any thoughts about where he might be?'

She shook her head. She put the cap on the pen and laid it down.

'Would you like to tell me about the last time you were with your father? Were you here when he left?'

She hesitated, then gave a nod. 'It was the second day of term after the Easter holidays. I was late home because I went to the library. They'd got a book in for me, a new book I'd put my name down for and they'd sent me a card to say it was in.' She lifted two books off the stack and handed him one from underneath. She was out to impress and the book was a learned work: Stern's *Principles of Human Genetics*. He didn't take much notice of that but he did look at the date stamp in the back. 'I rang the library to renew it,' she said defensively. 'I couldn't read it in three weeks. It's very difficult.' She smiled at last and became at once a beauty. 'I'm not saying it's too difficult for me but genetics is an abstruse subject. I've got my A-levels and they have to take priority.'

'You're interested in this sort of thing?'

'I've been offered a place in medical school, St Biddulph's.' Crocker had trained there, Wexford recalled. 'I shall get it, of course, but in theory it depends on my A-level results.' Her tone was such as to show she was in no real doubt that these would meet the standard. 'I have to get at least three Bs but an A and two Bs would be better.'

She must be a bright girl. A year or two back statistics had been published showing an excess of medical students and that at this rate there would be a surplus of forty thousand doctors by the end of the century. Medical schools were being instructed to raise their standards and cut their intake. So if Sara Williams had been offered a place at the highly prestigious St Biddulph's . . .

'Your mother and father must be proud of you.'

The sweeping glance she gave him told him he had said something stupid or at least wide of the mark.

215

'I can see you don't know my parents.'

'They'd prefer something else for you?'

'I could be a shorthand typist, couldn't I? I could be a nurse. I'd get paid while I was being those things, wouldn't I?' Her voice was full of scorn and anger. 'I can't be stopped, though. I'll get a grant anyway. I don't know what I'd have done in olden times.'

By 'olden times' he supposed she meant the days of his own youth when your parents paid for your education or you borrowed the money or worked your way. Things were different now. A father couldn't put his foot down with the same effect. He could only persuade or dissuade.

'The last time you saw your father,' he reminded her.

Her anger had died. She was practical again, crisply reciting facts. But there was something derisive in the way she spoke of her father, as if he were a joke to her – or an organism under a microscope.

'I came in and he was just leaving. I heard him talking to Mum about the route he was going to take. The A26 for Tonbridge, then the Dartford Tunnel on to the M25 and the M25 to the A12 which would take him to Ipswich.'.

'Why was he telling her the route? Would she be interested? I mean, wasn't it the route he normally took?'

'I said you didn't know my father. I'd say for a start he wouldn't be much concerned about the other person's *interest*. Dad talks a lot about cars and driving, roads, that sort of thing. I'm not interested but he talks to me about it. The car's a person to him, a woman, and she's got a Christian name. He calls her Greta. Greta, the Granada, you see.'

'So your father left and your mother went to Pomfret and you stayed here on you own studying?'

Was he imagining that hesitation, that brief wary flare in her eyes?

'That's right. I don't go out in the evenings at the moment. I haven't time.' She smiled again, this time with great artificiality. 'I heard they'd found his car.'

'In the process of being dismembered for its wheels and its radio.'

'Cannibalized,' she said, and she laughed the way her mother did. 'Poor old Greta.'

216

Could he have a look round the rest of the house? Notably through William's papers and clothes? Joy put up no objection. The television clack-clacked through the floor and the pop music thumped and droned through the wall. In the book of rules of human behaviour he kept in his head one of the first laws was the one about who got which bedroom. The British middle class mostly lived in three-bedroomed houses, one big bedroom, one slightly smaller, one little. In a family of parents, son and daughter, the daughter invariably got the second bedroom and the son the tiny one, irrespective of seniority. It was one aspect of life (the women's movement might have said if they'd noticed it) in which the female had the advantage over the male. Presumably it came about because girls from the first were conditioned into being more at home, more centred on home things and being confined within walls. In which case the women's movement wouldn't like it so much. But it was the girl in this household who had the smallest bedroom, even though her brother was now away most of the time. Of course, it might be that she had chosen this arrangement, but somehow he didn't think so.

He opened the door of the second bedroom and looked inside. There was a newish pine bedroom suite, two bright Afghan rugs, a fringed bedcover that was recognizably one of Marks and Spencer's designs. It looked as if someone with not much taste or money had done her best to make a 'nice' room of it and the sole personal touch its occupant had contributed was to hang a map of the world on the wall opposite the bed.

The main bedroom was like his own in size and proportions. The walls were even painted in the same colour as his own, Sevenstar emulsion Orange Blossom. There the resemblance ended. The Williamses slept in twin beds, each narrower than the standard three feet, he thought. He could tell hers was the one nearest the window by the nightdress case on it, quilted peach satin in the shape of a scallop shell. The rest of the furniture consisted of a wardrobe, dressing table, dressing-table stool, chest of drawers and two bedside tables all in some dark reddish wood with a matt finish and with rather bright gold chrome handles. There was also a built-in cupboard.

217

Wexford looked first in the drawer of the bedside cabinet between Williams's bed and the door. He found a box that had once held cufflinks but was now empty, a comb, a tube of antiseptic skin cream, an unused toothbrush, a packet of tissues, a tube of throat pastilles, two safety pins, several plastic collar stiffeners, a half-full bottle of nasal drops and an empty pill bottle labelled 'Mandaret. One to be taken twice daily. Rodney Williams'.

In the cupboard part of the cabinet were two paperback novels of espionage, an unused writing pad, a current British passport in the name of Mr R. J. Williams, a clean handkerchief initialled 'R' and two electric shavers.

The wardrobe contained Joy's clothes, a collection that had an unwashed, unclean smell about it with a whiff of camphor and some kind of disinfectant. Rodney Williams's clothes were in the cupboard. An overcoat, a sheepskin jacket, a plastic mac, two hip-length showerproof jackets, a shabby sports jacket and a new one, four suits, two pairs of slacks. All the clothes were good, all of much better quality than Joy's. Not a large wardrobe, Wexford thought, looking into the linings of coats and feeling in pockets. In the side compartments were underwear, pyjamas, on the floor three pairs of shoes and a pair of sandals. Whatever Rodney Williams had spent his surplus money on it wasn't clothes. Unless he had taken more with him than Joy or Sara knew. Maybe he had secreted a couple of bulging suitcases in Greta's boot during the course of the day.

The dining room, you could see, they hardly ever used. A light-coloured polished table stood in the dead centre of it with four light-coloured wood chairs with moquette seats around it. A sideboard with an empty Capo di Monte bowl on it nearly filled one wall and opposite this was a mahogany roll-top desk, perhaps a hand-down from a parent and certainly the nicest piece of furniture in the house. French windows, at which hung curtains of mustard-coloured rep – a favourite shade with Joy Williams – gave onto the back garden, a quarter acre of grass surrounded by close-board fencing and relieved by two small apple trees on which the blossom glimmered palely in the dusk. It didn't look as if the grass, several inches long now, had been mown since Williams did it five weeks before.

The desk wasn't locked. Wexford rolled back the top. There wasn't much inside. Writing paper, not the headed kind, envelopes, a bottle of ink in a cardboard box from which it had never been removed and never would be, a box of drawing pins, a glass jar of gum, a roll of Scotch tape. In one of the drawers was nothing but old Christmas cards, in the other a receipted electricity bill, a pocket calculator and a broken ballpoint pen.

If Williams had meant to go away for good wouldn't he have taken his passport?

He looked through the pigeonholes but found no cheque books, used or in use. Joy probably kept hers in her handbag. He went back to her. She was still watching television and now the programme was the everlasting serial *Runway* in which his daughter Sheila played the stewardess heroine. Had, in fact, played her for the last time the previous week. But this was a secret known to no one but her own family as yet. No newspaper had so far got hold of the story that a major air disaster would in the autumn end the career of Stewardess Charlotte Riley for ever.

Joy Williams didn't know it. If she knew Sheila was his daughter – and surely she must – she gave no sign. He had the curious experience of standing beside her while they both watched his daughter attempting to placate an ill-tempered passenger. Then he did what Crocker recommended – or nearly so. If he didn't go so far as to pull out the plug he did switch off the set. She blinked at him.

'Does your husband possess a typewriter, Mrs Williams?'

'A typewriter? No.'

'Is he still taking Mandaret?'

She nodded, looking at the blank screen as if she expected it spontaneously and without benefit of electricity to spring into cinematic life.

'It's a form of methyldopa, isn't it? A drug for high blood pressure?'

'He's had blood pressure for two or three years.'

'I found an empty Mandaret container in his bedside cupboard. I suppose he took a supply with him?'

'He wouldn't forget them. He didn't like to miss a day on them. He always took one when he got up and one with his tea.'

'I take it he had a bag with him? A suitcase? Something to put his clothes in?'

Again she simply nodded.

'What was he dressed in?'

'Pardon?'

'What clothes was he wearing when he left here to drive to Ipswich?'

It was plain she couldn't remember. She looked blank – and she looked bored. Wexford understood in that moment that she didn't love Rodney Williams, hadn't perhaps loved him for years. His presence or absence as a life companion were matters of indifference to her but his financial support and the status he gave her were not. Or were her feelings more subtle and diffuse than that? Of course they were. Feelings always are. There is never a simple clear analysis of a woman's reaction to her husband or his to her.

He pressed the point he had made.

'Sort of fawn trousers,' she said, screwing up her face with the effort of it. 'Cavalry twill, they're called. A dark blue pullover. Is his raincoat upstairs?'

'A plastic mac?'

'No, he's got a good raincoat. It's nearly new. He must have taken that. I expect he had a jacket in his bag too. He's got a brown suede one.'

'Did he like a wet or dry shave?'

'Pardon?'

'Did he use a razor with shaving cream and water?'

'Oh, yes. He couldn't get on with those electrics. He'd tried but he couldn't get on with them.'

And that accounted for the Remington and the Phillips upstairs. She was staring miserably at the blank, grey, shiny screen. Wexford felt it was cruel to deprive her of her solace, like keeping a dumb hungry dog from its plate of Kennomeat. He asked her for her sister's name and address and then he switched the television on again. She looked at him as if she thought him completely mad but she said nothing and her eyes were compelled back to the screen and to Sheila, dressing now in a hotel bedroom for an evening out with the Boeing 747 captain in Hong Kong.

Wexford walked home, thinking about Williams and money. What had he done with all that money? Even after tax and other deductions, after the stingy allotment to his household of £500 a month, he would have been left with at least £12,000 a year. He'd had a company car. It didn't go on cars. The passport, which was seven years old, showed a single visit to Majorca. It didn't go on foreign holidays. Of course, he had to keep his son Kevin at Keele and pay for his keep. He wouldn't get much of a grant on his salary . . .

And then, suddenly, Wexford understood what had been bugging him for the past hour. It had been a Thursday evening when Williams had left. Kevin Williams always phoned home of Thursday evenings. And that Thursday was certainly the first since he had returned to university after the Easter vacation. Yet his mother, who plainly adored him, who waited excitedly for his call and spoke proudly of his devotion to duty in regularly phoning at that time, had gone out on that particular Thursday evening and for no more pressing or life-enhancing appointment than a visit to her sister.

If she had visited her sister.

And how about his clothes? Was she lying when she said he had taken only a jacket and a raincoat with him? Or didn't she know? Somehow he couldn't imagine Williams leaving his car in Arnold Road and then humping huge bulging suitcases the quarter of a mile to Myringham station. Why go to Myringham anyway when, if he wanted to catch a train to London, Kingsmarkham station was eight miles nearer?

The following week the clothes, or some to them, turned up.

5

A lonely country road links Kingsmarkham with Pomfret.
Once Forest Road, Kingsmarkham, is past, the only houses
to be seen are those few up on the hillsides crowned by
Cheriton Forest. The forest is always rather dark and forbidding as coniferous forests are. On the horizon stands an
obelisk, a needle of stone, placed there by some local magnate
a hundred and fifty years ago.

Almost the last building in Kingsmarkham is the police
station. On the other side of the High Street Cheriton Lane
runs down to the buildings and courts of the Kingsmarkham
Tennis Club, and half a dozen other narrow roads compose
a small residential web. The gardens of houses in Forest Road
back onto open fields, and fields traversed by a footpath lie
between the club grounds and the town. The street lamps
stop two hundred yards on the Pomfret side of the police
station and after that there is an isolated one to light the bus
stop.

Roughly halfway between the towns, at the point of no
return, is the bus stop with bus shelter. The shelter was out
there because there are no trees at this point to break the
wind or provide cover from the rain. And on this night it
was raining as it had been for many nights. The fine rain
swept across the meadows in grey sheets.

The last bus from Pomfret to Kingsmarkham was due at
10.40. It came ten minutes late, rolling along not too fast
through the rain, sending up fountains of spray onto the
grass verges. The stop where the bus shelter was was a
compulsory one, not a request, so the bus pulled in to make
a token stop and prepared to pull out again, for there was

no one waiting. A shout from a woman passenger sitting in a front nearside seat alerted the driver. He had already taken off the brake but he put it on again and the bus juddered to a halt.

'There's a person crawling on the pavement!'

Here, where the shelter was, the lay-by was bordered by a few yards of pavement. The driver got down. Two or three of the passengers, disobeying the driver – who was he to tell them? – got down. There was no conductor on those single deckers. The rain was coming down in torrents, needles of it pounding the surface of the lay-by, the kerb, and the sodden bundle that crawled and whimpered with blood coming from its chest.

At first the conductor thought it a wounded dog. But the passenger was right, it was a man. It crawled up to the conductor and rolled over at his feet.

Next day, on the other side of Kingsmarkham, the Forby side, a firm called Mid-Sussex Waterways began dragging a pond. Green Pond Hall had stood empty for years but at the end of the previous January a buyer had been found for it and the purchase was completed by April. The grounds contained a pond and a stream and the new owner intended to turn the estate into a trout farm.

If the proper definition of a lake is a sheet of water covering the minimum of one acre, Green Pond was just too small to fit the requirement. But as a pond it was very large. It wasn't stagnant, for the small fast stream flowed through the middle of it, disappearing into a pipe which passed under a path and gushing out through a spout on the other side to fall away down to the Kingsbrook. In spite of this the pond was shallow and coated with the thick green slime of blanket weed. The purpose of the dragging was to clean it, increase its depth and rid the water of the algae Mid-Sussex Waterways believed might be caused by an influx of the nitrates which had been applied as fertilizer to the nearby meadows.

In the net, after the dragging, were found a wire supermarket basket minus its handle, a quantity of glass bottles, jars and light bulbs, the silencer part of a car exhaust system, wood in the form of twigs and chopped lengths, stones among which were flints and chalk pebbles, a rubber boot, a Pyrex casserole dish, chipped and cracked, a metal door handle and lock, a pair of scissors and a dark burgundy-coloured travelling bag.

The bag was coated with green slime and thin, fine-grained black mud, but when the clasps were undone and the zip unfastened it was seen that only water had penetrated the seams of the bag, soaking but hardly discolouring the clothes inside, the topmost of which was a brown suede blouson.

It was a piece of luck, Wexford thought, that William Milvey, the boss of Mid-Sussex Waterways, had found money inside the bag, £50 in fivers rolled up and fastened with a rubber band. If it had contained nothing but clothes, and damaged clothes at that, it was probable he would have tossed it into the pit which had been dug out by a mechanical digger for the purpose of receiving the rubbish caught in the dragnet. Money, Wexford had often noticed, has this kind of electric effect on people. Many a man who thinks himself honest, on finding an object bought with money will keep the object but not the money itself. It is as if the adage 'Finders keepers' applies to things but never to money, which has its own aura of sacredness, of being absolutely the pre-serve of him who has earned it.

But even so, Wexford might never have heard of the exist-ence of the bag were it not for a kidney donor card which was in the breast pocket of the blouson and which was signed R. J. Williams.

William Milvey knew who R. J. Williams was. He lived next door but one to him in Alverbury Road.

This fact it took Wexford some half-hour to find out. He questioned Milvey thoroughly about the bag. Had he seen it in the pond before he saw it in the net? Well, yes, he thought he had, now Wexford came to mention it. He fancied he had. At any rate he thought he could remember seeing a brownish-red lump of something up against the bank of the pond nearest to the path and the Kingsbrook. No, he hadn't touched it or attempted to pull it out. The dragnet had pulled it out.

Milvey was a shortish thick-set man with the heavy build

and big spread hands of someone who has done manual work for most of his life. He looked about fifty. The discovery of the bag seemed disproportionately to have excited him – or his excitement appeared disproportionate to Wexford at first.

'Fifty quid in it,' he kept saying, 'and that good jacket.'

'Did you see anyone about the grounds of Green Pond Hall?'

'Some fella up to no good, d'you mean?'

'I meant anyone at all.'

'We didn't have sight nor sound of no one.'

There might have been marks of car tyres on the drive in from the Forby Road or on the track that ran around the lower bank of the pond, the constant rain had turned these surfaces to mud, but any tracks there were had been obliterated by the heavy tyres of Mid-Sussex Waterways' mechanical digger.

Milvey simply couldn't remember if there had been any tyremarks on the track. They had the other man in and asked him, but he couldn't remember either.

'Fifty quid,' said Milvey, 'and that good jacket. Just chucked away.'

'Let me have your address, will you, Mr Milvey? I'll very likely want to talk to you again. Home or business?'

'They're one and the same. I operate from home, don't I?' He said this as if it were a fact he would have expected Wexford to know, and adding his address, used the same patient, mildly surprised tone. 'Twenty-seven Alverbury Road, Kingsmarkham.'

'Are you telling me you live next door but one to Mr Williams?'

Milvey's expression, though bland and innocent, had become a little uncomfortable. 'I reckoned you knew.'

'No, I didn't know.' Vaguely now Wexford recalled reading a planning application made to the local authority for permission to erect a garage – more a hangar really – large enough to house a JCB in the garden of 27 Alverbury Road. The area being strictly residential, the application had naturally been rejected. 'You must know Mr Williams then?'

'Pass the time of day,' said Milvey. 'The wife has a chat with Mrs Williams. My girl's in the same class at school with their Sara.'

'Mr Williams is missing,' said Wexford flatly. 'He's been missing from home for the past month or more.'

'Is that right?' Milvey didn't look surprised but he didn't say he knew either. 'Fifty quid in notes,' he said, 'and a jacket worth three times that.'

Wexford let him go.

'It has to be coincidence,' Burden said.

'Does it, Mike? It would be a hell of a coincidence, wouldn't it? Williams disappears because he's done something or someone's done something to him. His overnight bag is dumped in a pond and who should find it but the guy who lives two doors down the street from him? I haven't read any John Buchan for – well, it must be forty-five years. But I can remember in one of his books the hero's car breaks down and the house he calls at for help just happens to be the home of the master anarchist. A bit later on the hit man who's sent to get him turns out to be a burglar he's recently successfully defended in court. Now that's fiction and strictly for persons below fifteen, I'd say. But this that you call coincidence is comparable to those. Have you had any coincidences of that magnitude in your life?'

'Both my grandmothers were called Mary Brown.'

'Were they really?' Wexford was temporarily distracted. 'You never told me that before. And did they come from the same part of the country?'

'One from Sussex and one from Hertfordshire. I bet you the odds against that happening are a lot longer than against Milvey finding Williams's bag. You look at it and you'll see it's not that much of a coincidence. If it had been buried, say, or stuck in a hollow tree and Milvey had found it, that would be something else. But it was in a pond and Milvey's in the pond-dragging business. Once it got in the pond and the pond was due to be dragged – which whoever put it there wouldn't know, of course – the chances would be that Milvey *would* find it. You want to look at it like that.'

Wexford knew there was more to it than that; he couldn't dismiss it in the easy way Burden did. Milvey's behaviour had been a shade odd anyway and Wexford was sure he hadn't told all he knew.

'How long do you think the bag's been in the pond?'

It was on the floor between them, deposited on sheets of

newspaper, its contents, which Wexford had already examined, now replaced.

'Since the night he went, I suppose, or the next day.'

Wexford didn't go along with that either but he let it pass for the time being. As well as the brown suede blouson there was a raincoat in the bag, a trendy version of a Burberry, the fifty pounds, a toothbrush, tube of toothpaste and disposable razor wrapped up in a pair of underpants, a bottle of Monsieur Rochas cologne and a pair of brand-new socks with the label still on them. The underpants were a young man's Homs, pale blue and white, the socks dark brown, an expensive brand made of silk.

It was the kind of packing a man would do for an overnight stay somewhere, not for three nights, and the pants and socks and cologne seemed to indicate a night not spent alone. Or had there been more articles in the bag which had been removed? This could surely only have been done to prevent identification of the bag's owner. In that case why leave the donor card in the blouson pocket? 'I would like to help someone to live after my death', it stated somewhat naively in scarlet and white, and on the reverse side Rodney Williams had requested that in the event of his death any part of his body which might be required should be used in the treatment of others. Underneath this was his signature and the date a year past. The next of kin to contact was given, as might have been expected, as Joy Williams with the Alverbury Road phone number.

Men's natures were a mass of contradictions, there was no consistency, and yet Wexford marvelled a little that a husband and father could deliberately and ruthlessly deceive his wife over his income and pursue a course of skinflint meanness to her and his children yet want to donate his body for transplants. It would cost him nothing though, he would be dead after all. Was he dead?

'We're going to have to start looking for him. I mean really looking. Search the grounds of Green Pond Hall for a start.'

Burden had been pacing the office. He had taken to doing this lately and his restless pacing had a stressful effect on anyone he happened to be with, though he himself hardly seemed aware of what was going on. Twice he had been to the window, twice back to the door, pausing once to perch briefly on the edge of the desk. Now he had reached the window again where he stopped, turned and stared at Wexford in irritable incredulity.

'Search for *him*? Surely it's plain he's simply done a bunk to escape the consequences of whatever it is he's done.'

'All right, Mike. Maybe. But in that case what *has* he done? Nothing at Sevensmith Harding. He's as clean as a whistle there. What else could he have done? It's just possible he could be involved in some fraud that hasn't yet come to light but there's a strong case against that one. He got out. The only reason for that would be that discovery of the fraud was imminent. In that case why hasn't that discovery been made?'

Burden shrugged. 'Who knows? But it may just be a piece of luck for Williams that it hasn't been.'

'Why hasn't he come back then? If the outcome of this fraud has blown over why doesn't he come home? He hasn't left the country unless he's gone on a false passport. And why bother with a false passport when he'd got one of his own and no one started missing him till three days after he'd gone?'

'Doesn't it occur to you that leaving one's clothes on the river bank is the oldest disappearing trick in the world?'

'On the beach, I think you mean, not on the shores of a pond where the water's so shallow that to commit suicide you'd have to lie on your face and hold your breath. Besides, that bag has been in the pond only a couple of days at most. If it had been there since Williams went it'd be rotting by now, it'd stink. We'll sent it over to the lab and see what they say but we can see what they'll say with our own eyes and smell it with our own noses.'

'Williams is dead. This bag of his tells me he is. If he had put it into the pond for the purpose of making us think he was dead he'd have done so immediately after he left. And the contents would have been different. More identification, for instance, no scent and powder blue knickers. And I don't think the money would have been in it. He would have needed that money, he would have needed all the money he could lay his hands on. There's no reason to think he could easily spare fifty pounds – whatever he's done he hasn't robbed a bank.

'He's dead and, letter and phone call notwithstanding, he was dead within an hour or two of when his family last saw him.'

Next day the searching of Green Pond Hall grounds began.

The grounds comprised eight acres, part woodland, part decayed overgrown formal gardens, part stables and paddock. Sergeant Martin led the search with three men and Wexford himself went down there to have a look at the dragged pond and view the terrain. It was still raining. It had been raining yesterday and the day before and for part of every day for three weeks. The weather people were saying it would be the wettest May since records began. The track was a morass, the colour and texture of melted chocolate into which a giant fork had furrowed. There were other ways of getting down to the pond but only if you went on foot.

At three he had a date at Stowerton Royal Infirmary. Colin Budd had been placed in intensive care but only for the night. By morning he was sufficiently recovered to be transferred to a side room off the men's surgical ward. The stab wounds he had received were more than superficial, one having penetrated to a depth of three inches, but by a miracle almost none of the five had endangered heart or lungs.

A thick white dressing covered his upper chest, over which a stripped pyjama jacket had been loosely wrapped. The pyjama jacket was an extra large and Wexford estimated Budd's chest measurement at thirty-four inches. He was a very thin, bony, almost cadaverous young man, white-faced and with black, longish hair. He seemed to know exactly what Wexford would want to know about him and quickly and nervously repeated his name and age, gave his occupation as motor mechanic and his address a Kingsmarkham one where he lived with his parents.

'Tell me what happened.'

'This girl stuck a knife in my chest.'

'Now, Mr Budd, you know better than that. I want a detailed account, everything you can remember, starting with what you were doing waiting for a bus in the middle of nowhere.'

Budd had a querulous voice that always sounded mildly

indignant. He was one of those who believes the world owes him elaborate considerations as well as a living.

'That's got nothing to do with it,' he said.

'I'll be the judge of that. I don't suppose you were doing anything to be ashamed of. And if you were what you tell me will be between you and me.'

'I don't know what you're getting at!'

'Just tell me where you'd been last evening, Mr Budd.'

'I was at snooker,' Budd said sullenly.

What a fool! He'd made it sound at least as if he was having it away with a friend's wife in one of the isolated cottages on the hillside.

'A snooker club?'

'It's on Tuesday evenings. In Pomfret, a room at the back of the White Horse. It's over at ten and I reckoned on walking home.' Budd shifted his body, wincing a bit, pulling himself up in the bed. 'But the rain started coming down harder, I was getting soaked. I looked at my watch and saw the ten-forty bus'd be along in ten minutes and I was nearly at the stop by then.'

'I'd have expected a motor mechanic to have his own transport.'

'My car was in a crunch-up. It's in dock having a new wing. I wasn't doing no more than twenty-five when this woman came out of a side turning . . .'

Wexford cut that one short. 'So you reached the bus stop, the bus shelter. What happened?'

Budd looked at him and away. 'There was this girl already there, sitting on the seat. I sat down next to her.'

The bus shelter was well known to Wexford. It was about ten feet long, the seat or bench inside two feet shorter.

'Next to her?' he asked. 'Or at the other end of the seat?'

'Next to her. Does it matter?'

Wexford thought perhaps it did. In England at any rate, for good or ill, for the improving of social life or its worsening, a man of honourable intent who goes to sit on a public bench where a woman is already sitting will do so as far away from her as possible. A woman will probably do this too if a woman or man is already sitting there, and a man will do it if another man is there.

'Did you know her? Had you ever seen her before?'

Budd shook his head.

'You spoke to her?'

'Only to say it was raining.'

She knew that already, Wexford thought. He looked hard at Budd. Budd said, 'I said it was a pity we were having such a bad May, it made the winter longer, something like that. She pulled a knife out of her bag and lunged it at me.'

'Just like that? You didn't say anything else to her?'

'I've told you what I said.'

'She was mad, was she? A girl who stabs men because they tell her it's raining?'

'All I said was that normally at this time I'd have had my vehicle and I could have given her a lift.'

'In other words, you were trying to pick her up?'

'All right, what if I was? I didn't touch her. I didn't do anything to frighten her. That was all I said, that I could have given her a lift home. She pulled out this knife and stabbed at me four or five times and I cried out or screamed or something and she ran off.'

'Would you know her again?'

'You bet I would.'

'Describe her to me.'

Budd made the mess of that Wexford thought he would. He didn't know whether she was tall or short, plump or thin, because he only saw her sitting down and he thought she had a raincoat on. A thin raincoat that was a sort of pale colour. Her hair was fair, he did know that, though she had a hat on or a scarf. Bits of blonde hair showed under it. Her face was just an ordinary face, not what you'd call pretty. Wexford began to wonder what had attracted Budd to her in the first place. The mere facts that she was female and young? About twenty, said Budd. Well, maybe twenty-five or six. Pressed to be more precise, he said she could have been any age between eighteen and thirty, he wasn't good on ages, she was quite young though.

'Can you think of anything else about her?'

A nurse had come in and was hovering. Wexford knew what she was about to say, he could have written the script for her – 'Now I think that's quite enough. It's time for Mr Budd to have his rest . . .' She approached the bed, unhooked Budd's chart and began reading it with the enthusiastic con-

231

centration of a scholar who has just found the key to Linear B or some such.

'She had this sack with her. She grabbed it before she ran off.'

'What sort of sack?'

'The plastic kind they give you for your dustbin. A black one. She picked it up and stuck it over her shoulder and ran off.'

'I think that's quite enough for now,' said the nurse, diverging slightly from Wexford's text.

He got up. It was an extraordinary picture Budd's story had created and one which appealed to his imagination. The dark wet night, the knife flashing purposefully, even frenziedly, the girl running into the rain with a sack slung over her shoulder. It was like an illustration in a fairy book of Andrew Lang, elusive, sinister and other-worldly.

6

What had Burden meant when he said this amniocentesis had discovered something to worry Jenny? Wexford found himself brooding on that. Once or twice he had woken in the night and the question had come into his mind. Sitting in the car, being driven to Myringham, he saw a woman on the pavement with a Down's Syndrome child and the question was back, presenting itself again.

He hadn't liked to pursue it with Burden. This wasn't the sort of thing you asked a prospective father about. What small defect was there a father wouldn't mind about but a mother would? It was grotesque, ridiculous, there was nothing. Any defect would be a tragedy. His mind ranged over partial deafness, a heart murmur, palate or lip deformities – the test couldn't have shown those anyway. An extra chromosome? This was an area where he found himself floundering in ignorance. He thought of his own children, perfect, always healthy, giving him no trouble really, and his heart warmed towards his girls.

This reminded him that he had the National Theatre's programme brochure for the summer season in his pocket. Sheila was with the company and this would be the first season she had top lead roles. Hence the disengagement from further work on *Runway*. He got out the programme and looked at it. Dora had asked him to decide which days they should go to London and see the three productions Sheila was in. For obvious reasons it always had to be he who made those kind of decisions.

The new Stoppard, Ibsen's *Little Eyolf*, Shelley's *The Cenci*. Wexford had heard of *Little Eyolf* but he had never

233

seen it or read it, and as for *The Cenci*, he had to confess to himself that he hadn't known Shelley had written any plays. But there it was: 'Percy Bysshe Shelley' and the piece described as a tragedy in five acts. Wexford was making tentative marks on the programme for a Friday in July and two Saturdays in August when Donaldson, his driver, drew into the kerb outside Sevensmith Harding.

Miles Gardner had been watching for him and came rushing out with an umbrella. It made Wexford feel like royalty. They splashed across the pavement to the mahogany doors.

Kenneth Risby, the chief accountant, told him Rodney Williams's salary had been paid into the account Williams had with the Pomfret branch of the Anglian-Victoria Bank. From that account then, it would seem, Williams had each month transferred £500 into the joint account he had with Joy. Risby had been with the company for fifteen years and said he could recall no other arrangement being made for Williams, either recently or in the days when he was a sales rep. His salary had always gone to the Pomfret bank, never to Kingsmarkham.

'We've heard nothing,' Miles Gardner said. 'Whatever he meant by the PS to that letter he hasn't been in touch.'

'Williams didn't write that letter,' Wexford reminded him.

Gardner nodded unhappily.

'The first time we talked about this business,' Wexford said, 'you told me someone phoned here saying she was Mrs Williams and that her husband was ill and wouldn't be coming in. Would that have been on Friday, April the sixteenth?'

'Well, yes, I suppose it would.'

'Who took the call?'

'It must have been one of our telephonists. They're part-timers. I can't remember whether it was Anna or Michelle. The phone call came before I got in, you see. That is, before nine-thirty.'

'Williams had a secretary, I suppose?'

'Christine Lomond. He shared her with our assistant sales director. Would you like to talk to her?'

'Not yet. Maybe not today. It's Anna or Michelle I want. But which one do I want?'

'Michelle, I expect,' said Gardner. 'They tend to swop shifts a bit but it's usually Michelle on mornings.'

It had been, that Friday, and it was today. Michelle was a very young, very pretty girl with a vividly made-up face. The room where the switchboard was, not much more than a cupboard, was stamped with her personality (or perhaps Anna's) and there was a blue cineraria in a pot, a stack of magazines, a pile of knitting that had reached the bulky stage, and on the table in front of her, hurriedly placed face downwards, the latest diet paperback.

It was clear that Michelle had already discussed that phone call exhaustively. Perhaps with Anna or with Christine Lomond. Williams's disappearance would have been the talk of the office.

'I get in at nine,' she said. 'That's when the phone calls really start. But the funny thing was there weren't any that morning till Mrs Williams phoned at about twenty past.'

'You mean till someone phoned who *called* herself Mrs Williams.'

The girl looked at him. She shook her head quite vehemently. 'It was Mrs Williams. She said, "This is Joy Williams."'

Wexford let it go for the time being.

'What exactly did she say?'

' "My husband Mr Williams won't be coming in today." And then she sort of hesitated and said, "That's Mr Rodney Williams, I mean, the marketing manager." I said there was no one else in yet and she said that didn't matter but to give Christine the message he'd got flu and wouldn't be in.'

Whoever it was, it hadn't been Joy. At that time Joy didn't know her husband was Sevensmith Harding's marketing manager. Wexford had thanked Michelle and was turning away, diverting his mind to the matter of the firm's stock of typewriters, when he stopped.

'What makes you so sure the woman you spoke to was Mrs Joy Williams?'

'It just was. I know it was.'

'No, let me correct that. You know it was a woman who *said* she was Mrs Joy Williams. She had never phoned here before, had she, so you couldn't have recognized her voice?'

'No, but she phoned here afterwards.'

'What do you mean, afterwards?'

'About three weeks later.' The girl spoke with exaggerated patience now, as if to a very confused or simple minded person. 'Mrs Joy Williams phoned here three weeks after her husband left.'

Of course. Wexford remembered that call. It was he who had advised Joy to make it.

'I put her through to Mr Gardner,' Michelle said. 'I was a bit embarrassed, to be perfectly honest. But I know it was the same voice, really I do. It was the same voice as the woman who phoned that Friday morning, it was Mrs Williams.'

He picked up the girl at the roundabout where the second exit is the start of the Kingsmarkham bypass. She was standing on the grass verge at the side of the roundabout, holding up a piece of cardboard with 'Myringham' printed on it. Brian Wheatley pulled in to the first exit, the Kingsmarkham town-centre road, and the girl got into the passenger seat. Then, for some unclear reason, perhaps because he had already pulled out of the roundabout and it would not have been easy to get back into the traffic, Wheatley decided to continue through the town instead of on the bypass. This wasn't such a bad idea anyway, the anomaly being that the bypass which had been built to ease the passage of traffic past the town was often more crowded than the old route.

Wheatley was driving home from London where he worked three days a week. It was about six in the evening and of course broad daylight. He had moved to Myringham only two weeks before and was still unfamiliar with the byways and back-doubles of the area. The girl didn't speak a word. She had no baggage with her, only a handbag with a shoulder strap. Wheatley drove through Kingsmarkham, along the High Street, and became confused by the signposting. Instead of keeping straight on he began to think he should have taken a left-hand turn some half a mile back. He therefore – on what he admitted was a lonely and secluded stretch of road – pulled into a lay-by and consulted his road map.

His intention to do this, he said, he announced plainly to

236

the girl. After he had stopped and switched off the engine he was obliged to reach obliquely across her in order to open the glove compartment where the map was. He was aware of the girl giving a gasp of fright or anger, and then of a sharp pain, more like a burn than a cut, in his right hand.

He never even saw the knife. The girl jumped out of the car, slamming the door behind her, and ran not along the road but onto a footpath that separated a field of wheat from a wood. Blood was flowing from a deep cut in the base of Wheatley's thumb. He tied up his hand as best he could with his handkerchief but shock and a feeling of faintness made it impossible for him to continue his journey for some minutes. Eventually he looked at his map, found himself nearer home than he had thought, and was able to drive there in about a quarter of an hour. The general practitioner with whom he had registered the week before was still holding his surgery. Wheatley's wife drove him there and the cut in his hand was stitched, Wheatley telling the doctor he had been carving meat and had inadvertently pressed his hand against the point of the carving knife. Whether or not the doctor believed this was another matter. At any rate he had made no particular comment. Wheatley himself had wanted to tell the truth, though this would have meant police involvement. It was his wife who had dissuaded him on the grounds that if the police were called the conclusion they would reach would be that Wheatley had first made some sort of assault on the girl.

This was the story Wheatley told Wexford three days later. His wife didn't know he had changed his mind. He had come to the police, he said, because he felt more and more indignant that this girl, whom he hadn't touched, whom he had scarcely spoken to except to say he was going to stop and look at his map, should make an unprovoked attack on him and get away with it.

'Can you describe her?'

Wexford waited resignedly for the kind of useless description furnished by Colin Budd. He was surprised. In many ways Wheatley did not seem to know his way around but he was observant and perceptive.

'She was tall for a woman, about five feet eight or nine. Young, eighteen or nineteen. Brown hair or lightish hair, shoulder-length, sunglasses though it wasn't sunny, fair skin – I noticed she had very white hands. Jeans and a blouse, I think, and a cardigan. The bag was some dark colour, black or navy blue.'

'Did she give you the impression she lived in Myringham? That she was going home?'

'She didn't give me any sort of impression. When she got into the car she said thanks – just the one word "thanks", otherwise she didn't speak. I said to her that I thought I'd drive through the town instead of the bypass and she didn't answer. Later on I said I'd stop and look at the map and she didn't answer that either, but when I reached across her – I didn't touch her, I could swear to that – she gave a sort of gasp. Those were the only sounds she made, "thanks" and a gasp.'

The same girl as attacked Budd, one would suppose. But if Wheatley were to be believed, while there was some very slight justification for the attack on Budd, there was none for this second stabbing. Could the girl possibly have thought that the hand which reached across to open the glove compartment intended instead to take hold of her by the left shoulder? Or lower itself onto her knee? There was something ridiculous about these assaults, and yet two meant that they were not ridiculous at all but serious. Next time there could be a fatality.

Or had there been one already?

The manager of the Pomfret branch of the Anglian-Victoria Bank bore an extraordinary resemblance to Adolf Hitler. This was not only in the small square moustache and the lock of dark hair half covering Mr Skinner's forehead. The face was the same face, rather handsome, with large chin and heavy nose and small thick-lidded eyes. But all that would have passed unnoticed without the moustache and the lock of hair, so that it was impossible to avoid the uncomfortable conclusion that Mr Skinner was doing it on purpose. He knew whom he looked like and enhanced the resemblance. Wexford could only attribute one motive to a bank manager who wants to look like Hitler – a desire to intimidate his clients.

His manner, however, was warm, friendly and charming. All those, and implacable too. He could not consider either letting Wexford look into Rodney Williams's bank accounts or disclose any information about their contents.

'Did you say accounts plural?' said Wexford.

'Yes. Mr Williams has two current accounts here – and now I've probably said more than I should.'

'Two current accounts in the name of Rodney Williams?'

Skinner was standing up with his head slightly on one side, looking like Hitler waiting for Franco's train at Hendaye. 'I said two current accounts, Chief Inspector. We'll let it go at that, shall we?'

One for his salary to be paid into, Wexford thought as he was driven away, and the other for what? His Kingsmarkham household expenses were drawn from the Kingsmarkham account which he fed with £500 a month from Pomfret account A. Then what of account B? His wife didn't know of the existence of account A anyway. It alone was sufficient to keep his resources secret from her. Why did he need a third current bank account?

They were searching for him now on the open land, partly wooded, that lay between Kingsmarkham and Forby. But so far, since the discovery of the bag in Green Pond, nothing further had come to light. He's dead, Wexford thought, he must be.

Burden had been at Pomfret, talking to the Harmer family, Joy Williams's sister, brother-in-law and niece. John Harmer was a pharmacist with a chemist's shop in the High Street.

'They say Joy was with them that evening,' Burden said, 'but I wouldn't put that much credence on what they say. Not that they're intentionally lying – they can't remember. It was seven weeks ago. Besides, Joy often goes over there in the evenings. More or less to sit in front of their television instead of her own, I gather. But I suppose she's lonely, she wants company. Mrs Harmer says she was definitely there that evening, Harmer says it must be if his wife says so and the girl doesn't know. You can't expect a teenage girl to take much notice of when her aunt comes.'

Wexford told him what he had learned from the telephonist at Sevensmith Harding. 'Of course, the girl may be mistaken about the voices or she may have persuaded herself they were the same voice in order to get more drama out of the situation. But it's more than possible that the woman who phoned Sevensmith Harding the day after Williams left to say he was ill and the woman who phoned three weeks later to inquire as to his whereabouts are one and the same. And we know the second time was Joy. Now Joy was very keen to have me look for her husband when he first disappeared, but later on much less so – indeed, she was obstructive. That first time I talked to her she said nothing about having gone out herself that evening. That was only mentioned the second time. Joy is devoted to her son Kevin. Her daughter is nothing to her, her son everything . . . What on earth's the matter?'

Burden's face had set and he had gone rather pale. He had taken a hard grip on the arms of his chair. 'Nothing. Go on.'

'Well, then – her son always phones on Thursday evenings and that particular Thursday was the first one he had been back at college. Wouldn't a devoted mother have wanted to know all those things mothers worry about in such circumstances? Did he have a good journey? Was his room all right? Had he settled in? But this devoted mother doesn't wait in for his call. She goes out – not to some important engagement, some function booked months ahead, but to watch television at her sister's. What does all this suggest to you?'

Having struggled successfully to overcome whatever it was that had upset him, Burden forced a laugh. 'You sound like Sherlock Holmes talking to Watson.' Since his second marriage he occasionally read books, a change in him Wexford couldn't get used to.

'No,' he said, 'more "a man of the solid Sussex breed – a breed which covers much good sense under a heavy silent exterior".'

'I wouldn't say "silent". Was that from Sherlock Holmes?'

Wexford nodded. 'So what do you make of it?' he said more colloquially.

'That Joy is somehow in cahoots with her husband. There's a conspiracy going on. What for and why I wouldn't pretend to know but it's got something to do with giving everyone the impression Williams is dead. He left that evening and she went out later to meet him away from the house. Whatever they were planning was done away from the house

240

because it had to be concealed from the daughter Sara as much as from anyone else. Next morning Joy rang Sevensmith Harding to say her husband was ill. Of course, it's nonsense to say she didn't know that he was their marketing manager and the extent of his income. Next he or she typed that letter on a *hired* typewriter. She probably did that, not knowing what he called Gardner and making the mistake of addressing him as 'Mr Gardner'. The abandoned car, the dumped bag of clothes were all part of a plan to make us think him dead. But the increased police attention frightened Joy, she wanted things to go more at her pace. Hence the obstructiveness. I said I didn't know why but it could be an insurance fiddle, couldn't it?'

'Without a body, Mike? With no more proof of death than a dumped travelling bag? And if you wanted people to think you were dead, aren't there half a dozen simpler and more convincing ways of doing it?'

'You feel the same as me then? You don't think he's dead?'

'I know he's dead,' said Wexford.

Next day he was proved right.

It looked like a grave. It was in the shape of a grave, as clearly demarcated as if a slab of stone lay upon it, though Edwin Fitzgerald did not at first see this. In spite of its shape he would have passed it by as a mere curiosity, a whim of nature. It was the dog Shep who drew his attention to it.

Edwin Fitzgerald was a retired policeman who had been a dog handler. He lived in Pomfret and had a job as a part-time security guard at a factory complex on Stowerton's industrial estate. The dog Shep was not a trained dog in the sense of being police-trained – as a 'sniffer', for instance. Fitzgerald had bought him after his last dog died – a wonderful dog that one, more intelligent than any human being, a dog that understood every word he said. Shep could only follow humbly in that dog's footsteps and was often the subject of unfavourable comparisons. He didn't understand every word Fitzgerald said, or at any rate behaved as if he didn't.

On this particular morning in June, a dry one, the first really fine morning of the summer, Shep disregarded all Fitzgerald's words, ignored the repeated 'Leave it, sir' and 'Do as you're told' and continued his frenetic digging in the corner of what his master saw as a patch of weeds. He dug like a dog possessed. Indeed, Fitzgerald informed him that he was a devil, that he didn't know what had got into him. He shouted (which a good dog handler should never do) and he shook his fist until he saw what Shep had unearthed and then he stopped.

The dog had dug up a foot.

Fitzgerald had been a policeman, which had the double advantage of having taught him not to be sickened by such a discovery and not to disturb anything in its vicinity. He attached Shep's lead to his collar and pulled the dog away. This took some doing as Shep was a big young German Shepherd intent on worrying at the protruding thing for some hours if possible.

As far as Fitzgerald could see, now he had got the dog clear, the foot was still attached to a limb and the limb probably to a trunk. It was inside a sodden, blackened, slimy shoe caked with mud, and about the ankle clung a bundling of muddy wet cloth, once the hem of a trouser leg. Shep had dug it out from one of the corners of this curious little plot of ground. All around, on this edge of the meadow, grew tall grass ready to be cut for hay, high enough to hide the dog when he plunged in among it, but the rectangle – seven feet by three? – which Shep had found in there and had dug into was covered closely and in a neat rather horticultural way with fresh green plants. Weeds they were, but weeds attractive enough to be called plants, red campion, clover, speedwell, and they covered the oblong patch as precisely as if they had been sown there in a seed bed.

The grass which surrounded it, gone to seed, bearing light feathery seed heads of brown and greyish-cream and silvery-gold, hid it from the sight of anyone who kept to the footpath. It took a dog to plunge in there and find the grave. A day or two of sunshine, Fitzgerald thought, and the farmer would have cut the hay, cut those weeds too without a thought. Shep was a good dog after all, even if he didn't understand every word Fitzgerald said.

He retraced his steps to the branch of the lane that led to Myfleet and hurried down the hill to his bungalow where he phoned the police.

7

From the Pomfret road a narrow lane winds its way up into the hills and to the verge of the forest. All down the hedges here grows the wayfarer's tree with its flat creamy bracts of blossom, and beneath, edging the meadows like a fringe of lace, the whiter, finer, more delicate cow parsley. There are houses, Edwin Fitzgerald's among them, approached by paths, cart tracks or even smaller narrower lanes, but the lane gives the impression of leading directly to the obelisk on the hill.

It is like downland up here, the trees ceasing until the forest of conifers begins over there to the east, chalk showing in outcroppings and heather on the chalk. And all the way the obelisk looming larger, a needle of granite with its point a tetragon. The road never reaches it. A quarter of a mile this side it swerves, turns east and divides, one fork making for Myfleet, the other for Pomfret, and soon there are meadows again and the heath is past. It was in one of these meadows, close to the overhang of the forest, traversed by a footpath leading from the road to Myfleet, that the discovery had been made. Over to the west the obelisk stabbed the blue sky, catching a shred of cloud on its point.

The grave was in a triangle formed by the wood, the lane and the footpath, in a slightly more than right-angled corner of the field. It was near enough to the forest for the air to smell resinous. The soil was light and sandy with an admixture of pine needles.

'Easy enough to dig,' said Wexford to Burden. 'Almost anyone not decrepit could dig a grave like that in half an hour. Digging it deep enough would have taken a little longer.'

They were viewing the terrain, the distance of the grave from the road and the footpath, while Sir Hilary Tremlett, the pathologist, stood by with the scene-of-crimes officer to supervise the careful unearthing. Sir Hilary had happened to be at Stowerton when Fitzgerald's call came in. By a piece of luck he had just arrived at the infirmary to perform a postmortem. It was not yet ten o'clock, a morning of pearly sunshine, the blue sky dotted with innumerable puffs of tiny white cloud. But every man there, the short portly august pathologist included, had a raincoat on. It had rained daily for so many weeks that no one was going to take the risk of going without; no one anyway could yet believe his own eyes.

'The rain made the weeds grow like that,' said Wexford. 'You can see what happened. It's rather interesting. All the ground here had grass growing on it, then a patch was dug to receive *that*. It was covered up again with overturned earth, the weed seeds came and rain, seemingly endless rain, and what grew up on that fertile patch and that patch only were broad-leaved plants. If it had been a dry spring there would have been more grass and it would all have been much less green.'

'And the ground harder. If the ground hadn't been soft and moist the dog might not have persisted with its digging.'

'The mistake was in not digging the grave deep enough. It makes you wonder why he or she or they didn't. Laziness? Lack of time? Lack of light? The six-foot rule is a good one because things of this kind do tend to work to the surface.'

'If that's so,' said Dr Crocker, coming up to them, 'why is it they always have to dig so far down to find ancient cities and temples and so forth?'

'Don't ask me,' said Wexford. 'Ask the dog. He's the archaeologist. Mind you, we don't have any lava in Sussex.'

They approached a little nearer to where Detectives Archbold and Bennett were carrying out their delicate spadework. It was apparent now that the corpse of the man that lay in the earth had been neither wrapped nor covered before it was buried. The earth didn't besmear it as a heavier clayey soil might have done. It was emerging relatively clean, soaking wet, darkly stained, giving off the awful reek that was familiar to every man there, the sweetish, fishy, breath-catching, gaseous stench of decomposing flesh. That was what the dog had smelt and liked and wanted more of.

'I often think,' said Wexford to the doctor, 'that we haven't much in common with dogs.'

'No, it's at times like this you know what you've always suspected, that they're not almost human at all.'

The face was pale, stained, bloated, the pale parts the colour of a dead fish's belly. Wexford, not squeamish at all, hardened by the years, decided not to look at the face again until he had to. The big domed forehead, bigger and more domed because the hair had fallen from it, looked like a great mottled stone or lump of fungus. It was that forehead which made him pretty sure this must be Rodney Williams. Of course, he wasn't going to commit himself at this stage but he'd have been surprised if it wasn't Williams.

Sir Hilary, squatting down now, bent closer. Murdoch, the scene-of-crimes officer, was beginning to take measurements, make calculations. He called the photographer over but Sir Hilary held up a delaying hand.

Wexford wondered how he could stand that stink right up against his face. He seemed rather to enjoy it, the whole thing, the corpse, the atmosphere, the horror, the squalor. Pathologists did, and just as well really. It wouldn't do if they shied away from it.

The body was subjected to a long and careful scrutiny. Sir Hilary looked at it closely from all angles. He came very close to touching but he did not quite touch. His fingers were plump, clean, the colour of a slice of roast pork. He stood up, nodded to Murdoch and the photographer, smiled at Wexford.

'I could have a poke-about at that after lunch,' he said. He always spoke of his autopsies as 'having a poke-about'. 'Not much doing today. Any ideas who it might be?'

'I think I have, Sir Hilary.'

'I'm glad to hear it. Saves a lot of hassle. We'll smarten him up a bit before his nearest and dearest come for a private view.'

Joy Williams, Wexford thought. No, she shouldn't be subjected to that. He felt the warmth of the mounting sun kind and soft on his face. He turned his back and looked across the sweep of meadows to the Pomfret road, green hay gold-brushed, dark green hedgerows stitched in like tapestry, sheep on a hillside. All he could see was that face and a wife looking at it. This horrid image doth unfix my hair and make my seated heart knock at my ribs . . .

It occurred to him that the nearest point on the main road to this place was the bus stop where Colin Budd had been attacked. Did that mean anything? The lane that passed within yards of the burial place met the road almost opposite the bus stop. The brother-in-law might do the identification instead. John Something, the chemist. John Harmer.

He seemed a sensible man. Younger than Williams by five or six years, he was one of those tailored people, a neat, well-made, smallish man with regular features and short, crisply wavy hair. He had closed up his dispensary and left the shop in the care of his wife.

Having taken a deep breath, he looked at the body. He looked at the face, his symmetrical features controlled in blankness. He wasn't going to show anything, not he, no shock, disgust, pity. You could almost hear his mother's voice saying to a small curly-haired boy: Be a man, John. Don't cry. Be a man.

Harmer remembered and was a man. But he might have said with Macduff that he must also feel it like a man, for his face gradually paled until it became as sickly greenish white as the corpse's. His stomach, not his will, had betrayed him. Or threatened to. He came out into the air, into the sunshine, away from charnel-house corpse rot, and smelt the summer noonday, and the bile receded. He nodded to Wexford, he nodded rather more and longer than was necessary.

'Is that your brother-in-law, Rodney Williams?'

'Yes.'

'You are quite certain of that?'

'I'm certain.'

Wexford had thought of asking him to be the bearer of the news to Joy but he had quickly seen Harmer wouldn't be a suitable, let alone a sympathetic, messenger. He went himself, walking to Alverbury Road, thinking as he walked. There wasn't much he personally could do until the pathologist's report came and the lab had been over Williams's clothes. With distaste he recalled the bloodied mass of cloth that had wrapped the wounds. He felt glad now he had had the lab go over that car so carefully and at a time when it looked as if Williams might have been guilty of some misdemeanour and have done a moonlight flit.

Those crumbs of plaster in the boot could be vital evidence. At first he had supposed they derived from some routine of Williams's work. But Gardner had told him there was never a question of Williams having handled the stuff he sold. More likely the truth was that those plaster crumbs had been caught up in the folds of that bloodstained cloth and the body itself had been in the boot of the car . . .

In the front garden of 31 Alverbury Road someone had mown the bit of lawn and cut the privet hedge. It looked as if both these tasks had been performed with the same pair of blunt shears. Rodney Williams had been in one respect domestically adequate – he had kept his garden trim.

Sara opened the front door to him. He hadn't expected her to be there and he was a little taken aback. He would have preferred breaking the news to her mother alone. The school term wasn't yet over but A-levels were and with those examinations behind her there was perhaps nothing for her to go to school for.

She had on a white tee-shirt, pure unrelieved white, short-sleeved and showing felt-tipped pen drawings on her arms and hands, the snake again in green, a butterfly with a baby face, a raven woman with aggressive breasts and erect wings, somehow obscene on those smooth golden arms, childish and rounded.

'Is your mother in, Sara?'

She nodded. Had the tone of his voice told her? She looked sideways at him, fearfully, as they went down the short passage to the kitchen door.

Joy Williams anticipated nothing. On the table at which she was sitting were the remains of lunch for two. She looked up with a mildly disagreeable inquiring glance. They had been eating fish fingers with baked beans – an infelicitous mixture, Wexford thought. He could tell the constituents of their lunch by the quantity of it Sara had left on the plate. Joy had been reading a women's magazine of the royalty-sycophantic-crocheted-tea-cosy kind which was propped against a bottle of soy sauce, pathetic import surely of Sara's. What does a daughter do for her mother in a situation such as this? Go to her and put an arm round her shoulders? At least stand behind her chair? Sara went to the sink, stood with her back to them, looking out of the window above it at the grass and the fence and the meagre little apple trees.

Wexford told Joy her husband had been found. Her husband's body. More than that he couldn't tell her, he knew no more. The girl's shoulders twitched. Mrs Williams leaned forward across the table and put her hand heavily over her mouth. She sat that way for a moment or two. The whistling kettle on the stove began to screech. Sara turned round, turned the gas off, looked at her mother with her mouth twisted up as if she had toothache.

'D'you want a coffee?' Joy said to Wexford.

He shook his head. Sara made the coffee, instant in two mugs, one with a big 'S' on it and the other with the head of the Princess of Wales. Joy put sugar into hers, one spoonful, then after reflection, another.

'Shall I have to see him?'

'Your brother-in-law has already made the identification.'

'John?'

'Have you any other brothers-in-law, Mrs Williams?'

'Rod's got a brother in Bath. "Had", I should say. I mean he's still alive as far as I know and Rod's not, is he?'

'Oh, Mum,' said Sara. 'For God's sake.'

'You shut your mouth, you little cow!'

Joy Williams screamed it at her. She didn't utter any more words but she went on screaming, drumming her fists on the table so that the mug bounced off and broke and coffee went all over the strip of coconut matting on the floor. Joy screamed until Sara slapped her face – the doctor already, the cool head in an emergency. Wexford knew better than to do it himself. Once he'd slapped a hysterical woman's face and later been threatened with an action for assault.

'Who can we get hold of to be with her?' he asked. Mrs Milvey? He thought of Dora and dismissed the thought.

'She hasn't any friends. I expect my Auntie Hope will come.'

Mrs Harmer that would be. Hope and Joy. My God, he thought. Although the girl was sitting beside her mother now, holding her hand, while Joy leaned back spent, her head hanging over the back of the kitchen chair, the tears silently rolling out of her eyes, he could see that it was all Sara could do to control her repugnance. She was almost shaking with it. The need to be parted, the one from the other, was mutual. Sara, no doubt, couldn't wait for those exam results, the confirmation of St Biddulph's acceptance of her, for October and the start of term. It couldn't come fast enough for her.

'I'll stay with Mum,' she said, and there was stoicism in the way she said it. 'I'll give her a pill. She's got Valium. I'll give her a couple of Valium and find something nice for her on the TV.'

The ever ready panacea.

It was too late for lunch now. He and Burden might have something in the office, get a sandwich sent down from the canteen. He had said he'd see the press at 2.30. Well, young Varney of the local paper who was a stringer for the nationals . . .

There was a van on the police station forecourt marked TV South and a camera crew getting out of it.

'They've been up at the forest getting shots of the grave and Fitzgerald and the dog,' Burden said, 'and they want you next.'

'Good. I'll be able to put out an appeal for anyone who may have seen that car parked.' A less encouraging thought struck Wexford. 'They won't want to make me up, will they?' He had never been on television before.

Burden looked at him morosely, lifting his shoulders in a shrug of total indifference to any eventuality.

'It's not the end of the world if they do, is it?'

There was no time like the present, even a present that would end in ten minutes with his first ever TV appearance.

'What's happened to end your world, Mike?'

Burden immediately looked away. He mumbled something which Wexford couldn't hear and had to ask him to repeat.

'I said that I supposed I should tell you what the trouble is.'

'Yes. I want to know.' Looking at Burden, Wexford noticed for the first time grey hairs among the fair ones. 'There's something wrong with the baby, isn't there?'

'That's right.' Burden's voice sounded very dry. 'In Jenny's opinion, mind you. Not in mine.' He gave a bark of laughter. 'It's a girl.'

'*What?*'

Wexford's phone went. He picked up the receiver. TV South, the *Kingsmarkham Courier* and two other reporters were downstairs waiting for him. Burden had already gone, closing the door quietly behind him.

8

She was laying the table with their wedding present glass and silver. The lace cloth had been bought in Venice where they went for the first holiday after their honeymoon. Domesticity had delighted her when, as soon as she knew she was pregnant, she gave up teaching. It was the novelty, of course, being at home all day, playing house. Since then she had grown indifferent, she had grown indifferent to everything. Except to the child, and that she hated.

Sometimes, walking about the house after Mike had gone to work, pushing the vacuum cleaner or tidying up, the tears fell out of her eyes and streamed down her face. She cried because she couldn't believe that she who had longed and longed for a baby could hate the one inside her. All this she had told to the psychiatrist at their second session. She had listened to her in almost total silence. Once she said, 'Why do you say that?' and once 'Go on', but otherwise she simply listened with a kind interested look on her face.

Mike had suggested the psychiatrist. She had been so surprised because Mike usually scoffed at psychiatry that she said yes without even protesting. It was somewhere to go anyway, something different to do from sitting at home brooding about the future and her marriage and the unwanted child. And inevitably crying, of course, when she remembered as she always did what life used to be – when the days seemed too short, when she was teaching history to sixth formers at Haldon Finch, playing the violin in an orchestra, taking an advanced art appreciation course.

Jenny despised herself but that changed nothing. Her self-pity sickened her.

The sound of his key in the door – time-honoured heart stopper, test of love sustained – did nothing for her beyond bringing a little dread of the evening in front of them. He came into the room and kissed her. He still did that.

'How did you get on with the shrink?'

She resented the haste he was in. He wanted her cured, she felt, so that life could get back to normal again. 'What do you expect? A miracle in two easy lessons?'

She sat down. That always made her feel a little less bad because the bulge was no longer so apparent. And, thank God, the child was still, not rolling about and kicking.

'Don't let him give you drugs.'

'It's a woman.'

She wanted to scream with laughter. The irony of it! She was a teacher and this other woman was a psychiatrist and Mike's daughter Pat was very nearly qualified as a dentist, yet here she was reacting like a no-account junior wife in a harem. Because the baby was a girl.

He gave her a drink, orange juice and Perrier. He had a whisky, a large one, and in a minute he would have another. Not long ago he hadn't needed to drink when he got home. She looked at him, wishing she could bring herself to touch his arm or take his hand. An apathy as strong as energy held her back.

'Mike,' she said, and said for the hundredth time, 'I can't help it, I wish I could. I have tried.'

'So you say. I don't understand it. It's beyond my understanding.'

In a low voice, looking down, she said, 'It's beyond mine.' The child began to move, with flutters only at first, then came a hearty kick right under her lower ribs, giving her a rush of heartburn. She cried out, 'I wish to God I'd never had the thing done. I wish I'd never let them do it. They shouldn't have told me. Why did I let them? If I'd been ignorant I'd have gone on being happy, I'd have had the baby and I wouldn't have minded what it was, I'd have been pleased with any healthy baby. I didn't even specially want a son, or I didn't know I did. I didn't mind what it was, but now I know what it is I can't bear it. I can't go through all this and all through having it and the work and the pain and the trouble and a lifetime of being with it, having it with me, for a *girl*!'

He had heard it all before. It seemed to him that she said it every night. This was what he came home to. With slight variations, with modifications and changed turns of phrase, that was what she said to him on and on every evening. Until she grew exhausted or wept or slumped spent in her chair, until she went away to bed – earlier and earlier as the week's passed. In vain he had asked why this prejudice against girls, she who was a feminist, a supporter of the women's movement, who expressed a preference for her friends' small girls over their small sons, who got on better with her stepdaughter than her stepson, who professed to prefer teaching girls to boys.

She didn't know why, only that it was so. Her pregnancy, so long desired, at first so ecstatically accepted, had driven her mad. The worst of it was that he was coming to hate the unborn child himself and to wish it had never been conceived.

The wine bar was dark and cool. The restoration of an old house in Kingsmarkham's Queen Street had revealed and then opened up its cavernous cellars. The proprietor had resisted the temptations of roof beams, medieval pastiches, flintlocks and copper warming pans and simply painted the broad squat arches white, tiled the floor and furnished the place with tables and chairs in dark-stained pine.

Wexford and Burden had taken to lunching at the Old Cellar a couple of times a week. It had the virtue of being warm on cold days and cool on hot ones like this. The food was quiche and salad, smoked mackerel, coleslaw, pork pie, quiche, quiche and more quiche.

'What did they serve in these places before quiche caught on? I mean, there was a time not long ago when an Englishman could say he'd never heard of quiche.'

'He's always eaten it,' said Wexford. 'He called it cheese and onion flan.'

He had the morning papers with him. The *Kingsmarkham Courier* was a weekly and wouldn't be out till Friday. The national dailies had given no more than a paragraph to the discovery of Rodney Williams's body and had left out all the background details he was sure Varney had passed on to them. The *Daily Telegraph* merely stated that the body of a man had been found in a shallow grave and later identified as Rodney John Williams, a salesman from Kingsmarkham in Sussex. Nothing about Joy, his children, his job at Sevensmith Harding or the fact that he had been missing for two months. True, they had put him, Wexford, on TV but only on the regional bit that came after the news and then only forty-five seconds of the half-hour-long film they'd made.

The corpses of middle-aged men weren't news as women's were or children's. Women were always news. Perhaps they would cease to be when the day came that they got their equality as well as their rights. An interesting speculation and one which reminded him . . .

'You were going to tell me but we were interrupted.'

'It's not that she's anti-girls usually,' Burden said. 'For God's sake, she's a feminist. I mean, it's not some stupid I-must-have-an-heir thing or every-woman's-got-to-have-a-son-to-prove-herself. In fact I think she secretly thinks women are better than men – I mean cleverer and more versatile, all that. She says she doesn't understand it herself. She says she had no feelings about the child's sex one way or the other, but when they told her, when she knew, she was – well, dismayed. That was at first. It's got worse. It's not just dismay now, it's hatred.'

'Why doesn't she want a girl?' Wexford remembered certain sentiments expressed by his daughter Sylvia, mother of two sons. 'Is it that she feels women have a raw deal and she doesn't want to be responsible for bringing another into the world?' By way of apology for this crassness, he added, 'I have heard that view put.'

'She doesn't know. She says that ever since the world began sons have been preferred over daughters and now it's become part of race memory, what she calls the collective unconscious.'

'What Jung called it.'

Burden hesitated and then passed over that one. 'She's mad, you know. Pregnancy has driven her mad. Oh, don't look at me like that. I've given up caring about being disloyal.

I've given up damn well caring, if you must know. Do you know what she says? She says she can't contemplate a future with a daughter she doesn't want. She says she can't imagine living for twenty years, say, with someone she hates before it's born. What's my life going to be like with that going on?'

'At the risk of uttering an old cliché, I'd say she'll feel differently when the baby's born.'

'Oh, she will? You can be sure of that? She'll love it when it's put into her arms? Shall I tell you what else she says? That she never wants to see it. We're to put it up for adoption immediately without either of us seeing it. I told you she was mad.'

All this made Wexford feel like a drink. But he couldn't start drinking at lunchtime with all he'd got ahead of him. Burden wasn't going to drink either. Judging by the look of him some mornings, he saved that up for when he got home. They paid the bill and climbed up the stone steps out of the Old Cellar into a bright June sunshine that made them blink.

'She's seeing a psychiatrist. I pin my faith to that. Me of all people! I sometimes wonder what I've come to, saying things like that.'

Sir Hilary Tremlett's report of the results of the post-mortem had come. To decipher the obscurer bits for Wexford, Dr Crocker came into the office as Burden was departing. They nearly passed each other in the doorway, Burden long-faced, monosyllabic. The doctor laughed.

'Mike's having a difficult pregnancy.'

Wexford wasn't going to enlighten him. The other chair had been pushed under the desk. He shoved it out with his toe.

'He says here he found three hundred and twenty milligrammes of cyclobarbitone in the stomach and other organs. What's cyclobarbitone?'

'It's an intermediate-acting barbiturate – that means it has about eight hours duration of effect – a hypnotic drug, a sleeping pill if you like. The proprietary brand name would be Phanodorm, I expect. Two hundred milligrammes is the dose. But three hundred and twenty wouldn't kill him. It sounds as if he took two tablets of two hundred each.'

'It didn't kill him, though, did it? He died of stab wounds.'

256

Wexford looked up to see the doctor looking at him. They were both thinking the same thing. They were both thinking about Colin Budd and Brian Wheatley.

'What actually killed him was a wound that pierced the carotid.'

'Did it now? The blood must have spouted like a fountain.'

'There were seven other wounds in the neck and chest and back. A lot of stuff here's about fixed and mobile underlying tissues.' Wexford handed the pages across the desk, retaining one. 'I'm more interested in the estimate he makes of the proportions of the knife. A large kitchen knife with a dagger point, it would seem to have been.'

'I see he suggests death occurred six to eight weeks ago. What d'you reckon? He took two sleeping pills and someone did him in while he was away in the land of nod? If it happened as you seem to think soon after he left his house at six that evening, why would he take sleeping pills at that hour?'

'He might have taken them,' said Wexford thoughtfully, 'in mistake for something else. Hypertension pills, for instance. He had high blood pressure.'

While the doctor was reading Wexford picked up the phone and asked the telephonist to get him Wheatley's number. Wheatley had said he worked in London on only three days a week so there was a chance he might be at home now. He was.

'I didn't think you showed much interest,' he said in an injured way.

That one Wexford wasn't going to answer. It was true anyway. They hadn't shown all that much interest in a man getting his hand scratched by a girl hitchkiker. Things had taken on a different aspect since then.

'You gave me a detailed description of the girl who attacked you, Mr Wheatley. The fact that you're a good observer makes me think you may have observed more. Will you think about that, please, and try and remember everything that happened? Principally, give us some more information about what the girl looked like, her voice and so on. We'd like to come and see you.'

Mollified, Wheatley said he'd give it some thought and tell

257

them everything he could remember and how about some time that evening?

The doctor said, 'It couldn't have happened inside a car, you know, Reg. There'd have been too much blood.'

'Perhaps in the open air?'

'And tied his neck up in a Marks and Spencer's floral-printed teatowel?'

'It doesn't say that there!'

'I happened to notice it when the poor devil was resurrected. We've got one like it at home.'

The phone rang. The telephonist said, 'Mr Wexford, there's a Mrs Williams here wanting to talk to someone about Mr Rodney Williams.'

Joy, he thought. Well.

'Mrs Joy Williams?'

'Mrs Wendy Williams.'

'Have someone bring her up here, will you?'

The sister-in-law? The wife of the brother in Bath? When you don't know what to do next, Raymond Chandler advised writers of his sort of fiction, have a man come in with a gun. In a real-life murder case, thought Wexford, what better surprise visitor than the mysterious Wife of Bath?

He looked up as Burden re-entered the room. Burden had been going through the clothes found on Williams's body: navy blue briefs – very different from the white underwear in the cupboard in Alverbury Road – brown socks, fawn cavalry-twill slacks, blue, brown and cream striped shirt, dark blue St Laurent sweater. The back pocket of the slacks had contained a cheque book for one of the accounts with the Anglian-Victoria at Pomfret (R. W. Williams, private account), and a wallet containing one fiver, three £1 notes and two credit cards, Visa and American Express. No car keys, no house keys.

'He probably kept his house key on the same ring as his car keys,' Burden said. 'It's what I do.'

'At any rate, we'll get at that bank account now. The doctor here says there was a teatowel wrapped round his neck. To staunch the blood presumably.'

There came a knock at the door. Bennett came into the room with a young woman, not anyone's idea of a Wife of Bath.

'Mrs Wendy Williams, sir.'

She looked about twenty-five. She was a pretty girl with a delicate nervous face and fair curly hair. Wexford asked her to sit down, the doctor having sprung to his feet. She slid into the chair, gripping the arms of it, and jumped as Crocker passed behind her on his way to the door. Burden closed the door behind him and stood there.

'What did you want to see me about, Mrs Williams?'

She didn't answer. She had fixed him with a penetrating stare and her tongue came in and out, moistening her lips.

'I take it you're Rodney Williams's sister-in-law? Is that right?'

She moved her body back a little, hands still tight on the chair arms. 'What do you mean, his sister-in-law?' She didn't wait for a reply. 'Look, I . . . I don't know how to say this. I've been so . . . I've been nearly out of my mind.' Mounting hysteria made her voice ragged. 'I saw in the paper . . . a little bit in the paper and . . . Is that, that *person* they found . . . ? Is that my husband?'

9

It was seldom he could give people reassuring news. He was tempted to say no, of course not. The body has been identified. She was holding on to the arms of the chair, rubbing her fingers up and down the wood.

'What is your husband's name, Mrs Williams?'

'Rodney John Williams. He's forty-eight.' She spoke in short jerky phrases, not waiting for the questions. 'Six feet tall. He's fair going grey. He's a salesman. It said in the paper a salesman.'

Burden stared, then looked down. She swallowed, made an effort against panic, an effort that concentrated on tensing her muscles.

'Could you . . . please, I have a photo here.'

Her hands, unlocked from the chair, refused to obey her when first she tried to open her bag. The photograph she handed to Wexford fluttered, she was shaking so. He looked at it, unbelieving.

It was Rodney Williams all right, high domed forehead, crack of a mouth parted in a broad smile. It was a more recent picture than the one Joy had and showed Williams in swimming trunks (flabby hairless chest, spindleshanks, a bit knock-kneed) with this girl in a black bikini and another girl, also bikini'd but no more than twelve years old. Wexford's eyes returned to the unmistakable face of Williams, to the head you somehow wanted to slap a fringed wig on and so transform it.

She was waiting, watching him. He nodded. She brought a fluttery hand up to her chest, to her heart perhaps, froze for a moment in this tragic pose. Then her eyelids fell and she sagged sideways in the chair.

Afterwards he was to think of it as having been beautifully done but at the time he saw it only as a genuine faint. Burden held her shoulders, bringing her face down onto her knees. Picking up the phone, Wexford asked for a policewoman to come up, Polly Davies or Marion Bayliss, anyone who was around. And someone send a pot of strong tea and don't forget the sugar basin.

Wendy Williams came out of her faint, sat up and pressed her face into her hands.

'You are the wife of Rodney John Williams and you live in Liskeard Avenue, Pomfret?'

She drank the tea sugarless and very hot, at first with her eyes closed. When she opened her eyes and they met his he noticed they were the very clear pale blue of flax flowers. She nodded slowly.

'How long have you been married, Mrs Williams?'

'Sixteen years. We had our sixteenth wedding anniversary in March.'

He could hardly believe it. Her skin had the clear bloom of an adolescent's, her hair was baby-soft and the curl in it looked natural. She saw his incredulity and in spite of her emotion was flattered, a little buoyed up. He could tell she was the sort of woman to whom compliments, even unspoken ones, were food and drink. They nourished her. A faint, tremulous smile appeared. He looked again at the photographs.

'My daughter Veronica,' she said. 'I got married very young. I was only sixteen. That picture was taken three or four years back.'

A bigamist he had been, then. Not a common or garden wayward husband with a girlfriend living in the next town, not a married man with a sequence of pricey mistresses, but your good old-fashioned true blue bigamist. There was no doubt in Wexford's mind that Wendy Williams had as good-looking a marriage certificate as Joy's and if hers happened not to be valid she would be the last to know it.

That, then, was why he had taken no change of clothes

with him. He had those things in his other home. And more than that, much more. Wexford now saw the point of those bank accounts: one for his salary to be paid into and two joint accounts to be fed from it, one for each household, R. W. Williams and J. Williams; R. W. Williams and W. Williams. There had been no need to assume a different name on his second marriage – Williams was common enough to make that unnecessary. He had been like a Moslem who keeps strictly to Islamic law and maintains his wives in separate and distinct dwellings. The difference here was that the wives didn't know of each other's existence.

That Williams had had another wife, what one might call in fact a chief wife, was something this girl was going to have to be told. And Joy was going to have to be told about her.

'Can you tell me when you last saw Mr Williams?' Not calling him 'your husband' any more was the beginning of breaking the news.

'About two months ago. Just after Easter.'

This wasn't the time to ask her to account for that eight week gap. He told her he would come and see her at home that evening. Polly Davies would look after her and see she got home safely.

Something had at last happened to distract Burden temporarily from his private troubles. His expression was as curious and as alerted as a little boy's.

'What did he do at Christmas?' he said. 'Easter? What about holidays?'

'No doubt we shall find out. Other bigamists have handled it. He probably had a Bunbury as well.'

'A *what*?'

'A nonexistent friend or relative to provide him with alibis. My guess is Williams's Bunbury was an old mother.'

'Did he have an old mother?'

'God knows. Creating one from his imagination wouldn't have been beyond his capacity, I'm sure. You know what they say, a mother is the invention of necessity.'

Burden winced. 'That night he left Alverbury Road, d'you think he went to his other home?'

'I think he set off meaning to go there. Whether he reached it is another matter.'

Fascinated by Williams's family arrangements, Burden said, 'While Joy thought he was travelling for Sevensmith Harding in Ipswich he was with Wendy and while he was with Joy Wendy thought he was where?'

'I don't suppose she knew he worked for Sevensmith Harding. He probably told her a total lie about what he did.'

'You'd think he'd have got their names muddled – I mean called Wendy Joy and Joy Wendy.'

'There speaks the innocent monogamist,' said Wexford, casting up his eyes. 'How do you think married men with girlfriends manage? Wife and all get called "darling".'

Burden shook his head as if even speculating about it was too much for him. 'Do you reckon it was one of them killed him?'

'Carried his body and stuck it in that grave? Williams weighed a good fifteen stone or two hundred and ten pounds or ninety something kilos or whatever we're supposed to say these days.'

'It might have been Wendy made that phone call.'

'You reckon her voice sounds like Joy's?'

Burden was obliged to admit that it didn't. Joy's was monotonous, accent-free, uninflected; Wendy's girlish, rather fluting, with a faint lisp. Wexford was talking about voices, about the rather unattractive but nevertheless memorable quality of Joy's voice when his phone rang again.

'Another young lady to see me,' he said to Burden, putting the receiver back.

'Bluebeard's third wife?' it was the first attempt at a joke he had made in two months.

Wexford appreciated that. 'Let's say a fan, rather. Someone who saw me on the telly.'

'Look, why don't I take Martin and get on over to Wheatley? Then I'll be able to come to Wendy's with you tonight.'

'OK, and we'll take Polly along.'

The girl walked into his room in a breeze of confidence. She was seventeen or eighteen and her name was Eve Freeborn. Apposite names of the Lady Dedlock-Ernest Pontifex-Obadiah Slope kind that Victorian novelists used are in real life less uncommon than is generally supposed. That Eve Freeborn was aptly named Wexford came quickly to understand. She might have been dressed and cast for the role of

Spirit of Freedom in a pageant. Her hair was cropped short and dyed purple in parts. She wore stretch jeans, a check shirt and thongs.

The story she told Wexford, sitting with legs wide apart, hands linked, forearms making a bridge from the chair arms to rest her chin on, was delivered in a brisk and articulate way. Eve was still at school, had come there straight from school. President of the debating society no doubt, he thought. As she turned her hands outwards, thumbs on her jaw, he noticed the felt-tipped pen drawing on her wrist, a raven with a woman's head, and then as she moved her arm the shirtsleeve covered it.

'I realized it was my duty as a citizen to come to you. I delayed just long enough to discuss the matter with my boyfriend. He's at the same school as me – Haldon Finch. In a way he's involved, you see. We have the sort of relationship where we believe in total openness.'

Wexford gave her an encouraging smile.

'My boyfriend lives in Arnold Road, Myringham. It's a single-storey house, number forty-three.' Opposite Graham Gee who had reported the presence of poor old Greta, Wexford thought. 'His mother and father live there too,' said Eve in a tone that implied enormous condescension and generosity on the part of the boyfriend in allowing his parents to live in their own house. 'The point is – and you may not believe this but it's the honest truth, I promise you – they don't like him having me to stay the night with him. I mean, not me personally, you could understand that if they didn't like me, but any girl. So what we do is I come round after he's gone to bed and get in the window.'

Wexford didn't gape at her. He merely felt like doing this. He couldn't resist asking, 'Why doesn't he come to you?'

'I share a room with my sister. Anyway, I was telling you. I went round to his place around ten that Thursday night. There wasn't all that much space to park and when I was reversing I went into the car behind. I just bashed the wing of it a bit, not much, it wouldn't have had to have a new wing or anything, but I did think it was my duty to take responsibility and not just leave it, so I . . .'

'Just a moment. This was the night of April the fifteenth?'

'Right. It was my boyfriend's birthday.'

And a charming present he must have had, Wexford thought.

'What was this car you went into?'

'A dark blue Ford Granada. It was the car you asked about on TV. I wrote a note and put it on the windscreen, under a wiper. Just with my name and address on and phone number. But it blew away or got lost or something because the car was still there a long while after that and the driver never got in touch with me.'

At ten that night. Greta the Granada had been there at ten but how long had it been there?

'Just as a matter of curiosity, whose car were you driving?'

'My own,' she said, surprised.

'You have your own car?'

'My mother's technically. But it comes to the same thing.'

No doubt it did. They were amazing, these young people. And the most amazing thing about them was that they had no idea previous generations had not behaved as they did. People got old, of course, became dull and staid, they knew that, but in their day surely teenage girls had slept with their boyfriends, appropriated their parents' cars, stayed out all night, dyed their hair all colours of the spectrum.

He thanked her for her help and as she got up he saw the little drawing or tattoo again. He realized that he didn't know which of the local schools Sara Williams attended. And there remained the as yet unknown quantity, Veronica Williams . . .

'Do you know a girl of your own age called Sara Williams? Is she perhaps at school with you?'

He was positive she hadn't made the connection before, was making it now for the first time. 'Do you mean Sara is the daughter of this man who was murdered?'

'Yes. You go to the same school?'

'No, we don't,' she said carefully, 'but I know her.'

Wheatley lived on an estate of new houses on the Pomfret side of Myringham. They had been built, Burden recalled, by a company so anxious to sell their houses that 100 percent mortgages had been guaranteed with them and a promise given to buy a house back for its purchase price if after two

265

years the occupier were dissatisfied. The place had a raw look, oddly cold in the June sunshine. Wheatley's pregnant wife came to the door. A child of about three, a girl, was behind her, holding on to her skirt. Burden registered the fact of the pregnancy and the sex of the child with his heightened sensitivity to such matters and then he thought that his wife's pregnancy might have affected Wheatley's attitude to the girl he picked up. For instance, he might be sexually frustrated. Burden knew all about that. Wheatley too might have exaggerated the purity of his attitude towards the girl because he dared not risk the possibility of his pregnant wife finding out he was capable of putting his hand on other women's knees – or, in this instance no doubt, on other women's breasts.

The third bedroom of this very small house had been turned into a study or office for Wheatley. He was on the phone but rang off within seconds of Burden's and Martin's arrival. Yes, he had remembered some more about the girl. He was sure he could give them a more detailed description. There was no question of his remembering more of what the girl had said to him because she hadn't said any more. 'Thanks' and a gasp had been the only sounds that had come from her.

'I told you she was tall for a woman, at least five feet nine. Still in her teens, I'm sure. She had dark brown shoulder-length hair with a fringe, very fair skin and very white hands. I think I can remember a ring, not a wedding or engagement ring or anything, but one of those big silver rings they wear. I wouldn't call her pretty, not a bit.' Was that a sop to the wife who had come quietly into the room, carrying the little girl? 'Sunglasses, a dark leather shoulder bag. She had blue denim jeans on and a grey cardigan. She was thin – really skinny, I mean.' Another matrimonial sop. 'And underneath the cardigan she had a tee-shirt on. It was a white tee-shirt with a crazy picture on it – some sort of bird with a woman's head.'

'You didn't mention that before, Mr Wheatley.'

'I didn't mention the ring before or what colour her clothes were. You asked me to think about it and I thought about it and that's what I remember. You can take it or leave it. A white tee-shirt with a bird on it with a woman's face.'

*

266

'I don't believe it!'

She stared at Wexford, her mouth open in an appalled sort of way, her eyelids moving. She brought her hands up and scrabbled at her neck.

'I don't believe it!' Now there was defiance in her tone. Then, by changing one word, she showed him she accepted, she understood that what he had told her was true. 'I *won't* believe it!'

Polly Davies was with him, sitting there like a good chaperone, silent but attentive. She glanced at Wexford, got a nod from him.

'I'm afraid it's true, Mrs Williams.'

'I don't – I don't have a right to be called that, do I?'

'Of course you do. Your name doesn't depend on a marriage certificate.' Wexford thought of Eve Freeborn. There was a world between her and Wendy Williams, though a mere fourteen years, less than a generation, separated them. Would Eve know such a thing as a marriage certificate existed?

'Mrs Williams,' said stalwart Polly, 'why don't you and I go and make some coffee? We'd all like coffee, I'm sure. Mr Wexford will want to ask you some questions but I know he'd like you to have time to get over the shock of this.'

She nodded and got up awkwardly as if her bones were stiff. A glazed look had come across her face. She walked like a sleepwalker and no one now would have mistaken her for a twenty-five-year-old.

Burden shrugged silently as the door closed behind them and subsided into one of his typical morose reveries. Wexford had a look round the room they were sitting in. The house was newer than the Williams home in Kingsmarkham, a small 'town house' with an integral garage, built probably in the late 1960s. Wendy was a thorough meticulous and perhaps fanatical housekeeper. This was a through room with a dining area and it had very recently been redecorated in gleaming white with an undertone of palest pink. One of the colours in the Sevensmith Harding 'Ice Cream' range? The carpet was deep strawberry pink, some of the furniture mahogany, some white canework, cushions in various shades of pink and red. It was tasteful, it was a far cry from the stereotyped shabbiness of Joy's home, but somehow it was also uncomfortable, as if everything had been placed there – hanging baskets, little tables, red Venetian glass – for effect rather than for use.

He remembered that a young girl also lived here. There were no signs of her. But what sign did he expect or would he recognize if he saw it? She had been twelve in the picture . . .

'My daughter is sixteen now,' Wendy said when the coffee was brought. A slightly defiant note came into her voice as she added, 'She was sixteen three weeks ago.'

Her gaze fell. He did some calculations, remembering what she had said about her wedding anniversary taking place in March. So Williams had 'married' her three months before the child was born. He had had to wait until she reached the legal age for marriage.

'Where were you married, Mrs Williams?'

'Myringham Registry Office. My mother wanted us to have a church wedding but – well, for obvious reasons . . .'

Wexford could imagine one very obvious reason if she had been six months pregnant. The nerve of Williams, a married man, 'marrying' this child, as she had been, a mere dozen miles from his home town! The wedding to Joy, Dora had told him, had been at St Peter's, Kingsmarkham, the bride in white slipper satin . . .

Wendy was thrusting a paper at him. He saw it was her marriage certificate.

In the Registration District of Myringham, at the Registry Office, Rodney John Williams, aged thirty-two. In some respects, at any rate, he had been honest. Though he could hardly have distorted those facts. They had been on his birth certificate. A Bath address, his brother's probably, his occupation sales representative. Wendy Ann Rees, aged sixteen, Pelham Street, Myringham, shop assistant. The witnesses had been Norman Rees and Brenda Rees, parents presumably, or brother and sister-in-law.

He handed it back to her. She looked at it herself and her tongue flicked out to moisten her lips. For a moment, from the way she was holding it, he thought she was going to tear the certificate across. But she replaced it in its envelope and laid the envelope on the low white melamine table that was close up against the arm of her chair.

She pressed her knees together and folded her hands in

her lap. Her legs were very good with elongated slim ankles. To come to the police station she had worn a grey flannel suit with a white blouse. He had a feeling she was a woman who attached importance to being suitably dressed. The suit was changed now for a cotton dress. She was the type who would 'save' her clothes, not sit about in a straight skirt or risk a spot on white silk. In her sad wistful look youth had come back into her face.

'Mrs Williams,' he began, 'I'm sure you won't mind telling me how it was you weren't alarmed when your husband was away for so long.'

She did mind. She was reluctant. Patience, simply waiting quietly, succeeded with her where pressing the point might not have.

'Rodney and I . . .' She paused. It was always 'Rodney' with her, Wexford noted, never 'Rod'. 'We – we quarrelled. Well, we had a very serious quarrel. That must have been a few days after Easter. Rodney spent Easter with his mother in Bath. He always spent Christmas and Easter with her. He was an only child, you see, and she's been in an old people's home for years and years.'

Wexford carefully avoided looking at Burden. Wendy said, reminded by her own explanation, 'Has she been . . . ? I mean, has anyone *told* her?'

Enigmatically, Wexford said that had been taken care of. 'Go on please, Mrs Williams.'

'We quarrelled,' she went on. 'It was a very private thing we quarrelled about. I'll keep that to myself if you don't mind. I said to him that – well, I said that if he – if *it* didn't stop, if he didn't promise me faithfully that never – well, I said I'd take Veronica away and he'd never see us again. I – I struck him, I was so angry, so distressed, I can't tell you – well, he was angry too. He denied it, of course, and then he said I needn't trouble about leaving him because he'd leave me. He said he couldn't stand my nagging any more.' She lifted her head and looked Wexford straight in the eye. 'I did nag him, I'll be honest about it. I couldn't bear it, never seeing him, his always being away. We'd never had a single Christmas together. I always had to go to my parents. We hardly ever had a holiday. I used to *beg* him . . .' Her voice faltered and Wexford understood that realization was dawn-

269

ing. She was beginning to see what the real reason was for those absences. 'Anyway,' she said, making an effort at control, 'he – he calmed down after a while and I suppose I did too. He was going away again and he was due back on the Thursday – the fifteenth, that is. I was still very sore and upset but I said goodbye to him and that I'd see him on Thursday and he said maybe I would and maybe he'd never come back, so you see, I – when he didn't come back I thought he'd left me.'

It wasn't a completely convincing explanation. He tried to put himself in her shoes. He tried to think how he would have felt years ago when he and Dora were young if they'd had a row and she, going away to visit her sister, say, had told him maybe she wouldn't come back. Probably such a thing had actually happened. It did happen in marriages, even in excellent ones. But if she hadn't come back on the appointed day, if she'd been a couple of hours late even, he'd have started going out of his mind with worry. Of course, much depended on the seriousness of the quarrel and on the reasons for it.

'Tell me what happened that Thursday.'

'In the evening, do you mean?'

'When he didn't come.'

'I was at work. Thursday's our late night. I didn't tell you, did I? I'm manageress of the fashion floor at Jickie's.'

He was surprised. Somehow he had taken it for granted she didn't work. 'In Myringham?' he asked. 'Or the Kingsmarkham branch?'

'Oh, Kingsmarkham. In the Precinct.'

Jickie's was Kingsmarkham's biggest department store and the largest area of the Kingsbrook Shopping Precinct was given over to it. Doubtless Rodney Williams had taken care never to accompany Joy when she went shopping there for a jumper or a pair of tights on a Saturday afternoon. Had he risked walking arm in arm down Kingsmarkham High Street during shopping hours? With his son or daughter in the car, had he risked parking in the precinct car park? It was a tightrope he had walked and no doubt, for such is the nature of people like him, he had enjoyed walking it, but he had fallen off at last. Because of the tightrope or for some entirely different reason?

270

'We stay open till eight on Thursdays but I can never get away till nine and it takes me a quarter of an hour to get home. When I did get back Veronica was here but Rodney hadn't come. I thought there was still a chance he might come but he didn't and then I knew. Or I thought I knew. I thought he'd left me.'

'And in all the weeks that followed,' Burden put it, 'you weren't anxious? You didn't wonder what could happen to you and your daughter if he didn't come back?'

'I'd be all right financially without him. I've always had to work and now I'm doing quite well.' There was a note of self-esteem in the little soft voice now. Inside the white and pink and fair curls and underneath the lisp and diffidence, Wexford thought there might be a core of steel. 'We had a ninety per cent mortgage on this house and up till five years ago it was all Rodney could do to keep us. He got promotion then and things were easier but I kept on working. I needed a life of my own too, he was away so much.'

'Promotion?' hazarded Wexford, feeling his way.

'It's quite a small company and they haven't been doing too well lately – bathroom fittings and furniture, that sort of thing. Rodney was made sales manager for this locality.'

Polly Davies picked up the tray and took it away into the kitchen. Wexford thought how easy it was to imagine Rodney Williams – or his idea of Rodney Williams – in his other home but next to impossible to imagine him here. Seated at that glass-topped dining table, for instance, with its bowl of pink and red roses or in one of those pink chintz armchairs. He had been a big coarse man and everything here had a daintiness like a pink shell or the inside of a rose.

'I have to know what you quarrelled about, Mrs Williams.'

Her tone became prissy, very genteel. 'It has nothing whatsoever to do with Rodney's death.'

'How do you know?'

She looked at him as if this were unfair persecution.

'How could it be? He got killed because he picked up someone hitching a lift and they killed him. Something like that . . . It's always happening.'

'That's an interesting guess but it's only a guess, isn't it? You've no evidence for it and there's plenty of evidence against it. The car being returned to Myringham, for instance. A phone call was made to your husband's employers and a letter of resignation sent to them. Do you think that phone call was made by some homicidal hitchhiker?'

She sat rigid, keeping her eyes obstinately averted. Polly came back.

'Are you all right, Mrs Williams?'

A nod. An indrawn breath and a sigh.

'What did you quarrel about?'

'I could refuse to tell you.'

'You could. But why take a stand like that when what you tell us will be treated in the strictest confidence? Ask yourself if it's so awful that we won't have heard it before. And don't you think that if you don't tell us we may come to think it is something worse than it really was?'

She sat silent. She wore an expression like someone who expects at any moment to see something nasty and shocking on television. It was an anticlimax when she said almost in a whisper, 'There was another girl.'

'You mean your husband had a woman friend he'd been seeing?'

' "Seeing",' she said, 'I like that expression – "seeing". Yes, he'd been seeing a woman friend. That's one way of putting it.'

'How would you put it?'

'Oh, like that. The way you do. What else does one say? Something crude, I suppose.' The repressive lid suddenly jumped and let out a dribble of resentment, of bitterness. 'I thought no one else but me would ever matter to him. I look young, don't I? I'm pretty enough, I don't look my age. People say I look eighteen. What was the matter with him that he . . . ? Yes, we quarrelled about that. About a girl. I wanted him to promise me it would never happen again.'

'He refused?'

'Oh, he promised. I didn't believe him. I thought it would start up again when he got the chance. I couldn't stand it, I didn't want him if he was going to do that. I was glad when he didn't come back. Don't you see? I was *glad*.'

'I'll have to have this girl's name.'

Quick as a flash: 'I don't know her name.'

'Come now, Mrs Williams.'

272

'I don't know it. He wouldn't tell me. Just a girl. What does it matter?'

She had said too much already, she was thinking. He could read that, plain in her face, the look in her eyes of being appalled at her own indiscretion. At that moment, before he could say any more, the door opened and a young girl came in. Just before this happened there had been a sound downstairs and footsteps on the stairs – the living room was on the middle floor – but it had all taken place very quickly, within a few seconds. And now, without warning, the girl was here among them.

What first struck Wexford was that although she was not so tall and her hair was shorter she looked exactly like Sara Williams. They might have been twins.

10

Her hair was the same pale fudge colour, not curly but not quite straight either, the tips just touching her shoulders. Brown eyes, ellipse eyebrows, small straight nose, fine white skin sprinkled with freckles. Rodney Williams's high domed forehead and his small narrow mouth. But instead of jeans she wore a summer dress with white tights and white sandals. She stood in the doorway looking surprised at the sight of them, a little more than just startled.

Wendy Williams was taken aback.

In a flustered way she said, 'This is my daughter Veronica,' and to the girl, 'you're home early.'

'Not much. It's after nine.'

The voice was her mother's, soft and slightly affected but without the lisp. It was quite unlike Sara's abrupt uninflected tones. Recovering poise Wendy said to her, 'These are police officers. They'll only be a few minutes.' She lied fluently, 'It's to do with trouble at the shop. You won't mind leaving us alone for a bit, will you, darling?'

'I'm going to have a bath anyway.'

Closing the door with the sort of precision her mother might use, she went off up the spiral staircase that was the core of this house.

'I don't know why she's so offhand with me lately. This past year . . .'

Wexford said, 'You haven't told her?'

'I haven't seen her. She always goes to her friend's straight from school on a Tuesday. Or so she says, she's so secretive . . .'

'Which school, Mrs Williams?'

274

'Haldon Finch Comprehensive. I'll tell her about her father after you've gone. I suppose I shall have to tell her what he was – a bigamist, with another wife somewhere. It won't be easy. I don't know if you appreciate that.'

Wexford, when interrogating, would allow any amount of digression but never total distraction. Those he questioned were obliged to come back to the point sooner or later. It was hard on them for often they believed they had escaped. The leash had snapped and freedom was surely there for the taking, but the hand always came down and snatched up the broken end.

'We were talking about this woman friend your husband had. He may have gone to her on the night he died.'

'I don't know any more about her!'

Fear had come into her voice now. It was what many would have called caution or apprehensiveness but it was really fear.

'You called her a girl. You implied a young girl.'

A panicky jerky rapid way of speaking – 'A young single girl, very young, that's all I know. I told you, I don't know any more!'

Wexford recalled the overtures Williams had once made to Sylvia. When Sylvia was fifteen. Was it something like that that Wendy had implied when she asked so pathetically if she didn't still look young? That she at thirty-two to his forty-eight might not be young enough for him?

'Do you mean she's young enough to live at home with her parents?'

A nod, painful and perplexed.

'What else do you know of her, Mrs Williams?'

'Nothing. I don't know any more. Do you think I wanted him to talk to me about her?'

That was reasonable enough. At first he thought she was lying when she said she was ignorant of the girl's name. Now he was less sure. How often had he heard people say, 'If my husband (my wife) were unfaithful to me I wouldn't want to know', and when they were forced to know, 'I don't want to hear anything about it'? The knives of jealousy are honed on details.

The question he sensed she would hate but which must be asked he had saved till last.

'How did you know it was happening at all? How did you know of her existence?'

He had been wrong. She didn't mind. She didn't mind because her answer was a lie that she had been rehearsing in her mind, silently and busily while they talked, waiting for the past half-hour for the question to come.

'I had an anonymous letter.'

Eventually he would get at the truth. It could wait.

'Now, Mrs Williams, your daughter . . .'

'What about her?' Very quick and defensive.

'I shall want to talk to Veronica.'

'Oh no, not that. Please.'

'When you have told her and she has had a day or two to get over the shock.'

'But why?'

'Her father has been murdered. He was due to come here and she was here, alone here. It's possible he did come and she was the last person to see him alive.'

'He didn't come here. She would have told me.'

'We'll see, Mrs Williams. We shall also want to look over this house, particularly at any of your husband's personal property.'

'We keep coming back to these young girls,' Burden said.

'And to ravens with women's faces.'

'That too. Budd and Wheatley were both attacked by a young girl – not very seriously, either of them, but they were attacked and the assault was with a knife. Rodney Williams liked young girls – I mean, he seems especially to have liked them very young – and he had a very young girlfriend. He died as the result of a knife attack, he was stabbed to death. Now Wheatley says the girl who attacked him was wearing a white tee-shirt with a design on it of a sort of bird with a woman's head . . .'

'And Sara Williams,' said Wexford, 'possesses just such a tee-shirt and has a poster with a similar motif on her bedroom wall.'

'Does she? You're kidding.'

'No. It's true. And Eve Freeborn has a raven with a woman's head tattooed or drawn on her left wrist, and since the sun came out, Mike, and women aren't bundling themselves up in cardigans and jackets I've seen no less than five girls around Kingsmarkham and Pomfret wearing white tee-shirts with ravens with women's faces on them. How about that?'

'God, and I thought we were really getting somewhere. It's like that bit in Ali Baba and the Forty Thieves when the woman says he'll know the right oil jar because it'll have a cross on it and when he gets there someone's put crosses on all the oil jars.'

'You've been reading again. Or going to pantomimes. It looks to me as if these raven-harpy pictures are the motif or symbol of some sort of society or cult. Latter-day anarchists or some sort of spurious freedom fighters.'

'Animal Rights?' said Burden doubtfully.

'It could be, I suppose. The implication being that the animal – or in this case bird – has the feelings and rights of a human being? The poster Sara Williams has in her bedroom has some letters on it as well as the picture. An acronym, I think, a, r, r, i, a, Arria.'

'Animal Rights something or other?'

'There was a woman called Arria, in Roman history, I seem to remember. I'll try and find out. If it's animal rights, Mike, you would expect its members to make their attacks on people who in their view were being cruel to animals. Factory farmers, for instance, or masters of foxhounds. I don't suppose Wheatley keeps calves chained up in boxes in his back garden, does he? We'll ask Sara. But first I want to leave her and Joy to get over the shock of Williams having another wife and another child.'

'You've told them?'

'Yes. It was the money aspect that seemed to mean most to Joy. She had been deprived in order that he could maintain another household. She gave that bitter laugh of hers. If I'd had to live with that laugh it would have got horribly on my nerves.'

'How's Martin getting on with his typewriter inquiries?'

Wexford threw the report across the desk. It was no Sevensmith Harding machine that had been used to type Williams's letter of resignation. All the typewriters in use in the Myringham office were of the sophisticated electronic

277

kind. Neither of the Williams households contained a typewriter of any sort. The Harmers had a typewriter in the two-
storey flat over the shop where they lived and both Hope
Harmer and her daughter Paulette used it. It was a small
Olivetti, an electric machine.

'His new young lady typed that letter,' Burden said. 'Find
her and we find the typewriter.'

'Find her and it won't matter whether we find the typewriter or not.'

Sergeant Martin had also been to Bath.

There, it seemed, Rodney Williams had had his origins.
On an estate of houses some few miles outside the city, in a
house very like the one Rodney had bought for his second
bride, lived his brother Howard. It was Howard's address
that appeared on Wendy's marriage certificate.

His parents had also once lived in Bath but his father had
died when he was a child and his mother when Rodney was
twenty-seven. That dead mother Rodney in his calculating
way had used to his advantage. No doubt he had told Wendy
that old Mrs Williams disapproved of his marriage to a
young girl, would never wish to meet her, but the good son
would be obliged to pay the occasional duty visit . . .

The brother seemed honest and straightforward. There
was very little contact between him and Rodney. Years ago,
fifteen or sixteen at least, some of Rodney's mail had been
sent to his address by mistake. He had simply sent it on.
Communications from the registrar at the time of the marriage to Wendy, Wexford thought. Howard Williams was
also a salesman and on 15 April he had been in Ireland on
business for his firm.

Joy hadn't told him of his brother's death. He had seen it
in the papers and seemed to have reacted with calm indifference.

Wendy Williams's home was on the outskirts of Pomfret
and a mile from the Harmers' shop. Had the relative nearness
of his in-laws to his second and bigamous home worried
Williams? Had he only agreed to buy a house there to placate
Wendy or gratify some wish of hers? Or did he see this sort
of risk as just part of the tightrope walk?

Between the estate and the nucleus of the town, that which
not long ago *was* the town, lay the sports grounds of the

Haldon Finch Comprehensive School, playing fields, tennis courts, fives courts, running track. The Haldon Finch, though new and an example of the new education with its two thousand pupils of both sexes housed in no less than six buildings, was as much 'into' games as any public school of the past. You might get ten O-levels but you were nothing if you weren't good at games.

At 5.30 in the afternoon twelve girls were playing tennis on the courts adjacent to Procter Road.

'It must be a match with another school,' Burden said. 'They start after school's finished.'

He and Wexford were in the car, on their way to see Veronica Williams. Donaldson had taken a short cut, or at least a traffic-avoiding cut, and they had found themselves amid this complex of sports fields.

'We'll get out and watch for a minute or two.'

Burden got out, though demurring.

'It makes me feel funny standing about watching girls. I mean, you ask yourself – *they* ask *them*selves – what sort of blokes would do that?'

'What would you think if you saw two middle-aged women watching young men playing squash?'

Burden looked sideways at him.

'Well, nothing, would I? I mean, I'd think they were their mothers or just women who liked watching sport.'

'Exactly. Doesn't that tell you something? Two things? One is that, whatever the women's movement says, there is a fundamental difference between men and women in their attitude to sex, and the other that this is an area in which women might claim – if it's occurred to them – to be superior to us.'

'It's changing though, you have to admit. Look at all those clubs up north where men do strips for women audiences.'

'The attitude is still different. Men go to strip shows and gawp in a sort of seething silence.'

'Don't women?'

'Apparently women laugh,' said Wexford.

One of the tennis players was Eve Freeborn. He spotted her from the purple slick in her hair. Her partner was a thin dark girl, their opponents a big heavily built blonde and another thin dark girl, this one wearing glasses. This four was on the court nearest to the road. Wexford could see enough of the other two courts and the other four couples only to be sure that Sara Williams was not among them. Sara didn't attend the Haldon Finch, of course – that would have been too great a risk even for Rodney Williams – but if this was a match six of the girls must come from another school. Seated on the three umpire chairs were three young women who had the look of games teachers.

He was aware at once that no one was playing very well. Had the standard deteriorated since the days when he had watched Sylvia and Sheila playing tennis? No, it wasn't that. It was television. These days you saw tennis played on TV. Top championships week after week, it seemed, here or in Europe or in America, and it spoiled you for the real thing, the local article. A pity really. It made you irritated at how often they missed the ball. Eve Freeborn had a good hard service. She would have served aces – only they were always on the wrong side of the line. Her opponent in the glasses was the worst player of the twelve, slow on her feet with a weak service and a way of scooping the ball up into the air, making it easy prey for Eve's slamming racket.

'Two match points,' said Burden, who had been attending more closely to the progress of the set.

Eve served a double fault. One match point. She served again, weakly, and the blonde shot it back like an arrow down the tramlines. The umpire announced deuce. Eve served another double fault.

'Van out,' said Wexford.

'My God, but that shows your age. That's what they said at tennis parties in the thirties.'

The umpire corrected him by saying crisply that the score was 'advantage Kingsmarkham'. So it was Kingsmarkham High who were the visitors here, once a grammar school, now private and fee-paying, no longer state-aided.

Kingsmarkham won the game. They changed ends, the girls paused by the umpire's chair and wiped faces and arms, drank Coke out of cans. Eve was standing only a few yards from Wexford. The little flame-coloured badge he had till now seen only as an orange spot near the neckline of her white tee-shirt showed itself at closer quarters to be a badge. He could make out spread wings on it and the letters ARRIA.

280

Eve didn't or wouldn't look at him. Perhaps he wasn't recognizable out of his office, in shirt-sleeves. He peered more closely. The umpire got down from her chair and came to the wire fence. She was a stocky, muscular young woman with a cross face and flashing eyes. In a voice full of crushed ice she said, 'Was there something you wanted?'

Wexford inhibited all the possible replies, improper, provocative, even mildly lecherous, that sprang to mind. He was a policeman. Anyway, Burden got in first with the flasher's classic caught-before-the-act answer.

'We were just looking.'

'Well, perhaps you'd like to get on with whatever you're supposed to be doing.'

'Move along, Mike,' said Wexford.

They went quickly to the car. The games mistress glared after them.

'Do they still call them that?'

'Call them what? Games mistresses?' Burden was silent for a moment. Then he said, screwing up his face, 'I'll tell you when my new daughter's eleven. If she gets to exist. If she gets to be eleven. If she and I are together when she does.'

'It's not as bad as that.'

'No? Maybe not. Maybe it's she and I that'll be together and not Jenny and I.'

Things must be bad with Burden for him to burst out with that in Donaldson's hearing. Not that Donaldson would say a word. But he would hear and he would think. Wexford said nothing. He watched Burden's face close up, the eyes grow dull and the mouth purse, the frown that was hardly ever absent re-establish itself in a deep double ridge. The car drew away. He looked behind him and saw Eve leaping to achieve her best volley of the match.

'Veronica was supposed to be playing in a tennis match,' said Wendy Williams, 'but of course she was too upset. She hasn't been to school today and I had to take the day off. I had to tell her her father had another wife and family. It was bad enough telling her he was dead.'

The second Mrs Williams, whom Wexford had at first thought of as rather sweet and gentle, he now saw had other

281

sides to her nature, among them a rather unpleasant habit of laying the blame for her misfortunes on whomsoever else might be present.

'I told her everything and at first she wouldn't speak and then she became very distressed.' The soft little voice trickled round the phrases. The eyes opened wide and wistful, like a Pears Soap child seeing distant angels. Wexford had the disturbing thought that perhaps she had cultivated all this because Williams had fancied little girls. 'You'll be gentle with her, won't you? You'll remember she's only sixteen? And it's not just that she's lost her father, it's worse than that.'

No question here of being sent up to the girl's bedroom. Veronica would come down. And Wendy would be there. He supposed Veronica must have been the missing tennis player for whom the dark girl not wearing glasses had substituted. While he was speculating Veronica came in, walking diffidently, a dead look still on her face. She had been crying but that was a long while ago now. Her eyes were dry and the lids pale, but a puffiness remained. Nevertheless she had dressed herself carefully for this encounter, as had her mother. Such things, which would have been lost on many men, never escaped Wexford. Wendy was in a black cotton dress with big sleeves that was a little too becoming to qualify as true mourning and Veronica in a pink pleated skirt, sweat shirt with a gold V on it and pink and white running shoes. Probably Wendy got their clothes from Jickie's at a discount.

'This is Chief Inspector Wexford and Inspector Burden, darling. They want to ask you one or two questions. Nothing difficult or complicated. They know what a bad shock you've had. And I shall be here all the time.'

For God's sake, she's not ten, Wexford thought. The girl's dull staring look disconcerted him.

'I'm sorry about your dad, Veronica,' he began. 'I know you're feeling unhappy and you'd probably like to be left alone. But your mother's told you what's happened. Your father isn't simply dead. He was killed. And we have to find out who killed him, don't we?' A not unfamiliar doubt assailed him. Did they? *Cui bono?* Who would be satisfied, avenged, recompensed? He was a policeman and it wasn't for him to think such thoughts. Not a hint of them was in

282

his tone. He looked at the girl and wondered what had been going on in her mind all those weeks her father was missing. Had she believed, like her mother, that he was with another woman? Or had she accepted his absence as she must have accepted all his other absences when he was allegedly away travelling for his firm or paying filial visits in Bath? She was no longer looked at him but down at the floor, her head drooping like a tired flower on a stalk.

'Do you think we could go back to April the fifteenth?' he said. 'It was a Thursday. Your mother expected your father home that evening but she had to stay on late at work. You were here though, weren't you?'

The 'yes' came very quietly. He might not have understood it for what it was if she hadn't nodded as well.

'What did you do? You came home from school when – at four?' He too was talking to her as if she were ten, but something in her attitude, her bowed head, feet crossed, hands in lap, seemed to invite it. Again that nod, the head lifted a little to make it. 'And then what happened? What sort of time did you expect your father to come?'

She murmured that she didn't know.

'We never knew what time to expect him,' Wendy said. 'We never knew. It might have been any time.'

'And did he come?' said Wexford.

'Of course he didn't! I've told you.'

'Please, Mrs Williams, let Veronica answer.'

The girl was shy, nervous, perhaps also unhappy. She was certainly in shock still. But suddenly she made an effort. It was as if she saw that there was no help for it, she was going to have to talk, she might as well get it over. Sara's tortoiseshell brown eyes looked in his and Sara's Primavera lips parted with a quiver.

'I had tea. Well, a Coke and some stuff Mummy left me in the fridge.' Yes, Wendy for all her own youth was the kind of woman who would be smotheringly protective, even to the extent of preparing meals in advance for a sixteen-year-old as if she were an invalid. Veronica said, 'I'd asked my friend round – the one whose place I was at when you came before – but she rang up and said she couldn't come. She said I could go to her.'

'But you wanted to wait in for your father?'

She was no Sara, no Eve Freeborn. She turned her head and looked to her mother for help. It came, as no doubt it always did.

'Veronica had no need to wait in for Rodney. I've told you, we never really thought he'd come at all.'

' "We", Mrs Williams?'

'Well, I don't really know what Veronica thought. I hadn't said anything to her then about the possibility of our splitting up. I was waiting to see what would happen. But the point is Veronica had no need to wait in for him and I wouldn't have . . . well, she's got her own life to lead.'

What had she been going to say when she broke off and made that extraordinary statement about this little creature's obviously nonexistent independence?

'You went out then?'

'I went to my friend's. I didn't stop there long. We played records. I wanted her to come out for a coffee but she couldn't, she was baby-sitting with her brother. She's got a brother who's only two. That was why she couldn't come over to me.'

'So you went back home. What time?'

'I didn't go straight home. I had a coffee on my own at Castor's. I got home about nine and Mummy came in ten minutes after.'

'You must have been disappointed your father wasn't there.'

'I don't know,' she said. 'I didn't think about it,' and surprisingly, for this wasn't really at issue, 'I don't mind being alone. I like it.'

'Well, my goodness,' said Wendy, not letting that one pass, 'you're never left alone if I can help it. You needn't talk as if you'd been neglected.'

Wexford asked the name of the friend and was told it was Nicola Tennyson and given an address that was between here and the town centre. No objection was put up by Wendy to their examining such of his personal property as Rodney Williams had in this house. It left Wexford with the feeling that this was because she rather wanted them to see over her house, its cleanliness, its elegant appointments and the evidence of her skill as housekeeper.

Here, at any rate, was the rest of Williams's wardrobe. It

was interesting to observe how he had kept his more stylish and 'in' clothes for this household. Jeans hung in the gilt-decorated white built-in cupboard, Westerner shirts, a denim suit and another in a fashionably crumpled stone-coloured linen mixture. There were two pairs of half-boots and a pair of beige kid moccasins. And the underwear was designed for a younger man than the part-time occupant of 31 Alverbury Road.

'He was two different men,' Wexford said.

'Perhaps three.'

'We shall see. At any rate he was two, one middle-aged, set in his ways, bored maybe, taking his family for granted, the other young still, even swinging – take a look at these underpants – making the grade with a young wife, living up to this little bandbox.'

Wexford looked around him at the room, thinking of Alverbury Road. There were duvets on the beds here, blinds at the windows, a white cane chair suspended from the ceiling, its seat piled with green, blue and white silk cushions. And the bed was a six-foot-wide king-size.

'He probably called it the playpen,' said Burden pulling a face.

'Once,' said Wexford.

In this house Williams had had no desk, only a drawer in the gilt-handled white melamine chest of drawers. This had been Wendy's house, no doubt about it, the sanctum where Wendy held sway. Girlish, fragile, soft-voiced though she might be, she had made this place her own, feminine and exclusive – exclusive in a way of Rodney Williams. He had been there on sufferance, Wexford sensed, his presence depending on his good behaviour. And yet his behaviour had not been very good even from the first. There had always been the travelling, the Bunbury of a mother, the long absences. So Wendy had made a home full of flowers and colours and silk cushions in which he was allotted small corners as if – unconsciously, he was sure it was unconsciously – she knew the day would come when it would be for herself and her daughter alone. Wexford looked inside the drawer but it told him little. It was full of the kind of papers he would have expected.

Except for Williams's driving licence with the Alverbury Road address.

'He was taking a risk leaving that about,' said Burden.

'Taking risks was his life. He took them all the time. He enjoyed the high wire. Anyway, suspicious wives read letters not driving licences.'

There were bills in the drawer, the counterfoils from credit-card chits, an American Express monthly account. Which address had that gone to? Yes, this one. It fitted somehow. Visa and Access were the workaday cards, American Express more cosmopolitan, more for the playboy. No doubt it was Wendy who paid the services' bills from the joint account. There was none in the drawer, only a rates demand, a television rental account book, an estimate from Godwin and Sculp, builders, of Pomfret, dated 30 March, for painting the living room, and an invoice from the same firm (stamped *Paid*) for renewal of a bathroom cistern. Under this lot lay Rodney's joint account cheque book, a paying-in book for the joint account, and a small glass bottle, half full of tablets, labelled 'Mandaret'.

On this the top floor of the house were two more bedrooms and a bathroom. Veronica's room was neat as a pin, white with a good deal of broderie anglaise about it and owing much to those magazine articles prevalent in Wendy's own childhood on how to make a dream bedroom for your daughter. No doubt poor Wendy had never had a dream bedroom of her own, Wexford thought, and he sensed that her youth had been nearer to that of Sara. No posters here, no home-made mobiles and no books either. It was designed for a girl who would do nothing in it but sit in the window seat looking pensive and wearing white socks.

The spiral staircase, a contraption of hideous discomfort and danger to all but the most agile, went through the middle of the house like a screw in a press. Down on the ground floor was a shower room, a separate lavatory, the third door on that side opening into the integral garage, and at the end of the passage a room the width of the house that opened through french windows onto patio and garden roughly the size of a large dining table. The room, that might have been for dining in or a study for Rodney Williams if he had been allowed one, was plainly devoted to Wendy's interests. She had a sewing machine in it and a knitting machine, an ironing board set up with two irons on it, one dry and one steam, and there were clothes everywhere, neatly hung or draped, sheathed in plastic bags.

Mother and daughter were still sitting upstairs at the glass-topped table. Wendy had taken up some sewing, a handkerchief or possibly a traycloth into which she was inserting tiny stitches, her little finger crooked in the way it used to be said was vulgar to hold a teacup. Veronica nibbled at dry roasted peanuts out of a foil packet. The dry kind it would be, the other sort tending to leave grease spots. They were both as tense as compressed springs, waiting for the police to go and leave them alone.

'Have you heard of a society or club called ARRIA?' Wexford said to Veronica.

The spring didn't leap free of its bonds. There was no shock. Veronica merely nodded. She didn't screw up the empty peanut packet but flattened it and began folding it very carefully, first into halves, then quarters.

'At school?'

She looked up. 'Some of the girls in the sixth and seventh years belong to it.'

'But you don't?'

'You have to be over sixteen.'

'Why girls?' he said. 'Haldon Finch is co-ed. Don't any boys belong?'

She was a normal teenager really. Underneath the prissy looks, the shyness, the Mummy's girl air, she was one of them. The look she gave him seethed with their scorn for the cretinous incomprehension evinced by adults.

'Well, it's all women, isn't it? It's for women. They're – what d'you call it? – feminists, militant feminists.'

'Then I hope you'll keep clear of it, Veronica,' Wendy said very quickly and sharply for her. 'I hope you'll have nothing to do with it. If there's anything I really hate it's women's lib. Liberation! I'm liberated and look where it's got me. I just hope you'll do better than I have when the time comes and find a man who'll really support you and look after you, a nice good man who'll – who'll *cherish* you.' Her lips trembled with emotion. She laid down her sewing. 'I wasn't enough of a woman for Rodney,' she said as if the girl

287

wasn't there. 'I wasn't enough of a girl. I got too hard and independent and – and *mature*, I know I did.' A heroic effort was made to keep the tears in, the break out of the voice, and a victory was won. 'You just remember that, Veronica, when your turn comes.'

Sergeant Martin was handling the complaint though, as he told Wexford, he hadn't much to go on. Nor had any harm been done – yet.

'A Ms Caroline Peters who's a physical education instructor at the Haldon Finch Comprehensive,' Martin said. 'Miz not Miss. She got very stroppy, sir, when I called her Miss. I called her an instructress too and had a job getting my tongue round it but that wasn't right either. She says two men were hanging about watching the girls playing a tennis match. Acting in a suspicious manner, she says. Came in a car which was parked for the express purpose of them getting out to watch. Voyeurs she called them. Afterwards she asked the girls if any of them knew the men but they denied all knowledge.'

Thank you Miss Freeborn, thought Wexford.

'Leave it, Martin. Forget it. We've better things to do.'

'Leave it altogether, sir?'

'I'll handle it.' A note to the woman or a phone call explaining all, he supposed. She had a right to that. She was a good conscientious teacher acting in a responsible manner. He mustn't laugh – except later perhaps with Burden.

There had been much food for thought picked up on his visits to Liskeard Avenue. And there had been something to make him wonder, something that was neither a piece of information nor the germ of an idea but entirely negative.

Wasn't it extraordinary that during those visits, those long talks, and during his initial interview with her, Wendy Williams had shown not the slightest interest in Rodney's other family? She had asked not a single question about the wife she had supplanted but not replaced, nor about the children who were siblings by half-blood of her own Veronica. Because she was inhibited by intense jealousy? Or for some other reason more germane to this inquiry?

11

Kevin Williams looked more like his mother than his father. He wouldn't have been recognizable as Veronica's half-brother. The genetic hand-down which was so distinctive a feature in Sara and Veronica had missed him and his forehead was narrow with the hair growing low on it. His manner was laconic, casual, indifferent.

Wexford, who had Martin with him, had interrupted what seemed to be a family conclave. For once the television was off, sight and sound. Joy Williams introduced no one but her son and his introduction she made proudly and with abnormal enthusiasm. Wexford was left to deduce that the woman and the girl who sat side by side on the yellow sofa must be Hope Harmer and her daughter Paulette.

Mrs Harmer, though plumper, fairer and better cared for than her sister, looked too much like her for her identity to be in doubt. She was a pretty woman and even in the present crisis she looked pleased with life. But the girl – to use an expression favoured by Wexford's grandsons – was 'something else again'. She was beautiful with a beauty that made Sara and Veronica merely pretty young girls. She reminded Wexford of a picture he had once seen, Rossetti's portrait of Mrs William Morris. This girl was dark and her face had the same dark glow as the face in the picture, her features the same symmetry and her large dark eyes the same otherworldly soulfulness. When he asked her if she was who he thought she was she raised those dark grey dreaming eyes and nodded, then returned to what she had been looking at, a magazine that seemed entirely devoted to hairstyles.

Kevin's term had ended the day before and he had come

straight home. Not to stay, though, he made clear to Wexford when they were alone in the stark dining room. He owed it to his mother to stay a few days, but next week he intended to stick to the plan he had made months before of going down to Cornwall to stay with a friend and later he would be camping in France. He seemed astonished when Wexford asked him for the address of the Cornish friend.

'We'd rather you didn't leave the country at present.'

'You can't keep me here. My father's death has nothing to do with me.'

'Tell me what you did on the evening of Thursday, April the fifteenth.'

'Was that when he died?' The casual manner had grown sullen. He was his mother in truculent mood all over again.

'I'll ask the questions, Kevin.'

It wasn't said roughly, but nevertheless the boy looked as if no one had spoken like that to him before. His low forehead creased and his mouth pouted.

'I only asked. He was my father.'

In his tone, that of contrived, badly acted sentiment, Wexford suddenly understood that no one in this household had cared a damn for Rodney Williams. And they hadn't in the other household either. People didn't care for him for long. In this area he had, at any rate, got his deserts.

'What happened that evening? What did you do?'

'Phoned home, I suppose,' he said, careless again. 'I always do on Thursdays or my mother goes bananas.'

'You phone from college?'

'No, the phones are always out of order or it's a hassle finding one that's free.' Kevin seemed to have decided he might as well give in to Wexford's questioning if not with a good grace. 'I go out to phone. Well, two or three of us do. To a pub. I phone home and transfer the charge.'

'You'll remember that Thursday if I tell you it was the first Thursday after you got back to college from the Easter vacation.'

The boy thought about it, seeming to concentrate. Wexford had no doubt he had known perfectly well all along.

'Yeah, I do remember. I phoned home around eight, eight-thirty – I don't reckon you want to know to the minute, do you? My mother was out. I talked to Sara.'

'That must have surprised you, your mother being out when you phoned.'

'Yeah, it was unusual. She thinks the sun shines out of my arse, as you've maybe noticed.' He jerked his shoulders in an exaggerated shrug. 'Unusual,' he said, 'but not unknown.'

More indignation came when Wexford asked for the names of Kevin's companions on the trip to the pub where the phone was. But it was hot air, pointless obstructiveness. The names were forthcoming after some expostulation.

'How did you get on with your father?'

'There was no communication. We didn't talk. The usual sort of situation, right?'

'And your father and Sara?'

The reply came sharply. It was incredible. It was exactly the reply a boy of Kevin's age might have made a hundred years before – or, according to literature, might have made.

'You can leave my sister out of this!'

Wexford tried not to laugh. 'I will for now.'

He found Joy and her sister questioning Martin in depth about Wendy Williams. The girls, the two cousins, had gone. Martin was answering in monosyllables and he looked relieved when Wexford came in. Joy broke off at once and, having seen he was alone, said, 'Where's my son?' as if Wexford might have arrested him and already stowed him away in a police car.

This would be his first encounter with Miles Gardner since the discovery of Rodney Williams's body. He and Burden waited for him in the managing director's office. The panelled room was dim and shadowy in spite of the bright day outside. A copper pot filled with Russell lupins stood on the window-sill. Wexford picked up the desk photograph of Gardner's family and looked at it dubiously.

'I suppose I'm sensitized to adolescent girls,' he said. 'I see them everywhere.'

'Just remember what the games mistress said.'

'I don't think I'm in danger, though they're a very pretty lot we're in contact with. One can almost see Williams's point of view.'

'He was just a dirty old lecher,' said Burden, apparently forgetting Williams had been a mere three years his senior.

'The primrose way to the everlasting bonfire.'

Gardner came in, apologizing for having kept them waiting. He began on some insincere-sounding expressions of sorrow at Williams's demise which Wexford listened to patiently and then cut short.

'If you're free for lunch we might all go over to the Old Flag.'

But this was something Gardner, regretfully, couldn't manage. 'I've promised to give my daughter lunch, my youngest one, Jane. She's got the day off school to go for an interview at the university here. A bit of an ordeal, she's a nervous kid, so I bribed her with the offer of a slap-up lunch.'

The University of the South was situated at Myringham. Another eighteen-year-old then . . .

'She should get a place,' Gardner said, and with a kind of rueful pride, 'There go our holidays abroad for the next three years.'

Wexford said he would like to talk to Christine Lomond, and in the room that had been Williams's if possible. Gardner took him there himself, up in the small slow lift. There were two desks and two typewriters, a Sierra 3400 and an Olympia ES 100. But this place was 'clean' as far as typewriters went. Martin had seen to that. The girl who came in was fresh-paint glossy in a suit of geranium-red linen, dark green cotton blouse, green glass rhomboid hanging on a chain and on her left wrist a watch with a red and green strap. Her hair had been touched with what his daughter Sylvia assured him were called 'low lights', though Wexford couldn't quite believe this and thought she must have been having him on. Christine Lomond's fingernails were the brilliant carmine of the latest Sevenshine front-door shade Pillarbox ('A rich true red without a hint of blue, a robust high gloss that stands up ideally to wind and weather'). They scuttled over the filing cabinet like so many red beetles.

Wexford had asked her to see what she could find him as samples of Williams's own typing, any report, assessment, rough notes even, he might have brought to the office with him. She said she was sure anything of that sort would have been handwritten, and it was two or three handwritten sheets that she produced for him, and then several more which she told him had probably been typed on the Olympia machine but using a different daisywheel, thus altering the typeface. Wexford was particularly interested because there seemed to him to be a flaw in the apex of the capital A.

The experiment, however, showed nothing but his own ignorance of typewriters or at any rate of recent technological advances made in typewriters. The red-tipped white fingers whipped a sheet of paper into the machine, switched it on, switched it off, whipped out the daisywheel, inserted another, and rapidly produced a facsimile of the first four lines of Williams's sales forecast for the first three months of the year.

'It's getting a bit ragged,' Christine Lomond said. 'We need a new wheel,' and she pulled the damaged one out and dropped it into the wastepaper basket.

'Where do you live, Miss Lomond?'

'Here. In Myringham. Why?' She had a rather abrupt manner, of the kind that is usually called 'crisp'.

'Did you like Mr Williams?'

She was silent. She seemed affronted, having anticipated perhaps nothing more than an investigation of papers and machines. How old was she? Twenty-six? Twenty-seven? She could be a good deal less than that. The heavy make-up and elaborate hairstyle aged her.

'Well, Miss Lomond?'

'Yes, I liked him. Well, I liked him all right. I didn't think about liking or disliking him.'

'Would you think back, please, and give me some idea of what you were doing on the evening of April the fifteenth?'

'I can't possibly remember that far back!'

Her eyelids flapped. They were a gleaming laminated sea blue ('Delicate turquoise with a hint of silver, ideal for that special ceiling, alcove or display cabinet').

'Try and pinpoint it,' said Burden, 'by thinking of what you were doing next day. That was the morning someone phoned to say Mr Williams was ill and wouldn't be in. Does that help?'

'I expect I was at home on my own.'

She didn't sound defensive, guilty, afraid. She sounded

293

sullen, as if the clothes and the make-up, the 'grooming' had not been effective.

'Do you live on your own or with someone?'

Surely the most innocent of questions. She pounced on it as surely as if those red nails had seized and clutched.

'I certainly do not live with someone! I was at home on my own watching the TV.'

Another one. What had they done in the old days before the cathode conquest? He ought to be able to remember pre-television alibis but he couldn't. I was reading, sewing, putting up shelves, fishing, listening to the radio, out for a walk, in the pub, at the pictures? Maybe.

Unwillingly, even grudgingly, she gave them her address. She admitted to possessing a typewriter, an old Smith Corona, though not a portable, and insisted it was in her parents' house in Tonbridge and she had never had it with her in the Myringham bedsit.

Downstairs in the reception area they encountered a young girl undressing. Or so to Wexford's astonished eyes it at first appeared. She was talking to the telephonist (Anna today) and in the act of pulling a cotton dress off over her head. Long slim legs in white tights, pale blue pumps with curly heels, and yes, a skirt which dropped to its former just-above-the-knee length when the garment, evidently a middy blouse, was off. Underneath it was a white tee-shirt. Her back was to Wexford. She kicked off the blue pumps, sending one flying across the room and leaving no doubt in the mind of an observer that this was a cathartic shedding of a hateful costume after an ordeal was over.

'Jane,' said Anna in a warning tone, 'there are some . . .'

She spun round. On the front of the tee-shirt were printed the letters ARRIA.

The first thing that struck Wexford about the house in Down Road, Kingsmarkham, was that there was no question of any of its occupants being obliged to share a bedroom. It was a very large, castellated, turreted, balconied Edwardian pile. Most houses like it had been converted into flats but not this one. A single family inhabited it and its (at least) eight bedrooms. Yet Eve Freeborn had given him the reason for going to her boyfriend in Myringham instead of his coming to her that she shared a bedroom with her sister. Perhaps she hadn't a sister either. He would soon see.

At first he thought the girl who opened the front door to him *was* Eve. After all, the fact that this one had green hair meant nothing. They changed their hair colour these days as fast as they used to change their lipstick. A second look told him they weren't even identical twins. Twins, yes, fraternal twins with the same build of body and the same eyes. That was all. God knew what colour their hair really was. They had probably forgotten themselves.

The house smelt faintly of marijuana. An unmistakable smell that was like woodsmoke blended with sweet cologne.

'Eve?' Eve's sister said with incredulity. 'You want to see Eve?'

'Is that so difficult?'

'I don't know really . . .'

He had shown her his warrant card. After all, she was a young girl and it was evening. She shouldn't admit unidentified men into the house. But she was looking at it as if it were a warrant for her arrest. He felt impatient.

'Perhaps I should fill in a form or produce a sponsor.'

'Oh, no, come in. I'm sorry. It's just that . . .'

She had an irritating way of leaving her sentences unfinished. He followed her into the hall, darkly panelled like the offices of Sevensmith Harding, and up a big elegant winding staircase with a gallery at the top. The marijuana smell was fainter but it was still there. What astonished him about the house was the aura of the sixties that pervaded it. On the wall here was a poster (albeit a glazed and framed poster) of John Lennon seated at a white grand piano. A vase stood on a side table filled with dried grasses and shabby peacock's tail feathers. And hanging up as an ornament, not because it had been left there by chance, was an antique red silk dress embroidered with gold, its red and its gold tattered and shredded by time and moths. He said, 'Are your parents at home?'

'They've got a flat in London. They're there half the time.'

Impossible to tell if she minded or was glad. Those parents need not be more than forty themselves, he thought, and

Mother might be less. Eve's twin said, 'Perhaps you'd better wait here. I'll just see if . . .'

All the bedroom doors were open. Only they weren't bedrooms, not exactly. Each one, as far as he could see, had the look rather of a bedsit, with chairs and tables and floor cushions and a couch or divan with an Indian bedspread flung artlessly over it, posters on the walls and postcards pinned up higgledy-piggledy. He sat down to wait in a rocking chair that had its rockers painted red, black and white and a dirty lace veil draped over its back, and wondered how to explain this mysterious house.

Then he understood. It wasn't the girls who were living in the past, who were twenty years out of date, or purposely living in an anachronism. Those parents had been young in the sixties, had revelled probably in that new inspiring freedom, and now the spirit of the sixties, the flavour, the mores would never leave them. Not the girls but the parents were the marijuana users. He would have to do something about that . . .

How long was she going to keep him waiting?

He got up and went out into the passage. There was no one about. But from somewhere he could hear the sound of female voices – a sound that was not in the least like the twittering of birds, strong earnest talk rather than a murmuration. A staircase led to the attic floor but it wasn't from up there that the voices came.

There was a burst of laughter, some sporadic clapping. He walked down the passage towards the sound, came out into another smaller, squarer landing, a map of the heavens painted on its ceiling by a trained but unsure hand. An amateur astrologer who had been to art school, he thought, which brought the sixties once more to mind. As he stood there, doubtful of the wisdom of bursting into a room full of women, the door opened and two girls came out. They stopped in the doorway, looking at him in astonishment. One was unknown to him, the other was Caroline Peters, physical training instructor.

Before anyone spoke Eve Freeborn came out of the room, shouldering her way past the two who blocked the doorway. She was once more in the pelvis-crusher jeans but this time with a purple satin blouse to match her hair. Caroline Peters, on the other hand, was dressed exactly like a boy – or like boys used to dress before punk apparel came to stay: blue jeans, brown leather jacket, half-boots; no make-up, hair cropped in a crewcut.

'Sorry,' Eve said. 'Have you been waiting long?'

'*They* kept *us* waiting,' said Caroline Peters with the maximum venom, 'for four thousand years.'

She had recognized him and wasn't pleased. Or had he been recognized for what he was in addition to being a policeman – a man? Wexford had never before personally encountered the kind of militant feminist who advocates total separatism. Enlightenment broke upon him.

'Have I by any chance interrupted a meeting of ARRIA?'

'It's over,' said Eve. 'It's just over.'

'We wouldn't have permitted interruption.'

Wexford looked at Caroline Peters. 'Don't go yet, please. I'd like to talk to you too.'

She lifted her shoulders, went back into the room. Eve waved a hand at the other girl, a pretty, sharp-faced redhead.

'This is Nicky.'

Inside the room, another, larger, bedsit hung with striped bedspreads on ceilings and walls like a Bedouin tent, half a dozen more girls were standing about or preparing to leave. Sara Williams was there and her cousin Paulette, the two of them talking to Jane Gardner, and all of them wearing ARRIA tee-shirts. A black girl, thin and elegant as a model, sat crosslegged on a floor cushion.

Eve said to the company, 'I don't remember what he's called,' as if it hardly mattered, 'but he's a policeman.' She pointed at one girl after another: 'Jane, Sara, Paulette, Donella, Helen, Elaine, and Amy, my sister, you've met.'

Caroline Peters pushed her hands into the pockets of her leather jacket.

'What is it you want?'

'I'd like to know more about ARRIA for a start.'

'For a *start* it was *started* by me and a like-minded woman, a classical scholar now at Oxford.' She paused. 'Arria Paeta,' she said, 'was a Roman matron, the wife of Caecina Paetus. Of course she was obliged to take his name.' Wexford could tell she was one of those fanatics who never miss a trick. 'Ancient Rome was known for its gross oppression and exploitation of women.' Teacher-like, she waited for his comments.

They came – perhaps to her surprise. 'The Emperor Claudius,' said Wexford who had done his homework, 'ordered Paetus to commit suicide but he proved too cowardly, so his wife took the sword and plunging it into her own heart, said, "See Paetus, it does not hurt . . ." '

'You've been reading Graves!'

'No. *Smith's Classical Dictionary*.' The girl called Nicky laughed. 'But I don't know what the letters stand for,' he said.

'Action for the Radical Reform of Intersexual Attitudes.'

'A case of making the nym fit the acronym? Or is it a deliberate obscuration?'

'Perhaps it is.'

'How many schools are involved?'

It was Eve who answered him. 'Kingsmarkham High, Haldon Finch, St Catherine's . . .' but Caroline Peters interrupted her.

'I teach at Haldon Finch. ARRIA had its inception just over a year ago at St Catherine's. We admitted as members only those women over sixteen, those in fact in the sixth and seventh years. I'm glad to say it had an immediate appeal – how could an organization designed expressly for women, designed to give men no quarter – be otherwise?' She turned on him a glacial look of distaste and it gave him a most unpleasant feeling. He didn't belong to a minority, there was no way he could be categorized into a minority, yet the sensation she gave him was of doing so and of an oppressed one at that. 'Our very well-organized propaganda machine,' she said, 'spread the good news through the other schools in the area and we soon had considerable cells at Pomfret College of Further Education and Kingsmarkham High.' The good news, he thought, the 'gospel' no less. She astonished him by saying, 'We now have a membership of just over five hundred women.'

He suppressed the whistle he wanted to give. What must the local population of seventeen- and eighteen-year-old girls be? All of them, including those who had left school, could surely hardly amount to more than a couple of thousand and that meant 25 per cent in ARRIA. Why, they could almost start a revolution!

'All right, you've got badges, you've had tee-shirts printed, you hold meetings, but what do you *do*?'

Caroline Peters answered readily. 'Basically, have as little contact with men as possible. Defy men by intellectual and also by physical means.'

He pricked up his ears at that. She wasn't carrying a bag but she had pockets. Most of the other girls had bags. He hadn't got a warrant and, almost more to the point, hadn't a woman with him to carry out a search.

'We have a constitution and manifesto,' she said. 'I expect there's a copy about and I see no objection to your having one. Would you women agree to that?' There was a murmur of assent, some of it amused. 'But I must point out that our aim isn't to meet men on equal terms. It isn't to come to a truce or compromise with them nor to reach that uneasy détente which in past revolutions has sometimes come into being between a proletariat and a bourgeoisie. As Marx said in another context: Philosophers have tried to explain the world. The point surely is to change it. Good night, everyone.' She went out of the room, closing the door with a somewhat sinister quietness behind her.

Silence. The black girl, Donella, cast up her eyes, rolling sloe-brown pupils in moon-white whites. Eve said, 'By physical means, she only meant self-defence stuff. It's compulsory when you join to take a self-defence course, karate or judo or tai chi or whatever.'

'Personally,' said Donella, 'I think that's one of the things that attracts people – the sport, you know.'

'You may have noticed, there've been three times as many evening courses in martial arts started since ARRIA began. That's in response to increased demand, that's ARRIA.'

Nicky had spoken with pride, not aggressively. She made a swift chopping movement with one arm. Wexford, a large man over six feet tall, felt relieved he wasn't on the receiving end of that blow. It was true about the judo and karate courses, he had remarked on it himself to Burden, pleased that women were at last taking steps to defend themselves against the muggings and rapes which in the past few years had so disproportionately increased.

299

'All right,' he said, 'that's for self-defence. How about aggression? I don't suppose anyone's going to admit to carrying an offensive weapon?'

Nobody was. They didn't look scared or guilty or even alert. He fancied he saw wariness in one or two faces.

'I'll give you a copy of the constitution,' Eve said. 'There's nothing private about it. Everyone's welcome to know what we do, men as well as women. Do you have daughters?'

'They're a lot older than you.'

She looked at him in a not unkindly way, assessing. 'Well, they would be, wouldn't they? You can't be too old for ARRIA, though.'

The constitution was typed and photocopied. He noted that there were no flaws in the apexes of the capital As or the ascenders of the lower-case ts. It went into his pocket to be read at leisure. Sara Williams, he observed, was watching his every movement. The big fair girl called Helen he now realized had been Eve's partner in the tennis match. He said to Eve, 'If everyone is in fact going I'd like to talk to you alone for five minutes.'

The brisk policeman's tone replacing the one of easy jocularity seemed to jolt her. She pushed fingers through the purple crest of hair.

'OK, if that's the way you want it. Everybody out, right?' She gave a hiccuping giggle. 'Home, women!'

Amy said, 'Well, I think I'll just . . .' and drifted vaguely towards the door.

They all began to take their leave in ways peculiar to young girls, whether feminists or reactionaries. Helen and Donella closed in upon each other with a tight bear hug which ended in giggles and heads subsiding on each other's shoulders. Sara wrapped her arms round herself and moved across the floor with vague dancing steps. Jane humped her bag, filled with ARRIA constitution sheets, as if it weighed a ton, making agony faces. Nicky was lost in a dream that seemed to turn her into a sleepwalker so that she neither paused in her exit nor spoke but merely raised a languid flapping hand in farewell as she passed through the doorway.

Alone with Eve, Wexford said, 'You've been telling me lies.'

'I have not!'

300

'Why did you tell me your boyfriend couldn't come here because you had to share a bedroom with your sister? This is an enormous house and as far as I can see your parents mostly aren't here anyway. But you told me lack of space – and you implied lack of privacy – stopped him coming here.'

'Well,' she said, a sly look in her eyes, 'I can explain that. You'll see the answer in our constitution actually. Rule 4.'

He pulled the constitution out of his pocket. Here it was, Rule 4. 'Women' – not ARRIA members, he saw, but always 'women' as if the society contained the world's entire female population – 'Women shall avoid the company of men wherever possible but should their presence be required for sexual, biological, business or career purposes, it is expedient and desirable for women to go to them rather than permit them to come to us.'

'But why?'

'Caroline and Edwina – she's the classical one who's at Oxford – they said it smacked of the sultan visiting his harem. You've got to think it through, you know. When you do you can see what they mean.'

'So that's why you went to your boyfriend in Arnold Road? You required his presence for sexual or even biological purposes?'

'Isn't that why women usually require men?'

'There are other ways of putting it. More aesthetic ways, I'd say. Maybe more civilized.'

'Oh, *civilized*. Men made civilization and it's not up to much, is it? It's no big deal.'

He left it. 'Did you know Sara Williams was the daughter of the murdered man whose car you saw in Arnold Road?'

'Not then I didn't. I do now. Look, I only know her through ARRIA and I didn't know her father. For all I knew, she mightn't have had a father.'

He accepted that. 'Miss Peters didn't tell me much about this society of yours, did she? Only that it's a wildfire movement, it's caught on in all the local schools. How about the – what shall I call it? – esoteric stuff? How do you join? Do you pay a subscription? Is there any sort of ritual – like freemasons, say?'

'We don't need money,' she said, 'so there's no sub. Where would they get it from anyway? Most of our members are still at school. They'd have to get it from their fathers and that's out. See Rule 6 on dependence. The only thing that costs us is the photocopying, only it doesn't because Nicky does it on her dad's Xerox in the night, when he's asleep.'

There was an irony there but Wexford didn't point it out. 'Anyone can join?'

'Any woman over sixteen who's not married. Obviously a married woman has already capitulated. Anyway, it wouldn't be possible for her to keep to the rules.'

'That would let my daughters out.'

She ignored him. 'I'm a founder member. When we started there was a lot of really wayout stuff going on. Edwina wanted initiation ceremonies, sort of baptisms of fire if you can imagine.'

'What sort?'

He was deeply curious. At the same time he was afraid she would soon realize she was spending too much time unnecessarily in the society of a man. She considered his question in thoughtful silence. She was not a pretty girl. But perhaps this didn't matter in these days when beauty was no longer at a premium. She had one of those chinless faces, long-nosed, full-lipped, but with creamy delicate skin. A frown creased, or rather crumpled, her forehead. Creasing was for older people. Eve's frown was like the bunching of a piece of cream velvet.

'Some of the others went along with her ideas,' she said. 'I mean, she was a radical feminist. For instance, she used to say we couldn't make revolution on Marxist principles on account of Marx having been a man. She said sexuality was politics and the only way to get freedom was for all women to be lesbians. Any hetero behaviour was collaborating with the enemy. Even Caroline Peters never went as far as that.'

'You were going to tell me about initiation.'

Eve seemed reluctant to reach the subject. 'They actually formed a splinter group over it. Sara, the one whose father was murdered, she was one of them and Nicky Anerley was another. One of the things they objected to was being educated along with the other sex. They wanted schools and colleges run by women and with women teachers. Of course, it would be best, it's the ideal if you know what I mean, but it's a bit fantastic.'

'Particularly as it's only in very recent years that women have gained admission to certain men's colleges, notably at Oxford.'

'That's beside the point. This would be a question of getting the men out altogether. Edwina and the rest of them who were at mixed schools wanted to go on strike until they agreed not to admit boys. But Caroline wouldn't have that. I suppose she was afraid of losing her job.'

'And that's what caused the rift in the party?'

'Well, partly. This was all last summer and autumn. It more or less stopped when Edwina went up to Oxford in October and the others drifted back. I may as well tell you. It was all a sort of fantasy anyway. Edwina said in order to prove herself a true feminist a woman ought to kill a man.' Eve looked at him warily. 'I don't mean everyone who joined ARRIA was to have to kill a man to get to be a member. The idea was for groups of three or four to get together and . . .

'But that's not an initiation ceremony really, is it? I could tell you about some of those if you want.'

12

With inscrutable face Jenny Burden sat reading ARRIA's manifesto. She was past the stage now of prettifying disguises of her pregnancy. It was beyond disguise and her condition didn't flatter her. Younger than her years though she had always looked, she now appeared too old to be having a baby. Her face was not so much lined as lacking in its former firmness, caverns hollowed out under the eyes and chin muscles sagging. She had no lap now so she held the flimsy sheets against a book propped up on the table in front of her.

But Wexford could tell by Burden's pleased expression that he was content to see his wife making even this small effort to escape from the apathy that had settled on her as the psychotherapy she was having progressed. No longer in revolt, no longer violent in her hatred of the child, she had become resigned. She waited in hopeless passivity. When Wexford arrived she had taken his hand, put up her face for a kiss, inquired in a limbo voice after Dora and the girls. And he had thought: when the baby is born she could go completely mad, enter a schizophrenic world and pass the rest of her life in hospital. She wouldn't be the first to whom such a thing had happened.

Still, now she was reading ARRIA's constitution, and apparently reading every word with care. Wexford wouldn't talk about the Williams case in her presence and Burden knew that. Suddenly she began reading aloud.

'Rule 6: With certain limited exceptions, no woman shall be financially dependent on a man. Then they list the exceptions. Rule 7: All women shall take a course in some martial art or self-defence technique. Rule 8: All women shall carry a permitted weapon for self-defence, i.e. ammonia spray, pin, penknife, pepper shaker, etc. Rule 9: No member shall marry, participate in the bourgeois concept of becoming 'engaged' or share accommodation with a man in a cohabiting situation. Rule 10 . . . Do you want Rule 10?'

'Oh, I have read it,' Wexford said. 'It is heresy!'

She didn't recognize the quotation. 'You're bound to think that way, aren't you? Perhaps I should have read all this before I met you, Mike.'

He took the blow with a physical flinch.

'ARRIA didn't exist then. It was around earlier this year before I gave up work, though. I always wanted to get hold of their manifesto but no one would even talk to me about it. I was a married woman, you see.'

'I suppose I was lucky to get it,' Wexford conceded.

Burden was making an effort to recover from the pain she had given him. 'I want to hear Rule 10.'

'All right. Rule 10: Women wishing to reproduce should select the potential father for his physique, health, height, etc., and ensure impregnation in a rape or near-rape construct.'

'In a *what*? What the hell does it mean?'

Wexford said, 'Margaret Mead says men of the Arapesh fear rape by women just as women in other cultures fear rape by men.'

'The mind boggles.' By this, Wexford knew, Burden meant he would dearly have loved to inquire further into the mechanics and techniques but was hampered by inhibition. 'The trouble is surely that most of this was written by lesbians like Edwina Klein and Caroline Peters. It doesn't seem to cater for women who actually *love* men – and those are surely in the vast majority.'

Jenny looked coldly at her husband. 'In the sort of explanation bit that comes after the rules it says the authors realize woman may feel affection for men and even – I quote – "what is termed sexual love" but it is necessary that something must be given up for the cause. Other women in the past have denied themselves this indulgence and been amply compensated. It goes on: "After all, what does this so-called 'love' amount to when a woman sets it against its concomi-

305

tants: gross exploitation, pornography, degradation, career prohibition or curtailment, rape, father-daughter incest and the still-persisting double standard?" '

'It doesn't seem to bear much relation to our own home lives, does it?' said Burden.

Jenny had tears in her eyes, Wexford saw. They shone there, unshed. 'Revolutionaries are always extreme,' she said. 'Look at the Terror of 1793, look at Stalinism. If they're not, if they compromise with liberalism, all their principles fizzle out and you're back with the status quo. Isn't that what's happened to the broader women's liberation movement?'

The men looked at her with varying expression of doubt and dismay. Burden had gone rather pale.

'If these girls,' said Jenny, 'can accomplish just a fraction of what they're setting out to do, if they can begin to make people see what "inequitable arbitration" really amounts to, perhaps – perhaps I shan't so much mind my daughter being born.'

This time she didn't break down into tears. 'I know you want to talk. I'll leave you.' She turned to her husband, kissed his forehead, carried herself clumsily to the door. There was no dignity there and no beauty because the child that made her heavy was unwanted ... Burden put out one finger to touch the ARRIA manifesto like someone steeling himself to make contact with something he has a phobia about.

'I feel it threatens me, all this. I'm frightened of it.'

'It's good that you're honest enough to admit it.'

'Do you really think there's anything in this killing a man stuff?'

He had done so at first. It had seemed the obvious answer and for a moment or two the only possible answer. At that point his whole tone towards Eve had changed. He had been dancing lightly with her and then, suddenly, the music stopped and he seized hold of her. That was what it was like. Of course, he had frightened her with his quick rough questions ...

'But nobody ever did it! It was a fantasy – like group sex or something. Like an orgy. You think about what it would be like, you fantasize, but you don't *do* it.'

'Many do.'

'Well, OK, that wasn't a very good comparison. The point is fantasy doesn't become reality, the two don't mix.'

'Don't they? Isn't that what a psychopath is? Someone who confuses fantasy with reality?'

She had insisted, with the panic of someone who realizes she has said too much, that Edwina Klein's idea had been hers alone, even the splinter group had opposed it. Knives next. He had gone on to ask her what was meant by 'permitted weapons'. Did this category include knives? Not *real* knives, she said, and she had looked at him as a child might, round-eyed, afraid of something it doesn't understand.

'It's tempting,' he said to Burden, 'to think of a group of those ARRIA girls grabbing hold of poor old Williams like the Maenads with Orpheus and doing him in on the Lesbian shore.'

Burden looked at him, mystified. 'Shall we have a beer?' he said.

'Good idea.'

> ' "Malt does more than Milton can
> To justify the ways of God to man". '

'You're right there,' Burden said feelingly.

He came back with two cans and two tankards on a tray. Poor chap, Wexford thought, he's had enough. And how curious it was that all these dramatic things happened to Burden, who was such an ordinary, unimaginative, salt-of-the-earth person. The prototype surely of Kafka's man to whom who, though he shut himself up in his room, hid himself, lay low, life nevertheless came in and rolled in ecstasy at his feet. Whereas for him, Wexford, nothing much came along to disturb his private peace. Thank God for it!

'Just the same,' he said, 'we're going to have our work cut out checking out every one of ARRIA's members. There are said to be five hundred of them, remember.'

'The girl who stabbed Budd may not be the same girl who stabbed Wheatley who may not be the same girl as the one that killed Williams, but on the other hand they may be one and the same.'

'Right,' said Wexford. 'But don't let's talk of the "one" that killed Williams. No girl on her own could have carried

307

his body into that car and then carried it out again and buried him.'

'The way I see it, we have to think of it along these lines. On the one hand we have the radical feminists of whom we know (a) that the notion of killing a man was at any rate considered by them and (b) that they are required by their own rules to carry offensive weapons. We also know that Wheatley certainly and Budd probably were stabbed by ARRIA members. We've been told too that Williams, pursuing his well-known tastes, had a very young girl-friend. Now is this girlfriend a member of ARRIA?'

'Whatever the ARRIA rules may say,' said Wexford, 'we know members do have to do with the opposite sex. Look at Eve climbing in through her boyfriend's window. She hasn't made the supreme sacrifice of giving up men. And if you want to kill a man what better way of doing it than in what ARRIA would probably call a libido-emotional construct – in other words a love affair?'

Burden finished the last of his beer. In the next room Jenny had put a record on, Ravel's *Pavane on a Dead Infanta*. 'Who said that about malt and Milton?'

'Houseman. His life was ruined by an unrequited love.'

'Blimey. Why ravens?'

'In ARRIA's logo, d'you mean? They're predatory birds, aren't they? No, I suppose not. Harsh-tongued? I really don't know, Mike. At any rate, they're not soft and submissive. The collective noun for them is an "unkindness". An Unkindness of Ravens. Appropriate, wouldn't you say? In their attitude to the opposite sex anyway. They stab at us with knives rather than beaks.'

'Not without provocation, of course.'

'That's true. Budd on his own admission tried to get fresh with the girl who attacked him. He may have got fresher than he says. Wheatley says he didn't get fresh at all but I'm not inclined to believe him. They made passes and got themselves stabbed. Makes you wonder what Williams did, doesn't it?'

As Wexford walked home he thought about what he had had to do as a result of his visit to the Freeborns' house.

Sergeant Martin and Detective Bennett had paid a follow-up call and this morning Charles Freeborn, the girls' father, had appeared at Kingsmarkham Magistrates' Court charged with possessing cannabis and with permitting cannabis to be smoked upon his premises. Bennett, who detected the stuff in a positively cat-and-mouse way – or cat-and-catmint way – had begun a methodical search of the big overgrown garden, starting at the conservatory, following the crazy-paving path through a copse of unpruned dusty shrubs. This path curved all round the perimeter of the garden, winding its way between ghosts of flowerbeds where a few attenuated cultivated plants thrust their heads through a matting of bindweed, ground elder and thistles. A gate in the fence at the garden's foot afforded a shortcut into a path to the High Street. Bennett had been wondering if he was getting obsessional imagining *Cannabis sativa*, which requires sunlight and space, might even flourish here when he suddenly came upon the only tended flowerbed in the whole half acre.

He was nearly back at the house again, the stifling, shadow-spreading trees behind him. A neat rectangular clearing had been made in the shaggy grass here, the soil well watered, weeded, and the bed bordered with bricks. Martin had declared the vigorous young plants to be seedling tomatoes but Bennett knew better. Infra-red light is essential to the Indian hemp if its effect when ingested is to be the characteristically hallucinogenic one, and these plants were basking in it, for their bed was in the only part of the garden to enjoy day-long uninterrupted sunshine.

Wexford pondered, not for the first time, on the ethics of going into someone's house for a check and a chat, while there detecting a forbidden drug and immediately, scarcely with a qualm, taking steps to prosecute the offender. One's host *in absentia*, so to speak. Of course he was right, *it* was right. He was a policeman and that came first. That must always come first or chaos would come instead . . .

By the time the schools broke up towards the end of July Wexford's men had vetted and cleared something like 50 per cent of the ARRIA membership. Tracking them down was the difficulty, for Caroline Peters denied the existence of a list of members. Why should a list be needed when there was no subscription, and dates and venues of meetings were passed on by grassroots?

Paulette Harmer, Williams's niece, a sixth-form-college student, was cleared. She had been out with her boyfriend, to whom she would become engaged at Christmas – thereby abrogating ARRIA membership? – on the evenings Budd and Wheatley were stabbed, and at home with her parents and her aunt Joy on 15 April. Eve Freeborn, before going to her boyfriend in Arnold Road, had spent the evening at home with her parents and her sister. This alibi also accounted for Amy. Neither could be cleared of the Budd and Wheatley stabbings. Nor could Caroline Peters who, however, had been at a meeting in London on the evening of the 15th. The redheaded Nicky turned out to be Nicola Anerley and not the Nicola Tennyson who was Veronica Williams's friend. She had been at a party on 15 April, Helen Blake's eighteenth party, which had also been attended by another twelve members of ARRIA, all of whom Wexford was able to discount as far as the murder of Williams was concerned.

Jane Gardner he questioned himself. She was the right age, pretty and lively, an active member of ARRIA. He owed it to the cordial relationship he had had with her father to go himself and not send Bennett, say, or Archbold.

Miles was at home, had made a point evidently of being at home. He was affronted and preparing to be bitterly offended. He and his tall wife were in the drawing room (walls of Sevenstar Chinese yellow, black carpet, *famille jaune* porcelain) and Wexford was shown in by the cleaning lady masquerading as a maid. They spoke to him, he thought, in the aghast tones of parents asking a headmaster why he intends to expel their daughter from his school. Pamela Gardner called him 'Mr Wexford' though it had been 'Reg' in the past. Since she had no means of summoning the cleaning lady except by shouting, she went to fetch Jane herself.

'This is so entirely unnecessary,' Gardner said in a hard voice.

Wexford said it was routine and felt like a cop in an ancient Cyril Hare detective story.

The girl came in smiling and perfectly at ease. Then he had to ask the parents to go. They did but with a very ill grace. At first Pamela Gardner pretended she didn't understand what he meant. Light dawned, then came incredulity, lastly disgusted acceptance. She took her husband's arm as if the very cornerstones of their home life had been threatened.

'Did you get a university place? Wexford asked Jane as soon as they were alone.

'Oh, yes, thanks. We met before, didn't we? At Dad's office? I never thought I would actually. I'd even enrolled at secretarial college in London just in case. My school doesn't have a commercial department.'

There came back to him a recollection of this girl changing her clothes in full view of the street. In 'Dad's office'. And when she had turned round to see him looking at her she hadn't turned a hair.

'Did you know Rodney Williams, Jane?'

'I'd met him. At the office. Dad introduced us. He had a lot of charm, you know.' She smiled, reminiscently, a bit sadly. 'He could make you feel you were the only person there worth talking to.'

It struck Wexford that this was the first person he had spoken to with a good word to say for Rodney Williams. She spoiled it a little.

'I expect he was like that with all girls of my age.'

Was she an enthusiastic member of ARRIA? Had she been in the splinter group? Did she carry a weapon? Where had she been when Budd was stabbed, when Wheatley was stabbed, when Williams was killed? Yes to the first and second questions, an indignant no, wide-eyed and law-abiding, to the third. A baby-sitting alibi for 15 April, a visit to her newly married sister for a Budd alibi, no memory of what she had been doing on the evening of the Wheatley stabbing. Apropos of none of this, surprising her with what seemed inconsequential, he said, 'Which schools do have commercial departments?'

'Haldon Finch, Sewingbury Sixth Form.' She gave him an earnest look. 'Dad's really upset that you suspect me.'

'There's no question of that. This is routine.'

'Well . . .' Suddenly she was the good daughter, dutiful, compliant, obedient. 'He and Mummy are dead against you taking my fingerprints.'

'You' presumably implied the Mid-Sussex Constabulary

or did she think he had come armed with pads and gadgets? The cleaning lady showed him out, her apron changed for rather smart dungarees. There was no sign of Miles or Pamela. Donaldson drove him back to Kingsmarkham and dropped him outside his own house. Dora, dressed up, was on the phone to Sylvia.

He passed close by her and touched her cheek with his lips. She responded to the kiss, mouthed something about getting a move on, went on talking to Sylvia. He went upstairs, changed into what he called his best suit, grey like the others but the latest and least shabby. When he retired he would never wear a suit again – not even to the theatre.

In the train he told Dora about the Gardners and said he had a feeling they wouldn't be asked to any more garden parties. She said that didn't matter, did it? she didn't care. And he shouldn't care either, he should relax, especially tonight.

'I wish I'd read the play.'

'You haven't had time.'

'You can always make time for things you want to do,' he said.

As it was he didn't even know what *The Cenci* was about and of its history only that it had for a long time been banned from the English stage. He and Dora, on holiday in Italy, had seen Guido Reni's portrait of Beatrice Cenci in the Galleria Nazionale in Rome, though he wouldn't have connected that with the play but for Sheila's saying it would be reproduced in the programme. It would have been a good idea to have read the play – or to have read Moravia's *Beatrice Cenci*, a novel that might be more entertaining.

The play threatened at first not to entertain at all. Shelley, Wexford thought to himself while aware he was no informed critic, wasn't Shakespeare. And wasn't he, in writing this sort of five-act tragedy in blank verse, some two hundred years out of date? Then Sheila came on, not looking like the portrait but with a small cap on her golden hair and dressed in white and grey, and he forgot everything, even the play, in his consuming pride in her. She had a peculiar quality in her acting, which critics as well as he had remarked on, of bringing clarity to obscure or periphrastic lines, so that her entrances always seemed to let light in upon the arcane. It was so now, it continued to be so . . . He saw and understood. The plot and purpose of the play began to unfold themselves for him and Shelley's style ceased to be an anachronism.

The effect on Dora was less happy.

She whispered to Wexford while they were having a glass of wine during the interval, 'There's more to it than I can see, I know that. It's not just that they can't stand the old man's harshness any longer, is it? I mean, why did Sheila come tearing in screaming about her eyes being full of blood?'

'Her father raped her.' Wexford realized what he had said and corrected himself. 'Count Cenci raped his daughter Beatrice.'

'I see. Oh yes, I do see. It's not made very clear, is it?'

'I imagine Shelley couldn't afford to spell it out. As it was, it must have been the incest theme that got the play banned.'

While waiting for the curtain to go up on Act Four he read the essay on the historical facts on which the play was based which had been written for the programme by an eminent historian. Beatrice, her stepmother and her brother had been put to death for the murder of Count Cenci. They really had. It had all happened. Guido had painted the portrait while Beatrice was in prison. Later they had tortured her to extract a confession.

It wasn't the kind of piece, he decided, that one would ever want to see again or read or remember a line from. When it was over they went backstage. They always did. Sheila, though in jeans and sweater now, still had a mask of gleaming white paint on her face and her hair top-knotted for execution as when she had cried:

> '. . . Here, Mother, tie
> My girdle for me . . . My Lord,
> We are quite ready. Well, 'tis very well.'

Going home, Dora fell asleep in the train. Wexford found his mind occupied with the prosaic subject of typewriters.

It was the caretaker of the Haldon Finch Comprehensive School, primed by a phone call from the County Education

313

Department, who showed them round. Wexford had been inside the school before, years ago when the nucleus of these buildings had been the old county high school. Incorporated into it now were the buildings next door, a former clinic and health centre, as well as a vast new assembly hall and the glass, concrete and blue-slate complex of classrooms, music room and concert hall, with the sports centre a gilt-roofed rotunda that the sun set ablaze.

'It reminds me,' Wexford said to Burden, 'of a picture I once saw of the Golden Temple at Amritsar.'

But the commercial department had no new building to house it. It was pushed away into three rear classrooms at the top of the old high school, as if the education authority had half-heartedly accepted the recent remark of a government minister that shorthand and typing were no part of education and should not be taught in schools. Wexford followed Burden and the caretaker up a remarkable (and remarkably battered) Art Deco marble staircase and along a wide vaulted passage. The caretaker unlocked and opened the double doors into the commercial department. These too were Art Deco, with parabolas and leaves in green ironwork on their frosted glass. The old high school had been built in 1930 and the classrooms inside looked as if they had received no more than one coat of paint since then. They were shabby, typically green and cream, with a view of rooftops and a brick well full of dustbins.

It was in the farthest room that the typewriters were. Wexford asked himself what he had expected. The latest in word processors? Obviously here the country's resources were mainly devoted to science and sport. Nor presumably would ARRIA encourage its members towards a secretarial career. There was not an electric typewriter among the machines and some of them looked older than the building itself. Burden, walking between the tables, had a piece of paper in his hand, probably with the faults of the typewriter they were looking for written on it. As if he couldn't remember without that! A break in the head of the uppercase A and the ascender of the lower-case t, a comma with a smudged head.

He felt a small flicker of excitement when he spotted the first of the Remington 315s.

314

'Can you type?'

'Enough to test these,' said Burden and impressed Wexford by getting to work and using all his fingers.

Nothing wrong with the A, the t and the comma on the first one. Burden slipped his paper into the roller of the second. The capital A wasn't all it might have been but neither was the B or the D or a lot of others. The lower-case faces and the comma seemed unflawed. He tried the third machine, the caretaker watching with the fascinated awe of one who expects the litmus paper to turn not red but all the colours of the spectrum. This typewriter, however, seemed without faults. It produced the best-looking copy so far. There was only one more. Burden slipped his paper in and this time, instead of 'Now is the time of All good men to come to the Aid of the party', typed 'A thousand ages in Thy sight are like an evening gone'. If he had been a Freudian, Wexford thought, he would have wanted to know why. Perhaps it was just done to astonish the caretaker. Anyway, whatever the reason, this wasn't the machine Rodney Williams's letter of resignation had been typed on.

'That's it then.'

'Show my four samples to the experts. We could be wrong.'

'We're not wrong. These are all the typewriters the school has?'

'Apart from them as has gone away to be serviced.'

'Now he tells me,' said Wexford.

'There's always some go away in the summer holidays. It's never the lot of them. They go in, like, rotation.'

'Do you know how many have gone and where?'

The caretaker didn't know the answer to either question. No more than, say, five, he thought. He had never heard the name of any firm which might be servicing the machines or seen a van arrive to take them away.

'We must be thankful,' Wexford said as they came out of the school, 'that at least it's an old manual portable we're looking for and not one of the modern kind with a golfball or daisywheel.'

'A what or a *what*?'

'Let's say with a detachable typeface that our perpetrator could simply have taken out and thrown away.'

315

School might have broken up but sport went on. Half a dozen boys in shorts and tee-shirts were running laps round the biggest playing field and on the tennis courts a doubles game and a singles were in progress. The umpire seats were empty but Caroline Peters was there in the role of coach, and as they approached the wire fencing Wexford saw that what he had supposed to be a singles match was in fact instructor and instructed, the pupil here being Veronica Williams.

The four doubles players were Eve and Amy Freeborn, Helen Blake and another girl he had never seen before. So there were actually seventeen- and eighteen-year-olds in this corner of Sussex he had never seen before? He was beginning to think he knew them all by sight and usually by name too. He and Burden went over to the fence and watched, as they had done that previous time. Caroline Peters glared but didn't come over to admonish. She knew who they were now.

It was clear from the first that Veronica was streets ahead of the other players, though two years younger than any of them. She was the best tennis player Wexford had ever seen on a local court. This time the discrepancy between what he saw on TV and what he saw at home did not seem quite so wide. She was a strong, lithe, fast player with a hard accurate backhand and a powerful smashing action. When Caroline Peters made her serve her service was as hard as Eve's but the balls struck the court well inside the line.

The doubles players changed ends. Eve looked in Wexford's direction and then ostentatiously away. Loyalty to the father he had had charged with possessing cannabis, he supposed. He had been getting a lot of stick of that kind lately. All part of a policeman's lot, no doubt. Veronica returned Caroline Peter's lob with a hard transverse drive which Caroline ran for but couldn't reach. It was a mystery, Wexford thought, where somebody got that kind of talent from. You couldn't imagine that finicking Wendy playing any sort of game or even walking more than half a mile, while Rodney Williams had been out of condition for years. Did the other Williams family play games? There had been a tennis racket up on Sara's bedroom wall, he remembered. Of course, the probable answer was that any healthy young

316

girl keen on tennis could be coached to the standard of Veronica Williams. She was already sixteen. It was already too late for her to begin competing in anything much more significant than inter-school matches.

The girl whose face and name he didn't know served a double fault. One more of those and the set would be lost. She served one more of those and threw her racket down in the kind of petulance she wouldn't have known about if she hadn't watched Wimbledon on TV. Wexford and Burden walked back to the car.

'Have we got anything on the fingerprints found in Williams's car yet?' Burden asked.

'They took about sixty prints,' Wexford said, 'all made by nine people. By far the greater proportion were made by one man and they've more or less established that man was Williams.'

'I don't suppose his fingers were in very good shape after being in the ground for nine weeks.'

'Exactly. They matched the car ones to prints in his bedroom – well, bedrooms – of course. The other prints were made by two unknown men, and may well belong to whoever began the dismantling of Greta, by Joy, Wendy, Sara, Veronica, and two more women or girls who might be friends of the wives and daughters – or who might not. The steering wheel had been wiped.'

'Much what you would expect really,' said Burden.

Nicola Tennyson, Veronica's friend, was thrilled to have her fingerprints taken. She was unable to remember much about 15 April. Certain it was that she had been babysitting her brother that evening and Veronica had come in, but she couldn't remember times. Veronica and she were often in each other's homes, she said.

One of the two unidentified sets of fingerprints on Greta turned out to be hers.

13

Wheatley said that the woman who stabbed him had been more than commonly tall. Budd said that because he had only seen her sitting down he couldn't tell her height. That wasn't strictly true. He had seen her running off with the sack over her shoulder. The sack was the only thing he could really remember, that and the fact she had blonde hair. The girl who attacked Wheatley had 'brown or lightish' hair. She was eighteen or nineteen. Budd thought his assailant was twenty. Or twenty-five or-six. Or any age between eighteen and thirty.

In each case their wounds had been made with the blade of a large penknife. Not necessarily the same penknife, though. Not necessarily the same woman. Wexford asked himself what had been in the sack. He didn't think Budd had invented the sack. Budd wasn't endowed with enough imagination for that. There had been a sack all right, a black plastic dustbin liner. What had she been carrying it for and why?

It had been pouring with rain. Those plastic sacks were very good for keeping things dry. Keeping what dry? The bus stop was the nearest one to the place where they'd found Rodney Williams's body. But he had been dead six weeks by the night Budd was attacked. Wendy Williams wasn't particularly tall but she was blonde and she looked much younger than she was. To Budd she might seem in her early twenties.

She had begun a fortnight of her annual holiday. Wexford

318

thought to himself that she might be spending the major part of it at Kingsmarkham Police Station. He went with the car to fetch her.

Veronica was in the raspberry-ice-cream living room, seated at the glass-topped table, turning the pages of *Vogue*. He thought she looked like a teenage girl in a French film of the sixties. He hadn't seen many French films of the sixties but nevertheless the impression was there in Veronica's band-box look, the beautifully cut, newly washed, pageboy hair, the clothes – primrose pinafore dress, starched white blouse, blue bootlace tie, white ankle socks, sky-blue sandals – that were just a little too young for her, the expression on her face that was 99 per cent innocence and 1 per cent calculation.

'I saw you playing tennis the other day.'

'Yes, I saw you too.'

Why the wary look suddenly, the shade of unease across that naivety?

'You're very good.'

She knew that already, she didn't need to be told. A polite smile and then back to *Vogue*. Wendy Williams came down the spiral staircase, walking slowly, giving him a voyeur's look if he had wanted it of shapely legs in very fine pale tights all the way up to a glimpsed border of cream lace. He wasn't looking, but out of the corner of his eye he saw her hold her skirt down as if he had been.

She had dressed up. Women these days didn't bother with fancy dressing except for special occasions, except when it was fun. That was general, not just the ARRIA view of things. For going down the cop shop, Wexford thought, you went in the jeans and shirt you wore around the house. But this was something that hadn't yet got through to Wendy Williams and maybe never would. She probably didn't possess a pair of jeans. And Veronica's would be the designer kind with Vidal Sassoon or Gloria Vanderbilt on the backside. Wendy had a pretty cotton dress on, the kind that needs a lot or ironing, a wide black patent belt to show she still had an adolescent waist and red wedge-heeled shoes that pinched where they touched.

The car filled with her perfume. Estée Lauder's White Linen, decided Wexford, who was good on scent. He made up his mind to take her up to his office, not into one of the interviewing rooms.

'You haven't told me much about this girlfriend of your husband's, Mrs Williams,' he said when they were there.

'I've told you all I know. I've told you it was a very young girl and that's all I know.'

'I don't think so,' he said. 'There's more if you search your memory.'

A secretive look was closing up her face. Why? Why should she want to conceal this girl's identity from him?

'I wish I'd never mentioned any girl to you!' Exasperated. The tone of a mother to a child who keeps nagging her about a treat she had promised him.

'You had an anonymous letter, you said.'

She hesitated. She opened her mouth to begin an explanation. He cut her short.

'You didn't keep it though. You burned it.'

'How did you know?'

'Mrs Williams, let me tell you what I do know. First, it's only in books that people burn anonymous letters. In real life they may not care much for them, they may even recoil from them in disgust, but they don't burn them. Most people don't have fires any more, for one thing. Where would you burn something?'

She didn't say anything. A sullen crushed look made her almost ugly.

'People who get anonymous letters may not like looking at them. Usually they put them away in a drawer in case or until we want to see them. Or there's the dustbin. You read somewhere that the requisite thing to do with an anonymous letter was burn it, didn't you? In a detective story probably. The truth is you never received one.'

'All right, I didn't.'

'Hasn't anyone ever told you you mustn't tell lies to the police?'

He hadn't spoken harshly. His tone was almost bantering. It was mockery, even as mild as this, she couldn't stand. She flushed and her mouth set mulishly.

'I didn't tell lies. There was a girl.' Perhaps she could see he wasn't going to say anything for a moment or two. 'He was perverted about young girls, that's what it amounted to

320

and it ruined my life.' Her voice rose, edgy and plaintive. 'I thought he was in love with me when we first met. I thought he loved me but now I know he just fancied me because I was young. And when Veronica was coming he had to marry me. Well, *marry*. It's easy to marry, isn't it? You can do it over and over again.

'I never had any life, I never had any youth. Do you know something? I'm thirty-two and I've never so much as been taken out to dinner in a decent restaurant by a man. I've never been abroad. I've never had a thing to wear that didn't come discount from Jickie's. I never even had an engagement ring!'

He asked her how she knew of the girl's existence. Just at this point Marion came in with coffee on a tray, three unprepossessing cheese sandwiches and three custard-cream biscuits. Wendy looked at the sandwiches and shook her head in a shuddery genteel sort of way.

He repeated the question.

'Rodney confessed.'

'Just like that? Out of the blue? You didn't suspect anything but he confessed to you he had a young girlfriend?'

'I told you.'

'Why did he confess? Was he intending to leave you for her? As in fact you thought he had done?'

That made her laugh in the way someone does who has knowledge of a secret you will never guess. He persisted and she looked exasperated, answering that she had told him already. She ate nothing, he ate a sandwich, leaving the rest for Marion, who had a hearty appetite. Afterwards, he thought, Wendy Williams would probably tell people she was kept at the police station for hours and not given a thing to eat or drink.

He asked her once more about 15 April. The evening. What time had she left Jickie's to drive home to Pomfret? all the staff at Jickie's had been questioned by Martin and Bennett and Archbold. They had forgotten. Why should they remember that particular evening? One of the girls on the fashion-floor pay desk said that if Mrs Williams hadn't actually left the building before nine, that would have been very late for her. On Thursdays she usually left as soon after eight as possible and had been known to leave at 7.30.

Wendy insisted she left at nine. She stuck to that. He left it. He said there was something he had to ask her. Seeing that her husband consistently neglected her and for two months she believed he had finally left her, had she formed a friendship with any other man?

'It would be a natural and normal thing to you. You're a very young woman still. You said yourself that you felt life and youth had been denied you.'

'Are you suggesting I was having a – a relationship with someone?'

'It would be very understandable.'

'I think that's disgusting! That's really immoral. I've got my daughter to think of, haven't I? I've got Veronica to set an example to. Just because Rodney behaved in that horrible way, that's no reason for me to do the same. Let me tell you, I've always been absolutely faithful. I've never looked at another man, it would never have entered my head.'

He was beginning to know her and her protests. He said not another word on that one but thought the more. It was afternoon now and Burden would be setting in motion their prearranged plan. It might not work, of course – and if it did what would it show or prove? He didn't even know if he expected it to work.

In the meantime he questioned her about her life, her feelings, her reactions. Still she hadn't said a word about the other Williams family. She was prepared to acknowledge Rodney Williams had married her bigamously while ignoring the existence of his first or true wife. You would have expected her natural curiosity to get the better of her. Was she rising above such human failings? That was a possible explanation.

'Mrs Joy Williams,' he said deliberately, 'has a son and daughter. Her daughter and Veronica are very much alike. Do you have any feelings about these people?' He was aware he sounded like a psychotherapist, though any interrogating policeman was one of those. But nevertheless he made a slight correction. 'Aren't you interested in knowing something about them?'

'No.' Once more she had flushed. She looked mulish. 'Why should I be? They're nothing to me. Rodney can't have cared much for them.'

'Why do you say that?'

She made a little gesture with her hands to indicate that the answer was obvious. Wexford said that was enough for today and he'd organize a car to take her home. They went down in the lift, timing it perfectly, for as the lift came to a stop and the doors opened Burden came walking across the black and white checkerboard floor towards it with Joy Williams beside him. Wexford spoke to Burden for the sake of stopping and saying something. The two women stood there, Joy staring at Wendy, Wendy contemplating the wall ahead of her as if it were the most fascinating example of interior decor since the cave paintings of Trois Frères.

They presented a contrast, pathetic and grotesque. It was almost too marked to be quite real. They were like a cartoon for an old-fashioned advertisement, the wife who doesn't use the face cream, floor polish, deodorant, stock cubes, and the wife who does. Joy had a cardigan on over a cotton dress with half its hem coming down. All her shoes had a curious way of looking like carpet slippers though they weren't. Wendy swayed a little on her high heels, craning her neck and putting on a winsome look. Wexford smelt a gush of White Linen from her, perhaps because she was sweating. The irony was that both these women had been rejected.

Burden and Joy went into the lift. The doors closed.

'Do you know who that woman was?'

'What woman?' said Wendy.

'I'm not talking about Detective Bayliss. The woman who has just gone up in the lift with Inspector Burden.'

She raised her eyebrows, moved her shoulders.

'That was Mrs Joy Williams.'

'His wife?'

'Yes,' said Wexford.

'She looked about sixty.'

Upstairs Burden was asking Joy about the phone call, the letter of resignation. Why had she gone out on the evening of 15 April instead of remaining at home to await her son's phone call?

'I can't be always at his beck and call,' she said, her voice full of bitterness. 'It's all one to him whether I'm there or not. He's his father all over again – indifferent. I've done everything for him, worshipped the ground he walked on.

323

Might as well not have bothered. Do you know where he is now? In Cornwall. On holiday. That's all it means to him that his mother's a widow.'

It could just be true. It could just be that she had at last seen the results of spoiling a son. A quarrel, Burden thought, the day before Kevin returned to university. He could hear the things that would have been said – all right, just wait till next time you want something; you phone, my lad, but don't count on me being here . . . Yet there had been no sign since then of adoration flagging.

'Do you know who that woman was with Chief Inspector Wexford?'

'I can guess.' The harsh clattering laugh. 'Cheap little tart. I don't admire his taste.'

He asked her if Sara had a boyfriend. Incredibly, she said she didn't know. It was plain she didn't care. Hatred came into her eyes when her daughter's name was mentioned.

'And after all I've done for her,' said Joy as if their discussion had been on the subject of the host of services she had performed for Sara and the girl's ingratitude. Burden had her driven home. He felt as if he had been brought up against a wall, the solid brick an inch from his face.

Carol Milvey was not a member of ARRIA but she was eighteen years old and lived next door but one to Joy Williams. And it was her father, the boss of Mid-Sussex Waterways, who had found Rodney Williams's travelling bag in Green Pond, a coincidence which had never been explained. Sergeant Martin saw her. The interview was a brief one, for Carol Milvey had been ill in bed with tonsillitis on 15 April and had taken two days off school.

A further ten members of ARRIA were cleared, both for 15 April and the evening on which Brian Wheatley had been stabbed in the hand. It was August now and people were beginning to go away on holiday, ARRIA members surely included. The Anerley family and their daughter, the red-headed Nicola, had been in France since the end of the school term and were not expected back until 12 August. On this date too Pomfret Office Equipment Ltd were due to reopen after two weeks' holiday closure, a southern version of North

Country wakes weeks, as Wexford remarked. If the typewriters missing from Haldon Finch were serviced in the neighbourhood it was with Pomfret Office Equipment they had to be. No other firm of typewriter engineers admitted to knowledge of their whereabouts.

The commerce department at Sewingbury Sixth Form college had been checked out. They had microcomputers, ACT Apricots, as well as four dedicated word processors, and their typewriters were ten highly sophisticated Brother machines. Kingsmarkham High School had one typewriter only in the building and that in the school secretary's office.

Kevin Williams came back from Cornwall and left again with six like-minded students to camp in the Channel Islands. The Harmers with Paulette's boyfriend went to North Wales for a week, leaving an Indian pharmacist and his wife, both highly qualified but jobless, in charge of shop and dispensary. Sara went nowhere. Sara stayed at home, awaiting no doubt the A-level results due the second or third week of the month, after the degree results and before the O-levels.

'I can't help wondering if there'll still be A-levels when this new baby of ours grows up,' said Burden. Nowadays he talked gingerly and awkwardly about the coming child but as if its birth were a certainty and its future more or less assured. 'I'll be an old man by the time she wants to go to university. Well, I'll be in my sixties. I'll be retired. Do you remember filling in those grant forms? Getting one's employer to vouch for one's earnings and all that? Still, by then they'll do it all on a computer, I suppose, a kind of twenty-first-century Apricot.'

'Or an Apple,' said Wexford. 'Why do computer makers call their wares after fruit? There must be some unexpected Freudian explanation.' A glazed look of boredom blanked Burden's face. 'Talking of unexpected explanations.' Wexford said quickly, 'do you realize there's one aspect of this case we've given no thought to? Motive. Motive has scarcely been mentioned.'

Burden looked as if he were going to say that the police need not concern themselves with motive, that perpetrators in any case often stated motives that seemed thin or incredible. But he didn't say that. He said hesitantly, 'Aren't we concluding Williams was killed in what ARRIA would call self-defence?'

'Surely the difficulty there is that if we assume – which we are doing – that the woman or girl who made the phone call and wrote the letter was Williams's girlfriend, why should she need to defend herself against him? Budd and Wheatley were attacked because they made sexual advances. But this girl, being his girlfriend, presumably welcomed his sexual advances.'

Burden said in his prudish way, 'That might depend on their nature.'

'You mean they were sadistic or he wanted to wear one of her nightdresses? We've no evidence Williams was funny in that way. And aren't you forgetting something? It looks as if this murder was somewhat premeditated. Williams was given a sleeping drug before he was stabbed. I don't see my way to accepting a theory that one day Williams suggested to his girlfriend that they have sex in this new naughty way, whereupon she substitutes a sedative for his blood-pressure pill and when he's asleep stabs him eight times with a French cook's knife.'

'Then what motive do you suggest?'

'I don't. I can't see a girlfriend killing him to be rid of him because surely all she had to do was give him the out, tell him to go back to his wife or wives. And although a girl could have killed him on her own, she couldn't have disposed of his body on her own. A girl with a jealous husband or boyfriend? ARRIA members don't have husbands. ARRIA members aren't supposed to get sufficiently involved with men for a triangular jealousy situation to arise. But is she an ARRIA member? Does she exist?'

'If one could only read the book of fate,' said Burden, unaware that he was quoting and no longer thinking about the Williams case anyway.

'If this were seen,' said Wexford, 'the happiest youth, viewing his progress through, would shut the book and sit him down and die . . .'

He went home to fetch Dora and the two of them went to see Sheila in *Little Eyolf* at the Olivier.

14

Pomfret Office Equipment Ltd was open for business by 9.30 on the morning of 12 August. It was a shopfront with a big storage shed behind. The business was run by two men called Ovington, father and son. Edgar Ovington, the father, acknowledged at once that his firm serviced typewriters for the Haldon Finch Comprehensive School. The machines were usually attended to during the long summer holiday. His son had fetched the Haldon Finch machines the day before term ended, 26 July.

Wexford and Burden followed him into the shed at the back. It was full of typewriters, manuals, electric and electronic machines. They stretched away, rows of them ranked on slatted shelves, all labelled with tie-on luggage labels. Ovington pointed out the Haldon Finch typewriters, three on the lower shelf, two on the upper. The label on each said: H. Finch. Three portable Remington 315s, two Adler Gabrielle 5000s. Burden gave Ovington a condensed explanation of why they were looking for a particular typewriter and what made it particular. He asked for a sheet of paper. Ovington broke open a packet of 70-gramme white bond and peeled off two sheets from the top.

A flaw in the upper-case A, the ascender of the lower-case t and the head of the comma smudged. Burden slipped a sheet of paper into the roller of the first machine and typed a few lines from 'O God Our Help in Ages Past', the only hymn he knew by heart. No flaws. No flaws in the second machine either.

'You haven't put a new typeface on any of these machines?' Wexford asked.

'I haven't so much as touched them yet,' said Ovington.

Burden tried the third Remington. It was perfect, a better face than the others had, its need of servicing apparent only in the tendency of one or two of the keys to stick.

'These were the only typewriters fetched from the Haldon Finch Comprehensive School?'

'That's right. I label everything the minute it comes in to be on the safe side.'

'Yes, I see. So there's no possibility one of these machines could accidentally have been returned to a private customer?'

'It wouldn't go to a private customer if it was labelled Haldon Finch, would it?' said Ovington truculently.

He was a dour, prickly, suspicious man, always on the lookout for slurs anyone might cast on his ability or efficiency. Burden's request to try out any other Remington 315s there might be among the two hundred or so machines in the shed started him arguing and might have held them up but for the arrival, smiling and anxious to please, of the son, James Ovington. He was a tall, big-built young man with a toothy smile and a head as bald as an egg.

'Help yourselves. Be my guest.' The big white teeth glared as the lips stretched. 'Would you like me to have a sample of typing done from every machine here?' He meant it too, there was no sarcasm.

'We'll do it,' said Burden. 'And it's only the 315s we're interested in.'

Two more stood on the shelves besides the three he had tested. 'Sufficient is Thine Arm alone,' he typed, 'And our defence is sure'. Nothing wrong with that one. 'The busy tribes of flesh and blood. With all their cares and fears, Are carried downward by the flood, And lost in following years.' No flaws.

'Thanks for your help,' said Wexford.

James Ovington said it was his pleasure and smiled so widely that his dragon-seed teeth threatened to spill out. His father scowled.

'It's going to be in a ditch somewhere or a pond,' said Burden.

'Not in Green Pond, anyway. Or Milvey would have found it.' Wexford was reminded again of the as yet unexplained coincidence. The connecting link between Milvey and

Rodney Williams wasn't Carol Milvey, for Carol Milvey had been ill with tonsillitis on the evening of Williams's death. So what was it? Connecting link there must be. Wexford refused to believe that it was by pure chance that Milvey had discovered his neighbour's overnight bag in Green Pond.

And coincidence became remarkable beyond any possible rational explanation, entering the realms of magic or fantasy, when a call came in from Milvey himself next day to say he had found not the typewriter but a long kitchen knife, a French cook's knife, in a small ornamental pond on the Green Pond Hall estate.

The three ponds in the old water garden, now a wilderness, had been silted up with soil and fine sand washed down by springs from Cheriton Forest. Wexford's men had cleaned out those ponds during their search of the estate but since that time a further silting-up had taken place. The prospective trout farmer had called Mid-Sussex Waterways in once more to attempt to find a solution to the problem of the clogged water course.

Had the knife been placed there since the police search? Or had it been washed down from a hiding-place upstream? It was a large knife, the handle of ivory-coloured plastic six inches long, the blade nine inches, a right-angled triangle with the hypotenuse the cutting edge. It had a sharp and vicious-looking point. There were traces of grey mud in the rivet sockets of the handle but not a streak or pinpoint of rust anywhere. Wexford had the knife sent to Forensics at Stowerton. The Milvey link was still a mystery to him. He confronted Milvey across his desk, at a loss for what to ask him next. The wild thought entered his head that Milvey and Joy Williams might have been lovers. It was too wild – not fat dull Milvey and draggle-tailed Joy. And if Milvey were involved in Williams's death, why should he produce the weapon?

He found himself reduced to saying, 'You do see, don't you, Mr Milvey, that this situation and your position in it is a very mystifying one. The man who lives next door but one to you is murdered. You find first the bag he had with him when he disappeared, then a knife that in all probability is the murder weapon.'

'Somebody,' said Milvey who didn't seem to see the point, 'had to find them sooner or later.'

'The population of Kingsmarkham is somewhere in the area of seventy-eight thousand souls.'

Milvey stared at him with bull-headed stupidity. At last he said with truculence, 'Next time I find something I reckon will help the police with their inquiries I'll keep quiet about it.'

While Forensics were testing the knife against Williams's wound measurements Sergeant Martin with Bennett and Archbold made inquiries as to its provenance. They listed thirty-nine shops and stores in the area where similar knives were sold. Only Jickie's however, stocked that particular brand of French cook's knife.

'Wendy Williams may work there,' Wexford said, 'but everyone shops there. We do. You do. Martin's asking the staff in the hardware department if they can remember anyone recently buying a French cook's knife. You know how far that'll get us. Besides, they've stocked the things for the past five years. There's no reason to believe the knife was bought specifically to kill Williams. In fact, the chances are it wasn't.'

'Yes, we're still at square one,' Burden said.

'You're being faint-hearted. Come and spend an afternoon among the typewriters. I've a hunch I want to put to the test.'

Ovington senior was on his own. He tried at first to fob them off with pleas of pressure of work. Wexford suggested gently that this might be construed as obstructing the police in the course of their inquiries. Ovington, grumbling under his breath, led them once more into the shed at the back of the shop.

· Walking between the rows, Wexford examined the labels tied to the machines.

'You always used this method of labelling?'

'What's wrong with it?'

'I didn't say there was anything wrong with it. I don't think it's very clear, that's all. For instance, what does "P and L" stand for?' He pointed to the labels on a pair of Smith Corona SX 400s.

'Porter and Lamb on the estate,' said Ovington gruffly. He meant the industrial estate at Stowerton.

'And TML?'

'Tube Manipulators Limited.'

'And you know absolutely what those initials – I might say codes – mean when you're returning machines? You know that "P and L" stands for Porter and Lamb and not, for instance, for Payne and Lovell, the hardware people in the High Street here?'

'We don't do any work for Payne and Lovell.' Ovington looked astonished.

'I think you understand me though. With this system of labelling mistakes could be made. I'll come to the point. "H. Finch" is rather a rough and ready way of indicating the Haldon Finch Comprehensive School.'

'It serves its purpose.'

'Suppose you had a customer called Henry Finch. What would stop his machine getting mixed up with the Haldon Finch ones?'

'We don't have a customer called Henry Finch, that's what.'

Burden said sharply, 'D'you have any customers called Finch?'

'We might have.'

It was the curious reply, or a version of it, Wexford had so often heard witnesses give in court when they did not want to commit themselves to a positive 'yes'. 'I might have', 'I may have done'. Ovington, in his greasy old suit, open-necked shirt, his chin pulled back into his neck and his lips thrust forward, looked shifty, guilty, suspected and suspicious, truculent for the mere sake of truculence.

'I'd like you to check, please.'

'Not Henry,' said Ovington. 'Definitely not. A lady. Not an H at all.'

'You're wasting my time, Mr Ovington.'

He was enjoying it, with sly malice. 'We did some repairs on a Remington for her a while back. Not a 315 though.' At last, scratching his head, 'I could look in the book.'

'This could be it,' Wexford said when he and Burden were

alone for a moment. 'They could have got mixed up and sent the wrong one back.'

'Wouldn't she have noticed?'

'She might not be a regular typist. She might not have used the machine since its return.'

He began looking at labels on all the typewriters on the lower shelf on the left-hand side. P and L, E. Ten (what could that mean?), TML, HBSS, H. Finch, J. St G, M. Br . . . Ovington came back with a ledger.

'Miss J. Finch, 22 Bodmin Road, Pomfret. She collected the machine herself on July the twenty-sixth.' He slammed the book shut as if he had just proved or disproved something to his triumphant satisfaction.

July 26. The day the Haldon Finch machines were collected and brought here, Wexford thought. Did all this mean anything or nothing? Were the girlfriend and the girlfriend's typewriter after all sitting pretty somewhere in London or Brighton?

Neither he nor Burden knew where Bodmin Road was.

'You know something?' Burden said. 'Wendy Williams lives in Liskeard Avenue and Liskeard's a place in Cornwall. Bodmin's the county town of Cornwall. It may be just round the corner.'

'We'll look it up as soon as we get back.'

It was just round the corner. Liskeard Avenue, Falmouth Road, Truro Road, with Bodmin Road running crossways to connect them all.

'She was practically a neighbour of his,' Burden said, sounding almost excited. 'An ARRIA member, I bet you. Here she is on the Electoral Register. Finch, Joan B.'

'Wait a minute, Mike. Are we saying – are we assuming rather – that a Haldon Finch typewriter was collected by her in error or that it's her own typewriter she has, that this is the machine we're looking for, and we've stumbled upon her not by deduction but by pure luck?'

'What does that matter?' Burden said simply.

Twenty-two Bodmin Road was a small purpose-built block of four flats. According to the doorbells, J. B. Finch lived on the first floor. However, she was not at home either in the afternoon or at their two further calls at seven and eight in the evening. Wexford had been home an hour when a call came through to him to say a fourth man had been stabbed, this time in the upper arm, not a serious wound, though there had been considerable loss of blood.

The difference was that this time his cries were heard by two policemen sitting in a patrol car in a lay-by on the Kingsmarkham bypass. It was after sunset, the beginning of dusk. They had found the victim of the attack lying half across a public footpath, bleeding from a wound near his shoulder. While they were bending over him a girl came out from among the trees of the woodland on the north side of the path, announced her name as Edwina Klein and handed them a penknife from which she had wiped most of the blood.

15

ARRIA expected a show. Its members were in Kingsmarkham Magistrates' Court in force. Wexford had never seen
the small wood-walled area that passed for a public gallery so
full. Caroline Peters was there and Sara Williams, redhaired
Nicola Anerley, Jane Gardner and the Freeborn twins, Helen
Blake and Donella the black girl, the tennis player who wore
glasses and the tennis player who did not.

It was to be a test case, of course. Wexford had guessed
all of it pretty well before he talked to Edwina Klein. She
had not exactly been an *agent provocateur*. It was a terrible
world we lived in if a woman who chose to walk alone along
a field path at dusk could be called that. But the truth was
that Edwina had set out to walk there, and to do so evening
after evening since she came down from Oxford at the end
of June, in the expectation of being attacked. She had been
frank and open with him, hiding nothing, admitting, for
instance, that it was she who while home for a weekend had
been Wheatley's assailant. For this reason he had decided
not to oppose bail. She would talk freely to him again, she
had promised and, with a faith that would have set the Chief
Constable's hair standing on end, he believed her.

With Caroline Peters a founder member of ARRIA, she
was a thin straight girl of medium height, fiercely intelligent,
a pioneer and martyr. She was dressed entirely in black,
black trousers, black roll-neck sweater, her hair invisible
under a tightly tied black scarf. A raven of a woman, the
only colour about her the tiny orange ARRIA badge pinned
on near her left shoulder.

What did the girls in the public gallery expect? Something

334

like the trial of Joan of Arc, Wexford supposed. All were ignorant of magistrates' court procedure, all looked disbelieving when in five minutes it was all over and Edwina committed for trial to the crown court. The charge was unlawful wounding. She was released on bail in her own surety of £1000 and for a similar sum in that of an elderly woman, her great-aunt, not old enough to have been a suffragette but looking as if she might regret having missed the chance.

The ARRIA contingent filed out, muttering indignantly to each other. Helen Blake and Amy Freeborn picked up the orange banner with a woman-raven on it that they had been obliged to leave outside. The others fell in behind them and what had been a group became a march. 'We shall overcome,' they sang, 'we shall overcome some day.' They marched behind the banner up to the police station forecourt and across it and out into the High Street.

Joan Finch was sixty-five years old, perhaps more. Wexford wasn't surprised. There must be a few women called Joan under fifty, and even fifty years ago Joan was becoming an old-fashioned name. It was Burden who had built so much on the chance of her being the girl they were looking for.

She took them into the poky little den, designed for surely no more than luggage storage, where she worked, and showed them the typewriter, a big manual Remington at least as old as herself. Fingers today would flinch at that iron forest of keys that took so much muscle power to fell it.

As Ovington had told them, she had collected it from Pomfret Office Equipment on 26 July. There was no doubt at all that it was hers. It had been her mother's before her and seemed as much of a family heirloom as any clock or piece of china.

Of sole significance to Wexford and Burden was the fact that it wasn't a Remington 315 portable machine. This was something Miss Finch seemed unable to grasp. She insisted on sitting down at the typewriter and producing for them a half page of men coming to the aid of the party and quick brown foxes. The Ovingtons had done a good job. There wasn't a flaw or an irregularity to be seen.

335

They had lunch at the little bow-fronted wine bar two doors away. Pamela Gardner was at a corner table lunching with a woman friend. She looked through Wexford with a contemptuous stare. Her daughter had bounced along that morning, singing as heartily as anyone and a good deal more loudly, waving to him as if they were old friends. Edwina Klein was coming to the police station at 2.30 to talk to him. It was no part of the conditions of her bail that she should do this but he felt sure she wouldn't fail him. Burden said, 'Only three weeks to go now.' He was talking of the coming baby. 'They say it'll be on time. They don't really know though.'

'There's more they don't know than they ever let on.'

Burden picked at his quiche. 'She had the heartburn at the beginning and I'm getting it now.' He was pale, bilious-looking.

'We'll see if the Harmers can supply you with an indigestion remedy.'

The Pre-Raphaelite head of Paulette could be seen through the window of the dispensary where she was evidently helping her father. It was Hope Harmer who served Burden. She seemed discomfited by their visit, unable perhaps to realize that policemen too have private lives and are as liable to bodily ills as anyone else.

'Did you have a good holiday?' Wexford asked her.

'Oh yes, thank you, very nice. Very quiet,' she added as people do when describing their Christmas celebrations as if to admit to liveliness and merriment were to deny respectability. 'All good things come to an end though, don't they? We could have stayed away another week only my daughter's expecting her A-level results. They're due any day.'

Sara Williams must also be on tenterhooks then . . . 'Another would-be doctor in the family?'

'No, no. Paulette's hoping to follow in her Daddy's footsteps.'

She was all bright placatory smiles, accompanying them to the door when they left like an old-fashioned shopkeeper. Wexford walked into the police station just before 2.30. Edwina Klein was waiting for him, shown upstairs to his room, and he felt relief at the sight of her in spite of his confidence that she would keep her word. With her, seated in the other visitor's chair, like a chaperone, was the aunt.

Wexford was surprised. He had seen Edwina as the very epitome of independence, of self-reliance.

'I happen to be a solicitor as well as an aunt.'

'Very well,' said Wexford, 'but this won't be an interrogation, just a talk about various aspects of this case.'

'That's what they all say,' said the aunt whose name was Pearl Kaufmann. In appearance she was rather like Virginia Woolf in her latter days, tallish, thin, long-faced, long-nosed, with a full mouth. She wore a navy blue silk dress, mid-calf length, and clumpy white sandals that made her feet look large.

Edwina was still in the black she had worn in court but with the roll-necked sweater changed for a sleeveless black tee-shirt that was better suited to the heat of the day. The ARRIA badge had been transferred to this. Edwina had sunglasses on which turned her face into an expressionless mask.

'He treated me exactly as if I was a prostitute,' she had said to him of Wheatley at that earlier conversation. The black glasses hadn't covered her eyes then. They had been bright with eagerness, with earnestness, with the zeal of youth. 'Not that there's anything wrong with being a prostitute. That's OK, that's fine if that's where you're at. It's just the way men *assume* . . .'

'Only some men.'

'A lot. He didn't even talk to me. I tried to talk to him. I asked him where he worked and where he lived. When I asked him where he lived he gave a strange sort of laugh as if I'd said something *wrong*.'

'Why did you ask him for a lift? To provoke exactly the sort of situation that arose?'

'No, I didn't. Not that time. I admit I did last night but it was different with the man in the car. I'd had a lift from London to Kingsmarkham and the guy couldn't take me any farther.' She seemed to consider. 'It was because of what happened in the car that I decided to try walking in the forest and see.'

'You'd better tell me what happened in the car, hadn't you?'

'He pulled into a lay-by. He did talk then. He said, "Come

on, we'll go in the wood". I didn't know what he meant, I really didn't. Do you know what he thought? He thought I wanted paying first. He said, "Will ten pounds do?" And then he touched me.' Edwina Klein laid her right hand on her left breast. 'He touched me like I'm doing now. Like it was a tap or a switch. He didn't try to put his arms round me or kiss me or anything. It was just offering to pay and feeling the switch. I took out my knife and stuck it in his hand.'

There had been no aunt present when she talked to him then and no black circles to take the character from her face. Her manner now was more subdued, less indignant. Her experience of the court had perhaps chastened her. She waited almost meekly for him to begin questioning her. Miss Kaufmann sat looking at Wexford's wall map with simulated interest.

'Have you stabbed any other men?' he said abruptly, knowing the remark would be objected to.

Edwina shook her head.

'We won't mind about that, Mr Wexford.' It seemed highly suitable to the aunt's manner and appearance that she should use this obsolete Victorian phrase. She elucidated with something more contemporary. 'We'll forget you said that.'

'As you please,' said Wexford. 'When the police use *agents provocateurs* – as, for example, in the case of a policewoman sitting in a cinema where a member of the audience is suspected of assaulting women – the public, particularly the public of your sort of persuasion, gets up in arms. There's an outcry when a young policeman deliberately uses a public lavatory frequented by homosexuals. In other words, it's not all right for them to do this in the interests of justice but it's all right for you to in the mere interest of a principle. There's rather a crude name for what you did and were, isn't there?'

He had been too mealy-mouthed, too gentlemanly, he quickly saw.

'A pricktease,' she said flatly. The aunt didn't move an eyelid. 'I didn't do that. I didn't do anything but go for a walk in a wood. I wasn't provocatively dressed.' Scorn came into her voice now and she lifted up her head. 'I wouldn't be! I had jeans on and a jacket. I never wear make-up, not ever. The only thing I did to provoke anyone was *be* there and be a woman.'

'I think my niece is saying,' said Miss Kaufmann dryly, 'that it isn't possible to be a woman in certain places with impunity. She was out to prove this and she did prove it.'

He let it go. He left it. He felt the force of what the two women said and he knew it was true, and that this was an instance of a policeman knowing that the opposing argument is sounder than his own but of having to stick to his own just the same. That all women who intended to go about by themselves at night should learn self-defence techniques seemed to him the best answer. The alternative was that men's natures should change and that was something which might slowly happen over centuries but not in years or even decades. He wrote busy nothings on the sheet of paper in front of him to fill thirty seconds of time and keep them temporarily silent. At last he lifted his head and looked at Edwina Klein. For some reason, perhaps because his eyes were naked, she took off her glasses. Immediately she looked earnest again and very young.

'You know the Williams family, I think?'

She was prepared for this. Somehow she knew that this was what she was really there for. Her answer surprised him.

'Which Williams family? There are two, aren't there?'

'There may be two hundred in this neighbourhood for all I know,' he said sharply. 'It's a common name. I'm talking about the Williams family that live in Alverbury Road, Kingsmarkham. The girl is called Sara. She was in court this morning. I think you know her.'

She nodded. 'We were at school together. She's a year younger than I am.'

'Did you know Rodney Williams, the dead man?'

She was very quick to reply. Miss Kaufmann looked up as if warningly. 'Him and Mrs Williams, yes. Sara and I used to do ballet together.' She smiled. 'Believe it or not.' Miss Kaufmann cast up her eyes as if she could hardly believe it. 'They'd come for Sara or one of them would. I remember him because he was the only father who ever came. Sometimes he'd come and sit through the whole class.'

Watching pubescent girls in little tutus, thought Wexford, or more likely leotards these days.

339

'You asked me which family I meant,' he said.

'I slightly know the other one.' She lifted her shoulders. 'Veronica Williams looks exactly like Sara.'

He felt a tightening of nerves. She might be a link between the two families. She was the only person he had yet talked to who knew – or admitted to knowing – both sets of Williamses.

'You were aware that they were half-sisters then? You knew Williams was their father?'

'No. Oh no. I suppose I thought – well, I didn't think about it. I honestly don't know, really. Perhaps that they might be cousins?'

'When did you last see Rodney Williams?'

'Years ago.' She was becoming nervous, frightened. It meant nothing, it was evidence only of her realization that she had been brought her to face one sort of ordeal and, that over, was being subjected to another of an unexpected kind. 'I haven't seen him for years.'

'Then how do you know Veronica?'

No dramatic *crise de nerfs* and no hesitation either. 'I played tennis against her. When I was at school.'

'She's three years younger than you.'

'OK. Sure. She was a sort of child prodigy. She was in Haldon Finch's first six when she was under fourteen.'

It was all reasonable, more than plausible. She had been in Oxford the night Rodney Williams died, having gone up early, a week before her term began. She had told him so last evening and told him, in grave and careful detail, whom to check this with. Bennett was in Oxford checking now but Wexford had little doubt Edwina hadn't lied to him.

'You knew both families,' he said now, 'but you didn't know, so to speak, they were one family? You didn't know Rodney Williams was the father of Veronica as well as of Sara and Kevin?'

'Kevin? I've never even heard of him before.'

'Sara's older brother.' He decided to be entirely frank with her. Miss Kaufmann sat watching him, an acid twist to her mouth. 'They didn't know of the existence of the others,' he said. 'The Pomfret family didn't know of the existence of the Kingsmarkham family and the Kingsmarkham family didn't know the existence of the Pomfret family until quite a while after Rodney Williams was dead. So if you knew, that must mean you also knew Rodney Williams was a bigamist or at least a married man maintaining two households. And if you knew that how did you know it?'

'I didn't.'

The cool negative disappointed him. He had felt on the brink of a breakthrough. But she qualified it.

'I didn't know. I said they looked alike, I'd noticed that, and I remember once saying to my aunt that they must be cousins.' Edwina looked at Miss Kaufmann and Miss Kaufmann nodded in a rapid impatient way. 'I didn't know either of them well,' Edwina said. 'You've got to remember that. I'd never spoken more than a few words to Veronica. And Mrs Williams, that's the real wife, I've seen her about but she's forgotten who I am or something, and as far as the other one goes I was just a customer.'

He had nothing else to ask her. She had stabbed Brian Wheatley and Peter John Hyde, her assailant in the wood, but he was certain she hadn't killed Williams. If a woman had done that she would have needed a second to help her.

'That's all then, thank you, Miss Klein.'

She got up and walked slowly and gracefully to the door, holding herself erect but with her head slightly bowed. They had the same figure, the same walk, this aunt and niece, though fifty years separated them. What would become of Edwina Klein now? It was inevitable she would be found guilty. Would her college have her back? Or was her whole future spoiled? Had she blown it for the sake of a lost cause? At the door, just before he opened it for her, she said, 'There's one thing. You said the Pomfret Williamses and the Kingsmarkham Williamses didn't know about each other. For the sake of setting the record straight, that's not right.'

The excitement was back, drying his throat. 'What do you mean?'

'What I say. They did know about each other.'

He took his hand from the door and leaned against it like someone barring egress. But Edwina Klein stood there willingly, looking a little puzzled, the aunt bored but patient.

'How do you know that?'

'Because I've seen them together,' she said.

341

Relief ran over him like sweat. He felt cool and lightheaded with it. She was aware now that she had told him something revelatory, unguessed at, and her face, close to his, was full of alert inquiry.

'Whom did you see together?' he asked her.

'Those two women. I saw them in the Precinct Café in Kingsmarkham having coffee together.'

'When? Can you remember when?'

If it were a week ago or even a month ago it meant nothing.

'Last Christmas, I think. It must have been Christmas or Easter for me to have been home. The only weekend I've been home was when *Wheatley* gave me that lift.' Edwina put infinite scorn into the pronunciation of his name. 'It wasn't then and it wasn't Easter. I know it can't have been because there was snow on the ground.'

'Snow fell,' said Miss Kaufmann, helpful now her niece was not directly threatened, 'during the first week of January.'

'It must have been then,' said Edwina.

She smiled, as if pleased to have been of help at last. He knew she hadn't lied.

16

As Wexford opened the gate of 31 Alverbury Road the post-
man was coming down the path, a wad of mail fastened with
a rubber band in his left hand. None of it apparently was
for 29 and his next call was at Milvey's, two doors down.
Watching him, Wexford suddenly understood how Milvey
came into the case. There was no coincidence at all, it was
all simple and logical, only he had been putting the cart
before the horse . . .

He rang the bell. As he did so St Peter's clock struck nine.
It was Sara who opened the door and so quickly he knew
she must have been standing directly behind it. She was
holding a paper.

'Two As and a B,' she said, and smiled with gratification.
She had spoken as if the sole purpose of his call had been
to hear about her A-level results. Before she closed the door
she must have seen the police car outside with Donaldson at
the wheel and Marion Bayliss in the back.

'Congratulations,' Wexford said. 'Where's your mother?'
She didn't answer. She might not have heard for all the
notice she took.

'St Biddulph's told me they'd take me with three Bs or two
Bs and an A, so this is rather better.'

Frenetic excitement was in the girl's eyes, an excitement
that was manic and all the more disconcerting for being
under such tight control. He had seen her as a Botticelli girl,
mild-faced, tranquil, with a spring-like innocence. Primavera
should not tremble with triumph nor Venus's eyes glitter.

'I'm going to phone my cousin Paulette, find out how she
did.'

To crow a little? Or to be kind? Joy Williams came out from the kitchen, dressed as he had never seen her before. He hadn't told her but perhaps she had guessed she would be meeting Wendy again. Or Wendy herself had told her the evening before? He was prepared for that. He rather hoped they realized he knew of their prior acquaintance. Joy wore a clean, tidy skirt and blouse. She had washed her hair and smudged lipstick on her mouth, in the uncertain slapdash way women do who seldom wear it and somehow feel ashamed to do so. Probably she always dresses up when she and Wendy meet, he thought. There would be rivalry there even if they were allied in a common hatred of Williams. Besides, an alliance would not mean they actually *liked* each other . . .

Sara could be heard on the phone. 'Have they come? Well?'

Not much of a bedside manner. He imagined her talking in that hectoring way to a patient. A hard, neurotic little go-getter, he thought her, without an atom of concern for the mother whom the police suspected of murdering her father.

'That's not bad though, is it?' she was saying. 'It's not as if you need As or even Bs.'

Patronizing. Somewhat lofty. The pharmacist, of course, was the poor man's doctor, or the doctor for the faint-hearted. 'I'll ask the chemist to give me something for my throat.' Or my head, back, cystitis, bleeding, lump in the breast . . . He took Joy out and closed the front door behind them.

Sergeant Martin and Polly Davies brought Wendy in. The evening before she had been in tears of vexation at missing a day's work but that she could have refused to come – that the police were still in a position only to ask and persuade – seemed no more to have occurred to her than to Joy. They were not blessed with lawyers for aunts. The senior wife – the Sultana Valideh – was already seated in the interview room when Wendy was brought in, the expressionless face averted, the dark brown animal eyes staring past her at the window.

Wendy wore a printed smock dress, Kate Greenaway-like,

in a Laura Ashley print, at the neck and wrists frills tied with bows. She had white tights on and white shoes. While the sergeant and Polly stood by (Polly told Wexford later) Wendy had taken her daughter Veronica in her arms and hugged her in a highly emotional way, bringing a fresh rush of tears. Veronica had looked very taken aback. But Wendy had pressed her close to her, stroking her hair, almost as if she expected never to see her again. And Polly, who was a reader of romantic period fiction, said it was like Marie Antoinette setting off in the tumbril.

'Farewell, my children, for ever! I am going to your father.'

Now all that remained as evidence of this scene was the swollen pinkness of Wendy's face. She gave Wexford a piteous look. She would have preferred Burden to interrogate her, she found him more sympathetic than this elderly, hard, sardonic man, but Burden wasn't there. He was in Alverbury Road in conversation with Mrs Milvey.

Wexford said, and he seemed to be addressing either or both of them, 'Which of you first found out the other existed?'

It was Wendy who answered. Her voice was even more fretful than usual. 'I don't understand what you mean.'

'I'll put it another way. When did you first discover Rodney Williams had a wife? And you, Mrs Williams, when did you find out your husband had "married" again?' He put very audible inverted commas round that past principle. 'Well?' he said. 'I know you haven't been truthful with me. I know you knew each other. The question is when did you first know?'

'I never knew she existed till you told me.' Joy spoke in her weary lifeless way. 'When you told me my husband was a bigamist on top of all the rest.'

'All what "rest", Mrs Williams?'

'Lying to me about his job for a start.'

Wendy murmured something.

'I'm sorry, Mrs Williams, I didn't catch that.'

'I said, "having other women". I meant that's what the rest was, having other women.'

'He never had other women,' said Joy. She was responding to Wendy's prompting but she wasn't speaking to her. It was

345

Wexford she was addressing. 'He had *her* but he never had others.'

'Let her delude herself if she wants,' said Wendy to no one in particular, lifting her shoulders and smiling very faintly.

'When did you first meet her, Mrs Williams?' Wexford was finding it a shade awkward, their both sharing the name. He got up and came round the table to address the words specifically to Wendy. Joy burst out, 'You've no business to call her that! She's no right to that name. She's Miss What-ever-she-used-to-be. You call her that!'

'The manners of a fishwife,' said Wendy. 'She's as common as dirt. No wonder he came to me.'

'Nasty little bitch! Look at her, dressed up like a kid!'

They're staging it, Wexford thought, they must be. It's all set up for my benefit, rehearsed as like as not. He called the two women quietly to order.

William Milvey was at home that day. The offices of Mid-Sussex Waterways were in his house and he was awaiting the visit of the VAT inspector. That was who he thought Burden was and for some moments they talked at cross-purposes, having one of those conversations so amusing to hearers and so frustrating to the participants.

Their hearer in this case was Mrs Milvey, a big-built lady, very ready with her laughter. She laughed merrily at their discomfiture. But Burden's troubles were quickly over. After that all went smoothly and it turned out to be as Wexford had supposed.

'The wife's a director of our company just as much as me,' Milvey said importantly. 'And naturally she knows the ins and outs of the business equally to what I do.'

'I have to know where he's going to be every day in case there's phone calls,' said Mrs Milvey, who was less pompous than her husband. 'The fifteenth of April? I'll have a look in the book, shall I, Bill?'

At this point the VAT inspector did arrive, a man in his early twenties by the look of him, carrying a briefcase. Milvey seemed reluctant to absent himself from the more interesting (and perhaps less alarming) examination but he was obliged to go. He took the VAT man into his office and closed the door. Mrs Milvey smiled comfortably at Burden.

'From Easter right up till the end of April they was working up Myringham way, she said, referring to the ledger she was holding. 'They never started on Green Pond till a month later.'

'Are you sure?'

'Positive. No doubt about it. It's down here in black and white. Green Pond, May the thirty-first. Besides, I remember it all now. Bill had a job lined up for the end of May, a big drainage job over to Sewingbury, and the chap cancelled at the last minute. But as luck would have it, this trout farm chap at Green Pond had been given his name and he rung up and said could he drag the pond? Well, Bill happened to be free on account of the cancellation. Must have given the trout farm fella a bit of a surprise, him saying yes, I'll start prompt on Monday.'

The office door opened again and Milvey put a hand out for his book. His wife gave it to him.

'Did you tell anyone?'

'I expect so. There was no secret about it, it was open and above board. You like to have a bit of news to tell folks, don't you? Now you're wanting to know if I told my neighbour Mrs Williams, aren't you?'

'Did you?'

'I never knew a thing about her husband then, mind you. I met her going down to the shops. Bill was getting the van out. I said something like, Monday he'll be doing a job at Green Pond Hall. There's going to be a trout farm, did you know? Something like that.'

'But you definitely told her your husband would be dragging the pond on Monday, May the thirty-first?'

'I couldn't see it would do any harm, could I?'

Had it? Wexford hadn't been entirely correct in his supposition, which was that Mrs Milvey had told Joy the pond had already been dragged or was not to be dragged until a much later date. But this gave a different – and incomprehensible – look to thing. If Joy had known Green Pond was to be dragged on the following Monday, the pond into which she had dumped her husband's travelling bag, wouldn't she have retrieved it during the weekend? The alternative possibility was that she had hidden it elsewhere and only put it in Green Pond when *she knew it was to be immediately dragged*. Why should she do such a thing, why behave so absurdly?

This was a hunch of Wexford's that had gone awry. Burden was on his way to put the second one to the test. They seemed no nearer, as far as he could see and in spite of Edwina Klein's revelation, to breaking the case. Next week he would probably start his paternity leave . . .

Bald-headed James Ovington, the son, was alone in charge of Pomfret Office Equipment. His ingratiating smile was as broad as ever. Burden noticed a new mannerism, a nervous way he had of rubbing his hands together. At any rate, the dour and obstructive father was nowhere around.

'Now can I help? Tell me what I can do.'

'You have a method of labelling your machines here,' said Burden. 'Not exactly a code, a kind of speedwriting. Last time we were here we noticed one labelled "E. Ten". I wondered what that stood for. It wasn't a Remington 315, of course, we'd have pounced on it if it had been. This is a kind of shot in the dark and I daresay I'm not making myself too clear.'

'It's clear enough you want to know what "E. Ten" stands for and that's easy.' Nevertheless, he hesitated and Burden wondered why a shade of unease seemed to cross his face.

'Eric Tennyson,' Ovington said. 'That's who it is, that's who "E. Ten" stands for.'

Second time lucky . . . 'I don't suppose you know if he has a daughter called Nicola?'

'Well, I do know as a matter of fact. The answer's yes.'

Veronica Williams's friend, her home the house to which Veronica regularly went on Tuesdays. But the typewriter labelled 'E. Ten' wasn't a Remington 315. Unless . . .

'An Olivetti,' said Ovington. 'They've got another machine. I don't rightly remember what. She types stuff for people, I mean does it for a living.' The uneasy look was back again. 'I may as well tell you,' he said as if about to make a confession of something that for a long while had weighed heavily on him. 'They're friends of mine. I knew I ought to tell you last time you were here.'

'But why shouldn't they be friends of yours, Mr Ovington?'

'Well . . . They're friends of Mrs Williams too. I mean the Mrs Williams whose husband got killed, the one you're making inquiries about. I mean that's where I met her, in their house.'

'Are you trying to tell me something, Mr Ovington?'

This fresh smile, a forced straining of the muscles, turned his face into a gargoyle. He rubbed his hands briskly, then clasped them behind his back to prevent a repetition of the gesture. Light from the shallow overhead lamps in the shed shone with a yellow gleam on the hairless head. Why were the heads of bald men compared to eggs? Ovington's head more than anything resembled a polished pebble.

'What is it you're saying, Mr Ovington?'

'I've been getting friendly with her. With Mrs Williams. There was nothing wrong, I don't mean that. I met her at Eric's and we'd have a drink sometimes, go for a walk, that sort of thing. When it looked as if that husband of hers had finally – well, when it looked as if he'd gone for good, I – I hoped things could get more serious.' He spoke jerkily, floundering, hopelessly unable to handle the situation he had got himself into. 'There was nothing *wrong*. I'd like to repeat that.'

Burden thought irrelevantly that Wendy Williams must be attracted by bald men, first Rodney with his exaggerated forehead, naked as an apple, then this pebble-head.

'But I thought,' Ovington said earnestly, 'that it would be wrong of me – disloyal, you know – to deny the relationship at this juncture, sort of deserting the sinking ship when you hear the cock crowing, if you get my meaning.'

More or less Burden did get it. He thought of the joy Wexford would have in that gloriously mixed metaphor. Now for the Tennysons. Half an hour later he was in their house on the Haldon Finch side of Pomfret, being told by Mrs Tennyson that her daughter was camping in Scotland till the end of the month but could she help him?

Her husband had fetched the repaired and serviced Olivetti from Pomfret Office Equipment three days before. Yes, she had her small portable for use when the other one was away for its annual overhaul. She showed it to him: a Remington 315.

Burden stuck the sheet of paper she gave him into the roller. 'A thousand ages in They sight, Are like an evening gone . . .' A flaw in the apex of the capital A, the ascender of the lower-case t, the head of the comma . . .

'I'd never seen her in my life till you had us meet here.'

That was Wendy. Joy said nothing.

'I put it to you that you'd known each other for a long time. I suggest it was like this: Mrs Joy Williams came into Jickie's as a customer one day and in conversation you discovered the link between you. This happened a year ago. You've been in touch with each other ever since.'

Joy gave one of her cold rattling laughs that had something in it of the cackle of a game bird.

'If I'd known about her why should I pretend I didn't?' said Wendy.

Joy answered. She didn't exactly address Wendy, she hadn't yet done that except to abuse her, but she made her first statement not inimical to the other Mrs Williams.

'If her and me knew each other he thinks we might have murdered Rod.'

'I'm more likely to have murdered *her*,' said Wendy in a lofty voice. She looked down and noticed a ladder in her pale milk-coloured tights. It crept up the outside of her right leg like a millipede. Joy noticed it too. She fixed her eyes on the slowly mounting run and her mouth moved. It was nearly a smile.

Wexford said, looking at Joy, 'Someone phoned Sevensmith Harding on Friday, April the sixteenth, to say Rodney Williams was ill and wouldn't be coming to work. The girl who took the call isn't in much doubt that it was your voice, Mrs Williams.'

'She doesn't know my voice. How could she, whoever she is? Aren't you forgetting, I didn't know Rod worked there?'

The door opened and Burden put his head round. Wendy was licking her finger and dabbing at the ladder with her wet fingertip, dabbing as it happened in vain, for the ladder quite suddenly crept another half-inch. It was this which might have occasioned Joy's rattle laugh. Wexford got up and went out of the room, leaving the two women with the two women detectives.

Burden had sent his typing sample to the forensics lab. He told Wexford the substance of his interview with Mrs Tennyson. She had typed no letter of resignation herself and no one had asked her to do such a thing. Wendy Williams she had known for years, though her acquaintance with Rodney had been slight. Their daughters were the same age, were at school together, were 'best friends'.

'Could Wendy have typed it?' Wexford asked him. 'I mean, could she have had access to this machine? If this killing was premeditated, and it looks as if it was, she could have typed that letter days or even weeks before.'

'The Tennyson woman shuts herself up in a room she uses as an office and types for three or four hours a day. As a regular thing she uses the Olivetti and the Remington isn't even kept in there. It's usually in a cupboard in the hall unless the husband Eric wants it or the daughter Nicola uses it to type a school essay. Apparently, they're allowed to do that at the Haldon Finch. Could you credit it?'

'It seems a sensible and harmless practice,' said Wexford. 'Was Wendy ever alone in that house?'

'Early in April she came to call for Veronica, take her home or something. It was dark or late or she was passing. Anyway, the two girls were still out and Mrs Tennyson was typing something. She left Wendy alone for at most ten minutes, she says, until she finished off what she was doing.'

'Wendy would have to know the machine was there. She would have to have paper. But I agree it goes a long way to answering the question of how and where the letter was typed. As to typewriters, what better than to use one that was normally kept shut up in a cupboard? It was by the merest luck that we got on to it.' He listened while Burden told him about Ovington. 'Is that a motive, Mike? We keep coming back to that, the lack of motive. But if Wendy wanted to marry Ovington . . .'

'Who did Joy want to marry?'

'Yes, OK, I see your point. If they did it they did it together and Joy wouldn't be likely to help murder Rodney so that Wendy could marry someone else.' Wexford brought his fist

351

to his forehead and drummed against it. 'I'm a fool! There's no motive. If Wendy knew about Joy she also knew she wasn't married to Rodney, so there was no legal bar to her marrying someone else . . . What about the knife, the weapon we're never going to prove *was* the weapon beyond a doubt? It could have been Joy's or Wendy's.'

'Wendy works at Jickie's and Jickie's stock those knives.'

'Wendy works there but the whole neighbourhood shops there.' Wexford thought for a moment. 'Among the stuff we found in Rodney Williams's bedroom in Liskeard Avenue,' he said, 'was an estimate from a firm of decorators for painting Wendy's living room. When we saw that room it had obviously been painted very recently. By that firm? By another? By Wendy herself? I think we ought to find out, don't you?'

Burden looked at him. They were both thinking that Rodney Williams had been stabbed to death. One of the knife thrusts had pierced the carotid. 'Yes, I do,' he said.

The day was very warm and close, a heavy, sultry, almost sunless day of the kind that only comes as August wanes. For the few moments he and Burden were in his office, the window open and the half-closed blinds swaying slightly in a hint of breeze, he had kept his jacket off. Now he put it on again and went back downstairs to the interview room where the two women were.

17

A picture of Joy and Wendy leaving Kingsmarkham Police Station was on most front pages of the national press next day. The more sensational of the newspapers managed to give the impression that they were not leaving but entering and that readers would not be too wide of the mark in concluding they had never left. Joy had her hand up over her face, Wendy looked piteously into the cameras, a distraught waif in her little-girl smock. The ladder in her tights was cruelly evident. Burden stood by, cool and rather aloof in a newish suit.

'You look young and handsome,' said Jenny at the breakfast table. 'You look so thin!' She shifted her huge weight, pushing back her chair.

'It's the worry.'

'I expect it is, poor Mike.' She put up her arms and hugged him. It was now only possible for her to do this while sitting down. He held her and thought, It may still be all right, we may still survive.

He went out before nine into a morning that was anything but fresh, a grey, sultry, sticky day. The sky was a flat, very pale grey with the sun a puddle of white glowing through it. This was the kind of day, he thought, that only England knows. Fifty of them can compose a summer.

How many builders and decorators were there in Pomfret? In Kingsmarkham? Not just the established firms but the one-man bands, the man who works in his spare time for money in the back pocket? With luck the Pomfret Williamses had availed themselves of the services of the firm who sent Rodney the estimate.

He didn't go to the police station first, so he was not present when Hope Harmer phoned to say her daughter was missing, had not been home all night or reappeared that morning.

John Harmer was in his dispensary and business was as usual. That is, when customers wanted soap or disposable razors instead of a prescription made up he came out and served them. He refused to believe anything had happened to his daughter. She was a grown woman well able to take care of herself as her prowess at that judo stuff evinced. Her absence probably had something to do with this women's movement nonsense.

Paulette's mother had come to work but only perhaps because of the pressures put on her by her husband. It was from there that she had phoned, the culminating act of a scene between them, Wexford guessed. She was in a piteous state. Hope Harmer was a woman whom it suited only to be happy. She was easily content and in contentment her plump, fair good looks bloomed. Unease affected her as it does an animal, drawing her face, freezing her features, mysteriously making bright hair lank and placid eyes stark with fear.

Wexford had Martin with him, the two of them top brass for the mere matter of a missing girl – but circumstances alter cases.

'My husband says what do I expect when I let her go out with her boyfriend at all hours and stay the night at his place. But they all do it these days and you can't be different. Besides they're engaged and I always say if you really love each other . . .'

She was talking for the sake of talking but her voice faltered. She began twisting her hands.

'Did Paulette go out with her fiancé last night?'

'No, he's in Birmingham. He had to go to Birmingham for his firm.'

Not for the first time Wexford marvelled at how illogical human thinking can be.

'But she did go out? Where did she go?'

354

'I don't know. She didn't say. She just went out at about seven.'

Martin said, 'You didn't want to know where she was going?'

'Want to know! Of course I wanted to know. If I had my way I'd know where she was every minute of the day and night. I mean I didn't ask her, I'd forced myself to that. When she was younger her father used to say: I want to know where you're going and who with but once you're eighteen you're legally grown-up and you can do what you like. Well, she's eighteen and she remembered that and my husband remembers it and he stops me asking and Paulette wouldn't answer anyway.'

The poor woman was wretchedly caught between husband and daughter, and bullied, doubtless, by both – or had she been happy to have decision-making taken out of her hands?

'Tell me what happened later on. Of course you didn't wait up for her?'

'I would have. I knew Richard was in Birmingham, you see. John said he wasn't having me get in a hysterical state. He took a sleeping pill and he made me take one.'

Presumably sedatives were unlimitedly on tap *chez* Harmer ...

'This morning I – well, I left her bedroom door open before I went to sleep. That way – if it was shut, you see, I'd know she'd come in. I – I had to make myself open my own bedroom door and look. Her door was still open, it was such a shock, I ... Well, I went to look, in case she'd come in and left her door but, of course, she hadn't. John still wasn't alarmed. Somehow I couldn't make him see that if Richard was in Birmingham Paulette couldn't have been with him ...'

Mrs Harmer burst into raging tears. Instead of falling forward onto her arms to cry she lay back, let her head hang back and wailed. Martin went into the dispensary and fetched John Harmer. He came in looking cross and harassed. The noise his wife was making had the effect of causing him to put his hands over his ears in the manner that does nothing to block out sound but indicates that the sound is in some way distasteful or irritating.

'She'd better have a Valium. That'll help her pull herself together.'

'What she had better do, Mr Harmer,' said Wexford, 'is get off home. And you had better take her. Never mind the shop.'

Godwin and Sculp had not done Wendy Williams's decorating but they knew who had – a man who had once worked for them, who had left to set up in business on his own and who undercut them, Burden was told, at every opportunity. Running Leslie Kitman to earth was less simple. He had no wife and his mother was no Mrs Milvey to have his precise location at her fingertips. She gave Burden five possible addresses at which her son might be found: a farmhouse between Pomfret and Myfleet, a block of flats in Queen Street, Kingsmarkham, a cottage in Pomfret, and two houses on new estates outside Stowerton. Kitman was at none of them but the second Stowerton household told Burden he might just be lucky and find him in – Liskeard Avenue.

And it was there, three houses away from Wendy Williams's, that Burden discovered Kitman on top of a ladder. The house was like Wendy's, grey bricks and white weatherboard and picture windows. Kitman was painting a top-floor window frame. When Burden, standing at the foot of the ladder, shouted up who he was, Kitman launched immediately into a catalogue of reasons for not renewing his car tax. Burden hadn't even noticed his car, still less that the tax disc showed an expiry date of the end of June. At last, though, Kitman was made to understand and he came quickly down the ladder, his brush dripping white paint onto the lawn beneath.

The evening before Wendy Williams had spent in bed where she had retired, worn out, as soon as she returned from the police station. Veronica had brought her tea and bread and butter. It was all she ever seemed to fancy when upset. Joy Williams had also been at home with her daughter. At any rate they had been in the same house, Sara in her room as usual, Joy watching television and intermittently struggling

356

to complete the form of application for a grant that would take Sara through medical school. And although it was a Thursday evening there had been no phone call from Kevin who extended this courtesy to his mother only when he was at college and not while junketing around holiday resorts.

These were the alibis Wexford was given by his two principal suspects. Richard Cobb came back from Birmingham in the course of the afternoon and furnished Wexford with a very detailed and apparently satisfactory account of where he had been the night before. Police in Birmingham would help with a check on that. By six Paulette hadn't come home and Wexford knew she never would, he felt in his bones she wouldn't.

The day was sultry and overcast. For hours the thunder had been growling and rumbling and gradually a wind had risen, a dry gusty wind that did nothing to lower the temperature. It still remained hot and stuffy. Wexford and Burden sat in Wexford's office. A search for Paulette hadn't begun yet. Where would one search?

'The lines I'm thinking along,' said Wexford, 'are that Paulette Harmer procured the Phanodorm with which Rodney Williams was sedated. She was in a position to do that, she could easily have done it. I'm wondering if she lost her nerve and told someone – well, Joy – she was going to admit it before we found out.'

'Of course, there's another possibility . . .' Burden left the suggestion suspended.

Wexford looked abstractedly out of the window. It was time to go home but he had no inclination to go. The weather, the atmosphere, the late day, hung heavy with expectation. The thunder, of course, was a threat in itself, a sign of imminent storm, yet it seemed to contain some kind of emotional menace as well, as of looming tragedy.

'Tell me about Kitman,' Wexford said. 'In detail.' Burden had already given him an outline of his talk with the painter.

'He started doing that job for Wendy on April the fourteenth. There was paper on the walls, he said, and he had a job stripping it off. He was doing it all through the fourteenth and the fifteenth and he still hadn't finished by the time he knocked off on the fifteenth.'

'Should have used Sevensmith Harding's Sevenstarker,

357

shouldn't he?' said Wexford and quoting, ' "The slick, sheer, clean way to strip your walls". '

'Maybe he did. He says the room was still furnished but he had covered the pieces of furniture up with his own dustsheets. When he came back in the morning – the morning of Friday the sixteenth, that is – some of the sheets were off and folded up. But that was also on the morning of the fifteenth and other mornings, I gather. Wendy and Veronica were to some extent still living in that room.'

'Did he notice anything else that Friday morning?'

'A stain on the wall is what we want, isn't it? A great bloodstain? And blood all over his dustsheets? There wasn't anything like that or if there was he didn't notice or can't remember. The walls were splashed and marked and patchy anyway, you can imagine. And on the sixteenth he covered up whatever might have been there by putting his first coat of paint on. Sevenstar emulsion, no doubt. One thing he did notice, though, and I didn't ask him about this, he volunteered it. Apparently it's been vaguely preying on his mind ever since. One of the dustsheets wasn't his.'

'*What?*'

'Yes. I thought that'd make you sit up. He has a few dustsheets he takes about with him. Some of them are old bed sheets and there are a couple of curtains and a candlewick bedspread too. Well, according to him, when he left on the fifteenth all seven of his sheets were covering the furniture and part of the carpet. Next morning he came in to find that three of the sheets had been taken off the furniture and were folded up on the floor. He thought nothing much of it but later he noticed that one of the folded sheets wasn't his. It was newer than his and in better condition.'

'Did he ask Wendy about it?'

'He says he did. On the Saturday. She told him she knew nothing about it. And what did it matter to him, after all? He had the right number of dustsheets. You don't go to the police because someone has taken one of your dustsheets and substituted another. But he wondered about it, he says. It niggled him is the way he puts it. Are we going to have those two women back?'

'Of course we are.'

It was Friday, the last Friday in the month. ARRIA met

on the last Friday of the month, Wexford thought. No, the last Thursday. It was two months ago yesterday that he had gone to the Freeborns' house and interrupted a meeting.

He picked up the phone and spoke to John Harmer. Paulette's father was anxious now, no longer calm and scathing. He said his wife was asleep. Heavily sedated, Wexford guessed.

'The place is crawling with police,' said Harmer.

Wexford replied dryly, 'I know.'

He thought it an unfortunate way of describing the initial search he had mounted in the environs of the Harmers' home. The man's breathing at the other end of the line was audible. His voice had been rough and shaky. If insulting the police helped him, well . . .

'I can't tell you I don't think this a serious cause for concern, Mr Harmer. I'm very sorry. I think you should prepare yourself for bad news. Perhaps it would be best to say nothing to your wife as yet.'

'I'm not likely to wake her up and tell her you think her only child's dead, am I?'

Wexford said a polite goodbye and rang off. Harmer's rudeness gratified him a little. It was more than excusable in the circumstances and at least it showed Harmer wasn't the unfeeling husband he had thought him. Tomorrow morning they would widen the search for Paulette. By then he might have some idea of where and how to widen it.

A few drops of rain struck the windows, needles on the glass. The thunder thudded and cracked over Myringham way. Martin and Marion Bayliss brought the two Mrs Williamses in and Wexford went down to the interview room to confront them. Wendy in her Jickie's suit, hair freshly set – in Jickie's hairdressing department? – was in tears, dabbing at her eyes with a pink tissue. Joy had never looked so down at heel, broken sandals on her bare feet, a button missing from her button-through creased cotton dress, a scarf tied round her head. She looked like a refugee, such as have passed in streams across Europe at frequent times in modern history. Her face was grey and drawn.

Burden came in and sat beside him. The room had got so dark they had to have the light on. Still it wasn't really raining. When no one attempted to comfort Wendy and no offers of cups of tea were made she stopped crying. Rather defiantly, she produced the box of pink tissues from her bag and set it on the table in front of her.

'Was Paulette Harmer the girl your husband was seeing?'

Wexford addressed the question to both women. It was awkward. It seemed to treat polygamy as a legal state. Joy gave a dry cackle, more than usually scornful. Wendy said she didn't know who Paulette Harmer was, she had never heard of her.

'Who was it then?'

'He didn't have a young girlfriend,' said Joy. 'He didn't have any girl.' She nodded at Wendy. 'Unless you count her. And that's not the word I'd use for her.'

Wendy sniffed and pulled a tissue out of the box.

'Well, Mrs Williams?' Wexford said to her.

'I told you, I don't know.'

'On the contrary, you told me you knew there was one. This very young girl living around here with her parents – you never heard of her, she doesn't exist?'

Wendy looked at Joy. Their eyes met. For the first time Wexford thought he sensed a rapport between them. Then Wendy turned sharply away and shook her head violently.

'Rodney Williams was attracted by young girls,' Wexford said. 'You're an example yourself, Mrs Williams. How old were you when you and he met? Fifteen? Is that why you invented a young girlfriend for him? You knew it was in his nature?'

'I didn't invent it.'

He was suddenly aware of a change taking in place in Joy. She was shaking with emotion. Her hands held the table edge. Rain had begun to patter on the windows. Burden got up and closed the fanlight. Joy leaned forward.

'Has Sara been talking to you?' she said.

It was on the tip of his tongue to say he would ask the questions. But he didn't say it. He felt his way. 'It's possible.'

'The little bitch!'

How was it he sensed that the two women were at last united by some common bond? And that bond wasn't the dead man. The noise of the rain was intense now, a crashing cloudburst. He thought, they did know each other. The Klein girl was telling me the truth. They were close in a conspiracy and they're back in it again, the acting is over ... He turned to Joy and it was as if his approaching, ultimately fixed gaze lit the fuse.

She spoke in a raucous throaty voice.

'You may as well have it. It wasn't young girls he was attracted to, not *any* young girls. It was his own daughter.'

18

It happened, it wasn't even uncommon. Lately it had been the modish subject for the pop sociology paperback. Yet that father-daughter incest might be a motivating factor in this case had not crossed Wexford's mind. Afterwards he was to ask himself *why* it hadn't crossed his mind, knowing his mind and the way it worked, but now in the interview room with the two women across the table from him he could only recall *The Cenci* and Beatrice – his own daughter playing Beatrice – running onto the stage crying:

'O World! O life! O day! O misery!'

That should have told him. Wendy had covered her face with her hands. Joy stared at him, her lips sucked in. A bead of saliva had appeared at the left corner of her mouth. She put her hand out for one of Wendy's tissues, tentatively, cautiously, watching Wendy, like an old dog approaching the food bowl but uncertain as to what the young dog will do. Wendy took her hands down. She didn't speak. She gave the tissue box a little push in Joy's direction. Burden sat, wearing his stony, contemptuous look.

Wexford was framing a question. Before he could utter it Joy spoke.

'She came and told me. Her own mother! His own wife! She said he'd come into her bedroom in the middle of the night. He said he was cold, he never seemed to get warm since we'd slept in twin beds. That's what he said to her. He said she could make him warm. Why didn't she scream out? Why didn't she run away? He got into bed with her and did it to her. I'm not going to repeat the word she used, they all use it for *that*. It was while I was asleep. I was asleep and he was doing that with his own daughter.'

She laughed. The sound was drier than ever with more of a rattle in it but it was a laugh. She looked at Wendy and directed the laugh at her. And, Wexford thought, she may have been in cahoots with her, she may have told her all this before in womanly confidence, in sisters-under-the-skin conspiracy, but she enjoys telling it now – in our presence, a public triumphant putdown.

Like the therapist to whom he had compared himself, he would let her talk without interruptions, without breaking in to question. If she would talk. The pause endured. Wendy looked away and at the screen of water, curiously claustrophobic, the rain was making down the panes. She had pushed her fingers so hard into the skin of her face that they left pink pressure marks. Without prompting, Joy went on.

'She waited till he'd gone to work and then she told me. I was ironing her a blouse for school.' Insult had been thus added to injury, she implied. The father's rape would have been less offensive to the mother if the news had been imparted to her while she was ironing a shirt for Kevin. 'She burst right out with it. There wasn't a question of being tactful, mind, of – well, breaking it gently. He was only my husband. It was only my husband she was telling me about being unfaithful to me.' The laugh came again, but a ghost of it this time. 'I wouldn't listen to her. I said, don't tell me, I don't want to hear. I put my hands over my ears.'

A rejecting gesture not unknown in the Harmer-Williams families, Wexford thought. He nodded at Joy, feeling it was necessary to give some sign.

'I put my hands over my ears,' she said again. 'She started shouting at me. Didn't I care? Wasn't I upset? I answered her then. I said of course I was upset. No mother wants to hear her daughter's like that, does she? I said to her, You spread that about and you'll split us up, your father'll go to prison and what are people going to think of me? What's Kevin going to say to them at college?'

Burden said quietly, 'What did you mean by that, Mrs Williams, your daughter was "like that"?'

'It's obvious, isn't it? I'm not saying he wasn't weak.' A

glance for Wendy and a quick withdrawal of the eyes. 'Well, we know he was. But he'd never have done that without . . .'

She stopped and looked at Wexford. He remembered when he had first talked to Sara and her mother had sent him up to her bedroom saying she wouldn't object – 'Rather the reverse if I know her.'

'Encouragement?' he said flatly.

She nodded impatiently. 'Putting her arm round him, trying to get his attention. She wasn't *ten*. I said to her, you're not ten any more. Sitting on his knee – what did you expect? Now the least you can do is keep quiet about it, I said, think of my feelings for a change.'

'When did all this happen?'

'It was before Christmas. I know it was because I remember saying that she'd picked a fine time, hadn't she, just when we were all going to be together for Christmas.'

Wendy, whose face had been impassive, winced slightly. Had she realized at last where and how Rodney Williams spent his Christmases? It was soon after that, probably in the first week of January, Wexford recalled, that Edwina Klein had seen the two women together.

'Did you tell anyone?' Burden asked.

'Of course I didn't. I wasn't going to broadcast it.'

He turned on Wendy. 'When did she tell you? Or should I say warn you?'

Wendy had looked shocked by none of this. Not even surprised. But she shook her head. 'She never did.'

'Come on, Wendy . . .' Wexford had solved the names problem at last. 'Joy found out you existed, sought you out especially to tell you what Rodney was really like. To tell you, in fact, to have a care to your own daughter.'

'Tell her?' said Joy. 'Why should I care?'

'Wendy,' Wexford said more gently, almost insinuatingly, 'you're not going to tell us you didn't know about Rodney and his daughter Sara. You're not going to make believe what we heard just now was all news to you. You couldn't have looked less surprised than if I told you it was raining. Joy came into Jickie's, didn't she, and told you who she was? I'll make a guess at the week before Christmas. How did she know who you were? She'd seen Veronica in the street and spotted the resemblance to Sara – a likeness no one could mistake . . .'

That they were surprised now, both of them, he couldn't doubt. He had been wrong there then. Never mind. There were other ways – following Rodney, seeing him and Wendy together, a host of ways.

'You met at Jickie's, went on to meet again after Christmas. No doubt there were many meetings . . .'

Wendy jumped up, eyes full of tears, grabbing a handful of tissues.

'I want to talk to you alone! Just you and me quite alone!'

'Surely,' said Wexford.

He got up. Burden didn't wait for them to leave the room before starting on Joy with his questions. When did she first suspect Rodney had a second home? Did she ever ask him? Joy was laughing at this second suggestion when Wexford closed the door. He took Wendy upstairs to his own office. The rain had abated, was now merely trickling, slipping, spilling, down the washed gleaming glass. Twilight hadn't yet begun and the sky was a clear grey, light from cloud-coated sunshine. Wendy stumbled a little going into the room. He thought it might be unwise to touch her, even to the extent of steadying her. She held on to the door frame and shot him a look of grievance.

In the chair he held out for her she sat down gingerly, treating herself as if she had become fragile. She had turned into a convalescent, tentatively putting out feelers to the world. Her shoulders she was keeping permanently lifted.

'What did you want to say to me, Wendy?' He had dropped the 'Mrs Williams' altogether now.

She whispered it, sustaining the invalid image, a broken woman, wan-faced, such as might fittingly inhabit the Castle of Petrella and be called Lucretia.

'The same as what she said.'

'I'm sorry, Wendy. You must make yourself plainer than that.'

'It was the same for us. The same as what she said. Or – well, it would have been. I mean, he would have done but he went away and got himself killed.'

Light penetrated. 'You mean Rodney also made advances

to Veronica? Only, if I interpret what you're saying correctly, it was merely advances?'

She nodded, tears splashing now, wads of tissues held to her eyes like swabs.

'Before Joy warned you or afterwards?'

A shrugging, then a shaking, of the whole body. Make-up scrubbed off with that cheapest and most readily available cleanser, tears. Wendy presented to Wexford a youthful, naked, desperate face.

'He had been a little more attentive to her, had he, than we in our society expect of a father to a teenage daughter? Did she tell you or did you see? Kissed her and said it was good to be alone with her and you out of the way?'

She jumped up. 'Yes, yes, yes!' she shouted.

'So on April the fifteenth, although you didn't think there was much chance of Rodney coming back, you encouraged your daughter to go out so as not to be alone with him? You told her not to run the risk of being alone with him but to stay out until you came home?'

Guilt was heavy on her face now, driving away indignation. He felt she was on the brink of a confession.

'Or did you send her out so that *you* could be alone with Rodney – you and Joy?'

The air was sharply clear, the rain past, the sky two shades of blue, a dark clean azure and the smoky blue of massed cloud. Nine o'clock and growing dark. Water lay in glassy pools, reflecting the sky. There was an unaccustomed coolness, almost a nip in the temperature. Before morning there would be more rain. Wexford could see it in the clarity and smell it in the atmosphere. He walked from the police station and kept on walking, just to get away from the enclosing four walls, the stuffiness, the millions of uttered words, the weariness of lies.

People used to tell him when they needed an alibi – now they cited television – that they had been for a walk. They didn't know where, just for a walk. He hadn't believed them. Everyone knew where they had been on a walk. Now he thought he might not be able to say where he had been tonight. His progress was aimless, though not slow, a fairly brisk marching in the fresh cold air, a thinking walk to dwell on what had passed.

So inconclusively. So unsuccessfully. He had wrung those two women, turned the handle and ground them through the rollers. Joy had laughed and Wendy had wept. He had kept on repeating over and over to himself: Edwina Klein saw them together. Why should she lie? Why should she invent? He had to let them go at last. Wendy was near collapse – or feigning it beautifully.

It was clear, the whole case, Burden said. A motive had at last emerged. Joy killed out of bitterness and jealousy, Wendy out of fear Rodney would serve Veronica the same way as he had served Sara. An unfortunate verb in the circumstances, but perhaps not inept . . . A conspiracy laid just after Christmas, brooded over through the early spring, hatched out in April. Murder in the room that would be decorated tomorrow. Staunch the blood with Kitman's dustsheet, realize too late what you have used.

It must have happened that way, there was no other. Perhaps they hadn't intended to kill, only confront him jointly, threaten and shock. But the French cook's knife had been handy, lying on the table maybe. That didn't explain drugging him with Phanodorm. The knife Milvey had found? Its blade matched with the width and depth of the wounds. So would a thousand knives.

He was in Down Road, under the dripping lime trees. Perhaps, all along, he had known he was making his way here. The big old houses, houses that could justly be called 'piles', seemed sunken tonight in dark, still, sodden foliage. A dark green perfume arose from grass and leaf and rain-bathed flowers. Somewhere nearby a spoilt dog, left alone for the evening, vented its complaints in little bitter whimpering wails. Wexford opened the gate to the Freeborns' house. Lights were on, one upstairs and one down. The dustmen had been that morning, long before the rain started, and left the scattering of litter they didn't bother to remove from places where the occupants failed to tip lavishly. A sodden sheet of paper, pasted by rain onto the gravel, bore the ARRIA logo and a lot of printing it was too dark to read.

Both twins came to the door. He approved their caution. Once more they were alone in the house, left to their own devices, the switched-on parents far away at some veteran hippies' haunt. Both had pale blue hair tonight, pink stuff on their eyelids, otherwise the nearly identical faces were bare. And identical on both faces was dismay at the sight of him. Eve spoke.

'Do you want to come in?'

'Yes, please.' The house no longer smelt of marijuana. That was one thing he had achieved, a dubious success. The girls seemed not to know where to take him. They stood in the hall. 'There was a meeting of ARRIA last night,' he said. 'Where was it? Here?'

'They're mostly held here,' said Amy.

'And it was here last night?'

'Yes.'

He pushed open a door and switched a light on. It was a huge living room, floor cushions making islands on parquet that hadn't been polished for two decades, a divan with thrown over it something that might have had its origin in Peru, the only chair a wicker hemisphere hanging from the ceiling. French windows, uncurtained, gave onto what seemed an impenetrable wood.

He sat in the hanging chair, refusing to be alarmed by its immediate swinging motion.

'Who was at the meeting?'

They exchanged glances, looked at him. 'The usual crowd,' said Amy, and conversationally, 'It's always the same lot that turn up, isn't it?'

The names he ran through got a nod at every pause. 'Caroline Peters? Nicola Anerley? Jane Gardner? Paulette Harmer?' Eve nodded. She nodded in the same way as she had at the other names. 'Edwina Klein?'

There must have been a note of doubt in his voice.

'Yes, Edwina was here. Why not?'

'Why not indeed. And why not Sara Williams, come to that?'

'Sara didn't come,' said Amy. 'She had to stay home with her mother.'

So John Harmer hadn't been so far out when he suggested his daughter's disappearance had something to do with this 'women's movement nonsense'.

'What time did the meeting end?'

'About ten,' said Amy. 'Just about ten.' She had forgiven them if her sister never would. She had altogether put off that distant manner. 'Someone told me today that Paulette didn't go home all night and . . .' She left the sentence hovering.

'You never told me,' Eve said sharply.

'I forgot.' Amy turned her eyes back on Wexford. 'She was a bit late. She didn't say why. Edwina brought her aunt – not to join, just to see what went on, though she's eligible of course, never having married. It was good seeing someone old who'd had principles and stuck to them.'

'I have fought the good fight,' said Wexford. 'I have run a straight race. I have kept the faith.'

'That's right. That was exactly it. How did you know?'

He didn't answer her. The Authorized Version was unknown to them, lost to their generation as to the one before, a dusty tome of theology, in every way a closed book.

'Was Paulette alone when she left?'

'The meeting was upstairs.' Eve was chilly and unbending but she had spoken. 'We didn't see people out. They went downstairs and let themselves out. Paulette left with Edwina and her aunt.'

'They may have left together,' said Amy, 'but they didn't go off together. I looked out of the window and saw Edwina and her aunt getting into the aunt's car and Paulette wasn't with them.'

'What's out there?' Wexford said abruptly. He pointed at the long windows beyond which was visible only a mass of foliage.

'The conservatory.'

Amy opened the doors, swung them open and put her hand to a switch. Unconventional the Freeborn family might be; they were not feckless. The old domed conservatory, its upper panes of stained glass, claret and green in an Art Nouveau design of tulips, was full of dark green leafy plants, some of which looked subtropical, all demanding ample water and getting it. It must cost a fortune to heat in winter, Wexford thought, coming closer, entering the conservatory and spotting an orchid or two, the velvety mauve trumpet of a *brunfelsia*.

Eve, without being asked, flooded the garden beyond with

light. Touching another switch brought on arc lamps, one on the conservatory roof, another in the branches of an enormous ilex. The garden, so-called, hardly deserved floodlighting. It was a wilderness of unmown grass, wild roses, brambles, the occasional hundred-year-old tree. And it was huge, the kind of garden whose owners might justly say they were never overlooked. Shrubs that appeared dense black at this hour made an encircling irregular wall round its perimeter.

'We don't any of us go in it much,' said Amy. 'Except as a shortcut to the High Street. And when it's muddy or whatever . . .' Another sentence was left hanging. She went on vaguely, 'Dad's keen on the conservatory. It's him that grows the plants.'

The *Cannabis sativa*, thought Wexford, but hardly in here. You need infra-red light for that and plenty of it. He opened the door into the garden, a glass door of slender green and white panels. The cold damp air breathed water in suspension at him. He noticed a path among the grass, pieces of crazy paving let into what had once been turf, was now wet hay. The girls weren't coming with him. Eve wound her arms round her body, hugging herself against the cold. Amy breathed on the glass and with her fingertip began drawing a raven with a woman's face. Wexford went down the path. The arc lamps reached no further than thirty feet or so. He took his torch out of his pocket and switched it on.

The path led to the gate in the far fence, he thought. That was what Amy meant by a shortcut to the High Street. First it wound through a copse of dark shrubs, laurels, rhododendrons, all glistening and dripping with water. He was curiously reminded of walking in a cemetery. Cemeteries were like this, untended often, places of ornamental shrubs, funereal trees, like this without flowers, unlike this with gravestones.

He came upon the fence and the gate quite suddenly, almost bumping into the gate which was in a break in the untrimmed hedge that followed the line of the close-boarding. From here the backs of other big houses could just be seen, two of them with yellow rectangles on black that were lights in their windows. The light didn't reach here and no moon had appeared. The path curved its way all round the garden. He followed its ellipse, returning on the right-hand side. Bamboo here, half dead most of it, a mass of canes. Then something prickly that caught at his raincoat. He pulled and heard the tearing sound. Turn the torch on it to see what had happened . . .

Turn the torch into the midst of this circle of briar roses, brambles with wicked thorns – onto an outflung arm, a buried face, a logo and an acronym, red on white cotton – ARRIA and the raven-woman.

It was more like a cemetery here than he had supposed . . .

19

The scene-of-crimes officer. Dr Crocker. Sir Hilary Tremlett fetched out of his bed and wearing a camelhair coat over pyjama top and grey slacks. Burden as neat and cool as at mid-morning. And the rain coming down in summer tempests. They had to rig a sort of tent up over the body.

She had been strangled. With a piece of string or cord perhaps. Wexford himself could see that without reference to Dr Crocker or Sir Hilary. The photographer's flash going off made him blink. He didn't want to look at her any more. It sickened him, though not with physical nausea, he was far beyond that. No pharmacology degree now, no marriage to Richard Cobb, no full flowering of that strange beauty that had been both sultry and remote.

The girls worried him, Eve and Amy, alone in that house with a young girl, a contemporary, dead in the garden. Marion Bayliss had tried to reach their parents but they were at none of the phone numbers the twins could produce. Neighbours shunned the Freeborns. With the families immediately next door they weren't even on speaking terms. Eve thought of Caroline Peters and it was she who came to the house in Down Road and stayed for the rest of the night. Wexford crawled into bed at around three. There was a note for him from Dora which he read but did not mark or inwardly digest: 'A man called Ovington keeps phoning for you.' She was deeply asleep and in sleep she looked young. He lay down beside her and the last thing he remembered before sleeping himself was laying his hand on her still-slender waist.

372

'She'd been dead about twenty-four hours,' said Crocker, 'which is about what you thought, isn't it?'

When you don't get enough sleep, Wexford thought, it's not so much tired that you feel as weak. Though perhaps they were the same thing. 'Strangled with what?' he asked. 'Wire? Cord? String? Electric cable?'

'Because it's easily obtainable and pretty well impossible to break I'd guess the kind of nylon cord you use for hanging pictures. And where were your suspects – ' Crocker looked at his watch ' – thirty-six hours ago?'

'At home with their daughters, they say.'

Wexford began going through the statement Burden had taken from Leslie Kitman, the painter. A description of the missing dustsheet was gone into in some detail. Useless now, of course. It was four months since that dustsheet, concealed in a plastic bag, had been removed by the council's refuse collectors. And the knife as likely as not with it. Somehow he couldn't believe in Milvey's knife, he couldn't take two Milvey coincidences . . .

The walls had been stained and pitted, Kitman said. He couldn't remember if the stains had looked any different on the morning of 16 April from the afternoon of 15 April. Some of the holes, he thought, might have been filled in by someone else. He had made good some of the cracks and holes with filler which, when it dried, left white patches. On 16 April and the morning of the 17th he had lined the walls with wood-chip paper and on the Monday following begun painting over the paper.

Was he going to have those women in again? One of them had killed the girl the night before last. To keep her from confirming their guilt in the matter of the Phanodorm. Only one of them or both? Joy could easily have known where she would be and that she left by the shortcut to the High Street where she would catch the Pomfret bus.

Burden was late. But then he too had been up and on the go since early yesterday morning, finally getting to bed even later than Wexford. To be up after midnight, thought Wexford, is to be up betimes. He had always liked that, only no one knew what 'betimes' meant any more, which rather spoiled the wit of it. Thinking of going to bed reminded him of Dora's note and he was about to pick up the phone and get hold of Ovington when Burden walked in.

He didn't look tired, just about ten years older and a stone thinner. He was wearing his stone-coloured suit with a shirt the same shade and a rust tie with narrow chocolate lines on it. Might be going to a wedding, thought Wexford, all he needed was a clove carnation.

'Jenny's started,' he said. 'I took her to the infirmary this morning at eight. There's not going to be anything doing much yet awhile but they wanted her in promptly.'

'You'd better start your leave as from now.'

'Thanks. I thought you'd say that. I must say these babies do pick their moments. Couldn't she have waited a week? She's going to be Mary, by the way.'

'After your grandmothers, no doubt.'

But the coincidence he had related to Wexford had slipped Burden's memory. 'Do you know that never crossed my mind? Perhaps Mary Brown Burden then?'

'Forget it,' said Wexford. 'It sounds like an American revivalist preacher. Keep in touch, won't you, Mike?'

Later in the day, with luck, the pathologist's report on Paulette Harmer would come and also perhaps something from Forensics on the murder weapon. He had Martin go to a magistrate and swear out a warrant to search the Williams home in Liskeard Avenue, and he wasn't anticipating any difficulties in getting it. In the meantime he had himself driven to the other Williams home. He didn't feel up to walking, whatever Crocker might advise.

Sara was mowing the front grass with one of those small electric mowers that cut by means of a line wound on a spool and are principally intended for trimming edges. As he got out of the car the motor whined and stopped cutting and the girl, crimson with bad temper, up-ended the flimsy machine and began tugging furiously at the line. He heard a hissed repetition of the word Joy disliked so much that she had used of her father's assault.

'Fuck, fuck, fuck, fuck!'

'If you do that with the current switched on,' Wexford said, 'one day you're going to cut your hand off.'

She cooled as rapidly as she had become incensed.

'I know. I've promised myself I'll always switch it off

before I fiddle with it. But these god-damned things never work for long.' She pulled prongs out of a socket to oblige him and smiled. An ARRIA tee-shirt today, identical to the one on dead Paulette. 'This is the fourth of these spools we've had this summer. Do you want to see my mother?'

And yet she couldn't know about Paulette. He remembered her thinly veiled boasting to her cousin on the phone and he didn't think she would much care. Nor would she much care when her mother was arrested for the murder. But perhaps it was natural for victims of incest not to care much about anything. He felt a wrench of pity for her.

'I want to talk to you first.'

The garage, now there was no car to occupy it, had become a toolshed and repository for rather battered garden furniture. Sara indicated a deckchair to Wexford. For her part she sat down on an upturned oil drum and set about struggling with the stubborn spool. This looked as if it might go the way of its fellows, three of which lay on a shelf next to a dozen half-used Sevenstar paint tins. He supposed she was busying herself so as not to have to look at him while he talked to her about her father.

At his first mention of incest, a tactful broaching of what her mother had told him, she didn't flush but turned gradually whiter. Her skin, always pale, grew milk-like. And he noticed a phenomenon, perhaps peculiar to her. The fine gold down on her forearms erected itself.

He asked her gently when it had first happened. She kept her head bent, with her right hand attempting to rotate the spool while with her left forefinger and thumb she tugged at the slippery red line.

'November,' she said, confirming his own ideas. 'November the fifth.' She looked up and down again quickly. 'There were only two times. I saw to that.'

'You threatened him?'

She hesitated. 'Only with the police.'

'Why didn't you tell your brother? Or did you? I have a feeling you and your brother are close.'

'Yes, we are. In spite of everything.' She didn't say in spite of what but he thought he knew. 'I *couldn't* tell him.' Like a different girl speaking, her face turned away, 'I was ashamed.'

375

And she hates her mother, so it was a pleasure to tell *her*? She gave a final tug and the line came through, far too much of it, yards of loosely-coiled scarlet flex.

Kevin was indoors, having unexpectedly arrived that morning by means of some comfortless and inefficient transport. He was lying spent, exhausted, dirty and unkempt, on the yellow sofa, his booted feet up on one of its arms. Joy had answered Wexford's knock with refreshments for Kevin in her hands, a trayful of sandwiches, coffee, something in a carton that was ice cream or yogurt. Wexford shut the door on him, hustled Joy into the kitchen. She was dressed exactly as she had been the day before, even to the headscarf – had she tied it on to run to the shops for Kevin-provender? – and gave the impression of having never taken her clothes off, of sleeping in them. He told her, quite blandly, about Paulette, but she knew. John Harmer had phoned her while Sara was in the garden. Or that was the explanation she gave Wexford for knowing. He said he would want her later at the police station, she and Wendy. He would send a car for her.

'What's my son going to do about his evening meal?'

'Give me a tin opener,' said Wexford, 'and I'll teach him how to use it.'

She didn't observe the irony. She said she supposed he could have something out of a tin for once. At least she didn't suggest his sister might cook for him, which was an improvement (if that was the way you looked at things) on twenty years ago.

The next stop was Liskeard Avenue, Pomfret. Martin had got his warrant and was there with Archbold and two uniformed men, PC Palmer and PC Allison, Kingsmarkham's only black policeman. A tearful Wendy was trying to persuade them it wouldn't be necessary to strip the paper off her living-room walls.

At the glass table sat Veronica. Evidently she had been at work on the hem of a white garment that lay in front of her but had laid down her needle when the policemen arrived. Wexford thought of the girl in the nursery rhyme who sat on a cushion and sewed a fine seam, feeding on strawberries, sugar and cream. It must have been her dress which suggested it to him with its pattern of small wild strawberries and green leaves on a creamy ground. Tights again, dark blue this time, white pumps. Another thing that made those girls look alike was the way neither of their faces showed their feelings. They were the faintly melancholy, faintly smug, nearly always impassive faces of madonnas in Florentine paintings.

Wexford's daughter Sylvia had a cat which uttered soundless mews, going through the mouth-stretching motion of mewing only. Veronica's 'hello' reminded him of that cat, a greeting for a lip-reader, not even as audible as a whisper. Wendy renewed her appeals as he came in, now making them to him only.

'I'm sorry, Wendy. I understand your feelings. We'll have the room redecorated for you.' Or for someone, he thought but didn't say aloud. 'And there'll be as little mess as possible.'

And it really was Sevensmith Harding's Sevenstarker they intended to use for the job, four large cans of it, each labelled in red italic script that this was the slick, sheer, clean way to strip your walls. Wexford found himself hoping this wasn't too gross an exaggeration.

'But what for?' Wendy kept saying, at the same time, curiously enough, picking up ornaments and pushing them into a wall cupboard, loading a tray.

'That I'm not at liberty to say,' said Wexford, falling back on one of the stock answers of officialese. 'But there's plenty of time. Please clear the room yourself if you want to.'

In silence Veronica picked up her sewing. She threaded her needle, using a small device manufactured for that purpose, and slipped a pink thimble onto her forefinger.

'She's doing the hem of her tennis dress. She's playing in the women's singles final at the club this afternoon.' Wendy spoke in tragic tones, only slightly modified by a faint proud stress on the word 'club'.

Kingsmarkham Tennis Club, presumably, or even Mid-Sussex. 'We shan't stop her,' Wexford said.

'You'll upset her.' She drew him into the kitchen, through the already open doorway. 'You're not going to say anything to her about you-know-what? I mean you're not going to go into it?'

'I'm not a social worker,' he said.

'Nothing actually happened anyway. I saw to it nothing happened.'

Impossible, though, not to see Rodney Williams, hitherto no more than liar and con-man, as some sort of monster. To make a sexual assault on one daughter was heinous enough, but almost immediately to have designs on her younger half-sister?

'Of course, you wouldn't have suspected anything *might* happen if Joy hadn't warned you.'

'How many times do I have to tell you I never saw the woman till you – introduced us?'

'Something you haven't told me is how you knew Rodney made sexual advances to Veronica. He didn't tell you but you knew. Veronica was the young girl living at home with her family you led us a wild goose chase about, wasn't she?' He closed the door between the rooms and leaned against it.

Wendy nodded, not looking at him.

'How did you know, Wendy? Did you see something? Did you notice something in his behaviour when he thought you weren't looking? Was that after or before Joy warned you?'

She mumbled, 'I didn't see anything. Veronica told me.'

'*Veronica*? That innocent child in there who's more like twelve than sixteen? That child you've very obviously sheltered from every exposure to life? She interpreted her father's affectionate kisses, his arm around her, his compliments, as sexual advances?'

A nod. Then a series of vehement nods.

'And yet you say "nothing actually happened". By that I take it you mean there was no more than a kiss and a touch and a compliment. But she – *she* – saw this as an incestuous approach?'

Wendy's response was characteristic. She burst into tears. Wexford pushed up a stool for her to sit on and found a box of tissues, never a difficult task in that house. He returned to the living room where the carpet was now covered with sheets and from which Veronica had disappeared. Allison was daubing the walls with Sevenstarker, Palmer already at work with a metal stripping tool. The hunch he had about what was under that paper was probably crazy, but besides that it was just possible an analysis of old plaster might show

378

traces of Rodney's blood. And might not. Anyway, it was work for Leslie Kitman. He could come in next week and put it all back again at the expense of the Mid-Sussex Constabulary.

The rain had started again. That would put paid to Veronica's match in the afternoon as neither the Kingsmarkham Tennis Club nor the Mid-Sussex County at Myringham had covered courts. Wexford, back in his office though it was Saturday, noted the time. Twelve-thirty. Getting on for three hours since Mike had been in and announced the imminence of his new daughter. Well, it was too soon yet to expect much, early days.

Something kept nagging at the back of his mind, something Wendy had said. About the tennis match, he thought it was. But she hadn't said anything except that Veronica would be playing that afternoon. Why did he have this curious feeling then that in what she said lay the whole answer to this case? He often had feelings like that about some small thing when a case was about to break, and the small thing always turned out to be vital and his hunch seldom wrong. The difficulty was that he didn't know what he had a hunch about.

All the available men he had were either at Wendy's taking her room apart or else, the far greater number of them, conducting a house-to-house in Down Road and interrogating every girl who had been at the ARRIA meeting. A mood of loneliness and isolation enclosed him. Dora had gone to London and to stay the night with Sheila in Hampstead. His elder grandson Robin would be nine today, his birthday party due to begin three hours from now. Crocker played golf all day on Saturdays. Wexford would have liked to sleep but he found it hard to sleep in the daytime. What the hell was it Wendy had said? What *was* it? Tremlett was probably still at work on that poor girl's body . . . She had got Phanodorm for Joy and threatened to tell that she had. Well, not threatened, warned rather that she would have to, she would be scared not to. Joy had given Rodney the Phanodorm, substituting it for his blood-pressure pills, and it took just the time of a drive to Pomfret to act. Follow him by bus to Wendy's. He's asleep when you get there and you look at him and remember what he's done to you by way of what he's done to your daughter. Married another woman too, like a bloody sheikh. And the other wife goes along with you, though you hate her. It's her daughter at risk now since you told her where his tastes lie. Why let him ever wake up again? If there's a mess she says the room's going to be decorated tomorrow. And if you hide the body for long enough . . .

In the morning phone the office, say he's ill, disguising your voice a bit. She'll type his letter of resignation for you, she's got access to a typewriter in a friend's house that no one's going to trace. You're both in it equally, you and she, the two wives of Rodney Williams, for better for worse, till death parts you. She stabbed him too, though you gave him the sleeping pill. You and she together carried the body down that crackpot spiral staircase, through the doorway into the integral garage. Laid him in the car with his travelling bag. She drove because you never learned, but you did most of the grave digging. Soiling your hands never bothered you the way it did her. Two wives, in it together equally, and whom murder has joined let no man put asunder.

Wexford had got himself under Joy's skin and he very nearly finished this internal monologue with one of her awful laughs. The chances were Burden wouldn't phone before evening. And then surely he'd phone him at home. He drove to the Old Cellar and had himself a slice of quiche, broccoli and mushroom, a pleasant novelty, one small glass of Frascati to go with it – it was Saturday, after all, though with nothing to celebrate – and then back again to the estate where the streets were named for Cornish towns, Bodmin, Truro, Falmouth, Liskeard. A cold grey rain fell steadily. They were back to the weather they had had between Rodney Williams's disappearance and the discovery of his body.

In Wendy's living room considerable progress had been made. Three walls were more or less stripped. It wasn't what Wexford would have called slick, sheer and clean but it wasn't bad. Martin had got hold of someone from Forensics, a shaggy girl in navy all-in-ones, who nevertheless had the air of an expert and was painstakingly scraping samples of brownish plaster off the walls.

Wendy was downstairs in her sewing-ironing-laundry

room or whatever, cutting patterns out of magazines. For therapy, no doubt. Veronica was with her, Miss Muffet on a velvet pouffe. No match for her today as he had predicted. He suddenly remembered his threat to send a car for Joy 'later' and the crisis over Kevin's dinner this had precipitated. Well, it would have to be much later . . . Or tomorrow. Or every day on and for ever. No, he mustn't think that way.

Wendy had changed her dress for a linen suit. Perhaps she had been going to watch her daughter play, for Veronica, as though not resigned to the cancellation until the last moment, was in her tennis whites, pleated miniskirt – who could imagine her in shorts? – and a top almost too well finished to be called a tee-shirt.

'I suppose they'll postpone it till Monday night,' said Wendy in a high rather mad voice, 'and that means half the spectators won't come.'

Down the spiral staircase came the expert with her case of samples, the scraper in her hand.

'I think I'm going to be sick,' whispered Veronica.

Her mother was all care, all solicitude, jumping up, hastening her to the ground-floor bathroom.

Wexford went back upstairs. Archbold had gone. The expert had gone. Martin was drinking tea from a flask and the other two Coke from cans while they waited for the Sevenstarker on the fourth wall to do its stuff. Wexford felt something very near a qualm. The room, which had been a shell-pink sanctuary, was a nasty mess. A shambles, Martin called it, but a shambles, meaning a slaughter house, was just what Wexford thought it had been used for, the reason for this destruction. Suppose he was wrong? Suppose the killing of Rodney Williams had taken place elsewhere?

Too late now.

The police's loss would be Kitman's gain. It is the business of the thinking man, he paraphrased, to give employment to the artisan.

'Let me have one of those, will you?' he said to Martin, pointing to the scrapers. The white patches of plaster among the brown were the areas Wendy herself had filled before Kitman began papering.

It wouldn't budge the white plaster.

'Want me to have a go, sir?' Allison produced what Wexford thought might be a cold chisel.

'We'll all have a go.'

It made Allison's day. He had never before distinguished himself in any way since joining the force two years before. Sometimes he thought – and his wife – that they had only taken him on because he was black and not because he was suitable or any good. They were inverted race snobs. For weeks everyone had bent over backwards to treat him with more kindness, courtesy and consideration than they would show, for instance, to a millionaire grandfather on his deathbed. That had worn off after a while. He was a bit lonely too in Kingsmarkham where only his wife, his kids and two other families were West Indian like him. But today paid for all that. It was what made him in his own eyes an officer of the law.

'Sir, I think I've found . . .' he began.

Wexford was there beside him like a shot. Under his eyes Allison dug in carefully, thanking his stars he'd remembered to put his gloves on. The object was stuck in the fissure wrapped up in newspaper, plastered over. He chipped and dug and then put his hand to it, looking at Wexford, and Wexford nodded.

The knife didn't clatter out. It was unveiled as reverently as if it were a piece of cut glass. They all looked at it lying there on its wrappings, clean as a whistle and polished bright as a long prism in a chandelier.

20

Wexford had them with him all day Sunday and Monday morning's papers said an arrest was imminent. But Wexford wanted the two women, not just one, Joy as well as Wendy. Charging Wendy with Rodney Williams's murder was an obvious act. The knife buried in her living-room wall had a blade which exactly matched the knife wounds on the body and it was wrapped in part of the *Daily Mail* of 15 April. Still, he wanted Joy as well and Joy had no apparent connection with the crime. The only evidence he had was a witness who claimed to have seen the two women together and a voice on the phone that was probably hers.

Joy also had an alibi. Wendy didn't. All day long nails were going into Wendy's coffin, or at least the shades of the prison house were closing about her. Until Ovington came. That is, until Ovington's second visit.

Alone in the house, eating a junk food supper, Wexford got a call from Burden late on Saturday evening. Jenny's labour hadn't exactly been a false alarm but it had gradually subsided during the day. They were keeping her in, though, and considering some method of induction...

'You wanted her to wait a week,' said Wexford nastily. 'You'd better come back to work.'

He phoned Ovington first thing in the morning. Never mind about Sunday and all that. By the time Ovington arrived at the police station he and Sergeant Martin and Polly Davies had Joy and Wendy in an interview room, the demented refugee and the broken doll. The curious thing was they had come closer to each other. In appearance that is. There had been a sort of blending, and he thought of

383

Kipling's hedgehog and tortoise, combining to make an armadillo. Joy and Wendy hadn't gone that far, but anxiety and harassment had done their work on the younger woman and the older had smartened herself up, perhaps because her son was back. At any rate the headscarf was gone and she had proper shoes on. But Wendy's make-up was stale, she had hairs all over the shoulders of her black cotton dress and the ladder that sprang in her tights didn't fidget her.

He left them to go and talk to Ovington. Smiling as usual, absurdly ingratiating, he could hardly have persuaded even the most gullible to believe him, certainly not a hard-headed policeman.

'She was with you on April the fifteenth?' Wexford said. 'She came to your place after work for a drink? Why hasn't she so much as mentioned this to me?'

'She doesn't want anyone to know she was seeing me while her husband was still alive.'

That was in character. Wifely virtue was one of the aspects of the image Wendy liked to present. That didn't mean Ovington's story was true. Ovington was trying it on, a kind, stupid man with a misplaced idea of duty. Absently Wexford thanked him for coming. Then, as he was going back to the Williams wives, it occurred to him Ovington might have been in it with Wendy instead of Wendy with Joy. In that case who had made the phone call?

Wendy was crying. She said she was cold. It was true that the weather had turned very cold for the time of year but she should have been prepared for that, sacrificed vanity and brought a coat. He thought of all the places in the world and all the policemen in them where Wendy would have been allowed to shiver, where the temperature would have been lowered if possible, a little hypothermia encouraged. You couldn't call it torture, cooling someone into admissions . . .

'Get her something to put on,' he said to Polly.

He took them through the incest again and he got more stories full of holes. Joy hadn't believed Rodney would do that, yet she insisted Sara had led him on, insisted too that he would have gone to prison if she had breathed a word. Wendy now said Veronica had told her Rodney had started coming into her bedroom to kiss her good night and it wasn't

384

'nice'. That, said Joy, forgetting her former statement, was just how it had begun with Sara. Polly came back into the room with a grey knitted garment, something from Marks and Spencer's range for old ladies – God knows where she found it – which Wendy put on with a show of reluctance.

Sandwiches were brought in to them at lunchtime, one lot corned beef, the other egg and cress. Not exactly the Sunday joint, two veg and Yorkshire pudding. By that time Wexford had taken them through 15 April and was getting on to last Thursday night. Wendy had forgotten her coat but not her box of tissues, shades of peach this time. She sat snivelling into handfuls of them.

Just before three Joy broke at last. She started to howl like a dog. She rocked back and forth in her chair, howling and drumming her fists on the table. Wexford stopped the proceedings and sent for a cup of tea. He took Wendy into the interview room next door and asked her about Ovington. Rather to his surprise she agreed without much reluctance that she had been in Ovington's flat on 15 April from about 7.45 until about 9.15. Why hadn't she said so before? She gave the reason Ovington had given for her. They had hatched this up together, Wexford thought.

'I thought I might as well tell you,' she said with an aplomb that almost staggered him. 'I didn't before because you've all got minds capable of anything. But there's been so much real dirt dug up I don't think my innocent little friendship amounts to much.'

What did any of it weigh against that knife in the wall?

Late in the afternoon Burden walked in, looking a hundred years old.

'For God's sake,' said Wexford. 'I wasn't serious.'

The truth was Burden didn't know how otherwise to pass the time. He started on Joy, trying to break her alibi. But the tea had done wonders for her. She stuck to her story about watching television at the Harmers' and after half an hour of that had the brainwave that might have struck her days ago. She didn't have to talk at all if she didn't want to. Nobody had charged her with anything.

Unfortunately, by this time Wendy was back in the room with her and heard what she said.

Through her tears she smiled quite amicably at Joy. 'Good idea. I'm not talking either then. Pity I didn't think of it before.'

Joy uttered one last sentence. 'It was me thought of it, not you.'

United in silence, they stared at Wexford. Why not charge them both? With murdering Rodney Williams and, if he couldn't make that stick, with murdering Paulette Harmer? Special court in the morning, a remand in custody . . . Archbold came in and said there were three people to see him. He left the silent women with Burden and Martin and went down in the lift.

James Ovington was sitting there with his taciturn father and an elderly woman he introduced as his mother. Somehow Wexford had never thought of Ovington *père* as having a wife but, of course, he would have; James Ovington must have come from somewhere. He only looked like a waxwork. More so than ever this afternoon, his complexion fresher, his cheeks pinker, his smile flashing.

'My parents want to tell you something.'

That was one way of putting it. They didn't look as if they had any desire beyond that of going home again. Wexford asked them to go up to the first floor with him to his office but Mrs Ovington said she'd rather not, thank you, as if any suggestion of going upstairs in the company of men was indecent. They compromised with an interview room. Mrs Ovington looked disparagingly about her, evidently thinking it wasn't very cosy. James Ovington said, 'What were you going to tell the chief inspector, Dad?'

Nothing apparently.

'Now you know you were willing to come here and tell him.'

'Not willing,' said Ovington senior. 'If I must I must. That's what I said.'

'Is this something about Mrs Wendy Williams, Mr Ovington?' prompted Wexford.

Very slowly and grudgingly Ovington said, 'I saw her.'

'We both did,' said Mrs Ovington, suddenly brave. 'We both saw her.'

Wexford decided patience was the only thing. 'You saw her, yes. When was this?

James opened his mouth to speak, wisely shut it again. His father pondered, at last said, 'She's got a car. She'd parked it outside the shop on the yellow line. That don't matter after half six. We never saw her go in.'

Silence fell and endured. Wexford had to prompt.

'Go in where?'

'My son's place, of course. What else are we talking about? He's got the bottom flat and we've got the top, haven't we?'

'Up four flights,' said his wife. 'Wear the old ones out first, that's what it is.'

'We saw her come out,' said Ovington. 'Out of our front window. Round a quarter past nine. Tripped over and nearly fell in them heels. That's how Mother come to see her. I said, Here, Mother, look at this, them heels'll have her over.'

'It was April the fifteenth!' said James, unable to contain himself any longer.

'I don't know about that.' His father shook his head. 'But it was the first Thursday after Easter.'

That night he went to bed early and slept for nine hours. He didn't let himself think about the two women, Joy with no evidence against her, Wendy exonerated by the Ovingtons. They had been sent home with the warning that he would very likely want them back again on Monday morning. Old Ovington hadn't been lying but still his story didn't militate against the possibility that while Joy had done the deed in Wendy's house Wendy had later met her in time to help her dispose of the body, the clothes and the car.

In the morning he awoke clear-headed and calm. Immediately he remembered what it was Wendy had said to him. It had been when she told him Veronica was to play in a tennis singles final. The significance was in what it reminded him of, and now he remembered that too and as he did so everything began to fall gently and smoothly into place, so that he felt like one recalling and then using the combination of a safe until the door slowly swings open.

'But what a fool I've been,' he said aloud.

'Have you, darling?'

387

'If I'd got on to it sooner maybe that poor girl wouldn't have died.'

'Come on,' said Dora. 'You're not God.'

The phone was ringing as he left the house. It was Burden but Wexford wasn't there to answer it and Dora spoke to him.

A report on the postmortem, rushed through by Sir Hilary Tremlett, was awaiting Wexford. He went through it with Crocker beside him. Strangling had been with a fine powerful cord and whatever this was had left a red staining in the deep indentation it had made around the victim's neck.

'The nylon line from the spool of an electric edge trimmer,' said Wexford.

Crocker looked at him. 'That's a bit esoteric.'

'I don't think so. Joy Williams has three such spools in her garage and one of them, unless I'm much mistaken, will be empty.'

'Are you going to go there and check that?'

'Not just at the moment. Maybe later. Do you think it wrong to encourage a child to inform against its immediate family?'

'Like what happens in totalitarian societies, d'you mean? Or what I suppose happens. Extremists always believe the means are justified by the end. It depends what you mean by immediate family too, I mean, against a parent is a bit grim. That sticks in one's throat.'

'Drugging a man and stabbing him and burying the knife in a wall sticks in one's throat too.' Wexford picked up the phone and put it down again. 'I've got two women to arrest,' he said, 'and the way things are I'll never make the charges stand up. When do the schools go back?'

Crocker looked a little startled at this apparent *non sequitur*. 'The state schools – that is, the older kids – sometime this week.'

'I'd better do it today if I'm to catch her without her mother.' He lifted the phone again, this time asked for an outside line. It rang for so long he began to think she must be out. Then at last Veronica Williams's soft, rather high voice answered, giving the number in all its ten digits. Wexford spoke her name, 'Veronica?' then said, 'This is Chief Inspector Wexford of Kingsmarkham CID.'

'Oh, hello, yes.' Was she afraid or did she always answer the phone in this cautious breathless way?

'Just one or two things to check with you, Veronica. First, what time is your match tonight and where is it?'

'Kingsmarkham Tennis Club,' she said. 'It's at six.' She gathered some courage. 'Why?'

Wexford was too old a hand to answer that. 'After that's over I'd like to talk to you. Not you and your mother, just you alone. All right? I think you have quite a lot of things you'd like to tell me, haven't you?'

The silence was so heavy he thought he'd gone too far. But no. And it was better than he had hoped. 'I have got things to tell you. There are things I've *got* to tell you.' He thought he heard a sob but she might only have been clearing her throat.

'All right then. When you've finished your match come straight here. D'you know where it is?' He gave her directions. 'About ten minutes' walk from the club. I'll have a car to send you home in.'

She said, 'I'll have to tell my mother.'

'By all means tell your mother. Tell anyone you like.' Did he sound too eager? 'But make sure your mother knows I want to see you alone.'

The enormity of what he was doing hit him as he put the phone down. Could anything justify it? She was a sixteen-year-old girl with vital information for him. The last teenage girl with vital information for him had been strangled before she could impart it. Was he sending her to the same death as Paulette Harmer? If Burden had been there he would have told him everything but with the doctor he had reservations.

'You're not going round there, then?' Crocker said, a little mystified as much by Wexford's expression as by the cryptic phone conversation.

'That's the last thing I must do.'

Later, when the doctor had gone, Wexford thought, I hope I have the nerve to stick it out. Pity it's so many hours off. But the advantage of an evening match was that afterwards it would be dark . . . Advantage! She would be phoning her mother now at Jickie's to tell her, he thought, and somehow – hopefully – persuading Wendy not to come with her. He would have that girl watched every step of the way.

389

The phone rang.

He picked it up and the telephonist said she had a Miss Veronica Williams for him. What a little madam she was giving her name as 'Miss!'

'I could come and see you now,' the childish voice said. 'That might be easier. Then I wouldn't have to upset Mummy. I mean I wouldn't have to tell her I don't want her with me.'

He braced himself. He hardened his heart. 'I'm too busy to see you before this evening, Veronica. And I'd like you to tell your mother, please. Tell her now.'

If she called back, he thought, he'd relent and let her come. He wouldn't be able to hold out. Would she recognize Martin? Archbold? Palmer? Certainly she'd know Allison. But would it matter if she did recognize them? He'd be there himself anyway. There was no way he was going to let her take that ten-minute walk in the half-dark from the club down a lane off the Pomfret Road to the police station, especially in the case of her following his directions and taking the footpath across one and a half fields.

The phone rang again. That's it, he thought. I can't keep it up. I'll go round there and she'll tell me and that'll be evidence enough . . . He picked up the receiver.

'Inspector Burden for you, Mr Wexford.'

Burden's voice sounded strange, not really like his voice at all.

'It's all over. Mother and baby are doing fine. Jenny had a Caesarean at nine this morning.'

'Congratulations. That's great, Mike. Give my love to Jenny, won't you? You'd better tell me what Mary weighed so that I can tell Dora.'

'Eight pounds nine ounces, but it's not going to be Mary. We're changing just one letter in the name.'

Wexford didn't feel up to guessing. Jenny's persuaded him into something fancy against his better judgement, he thought.

'Mark, actually,' said Burden. 'I'll see you later. Cheers for now.'

21

A woman had once been found murdered on that very footpath.* They would all have that in their minds, even Palmer and Archbold who hadn't been there at the time, who had probably still been at school. As Veronica Williams still was. Had she ever heard of the murder? Did people still talk about it?

That woman had lived in Forest Road, the last street in the area to bear the postal address Kingsmarkham. The Pomfret boundary begins there, though it is open country all the way to Pomfret in one direction and nearly all the way to Kingsmarkham Police Station in the other. The tennis club, however, is not in Forest Road but in Cheriton Lane which runs more or less parallel to it on the Kingsmarkham side. Smallish meadows enclosed by hedges cover the few acres between the club and the town, and the footpath runs alongside one of these hedges, at one point skirting a little copse. It emerges into the High Street fifty yards north of the police station and on the opposite side.

Wexford had Martin and Palmer in a car in Cheriton Lane, would station himself and Archbold in the copse, Loring among the spectators at the match, Bennett to start walking from the High Street end, Allison to follow her at a discreet distance.

'One black man'll look very like another to her, sir,' Allison had said. 'That mightn't be so in a city but it is out here.'

'Don't tell me Inspector Burden and I look alike to you.'

* See *A Sleeping Life*.

'No, sir, but that's a question of age, isn't it?'

Which puts me firmly in my place, thought Wexford. Burden was in his office, sitting beside him, anxious to take part in the protection-of-Veronica exercise. Can't keep away from the place for more than five minutes, Wexford had grumbled at him. At least Burden had supplied a diversion in the lull of the long afternoon.

'I don't understand how they could make a mistake over the sex like that. God knows I don't know much about it, but if a man has an XY chromosome formula and a woman XX surely they must always have it from embryo to old age?'

'It's not that. It's like this. In an amniocentesis they extract cells from the amniotic fluid the foetus is in. But occasionally they make a mistake and once in about ten thousand times they take cells from the mother not the child. And even then they aren't always going to know their error. Because if the child does happen to be a girl... In this case, though, I gather someone's head is going to roll.'

'It caused a lot of unnecessary misery.'

'Misery, yes,' said Burden, 'but maybe not unnecessary. Jenny says it's taught her a lot about herself. It's taught her she's not what you might call a natural feminist and now she has to approach feminism not from an emotional stand-point but from what is – well, right and just. We didn't know, either of us, what a lot of deep-rooted old-fashioned prejudices we had. Because I felt it too, you know, I also wanted a son though I never said. It's taught us how much we've concealed from the other when we thought we were frank and open. All this has been – well, not far from – what does Jenny call it? – Guided Confrontation Therapy.'

With difficulty Wexford kept a straight face. 'So long as now you've got a son you don't wish it was a girl.' He said 'you' but he meant Jenny whom he thought the kind of woman for whom the unattainable grass might always be the greener.

'Of course not!' Burden exclaimed, looking very sour. 'After all, as Jenny says, what does it really matter so long as it's healthy and has all its fingers and toes?'

This was a cliché Wexford didn't feel he could compete with. Now Burden was here how would he feel about taking

392

part in the Veronica watch? Not much, said Burden, he had to be back at the hospital. Then Wexford thought it might start raining. If it rained the match would be cancelled and in all probability Veronica would simply take the bus to the police station from Pomfret.

But the sky lightened round about 5.30. He wondered what those two women were thinking. How had they reacted to being left all day to their own devices? Unless the match was over in two straight sets Veronica could hardly expect to leave the club before seven. Should he fill in the time by seeing what he could get out of Kevin Williams? But he didn't really want to get anything out of him. He knew it all already. Why not simply go and watch the match?

It hadn't occurred to him to ask himself – or anyone else for that matter – if the tournaments of the Kingsmarkham Tennis Club were or were not open to the public. And it wasn't until he walked through the doors of the clubhouse that the question came into his mind. But a hearty elderly man with the air of a retired Air Force officer who said he was the secretary welcomed him with open arms. They loved spectators. If only they could get more spectators. It provided such encouragement for the players.

He had already spotted Martin and Archbold sitting in the car a discreet distance from the gates. Now if Veronica saw him, as it was most likely she would do, his best course would be to leave. Then, later, she wouldn't fail to follow. The great thing was not to give her a chance to speak to him. Therefore, to the bar, a refuge which was also the last place to which a sixteen-year-old competitor was likely to retreat before a match. The secretary, seeing him headed in that direction, trotted up to say that as a non-member he wasn't allowed to purchase a drink but if he would permit a drink to be bought *for* him . . . ? Wexford accepted.

The bar was semicircular, with a long curved window offering a view of three of the club's nine hard courts. Wexford had a half of lager, the club like most places of its kind being unable to provide any sort of draught beer or 'real ale'. The secretary talked rather monotonously, first about the bad public behaviour of certain international tennis stars, then their own disappointment at Saturday's rain and the enforced cancellation of this singles final. There would have been more spectators on a Saturday, he said sadly. In fact, nine people had actually come along – he had counted – but had had to be turned away. Of course, they were most unlikely to come back tonight. Wexford had the impression that if any of them had turned up the secretary would have bought them drinks too.

It got to six, to ten past. She's not going to come, Wexford thought. Then an umpire arrived and climbed up into the high seat. Five canvas chairs and a wooden bench had been arranged for a possible audience. It looked as if they would remain empty but after a while two elderly women with white cardigans over their tennis dresses came and sat down and at the same time, approaching by the path that led from the farther group of six courts, Loring sauntered up. In sound English fashion the women sat in the canvas chairs on the left-hand end of the row and Loring at the extreme right-hand end of the bench. Colin Budd should have been so wise.

Veronica and a taller, older, altogether bigger girl appeared outside the court and let themselves in by the gate.

'Well, best get out there and give them some moral support,' said the secretary, rubbing his hands together.

It was certainly cold. A gust of wind whipped across the court, tearing at Veronica's short pleated skirt. In classic style they began with a knock-up.

'I don't think I will,' said Wexford. 'D'you mind if I watch from in here?'

The secretary was terribly disappointed. He gave him a look of injured reproach.

'You mustn't buy any drinks, you do know that, don't you? And you're not to serve him, mind, Priscilla.'

Loring, his jacket collar turned up, was smoking a cigarette. The secretary appeared, running up to the two women, and sat beside them. The knock-up, in which Veronica had had the best of it, was over and the match began.

Dark would come early because the day had been so dull. Wexford wondered if the light would hold long enough for the match to be played to the finish. Veronica, whose service it was, won the first game to love but had a tougher time when her opponent came to serve.

'You can have a drink if you like,' said Priscilla. 'I work it like this. I give it to you for free and next time a member buys me a drink I'll charge yours up to him. I'm a total abstainer actually but I don't let on to this lot.'

Wexford laughed. 'Better not, thanks all the same.'

'Suit yourself.' She came over and stood beside him and watched.

Three games all. It looked as if it would go on and on and then quite quickly it was all over, Veronica having won her own two service games and broken her opponent's.

'She's a little cracker, that kid,' said Priscilla. 'Strong as a horse. She's got arms like whipcord.'

It was twenty to seven and the edge of dusk. Veronica won the first two games but the other girl was fighting back for all she was worth. Perhaps she had never played against Veronica before. At any rate, it had taken her all this time to find her weakness but she had found it at last. Veronica couldn't handle long swift diagonal drives to her forehand, though backhand presented her with no problems. It was half a dozen of those forehand drives that won her opponent the next game and the next and the next two until she was leading 4–2. The light had grown bluish but the white lines on the court were still clearly visible, seeming to glow with twilight luminosity.

And then it was as if Veronica mastered the craft of dealing with those hard cross-court strokes. Or, curiously, as if some inspiration came to her from an external source. Certainly it was not that she had spotted him or had recognized Loring, whom she had never previously seen. But a charge of power came to her, a gift of virtuosity she had not known before. She had never before played like this, Wexford was sure of it. For a brief quarter of an hour she played as if she were on the centre court at Wimbledon and was there not by a fluke but by a hard-won right.

Her opponent couldn't withstand it. In that quarter hour she gained only four points. Veronica won the set by 6 games to 4 and thus secured the match. She threw her racket into the air, caught it neatly, ran to the net and shook hands with her opponent. Wexford said good night to Priscilla and left the way he had come, having watched the players go into the pavilion where the changing rooms were. Loring was still sitting on the bench.

Allison he spotted as soon as the footpath entered the field. He was lying very still in the long grass by the hedge and mostly covered by it. But Wexford saw him without giving any sign that he had done so. He was pretty sure Veronica wouldn't. The path wound on parallel to the hedge, then began to skirt the copse.

The false dusk hung still, suspended between light and dark. If it had been much darker no prudent young girl would have dared walk this way. Veronica Williams, of course, in spite of the impression she gave, was not a prudent young girl.

The air was still and damp and the grass moist underfoot. Wexford made his way along the path, under the high hedge, certain as he had been all along that Veronica's assailant would wait for her in the copse. Archbold had been there since 5.30 to be on the safe side. It was too late now for Wexford to join him without taking the risk of being seen. As it was, by staying to watch the match, he was taking a chance of spoiling the whole plan. Ahead of him a maple tree in the hedge spread its branches in a cone shape, the lowest ones almost touching the ground. He lifted them, stood against its trunk and waited.

By now it was 7.30 and he had begun to wonder if she would come at all. Though members had been thin on the ground there might have been some plan to fête her in the clubhouse. Hardly with drinks though. And she would have got out of it, she needed to see him as much as he her. Then he remembered she was her mother's daughter; it would take her longer than most girls to change her clothes, do her hair. She might even have a shower. Wendy was the sort of woman who would get a dying person out of bed to change the sheets before the doctor comes.

He stood under his tree in the silent dusk which was growing misty. Occasionally it was possible to hear in the distance a heavy vehicle on the Kingsmarkham to Pomfret road. Nothing else. No birds sang at this season and this hour. He could see the path about ten yards behind only and perhaps fifty yards ahead and it seemed to him then the emptiest footway he had ever contemplated. Allison would get rheumatism lying there on the damp ground, the cold seeping into his bones. Archbold, wrapped in his padded jacket, had probably fallen asleep . . .

She appeared quite suddenly. But how else could she have come but noiselessly and walking quite fast? She didn't look afraid though. Wexford saw her face quite clearly for a moment. Her expression was – yes, innocent. Innocent and trusting. She had no knowledge that there was anything to fear. If Sara, her half-sister, was a Florentine madonna, she was a Medici page, her small face grave and wistful in its gold-brown frame of bobbed hair and fringe. She wore her pink cotton jeans, beautifully pressed by Mother, her pink and white running shoes, a powder blue and white striped anorak that hung open over a white fluffy pullover, and she was carrying her tennis racket in a blue case. Wexford took all this in as she passed him, walking quickly.

He didn't dare come out. She might look back. Instead he dropped down into the field at the other side of the hedge. There had been a crop growing here, wheat or barley, but the grain had been cut and all that remained was a stubble that looked grey in this light. He ran along the hedge side, some few feet above the footpath. A long way ahead now he could just see the top of her head bobbing along. She had reached the corner of the copse.

There was a barbed-wire entanglement here that threatened to bar his passage, the spaces between the wires too narrow to squeeze through, the top wire too high to sling a leg over without terrible detriment to trousers. There was nothing for it but to retrace steps, pass through the hedge and clamber up the bank onto the footpath. She was too far away to see him even if she did look back. He jumped down, rounded the bend in the path, but now, though the copse was in full view, he couldn't see her at all.

His heart was in his mouth then. If she had met her assailant and gone into the wood, if Archbold truly had gone to sleep . . . He left the path and plunged into the copse. It was dark and dry in there, a million needles underfoot from the firs and larches. He ran through the trees and met Archbold head on.

'There's no one here, sir. I haven't seen a soul in three hours.'

'Except her,' said Wexford breathlessly.

'She just walked past. She's on her own, heading for the High Street.'

He came out of the wood on the Kingsmarkham side, Archbold behind him. She was nowhere to be seen, the hedges too high, the foliage on the trees too thick and masking. And then he forgot discretion and catching a murderer and ran along the path in pursuit of her, afraid for her and for himself. A moment before he had been praying Bennett wouldn't appear, walking from the Kingsmarkham end, and spoil it all. Now he hoped he would.

There was one more field and that low-lying, the path passing diagonally across it and then running beside a hedge at right angles to the road. No sign of Bennett. Because he had seen her? Or seen her attacker? Would he be capable of that in this fast-fading light? The meadow was grey and the hedges black and the air had the density of fallen cloud. Through the mist you could just see a light or two from cars on the Pomfret road, behind that an irregular cluster of pale lights that was probably the police station.

She was nowhere. The meadow was empty. There was a movement just discernible on the far side of it, where the path met the hedge. She had crossed the diagonal and come to the last hundred yards, her pale clothes catching what light there was so that she gleamed like a night moth. And like a night moth fluttered along against the dark foliage.

Wexford and Palmer didn't take the diagonal. They dared not risk being seen. They kept to the boundary hedge, though there was no path here, and Palmer, who was thirty, outran Wexford who felt that he had never run so hard in his life. All the time he could see the pale fluttering moth moving down there, homing on the stile that would bring her to the wide grass verge of the Pomfret road.

She never reached it. The fluttering stopped and there was something else down there with her at the bottom of the field where the dead elms stood, their roots a mass of underbrush, of brambles and nettles and fuzzy wild clematis. The something or someone else had come out of that and barred her way. He thought he heard a cry but he couldn't be sure.

At any rate it was no scream but a thin shriek of – perhaps surprise. He cut the corner, running hell for leather, his heart pounding fit to burst, running the way no man of close on sixty should run.

And Archbold got there only just first. It was strange that the knife should catch a gleam on it even in this near darkness. Wexford saw the gleam and then saw it drop to the ground. Archbold was holding Veronica who had turned her face into his chest and was clinging to his coat. He went up to the other himself. She made no attempt to run. She clasped her hands and hung her head so that he couldn't see her face.

In that moment Bennett materialized, so to speak. He came out of the dark, running. Sara Williams looked up then with an expression of faint dull surprise.

'Take them both,' said Wexford. 'They'll be charged with the wilful murder of Rodney Williams.'

22

'It was they, not their mothers, who knew each other,' Wexford said. 'Edwina Klein told me but I misinterpreted what she said. "Those two women knew each other", she said to me. "I saw them together". I took her to mean Joy and Wendy. Joy and Wendy were women and Sara and Veronica were girls. Except that to a militant feminist founder member of ARRIA all females are women. Just as they are,' he added, 'to organizers of sports events. It's the women's singles even if both players are fifteen.'

Burden and the doctor said nothing. They were all sitting in Burden's grass widower's house, drinking Burden's grass widower's instant coffee. It was over. A special court for one and a special juvenile court for the other and the two girls had been committed for trial. Afterwards the press had caught Wexford, a camera crew springing out of their van with the agility of the SAS, and once again he would be on television. Looking a hundred years old, he thought, after being up half the night talking to Sara Williams. People would phone in suggesting it was time he retired.

'They met at a tennis match, of course. The second time I met Sara I noticed she had a tennis racket up on her bedroom wall. She wasn't anywhere near Veronica's standard, not in the high school's first or second six. She just scraped into their reserve. Still, one day she was called on to play and she met Veronica as her opponent. What happened then? I don't know and she hasn't told me. I'd guess that one of the other girls there commented that they looked alike and seeing they had the same surname, were they cousins? It was up to one of them to probe further and one of them did. Sara, probably. After that it wouldn't have been hard to find out, would it? "Look, I've got a photo, this is my mum and dad . . ." '

'Something of a shattering experience, wouldn't you say?' said the doctor.

'Also I think an exciting one.'

'That's a superficial way of looking at it,' said Burden. 'I'd almost say unfeeling. Both those girls were lonely, Veronica sheltered and smothered, Sara neglected, no one's favourite. Wouldn't it have been both shattering and immensely *comforting* to find a sister?'

The sensitivity which had developed in Burden late in life always brought Wexford a kind of affectionate amusement. It was so often misdirected. It resembled in a way those good intentions with which hell is paved.

He picked his words carefully. They were strong words but his tone was hesitant.

'Sara Williams doesn't have normal feelings of affection, need for love, loneliness. I think she would be labelled a psychopath. She wants attention and she wants to impress. Also she wants her own way. I imagine that what she got from her half-sister was principally admiration. Sara has an excellent brain. Intellectually, she's streets ahead of Veronica. She's a strong, powerful, amoral, unfeeling solipsist with an appalling temper.'

Crocker's eyebrows went up. 'You're talking about an eighteen-year-old who was raped by her own father.'

Wexford didn't respond. He was thinking about what the girl had said to him, presiding at the table in the interview room with Marion Bayliss at one end, himself opposite and Martin facing Marion. But Sara Williams had presided, holding her head high, describing her feelings and actions without a notion of defending herself.

'My sister looks just like me. I used to feel she was another aspect of me, the weaker, pretty, feminine part, if you like. I wanted ultimately to be rid of that part.'

Solipsism, according to the Oxford dictionary, is the view or theory that self is the only object of real knowledge or the only real thing existent.

'Why didn't you tell your parents you and Veronica had met?'

'Why should I?'

Her cool answers took the breath away.

'It would have been the natural thing to confront your father with what you had found out.'

She was honest in her way. 'I liked having the secret. I enjoyed knowing what he thought I didn't know.'

'So that you could hold it over him?'

'Perhaps,' she said indifferently, bored when the discussion was not totally centred on herself.

Was that what she had had to threaten him with in the matter of the incest? Was that how she had stopped it?

'You prevented Veronica from telling her mother?'

'She did what I told her.'

It was uttered the way a trainer speaks of an obedient dog. The trainer takes the obedience for granted, so effective are his personality and technique, so unthinkable would an alternative reaction be. Wexford thought Crocker and Burden would have had to hear and see Sara to appreciate all this. He couldn't even attempt to put it across to them. 'The two girls met quite often,' he went on. 'Sara even went to Veronica's home when Wendy was at work. Veronica came to admire her extravagantly. She followed her, she would have obeyed her in anything.'

'Would have?'

'Did. Psychiatrists call what overtook them *folie à deux*, a kind of madness that overtakes two people only when they are together and through the influence of each on the other. But in all such cases you'll always find one party who is easily led and one who is dominant.' Wexford digressed a little before returning to the point. 'Looking back, I don't think Sara Williams has ever addressed a sentence to me that didn't begin with "I" or wasn't about herself.'

He went on, 'The coming and going between the Williams homes led to a pooling of information. For instance, Sara had believed her father was a sales rep with Sevensmith Harding for the Ipswich area. Veronica thought he was a rep with a bathroom fittings company. They took steps to find out the truth and did. It's over a year now since they found out what Rodney really did, what his position was, and discovered – via some research into marketing managers' earnings on Sara's part – what his actual salary was.

'Sara also warned Veronica of their father's – proclivities. That, of course, is how Wendy came to fear an incest attempt. Not because she witnessed anything herself or because Veronica put two and two together from a kiss and a cuddle but because Sara told Veronica what to expect and Veronica passed it on without disclosing her source. One way and another Sara made Veronica into a very frightened girl. A very bewildered and confused girl. Think of her situation. First she discovers her father has a legal wife and a grown-up family, next that he could never have in fact married her mother and she must be illegitimate. Necessarily, therefore, he's deceitful and a liar. He doesn't even have the job he says he has. Worst of all, he has raped his other daughter and will certainly have the same designs on her. No wonder she was frightened.

'Telling Wendy her fears of a sexual attack had the effect only of causing trouble between her mother and father. Did Wendy accuse Rodney and Rodney hotly deny it? Almost certainly. The quarrel was at any rate bad enough to make Wendy believe Rodney would leave her but fear that if he didn't Veronica would be in danger. So we see that the reason she didn't want Veronica to stay in on the evening of April the fifteenth was that if Rodney did come back she would be alone with her father – and this would be the first time she would be alone with him after the disclosure was made.

'But Veronica had another confidante and friend now, apart from her mother. She had Sara. And Sara absolutely justified the faith she put in her. Sara had a good idea for diverting Rodney's attention from his daughter, diverting his attention from everything, in fact. Substitute sleeping pills for his blood-pressure tablets. It was something that could only be done once though and in an emergency.

'Now on April the fifteenth, however much their mothers may have been in ignorance, Sara and Veronica knew that when Rodney left Alverbury Road he would drive straight to Liskeard Avenue. So Sara herself made the exchange of tablets, two only remaining in the container. Don't forget we found an empty Mandaret container in Alverbury Road and a half-full one in Liskeard Avenue. Rodney took his two Mandaret as he thought, leaving the container in his bedroom, and drove to Pomfret. No doubt he began to feel droswy on the way.'

'But these were Phanodorm, supplied by Paulette Harmer?' said the doctor.

'I suppose they were supplied by her. It seems most likely. But Paulette didn't die because she illicitly provided a sleeping drug. She died because the turn events were taking made her concentrate her mind on the evening of April the fifteenth, made her remember in fact what had really happened. What she remembered was her mother speaking to her aunt Joy on the phone that evening and making some remark about being glad Kevin had settled in back at college. And she was going to tell us because she knew from the papers and television and her parents' conversation how strong was the suspicion against her aunt. She knew very well her aunt had been at home that evening, in at eight to receive Kevin's phone call and still in at eight forty-five to receive her mother's.'

The girl should have been strewing flowers or rising from the waves in a cockleshell. The face was bland, innocent and somehow secretive. Even now there was a tiny self-satisfied smile. Her hair was scraped back tight from that high forehead but wisps had come free and lay in gold tendrils on the white skin.

'I got a phone call from Veronica. It was just to tell me he'd gone to sleep like I said he would. I said I'd come over.'

He had interrupted her to ask why.

'I just thought I would. I wasn't going to get a chance like that again, was I?'

He stopped himself asking her what she meant. Her eyes seemed to enlarge, her face grow blanker.

'I saw him sleeping there and I thought, I've got him in my power. I thought of the power he had over *me*. I started to get angry, really angry.'

'And Veronica?'

'I didn't think about Veronica. I suppose she was there. Well, I know she was. I said to her, "We could kill him and stop all of it". I told her to get me a knife. I wasn't serious

404

then, it was fantasy. I was angry and I was excited – high like when you've had a drink.'

Folie à deux. Was Veronica excited too? He wouldn't get much about another's feelings out of this girl.

'I took the knife out of her hands and took off the cardboard guard that was on it. I went up to my father who was lying on the settee and I started playing around, waving the knife over him, pretending to stick it in him. I could tell he was sound asleep. I was making Veronica laugh because I was doing all this stuff and he was just oblivious of it. I don't remember what made me stop playing. I was so excited and high I don't remember. But that's how it was. One minute it was fantasy and the next it was for real.'

She looked down at the table at Marion and then the other way at Martin. It was as if she were gathering the attention of her audience. Once more her eyes met Wexford's in a steady gaze.

'I raised the knife and stuck it in his neck, right in hard with both hands. I'd made him wake up then and make noises, so I stabbed him a few more times to stop the blood spraying like that. I'm going to be a doctor so I knew the blood would stop when he was dead . . .'

It took Wexford, hardened as he was, a moment or two to collect words.

'Did Veronica stab him?'

'I gave her the knife and told her to have a go. I'd made a big wound in his neck and she stuck it in there and then she went off and was sick.'

'Completely mad,' said Burden. 'Bonkers.'

'Perhaps. I'm not sure. Let's not get into defining psychosis.'

'What happened next?' said the doctor.

'The room was covered for the most part in dustsheets. Rodney had come in half asleep, climbed the stairs and lain down on the settee which had a dustsheet over one end. The end, incidentally, where he laid his head. It was this sheet, the property of Leslie Kitman, which received most of the blood. Some went on an area of wall from which the paper had been stripped that day. Sara washed the wall and wrapped Rodney's head up in the dustsheet. Veronica, recovered and very much under orders from Sara, washed the knife and then had the idea of plastering it into the wall. This was the first weird too-clever thing the girls did. There were others. There were fissures in the walls needing to be filled in and in the garage was a packet of filler. Also in the garage was Rodney's car, Greta the Granada, which Sara, though not Veronica, was able to drive. They rolled up the dustsheet and wrapped two of Wendy's Marks and Spencer's teacloths round Rodney's neck. Having cleaned up the room, they carried Rodney down the spiral staircase, through the door from the hall into the garage and put him into the boot of the car. On their way out in the car they deposited the dustsheet in the dustbin. It was about seven-thirty.'

'Then,' said Burden, 'how did Kevin manage to speak to his sister when he phoned Alverbury Road at eight o'clock?'

'He didn't. He spoke to his mother. And, of course, he and Joy were both well aware it was his mother he had spoken to. They lied to protect Sara. Oh, I know Joy hasn't much affection for Sara but she was her daughter. Once she began to think about it she saw that Sara might have had something to do with Rodney's disappearance. At first she genuinely thought he had left her and she got me in to advise her. But then things changed. I think I know why. On my advice, she phoned Sevensmith Harding and they told her *she* had spoken to them on Friday, April the sixteenth, to explain Rodney was ill. Now Joy no doubt at first thought this a mere mistake but they had been so sure it was her voice. Joy knew someone whose voice sounded very like hers – her own daughter.

'Don't forget that she knew how Sara felt towards her father on account of the incest. She also knew Sara had been out of the house for hours on the evening of April the fifteenth. So she told us and got Kevin to agree – no difficulty there, he distrusts the police and is close to his sister – that it was she who had gone out and Sara who had been at home to take the phone call. Was there collusion with Sara? I doubt it. There was no real communication between her and her mother. My guess is Joy said it might be wiser to arrange things this way and Sara agreed with just a nod and a "yes" probably.'

'You're painting a picture of a self-sacrificing maternal type,' said the doctor, 'which doesn't at all accord with our concept of Joy Williams. Rather like the old story of the mother pelican tearing at its own breast to feed its young – and just as much of a myth.'

'No. Joy quite rightly believed there was no real risk in it for her. She thought it impossible we could arrest the wrong person. Her trust must have been sorely put to the test these past few days.'

Always happier on circumstantial details, Burden said, 'So the two girls took Williams's body up to Cheriton Forest and dug a grave for him with his own snow shovel?'

'A shallow grave because, having killed him, Sara didn't want it to be too long before the body was discovered. She wanted a couple of weeks to pass only, rightly believing that this was the sort of time which would be just about right to blur the evidence. In fact, things didn't go her way and it was two months before the body was found.

'I turned over and over in my mind the complication of the Milvey coincidence. But now it has come out quite clearly. There is no coincidence. Sara and Veronica hid Rodney's travelling bag – in the forest probably – hoping it would be found within, say, the next few days. But as it happened, no one found it. Then one day Mrs Milvey happened to say to Joy in Sara's hearing that Milvey would be at Green Pond next day, dragging the pool. Sara retrieved the bag and dumped it in the pool in time for Milvey to find it next day.'

'But why did she want the body found? What difference could it make to her?'

'I'll come to that later.'

'I don't see why go to all the trouble of phoning Sevensmith Harding and forging a letter to delay discovery, and then later try to accelerate it. Incidentally, I take it it was Sara who made the phone call? Her voice is very like Joy's.'

'She made the phone call and Veronica typed the letter. At her friend Nicola Tennyson's house, on Nicola's mother's typewriter.

'They buried the body, hid the travelling bag, and Sara drove Veronica back to Pomfret to be sure she got home before Wendy did. That was at about nine. Wendy, of course, didn't get home until nine thirty, being out doing some mild courting with James Ovington. Sara drove to Myringham and dumped the car in Arnold Road where no more than half an hour later it was seen and indeed bumped into by Eve Freeborn. If Sara had been a bit later and Eve a bit earlier those two members of ARRIA would have encountered each other and made our task a lot easier. But by the time Eve came Sara was on the bus for home.

'In the morning she shut herself in the living room and made the phone call before she went to school. Of necessity it was a very early call and she was lucky there was someone there to receive it. And that, I think, accounts for all the circumstances of the murder of Rodney Williams.'

Burden picked up the tray.

'Does anyone want more coffee?'

Neither did. Wexford said it was nearly beer time, wasn't it? The doctor frowned at him and he deliberately looked away, out into Burden's bright, neat garden, the flower borders like chintzy dress material, the lawn a bit of green baize. The sunshine was making Jenny's yellow chrysanthemums nearly too bright to look at. Burden opened the french windows.

'The sad thing,' said Crocker, 'is that all this is going to make it next to impossible for Sara Williams to make a career in medicine.'

Burden looked at him. He said sarcastically, 'Oh, surely St Biddulph's will overlook a little matter like stabbing her father to death with a carving knife.'

'You don't think it justification then, and more than justification, for a girl to make a murderous assault on the father who has raped her and shows signs of meting out the same treatment to her younger half-sister? Don't you think any judge or jury would see this as an extentuating circumstance?'

It was Wexford who answered him. 'Yes, I do.'

'Right, then there's not going to be any question of years of imprisonment, is there? She'll never have the dubious distinction of being a GP like your humble servant here, but at least there won't be punishment in the accepted sense.'

'I wouldn't be too sure of that.'

'On account of the planning and the covering of tracks, do you mean?'

'She killed Paulette Harmer,' Burden said.

'She did indeed but that wasn't what I meant. You see, Rodney Williams never committed incest with his elder daughter. He never showed signs of committing incest with his younger daughter. And I very much doubt if he ever sexually assaulted anyone, even in the broadest meaning of that term.'

23

Crocker had caught on quickly. Wexford left it to him to explain. The doctor began outlining Freud's 'seduction theory' as expressed in the famous paper of 1896.

Thirteen women patients of Freud claimed paternal seduction. Freud believed them, built on this evidence a theory, later abandoned it, realizing he had been too gullible. Instead, he concluded that little girls are prone to fantasize that their fathers have made love to them, from which developed his stress on childhood fantasy and ultimately his postulation of the Oedipus Complex.

'You're saying it was all fantasy on Sara's part?' Burden said. 'She's not exactly a *little* girl.'

'Nor were Freud's patients little girls by the time they came to him.'

Wexford said, 'I think Sara had a daughter's fantasy about her father. When she was older she read Freud. She read books on incest too – they're all there in her bedroom. There's a mention of father-daughter incest in the ARRIA constitution. Did she read that too or did she write it? At any rate, *in her mind* she was heavily involved with her father, far more involved with him than he was with her.'

'How do you know the seduction didn't really take place? Men do commit incest with their daughters. I mean, how could Freud have known one of those thirteen wasn't fantasizing but telling the truth?'

'I can't answer that,' Wexford said, 'but I can tell you it never happened to Sara. She isn't the kind of girl to whom it happens. She isn't ignorant or obtuse or cowed or dependent. This seduction, or apparent seduction, followed a classic pattern as laid down in the books. The girl doesn't struggle or fight or scream. She doesn't want to make a disturbance. At the first opportunity she tells her mother and mother reacts with rage, reproaches, accusations of the girl's provocative behaviour. Now Joy, as we might expect, fitted beautifully into the classic pattern. But Sara? If it had really happened wouldn't Sara, a leading member of ARRIA, a militant feminist, have fought and screamed? She was very handy with a knife, wasn't she? And she's the last person to care about making a disturbance in a household, either emotional or physical. As for telling her mother – Sara tell her mother? There's been no real communication between them for years. She despises her mother. If she'd told anyone it would have been her brother Kevin. No, there was no seduction, for if there had been she would have kept the experience secret to use against her father, not come running with it to Joy.

'It was Sara who stabbed Colin Budd, of course. It happened, if you remember, the night before Milvey started dragging Green Pond. Sara retrieved the bag after dark, went up to the forest to do it and put the bag inside a plastic sack. When Budd came along she was waiting to catch the bus that would take her to the other end of Kingsmarkham, near enough to the Forby road and Green Pond Hall. The last thing she wanted was Budd taking an interest in her. Besides, she had indoctrinated herself to be always on the watch for sexist approaches. What was she doing but going about her private business? And this man has to treat her as if her primary function in this world was to be an object for his diversion and entertainment. No doubt she also lost her nerve. She stabbed him with a penknife.'

'If it was all fantasy,' said Burden, reverting to the analysis of Sara Williams's character, 'why did she warn Veronica? Why warn her of something that would never happen?'

'You're supposing fantasy is something "made up", so therefore something the fantasizer herself doesn't believe in?'

'Well, does she? Did Sara convince herself.'

'Yes and no. She's admitted to me nothing ever happened. On the other hand, I wouldn't be surprised if tomorrow she says it did and believes it herself. Having this secret to communicate, this awful and horrifying secret, must have much increased her ascendancy over Veronica. It enhanced her power. Veronica was very frightened of her, you see, full of admiration, awe almost, but even before the killing of Rodney becoming unnerved by the whole set-up.'

Wendy had been sent for and for once had been calm, sensible, steady. He had considered the atmosphere of his office more relaxing than one of those stark interview rooms. Marion and Polly were seated side by side and Veronica a little apart from everyone until Wexford came in. Little Miss Muffet and the great spider who sat down beside her. Only there was no frightening her away. It would be a long time now before Veronica Williams could get away.

She was very pale. Her hair, he noticed, was a couple of inches longer than when he had first seen her, six inches longer than the crop of the beach photograph. Had she been growing it in imitation of her idol and model Sara? He had asked her when she first met her half-sister.

'It was September.' Her voice was so soft he had to ask her to repeat it. 'September – a year ago,' she said.

'And you met how often after that? Once a week? More?'

Very quietly, 'More.'

He extracted from her the information that they constantly spoke on the phone. It was like a game sometimes, Sara phoning and saying she would be in Liskeard Avenue in five minutes, she phoning Sara to say if Sara was careful not to be seen she could come and watch Rodney and Wendy watching *her* play tennis.

'It stopped being a game, though, didn't it? On April the fifteenth it stopped?'

She nodded and her body convulsed in an involuntary shiver. Wendy said, 'Why did you always do everything she said? Why did you tell her everything?'

How could she answer that?

'You told her you were coming here to confess your part in it, didn't you, Veronica?' Wexford spoke very gently.

Her eyes went to Wendy. 'I thought the police would arrest my mother.'

A small spark of triumph on Wendy's doleful face. In

412

these unbelievable circumstances her years of devotion were rewarded . . .

Wexford surfaced from his reverie to see Burden depositing three beer cans in front of them from a tray laden with the kind of junk food he lived on while Jenny was away.

'Wake up!'

'Sorry.'

'Look, if there was no incest and therefore no renewed assault from Rodney to be feared, if there was no threat to Veronica, what was the motive for killing him? All through this case we could never come up with any sort of solid motive. Or are you saying a psychopath doesn't need a motive – at any rate not a motive understood by normal people?'

Wexford said slowly, 'I've suggested to you that there was a good deal of calculation in Sara's behaviour, some of it of an apparently incomprehensible kind. Her original concealment of the body, for instance, and later her anxiety for it to be found. I've also made it clear – rather to your joint disapproval, I think – that I don't feel much sympathy towards Sara. And this is because I feel she had no justification for what she did.

'She had a motive all right, and as calculated and coldblooded a motive as any poisoner polishing off an old relation for his money.'

'But Rodney didn't have any money to leave, did he?' Burden objected.

'Not so's you'd notice, though the manager of the Anglian-Victoria has shown me how a nice little bit was accumulating in the account from which the two joint accounts were fed. Enough, anyway, for him to recommend that Rodney put it into investments. Still, it wasn't for a possible inheritance that Sara killed him, though money was her motive.'

'Not a cash gain though, I think,' said the doctor.

Wexford turned to Burden. 'You raised this very subject not long ago, Mike. That was when you thought you were going to have a daughter – and that's relevant too. You talked about her going to university and applying for government grants. Do you remember?'

'I suppose so. I don't see where the relevance comes in.'

'Sara wants to be a doctor,' said Wexford. 'Well, *wanted*

413

to be, I should say. It was a driving ambition with her. And increasingly hard though this is becoming, she knew she had the ability to get into medical school. Her parents, however, discouraged her. And it must have looked to her at that stage as if this was a classic case of opposition to daughter's ambitions simply because she was a daughter and not a son, because in fact she was a woman. On Joy's part it probably was. Very likely she wouldn't have cared for Sara to achieve greater success and have a more prestigious profession than Kevin.

'At first this parental opposition didn't much worry Sara. I'm speaking, of course, about this time last year. Sara remembered her brother getting a place at Keele and the form of application for a grant coming from Sussex County Council Education Committee to her father. At the time she didn't take much notice. Certainly she didn't see the completed form. But she knew that the greater the parental income the smaller the grant would be and that with the form there came a form of certificate of parental employment the parent's employer had to complete detailing his gross salary, overtime, bonus or commissions and his taxable emoluments. Now, Mike, you'll recall that certificate in your own case and sending it to the Mid-Sussex Constabulary when you applied for grants for John and Pat?'

Burden nodded. 'I'm beginning to see the light here.'

'Twelve months ago Sara met Veronica. Gradually, when the shock of that encounter began to recede, when it provided the solution to certain unexplained anomalies, shall we say, Sara saw the cold reality for what it was. Her father might talk about not wanting his daughter to be a doctor for aesthetic reasons, for reasons of suitability, she would get married and her education be wasted, et cetera. He might talk that way but the reason behind the talk was very different. Finding that he had lied both to her mother and Veronica's about what his position and his earnings were, she had taken steps to discover what he did and what he earned. Now she understood. If he filled in the grant application form for her he would have to declare to the Sussex County Council that his income was not £10,000 a year but two and a half times that, and there would be no way he could deceive the authority as he had deceived her mother because

414

his employers, Sevensmith Harding, would have to complete the certificate of parental income from employment.

'Now according to the grants department's contribution scales, a parent earning £10,000 per annum would have to contribute to medical school costs only something in the region of £470 but a parent earning £25,000 a sum of nearly £2000. Rodney had two homes and two families, he was already paying out this sort of sum for Kevin at Keele – remember he had to tell the grants department the truth, whatever he told his wives – and Sara could see the way the wind was blowing. She could see there was no way he would part with £2000 a year for her benefit. And when she asked him point blank if he would fill in the form when it came he told her he wouldn't – she would never make a doctor and he was doing her a kindness in not encouraging her.'

'What a bastard,' said Crocker.

Wexford shrugged. 'The mistake is ours when we deceive ourselves about parent-child relationships. When we keep up the belief that all parents love their children and want what's best for them.'

'Surely, though, if Sara had talked about this at school or discussed it with some sympathetic officer at the grants department, a way could have been found for her to get a grant, bypassing Rodney? There must be many cases where a parent withholds consent and won't complete a grant application.'

'Probably. But Sara is only eighteen. And remember that to have done what you suggest she would have to reveal that her father was a liar and a cheat, that he deceived her mother, that he was a bigamist. And how long would all this take? Would it mean her waiting a year? And what of her place at St Biddulph's, a teaching hospital where places are like gold dust and where they keep a reserve list bursting with applicants dying to be accepted? What she decided on instead was, first, persuasion and if that failed, blackmail.'

'She told him that if he didn't consent to fill in the form she'd tell Joy about Wendy and get Veronica to tell Wendy about Joy?'

'She was *going* to tell him that. She had a bit of time though. She hadn't even sat her A-levels. The grant form wouldn't come till July. And she also had the incest. Of course, it had never taken place but Joy thought it had, Veronica was scared stiff it had. If all else failed she might be able to use it as another weapon in the blackmail stockpile. That was why she was pleased to see how effective her warnings had been in Veronica's case. Veronica was beginning to be afraid of the affectionate attention Rodney paid her. Veronica didn't want to be alone with him and if she had to be she wanted him disarmed and immobilized. Sara saw to that with the Phanodorm, and increased Veronica's fear by the seriousness of taking such a step.

'But how much simpler, after all, to kill him! And there he was, lying asleep, the potential destroyer of her future. Kill him now, in this room which will soon be made pure and immaculate, cleansed of all signs of violent death. Rid the world of him, seize your opportunity. And perhaps it would also be a heroic act. Hadn't there almost been a clause in the ARRIA constitution demanding a man's death as qualification for entry? Veronica will help because Veronica also hates him now and is mortally afraid of him . . .

'But suppose they never find the body? Suppose the weeks go by and July comes and August and with them the grant application and you can't fill in the section that says "Father, if deceased the fact should be stated . . ." because only you and Veronica know he is deceased? You have finished your A-levels and the time is going by – the moment has come to take steps for that body to be found without more delay.'

'You might say,' said Crocker, 'that the murder was both coolly premeditated and carried out on an impulse.'

'You might. Because of what Sara is, a highly complex personality, this was all kinds of a murder. A ritualistic killing – remember that Veronica was required to stab him too. A revenge killing – Sara had more than half-convinced herself and wholly convinced Veronica of the reality of the incest. When she stabbed Rodney she was a woman out of classical myth, she was Beatrice Cenci. It was an *experimental* killing, a kind of vivisection, carried out by Sara the scientist, to see if it would work, to see if it could be done. It was murder from disgust, from disillusionment. Rodney, whom she had once worshipped, was just a squalid bigamist with another daughter, a copy of herself, he loved as much as or more than he had ever loved her. But above all, in spite

416

of all those other factors, it was murder for gain, carried out so that she might satisfy her ambition at all costs. All in all, I don't think that's the sort of person I'd care to have as my family physician, still less performing surgery on me and mine. So perhaps Rodney was right when he told Sara she was an unsuitable candidate for medical school. Who knows? Perhaps it wasn't simply meanness with him, he wasn't quite the bastard you make out. Perhaps he sensed in that daughter of his, without ever examining his conclusions, traits in her character that were abnormal, that were destructive, and it was to these he referred when he said she would never make a doctor.'

Wexford got up.

'I shall call it a day,' he said. 'I shall go to the wife of my bosom the same as I ought to go.'

Burden began tidying the room, putting things on a tray. 'And tomorrow the wife of my bosom comes home to me.' He looked pleased, satisfied, hopeful, as if there had been no five months' long disruption of his happiness. 'One of her old pupils at Haldon Finch went in to see her and the baby. An ARRIA member. She told Jenny the raven bit means they're cleaning up the carrion men have left behind in the world. We did wonder.'

'Ah,' Wexford paused in the doorway. 'Something I nearly forgot to tell you. About Williams's young girlfriend . . .'

They looked at him. 'Williams didn't have a young girlfriend,' Burden said.

'Of course he did. She had nothing to do with his death, nothing to do with this case, so she hardly concerned us. But a man like Williams – it was in his nature, inevitable. Both his wives knew it, they sensed it. Probably he's always had a young girlfriend, a succession of them.

'This one – hers were the other set of prints on the car. No wonder she said her dad didn't want me to take them. They met at Sevensmith Harding, of course. In the office.'

'Jane Gardner . . .'

'That's who he had his date with on April the fifteenth in Myringham. Join her for her baby-sitting, then spend the night together at the Cheriton Forest Hotel. Why else did he have a bag with him with a single change of underwear and a toothbrush and toothpaste? But the sleeping pills overcame him as he was driving through Pomfret, and instead of going on to meet Jane he was just able to make it to his own house. What she thought was that he'd stood her up. Then, when he disappeared, that he'd gone off with another woman. I had a word with her this morning and she admitted it – no more need to conceal it now we'd made an arrest.'

'What put you on to her?'

'I don't know. Guesswork. She was the only person I ever spoke to who had a good word for Rodney Williams.'

Wexford let himself out, closing Burden's blue front door behind him.

THE VEILED ONE

For Simon

I would like to thank Leonie Van Ness for an idea which she suggested to me in Ottawa and which contributed to the plot of this novel – Ruth Rendell

1

The woman was lying dead on the floor when he came in. She was already dead and covered up from head to toe but Wexford only knew that afterwards, not at the time. He looked back and realized the chances he had missed but it was useless doing that – he hadn't known and that was all. He had been preoccupied, thinking of an assortment of things: his wife's birthday present that was in the bag he carried, modern architecture, yesterday's gale which had blown down his garden fence, this car park that he was entering from the descending lift.

Even the lift was not as other lifts elsewhere, being of rattling grey metal undecorated except for graffiti. Irregular printing from whose letters the red paint had dripped like trails of blood, informed him that someone called Steph was 'a diesel dyke'. He wondered what that meant, wondered too where he could look it up. The lift was going down. Into the bowels of the earth, he thought, and there was something intestine-like about this place with its winding passages and its strictly one-way direction. Perhaps, though, it was better to excavate for this purpose than to erect above the ground, especially as any extraneous building would inevitably have been in the style of the shopping centre itself – ramparts, perhaps, or the walls of a city, some quaint attempt at a reconstruction of the Middle Ages.

He had just come from the Barringdean Centre, the new shopping complex built to look like a castle. That was the style modern planners thought suitable on the outskirts of an ancient Sussex town where nothing genuinely medieval remained. Perhaps that was why. Anyway the centre looked

421

less like a real castle than a toy one, the kind you have to assemble from a hundred plastic bits and pieces. Shaped like a capital 'I', it had four towers on the ends and a row of turrets along its length. Looking back at it, he half-expected bowmen to appear in the Gothic windows and arrows to fly.

But inside all was of the late twentieth century, only to be expressed in eighties words – amenities, facilities, enclaves and approaches. A great fountain played in the central concourse, its waterspouts almost reaching but not quite touching the pendent chandelier of shards of frosted glass. Wexford had entered at this point by the automatic doors and approach from the glass covered way. He had gone up the escalator where a breath of spray stung his fingers on the hand-rail, realized at the top that the shop he sought must be downstairs after all – was not Suzanne the hairdresser who also sold wigs and leotards, or Linen That Shows or Laceworks – and went down again by the escalator to the Mandala. This was a set-piece in the area at the other end with potted plants in concentric circles – brown chrysanthemums, yellow chrysanthemums, white poinsettias and those plants with cherry-like orange fruit that are really a kind of potato. The crowds were thinning out; it was getting on for six when the centre closed up. Shop assistants were weary and growing impatient and even the flowers looked tired.

A Tesco superstore filled the whole crosspiece of the 'I' on both floors at this end, British Home Stores the other. Between them was Boots the Chemist with W. H. Smith facing it, the Mandala in between. Down a side passage that led from the main above-ground car park, children still played on a fat zebra made of black and white leather, a hi-tech climbing frame, a dragon on wheels. Wexford found the shop where Dora, a week ago, had pointed out to him in the window a sweater she liked. Addresses it was called, with a chocolate shop next to it and a wool and craft place Knits 'n' Kits on the other side. Wexford was not a man to hesitate or deliberate over a matter like this. Besides, Demeter the health-food shop opposite was already closing and the jewellers next to it were lowering the fancy gilt latticework bars inside the window. He went into Addresses and bought the sweater, the transaction taking four minutes.

By now shoppers were being hustled out, even Grub 'n' Grains the café having someone suspiciously like a bouncer on its door. And the lights were dimming, the leaping spouts of the fountain slowing . . . subsiding, until the ruffled surface of the pool into which it played became glasslike. Wexford sat down on one of the wrought-iron benches that were ranged along the aisle. He let the crowd make its way out through the various arteries that led from this central column and then he too left by the automatic doors into the covered way.

A great exodus of cars from the above-ground car parks was under way. At the far end he looked back. Flags flew from all the turrets along the centre's spine, red and yellow triangular pennants which had fluttered all day in the tail-end of the gale but drooped now in the stillness of a dark, misty evening. Slits of light still showed in the narrow pointed-topped Gothic windows. Wexford found himself alone here at the entrance to the underground car park, the only evidence of those hordes of shoppers being their abandoned trolleys. Hundreds of these jostled each other in higgledy-piggledy fashion, and would no doubt remain here till morning. A notice informed their users that the police took a serious view of those who allowed a shopping trolley to obstruct the roadway. Not for the first time, Wexford reflected that the police had more important things to do – though how much more important he was only to realize later.

The planners had decreed that this car park must be subterranean. He came into the lift and the stairs by way of a metal door whose clanging reverberations could still be heard as the lift descended. Wexford heard its echoes and at the same time feet pounding up the stairs, the feet of someone running hard; that was something else he remembered later. Down here it was always cold, always imbued with an acrid chemical smell as of metal filings awash in oil. Wexford stepped out of the lift at the second of four levels and came into the wide aisle between the avenue of pillars. Most of the cars were gone by now and in their absence the place seemed more desolate, uglier, more of a denial. Of course it was foolish and fanciful to think like this – a denial of what, for instance? The car park merely served a purpose, filled a need in the most practical utilitarian way. What would he have had instead? White paint? Murals? Tiles on the wall depicting some episode of local history? That would have been almost worse. It was irrational that the place reminded him of a picture it did not in the least resemble – John Martin's illustration of 'Pandemonium' for *Paradise Lost*.

His car was parked at this end. He didn't have to walk the length of the place – under the low concrete ceiling, between the squat uprights, into the wells of shadow – but merely cross over the bays along the left-hand wall. There was an echo down here and the sound of his footsteps rang back at him. If his powers of observation, in general so sharp, were less acute than usual, at least he noticed the numbers of cars that remained and their makes and colours. He saw the three between him and the middle of the car park where one ramp came up and another went down: one on the left, a red Metro, and diagonally opposite it on the right, parked side by side, a silver Escort and a dark blue Lancia. The woman's body lay between these two, closer to the Escort, concealed by a shroud of dirty brown velvet which made it look like a heap of rags.

Or so they told him afterwards. At the time he saw only the cars, the colours of their bodywork not entirely drained by the cold strip lights but muted, made pale. He lifted the boot-lid and put inside it the dark blue bag with 'Addresses' stamped on it in gold. As he closed it a car went by him, a red car going rather too fast. There were more red cars than any other colour, he had read somewhere. Motorists are aggressive and red is the colour of aggression. He got into the car, started it and looked at the clock. This was something he always did quite naturally, looked at the clock when he started the ignition. Seven minutes past six. He put the automatic shift into drive and began the climb out of the earth's bowels.

On each level the way out wound round half the floorspace at the opposite end from where the lift and stairs were, wound round anticlockwise and turned right up the ramp to the next level. He passed the three cars – the two on the left first, then the red Metro. Of course he didn't look to the right where the woman's body was. Why should he? His exit route took him round the loop, on to the straight on the

424

other side. Not a car remained here; the bays were empty. He climbed up to the first level, looped round and out into the night. There might have been cars remaining on that level, but he hadn't noticed and he could only remember the red Vauxhall Cavalier with a girl in the driving-seat facing him as he came up the ramp. She pulled out and followed him, impatient to be off and exceed the speed limit. Teenage girls at the wheels of cars were worse then the boys these days, Burden said. Wexford emerged into the open air, up the ramp. Most of the shoppers were gone; it was ten past six, they closed the centre at six and only the last stragglers remained, moving towards cars in the above-ground parking areas. The girl overtook him as soon as she could.

Wexford had pulled in and slowed to allow her to do so and it was then that he saw the woman emerge from the glass-covered way. He observed her because she was the only person to approach the car park and because she wasn't hurrying but walking in a controlled, measured fashion threading her way between the trolleys, fending off with her foot one that rattled into her path. She was a small, slender, upright woman in coat and hat carrying two bags of shopping, both red Tesco carriers. The metal door clanged behind her and he drove on across the wide nearly empty car-less space where the mist hung as a glaucous clouding of the air, out of the exit gates and half a mile on into Castle Street and the town. The traffic lights in the High Street outside the Olive and Dove turned red as he approached. The hand-brake on, he looked down at the evening paper he had bought before he drove to the centre but so far had not even glanced at. His own daughter's famous face looked back at him, affording him only a mild jolt. Pictures of Sheila in the papers weren't unusual. Seldom, however, were they accompanied by revelations of this sort. There was another photograph beside the portrait; Wexford looked at that one too and with lips pursed drew in a long breath. The lights slipped through amber into green.

The Barringdean Shopping Centre was on the outskirts of Kingsmarkham but nevertheless within the town. It had been built on the site of the old bus station when the new bus station was put up on the site of the old maltings. Everyone went shopping there and the retailers in the High Street suffered. By day it was a hive of bees buzzing in and swarming out, but at night the centre was left to its fate – two break-ins during it first year of life. Apart from the security men and store detectives within the centre itself, there was a caretaker who called himself the supervisor and who patrolled the grounds or, more usually, sat in a small concrete office next door to the car-park lift-shaft, reading the *Star* and listening to tapes of *Les Misérables* and *Edwin Drood*. At six-fifteen each evening David Sedgeman performed his last duty of the day as Barringdean Shopping Centre supervisor. He put the trolleys into some sort of order, slotting one inside another to form long articulated carriages, and closed the gates of the pedestrian entrance in Pomeroy Road, fastened the bolts and attached the padlock. These gates were of steel mesh in steel frames and the fence was eight feet high. Then Sedgeman went off home. If anyone remained about the grounds, they had to leave by the traffic exit.

The residents of Pomeroy Road had benefited from the removal of the bus station. It was quieter now that no buses turned in and departed from six in the morning until midnight. Instead there were all the shoppers coming and going, but soon after six they had all left. On the opposite side of the street short terraces of Victorian houses alternated with small blocks of flats. Directly facing the gates, in one of these houses, Archie Greaves lived with his daughter and son-in-law. He spent a large part of his days sitting in the downstairs bay window watching the people; it was far more entertaining for him now than in the bus station era. He watched the people go into the phone box just outside the gates on the right-hand side and some of them must have seen him watching them, for more than once he had been approached, accosted by a tap on the window and asked for change for the phone. He watched the shoppers arrive and the shoppers leave; it amused him to make a mental note of arrivals and check on their departure. He recognized certain regulars and because he was a lonely man – his daughter and her husband out all day – thought of them almost as his friends.

This evening was misty. It had got dark very early and by six was black as midnight, the mist very apparent where lights caught it and made a greenish shimmer. The gutters of Pomeroy Road were clogged with fallen leaves, the plane trees almost bare. Beyond the open gates lamps lit the car parks that were fast emptying and in the shopping centre building itself, where the turrets were silhouetted black like the teeth of a saw against the streaked cloudy purple of the sky, the lights were beginning to dim. Before many more minutes had passed by, they would all have gone out.

Pedestrians had been coming out sporadically ever since Archie first went to sit there at four o'clock. His breath clouded the glass and he rubbed it with his jacket sleeve, taking his arm away in time to see someone running out of the gates. A young man it was – a boy to him – empty handed, going as if all the devils in hell were after him. Or store detectives, Archie thought doubtfully. Once he had seen a woman running with people pursuing her and he guessed she had been shoplifting. This boy he had never seen before; he was a stranger to him and he passed out of sight under the plane trees into the misty dark.

Archie hadn't put a light on because he could see better sitting in darkness. An old-fashioned electric fire made a glow in the room behind him. No one was pursuing the boy – perhaps he had only been in a hurry. The people who were leaving at a more leisurely pace had looked at him without much curiosity and, like Archie, expected to see retribution coming. But the darkness absorbed them as well. He saw a car come up out of the mouth of the underground park and then another. The lights that illuminated the shopping centre turrets went out. Then Archie saw David Sedgeman appear from behind the angle of the concrete wall with the padlock keys in his hand. Because of the mist and because Archie hadn't put his light on, Sedgeman had to peer to see the pale blur of the old man's face and then he nodded and raised his hand. Archie gave him a salute. Sedgeman closed the gates, looped the chain through the steel mesh, fastened and locked the padlock. Then he shot both bolts, one at the bottom and another a foot above his head. Before he went back, he gave Archie another wave.

This was the signal for Archie to get moving. He got up and went to the kitchen where he made himself a mug of tea with a tea-bag and took two chocolate chip cookies out of the biscuit tin. No potatoes to peel tonight because his daughter and her husband would be out at a friend's son's engagement party. There would be no cooked supper for Archie, but at his age he preferred little snacks of tea and biscuits and bits of chocolate anyway. Back in the front room he put the television on, though he had missed most of the six o'clock news and the bit he got was all about the trial of terrorists and some actress damaging Ministry of Defence property. He didn't turn it off but just turned down the sound and switched on the central light. Archie had read somewhere that watching television in the dark turns you blind eventually.

The light was also on in the phone box now. It came on at six-thirty when the box hadn't been vandalized and the lamp smashed as sometimes happened. Archie sat on the window once more, one eye watching the street and another the screen, hoping something more cheerful would come on soon. By now the shopping centre was in darkness, though two lamps were still alight in the open air car parks. A middle-aged man, one of the neighbours, came long with his dog which lifted its leg against the red metal door of the call box. Archie felt like banging on the window but knew it would do no good. Dog and owner went off into the mist while Archie drank his tea, ate the second biscuit and wondered whether he should get himself a third or wait an hour. Weather forecast now; he couldn't hear it, but he could see by all those little clouds and whirly lines that it was going to be a mixture as before.

Outside was silence, darkness, mist which moved and cleared and rolled sluggishly back, which the lights – half-obscured by plane-tree branches – turned to a watery, acid-green phosphorescence. The darkness was deep in the tarmac desert, nothing visible but two islanded spots of light and now these also went out . . . one, two . . . leaving blackness that met a dark grey but luminous sky. Only the lamps of Pomeroy Street and a ray or so from the mouth of the underground car park faintly lit the area behind the gates. And into this a little woman walked from behind the concrete wall, having perhaps come from the car-park lift, Archie thought. She walked a few yards in one direction to stare into the blackness, then she turned and gazed towards the gates and him. She seemed to be looking to see if there was anyone about, or looking for someone or something. There was anger, repressed and contained, revealed in the slow deliberate way she moved – he could tell that even in the dark.

She might have a car in there and be unable to get it started. There was nothing he could do and now she had gone again, the wall cutting her off from his view. Archie switched off the television, for he could stand no more of what had appeared silently on the screen – starving Africans with pot-bellied dying babies, more of those people that he in his impotence and penury could not aid. He looked back at the empty stillness outside. Fetching the third biscuit might be postponed for an hour or so. He had to find ways to fill up his evening, for he couldn't very well go to bed until nine which was more than two hours away. The chances were that nothing more would happen out there until eight next morning when the shopping centre opened, nothing at all except cars passing and maybe a couple of people coming to use the phone box. He was thinking this, reflecting on it, when the woman appeared again, walking now in the stalking single-minded fashion of a cat homing on it pray.

When she came up to the gates, she got hold of them as if expecting they would open, as if the padlock would fall apart and the bolts slide back. Archie got to his feet and leaned forward on the window sill. The woman was much too short to reach the top bolt; she seemed now to have realized that the padlock was fastened and the key gone, and she began to rattle the gates. Her eyes were not on him but on the phone box, which was only a few yards from her but tantalizingly outside those gates.

She shook the gates more and more violently and they clanged and rattled. Anyone could see it was useless doing that because of the bolts and the padlock, and Archie began to wonder, because of the sudden and violent change in her demeanour, if she wasn't quite all there, if she were a bit mad . . . crazy. His reaction to anything like that would usually be to ignore it, to shut his eyes or go away. But it was the phone box she wanted; all this frenzy was on account of not being able to reach the phone box. There were always the neighbours – let someone else attend to it, someone younger and stronger. Only no one ever did. Archie sometimes thought a person could be murdered in Pomeroy Street in full view, in broad daylight, and no one would do anything. The woman was shouting now – well, screaming. She was stamping her feet and shaking the gates and roaring at the top of her voice, yelling things Archie couldn't make out but which he heard all right when he had put his cap on and his raincoat round his shoulders and was making his way out on to the pavement.

'The police! The police! I've got to get the police! I've got to phone. I've got to get the police?'

Archie crossed the road. He said, 'Making all that fuss won't help. You calm down now. What's the matter with you?'

'I've got to phone the police! There's someone dead in there. I've got to phone the police – there's a woman and they've tried to cut her head off!'

Archie went cold all over; his throat came up and he tasted tea and chocolate. He thought, my heart, I'm too old for this. He said feebly, 'Stop shaking those gates. Now, come on, you stop it! I can't let you out.'

'I want the police,' she shrieked and fell to lean heavily against the gates, hanging there with her fingers pushed through the wire mesh. The final clang reverberated and died away, as she sobbed harshly against the cold metal.

'I can go and phone them,' Archie said and he went back indoors, leaving her sagged there, still, her hands hooked on the wire like someone shot while trying to escape.

2

The phone rang while he was in the middle of going through
it all with Dora. Supper had been eaten without enthusiasm
and the bag containing Dora's birthday sweater lay unre-
garded on the seat of the chair. He had turned the evening
paper front-page downwards but – unable to resist the horrid
fascination of it – picked it up again.

'Mind you, I knew things weren't going well with her and
Andrew,' Dora said.

'Knowing one's daughter's marriage is going through a
bad patch is a far cry from reading in the paper that she's
getting a divorce.'

'I think you mind about that more than about her coming
up in court.'

Wexford made himself look coolly at the newspaper. The
lead story was the trial of three men who had tried to blow
up the Israeli Embassy and there was something too about
a by-election, but the page was Sheila's. There were two
photographs. The top picture showed a wire fence – not
unlike the fence that surrounded the shopping complex he
had recently left, only this one was topped with coils of razor
wire. The modern world, he sometimes thought, was full of
wire fences. The one in the picture had been mutilated and
a flap hung loose from the centre of it, leaving a gaping hole
through which a waste of mud could be seen with a hangar-
like edifice in the middle of it. From the darkish background
in the other photograph his daughter's lovely face looked
out, wide-eyed, apprehensive, to a father's eye, aghast at the
headlong rush of events. Wisps of pale curly hair escaped
from under her woolly cap. The headlines said only 'Sheila

Cuts the Wire'; the story beneath told the rest of it, giving among all the painful details of arrest and magistrates' court appearance the surely gratuitous information that the actress currently appearing in the television serialization of *Lady Audley's Secret* was seeking a divorce from her husband, businessman Andrew Thorverton.

'I would have liked to be told, I suppose,' Wexford said. 'About the divorce, I mean. I wouldn't expect her to tell us she was going to chop up the fence around a nuclear bomber base. We'd have tried to stop her.'

'We'd have tried to stop her getting a divorce.'

It was then that the phone rang. Since Sheila had been released on bail, pending a later court appearance, Wexford thought it must be her at the other end. He was already hearing her voice in his head, the breathy self-reproach as she tried to persuade her parents she didn't know how the paper had got that report about her divorce . . . she was overcome . . . she was flabbergasted . . . it was all beyond her. And as for the wire-cutting . . .

Not Sheila though. Inspector Michael Burden.

'Mike?'

The voice was cool and a bit curt, anxiety underlying it, but he nearly always sounded like that. 'There's a dead women in the shopping centre car park, the underground one. I haven't seen her yet, but there's no chance it's anything but murder.'

'I was there myself,' Wexford said wonderingly. 'I only left a couple of hours ago.'

'That's OK. Nobody thinks you did it.'

Burden had got a lot sharper since his second marriage. Time was when such a rejoinder would never have entered his head.

'I'll come over. Who's there now?'

'Me – or I will be in five minutes. Archbold. Prentiss.' Prentiss was the Scene-of-Crimes man, Archbold a young DC. 'Sumner-Quist. Sir Hilary's away on his hols.'

In November? Well, people went away at any old time these days. Wexford rather liked the eminent and occasionally outrageous pathologist, Sir Hilary Tremlett, finding Dr Basil Sumner-Quist less congenial.

'There's no identification problem,' said Burden. 'We

432

know who she is. Her name's Gwen Robson, Mrs. Late fifties. Address up at Highlands. A woman called Sanders found her and got hold of someone in Pomeroy Street who phoned us.'

It was five-past eight. 'I may be a long time,' Wexford said to Dora. 'At any rate I won't be back soon.'

'I'm wondering if I ought to phone Sheila.'

'Let her phone us,' said Sheila's father, hardening his heart. He picked up the bag with Dora's present in it and hid it at the back of the hall cupboard. The birthday wasn't until tomorrow anyway.

The car-park entrance was blocked with police cars. Lights had appeared from somewhere, the place blazed with light. Someone had shot the linked shopping trolleys across the parking area to clear a space and trolleys stood about everywhere but at a distance, like a watching crowd of robots. The gates in the fence at the pedestrian entrance in Pomeroy Street stood wide open. Wexford pushed trolleys aside, spinning them out of his way, squeezed between the cars, opened the lift door and tried to summon the lift. It didn't come, so he walked down the two levels. The three cars were still there – the red Metro, silver Escort and dark blue Lancia – but the blue one had been backed out of its parking slot up against the wall and reversed into the middle of the aisle, no doubt to allow room for pathologist, Scene-of-Crimes officer and photographer to scrutinize the body that lay close up against the offside of the silver Escort. Wexford hesitated a moment, then walked towards the group of people and the thing on the concrete floor.

Burden got to his feet as Wexford approached and Archbold, who had old-fashioned manners, nodded and said, 'Sir!' Sumner-Quist didn't bother to look round. The fact that he happened at that moment to move his shoulder so that the dead woman's face and neck were revealed was, Wexford thought, purely fortuitous. The face bore the unmistakable signs of someone who has met her death by strangulation. It was bluish, bloated, horrified, and the mark on her neck of whatever was responsible for her asphyxiation was so deep that it had more the appearance of a circular cut, as if the blade of a knife had been run round throat and nape. Blazing lights in a place usually feebly lit showed up all the

433

horror of her and her surroundings – stained and discoloured concrete, dirty metal, litter sprawling across the floor.

The dead woman wore a brown tweed coat with fur collar and her hat of brown fawn checked tweed with narrow brim was still on her grey curly hair. Apparently small and slight, she had stick-like legs in brown tights or stockings and on her feet brown lace-up low-heeled walking shoes. Wedding and engagement rings were on her left hand.

'The Escort's her car,' Burden said. 'She had the keys to it in her hand when she was killed. Or that's the way it looks, the keys were under the body. There are two bags of groceries in the boot. It looks as if she put the bags in the boot, closed the boot-lid, came round to unlock the driver's door and then someone attacked her from behind.'

'Attacked her with what?'

'A thin length of cord, maybe. Like in thuggee.' Burden's general knowledge as well as sharpness of intellect had been enhanced by marriage. But it was the birth of his son, twenty years after his first family, that had made him abandon the smart suits he had formerly favoured for wear even on occasions like this one. Jeans were what the inspector had on this evening, though jeans which rather oddly bore knife creases and contrasted not altogether happily with his camel-hair jacket.

'More like wire than a cord,' Wexford said.

The remark had an electric effect on Dr Sumner-Quist who jumped up and spoke to Wexford as if they were in a drawing room, not a car park, as if there were no body on the floor and this were a social occasion, a cocktail party maybe: 'Talking of wire, isn't that frightfully pretty TV girl who's all over the paper this evening your daughter?'

Wexford didn't like to imagine what effect the epithet 'TV girl' would have had on Sheila. He nodded.

'I thought so. I said to my wife it was so, unlikely as it seemed. OK, I've done all I can here. If the man with the camera's done his stuff, you can move her as far as I'm concerned. Myself, I think it's a pity these people don't go cutting the wire in Russia.'

Wexford made no reply to this. 'How long has she been dead?'

'You want miracles, don't you? You think I can tell you

that after five minutes' dekko? Well, she was a goner by six, I reckon. That do you?'

And he had been there at seven minutes past . . . He lifted up the grubby brown velvet curtain that lay in a heap a few inches from the dead woman's feet. 'What's this?'

'It was covering the body, sir,' Archbold said.

'Covering it as might be a blanket, do you mean? Or right over the head and feet?'

'One foot was sticking out and the woman who found her pulled it back a bit to see the face.'

'Yes – who was it found her?'

'A Mrs Dorothy Sanders. That's her car over there, the red one. She found the body, but it was a man called Greaves in Pomeroy Street phoned us. Davidson's talking to him now. He found Mrs Sanders screaming and shaking the gates fit to break them down. She went raving mad because the phone box is outside the gates and she couldn't get out. Diana Pettit took a statement from her and drove her home.'

Still holding the curtain. Wexford tried the boot-lid of the red Metro. There was shopping inside that too, food in two red Tesco carriers and a clear plastic bag full of hanks of grey knitting-wool done up with string like a parcel. He looked up at the sound of the lift, an echo from it or reverberation or something; you could always hear it. The door to the lift had opened and a man appeared. He was walking very diffidently and hesitantly towards them and when his eyes met Wexford's he stopped altogether. Archbold went up to him and said something. He was a young man with a pale heavy face and dark moustache and he was dressed in a way which while quite suitable for a man of Wexford's own age, looked incongruous on someone of – what? Twenty-one? Twenty-two? The V-necked grey pullover, striped tie and gray flannel trousers reminded Wexford of a school uniform.

'I've come for the car,' he said.

'One of these cars is yours?'

'The red one, the Metro. It's my mother's. My mother said to come over and bring it back.'

His eyes went fearfully to where the body lay, the body that was now entirely covered by a sheet. It lay unattended – pathologist, photographer and policeman having all moved

435

away towards the central aisle or the exits. Wexford noted that awe-stricken glance, the quick withdrawing of the eyes and jerk of the head. He said, 'Can I have your name, sir?'

'Sanders, Clifford Sanders.'

Burden asked, 'Are you some relation of Mrs Dorothy Sanders?'

'Her son.'

'I'll come back with you,' Wexford said. 'I'll follow you; I'd like to talk to your mother.' He let Clifford Sanders, walking edgily, pass out of earshot and then said to Burden, 'Mrs Robson's next-of-kin . . . ?'

'There's a husband, but he hasn't been told. He'll have to make a formal indentification. I thought of going over there now.'

'Do we know who that blue Lancia belongs to?'

Burden shook his head. 'It's a bit odd, that. Only shoppers use the car park – I mean, who else would want to? And the centre's been closed over two hours. If it belongs to the killer, why didn't he or she drive it away? When I first saw it I thought maybe it wouldn't start, but we had to move it and it started first time.'

'Better have the owner traced,' said Wexford. 'My God, Mike, I was in here, I saw the three cars, I drove past her.'

'Did you see anyone else?'

'I don't know, I'll have to think.'

Going down in the lift, he thought. He remembered the pounding footsteps descending, the girl in the red Vauxhall following him, the half-dozen people in the above-ground parking areas, the mist that was visible and obscuring but really hid nothing. He remembered the woman carrying the two bags coming from the covered way, strolling, languidly kicking the trolley aside. But that was at ten-past six and the murder had already taken place by then. . . . He got into the car beside Archbold. Clifford Sanders in the red Metro was waiting a few yards along the roadway while a uniformed officer – someone new that Wexford didn't recognize – trundled the scattered trolleys out of their path.

The little red car led them along the High Street in the Stowerton direction and turned into the Forby Road. Archbold seemed to know where Sanders lived, in a remote spot down a lane that turned off about half a mile beyond the house and parkland called 'Sundays'. In fact it was less then three miles outside Kingsmarkham, but the lane was narrow and very dark and Clifford Sanders drove even more slowly than the winding obscurity warranted. Thick, dark, leafless hedges rose high on either side. Occasionally a pulling-in place revealed itself, showing at least that passing would be possible if they met another vehicle. Wexford couldn't remember even having been down there before, he doubted if it led anywhere except perhaps finally to the gates of a farm.

The sky was quite black, moonless, starless. The lane seemed to wind in a series of unneccessary loops. There were no hills for it to circumvent and the river to flow in the opposite direction. No longer were any pinpoints of light visible in the surrounding countryside. All was darkness but for the area immediately ahead, illuminated by their own headlights, and the twin bright points glowing red on the rear of the Metro.

But now Clifford Sanders' left-hand indicator was winking. Plainly, he was a kind of driver who would signal his intention to turn a hundred yards before the turning. A few seconds elapsed. There were no lights ahead, only a break in the hedge. Then the Metro turned in and Archbold followed, guided by the red tail-lights. With a kind of amused impatience Wexford thought how they might be in some Hitchcock movie, for he could just make out the house – a house which probably looked a lot less disagreeable by daylight but was now almost ridiculously grim and forbidding. Behind two windows only a pallid light showed. There was no other light either by the front door or about the garden. Wexford's eyes grew accustomed to the darkness and he saw that the house was biggish, on three floors, with eight windows here in the front and a slab of a front door. A low light of steps without rails led up to it and there was neither porch nor canopy. But the whole façade was hung, covered, clothed in ivy. As far as he could see it was ivy, at any rate it was evergreen leaves, a dense blanket of them, through which the two pale windows peered like eyes in an animal's shaggy face.

A garden surrounded the house – grass and wilted foliage at any rate, extending at the back to a wooden fence. Beyond that only darkness, fields and woods, and over the low hill the invisible town which might as well have been a hundred miles away.

Clifford Sanders went up to the front door. The bell was a very old-fashioned kind which you rang by turning the handle back and forth, but he had a key and unlocked this door, though when Wexford started to follow him he said in his flat chilly tone, 'Just a minute, please.'

Mother, evidently, had to be warned; he disappeared and after a moment or two she came out to them. Wexford's first thought was how small she was, tiny and thin; his second that this was the woman he had seen entering the underground car park as he had left it. Within moments then she had found the body that he had missed. Her face was very pale, as near a white face as you could find, very lined and powdered even whiter, a young girl's scarlet lipstick unbecomingly coating her mouth. She was dressed in a brown tweed skirt, beige jumper, bedroom slippers. Did her recent discovery account for the curious smell of her? She smelt of disinfectant, the apparent combination of lime and thymol which hospitals reek of.

'You can come in,' she said, 'I've been expecting you.'

Inside, the place was bleak and cavernous; carpets and central heating were not luxuries that Mrs Sanders went in for. The hall floor was quarry-tiled, in the living room they walked on wood-grain linoleum and a couple of sparse rugs. There was scarcely an ornament to be seen – no pictures, only a large mirror in a heavy mahogany frame. Clifford Sanders had seated himself on a very old, shabby horsehair sofa in front of the fire of logs. He now wore on his feet only grey socks; his shoes were set in the hearth on a folded sheet of newspaper. Mrs Sanders pointed out – actually pointed with an extended finger – precisely where they were to sit: the armchair for Wexford, the other section of the sofa for Archbold. She seemed to have some notion of rank and what was due to it.

'I'd like you to tell me about your experience in the Barringdean Centre car park this evening, Mrs Sanders,' Wexford began. He forced himself to shift his eyes from the newspaper on which his daughter's face looked out at him from between the pair of black lace-up brogues. 'Tell me what happened from the time you came into the car park.'

Her voice was slow and flat like her son's, but there was something metallic about it too, almost as if throat and palate were composed of some inorganic hard material. 'There isn't anything to tell. I came up with my shopping to get my car. I saw something lying on the ground and went over to look and it was . . . I expect you know what it was.'

'Did you touch it?'

'I pulled back the bit of rag that was over it, yes.'

Clifford Sanders was watching his mother, his eyes still and blank. He seemed not so much relaxed as sagging from despair, his hands hanging down between his parted legs.

'What time was this, Mrs Sanders?' Wexford had noted the digital watch she wore.

'Exactly twelve minutes past six.' To account for her leaving the shopping precinct so late, she gave an account of a contretemps with a fishmonger, speaking in the measured level way – too measured. Wexford, who had been wondering what her tone reminded him of, now recalled electronic voices issuing from machines. 'I came up there at twelve minutes past six – and if you want to know how I can be sure of the time, the answer is I'm *always* sure of the time.'

He nodded. Digital watches were designed for people like her who, prior to their arrival on the scene, had to make approximate guesses as to what time was doing between ten-past six and six-fifteen. Yet most of them were speedy people, always in a hurry, restless, unrelaxed. This woman seemed one of those rare creatures who are constantly aware of time without being tempted to race against it.

She spoke softly to her son. 'Did you lock the garage doors?'

He nodded. 'I always do.'

'Nobody always does anything. Anybody can forget.'

'I didn't forget.' He got up. 'I'm going into the other room to watch TV.'

She was a pointer, Wexford saw, a finger-post. Now the finger pointed into the hearth. 'Don't forget your shoes.'

Clifford Sanders padded away with his shoes in his hand and Wexford said to Dorothy Sanders, 'What were you doing between twelve minutes past six and six forty-five when you managed to attract the attention of Mr Greaves in Queen Street?' He had registered very precisely the time of the phone call Greaves made to Kingsmarkham police station: fourteen minutes to seven. 'That's half an hour between the time you found the body and the time you got down to the gate and . . . called out.'

She wasn't disconcerted. 'It was a shock. I had my shock to get over and then when I got down there I couldn't make anyone hear.'

He recalled Archbold's account, albeit at third hand. She had been screaming and raving inside those gates, shaking them 'fit to break them down' because the phone box was on the other side. Now the woman looked at him coldly and calmly. One would have said no emotion ever disturbed her equilibrium or altered the tone of the mechanical voice.

'How many cars did you see parked at that time on the second level?'

Without hesitation she said, 'Three, including mine.'

She wasn't lying; perhaps she hadn't been lying at all. He recalled how when he had passed through the second level there had been four cars parked there. One had pulled out, the one driven by the impatient young girl, and followed him fretfully. That had been at eight or nine minutes past six . . .

'Did you see anyone? Anyone at all?'

'Not a soul.'

She would be a widow, Wexford thought, nearly pensionable, without any sort of job, dependent in many ways and certainly financially dependent on this son who no doubt lived not far away. Later on, he reflected that he couldn't have been more wrong.

A wave of disinfectant smell hit him and she must have seen him sniffing.

'Coming in contact with that corpse,' she said, looking at him with steady, unblinking eyes, 'I had to scrub my hands with antiseptic.'

It was years since he had heard anyone use the word corpse. As he got up to go, she crossed the window and began to draw the curtains. The place smelt like an operating theatre. The better to observe Clifford's arrival with the car, Wexford supposed, the curtains – of brown rep, not velvet – had been left drawn back. He watched her pull them

440

together, giving each an impatient tug. Attached to the top of the door into the room was one of those extendable brass rails made to accomodate a draught-excluding curtain. No curtain, however, hung from it.

Wexford decided the time was not ripe to ask the question that came to his lips.

It had fallen many times to Michael Burden's lot to be the bearer of bad tidings of a particular kind, to break the news of a spouse's death. He, whose own first wife had died prematurely, flinched from this task. And it was one thing having to tell someone, for instance, that his wife had died in a road accident; quite another that her murdered body had been found. No one knew better than Burden that the majority of those who are murdered have been done to death by a near relative. The chances are that a murdered wife has been murdered by her husband.

It was only a few moments before Wexford's arrival that he had looked inside the dead woman's handbag. After the first photographs had been taken and the dirty brown velvet curtain lifted from the body, her handbag had been revealed lying under her, half concealed by her thigh. More photographs were taken, Sumner-Quist came and at last he was able to free the bag from where it lay and, holding it in gloved hands, undo the clasp and look inside. It was a standard cache of documents: driving licence, credit cards, dry-cleaning bill, two letters still in their envelopes. Her name and address presented themselves to him before he had even noted the other contents of the bag – chequebook, purse, pressed powder, packet of tissues, ballpoint pen and two safety-pins. Gwen P. Robson, 23 Hastings Road, Highlands, Kingsmarkham KM10 2NW. One of the envelopes was addressed to her as Mrs G. P. Robson, the other to Mr and Mrs R. Robson.

It might not be a shock to Robson; part of Burden's job was to observe whether it was a shock or not. He silently framed the words he would use as the car climbed the long hill that led up to the Highlands estate. All this had been countryside when Burden first came to Kingsmarkham, heathy hillsides crowned with woods, and from the top of

441

this incline by day you had been able to see the ancient landmark called Barringdean Ring. It was very dark tonight, the horizon defined only by an occasional point of light, and the circle of oaks was invisible. Nearer at hand Highlands was cosily lit. This was the way Gwen Robson had no doubt intended to come home, driving the silver Escort, entering Eastbourne Avenue and soon turning left into Hastings Road.

Burden had been there only once before, though the estate had been put up by the local authority some seven years ago. Street trees and garden trees had grown up and matured: the first newness of the houses had worn off and they looked less as if built from playbox bricks by a giant's child. Smallish blocks of flats no more than three storeys high, alternated with terraced or semi-detached houses, and opposite the block in which No. 23 was located stood a row of tiny bungalows designed as housing for the elderly. Not too far a cry from the old almshouses, thought Burden, whose wife had made him a lot more socially conscious than he used to be. On the doorstep of the Robson's house stood a rack made for holding milkbottles; it was of red plastic-covered wire, surmounted by a plastic doll in a white coat with 'Thank you, Mr Milkman' in red letters under it and a clip to hold a note in its outstretched hand. This absurd object made Burden feel worse, indicative as it was of domestic cheerfulness. He looked at DC Davidson and Davidson looked at him and then he rang the bell.

The door was answered very quickly. Anxious people fly to doors, to phones. Their anxiety, of course, may not be brought about by the obvious cause.

'Mr Robson?'

'Yes. Who are you?'

'Police officers, Mr Robson.' Burden showed his warrant card. How to soften this? How to ease it? He could hardly say there was nothing to be alarmed about. 'I am afraid we have very serious news. May we come in?'

He was a smallish, owl-face man, rather overweight; Burden noticed that he used a stick even to bring him this short distance. 'Not my wife?' he said.

Burden nodded. He nodded firmly, his eyes on Robson. 'Let's go in.'

442

But Robson, though they were in the hall now, stood his ground. He leant on his stick. 'The car? A car accident?'

'No, Mr Robson, it wasn't a car accident.' The bad part was that this could all be fake, all acting. He might have been rehearsing it for the past hour. 'If we could go into your . . .'

'Is she – is she gone?'

The old euphemism. Burden repeated it. 'Yes, she's gone.' and he added. 'She's dead, Mr Robson.'

Burden turned and walked through the open doorway into the well-lit, warm, over-furnished living room. A fire of gas flames licking beautifully simulated smokeless fuel looked more real than the real thing. The television was on, but more indicative of Robson's recent tension was the clock patience game laid out on a small appropriately round mar-quetry table in front of the armchair with its indented seat and crumpled pink silk cusions. Only a murderer who was also a genius would have dreamt up that one, Burden thought.

Robson had turned very pale. His thin-lipped mouth trem-bled. Still upright but leaning heavily on the stick, he was shaking his head in a vague, uncomprehending way. 'Dead? Gwen?'

'Sit down, Mr Robson. Take it easy.'

'Would you like a drink, sir?' DC Davidson asked.

'We don't drink in this house.'

'I meant water.' Davidson went off and came back with water in a glass.

'Tell me what happened.' Robson was seated now, no longer looking at Burden, his eyes in the circle of playing cards. Absently he took a minute sip of the water.

'You must prepare yourself for a shock, Mr Robson.'

'I've had a shock.'

'Yes, I know.' Burden shifted his gaze and found himself looking at the framed photograph on the mantel-shelf of a very good-looking girl who rather resembled Sheila Wexford. A daughter? 'Your wife was killed, Mr Robson. There is no way I can make this easier to hear. She was murdered and her body was found in the Barringdean Shopping Centre car park.'

Burden wouldn't have been surprised if he had screamed,

443

if he had howled like a dog. They came upon all sorts in their job. But Robson didn't scream; he merely stared with frozen face. A long time passed, a relatively long time, perhaps nearly a minute. He stared and passed his tongue over the thin lips, then he began mumbling very rapidly.

'We were married very young; we'd been married forty years. No children, we never had chick nor child, but that brings you closer; you're closer to each other without them. She was the most devoted wife a man ever had; she'd have done anything for me, she'd have laid down her life for me.' Great tears welled out of his eyes and flowed down his face. He sobbed and wept without covering his face, sitting upright and holding the stick with both hands, crying as most men only cried when they were very young children.

3

'It looks as if she was garroted.'

Sumner-Quist's voice sounded pleasurably excited as if he had rung up to impart a piece of gossip: that the Chief Constable had run off with someone else's wife, for instance.

'Did you hear me? I said she was garroted.'

'Yes, I heard,' Wexford said. 'Good of you to tell me.'

'I thought you might go for a tasty little titbit like that before I let you have the full report.'

Extraordinary ideas some people have about one's tastes, Wexford thought. He tried to assemble in his mind what he knew about garroting. 'What was it done with?'

'A garrote,' Sumner-Quist chuckled cheerfully. 'Search me what kind. Home-made, no doubt. That's your problem.' Still laughing, he told Wexford that Mrs Robson had met her death after five-thirty and before six and had not been sexually assaulted. 'Merely garroted,' he said.

'It used to be a method of execution,' Wexford said when Burden came into the office. 'An iron collar was attached to a post and the victim's neck placed inside. The mind boggles a bit when you start thinking how they *got* the victim's neck inside. Then the collar was tightened until asphyxiation occurred. Did you know this method of capital punishment was still in use in Spain as late as the 1960s?'

'And we thought it was only bull-fighting they went in for.'

'There was also a more primitive implement consisting of a length of wire with wooden handles.'

Burden sat on the edge of Wexford's rosewood desk. 'Haven't I read somewhere that if you were up for burning by the Inquisition the executioner would garrote you for a small fee before the flames got under way?'

'I expect that was where the wire-with-wooden-handles type came into its own.'

He wondered digressively if Burden's jeans were the kind called 'designer'. They were rather narrow at the ankle and matched the inspector's socks that were probably of a 'denim blue' shade. Unconscious of this rather puzzled scrutiny, Burden said, 'Is Sumner-Quist saying that's what was used on Gwen Robson?'

'He doesn't know, he just says "a garrote". But it had to have been something of that kind. And the murderer has to have had it with him or her, ready-made, all prepared – which when you come to think of it, Mike, is pretty strange. It argues unquestionably premeditated murder, yet in a situation where no one could have forecast the prevailing conditions. The car park might have been full of people, for instance. Unless our perpetrator carries a garrote about with him as you or I might carry a pen . . . I don't think we can say much more about that until we get the full forensic report. In the meantime, what's the sum total of our knowledge of Gwen Robson?'

She was fifty-eight years old, childless, a former home help in the employment of Kingsmarkham Borough Council but now retired. Her husband was Ralph Robson, also a former Borough Council employee, retired two years before from the Housing Department. Mrs Robson had been married at eighteen and she and her husband had lived first with his parents at their home in Stowerton, later on in a rented flat and then a rented cottage. Their names high on the borough housing list, they had been allocated one of the new houses at Highlands as soon as they were built. Neither was yet eligible for the state retirement pension, but Robson derived a pension from the local authority on which they had contrived to live in reasonable comfort. For instance, they had managed to run the two-year-old Escort. As a general rule they took an annual holiday in Spain and had been prevented from doing so this year only by Ralph Robson's arthritis, which was seriously affecting his right hip.

All this had been learned both from Ralph Robson himself

and from his niece Lesley Arbel, the original of the photograph that had so much reminded Burden of Sheila Wexford.

'This niece – she doesn't live with them, does she?'

'She lives in London, Burden said, 'but she spent a lot of time down here with them. More like a daughter than a niece, I gather, and an unusually devoted daughter at that. Or that's how it appears. She's staying with Robson now – came as soon as he told her what had happened to his wife.'

According to Robson, his wife had been in the habit of doing their weekly shopping every Thursday afternoon. Up until six months ago he had always gone with her, but his arthritis had made this impossible. On the previous Thursday, two days before, she had gone out in their car just before four-thirty. He had never seen her again. And where had he been himself between four-thirty and seven? At home alone in Hastings Road, watching television, making himself tea. Much the same as Archie Greaves, Wexford thought, whom he had been to see earlier that morning.

A policeman's dream of a witness, the old man was. The narrowness of his life, the confined span of his interests made him into a camera and tape device for the perfect recording of incidents in his little world. Unfortunately, there had not been much for him to observe: the shoppers leaving, the lights dwindling and going out, Sedgeman closing and locking the gates.

'There was this young chap running,' he said to Wexford. 'It was just on six, a minute or two after. There were a lot of people leaving, mostly ladies with their shopping, and he came running from round the back of that wall.'

Wexford followed his gaze out of the window. The wall in question was the side of the underground car-park entrance beside which stood a small crowd of ghoulish onlookers. There was nothing to see, but they waited in hope. The gates stood open, an empty food package rolled about the tarmac propelled by gusts of wind. The pennants on the turrets streamed in the wind, taut and fluttering. I was there, Wexford thought, almost with a groan, I came out of there at ten-past six and saw – nothing. Well, nothing but the Sanders woman.

'I reckoned he was in trouble,' Archie Greaves said. 'I reckoned he'd done something he shouldn't and been spotted and they was after him.' The man was so old that his face as well as the skin of his hands was discoloured with the liver spots that are called 'grave marks'. He was thin with age, his knitted cardigan and flannel trousers baggy on a bony, tremulous body. But the pale blue eyes, pink-rimmed, could see like those of someone half his age. 'He was just a boy with one of them woolly hats on his head and a zip-up jacket and he was running like a bat out of hell.'

'But there was in fact no one after him?'

'Not as I could see. Maybe they got fed up and turned back, knowing as they wouldn't catch him.'

And then he had seen Dorothy Sanders who was later to scream and rattle the gates, walking up and down searching the car parks for something or someone, her anger contained but her affronted indignation vibrating as later a demented terror was to stream from her, making Archie Greaves shiver and shake and fear for his heart.

An incident room had been set up in Kingsmarkham Police Station on Thursday night to receive calls from anyone who might have been in the Barringdean Shopping Centre underground car park between five and six-thirty. The local television station had broadcast an immediate appeal for possible witnesses to come forward and Wexford had managed to get a nationwide appeal on that night's ten o'clock news going out on the network. Calls started coming in at once – before the number to call had even disappeared from the screen, Sergeant Martin said – but of these the great majority were well-meant but misleading, or ill-meant and misleading, or were deliberate attempts to deceive. A call came from a young woman called Sarah Cussons who identified herself as the driver of the Vauxhall Cavalier which had followed Wexford's out of the car park, and another from a man beside whose car Gwen Robson had parked her red Metro. He had seen her drive in and was able to give her time of arrival at the centre as about twenty to five.

Throughout Thursday night the calls continued to come in, many of them from drivers of cars parked on all the levels who had seen nothing untoward. They were interviewed just the same. Early on Friday morning came a call on behalf of the owner of the blue Lancia. Mrs Helen Brook, nine months pregnant, had gone into labour while in the health-food shop in the shopping centre at about five on the previous evening. An ambulance had been called and she had been taken to the maternity wing of Stowerton Royal Infirmary.

None of the obviously genuine and well-intentioned callers was able to describe anyone else they had seen while parking or fetching their cars, though plenty of fantastic descriptions came in from those jokers who enjoy teasing the police. Two assistants from the Barringdean Centre shops phoned in to say they had served Gwen Robson, one just before five and the other, Linda Naseem – a checkout assistant at the Tesco supermarket – half an hour later. But by that time two of Wexford's officers were at the shopping centre questioning all the shop-workers, and Archbold had interviewed the man in charge of the fish counter in the Tesco superstore who confirmed he had had a row with a woman answering Dorothy Sanders' description 'at around six when they were closing up'. All that did was confirm her time of coming into the car park which Wexford could confirm himself.

That same morning Ralph Robson made a formal identification of his wife's body; the neck had been discreetly covered during this ordeal. He hobbled in on his stick, looked at the horror-stricken face from which some of the blue colour had faded, nodded, said, 'Yes,' but didn't cry this time. Wexford had not seen him on that occasion, hadn't yet seen him. He had interviewed David Sedgeman, the car park supervisor, himself. The man should have been a valuable witness, yet he seemed to have seen nothing or to have registered nothing he had seen. He could recall waving to Archie Greaves because he did this every evening, and for the same reason could recall locking the gates. But his memory offered him no worried woman or running man, no fast-driven car or suspicious escaper. Everything had been normal, he said in his dull way. He had locked the gates and gone home just as he always did, collecting his own car from where he always left it in a bay in one of the open-air parking areas.

The November air felt raw and the sky was a leaden grey.

449

A reddish sun hung over the roof-tops, not very high in the sky but as high as it would get. Burden had on a padded jacket, a pale grey Killy, warm as toast and turning him from a thin man into a stout one. His wife was away, staying with her mother who was convalescent after an operation, and that disturbed Burden, making him jumpy and insecure. He would spend tonight with her and their little son in his mother-in-law's house outside Myringham, but what he really wanted was his own family back home with him in his own house. His face took on a look both irritable and cynical as Wexford spoke.

'Did Robson strike you,' Wexford said in the car, 'as the sort of man who would sit himself down and with deliberation fashion a wire implement with a handle at each end for the express purpose of garroting his wife?'

'Now you're asking. I don't know what sort of a man that would be. He had no car, remember, his wife had the car. The centre's a mile away from Highlands . . .'

'I know. Is the arthritic hip genuine?'

'Even if it isn't, he had no car. He could have walked, or there's the bus. But if he wanted to murder his wife, why not do it at home like most of them do?'

Wexford couldn't keep from laughing at this insouciant acceptance of domestic homicide. 'Maybe he did, we don't know yet. We don't know if she died in that car park or the body was only dumped there. We don't even know if she drove the car.'

'You mean Robson himself may have?'

'Let's see,' said Wexford.

They arrived at Highlands and Lesley Arbel opened the front door to them. She didn't remind Wexford of his own daughter; to him she bore no resemblence to Sheila. He saw only a pretty girl who struck him at once as being exceptionally well-dressed, indeed almost absurdly well-dressed for a weekend of mourning in the country with one's recently bereaved uncle. She introduced herself, explained that she had not waited until the prearranged time for her visit but had come on Friday morning.

'My uncle's upstairs,' she said. 'He's lying down. The doctor came and said he was to get as much rest as he could.'

'That's all right, Miss Arbel. We'd like to talk to you too.'

450

'Me? But I don't know anything about it. I was in London.'

'You know about your aunt. You can tell us something of what sort of a person she was, better than your uncle can.'

She said in a rather pernickety way. 'That's right, he's my real uncle. I mean, my mother was his sister; she was my aunt because she married him.'

Wexford nodded, aware that his impatience showed. Mentally he cautioned himself against deciding too soon that a witness was irredeemably stupid. She took them into the Robsons' brightly furnished living room where a conflict of textile patterns dazzled Wexford – flowers on the carpet, flowers of a more formal design on the curtains, trees and fruits on the wallpaper, a rug with a sunburst pattern. The flames of a gas fire licked indestructible coals. The girl sat down and her own face smiled over her shoulder out of a silver frame. His question astonished her.

'These curtain, are they new?'

'Pardon?'

'Let me rephrase it. Were there ever different curtains at these windows?'

'I think Auntie Gwen once had red curtain, yes. Why do you want to know?'

Wexford made no answer but watched her while Burden asked about the telephone call her uncle had made to her on Thursday evening. Her clothes were remarkable, somehow evoking the unreal elegance of actresses in Hollywood comedies of the thirties, as sleek and as unsuitable for the wear and tear of living. A bunch of gold chains that looked too heavy for comfort hung against her cream silk shirt between the lapels of the coffee-coloured silk jacket. Crimson-nailed hands lay in her lap and she lifted one to her face, touching her cheek as she replied to his questions.

'You intended coming down for the weekend of Saturday as you often did?'

She nodded.

'But your uncle phoned you himself on Thursday evening and told you what had happened?'

'He phoned me on Thursday, on Thursday night. I wanted to come then, but he wouldn't have that. He had one of the neighbours, a Mrs Whitton, with him so I thought he'd be all right.' She looked from one to the other of them. 'You said you wanted me to talk about Auntie Gwen.'

'In a moment, Miss Arbel,' Burden said. 'Would you mind telling me what you were doing yourself on Thursday afternoon?'

'What do you want to know for?' She was more than astounded; her manner was affronted as if she had encountered insolence. Her long elegant legs, the feet encased in high-heeled cream leather pumps, drew close together, were pressed together. 'Why ever do you want to know that?'

Perhaps it was pure innocence.

Burden said blandly, 'Routine questions, Miss Arbel. In a murder enquiry, it's necessary to know people's whereabouts.' He attempted to help her along. 'I expect you were at work, weren't you?'

'I went home early on Thursday, I wasn't very well. Don't you want me to tell you about Auntie Gwen?'

'In a moment. You went home early because you weren't well. You had a cold, did you?'

A vacuous stare was turned on Burden, but perhaps not entirely vacuous for it seemed to contain an element of earnestness. 'It was my PMT, wasn't it?' she said as if she were famous for this disorder. as if all the world was aware of it. Wexford doubted if Burden even knew what those initials stood for, and now the girl seemed equally dubious. Frowning, she leaned towards Burden. 'I always have PMT and there's not a thing they can do about it.'

At this point the door opened and Ralph Robson came in, leaning on his stick. He had a dressing gown on, but with a shirt and pair of slacks underneath it. 'I heard voices.' His flat but beaky face was turned on Wexford with a puzzled look.

'Chief Inspector Wexford, Kingsmarkham CID.'

'Pleased to meet you,' Robson said, sounding anything but pleased. 'You coming here has saved me a phone call. Maybe one of you can tell me what's become of the shopping?'

'The shopping, Mr Robson?'

'The shopping Gwen got on Thursday, as was in the boot of the blessed car presumably. I can see I can't have the car back yet awhile, but the shopping's a different story. There's meat in those bags, there's a loaf and butter and I don't know what else. I don't say I'm poor, but I'm not so rolling in money as I can just let that lot go, right?'

Self-preservation or a tenacity for life overcame grief. Wexford knew this, but it never ceased mildly to surprise him just the same. It might be that this man felt no grief; it might be that he was responsible for his wife's death, but it might only be that he had ceased to feel much emotion for anyone or anything. That sometimes happened to people as they aged and Wexford had noticed it dispassionately but with an inner shiver. Yet Burden said he had wept when first told.

'We'll get it back to you later today,' was all Wexford said.

He had carefully gone over the contents of the shopping bag himself before having the perishable items placed in one of the police canteen fridges. There had been nothing among them to excite much interest: mostly food, but things from the chemist as well – toothpaste and talcum powder – and from the British Home Stores four light-bulbs; all of these contained in a BHS bag, indicating perhaps that she had stopped there first. Mrs Robson's handbag, which would also soon be returned and which Burden had first looked into in the car park, contained her purse with twenty-two pounds in it, plus some small change and a chequebook from the Trustee Savings Bank. The credit cards were a Visa and the card which the Barringdean Shopping Centre supplied for its patrons. Her handkerchief and the two folded tissues were unused. The letters which had provided the police with her identity and address were from a sister in Leeds and the other – scarcely a letter in any sense – an invitation to a Christmas fashion show at the shop where Wexford had bought Dora's sweater.

'Are you missing a brown velvet curtain, Mr Robson?'

'Me? No. What do you mean?'

'A curtain which might have been kept in the boot of your car for the purpose, say, of covering up the windscreen in frosty weather?'

'I use newspaper for that.'

Lesley Arbel said suddenly, 'Could you eat a bit of lunch, Uncle? A little something light?'

453

He had sat down and was leaning forward in the chair, pressing one hand on his thigh in what seemed genuine pain, his face twisted with it. 'There's nothing I fancy, dear.'

'But you're not still having those pills, are you? The ones that upset your tummy?'

'Doctor took me off the blessed things. There's some they don't suit, he said; they can give you ulcers.'

'You've got arthritis, have you, Mr Robson?'

He nodded. 'You listen,' he said, 'and you can hear the hip joint grind.' To Robson's evident agony there came a shift of bone in socket and Wexford did hear it, heard with dismay an unhuman ratchet-like sound. 'It's a bit of bad luck for me that I'm allergic to the painkillers. Got to grin and bear it. I'm in line for one of those replacement ops, but there's a waiting list round here of up to three years. God knows what sort of a state I'll be in three years. It'd be a different story if I could have it done private.'

This was no news to Wexford, that hip replacements could be carried out almost at once if the patient were prepared to pay but that the waiting time for National Health Service surgery might be very protracted. The unfairness of this was not lost on him, but he was more intent on trying to assess the genuineness of Robson's disability. He turned his eyes towards the girl and she looked at him artlessly, her face a beautiful blank.

'Where do you work, Miss Arbel?'

'*Kim* magazine.'

'Could you give me the address, please, and your own address in London too? Do you live alone or share?'

'I share with two other girls.' She sounded peevish, muttering the north-west London address. '*Kim*'s office is at Orangetree House in the Waterloo Road.'

Wexford had only once seen the magazine when Dora had bought it for the sake of some mail-order bargain it featured. A semi-glossy weekly, it had seemed aimed at a not very youthful market but at the same time making little provision for women past forty or so. The issue Wexford had seen had carried articles he thought dreary but which the magazine itself vaunted as controversial and lively, under such headings as: 'Is it OK to be a Lesbian?' and 'Your Daughter Your Own Clone?'

'Could you eat some scrambled egg, Uncle, and a little thin bread and butter?'

Robson shrugged, then nodded. Burden began speaking to him of Mrs Whitton, the neighbour who had come to sit with him before Lesley Arbel arrived. Had he seen anyone, spoken on the phone to anyone, while his wife was out?

Lesley got up, said, 'Well, if you'll just excuse me . . .'

While Robson told Burden about the Hastings Road neighbours, speaking in a wretched halting monotone and separating virtually every sentence from the next with a phrase to the effect that Gwen had known them all better than he did, Wexford left the room. He found Lesley Arbel standing in front of an electric stove, a printed tea-towel rather than an apron tied round her waist to protect the coffee silk skirt. Two eggs reposed in a bowl, a beater beside them, but instead of preparing her uncle's lunch she was examining her face in a handbag mirror and painting something on to it with a small, fat brush.

As soon as she saw Wexford she put brush and mirror away with extreme haste, as if this rapid manoeuvre would somehow render the prior activity invisible. She broke open the eggs, not very skilfully, got a piece of shell into the bowl and had to pick it out with a long red nail.

'Why would anyone want to murder your aunt, Miss Arbel?'

She didn't answer him for a moment, but reached up into a cabinet for a plate and put a cruet on to the tray she had laid with a cloth. Her voice when it came was nervous and irritable. 'It was some crazy person, wasn't it? There's never any reason for murders, not these days. The ones you read about in the papers, they're all people who say they don't know why they did it or they've forgotten or had a blackout or whatever. The one who killed her will have been like that. I mean, who would have wanted to kill her for a reason? There wasn't any reason.' She turned away from him and started beating the eggs.

'Everybody liked her?' he said. 'She wouldn't have had enemies?'

In her left hand she held the pan in which butter was smoking too strongly, in her other the bowl with the egg mixture. But instead of pouring one into the other, she stood

455

with the two vessels poised. 'It's a laugh really, hearing you talk like that. Or it would be if it wasn't such a tragedy. She was a wonderful, lovely lady – don't you understand that? Hasn't anyone told you? Look at Uncle Ralph, he's heart-broken, isn't he? He worshipped her and she worshipped him. They were just a lovely couple, like young lovers right up to when this happened. And this'll be the death of him, I can promise you that – this'll be the end of him. He's aged about twenty years since yesterday.'

She swung round, tipped the eggs into the pan and began rapidly cooking them. Wexford had the curious feeling that for all the apparent sincerity of her words what she was really trying to do was impress him with a kind of caring competent maturity – an ambition that went wrong when she seemed to realize that though the eggs were cooked she had forgotten about the bread and butter. Rather harassed by now, she cut doorsteps of bread and covered them with wedges of butter chipped from the refrigerated block. He opened doors for her, feeling something very near pity with-out exactly knowing what he pitied her *for*. The apron improvised from a tea towel fell off as she teetered into the living room on her stilt heels. But even so, as she passed the small wall mirror which hung between kitchen and living-room doorways, she was unable to resist a glance into it. Balanced on her pointed toes, holding the tray, flustered, she nevertheless took the opportunity of a narcissistic peep at her own face . . .

Robson was lying back in his armchair and had to be jolted out of his half-daze. This his niece did not only by propping him up with a cushion behind him and plumping the tray down on his lap, but also with the rough and some-how shocking, 'He asked me if Gwen had enemies! Can you credit it?'

Dull, bewildered eyes were lifted. Incredibly came the mumble, 'He's only doing his job, dear.'

'Gwen,' she said, and sentimentally, 'Gwen that was like a mother to me.' Suddenly her manner sharpened. 'Mind you, she wasn't soft. She had principles, very high principles, didn't she, Uncle? And she knew how to speak her mind. She didn't like that couple living together, the ones next-door-but-one, whatever they're called, the people that run a

456

business from home. I said times had changed from when she got married, but it didn't make any difference. I mean, everyone does that now, I said. But she wouldn't have it, would she, Uncle?'

They were all looking at her, Robson as well. She seemed to realize how animated her manner had been for one so recently bereaved and she flushed. Not much real love there, Burden thought, and said, 'Now we'd like to take a look round the house. Is that OK?'

She would have argued but Robson, having eaten almost nothing, pushing away his plate, nodded and waved one hand in an odd gesture of assent. Wexford wouldn't have bothered with the house; there was nothing relevant to Mrs Robson's life or death he expected to find. He was already half-adhering to the girl's view, that some badly disturbed person had killed Gwen Robson for no better reason than that she was there and a woman, unprepared and frail enough. However, he made his way into the bedroom she had shared with Robson and saw everywhere signs of domestic harmony. The bed was unmade. On an impulse aimed at no particular enlightening discovery, Wexford lifted up the flatter and less rumpled of the pillows and found underneath it Mrs Robson's nightdress just as it must have been folded and tucked away by her on Thursday morning . . .

A framed photograph showed her as she had once been, her hair dark and plentiful, mouth widely smiling, plumper than now. She was seated and her husband was looking over her shoulder, perhaps to give an illusion of the greater height he had not possessed. The books on her bedside cabinet were two novels of Catherine Cookson, on his the latest Robert Ludlum. On the dressing table a small container of Yardley 'Chique' perfume stood between his hairbrush and a pincushion in which were pinned three brooches. A surprising number of pictures covered the walls: more framed photographs of the two of them, a framed collage of postcards, sentimental mementoes of their own holidays, cat and dog pictures perhaps cut from calendars, a cottage in the flowery garden embroidered by someone – perhaps Gwen Robson herself.

The curtains in the room were as floral as this picture. In spite of her sober style of dressing, she had liked bright colours – pinks and blues and yellows. She might have worn brown, but she would not have furnished her house with it. A neatly stacked pile of *Kim* magazines occupied half the top of a long stool and on top of these lay last night's evening paper. Did that mean that the night after his wife had been murdered Robson had taken the evening paper up with him for his bedtime reading? Well, why not? Life must go on. And no doubt he had been given sleeping pills, had needed something to read while waiting for the drug to take effect. Wexford just glanced at the lead story and the photograph of the barrister Edmund Hope, as handsome and striking-looking as any of the Arab bombers he was prosecuting, then he turned away to study the view.

Beyond the window the Highlands estate presented a panorama of itself she must often have seen while standing here: Hastings Road where the house was, Eastbourne Road leading down to the town, Battle Hill mounting to the crown of the estate, pantiled roofs deliberately placed at odd angles to one another to give the illusion of some little hillside town in Spain or Portugal – coniferous trees bluish, dark green and golden-green because conifers are cheap and grow swiftly, winding gravel paths and concrete paths, windows dressed in Austrian blinds, looped-up festoons and frills, one solitary resident only to be seen: an elderly, very stout woman in long skirt and multi-coloured jacket who was breaking into pieces the end of a loaf of bread and putting them on to a bird-table in a garden diagonally opposite. The house she returned to was the first of those past the row of old people's sheltered housing. She looked back once at where Mrs Robson had lived, as anyone must look who lived here or came into this street. That was human nature. Her eyes met Wexford's and she immediately looked away. It was rather as Lesley Arbel had quickly put away her mirror and brush, as if this would negate the past act.

Wexford said, 'We may as well go. We'll give Mrs Sanders a ring and get her down to the station.'

'You wouldn't prefer to go to her?'

'No, I'd prefer to give her a bit of trouble,' said Wexford.

4

It was spread out on the table in the interview room — a curtain that had once been handsome, of a rich thick-piled tobacco-brown velvet, lined and weighted at the two corners of its lower hem. But splashed the centre of it was a large dark stain, a stain which might have been blood but which Wexford had already ascertained was not. Other stains had since been super-added; there was certainly an impression that the original splashings had ruined the curtain as a curtain, and that since the occurrence which had led to them any further damage to the velvet had been of no account.

Dorothy Sanders looked at it. Her eyes flicked and as she looked back at Wexford he noticed for the first time that they were of a curious pale fawn colour.

'That's the curtain that used to hang up on my door.' And then, after a long blank stare at Wexford had elicited no particular reaction, 'It's still got the hooks in it.'

He continued to stand and watch her, his face expressing nothing, but now he gave a small reflective nod. Burden was frowning.

'Where did you get it?' she said. 'What's it doing here?'

'It was covering Mrs Robson's body,' Burden said. 'Don't you remember?'

The change in her was electric. She jumped back, retracting arms and hands as if it were offal or slime her fingers had touched. Her face flushed darkly, her lips sucked in. She put a hand to her mouth — a characteristic gesture, he thought — and then flung the hand away, aware of what it had been in contact with. He had a glimpse then of how this slow, deliberate woman could become a screaming demented creature, and for the first time he understood that the old man called Archie Greaves might not have been exaggerating.

'You've touched it before, Mrs Sanders,' he said. 'You pulled it back to look at her face.'

She shuddered, her arms stretched out and shaking as if she could shake off her hands and so get rid of them.

'Come and sit down, Mrs Sanders.'

'I want to wash my hands. Where can I go and wash my hands?'

Wexford didn't want her to run away, but as he picked up the phone DC Marian Bayliss tapped on the door and came in. She began on a routine question and he nodded assent and said, 'Would you take Mrs Sanders to the ladies' loo, please?'

Dorothy Sanders was brought back after about five minutes, calm again, stony-faced and with more red lipstick on her mouth. He could smell the police station liquid soap ten feet away.

'Have you any suggestions, Mrs Sanders, as to how your curtain came to be covering Mrs Robson's body?'

'I didn't put it there. The last time I saw it was in a ...' she hesitated, went on more carefully, '... a room in my house. Folded up. In the attic, they call them attics. My son may have gone up there; he may have wanted it for something, though he'd no business ... without me saying he could.' A grim look cramped her features.

This hadn't occurred to Wexford as a possibility before, but it did now. 'Does your son live with you, Mrs Sanders?'

'Of course he lives with me.' She spoke as if, though it were possible there were some very few grown-up children who through general viciousness or perhaps being orphans lived apart from their parents, such situations were rare enough to provoke incredulity and even disgust. She spoke as if Wexford were a depraved ignoramus to suppose otherwise. 'Of course he lives with me. Where did you think he lived?'

'Are you sure this curtain was in a room in your house? It couldn't have been in the boot of your car?'

She was no fool. At least, she was sharp enough.

'Not unless he put it there.' The identity of 'he' was evident enough. She thought, reasoned, nodded her head. This was

460

not one of those women, Wexford thought with a kind of grim amusement, who even at the cost of their own lives would protect a child, criminal or otherwise – the kind who hid a wanted son or lied when questioned as to his whereabouts, who regarded a son not so much as an extension of herself, but as a precious superior. 'I expect he did put it there,' she now said. 'I'd sent through my catalogue for a proper nylon cover for the car. Nylon or fibreglass or one of those things.' Mail order she meant, Wexford decided. 'I'd sent for it a good two months ago, but they take their time, these people. I expect he couldn't wait.'

'She looked up at him, making him perform one of those about-turns in his assessment of human nature. For moment he felt he knew nothing; people and their ways were as much a mystery as ever they had been. She looked human at least, she spoke in a human way. 'He's not like me he hasn't got much patience. He can't help it. I expect he thought he'd just take that curtain and use it when we had a cold spell. You can't be kept waiting about for ever, can you?' She looked down at her watch, drawn to this recorder of time's passage by her references to its delays. Her wrist was like a bundle of wires, thinly insulated.

Burden had been pacing up and down. He said, 'It's your car but your son uses it?'

'It's my car,' she said. 'I bought it and paid for it and I'm the registered owner. But he has to go to work, doesn't he? I let him use it to go to work and then if I want to go shopping, he can take me and pick me up. He's got to have transport.'

'What does your son do, Mrs Sanders?'

She was one of those who expect their private arrangements to be intimately known by others, to need no elucidation, yet who show affront when those others reveal a knowledge gained by sensitivity or intuition. 'He's a teacher, isn't he?'

'You tell me,' Burden said.

She curled her nostrils in disgust. 'He teaches in a school for children who can't pass their exams without extra coaching.'

A crammer's, Wexford thought. Probably Munster's in Kingsmarkham High Street. It surprised him a little and yet

– why not? Clifford Sanders, he thought in the light of his new knowledge, would be one of those who lived at home while they attended university, going to and fro by bus. It would be interesting to find out if he was right there.

'Part-time,' she said, and astonished them both by saying in the same level, indifferent tone, 'He's inadequate in some ways.'

'What's wrong with him? Is he ill?'

Her old harshly censorious manner was back. 'They call it ill nowadays. When I was young, they called it lacking character.' A dark flush moved into her cheeks, mottling them. She was dressed in green today, a dark dull green, though her shoes and gloves were black. When the blush faded, the dull seaweed green seemed to show up the pallor of her skin. 'That's where he was, wasn't he, when he was supposed to be coming for me in the car park? He'd been to this psychiatrist. They call them psychotherapists; they don't have any qualifications.'

'Mrs Sanders, are you telling me that your son was in the Barringdean Centre car park when you were?'

Emotions warred behind the blush, the succeeding pallor, the muffling screen of green and black. She had not meant to let that out. Protecting her son was not as unknown to her as Wexford had at first believed: he could even see that in an intense, self-disgusted, incredulous way she loved her son, but perhaps she had not been able to resist that dig at a profession she disapproved of. She spoke with extreme care now, the pace of the voice electronically slowed to make understanding easier.

'He should have been there but he was not. He had come in, the car was there, but he . . .' she paused, breathing deeply, '. . . was not.'

An abrupt halting explanation followed. At first, when she saw the car and a body, she had thought it was Clifford lying there dead. She couldn't see the body because it was covered up and believing it to be Clifford, she pulled back the brown velvet covering. It wasn't Clifford, but it had been a great shock just the same. She had had to sit in her car and rest, recover herself. Clifford had been going to pick her up as he always did on Thursdays, always. It was an unvarying arrangement, though the school time might vary. She looked at her watch as she said this. Clifford brought her to the shopping centre, went to his session with the psychotherapist, returned to pick her up. She didn't drive. This Thursday they had arranged for him to be in the car park on the second level by six-fifteen. On her arrival she had had her hair done at Suzanne's on the upper floor of the centre – another inflexible arrangement – shopped, come back to the car park at twelve minutes past six.

After the shock of finding the body, after she had recovered somewhat – Wexford found this frailty of hers rather hard to believe in – she had gone up to look for Clifford. She had walked about looking for him, a statement that was confirmed by Archie Greaves. At last she had gone to the pedestrian gates . . .

'I broke down,' she said, giving each word equal monotonous weight.

'Where was your son, then? No, you needn't answer that, Mrs Sanders. You tell him we're interested and we'll have a talk with him later. We'll all take a break and he can do some thinking. How's that?'

She moved towards the door. Someone would drive her home. Her manner had in it something of the sleepwalker, or as if almost everything she thought and felt – perhaps momentous or amazing things – she kept veiled. She was so thin and wiry you would expect her to be a brisk woman, Wexford thought, but she was as languid as some slippery, rotund sea creature. Burden said as soon as she had gone, 'Is she saying he's potty?'

'I should think that depends on how strict you are and – ' Wexford looked up at Burden with a half-smile, 'how out of date. Apparently he can hold down a job and drive a car and carry on a normal conversation. Is that what you mean?'

'You know it isn't. He sounds very much like a candidate for Lesley Arbel's psychopath role to me.'

' "The outstanding feature is emotional immaturity in its broadest and most comprehensive sense. These people are impulsive, feckless, unwilling to accept the results of experience and unable to profit by them . . ." ' Wexford faltered for a moment, then went on, ' " . . . sometimes prodigal of effort but utterly lacking in persistence, plausible but insincere, demanding but indifferent to appeals, dependable only in their constant unreliability, faithful only to infidelity, rootless, unstable, rebellious and unhappy".'

Burden gaped a bit. 'Did you make that up?'

'Of course I didn't. It's David Stafford-Clark's definition of a psychopath – or part of it. I learned it by heart because I thought it might come in useful, but I can't say it ever has.' Wexford grinned. 'I liked the prose too.'

The expression on Burden's face rather indicated that he didn't know what prose was. 'I think it's very useful. It's good. I like that bit about dependable in their constant unreliability.'

'Oxymoron.'

'Is that another mental disease?' When Wexford only shook his head, Burden said, 'That bit you quoted – is it in a book? Can I get it?'

'I'll lend you my copy. I expect it's out of print; it must be twenty years since I read it. But you can't apply that to Clifford Sanders, you know. You've hardly talked to him.'

'That can be remedied,' said Burden grimly.

It was dark as Wexford drove along the street where he lived and approached his own house. A car was parked on his garage drive, Sheila's Porsche. He felt a tiny dip of the heart and immediately reproached himself. He loved his daughters dearly and Sheila was his favourite, but for once he wouldn't be elated to see her. A quiet evening was what he had looked forward to; it might be the last for a long time, for he had no faith in Burden's forecast of the straightforwardness of this case. And now it would be given over not only to talk, but talk on serious matters.

Irritation of a different kind succeeded this initial flash of dismay. She had parked her car on the garage drive because she supposed him to be home already, even supposed this to be his day off as it should have been, and expected his car to be inside the garage. Now he would have to leave it out in the street. Unburdening her heart to her mother would have taken priority over everything. He could imagine her saying every ten minutes or so how she must rush out and move the car before darling Pop got home . . .

Thinking like that cheered him, made him smile to himself, hearing with his mind's ear her enchanting, slightly breathless voice. He would say nothing, he resolved, of the wire-cutting, the reports of her coming divorce; he would utter no word of reproach, certainly no intimation of disappointment or upset, would cast on her no grave looks. He touched the Porsche lightly on its long, gleaming, nearly horizontal rear window as he passed it. Did she go to demonstrations in that? Well, it was only a small Porsche and black at that . . . Would she come and kiss his cheek or would she hang back? There was no knowing. He went in the back way, into the hall from the kitchen, hung up his coat, hearing her voice from the living room – hearing the voice of Beatrice Cenci, Antigone, Nora Helmer and now Lady Audley – falter and fall silent. He went into the room and immediately she was rushing to him and in his arms.

Over her shoulder he saw the small satirical smile on Dora's face. He hugged Sheila and as she relaxed, distanced her with his arms stretched and said, 'Are you OK?'

'Well, I don't know,' she giggled. 'Not really. I'm not really OK. I'm in an awful mess. And Mother's being very sniffy. Mother's being horrible, actually.'

Her rueful smile showed him this was only half-meant. Foolish this was, he knew it every time, but when he looked at her like this he could never help admiring afresh the beautiful, fair, sensitive face that would with luck defy time, the long, pale, soft hair, the eyes as clear as a child's and as blue, but not a child's. There was no wedding ring on her left hand, but often she wore no rings, just as she nearly always kept her fancy clothes for public or publicity appearances. The jeans she wore were shabby compared with Burden's. She had on a blue sweater of a similar shade and a string of wooden beads.

'Now you're home, darling,' said Dora, 'we can all have a drink. I'm sure I need it. In fact . . .' she looked from one to the other with a certain tact, with a knowledge that they might care for two minutes alone together, '. . . I'll get it.'

Sheila fell back into the chair she had jumped out of.

'Aren't you going to ask me why? Why, why, why everything?'

'No.'

'You have a blind faith in the rightness of everything I do?'

'You know I don't.' He was tempted to say of the husband she had left, 'I liked Andrew,' but he didn't say it. 'What are we talking about, anyway? Which of your sensational acts?'

'Oh, Pop, I had to cut the wire. It wasn't done hysterically or without thinking or for publicity or in defiance or anything. I *had* to do it. I've been psyching myself up to it for ever so long. People take notice of what I do, you see. I don't just mean *me*, I mean anyone in my position. They kind of say, "If Sheila Wexford does it there must be some meaning to it, there must be a point if a famous person like her does it".'

'What happened?' He was genuinely curious.

'I bought a pair of wire-cutters in a DIY place in Covent Garden. There were ten of us, all members of PANDA – Players Anti-Nuclear Direct Action – only I was the only well-known one. We went to a place in Northamptonshire called Lossington and we went in three cars, mine and two others. It's an RAF station where they have obsolete bombers. The importance of the place doesn't matter, you see, it's the gesture . . .'

'Of course I see,' he said a little impatiently.

'There was this bleak plain with a couple of concrete huts and some hangars and grass all round and mud and a wire fence gone rusty – miles of it, and high enough not to lose tennis balls if you were playing inside. Well, we all stood up against the wire and each of us cut a bit and a great flap of wire came down, then we went to the nearest town and the police station and walked in and told them what we'd done and . . .'

Dora came in with their drinks on a tray – beer for Wexford, wine for herself and her daughter. Having heard the last words, she said, 'You might have given a little more thought to your father.'

'Oh, Pop, the first idea was for us to cut the wire at RAF Myringford, but I stood out against that because of you, because it was on your patch. I did think of you. But I had to do it, I *had* to – can't you understand?'

His temper for an instant got the better of him. 'You're not Antigone, however much you may have played her. You're not Bunyan. Don't keep saying you *had* to do it. Do you really believe your cutting the wire round an obsolete bomber station or whatever is going to lead to a total ban on nuclear arms? I don't like them, you know, I don't believe anyone likes them; I'm afraid of them. When you and Sylvia were little I used to be – oppressed with fear for you. And if they've kept the peace for forty-five years, that doesn't mean a thing; it certainly doesn't mean they'll keep it for ninety. But I know better than to suppose this kind of thing is going to affect government.'

'What else can we do?' she said simply. 'I often think I don't believe that either, but what else can we do? They all think that banning Cruise missiles solves everything, but they're getting rid of less than ten per cent of the world's arsenal. The alternative is apathy, is pretending everything's solved.'

'You mean that "for evil to triumph",' Wexford said, ' "it is only necessary for good men to do nothing"?'

But Dora followed sharply with, 'Or do you mean that between the early warning and the bomb going off you'll have ten minutes in which to congratulate yourself on not being an ostrich?'

Sheila sat up, was silent for a while. It was as if what her mother said had not touched her, had gone unheard. Then she said very quietly, 'If you're a human being, you have to be against nuclear weapons. It's a . . . a sort of definition. Like . . . like mammals suckle their young and insects have six legs. The definition of a human being is one who hates and fears and wants to be rid of nuclear weapons. Because they're the evil, they're the modern equivalent of the devil, of Antichrist – they are all we'll ever know of hell.'

After that, as he remarked to Dora while Sheila made a mysterious secret phone call, there didn't seem any more to be said. Or not for the present. Dora sighed. 'She says Andrew's right wing and only interested in capitalism and he doesn't have an inner life.'

467

'Presumably she knew that before she married him,' Wexford said.

'She isn't in love any more and that always makes a difference.'

'It's not so much a depraved society that we live in as an idealistic one. People expect to remain in love with their partners all their lives or else break up and start again. Are you still in love with me?'

'Oh, darling, you know I love you very much, I'm devoted to you, I'd be lost without you, I – '

'Exactly,' said her husband, laughing, and he went outside to get himself another beer.

Nothing had been said about Sheila staying the night. She had arrived at four and in the usual course of things would have started back for London at about nine. It was less than an hour's drive. But the phone call she had made changed her mind, or so it seemed. She came back into the room looking pleased, looking happier than she had since Wexford arrived home, and announced that if they didn't mind – this with the self-confidence of the always-beloved child to whom parents' 'minding' was unknown – she would stay until tomorrow, she might even stay until after lunch tomorrow.

'Mother's the only person I know who still cooks roast beef and Yorkshire pudding for Sunday lunch.'

Wexford thought that asking her where she was living now could hardly be construed as interference, but he resisted saying how much he had liked the house in Hampstead.

'I had to move out, didn't I? I couldn't go on living in Downshire Hill, in Andrew's house that he'd paid for, and turn him out. Someone told him it was worth two million.' She sat down on the floor, hugging her knees. 'I can't cope with that kind of money. I've got this flat in Bloomsbury, Coram Fields, and it's OK, it's really quite grand.' She flashed a smile at her father. 'You'll like it.'

Dora had the *Radio Times* on her lap. 'Nearly time for Lady Audley. I don't want to miss it, so if you don't like watching yourself I'll have to send you to bed.'

'Oh, Mother. Do you really imagine I haven't seen it? I don't mind watching it again with you, but of course I saw a preview. Look, I must rush outside though and move my car so that Pop can put his in. No, I'll move mine, and put his in. It doesn't matter if I miss the beginning of – '

'I'll move the cars,' Wexford interposed. 'We've got five minutes. Keys, please, Sheila.'

She fished them out of her jeans pocket. His car was a little wide for the garage and he had made his offer less out of altruism than for fear of getting the new Montego scraped. Dora switched on the television. The wind had dropped and the night was dark and quiet, rather misty, each streetlamp a yellow blur. Between his garden and the empty site next door that had never been built on, the fence was sagging, in places laid flat on the flowerbed where the wind had felled it. The last few leaves on the cherry tree in his front lawn had been shrivelled by early frost and still clung to the nearly bare branches. Leaves lay everywhere, dark and wet, a blackened coating on path and pavement. Someone had found a child's Fair Isle glove on this mat of leaves and laid it on top of the low wall. The street was deserted. In a bay window opposite, between dark evergreen shrubs standing like sentries, between open curtains, he saw the blue glow of a screen suddenly flooded with colour and his daughter's face filling it in close-up.

Sheila hadn't locked the Porsche. Wexford opened the door and got into the driving-seat. It was an irony that his much cheaper and less prestigious car had automatic transmission, while this one had a manual gearbox. Presumably Sheila preferred it that way. The Montego had been his for only six months and it was the first automatic car he had ever possessed, but even so he was coming as near to forgetting about letting in clutches and shifting handles. So much so that when he switched on the ignition he failed to notice she had left the car in bottom gear. It jumped – being a powerful sports car it bounded like a spirited horse – and stalled. Wexford grinned to himself. So much for his conviction that he was the more careful driver. Another two inches and the Porsche would have hit his garage doors.

He moved the gear lever into neutral and switched on the engine once more. His foot on the clutch pedal, he was moving the lever into reverse when he became aware of a feeling of unparalleled strangeness, an unaccountable sensation of being more than usually alert and alive. It was as if he were young again, a young man with the vigour and carefree nature of youth. Some strengthening elixir seemed to surge through his veins. On this damp, dark night when he was tired at the end of a long hard day, he was visited with a renewal of youth and power, a springiness in muscle and nerves like a young athlete's.

All this was momentary. It came in a flash that was also a piercing ray of enlightenment. Did he hear anything? The ticking mechanism as of a clock – or was that imagination, some vibration in his brain? The thrusting gear slid into the reverse position, made contact, and without knowing why, without a pause for reasoning, he flung open the car door and precipitated himself with all his force horizontally out as the roar came behind him, the earthquake, the loudest most violent explosion he had ever known.

It happened simultaneously, all of it – the bomb going off, the leap from the doomed car, the fierce blinding pain as he struck his head on something cold and upright and hard as iron . . .

5

After Dorothy Sanders had been driven home, Burden meant to go to the Irelands' house at Myringford. But he would be too late now to see his son put to bed, too late to enjoy (as Wexford, quoting, had once expressed it) '. . . those attractions by no means unusual in children of two or three years old; an imperfect articulation, an earnest desire of having his own way, many cunning tricks and a great deal of noise.' His wife didn't expect him until later and the house would be full of visiting relatives.

Instead, after a lapse of ten minutes or so and without giving any warning of his intention, he followed Dorothy Sanders. Something in her son's appearance and manner told him this wasn't the kind of young man who went out on Saturday nights. And indeed it was Clifford himself who opened the door to him. His was a shut-in face, mask-like and inexpressive, with a pudginess about the features. He spoke lifelessly, showing no apparent surprise at another visit from a policeman. Burden was rather curiously reminded of a dog owned by a former neighbour of his. The owner had been inordinately proud of its submission, its total obedience, the subservience with which it had responded to his severe training. And one day, without warning, without any apparent prior change in its character, it had savaged a child.

Clifford, however, seemed to have the right idea and was leading Burden into that back room to which, on the inspector's previous visit with Wexford, he had retreated to watch television, when his mother opened the living-room door and said in her slow harsh voice to come in, as there could be

471

nothing the policeman had to say to her son which she couldn't hear.

'I'll have a word with Mr Sanders on his own for the time being, if you don't mind,' Burden said.

'I do mind.' She was rude in a way that wasn't even defiant; it was uncompromising, straight rudeness, with a straight look into her interlocutor's eye. 'There's no reason why I shouldn't be there. This is my house and he'll need me to get his facts straight.'

Clifford neither blushed nor turned pale; he did not even wince. He simply stared ahead of him as if thinking of something deeply sad. Long, long ago Burden had learned that you do not let the public get the better of you. Lawyers, yes, inevitably sometimes, but not the untrained public.

'In that case, I'll ask you to accompany me to the police station, Mr Sanders.'

'He won't go. He's not well, he's got a cold.'

'That's unfortunate, but you leave me no choice. I've my car here, Mr Sanders. If you'd like to get your coat on? It's a nasty damp night.'

She yielded, going back into the room she had come from and slamming the door with calculation, not from temper. Burden resisted the hackneyed maxim that bullies give way if you stand up to them, but he had found nevertheless that it was usually true. Would Clifford profit by his example? Probably not. It had gone too far with him; he needed help of a more expert kind. And it was of this that Burden first asked him when they were seated in the bleak dining room, furnished only with table, hard upright chairs and television set. On one wall hung a mirror, on another a large dark and very bad painting in oils of a sailing vessel on a rough sea.

'Yes, I go to Serge Olson. It's a sort of Jungian therapy he does. Do you want his address?'

Burden nodded, noted it down. 'May I ask why you go to . . . Dr Olson, is it?'

Clifford, who showed no signs of the cold his mother claimed for him, was looking at the mirror but not into it. Burden would have sworn he was not seeing his own reflection. 'I need help,' he said.

Something about the rigidity of his figure, his stillness and the dullness of his eyes stopped Burden pursuing this. Instead

472

he asked if Clifford had been to the psychotherapist on Thursday afternoon and what time he had left.

'It's an hour I go for, five till six. My mother told me you knew I was in the car park – I mean, that I put the car there.'

'Yes. Why didn't you tell us that at first?'

He shifted his eyes, not to Burden's face but to the middle of his chest. And when he answered Burden recognized the phraseology, the manner of speech, as that which people in therapy – no matter how inhibited, reserved, disturbed – inevitably pick up. He had heard it before. 'I felt threatened.'

'By what?'

'I'd like to talk to Serge now. If I'd had some sort of warning I'd have tried to make an appointment with him and talk it through with him.'

'I'm afraid you're going to have to make do with me, Mr Sanders.'

Burden was apprehensive for a moment that he was to be confronted with total silence against which even an experienced detective can do little. Sounds from Mrs Sanders could now be heard. She was in the kitchen, moving about, making an unnecessary noise by putting crockery down heavily and banging instead of closing cupboard doors. Whatever she was doing it seemed to be contrived to disturb. He winced at the sound of something breaking as it fell from her hands on to a stone floor. And then he heard another sound – he had got up to stand by the window – and this was far distant, the dull roar of an explosion. He stood quite still, his ear to the glass, listening to the reverberations die away. But he thought no more of it once Clifford began to speak.

'I'll try and tell you what happened. I should have told you before, but I felt threatened. I feel threatened now, but I'd be worse if I didn't tell you. I left Serge's place and I drove to the car park to pick up my mother. I saw there was a dead person lying there before I parked the car. I went to look at it – when I had parked the car, I mean – because I meant to call the police. You could see the person had been killed; that was the first thing you could see.'

'What time was this?'

He shrugged. 'Oh, evening. Early evening. My mother wanted me there at a quarter-past six. I think it was before

473

that; it must have been, because she wasn't there and she's never late.'

'Why didn't you call the police, Mr Sanders?'

He looked at the picture on the wall, then at the dark shiny window. Burden saw his reflection in it, impassive, one would have said devoid of feeling.

'I thought it was my mother.'

Burden turned his eyes from the reflected image in the dark glass. 'You what?'

With patience, in a heavy, almost sorrowful way, Clifford repeated what he had said. 'I thought it was my mother.'

And she had thought it was her son. What was the matter with the pair of them that each expected to find the other dead? 'You thought Mrs Robson was your mother?' There was a slight resemblance between the two women, Burden thought wonderingly – that is, to a stranger there might be. Both were of an age, thin, grey-haired, dressed in the same kind of clothes of the same sort of colour . . . but to a son?

'I knew it wasn't really my mother. Well, after the first shock I knew. I can't explain what I felt. I could tell Serge, but I don't think you would understand. First I thought it was my mother, then I knew it wasn't and then I thought someone was doing it to . . . to mock me. I thought they had put it there to get at me. No, not quite that. I said I couldn't explain. I can only say it made me panic. I thought this was an awful trick they were persecuting me with, but I knew it couldn't be. I knew both things at the same time. I was very confused – you don't understand, do you?'

'I can't say I do, Mr Sanders. But go on.'

'I said I panicked. My "shadow" had taken me over completely. I had to get out of there, but I couldn't just leave it lying there like that. Other people would see it like I had.' Dark colour had come into his face now and he held his hands clasped tightly. 'I had an old curtain in the boot of the car I'd used to cover the windscreen in cold weather. I covered it up with that.' Suddenly he shut his eyes, screwing them up as if to drive away the sight, to blind himself. 'It wasn't covered, you understand, when I found it, not when I found it. I covered it up and then I went away, I ran away. I left the car and ran out of the car park. Someone was in the lift, so I ran up the stairs. I went home, I ran out into the street at the back and then home.'

'It didn't occur to you then that you'd meant to phone the police.'

The eyes opened and he expelled his breath. Burden repeated his question and Clifford said, with a tinge of exasperation now, 'What did it matter? Someone would phone them, I knew that. It didn't have to be me.'

'You went out by the pedestrian gates, I suppose.' Burden remembered Archie Greaves' evidence, the running 'boy' he had taken for a scared shoplifter. And he remembered what Wexford had said about the sound of feet pounding down the car park stairs. That had been Wexford in the lift. 'Did you run all the way home? It's getting on for three miles.'

'Of course I did.' The voice held a tinge of contempt.

Burden left it. 'Did you know Mrs Robson?'

The blank look was back, the colour returned to normal – a clay pallor. Clifford had never once smiled; it was hard to imagine what his smile would be like. 'Who's Mrs Robson?' he said.

'Come now, Mr Sanders. You know better than that. Mrs Robson is the woman who was killed.'

'I told you I thought it was my mother.'

'Yes, but when you realized it couldn't be?'

He looked Burden in the eyes for the first time. 'I didn't think any more.' It was a devastating remark. 'I told you, I didn't think, I panicked.'

'What did you mean just now by your "shadow"?'

Was it a pitying look Clifford Sanders gave him? 'It's the negative side of personality, isn't it? It's the sum of the bad characteristics in us we want to hide.'

Not at all satisfied with what he had been told, finding the whole of this man's behaviour and much of his talk incomprehensible and even sinister, Burden resolved just the same to pursue it no further until the next day. It was at this point, though, that his determination began to take shape, a decision to get to the bottom of Clifford's disturbed mind and whatever motives had their source there. His behaviour was immensely suspicious; and more than that – disingenuous. The man was trying to make him, Burden, look a fool; he thought himself the possessor of an intellect superior to a policeman's. Burden was familiar with this attitude and the reaction it produced in himself – the chip on his shoulder, as Wexford called it – but he could not be persuaded that it was unjustified.

In the living room now, he talked to a rigid and sullen Dorothy Sanders, getting nowhere in his attempts to discover if Mrs Robson had been known to the family. Clifford brought in a basket of coal, fed a fire which did little to raise the temperature in the room, went away and returned with soap-smelling hands. Both mother and son insisted Mrs Robson had been unknown to them, but Burden had the curious feeling that though Dorothy Sanders' ignorance was genuine, her son was lying, or at least evading the truth for some obscure reason of his own. On the other hand, Clifford might have killed without motivation, or without the kind of motivation that would be understandable to a rational man. For instance, suppose he had not found a dead body and thought it was his mother's but had seen a woman who had suggested to him his mother in her worst aspects and for this reason had himself killed her?

After leaving them, Burden drove further down the narrow road which he now remembered – though there was nothing to show it – was called Ash Lane. The Sanders' house therefore was very likely Ash Farm. But as this passed through his mind and as he was thinking that they seemed to have no neighbours, he came to a bungalow set a little way back from the road which proclaimed itself as Ash Farm Lodge on a rustic board attached to wrought-iron gates. This he could see in his headlights. The bungalow itself was in darkness but as he paused, the engine running and the headlights beam undipped, a light came on in the house and a man appeared at the window.

Burden reversed and began turning the car, a lengthy process in that narrow defile. When he was once more pointing in the direction of Kingsmarkham he glanced to his right and with a start – more a jolt than an actual shock – he saw that the man had come outside and was standing on the doorstep looking at the car, his hand clutching the collar of a cowed-looking retriever. By now the whole place – with the two barns and tall silo behind it, plainly the present farmhouse – blazed with light. Burden drove off. He wouldn't have been surprised to hear a shotgun let off behind him, or to see the dog frenziedly pursuing the car. But nothing happened, there was only darkness and silence and an owl calling.

The news about Wexford reached Burden in a peculiarly horrible way. It was due to his own haste and keenness, he afterwards realized, behaving like some young ambitious copper instead of enjoying his day of rest. Of course, the point was that it would hardly have been a day of rest with Jenny's demanding mother and the Ireland aunts, and Jenny running up; and down stairs. Even if he had glanced at the Sunday paper before he left Myringford, he would only have read commentaries on the latest dramatic developments in the Israeli Embassy trial; there would have been nothing in it about the car bomb. The explosion had happened too late in the evening for that. And because the house was full of guests, no one had looked at television on Saturday night.

He phoned Ralph Robson before he left, but it was Lesley Arbel who answered, who agreed to his coming though telling him she couldn't think why as they had absolutely nothing more to tell him. Driving up the hill to Highlands, he told himself it was a pointless interview he had ahead of him, as the obvious thing was to wait until the next day and consult the Social Services department of Kingsmarkham Council. They might keep no records of those for whom their past home helps had worked, but they were more likely to put forward ideas and suggestions than Ralph Robson was.

The invalidism his niece fostered still kept the widower in his dressing gown. He seemed to have aged even in this short time, to hobble more painfully and be more bent. He sat by the gas fire with on his lap a little circular tray fancifully printed with wild birds in improbable colours, on which reposed a cup of tea and a plate of sugar-frosted biscuits. Burden had hardly been taken into the room by the girl – who this morning was dressed in a pink silk outfit, a kind of trouser suit with sarong top and harem pants, and very high-heeled pink shoes – when there came a ring at the doorbell and another visitor arrived. Lesley Arbel had no scruples about showing in the newcomer, though he must have been aware that Burden expected a private interview with her uncle. It was the neighbour opposite he and Wexford had seen from the window who had called, a Mrs Jago as far as Burden could gather from the mumbled introduction Robson made.

The reason for the visit seemed to be the usual one at a time of bereavement. She had come to see if there was anything she could do – any shopping, for instance, that she could get on the following day when Lesley Arbel had gone. Burden wasn't much interested in her, noticing only that she was a large stout woman, puffily overweight, dark and florid, and with a strong accent that suggested Central Europe to him. At least she seemed to have the tact or the good sense to realize Burden wanted privacy, and she left again as soon as Robson had said he would take up her offer and would she mind coming in again on the following morning?

The front door had scarcely closed and Lesley Arbel passed the hall mirror with an inevitable glance into it, when Robson said, 'It's time they did something for us. It's their turn, the lot of them. When you consider what my wife did for everyone in this blessed street, never spared herself, nothing was too much trouble. She'd only to hear someone was a bit under the weather and she'd be round seeing what she could do. Especially the old folks. I reckon she did more good on her own than all those so-called social services people. Isn't that right, Lesley?'

'She did a lot more good than my agony aunt,' Lesley said. 'Well, she was a sort of agony aunt herself, wasn't she? I used to call her that – joking, of course.'

Mystified, Burden echoed her words. 'Your agony aunt?'

'People brought her their troubles, didn't they?' It was Robson who answered for her. 'She works,' he said in a rather proud way, 'for the agony aunt on the magazine. For *Kim*. It's the problem page – you know, all those letters from readers about their troubles that the agony aunt answers. Lesley's her assistant.'

'Secretary, Uncle.'

'A bit more than a blessed secretary to my way of thinking. More a right hand. I thought you knew all that,' he said to Burden.

'No,' Burden shook his head. 'No, I didn't know. Your aunt – I mean your real aunt, Mrs Robson – I understand she'd been a council home help. Can you remember the names of some of the people she worked for?'

He addressed this question as much to Robson as his niece and Robson immediately took exception to it. 'Home helps don't work for people. They don't have employers, they have clients. They're more civil servants really.'

With an effort at patience Burden accepted this. He had to listen while Robson made out a case for his wife's having carried out her civil servant's function in the home of (it sounded like) every elderly, sick or deprived person in greater Kingsmarkham. Individual names, though, he couldn't recall. He enumerated the tasks his wife and performed gratuitously for the neighbours, and by association this recalled shopping to him and from here the two bags of groceries which the police still retained. With a slightly scathing edge to his voice, he said, 'I suppose you'll say you've got too much on your plates with last night's trouble to worry about a minor matter like that.'

'Last night's trouble?'

'The car bomb. One of your blokes got blown up, didn't he?'

Lesley Arbel said, 'The one that was here with you – or that's how I understood it from the TV. I'm sure it was his name they said.'

Practice at not showing one's feelings comes in useful. And it is true that shock stuns. Burden remembered now the dull and distant explosion he had heard on the previous evening while standing up against the french windows in the Sanders' dining room. Some sense of dignity, some knowledge that it would be wrong and a matter for later regret to do so, stopped him enquiring any more from Robson and his niece. But he was numbed with shock too, getting up almost mechanically, making routine remarks, the replies to which he found afterwards that he had totally forgotten. He was aware too – and this he did remember – of their faces looking at him curiously and with a mild, perhaps only imagined, malice.

Robson said something more about his groceries, something about wanting them before he gave his neighbour Mrs

479

Jago a shopping list, and then Burden had made his escape, was keeping himself from running to his car until the door had closed on Lesley Arbel's pink silk and high heels. He ran then.

Wexford's house was about as far from Highlands as it was possible to be, yet still be situated in Kingsmarkham. It wasn't wasting time, it was to calm himself, to make him a safer driver, that he went first into the phone box at the foot of the hill only to find it vandalized and the lead pulled from the wall. The second phone box he tried was the kind which, along with its fellows in the railway-station entrance, could only be operated with a Telecom card. Burden got back into the car, the palms of his hands damp and sliding on the steering wheel. He turned into Wexford's street with the feeling that he hadn't really breathed for five minutes; he seemed to have been holding his breath until his throat closed up. Yet all the time he was clinging to the hope that Robson and his niece might somehow be mistaken. Now he 'found the difference' as Wexford could have quoted him, 'between the expection of an unpleasant event, however certain the mind may be told to consider it, and certainty, itself.'

The sight of Wexford's house came as a second shock, and one not dulled by the first.

The garage was no longer there. The room over the garage was no longer there. The whole area between what remained of Wexford's house – the basic three-bedroomed structure – and the open ground next door was a heap of rubble, bits of car body, branches and twigs, shreds of fabric, twisted metal, broken glass. The side of the house from which the garage and the room above it had been torn was open to the weather – fortunately this morning mild and dry – and no attempt had yet been made to shroud in tarpaulins the gaping rooms in one of which a bed could be seen, in the other a picture hanging crooked on blue wallpaper. Burden sat in his car with the window down and stared at it. He stared in horror at the devastation and at the garden now revealed beyond, where fruit trees held leafless boughs against a tranquil pale blue sky.

In the middle of the front lawn the stout cherry tree still retained its branches – even, incredibly, some of its frost-bitten leaves. And the lavender hedge which Wexford had

480

so frequently in the past weeks promised to trim back as soon as he had the time was mostly still there, while looking as if the passage through it of a heavy missile had crushed some of it to the ground. The front wall was still there and undamaged, a child's woollen glove lying on one of the piers; Burden couldn't imagine how it came to be there. He looked back again at the wreck of the house, at what seemed to him only half or less of a house remaining. Then, slowly, he got out of the car and walked towards the front door, though he knew there could be no one living there now. If either of them survived, there could be no one there now . . .

He found himself numbed where he stood, paralysed and quite unable to think how next to act, when a man came out of the house next door, the house Wexford called next door though it was separated from his by a narrow open space that no one had ever been able to decide was large enough for a building site.

He said to Burden, 'How is he? Is he..?'

'I know nothing. I didn't even know . . .'

It was as if the street had been watching for him, took him necessarily for the bringer of news. A woman came out from opposite, a couple with a small child from further down on the same side.

The man next door said, 'He was in the car, his daughter's car. Sheila, you know. It was a hell of a bang, like the bombs in the war. I can just remember the war. My wife and I, we came out and there was smoke and you couldn't see a thing. I said to phone the police first thing and I did, but someone else had done it already. The ambulance got here like a shot. I must hand it to them, they didn't waste time. But we couldn't see what happened, only that they took someone away on a stretcher and then it was on the late-night news on telly about Mr Wexford and a car bomb, but they didn't know much, they couldn't tell you much.'

'He was lying on the lawn there,' said the woman with the child. 'He was lying there unconscious.'

'He was blown out of the car,' said her husband. 'It was the most amazing thing. We were watching Sheila in her serial and we heard this terrific bang and it was here, it was her car . . .'

'Where are they now, Sheila and her mother?' Burden asked.

'Someone said they went to the other daughter, wherever she lives.'

Burden said no more. Shaking his head, aware that he held one hand pressed against it as if it ached, he went back to his car and started the engine.

6

His dream was of cherry trees, notably the one George Washington was said to have chopped down and then been unable to tell a lie about when questioned by his father. A white cherry though, presumably that was, like the ones he had seen in a picture somewhere that were planted along the shores of the Potomac. Because of Washington's particular affinity with cherry trees? It must be. Probably those pink double cherries whose flowers looked as if made from crêpe paper weren't invented then. The one in his garden had been given him a year after he moved into the house by his father-in-law and he had never liked its papery blossoms and unnatural weeping branches. though he had liked his father-in-law very much. The tree was pretty for one week of the year, around the end of April . . .

He wasn't dreaming any more; this was more in the nature of a reverie. In some cherry-growing areas they put scarecrows in the trees, and in others sewed together sheets of netting large enough to protect the fruit from birds. Not that his tree was the kind that ever bore fruit but was sterile, those bright fluffy blossoms falling and leaving not a trace behind. He was aware now of a dull ache in his head above the forehead, a pain unaccountably associated with cherry trees. And yet not unaccountably . . . no. He opened his eyes, said to anyone who might be there, though for all he knew no one was, 'Did I hit my head on the cherry tree?'

'Yes, darling.'

Dora was sitting at his bedside and round the two of them the curtains were drawn. He tried to sit up but she shook her head, putting out her hand.

'What time is it?'

'About eleven. About eleven on Sunday morning.' She read what was passing through his mind. 'You haven't been unconscious all this time; you came round in the ambulance on the way here. You've been asleep.'

'I don't seem to remember anything except hitting my head on the cherry tree. Oh, and taking a sort of flying leap for some unknown reason . . . maybe from the front doorstep? I can't think why.'

'There was a bomb,' she said, 'underneath the car. It wasn't our car, it was Sheila's. Something you did set it off – I mean, whoever had driven it would have set it off.'

Wexford digested that. He couldn't remember; he wondered if he ever would. Dora and Sheila had been watching television and he came into the front garden for something and leapt into the darkness as a man who flies in a dream might, but the tree was in his way . . . Dora, though, was saying he was in a car, Sheila's car.

'I was in a car?'

'You went out to move Sheila's car and put ours away.'

'The bomb was meant for Sheila?'

She said unhappily, 'It looks like that. Well, it must have been. You mustn't distress yourself, you're supposed to rest.'

'I'm all right. I've only had a bang on the head.'

'You've got cuts and bruises all over you.'

'It was meant for Sheila,' he said. 'Oh, God, thank God I drove it. Oh, thank God! I don't remember, but I must have driven it. Am I in the Infirmary? In Stowerton?'

'Where else? The Chief Constable's downstairs and he wants to see you. And Mike's dying to see you; he thought you were dead. It was on television about you. Lots of people thought you were dead, darling.'

Wexford was silent, digesting it. He wouldn't think about Sheila at the moment and how near she had been to death, he wouldn't think of that yet. A sense of humour began creeping back.

'One thing, we shan't have to have the fence done,' he said and then he went on, 'A bomb. Yes, a bomb. Have we got any house left?'

'Well, you mustn't distress yourself. A bit more than half a house.'

Burden was temporarily in charge of the Robson case. It was his belief that Wexford would be off for at least a fortnight, though Wexford himself said that a day or two would do it. That was what he said to Colonel Griswold, the Chief Constable, whose sympathy was conveyed in incredulity that Wexford could remember nothing about the bomb and unreasonable anger against Burden for going away for the night without telling anyone.

'I'll make them let me go home tomorrow,' he told Burden.

'I shouldn't – not if I'd got your home to go to.'

'Yes. Dora says there's only about half of it left. I never liked that garage extension; I said it was jerry-built. No doubt that's why it fell down. I understand that people in our sort of situation usually go and live in a caravan.'

He had a large bandage round his head. Cuts on his left cheek were dressed with a white plaster. The other side of his face was turning black – before Burden's very eyes, it seemed. Sheila came in while he was still there and threw her arms round her father until he groaned in pain. And then the bomb expert from the Myringham Division of the Serious Crimes Squad came to question him and he and Sheila were obliged to leave. Now Burden, with Sumner-Quist's medical report in front of him, had to make up his mind whether it would be good for Wexford to be shown it later in the day. He would probably ask for it anyway, thus taking the power of showing it or withholding it out of Burden's hands.

In fact, there wasn't much in it Wexford didn't already know. The time of Mrs Robson's death was as firmly fixed as it ever could be at between five-thirty-five and five-fifty-five. And death had taken place on the spot where the body was found. She had died of asphyxiation as the result of a ligature being applied to her neck. Sumner-Quist went on to suggest that the ligature – he never once here used the term 'garrote' – was of wire probably in some kind of plastic coating, minute particles of such a substance having been found in the neck wound. This substance, presently being subjected to lab analysis, was most likely flexible polyvinyl chloride or polyvinyl chloride in combination with one of the polymers such as styrene acrylonitrile.

Burden winced a bit at these names, though he had a pretty good idea of the kind of stuff meant; no doubt it was much like the substance that insulated the lead on his desk lamp. It was suggested that the ligature had a handle at each end which the perpetrator must have grasped in order to secure a purchase on it and avoid cutting his or her own hands.

Gwen Robson had been a strong and healthy woman, five feet one inch tall, weight one hundred and ten pounds. Sumner-Quist estimated her age at three years less than what it had been in fact. She had never borne a child, suffered surgery of any sort. Her heart and other major organs of the body were in sound condition. She had lost her wisdom teeth and three other molars, but otherwise her teeth were present and healthy. If someone hadn't come up behind her in a car park with a garrote, thought Burden, she would very likely have lived another thirty years; she would long have outlived that arthritic, prematurely aged husband.

The Home Help Service was administered by the County Council, not the local authority, Burden soon discovered. It functioned from one of those bungalow buildings that house administrative offices in the grounds of once great private houses all over England. The great house in question was called Sundays on the Forby Road near the junction with Ash Lane. It had until recently been in private hands and, approaching it, Burden remembered the pop festival which had been held there back in the seventies and the murder of a girl during that festival. A huge sum had been spent on the purchase, causing anger among local ratepayers. But Sundays had been bought and these ugly single-storey buildings soon put up in the environs of the house. The mansion itself, though in part offices, was also available as a conference centre and for courses. Burden noted that a course in word processing was due to begin that day. His appointment was with the Home Help Supervisor, but it was her deputy who met him and began by telling him pessimistically that they could give him very little help. Their records went back only three years and Mrs Robson had been gone for two. The Deputy Supervisor could remember her, but the Supervisor herself had been in her present post less than two years. She produced for Burden a list of names, with addresses, of those men and women who had been Gwen Robson's 'clients'.

'What does a cross after a name indicate?'

'It means they've died,' she said.

Burden saw that there were more crosses than otherwise. On an initial glance no name or address leaped out significantly.

'What did you think of Mrs Robson?' he asked. This was Wexford's technique and although Burden did not altogether approve of it, he thought he might as well give it a go.

The reply came slowly, as if a good deal of thought and calculation was going into it. 'She was efficient and very reliable. A great one for phoning in, if you know what I mean. She'd warn you by phone if she was going to be even ten minutes late.'

Burden, irrepressibly, saw again the resemblance between the dead woman and Dorothy Sanders. Here was a new point of similarity – a shared obsession with time – but what he wanted was a meeting point, a location at which she and Clifford Sanders might have come into collision.

'I don't want to speak ill of her. That was a dreadful way to die.'

'It won't go any further,' said Burden, hope springing. 'What you say to me will be treated in confidence.'

'Well, then, she was a terrible gossip. Of course I didn't have that much to do with her, and to tell you the truth I used to avoid having much contact with her, but it seemed to me sometimes that she liked nothing better than finding out some poor old dear's private trouble or secret or whatever and spreading it round this place. Starting off always of course with that old one about it being within these four walls and she wouldn't say it to anyone else and so forth. I don't say there was any harm in it, mind, I don't say there was malice. As a matter of fact it was all done quite sympathetically, though she was a bit moralistic. You know the kind of thing – how wicked it was to have a baby without being married, how unfair on the child, and people living together not knowing the rewards of a happy marriage.'

'There doesn't seem much in that,' Burden said.

'Probably not. She was a great talker, she never stopped talking, and I don't suppose there's much in that either. I'll give her one thing, she was devoted to her husband. She was one of those women who are married to perfectly ordinary men and go about saying how wonderful they are – one in a million – and how lucky they are to have got a man like

487

that. I don't know whether it's sincere, or if they're trying to make out they've got an exceptional marriage or what. I remember her going on in here one day about someone she knew who'd had a Premium Bond come up. If that happened to her, she said, the first thing she'd do would be to buy her husband some special kind of car – I don't know what, a Jaguar maybe – and then she'd take him on holiday to the Caribbean. Anyway, you've got your list; it's the best I can do, and I hope it's of some help.'

Burden was disappointed. He wasn't sure what he had expected – some name on the list, perhaps, to tally with that of a witness in the case or with someone he had talked to in connection with it. As it was, because he had gone so far, everyone whose name was here would have to be seen. Archbold or Davidson could do that. Among those whose names were followed by a cross Burden noted that of a man who had lived in the sheltered housing at Highlands opposite the Robsons' own home: Eric Swallow, 12 Berry Close, Highlands. But what could that signify? The only difference between Eric Swallow and the others was that he was a 'client' who happened to have lived on the other side of the street from his home help.

The alibi of Clifford Sanders was the next important question of Burden's day. He saw from his notes that Clifford had told him he had left the psychotherapist Serge Olson at six p.m. Queen Street, where Olson had his premises in the flat over the hairdressers, was metered and except on Saturday mornings there were usually meters available. Burden, due to see Olson at half-past noon, stood in Queen Street observing that now, late on a Monday morning, three of the twelve meters were vacant. Clifford could easily have been in his car and away by two minutes past six if he left Olson at six. The worst of the Kingsmarkham rush hour traffic would have been over by then and he could have got into the Barringdean Shopping Centre car park with ease by ten-past six. But there was no way, if he was telling the truth, that he could have been there before five minutes to six.

Briefly calling in at the police station, Burden had phoned Stowerton Royal Infirmary to be told that Wexford was 'satisfactory and comfortable', a formula that conveys to the nervous caller the imminence of death. Burden had wasted no more time on the Infirmary, but phoned Dora at her elder daughter's. They had said that if Wexford continued to make good progress he could leave the hospital on Thursday. Wexford said he was going out tomorrow. Bomb experts were at the house, sifting through rubble and until they were finished nothing could be done about clearing up the mess. Burden was early for his appointment and he walked up and down looking in the windows of the newly refurbished Midland Bank, the shoe boutique and the toy-shop, but thinking about the bomb and wondering if it had really been meant for Sheila. Why would anyone want to blow up Sheila? Because she had cut the wire round a Ministry of Defence air base?

Burden strongly disapproved of the Campaign for Nuclear Disarmament and Greenpeace and Friends of the Earth and 'all those people'. This was one of the few issues on which he and his wife disagreed, or on which his wife had not won him over to her point of view. He thought they were all cranks and anarchists, either misguided or in the pay of the Russians. But it was quite feasible that other cranks, equally if not more reprehensible, might try to blow them up. Such a thing had been attempted – and indeed had succeeded – in the case of the Greenpeace vessel in the South Pacific. On the other hand, suppose some enemy of Wexford's – even if it were not too far-fetched, someone involved in the Robson case – knew that when Sheila stayed with him he was always in the habit of moving her car in order to put his own away? Whether or not this was true Burden was unsure but he thought it likely, knowing his chief. It had a been dark, misty evening. Would it have been possible to creep unseen across the wasteland and fasten that bomb to the underside of the Porsche? Burden found he knew very little about bombs.

The hairdressers was called Pelage which Wexford, who had looked it up out of curiosity, said was a collective noun for the fur, hair or pelt of a mammal. It had been open only six months and the interior décor was very hi-tech, resembling nothing so much as the inside of a computer. But the building in which it was housed was as ancient as anything in this part of Kingsmarkham High Street and the narrow steep staircase up which Burden made his way was a good hundred and fifty years old. By the look of the wormholes in the treads, it wouldn't endure much longer. If the woman descending hadn't been as thin as Burden they would have had difficulty in passing one another, for neither had been prepared to retreat. At the top a door was slightly ajar. There was no bell, so Burden pushed open the door and walked in, calling out, 'Hallo!'

He was in an ante-room, unfurnished but for floor cushions and something folded up to large suitcase size which reminded him of a mobile bench he had once borrowed for pasting wallpaper on, but was more likely to be a massage table. The ceiling was painted rather ineptly with signs of the zodiac and on the walls hung strange posters – one of a pair of boots with no legs in them but with distinctly separate toes and toenails, which Wexford could have told him was from a Magritte painting, and another of cats in cloaks and boots riding white horses. Burden remembered what Clifford Sanders had told him about his feelings and thought that this was what he felt here; he felt threatened.

A door at the opposite end of the room opened and a man came out in a very unhurried way. He stood just outside the door with his arms folded. He was a short man and extremely thickset without being fat; great breadth of shoulder and width of hip and thigh were not matched by a big belly. His hair – 'pelage', Burden could not help thinking – was dark and curly, long and thick as a woman's growing low over his forehead, linked by brown curly sideburns to his round bushy beard which itself was linked to a dense and rather more gingery moustache. Very little face showed, no more than a surprisingly fine-pointed nose, thin lips and a pair of dark eyes like those of a fierce animal.

On the phone Burden had given his full name, but Olson extended his hand and said, 'Come in here, Michael – or is it Mike?'

Burden had an old-fashioned and (his wife said) ridiculous antipathy to being called by his christian name except by friends. But he was aware too of how foolish it made him look to stand on his dignity with a contemporary, so he merely shrugged and followed Olson into . . . what? A consulting room? A therapy room? There was a couch and it was so much like the famous one in the Freud museum in London that Burden and Jenny had been to, even to the scattered oriental rugs, that he was sure a deliberate attempt at duplication had been made. Apart from the couch the room was cluttered with cheap ugly furniture and hung with posters, including an anti-nuclear one which pictured a devastated globe and above it a quote from Einstein: 'The unleashed power of the atom has changed everything except our modes of thinking and thus we drift towards unparalleled catastrophe'. This obscurely reminded Burden of Wexford and recalled to him with how much more of an open mind his chief would have approached this man . . . yet, how could you, at his age, conquer your prejudices?

Olson had sat down at the head of the couch, no doubt a customary position for him. He gazed at Burden in silence, again probably a habitual pose.

Burden began, 'I understand Mr Clifford Sanders is a patient of yours, Dr Olson.'

'A client, yes.' There it was again, that word. Patients, customers, guests – all in his contemporary world had become clients. 'And I'm not a doctor,' Olson went on.

This immediately recalled to Burden indignant articles he had read about purveyors of various forms of psychiatry being permitted to practise without medical degrees. 'But you have some sort of qualification?'

'A psychology degree; Olson spoke with a kind of calm economy. It was as if he would attempt to justify nothing, explain nothing; there he was, to be taken or left. Such a manner always gives an impression of transparent honesty and therefore made Burden suspicious. It was time for Olson to ask him precisely what it was that Burden wanted to see him about – they always did ask at this point – but Olson didn't ask, he merely sat. He sat and looked at Burden with a calm, mild almost compassionate interest.

'I am sure you have your own code of professional conduct,' Burden said, 'so I won't – at any rate, at this stage – ask you to divulge anything you may have diagnosed in Mr Sanders' . . . personality.' He frankly thought he was being magnanimous and rather resented Olson's faint smile and inclination of the head. 'It's a more practical matter I'm concerned with – the times of Mr Sanders' last appointment with you, in fact. Now as I understand it, he had a five o'clock appointment for a one-hour session and left you at six?'

'No,' said Olson.

'No? That isn't so?'

Shifting his gaze with what seemed perfect control, Olson turned his eyes on to the grey and cratered globe and the Einstein prediction. 'Clifford,' he said, 'comes at five as a general rule, but sometimes I've had to ask him to change and I did that last Thursday. I was giving a lecture in London at seven-thirty and I wanted to allow myself more time.'

'Do you mean to say Mr Sanders didn't come to you last Thursday?'

Olson was perhaps a man who would always smile indulgently at needless consternation. His smile was slight and a little sad. 'He came. I asked him to come half an hour earlier and in fact he came about twenty minutes earlier. And he left me at five-thirty.'

'Do you mean five-thirty, Mr Olson? Or with time for various parting remarks and fresh appointments and so on, would that be nearer twenty to six, say?'

Olson took off his watch, laid it on the table beside him and, indicating it, said, 'At five-thirty I pick up my watch and tell the client – in this case, Clifford – that time's up and I'll see him next week. There are no parting remarks.'

Jenny, Burden's wife, had been in analysis during her pregnancy. Had it been like this? Burden realized he had never exactly asked her. If you lay on that couch – did you? or wasn't it for lying on? – if you talked to this man, then, and opened your heart and spoke of your inmost secrets, he would be like an enormous impersonal ear . . . Burden, without liking or trusting him, suddenly understood that this of course was what was required.

'So Clifford Sanders left here at five-thirty sharp?'

Olson nodded indifferently; there was no question of Burden's disbelieving him. He said, 'You went to London? Where were you . . . lecturing?'

'I left here at six and walked to the station to get the six-seventeen train that arrives at Victoria at ten-past seven. My talk was on projection-making factors and I gave it before an audience of MAPT – that is, the Metropolitan Association

492

of Psychotherapists − at the Association's premises in Pimlico. I went there by taxi.'

The man seemed to have perfect assurance. Burden looked closely at him and said, 'Can you think of any reason, Mr Olson, why Clifford Sanders should have told us that his appointment with you was from five until six and that he left here at six?'

He's going to tell me he was threatened, Burden thought. He's going to talk about threats and defensiveness and projection. Instead, Olson got up and, moving to a very untidy desk which had perhaps once been a kitchen table, slowly turned the pages of an appointment book. He seemed to be examining some particular entry with care. Then he glanced at his watch and some inner reflection made him smile. He closed the book and still standing up, turned to face Burden.

'You may not know this, Michael. You may never have considered what a powerful figure time is in the human psyche. It might not be too presumptuous to suggest he could be another Jungian archetype in the collective unconscious. Certainly for some he can be an aspect of the Shadow.'

Burden stared at him with a failure of understanding as deep as disgust.

'Let's call him Time with a capital T.' said Olson. 'He has been depicted as a god in a chariot with wings and even been given a personification as Old Father Time − I expect you've come across that. Some people seem to be enslaved by time, by this old man with a skull for a face and a scythe in his hand, by this god in the winged chariot hurrying by behind them. They are his servants and they become very worried − very anguished, indeed − if they are not there, all present and correct, to bow down to him and do his bidding. But there are others, Michael, who hate time. They fear him and because this dread is so great and so omnipresent, they have no recourse but to drive him back into the unconscious. He is too frightening and so they banish him. The result of course is a total lack of knowledge of him, a world in which he is absent. His hours and half-hours for them to pass uncounted. These are the people − and we all know them − who can never get up in the morning and at night are always astonished that it should be three or four by the time they get to bed. To be on time for a date entails for them an almost superhuman effort. Their friends get to know this and invite them to come half an hour earlier than the party begins. As for a memory of time – to ask them to have any kind of accurate record is almost an act of violence.'

Burden blinked a little. He had seized on a point though.

'Are you telling me that these regular five o'clock appointments with Clifford Sanders were in fact made for four-thirty?'

Olson nodded, smiling.

'But I thought you said he had the five p.m. appointment?'

'I said that he *comes* at five; that isn't quite the same thing.'

'So last Thursday when you phoned him you must have asked him to come at four?'

'And he came about ten minutes late. That is, as I said, he came at about four-forty.' A genuinely good-humoured smile now broke across Olson's face. 'You're thinking I'm dishonest with my poor clients, aren't you, Michael? I'm pandering to their neurosis in a way perhaps that robs them of their basic human dignity – is that it? But I have to live, too, you see, and I have to recognize Time as a figure in my life. I can't afford to waste half an hour of him any more than one of his most abject slaves.'

Neither can I, thought Burden, getting up to take his leave. To his dismay, as he showed him out Olson laid an almost affectionate arm across his shoulder.

'You won't resent a lesson, I'm sure, Mike.'

Burden looked at him, then at the couch, and recovered some of his aplomb. He said with an edge of sarcasm, 'I expect it makes a change for you to talk.'

At first Olson, frowned, then his face cleared. 'That's for the Freudians, the silent listening therapist. I talk quite a lot; I help them along.' He had the happy man's simple unclouded smile.

It looks very much as if it was intended for your daughter, the Serious Crimes Squad man from Myringham said. You say your daughter hadn't given you any prior warning of her intention to visit you? She hadn't given me any prior warning, Wexford said. I don't know about my wife, I didn't ask.

494

You'll have to ask my wife. We have asked her, Mr Wexford, and no – your daughter's visit was a complete surprise to her.

What made the bomb go off?

You were about to back the car, weren't you? You were going to back it out of the garage drive in order to put your own car in, your wife says. We think it was activated by the reverse gear – triggered off by putting the gear into reverse. You see, your daughter says she never had the Porsche in reverse between getting into it outside her London flat and arriving at your home about an hour and a half later. And one can see, sir, that there would have been no occasion for her to use the reverse gear.

The bomber wasn't bothered, you can see that. It didn't bother him whether the bomb went off five minutes after she started and outside the Great Ormond Street Hospital for Sick Children, for instance, or down here on Sunday afternoon when she was backing out to go off home. It was all the same to him as long as she was in the driving-seat.

As long as she was in the driving-seat . . . Wexford lay in bed thinking about it. They got him up at four and made him have his tea with a lot of other men seated round a table in the middle of the ward. Some bomber had tried to kill Sheila and had failed – but he wouldn't stop, would he, because he had failed once? He would try again and again. It might be because of her anti-nuclear activities, but on the other hand it might not. Freaks and oddballs, were envious of the famous the successful, the beautiful. There were even people who equated actors with the parts they played and who were capable of seeing Sheila as Lady Audley, a bigamist and murderess. For that she must be punished, for her beauty and her success and her lack of morals; for acting a treacherous wife and for being one . . .

How was he going to live and go about his daily work with that ever-present fear of an assassin stalking Sheila? The newspapers were full of it; he had three daily papers lying on his bed, all of them speculating with a kind of merry cynicism as to what particular terrorists might have it in for Sheila. How was he going to stand all that?

Sylvia came after she had fetched her son Robin from his choir practice and then Burden came at evening visiting, full of the Robson medical report, his theories about Clifford Sanders as perpetrator, Gwen Robson as arch-gossip and ferreter out of secrets in the home help sorority and a curious interview he had had with a psychiatrist.

'This stuff about some people being unpunctual – because that's really what it amounts to – doesn't really effect the issue. Sumner-Quist gives the latest time at which Mrs Robson could have been killed as five to six. Clifford could easily have got there before five to six. Without hurrying he could have got there by a quarter to.'

Wexford made an effort. 'Intending to meet Mrs Robson there? You're saying it was premeditated? Because to keep in with your theory he certainly couldn't have encountered her by chance. He wouldn't have gone to that dreary car park to sit there for half an hour and wait for his mother. Or are you saying he was so lost to time that he didn't know whether it was a quarter to or half-past?'

'Not me,' said Burden, 'Olson the shrink. Anyway, I don't go along with that. I think Clifford has a perfectly normal attitude to time when he wants to have. And why shouldn't it have been premeditated? I don't believe Clifford thought or imagined or fancied or however you like to put it that Gwen Robson was his mother. Anyone would have to be a total banana truck to do that. And if he wanted to kill his mother, he could do that at home. No, the motive is likely to be a good deal more practical than that, as motives usually are.' He looked defiantly at Wexford, waiting for argument, and when none came went on, 'Suppose Gwen Robson was blackmailing him? Suppose she found out some secret about him and was holding it over him?'

'Like what?' said Wexford, and even to Burden his voice sounded weary and uninterested.

'He could be queer – I mean, gay – and afraid of Mum finding out. I mean, that's just a possibility since you ask.'

'But you haven't established any sort of link between them, have you? There's no evidence they knew each other. It's the kind of situation in which a son would only know a woman of her age if she were a friend of his mother's – and she wasn't. It's not as if Clifford has ever been in the market for a home help; he's not a housebound octogenarian or some

496

bedridden invalid. And while Mrs Robson *may* have been a blackmailer, have you any actual evidence that she was?'

'I will have,' Burden said confidently. 'Inquest in the morning. I'll give you a complete run-down on what's happened tomorrow.'

But Wexford seemed no longer to be following what he said – to be distracted by some action of his neighbour in the next bed, and then by the arrival of a nurse with a drugs trolley – and Burden, looking at him with slightly exasperated sympathy, thought how true it was that patients in hospital rapidly lose all interest in the outside world. The ward and its inmates, what they had for lunch and what sister said, these things are their microcosm.

The inquest opened and was adjourned, as Burden had expected. It could hardly have been otherwise. Evidence was taken from Dr Sumner-Quist, who was again making very free with the term 'garrote'. And a lab expert was able to treat the coroner to some very abstruse stuff about polymers and long-chain linear polyesters and a substance called polyethylene terephthalate. It was all by way of discovering what the wire of the garrote had been coated in and Burden wasn't much wiser when the expert had finished, though he gathered it all amounted to grey plastic.

Robson was not in court. There was no reason for him to have attended. Clifford Sanders and his mother were both there; Clifford due for a drubbing from the coroner, Burden thought, for his curious action in covering up the body and running away. But the first witness of all was Dorothy Sanders, who went into the box with deliberate self-assured deportment – having dressed herself, no doubt by chance, in clothes very like those found on the dead woman, even to the lacy brown stockings.

The man who had evidently come with them and who now sat beside Clifford he recognized as the farmer he had seen in Ash Lane, and who had come out on to the doorstep with his dog to stare after Burden's departing car.

7

Houses without women – Burden could always recognize them. It was not that such places were particularly dirty or uncared-for, but rather that the absence of a woman's hand showed in an asymmetry, a placing of objects in bizarre ways, clumsy makeshifts. The kitchen of Ash Farm Lodge – a large kitchen, since the bungalow had obviously been purpose-built for a farmer – was like that: the table littered with account books and pamphlets, a pair of boots standing on a magazine on top of the oven, a dishcloth spread out to dry on the back of a Windsor chair, a twelve-bore shotgun suspended from what was originally a saucepan rack.

The man Burden had seen in court said his name was Roy Carroll. He looked about fifty, perhaps more. His hands were particularly large, red and calloused, and the skin of his face was a darkly-veined red. The dog lay curled up not in a basket but a large drawer. Burden had the feeling that before it dared wake up it would have to indicate in some canine way a request for permission to do so.

Carroll was brusque and uncouth. He had admitted Burden to the house in a grudging fashion and his replies to questions were hardly fulsome, a 'Yes' and a 'No' and a 'Yes' and other grunted monosyllables. He knew 'Dodo' Sanders, he knew Clifford Sanders; he had lived in this house since it was built. When was that? Twenty-one years ago.

'Dodo?' Burden queried.

'That's what they called her, her husband and that. His mum. Dodo they called her, that's what I call her.'

'You're friends?'

'What does that mean? I know her, I've done odd jobs for her.'

Burden asked him if he was married.

'Never you mind that,' Carroll said. 'I'm not now.'

Gwen Robson? He had never heard of her until her death was on television. He had never had a home help in the house. Where was he on the previous Thursday afternoon? Carroll looked incredulous at being asked. Out shooting, he said, getting a rabbit for the pot. This time of the year he was out shooting most days at dusk. Burden noticed something that was interesting but surely of no importance. The magazine the boots stood on was a copy of *Kim*, the last kind of reading matter to associate with a man of Carroll's sort. It brought to mind the poster in Olson's room, the one with the boots that had five toenailed toes but no legs in them, and unaccountably he shuddered.

A weekday morning and Clifford very likely at work. Burden phoned Munster's, the school which ran crash courses for A levels, and asked to speak to Mr Sanders. He wasn't even sure Clifford worked there, but it turned out to have been an intelligent guess. Mr Sanders was teaching. Could they take a message? Wexford would have treated this more delicately, Burden knew that, but he didn't see why he should be tender towards the feelings of someone who was probably a layabout and certainly a liar, who was very probably homosexual, who had mixed-up feelings of confusion between his mother and dead women and was a psychopath anyway. He asked the woman who answered the phone to give Clifford Sanders a message that Detective Inspector Burden had called and would like him to come to the police station and ask for him as soon as his class was finished.

In the meantime, he made an application for a warrant to search the Sanders' house in the expectation of finding something in the nature of a garrote somewhere. Of course he could simply have asked Mrs Sanders' permission to search, most people don't refuse this request, but he felt she would. While he was waiting for Clifford he suddenly remembered Robson's shopping bags, so he summoned DC Davidson to find them, locate their contents and have the lot taken round to Highlands. The bags were red Tesco carriers and Burden had had intensive enquiries made at the Tesco store in the Barringdean Shopping Centre. Dressed in brown clothes similar to those worn by Mrs Robson, Marian Bayliss had retraced her possible steps through the centre. One of the checkout assistants remembered her passing through on the previous Thursday and put the time at about five-thirty. Burden began re-reading DC Archbold's report.

Linda Naseem knew Mrs Robson by sight, indeed knew her well enough to comment on the weather and ask after her husband. Gwen Robson was a regular shopper in the store and almost always came in on a Thursday afternoon, but what most interested Burden about this evidence was that Linda Naseem claimed to have seen Mrs Robson in conversation with a girl. This encounter, she said, took place immediately after Mrs Robson had paid and received her change, and when she was standing at the end of the check-out counter putting the goods she had bought into a carrier.

Describe the girl? She had been attending to her next customer and she hadn't taken much notice. Indeed, she hadn't seen the girl's face at all, only her back and the back of her head. She had been wearing a beret or some sort of hat. When Mrs Robson finished packing her bag, she and this girl went off together. At least, they went off. Linda Naseem couldn't absolutely say they went together.

Clifford came to the police station about half an hour after Burden had made his phone call; Munster's School was only about two hundred yards down the High Street. Burden's own office was rather a pleasant, comfortable place where any visitor might have felt he was paying a social call, so Burden didn't take him in there but into one of the interview rooms at the back on the ground floor. The walls were bare, painted the colour of scrambled eggs, and the floor was of grey vinyl tiles. Burden motioned Clifford into one of the grey metal chairs and himself sat down opposite him at the plastic-topped yellow table.

Almost without preamble, he began, 'You told me you didn't know Mrs Robson. That wasn't true, was it?'

Clifford looked truculent to Burden, his dull face sullen. He wasn't showing any obvious symptoms of fear as he spoke in his slow, monotonous voice. 'I didn't know her.'

There was a point in any interrogation or enquiry when Burden simply changed from using a suspect's surname and title to his or her first name. Wexford asked permission before he did this, but Burden never did. Using people's surnames and titles, in his opinion, was very tied up with feeling respect for them. This was why he needed to be called 'Mr' himself. He would have said he reached a stage when he lost respect for the person he was questioning and therefore pushed them a few rungs down the ladder of his esteem. If we had a language – where you could tutoyer and vouvoyer, said Wexford, you'd start thouing them.

'Now, Clifford, I'll be honest with you. Frankly, I don't yet know where you met her or how you knew her, but I know you did. Why not tell me and save me the trouble of finding out?'

'But I didn't know her.'

'When you say that, you're not helping yourself or deceiving me. All you're doing is wasting time.'

Clifford repeated doggedly now, 'I did not know Mrs Robson.' He laid his hands on the table and contemplated them. The nails were closely bitten, Burden noticed for the first time, this gave them the look of a child's hands, pink and pudgy.

'All right, I can wait. You'll tell me in your own good time.'

Did he really take that phrase literally or is he sending me up? Burden wondered. Not a gleam of humour showed on the round blank face when Clifford said, 'I don't have my own good time.'

A change of subject and Burden said, 'You must have been in that car park well before six. Mr Olson has told me you left him not at six but at five-thirty. You must have been there by five-forty-five at the latest. Would you like to know when Mrs Robson died? It was between five-thirty-five and five-fifty-five.'

'I don't know what time I got there,' Clifford said, speaking very slowly. 'It's no use asking me about times. I don't wear a watch, perhaps you've noticed.' He raised his arms in what Burden saw as an effeminate gesture, exposing plump white wrists. 'I don't think I went straight to the car park. I sat in the car and thought about what I'd been saying to

501

Serge. We'd been talking about my mother; hardly anyone calls my mother by her first name any more, not now, but when they did they called her Dodo. It's short for Dorothy, of course.'

Burden said nothing, perplexed as to whether he was being teased or whether Clifford generally talked to strangers like this.

'Dodos are large flightless birds, now extinct. They were all killed by Portuguese sailors on Mauritius. My mother isn't a bit like that. Serge and I talked about a man's anima being shaped by his mother and my mother having a negative influence on me. That can express itself in the man having irritable depressed moods, and when I was sitting in the car I thought about that and went back over it all. I like to do that sometimes. The car was on a meter and there was ten minutes to run. And I got out and fed the meter some more.'

'So you do take note of time sometimes, Clifford?'

He looked up and turned on Burden a troubled gaze. 'Why are you asking me questions? What do you suspect me of?'

'Suppose I said you went straight to the shopping centre, Clifford. Isn't that what you did? You parked the car in the car park and then you went in to the shopping centre and ran into Mrs Robson, didn't you?'

'I've told you the truth. I sat in the car in Queen Street. You ought to tell me what you suspect me of doing.'

'Perhaps you'd better go and sit in your car and think about that one,' said Burden, and he let him go.

Such mock naïvety angered him. Dodos, indeed, flightless birds! What was an anima anyway, or come to that a negative influence? Grown men didn't naturally behave and talk like children, not men who were teachers and had been to universities. He was suspicious of the childlike stare, the puzzled ingenuousness. If Clifford was sending him up, he would be made to regret it. In the morning they would search that house. Burden couldn't help thinking how satisfying it would be to have the case all wrapped up before Wexford was back at work.

Sheila, Wexford discovered on being driven from hospital to his other daughter's house, was staying at the Olive and

Dove, Kingsmarkham's principal hostelry. There was no room for her as well at Sylvia's, where her parents now occupied the only spare room.

'Anyway, I expect she feels it's easier to have her boyfriend there.'

There was rivalry between the two sisters of a never-quite-expressed kind. Sylvia cloaked her envy under the complacency of a happily married mother of sons. If she would have liked what her sister had – success, fame, the adoration of a good many people, lovers past and in the future – her covetousness was never explicit. But comments were made; a virtue was made of necessity. There was a tendency to talk about fame and money not bringing happiness and show-business people seldom having stable relationships. Married at eighteen, Sylvia would perhaps have liked at least a memory of lovers and the consciousness of something attempted, something done. Sheila, more open about her views, frankly said how nice it must be to have no worries, no fear of the future, reading in a leisurely way for an Open University degree, to be dependent on a loving husband. She meant she would have liked children, Wexford sometimes thought. Sylvia was waiting for him to ask for enlightenment, but he kept his enquiry to himself until she had gone to fetch the boys from school.

'I know there's someone,' Dora said. 'She was phoning someone she called Ned just before you went out and set that bomb off.'

'Thanks very much,' said Wexford. 'You make it sound as if I put a match to a fuse.'

'You know what I mean. When she comes over this evening, we can ask her about him.'

'I wouldn't ask her,' said Wexford.

But Sheila phoned to say she wasn't coming, that she was postponing her visit to her father until the following morning. Something had come up.

'Come down, I should say,' Sylvia said. 'Come down on the London train. I suppose he's an actor or a Friend of the Earth or both.'

' "Those who find ugly meanings in beautiful things",' said her father austerely, ' "are corrupt without being

503

charming." ' He returned to the copy of *Kim* magazine he had found lying about.

Sylvia had told him she took it occasionally and had supplied the little defensive explanation people in Jane Austen's day thought they had to give for reading novels. It was something to pass the time; you could pick it up and put it down; some of the stories were of a really high standard. Wexford liked the name of the magazine which seemed to him very avant-garde and appealing, for he confessed to himself that a part of him still lived in a world of *Home Knits* and *Modern Mother*. He turned to the page of enquiries from worried readers.

The 'agony aunt' Lesley worked for was a woman of the name, or alias, of Sandra Dale. At the head of the page was a photograph of her, a plump, middle-aged woman with fair curly hair and a sympathetic expression. Two of the letters were featured in bold-face type. One didn't appear at all, only the answer to it: 'T.M., Basingstoke: Practices like this may seem fun and I can understand they please your boyfriend, but is it worth risking your whole future sexual happiness? One day when you are married or in a permanent relationship, you may bitterly regret habits you can't break but which are keeping you from true fulfilment.'

Wexford wondered if the purpose of this sort of thing was simply the titillation of readers. It would be a very strongminded or deeply inhibited *Kim* reader who didn't speculate as to the nature of T.M.'s unbreakable habits. Very likely it was Robson's niece who had typed all these replies, having taken them down at Sandra Dale's dictation.

'There's a piece in there about Sheila,' Sylvia said, 'and some quite nice photos from the TV series.'

He turned to look at pictures of Sheila in a white ballgown, in her Victorian lady's black street dress and bonnet. The last instalment of *Lady Audley's Secret* was showing that evening; it would be repeated on Saturday, but who knew where they would be on Saturday? Neil wanted to watch a programme about finance on another channel and his elder son Robin was trying to persuade his mother to let him stay up and see Auntie Sheila. Rather surprisingly, Sylvia came down on her mother's side and in favour of watching this final episode. Had Neil forgotten they wouldn't be able to see the repeat because they were going out to dinner on Saturday night?

Neil lost and Robin lost. The little boy had come down for the third time in his pyjamas and was standing wistfully in the doorway. Wexford suddenly knew he wasn't going to be able to watch; he had re-read the novel while Sheila was rehearsing for the television adaptation, and he knew very well what was to happen to Lady Audley tonight: she was to be cast into the continental insane asylum. The way he felt, he would be unable to bear seeing Sheila even acting that stuff, to see her manhandled and screaming . . .

His head ached and he was tired. He got up and took the little boy's hand and said he was going to bed, too, so he would come up with Robin. The introductory music, melancholy-sweet, followed them softly up the stairs and then someone closed the door.

It was a dangerous feeling, this excitement born of hunting down a quarry – or born, rather, of creating a quarry fit to be hunted. Burden knew he was doing this and that it would be wise to pause and take stock. He did pause, briefly, and reminded himself how important it was not to tailor facts to fit a theory. On the other hand, he was growing very sure that Clifford Sanders was guilty of this crime. All he must be careful to do was to avoid pushing witnesses. Guide them, yes, but not give them enthusiastic shoves. In a frame of mind he told himself was cool and unbiased, he went very early in the morning to Highlands. There he got a surprise; as he turned into Hastings Road, he saw Lesley Arbel come out of Robson's house and approach his car, the silver Escort which was parked at the kerb. Burden pulled up behind the Escort.

'Not back at work, Miss Arbel?' he asked.

She was dressed with extreme severe formality in a black suit, white tie-necked blouse, black transparent seamed stockings and very high-heeled black patent shoes. With her glistening chestnut-coloured hair and painted eggshell face, she reminded Burden of one of those 'grown-up' dolls little girls have for birthday presents and which come with their own fashionable wardrobe.

'I'm not at work this week. I'm doing a course in word processors.'

'Ah,' said Burden. 'That would be the one at Sundays.'

'The Sundays Conference Centre, yes. The company have given me two weeks off to take the course and it happened to be very convenient to stay with Uncle.' She put a hand in a sleek black glove on the car door, remembered something. 'Uncle's got a bone to pick with you. Those bags of stuff you sent over, he said the piece of beef had gone off. It smelt disgusting, he said. I never saw it – he'd wrapped it up and put it in the bin before I ever got home.'

Taken aback, Burden had no rejoinder, but at that moment another car drew up and parked on the opposite side of the street. The woman called Mrs Jago came down to her front gate as a little girl of about three and a young woman got out of the car; there appeared to be another, bigger child sitting in the passenger seat. The visitor, though thin as a reed, was sufficiently like Mrs Jago as to leave no doubt this was a daughter. A mass of dark curly hair, rather resembling Serge Olson's but longer and glossier, covered half her back. The child, who also had long curly hair, ran to her grandmother and was taken up in her arms, where she clung to the massive bosom like a limpet to a domed, shiny, seaweed-clothed rock.

Ralph Robson was a long time coming to the front door. Burden could hear his stick making muffled thuds on the carpet. By the time the door opened, the two little girls and their mother had once more driven off. Robson was more owl-like than ever this morning, his nose apparently beakier, his mouth pursed, his eyes round and cross. A sports jacket of brindled brown tweed enhanced the effect and the hand on the stick gripped like a bird's claw round a twig. Burden was prepared for an exchange of courtesies, but Robson plunged straight into the bone-picking of which Lesley Arbel had forewarned him: he wanted compensation, he wanted reimbursement to the amount of four pounds fifty-two which was the price of the piece of spoiled sirloin.

Burden told him to put it all in writing and where to send his complaint. As soon as Robson had switched off that particular diatribe, he got on to the subject of his hip. The pain had intensified since his wife's death, it was ten times as bad as it had been a week ago and he could hear the joint grinding when he so much as shifted his position in a chair. Of course he was having to move about a lot more now that his wife was gone, she had saved him all that. There were areas in this country, he said, where you could get a hip replacement on the National Health Service in a matter of weeks. And he had heard that if you lived elsewhere they could transfer you to one of those places, but his doctor wouldn't have that – his doctor had said it couldn't be done. He had got himself to the surgery the day before, and that was what the doctor had said. It would have been different, he was sure, if he had had his wife to speak up for him.

'Gwen would have got things moving. Gwen would have told him what's what. If she'd known they could get me into some hospital on the other side of the country, she'd never have rested until she got some sense out of him. What's the use of talking now she's gone? I'm stuck with this for years maybe, until I can't stick another blessed day of it and take an overdose.'

It crossed Burden's mind that Robson was rather more than naturally obsessive about his arthritic hip. On the other hand, if you had a thing like that perhaps it would tend to exclude everything else from your existence. That physical pain might even distract you from the mental pain of losing your wife. Intent on not leading Robson (as the judges say), he asked him, once they were seated in front of the realistic blue flames, if he could remember any comments his wife might have made about her past 'clients'. Robson, as expected, immediately said it was a long time ago. Burden pressed him, which only had the effect of making him return to the subject of his hip and Gwen's remarks on what had brought it about and why he should have had arthritis when she didn't. This time Burden said he thought Robson was being obstructive and presumably he did not want his wife's killer found.

'You've no business talking to me like that,' Robson said, thumping his stick on the floor and wincing.

'Then cast your mind back and try to remember what your wife said to you about these people. She was a talkative woman, I'm told; she was interested in people. You're not going to tell me she'd come home at lunchtime or in the evening and not say a word to you about the old people she'd been working for? What, she never came back and said old Mrs So-and-So kept all her money in a stocking under the bed, or old Mr Whatever had a lady-friend? Nothing like that, ever?'

Burden need not have worried about leading Robson. These examples, far from stimulating him to invention or recall, seemed to provoke a truculent bewilderment. 'She never said about any old lady keeping money under the bed.'

'All right, Mr Robson,' Burden said, keeping his temper with difficulty, 'what did she talk about?'

An effort was made, as of a disused engine sparking into life with rusty wheels turning. 'There was that old boy over the road – Gwen was very good to him. She went on popping in there day after day long after she stopped working for the council. A daughter couldn't have done more.'

Eric Swallow of 12, Berry Close, Highlands, Burden thought, nodding encouragingly at Robson.

'Mrs Goodrich – that was the name. She wasn't so old, but she was crippled with one of those things they just give letters to, MS or MT or something. She'd been a lovely woman, a concert pianist Gwen said. She said she'd got some beautiful furniture in her place – valuable pieces, Gwen thought, worth a fair bit.'

Julia Goodrich of Paston Avenue, since moved from the district.

'I can't remember the rest of them; there was dozens and I can't remember them by name. I mean, there was one as told Gwen she'd had three kids by three different fathers and not married to any of them. That really upset Gwen. And there was an old boy as hadn't nothing but his pension, and used to give Gwen five-pound notes just for cutting his blessed toenails. She gave him a lot of her time, she'd be a good hour with him . . .'

'Someone gave your wife five pounds to cut his toenails?' Burden was intrigued and imagined Wexford's reaction to this bizarre picture. Was some sexual titillation or even satisfaction involved? Surely there must have been.

'There was nothing wrong in it,' Robson said, on the defensive at once. 'He just took his socks off and sat there and she did his nails with clippers. He never touched her,

508

she wasn't that sort. His feet were spotless, she said, clean as a baby's. And there was someone else – I can't remember names – as she gave a regular bath to. He was getting over some illness; he wasn't old, but he couldn't stand the district nurses bathing him and he said Gwen was a gentle as his own nanny when he was a little kid.'

Don't lead him, Burden said to himself. You must take your chance.

'Wait a minute, I've thought of a name: an old spinster called Miss Mac-something.'

'Miss McPhail,' said Burden, thinking this justified. Robson didn't seem interested in how he knew; like a lot of people, he took a degree of omniscience in the police for granted. They only asked questions to catch you out or for their own amusement. 'Miss McPhail of Forest Park.'

'That's her. She was wealthy, had a big house that was going to rack and ruin for want of looking after, and a blessed great garden. This young boy used to come in and do a bit to the garden in his college holidays. She wanted Gwen to come and work full-time for her. No thanks, Gwen said, I've got a husband to see to. I'll give you a hundred pounds a week, she said, and this was four years ago. You're joking, Gwen said, but she said no, that's what she'd give her to be her full-time cook and companion . . . and I reckon Gwen was tempted, only I put my foot down.'

Robson shifted his weight in the armchair and this time Burden thought he heard the hip joint grind. He heard something and saw Robson's face contort. Then Robson said, 'Is that all, then? Got enough, have you?'

Burden didn't answer but got up to go. Miss McPhail was dead now, he reflected as he was leaving, hers was one of the names on the list with cross after it. Passing his own home, he went in to use the phone and check up on Wexford's recovery, then continued to Ash Farm where a search had been in progress for the past two hours. Clifford wasn't there. Burden hadn't expected him to be, but Dorothy Sanders was waiting for him, her face tragic with woe, her eyes staring.

'They said two hours was the maximum. They said two hours at the outside, and they started at nine.'

'It's only ten-past eleven, Mrs Sanders,' said Burden, who should have known better.

'Why do people say these things and not stick to them?'

'They won't be long now. They'll put everything back as they found it; we do make a point of that.'

He made his way upstairs to Davidson and Archbold on the first floor. Archbold pointed up the narrow flight of stairs which led to the top storey and said the rooms up there were stuffed with old furniture – rubbish, junk, the accumulation of years. Going through all that had delayed them. Burden decided to investigate outside, where Diana Pettit had gone to search the garage and a kind of toolshed attached to the rear fence. He made his way along the passage that must lead to a kitchen and a back way out. Dorothy Sanders had her face pressed against the window, watching the search. Her back was rigid and her arms flexed and she was perfectly still, reacting to his arrival with not the faintest twitch of her body. Burden went out by the back door.

Beyond the Ash Farm ground – you could hardly call it a garden – farmland, drowned in rain, stretched away in all directions. There was no other house in sight. A hill shaped like a camels' hump cut off the view of Kingsmarkham and heavy clouds rested on the ridge of it.

Diana looked round when Burden came in and said, 'There's nothing here, sir.'

'That depends on what you're looking for, Diana. I suppose you've been told what you're looking for?'

'A garrote, though I'm not very sure what that is.'

Burden put his hands into the box of tools. It was one of those metal boxes divided into sections on two levels, in which the upper drawers can be drawn outwards by a kind of concertina motion. He picked out two objects, saying, 'These could answer the purpose very well.'

8

Diana Pettit and DS Martin both told Burden these were the kinds of things to be found in every toolbox in every garden shed. You might as well find a hammer or screwdriver in such a place and call it an offensive weapon. Everybody had a spool of plastic-covered wire and a great many people a garden line for making straight edges. Burden said he didn't; he had never even seen a garden line before. Was DC Pettit sure that's what it was?

Two metal pegs, ring-headed, were linked buy a length of twine. The twine was merely knotted on to the pegs and a piece of the plastic wire might well have temporarily replaced it, thus making a serviceable garrote. He took the things away, getting Diana to give Dorothy Sanders a receipt for them. The wire went to the lab for analysis and comparison with the particles of plastic found in Gwen Robson's neck wound. With a similar length of plastic wire which he had been out to buy tied to the iron pegs, Burden shut himself up in his office and practised garroting first the angled lamp and then one of the legs of his desk. Neither was the right size for a human neck.

Next morning Linda Naseem, who had Wednesdays off, was back on her checkout. Burden went to talk to her himself. It was exactly a week today since Gwen Robson had come in here, having parked her car underground on the second level, and walked under the glazed covered way to the Barringdean Shopping Centre, arriving inside at about four-forty. The next three-quarters of an hour were easily accounted for: a little window-gazing and the purchase of two items from Boots where an assistant remembered her.

The toothpaste and talcum powder had been in one of the carriers with the groceries and the light-bulbs from British Home Stores. No one remembered her in there, but that was to be expected. She had probably entered Tesco at about ten-past five, taken a trolley or perhaps only a basket and begun walking round the store picking out items from her list. Clifford Sanders at that time had certainly still been with Olson. Burden saw that he was putting Gwen Robson's visit to the store too early; it was far more likely that she had not gone into Tesco until twenty-past five. That way she wouldn't have reached the checkout until five-thirty-five or maybe a little later.

There were five girls on the Tesco checkouts. Burden was looking for an Indian and three of the girls appeared to be of vaguely Indian origin. He went up to one of them and she pointed down the line to where a small, slight girl of ethereal fairness, white-skinned and flaxen-haired, was changing the spool in her till. As he approached her, he noticed her wedding ring. Of course she was called Naseem because she was married to a Moslem from the East or Middle East. Burden reprimanded himself for jumping to conclusions as he knew Wexford would have admonished him. It was inexcusable in someone of his experience.

She took him into a side room or office marked 'Private' on the door.

'You knew Mrs Robson by sight, I think?' he began.

She nodded, looking slightly apprehensive.

'What time did you say she passed through your checkout last Thursday?'

She hesitated. 'I know I did tell the other policeman five-fifteen, but I've thought about it since and it could have been later. I remember looking at my watch and seeing twenty to six and thinking good, only half an hour to go. We close at six, but they're still going through after that.'

'How much later?' Burden asked.

'Pardon?'

'How long after you had seen Mrs Robson did you look at your watch and see five-forty?'

'I don't know. It's ever so hard to say, isn't it? Ten minutes?'

Ten minutes or five minutes, thought Burden, or even two

512

minutes. He asked her about the girl she had seen Mrs Robson talking to – was she quite sure it was a girl?'

'Pardon,' she said again.

'If you only saw the back of this person, who was in any case wearing a hat and presumably a coat or jacket as well, how did you know it was a girl and not a boy – a man, that is?'

She said slowly, as if reorganizing impressions and conclusions, 'Well, I just sort of knew – I mean I think it was. Oh, yes, of course it was. She had a hat on – a beret, I think.'

'It could have been a man, couldn't it, Mrs Naseem?'

'That just wasn't the impression I got,' said Linda Naseem.

Burden didn't ask her any more. Looking back on the interview, he felt he had been in the role of counsel who breaks down a witness's evidence by subtle questioning, leaving the jury to draw very firm conclusions from her uncertain replies. There had been no jury in Tesco's, but if there had been he had no doubt its members would have been thoroughly convinced of this fact: that on the previous Thursday Gwen Robson had been seen in the store talking to a young man at twenty minutes to six. He wandered back into the wide gallery of the lower level and stood in the Mandala concourse. It was all red and white poinsettias today and some sort of dark blue flower. Why these signs of patriotism on November 26? Probably those were simply the flowers the florist had most of.

Burden had a look in Boots, paused to examine the window of Knits 'n' Kits which today was full of tapestry canvases printed with dog and cat faces, glanced across at Demeter with its display of water filters and air ionizers. None of the assistants in any of these shops remembered seeing Gwen Robson. The fountain was playing, shooting up its jets of water to splash the lowest prisms of the chandelier. Burden went out through the main car-park exit, from the dry warmth and air freshener smell of the place into a cutting wind.

How long was he going to have to wait for a result from the lab? Several days probably. A phone call to Wexford's daughter's home obtained the engaged signal. Burden took his improvised garrote out of the desk drawer and practised flexing his hands round the pegs. One possibly got a better purchase by putting one's fingers through the rings and gripping the handles that way. He needed something more closely resembling a human neck than the desk leg. Into his mind's eye came an urn-shaped plant-pot container made of white polystyrene cunningly contrived to look like marble. DC Polly Davies had left it behind, with instructions as to the proper care of the cyclamen it contained, when she took her maternity leave and it had ended up in Wexford's office, the cyclamen long perished. The stem of that urn would be just about the right size and with a similar flexibility.

Still holding his garrote, Burden went up in the lift and along the corridor. The office door was slightly ajar and he pushed it open and went in. Wexford was sitting behind the desk, hunched up, wrapped in his old tweed overcoat. His head was plastered up and the bruises on his face had turned a sickly yellow-green. The small grey eyes that turned on Burden and his improvised weapon had a glassy look, atypically apprehensive, but his opening remark wasn't uncharacteristic.

'So it was you all along.'

Burden grinned. 'I've made this up and I was going to try it out on your plant-pot. Don't look like that; it's quite a reasonable idea.'

'If you say so, Mike.'

'What are you doing here, anyway? You're supposed to be off till the end of the week.'

'This is the end of the week.' Wexford said, shifting in his seat and flexing bruised hands. 'I've been reading all this stuff.' Every report made on the case so far had been sent up and lay on the desk in front of him. Burden, who loved reporting every interview in detail and even recording his own thoughts, had typed screeds. 'There are some quite interesting bits. I like Mrs Robson getting five quid for cutting the old boy's toenails.'

'I thought you would.'

'It makes me wonder how much of that sort of thing there was. This bath business, for instance. It's a fascinating line of enquiry.' Burden raised an eyebrow. Not quite certain what Wexford meant and somewhat repelled by the image, he picked the mock-marble urn off the windowsill and set about strangling it with his garrote. Wexford watched him speculatively. 'There are a lot of things I'd like to know which no one seems to have bothered with much,' he said. 'Lesley Arbel, for instance. Where was she last Thursday afternoon? We don't seem to know, though we do know that Gwen Robson was seen talking to a girl at five-thirty.'

'That was a man and it was five-forty,' said Burden, pulling on his handles, feeling the polystyrene crack and split, the wire digging into the spongy white flesh-like substance.

'I see. It would be a help to know why she was always down here and what she found so compelling about that not very exciting couple.' Wexford had picked up the only photograph they had of Gwen Robson – the snapshot, much blown-up, which the *Kingsmarkham Courier* had used. ' "One of those characteristic British faces",' he quoted, ' "that once seen are never remembered".'

'Those Sanderses say they don't remember her; both of them say they never saw her before. But I just know Clifford knew her, I feel it in my bones.'

'For God's sake give over doing that, Mike. I'm not squeamish, but it turns me up. Her home help visits are another interesting thing. You note how she never seems to have spent much time with those who had little or nothing to give. I wonder what old Mr Swallow had on offer, the one who lived opposite. Did she cut his toenails too – and did she perhaps have some particularly erotic technique with the scissors?'

'It's rather disgusting, isn't it?'

Wexford grinned, lifted his shoulders.

'Is it important?' Burden put the garrote into his pocket and came to sit on the edge of the rosewood desk. When Wexford made no reply to this but only sat there looking bemused, he said, 'You don't look well, you know. I doubt if you should be here.'

'I'm going to have a quiet day,' Wexford told him. 'I'm going to see how many cups of tea I can drink between two and five this afternoon.' Enlightening Burden, he added, 'it seems to me we haven't chatted up Robson's neighbours nearly enough.'

But he went on sitting there after Burden had gone. If he hadn't put out his hand to the radiator and felt it almost too hot to handle he could have sworn the central heating had

515

gone wrong. Without the comfort of his old overcoat, he would have been freezing. Sheila was back in London; he hadn't wanted her to go, but of course he hadn't said a word. What he would have liked was to shut her up somewhere for ever and stand guard over the door. But she had gone back to London in a rented car, back to the flat by Coram Fields that those people – whoever they were, those bombers, terrorists, fanatics – very well knew she occupied. Sylvia had the radio on most of the day, so Wexford got to hear every news bulletin, and every time he braced himself to hear the sentence that would start, 'An explosion . . .' That was why he had come back to work so soon really.

Bomb experts from Scotland Yard had come down to talk to him and the Myringham man had been back. Wexford had wanted to know what they were doing to protect Sheila and they had given him plenty of sturdy reassurance, only he wasn't reassured. He knew he wouldn't have felt so frightened if Sheila had been living with her husband, though that was illogical enough. If anyone had told him he would actually be glad to hear that his daughter was living with a man while married to someone else, he wouldn't have believed them. But that was how he felt now. It would comfort him to know that Sheila had that man Ned, whoever he might be, around night and day. What would comfort him most, of course, was what his son-in-law Neil advocated.

'Get her to stop doing acts of criminal damage. Take away her wire-cutters, or better still get her to make a public statement of guilt and her intention not to do it again.'

Surprisingly, it was Dora who countered, 'Would you have much respect for her if she did a thing like that?'

'Being alive's more important than respect, I should say.'

'Of course she won't do that,' Wexford had said. He was almost cross. 'She can't deny her principles, can she? She doesn't think she's guilty; she thinks the law's wrong – the law itself is guilty, if you like.'

Sylvia looked askance. 'Rather a strange commentary from a policeman, surely, Dad?'

He hadn't said any more. Apart from finding some way out of this anxiety, of making Sheila safe, he wanted more than anything to avoid a flaming row with Sylvia and Neil. The Chief Constable had said something to him on the phone

516

yesterday about the loan of a police house until his own was repaired – well, largely rebuilt, and at the pace at which builders worked nowadays that would be a year hence.

At any rate it was peaceful here. It was quiet and the cold he felt wasn't real. He had to 'struggle against a great tendency to lowness', as he put it to himself, and he went up to the canteen to get some lunch. Working his way through hot soup, hamburger and chips, comforting if not healthy food, he faced the prospect of getting into a car again and driving it. Neil had brought him to work and dropped him outside the gates. Donaldson, his driver, would take him up to Highlands. But sooner or later he was going to have to overcome the great barrier of inhibition that reared up between him and the driving-seat and the wheel of a car. He would have to conquer the paralysis he felt would descend upon his left hand as it tried to close over a gear shift, even in his case an automatic shift. Last night he had relived in a dream the explosion he thought he had no memory of, but had said nothing about it to anyone, not even Dora.

Patterns of life had changed subtly but radically during the years since Wexford had first become a policeman interviewing witnesses. In those early days all the men were out at work and all the women at home. Split-shift working, the advance in women's education and freedom, self-employment and of course unemployment had changed all that. He was not much surprised, at the first house where he called after leaving the car and Donaldson, to be admitted by a young man with a baby in his arms and a child of about three clinging to the legs of his jeans.

This was John Whitton, student and father of two, whose wife was a systems analyst in a full-time job. It was she who had spent time with Ralph Robson while he awaited the arrival of his niece. The house inside had that curious faint smell which all who have themselves been parents recognize – that of a compound of milk, infants' digestive processes, ammonia and talcum powder. This young parent had lived next door but one to Gwen Robson for three years since his marriage when the local authority had allocated him and his wife a house at Highlands, but he assured Wexford that their acquaintance had been slight. Knowing her to be a council home help and with a reputation for philanthropy (his own word), they had once ventured to ask her if she would baby-sit for them.

'Our regular sitter had let us down and it was a special occasion. As a matter of fact it was our third wedding anniversary, and Rosemary was expecting this one any day. We knew it would be months before we got out in the evening again. I asked Mrs Robson and it wasn't that she wouldn't do it; it was the amount she wanted paying. We couldn't run to that, living on one salary; we couldn't give her three pounds an hour. It wasn't as if Scott ever wakes in the evening – it would have been twelve quid for just sitting about watching telly.'

It was a long shot but Wexford thought he might as well try it, and he asked John Whitton about the previous Thursday. Had he seen Ralph Robson during the course of the afternoon, preferably after four-thirty? But Whitton shook his head. He had been at home, for his wife had the car that day, but it was a busy time for him with the children's tea to get and both of them to be bathed. He couldn't even recall having seen Gwen Robson go out.

Next door, between the Whittons and Ralph Robson, lived the couple Mrs Robson had so disapproved of, Trevor Morrison and Nicola Resnick. They were both in the house from which they ran a mail-order secondhand-book business which Wexford guessed was of a rather precarious kind. Here the first of that anticipated tea was offered, though of the herbal sort – crimson liquid with a floral-labelled bag loating in it. Wexford accepted a coarse, dark brown crunchy biscuit. Nicola Resnick, though young and liberated-looking in jeans and boots and Guernsey, turned out as much of a gossip as ever her grandmother could have been.

'She tried to get that old boy opposite to make his will in her favour. He used to tell everybody about the money he'd got in the bank. He was about a hundred, wasn't he, Trev?'

'He was eighty-eight when he died,' Trevor Morrison said.

'Yes, well, ancient. You see, he was always whingeing about not being able to manage, especially his fuel bills in the winter. And he liked to use his phone. He'd got this daughter in Ireland or somewhere and he liked to phone her;

no good waiting for her to phone him, he used to say. Well, I said to him you ought to apply for supplementary benefit. Why not? You've got a right to it and I believe in getting what you're entitled to. These old people are proud but it's just pointless, that sort of pride. You work all your life, you've got a right to anything the state will let you have. But it wasn't that with him. It's no good me applying, he said to me, I've got money in the bank and I'll have to tell them; I've got more than three thousand in the Trustee Savings Bank and when I let on about that, no way are they giving me benefit. And it was true.'

'This is Mr Eric Swallow we're talking about?' Wexford asked, making a valiant effort to drink his hibiscus tea.

'Old Eric, yes. I don't think I ever knew his other name, did you, Trev? Anyway, he used to tell everyone about this three thousand in the bank; he used to boast about it. And I heard him say his daughter was counting on getting that but she mustn't think it was automatic; it was his money to do as he liked with. Mind you, he was whingeing about her at the time, he hadn't had a word from her for weeks.'

'What was this about a will?'

'It must have been a year ago or more – at least that. She'd just given up being a home help, but she was in and out over the road every day. I was sitting here working on our catalogue and Trev was here too when she came to the door and asked if we would witness some document old Eric had got. It was quite a surprise – I mean, I'd hardly spoken to her before that and she'd ignore me if she saw me in the street. She said he had to sign this form and he needed two witnesses. And then do you know what she said? That we'd be better not being married, not being connected with each other! I was amazed. Well, I thought maybe it was something to do with this supplementary benefit and I was going to go, but Trevor asked Gwen what it was and all she said was it was nothing we need worry about, just a form. Well, naturally, that wasn't good enough for Trev and he said we had to know what we were signing before we went over there, and then she said it was Eric's will.'

'And that put me off quite a bit, as you can imagine,' said Trevor. 'It smelt, if you know what I mean.'

'That's absolutely right, it smelt. Anyway, I just said we

were a bit busy and to count us out. Gwen said that was OK; she'd soon find someone and anyway her niece would be down the next night. I expect you know that niece, don't you, the one that looks like she was modelling clothes?'

It was all interesting enough, and would have been useful if Gwen Robson had been suspected of murder and Eric Swallow and any of these other old people her victims. But it was she who had been the victim. Wexford asked his question about Ralph Robson's movements and Nicola Resnick was able to tell him that she had heard sounds from next door late on Thursday afternoon. The wall between the houses was thin and you could hear the click of lights being switched on and off, the thump-thump of Robson's stick and of course the television.

How could she particularly remember last Thursday?

Robson had had the children's programme *Blue Peter* on, she told him. That began at five-past five and was followed by a health programme about trace elements as food supplements. Nicola Resnick was interested in that and she had switched on her own set though Robson had his so loud she need scarcely have bothered.

Thursday afternoon once more, a week since the killing. Seven days ago Clifford Sanders had entered Queen Street from the High Street in his mother's car and parked it on the left-hand side on a meter, inserting into the slot, if he were to be believed, the forty pence that would ensure him one hour's parking. But it was already twenty minutes to five when he arrived, so that when he left Olson ten minutes on the meter still remained to run. And he had sat out those ten minutes, brooding on the things he had talked about to Olson, all that Dodo rubbish. Not that Burden believed that for a moment.

He went into all the shops on both sides of this part of Queen Street, the grocer's, a fishmonger, a fruiterer, a wine-shop, two cheap clothes boutiques and Pelage the hair-dressers. No one remembered seeing Clifford Sanders sitting in a car on the meter outside Pelage. The difficulty was that the red Metro was regularly parked on one of those meters on a Thursday afternoon, so it was hard to sort out when it had been there and when it hadn't, and when Clifford had been seen sitting in it and when he had not. One of the stylists at Pelage was very definite about having sometimes seen him sitting in the car in the driving-seat, just sitting there as if lost in thought, not reading or looking out of the window or anything.

From the cover of the wine supermarket window, Burden watched Clifford arrive at ten minutes to five. There was no meter free and he drove as far as where Castle Street cut across, then turned and came slowly back. By now someone was pulling out so Clifford waited, moved the Metro into the space, got out of the car and locked it. The day was damp and very cold and he wore a grey tweed overcoat and grey knitted hat pulled down well over his ears. From a distance, Burden had to admit, he looked not so much like a girl as an old woman. He put a couple of coins into the meter, which must still have had time to run from the previous insertion. Then he came quite slowly across the road as if he had all the time in the world instead of being, as was in fact the case, nearly twenty-five minutes late for his appointment. Burden felt a sneaking admiration for Serge Olson's technique in deliberately naming a time for this client half an hour in advance of the five o'clock when he knew he would arrive.

After Clifford had disappeared into the entrance at the side of Pelage, Burden went off along Castle Street to have a cautionary word with a jeweller he suspected of being a fence. Then into a call box to phone his wife and say he might be late but not very late – say around eight-thirty. A cup of tea and a cake in the Queen's Café and it was two minutes to six when he came back down Queen Street. An icy rain had begun to fall and the dark was the darkness of midnight, though brightly illuminated here by dripping, fuzzy yellow and white lights that turned the pavements a gleaming dirty gold and silver. Snowflakes started appearing among the silvery rods of rain.

Clifford came out of Olson's door at two minutes past six. He wasn't hurrying, but he was moving a good deal faster than when he had arrived. Burden sheltered from the rain and Clifford's view in the doorway of the greengrocer's; they were closing up and people kept pushing past him to carry in trays of chicory and aubergines. Clifford got into the car without even glancing at the meter; he started up and was away as the hands of Burden's watch moved to five-past six.

Wexford had read and heard about people seeing on someone else's arm the brand mark of the concentration camps, but he had not had that experience himself; and he didn't have it now – Dita Jago on this cold afternoon having her arms covered by a woolly garment that was itself a work of art: a knitted tapestry of greens and purples, rich reds and jewel blues. But when he glanced enquiringly at the great pile of manuscript which lay on the table in this strange cluttered room, the perhaps orderly muddle of notebooks and loose leaves, scrawled-on envelopes and works of reference, she had nodded to him.

'My great work,' she said. A smile made the remark a modest one. 'My memoirs of Oswiecim.'

'Auschwitz?' he said.

She nodded and, lifting up the topmost sheet of manuscript, turned it over so that only a blank side showed.

9

The room was of the same size and shape as the one in which he had talked to Robson and his niece; as the room Trevor Morrison and Nicola Resnick used as their office; as John Whitton's nursery. It was on the other side of the street and faced the opposite way, but the main difference from all those others lay in its rich clutter, the abundance of curious interesting things, the piles of books and papers and the adornment of its walls which was like nothing Wexford had ever seen before.

Unless you looked out of the window – seeing the trim little roadway, the trees in the pavement grass plots, the semi-detached houses – you might have believed yourself anywhere but on a local authority housing estate outside an English country town. What the walls were papered or painted with it was impossible to say, for they were covered all over with hangings which to Wexford had at first looked like lavish and elaborate embroideries but which, on examining them more closely, he saw to be knitted. Dora's efforts at what has been called 'the common art', resulting in jumpers for grandsons, at least told him that much. But this knitting was in all colours of the spectrum, those colours subtly matched and contrasted, creating abstract designs of immense complexity as well as pictures that in the execution of their strong primitive imagery reminded him of the paintings of Rousseau. In one a tiger crept through a jungle of green fronds and dark fruit-laden branches: in another a girl in a sarong walked with peacocks. The biggest, which covered the whole of one wall and had evidently been constructed in panels, was Chinese rather than tropical and showed a green landscape with little temples on the summits of hills and a herd of deer browsing between the woodland and the lake.

She was smiling at his wonderment. He only knew she was the creator of all this by the piece of work now in progress, another jungle picture taking shape from a circular needle, which lay on a round table beside Venetian glass animals and painted porcelain eggs. She had completed perhaps half of it.

'You're a busy woman, Mrs Jago,' he observed.

'I like to keep occupied.' Her accent was a rather unfamiliar guttural, Polish perhaps or Czech, but the English itself was grammatically and syntactically flawless. 'I have been writing my book for two years now and it's nearly done. God only knows if anyone will ever publish such a book, but I wrote it for my own satisfaction, to get it all down on paper. And it's true what they say.' She smiled at him again. 'Get it down, write it out and it's no longer such a terrible thing to remember. It doesn't cure but it helps.'

'The writer is the only free man, as someone said.'

'Whoever that someone was knew what he was talking about.'

She sat down facing him and picked up her knitting. Supplied with hibiscus tea by Nicola Resnick and Earl Grey by a Miss Margaret Anderson – who claimed never to have spoken to Mrs Robson or heard of her until she was dead – Wexford was rather relieved that Mrs Jago offered him no refreshment. Her fingers worked skilfully, moving with assurance a complex mass of coloured threads, selecting one, taking two or three stitches with it, abandoning this first shade and joining in another. Plump and tapering these fingers were, the wedding ring cutting deeply into the flesh. She was a mountain of a woman, yet somehow neither gross nor ungainly, her legs shapely with fine ankles and small feet in tiny black pumps. Remains of a gipsyish beauty showed in her full, pink-cheeked face. Her eyes were black, bright and in their cobweb wrinkles like jewels in a fibrous nest. Hair that was still dark was drawn back with combs into a large glossy bun.

'You came in and offered to do some shopping for Mr

524

Robson,' he began. 'That makes me think you must have known them fairly well.'

She looked up at him and the fingers were momentarily stilled. 'I didn't know them at all. I wouldn't be far wrong if I said that was only the second time I'd ever spoken to him except to say good morning.'

Wexford was disappointed. His hopes of this woman, though quite unjustifiable, had been high. Something about her made him feel she was essentially truthful.

'He was a neighbour,' she said. 'He'd lost his wife. She had been killed in a horrible way and it was the least I could do.' She remembered his name, though she had only briefly seen his warrant card. 'It was no trouble to me, Mr Wexford. I'm no Good Samaritan. My daughter takes me shopping or does it for me.'

'You may not have known him but you knew her, didn't you?'

She came to the end of her row, turned the linked needles. 'Hardly. Will you believe me if I tell you that was the first time I'd ever been in their house? Let me tell you something. I don't want you to waste your time on someone who can tell you very little. When I came out of the camp, they put me in a hospital the army ran. There was a man there, a soldier who was a ward orderly, and he fell in love with me. God knows why, for I was a skeleton and my hair had all fallen out.' She smiled. 'You wouldn't think that to see me now, would you? And I used to long and long to put on weight like they said I must. Well, this man – Corporal Jago, Arthur Jago – he married me and made me an English-woman.' She pointed to the pile of manuscript. 'It is all in the book!' Her knitting resumed, she said, 'But though I have tried I have never become very English, Mr Wexford. I have never quite learned to get on with the English way of always pretending everything in the garden is lovely. Do you under-stand what I mean? Everything in the garden is *not* lovely. There is a snake in the bush and worms under the stones and half the plants are poisonous . . .'

He smiled at the image she created.

'For example, Mr Robson – that poor man – he will say that what is to be will be; perhaps it is all for the best, life must go on. And Miss Anderson down the street who found a man who wanted to marry her at last when she was sixty years old . . . when he died a week before the wedding, what does she say? Maybe it was too late, maybe they'd both have regretted it. I cannot do with this.'

'But these are the tenets of survival, Mrs Jago.'

'Perhaps. But I cannot see that you survive any less if first you cry and rage and show your feelings. At least, it isn't my way and I am not comfortable with it.'

Wexford, who would have been quite happy to continue with this exploration of English emotion or lack of it, nevertheless thought it was time to move on. Weariness had come to take hold of him and his headache was back, a tight band wound around above the eyes. It was a piece of luck, sheer serendipity, that made him speak the name of the old man who had lived a few houses away in Berry Close.

'Eric Swallow,' he said. 'Did you have the same slight acquaintance with him?'

'I know who you mean,' she said, laying the knitting in her lap. 'That was rather amusing, but nothing to do with poor Mrs Robson being killed. I mean it couldn't be anything, really.'

'All right. But if it's amusing I'd like to hear it. There's little enough in this business to make us laugh.'

'The poor old man was dying. That isn't funny, of course. If I were English I would say maybe it was a merciful release, wouldn't I?'

'Was it?'

'Well, he was very old, nearly ninety. He had a daughter but she was in Ireland and she wasn't young, naturally. Mrs Robson used to do a lot for him; I mean, after she stopped being a home help and getting paid for it, she still went in there nearly every day. In the end when he got so that he couldn't get out of bed, they took him away and he died in the hospital . . .'

Wexford had had his eyes on the great landscape tapestry, but the sound of a car door slamming made him turn his head and then almost immediately the doorbell rang. Mrs Jago got up, excused herself and went out into the hall with a surprisingly light, springy tread. Voices could be heard, the clamorous treble of children. Then the front door closed again and Mrs Jago came back with two little girls: the younger of them, though too big to be carried, was in her arms; the other, who looked about five or six and who wore a school uniform of navy coat, yellow and navy scarf and felt hat with stripey band, walking by her side.

'These are my granddaughters, Melanie and Hannah Quincy. They live in Down Road, but sometimes their mummy brings them to me for an hour or two and we have a nice tea, don't we, girls?' The children said nothing, appearing shy. Dita Jago put Hannah down. 'Tea is all ready and we shall have it at five sharp. You can tell me when it is three minutes to five, Melanie; Mummy says you can tell the time now.'

Hannah went immediately to the table where the painted eggs and glass animals were. And though the older child had a book to read and had opened it, she was keeping a sharp cautionary eye on her sister's handling of the fragile things. Wexford, from personal experience, knew only too well the advantages and the pitfalls of that particular relationship, the stresses created in infancy that lasted a lifetime.

Dita Jago was placidly knitting once more. 'I was telling you about old Mr Swallow. Well, one afternoon – a Thursday I think it was, a year ago or a bit more – the front-door bell rang and there was Mrs Robson. She wanted me to come into Mr Swallow's with her and be a witness to something. In fact, she wanted two people and she'd seen my daughter's car outside, so she knew Nina was here. I found out afterwards that she had already been to a couple who live on the other side. He's called Morrison, I don't know her name, but anyway for some reason they wouldn't do it.

'As I've said, I don't suppose I'd ever spoken more than two words to her and she'd never met Nina. I had to introduce them. But that didn't stop her asking us both to go down there and witness this form.'

'Hannah, I'm going to be very cross if you break that little horse,' said Melanie.

A struggle ensued as the elder granddaughter did her best to prise from her sister's fingers a blue glass animal. Hannah stamped her foot.

'Grandma is going to be very unhappy if you break it. Grandma will cry.'

'No, she won't.'

527

'Give it to me, please, Hannah. Now do as you're told.'

'Hannah will cry! Hannah will scream!'

Shades of Sylvia and Sheila . . . Dita Jago intervened, drawing the younger child – who was by now carrying out her threat – on to her lap. Melanie looked mutinous, frowning darkly.

'Birds in their little nests should agree,' Mrs Jago said, not without irony, Wexford thought. She stroked the little girl's mane of dark curly hair. 'We thought it was something to do with the money he wanted to get from the what-do-you-call-it? DH-something – the supplementary benefit. There are always forms, aren't there? Anyway, we went down to Mr Swallow's with her and when we got there we found him asleep in bed. Mrs Robson was a little bit put out. My daughter said what was this form and had he already signed it? Well, you could see Mrs Robson didn't want to say. She said she'd wake Mr Swallow up; it was important and he'd want her to wake him.'

Hannah, her crying over, placed one thumb in her mouth and opening the other fist, showed her sister the blue glass horse, clenching her hand as soon as Melanie made a pounce for it.

Melanie turned away loftily. 'Five minutes to five, Grandma,' she said.

'All right. I said to tell me when it was three minutes to. Anyway, the piece of paper we had to sign was lying there on the table face-downwards. I mean we thought that's what it was and we were right. Nina just picked it up and took one look – and what do you think it was?'

Wexford had a pretty good idea, but he decided not to steal Mrs Jago's thunder and merely shrugged.

'It was a will, made out on a will form. Nina didn't get to read it because Mrs Robson snatched it away, but we could guess what was on it. It would have been leaving his money to Mrs Robson. Three thousand pounds, he used to boast he had; everyone here knew that. And she was after it – she liked money, there was no doubt about that. Well, we both shied away like anything. We told each other afterwards no way, absolutely not. Suppose that daughter had brought it up in court and we'd had to go there and say we'd signed it?'

'What was Mrs Robson's reaction to that?'

'Three minutes to five, Grandma,' Melanie said.

'I'm coming, darling. She didn't like it, but what could she do? I couldn't help having a laugh when we were outside. I heard later she went trying other people down the street, but she never struck lucky; she couldn't get anyone but her niece. It was only a few days after that they took Mr Swallow away and when he died there wasn't a will and his daughter got his money – being his real heir, you see, as was quite right. Now I must keep my promise to these children.'

Mrs Jago put the child on the floor and the knitting on the table and got up. 'You will stay for tea? We have Grandma's version of *sachertorte*.'

Wexford thanked her but shook his head. He had told Donaldson to come back for him at five and he thought of the deep pleasure of leaning back in the car and closing his eyes. Hannah had crept quietly to the table and replaced the little horse amongst the other animals with precision, with perfectly coordinated delicate fingers, her eyes all the while on her sister, her lips not quite smiling. It reminded him of Sheila playing all those years ago with a china ornament which Sylvia (though no one else) had forbidden her to touch. And Sheila had teased like this little one, peeping over a defiant shoulder with the faintest Gioconda smile.

'Of course, to do her justice she didn't want money for herself,' Dita Jago's voice interrupted his reverie. 'It was for him, it would have been all for him.' It was just as he was leaving, when they were out in the hall, that she said, 'Don't you want to know where I was last Thursday evening?'

He smiled. 'Tell me.'

'My daughter always goes shopping on Thursday afternoons and usually she takes me. But last week she dropped me off at the public library in the High Street and left the girls with me. She picked us up again at five-thirty.'

Why had she insisted on telling him that? he wondered. Perhaps merely to avoid a repetition of his visit. Or was he imagining things that the tone of her voice gave no hint of – reacting in a confused, almost fuddled, way because of the huge weariness which had overtaken him? Passing a wall mirror in the hall as he made his way out, he caught sight of his discoloured face, the bruised muzzle of a prize-fighter

529

recovering from a bout, and turned quickly away. He was no narcissist, no lover of his own image.

The front door closed on him. Her grandchildren's demands had cut short any parting pleasantries Mrs Jago might have made. It was just before five, for her clock had been fast, and Wexford waited for the car with the anxiety of a disabled pensioner expecting an ambulance. He had to lower himself into a sitting position on the low wall, feeling his bruised body creak. Going back to work had not been a wise idea, yet it hadn't seemed like work, more a matter of paying social calls. Mike ought to be left to himself to handle this case; he was quite capable of doing so. Someone like Serge Olson would say that he, Wexford, was at fault – only probably he wouldn't use a word like 'fault' – in being unable to delegate, in refusing to yield authority to the younger man. It was very likely a sign of insecurity, fear of seeing Mike usurp his place, even his job. Psychology, he thought, and not for the first time, often just wasn't true.

Cars passed. With a strong inner shudder, an actual shrinking, he tried to contemplate what it would be like to sit at the wheel again, start the ignition, move the shift into gear. That, of course, he wouldn't quite have to do, just manipulate from 'park' to 'drive'. But the notion of putting his hand to that lever brought a darkness before his eyes and made him hear a sound he had no recollection of hearing: the roar of the bomb. He closed his eyes, opening them to see Donaldson draw up at the kerb.

A hunch he couldn't quite believe in – it all seemed behaviour of the crassest, most unfeeling kind – led Burden to assume that Clifford Sanders was heading for the Barringdean car park. He couldn't follow him: he hadn't a car immediately to hand and, making his way there on foot, he told himself he was wasting his time. No one would do that. No one would return to the scene of so horrific a crime precisely seven days to the hour later, and there go through the same prescribed ritual. With, that is, one notable exception . . .

He entered the shopping complex by the pedestrian entrance where, a week before, Dodo Sanders had stood rattling the gates and screaming for help. But first he went

530

into the underground car park, descending to the second level in the lift. At least Clifford hadn't parked the car on precisely the spot where it had been the week before, but perhaps he had not done so only because that particular space and those next to it and opposite were already occupied. This time the Sanders' car was at the extreme opposite end to the lift and the stairs. It was empty which meant, presumably, that Clifford was somewhere in the shopping centre.

As he had been in the previous week, thought Burden, looking at his watch by the light of the glaring greenish strip-lights. Six-twenty-two, but he, of course, had walked here and taken some time to locate the car. Clifford's appointment had been at his normal time, five o'clock, so today his date to pick up his mother would be later. Six-thirty perhaps? With the centre closing at six and usually emptied by six-fifteen, would she be prepared to wait for him? But as he was speculating along these lines, watching the last cars backed out and driven away, he heard the clang of the descending lift. Clifford and his mother came out of it and Burden watched them walk towards their car, Clifford carrying two Tesco bags and a wicker basket. Burden thought he could easily be taken for a girl from the back; it was something to do with his plump hips and the rather short steps he took. He caught up with them as Clifford was lifting the boot-lid of the Metro.

Mrs Sanders turned and cast upon him a basilisk look. She was hatless, her hair set in a rather bouffant, cloudy way which didn't suit her. The red lipstick glistened in the pale face. He had wondered what that particular colour of skin reminded him of and now he knew: raw fish, a translucent, faintly pinkish white. She was perfectly calm and her voice was cold.

'I wish I'd never told anyone about finding that dead body. I wish I'd kept quiet.' Burden had an inkling then of the icy authority she exercised over her son and had no doubt exercised since he was an infant. There was an awful precision in that tone and it was backed by a great storehouse of nervous energy. 'I'm not usually a fool. I should have had the sense to stay out of it; I should have followed his example.'

531

'What example was that, Mrs Sanders?' Burden asked.

Her attention was on the time by her digital watch and that indicated on the clock in the Metro which she bent down to look at. Abstractedly, she said, 'He ran away, didn't he?'

'You tell me. I've got a very good idea what it was he did, and running away was only a small part of it.' While Clifford unlocked the driver's door, he said, 'You won't mind giving me a lift, will you? We can take your mother home first and then you and I will have another talk at the police station.'

Clifford didn't say anything. The only sign that he had heard was when he reached inside to release the lock on the passenger door. And on the way back to Ash Lane no one said a word. Half the carriageway of this end of the Forby Road was undergoing repairs, temporary traffic lights had been installed and a long queue of cars waited. Dodo Sanders, sitting in the front next to Clifford, pulled down her glove and lifted up her coat cuff to look at her digital watch. Why it should have been important to her to know the precise time they had left the car park and the precise time they began queueing at the lights, Burden couldn't guess. Perhaps, though, that wasn't the purpose of all this watch-gazing. It might be that she simply wanted to know the time, that all day long, every day, every five minutes, she had to know the time.

She spoke as Clifford drew up by the kerb. 'I can take the things in. There's no need to come with me.'

But he got out of the car, removed the bags from the boot and carried them up to the front door. He unlocked the door and stood back for her to pass in ahead of him. Burden understood it all. She was one of those people who say things like that but don't mean them. She was the sort who would say, 'Don't worry about me, I'll be all right on my own', or 'Don't bother to write me a thank-you letter', and then create hell when she got left alone or when no letter came. His mother-in-law was a bit like that, though Mrs Sanders was a thousand times worse.

Clifford got back into the driving-seat and Burden stayed where he was, in the back. He didn't care whether they talked or not; they would talk at the station. The driving was done with the slow care, the superfluous signals and excessive braking habitual to Clifford. He broke the silence as they turned in to find the last remaining parking space.

'What is it you suspect me of?'

Burden felt a reluctance to answer questions of that kind. They seemed to bring him down to Clifford's level of ingenuousness and simplicity. Simple-mindedness expressed it better, perhaps. 'Let's leave that until we're inside, shall we?' he suggested.

He called up Diana Pettit and together they shepherded Clifford into that grey-tiled interview room. It was dark now, of course, had been dark for two hours, and the lights in this room were as grim and uncompromising as those in the Barringdean Centre car park, but much brighter. The central heating was on in here, though, just as it was all over the building. Police officers just as much as those they interviewed, as Burden had once told someone without irony, were often obliged to sit there for hours. The immediate warmth, a much greater heat than he enjoyed in his own home, made Clifford ask to take off his hat and coat. He was one who would ask permission before he did almost anything; no doubt asking for leave had been a requirement of right conduct dinned into him from his earliest years. He sat down and looked from Diana to Burden and Burden back to Diana, like a puzzled new boy whom school rules bewilder.

'I'd like you to tell me what you're accusing me of.'

'I'm not accusing you of anything yet,' Burden said.

'What you suspect me of, then.'

'Don't you know, Clifford? Haven't you got a clue? What do you think it is – helping yourself out of the collection in church?'

'I don't go to church.' He essayed a faint smile and it was the first Burden had ever seen him give. The smile seemed contrived with difficulty as if a mechanical process had to be set in motion, a series of button-pressing and lever-pulling only half-remembered. It irritated Burden.

'Perhaps you stole a car then. Or nicked a lady's handbag.'

'I'm sorry. I don't know what you're getting at.'

Burden said abruptly. 'Have you any objection if I record this interview? Tape it, I mean?'

'Would it make any difference if I had?'

'Certainly it would. This isn't a police state.'

'Do as you like,' Clifford said indifferently and he watched Diana begin recording. 'You were going to tell me what I'm supposed to have done.'

'Let me tell you what I think happened. I think you met Mrs Robson inside the shopping centre, in Tesco's. You hadn't seen her for quite a while, but you knew her and she knew you – and she knew something about you you'd like kept secret. I wonder what it was. I don't know yet, I honestly don't know, but you'll tell me. I hope you'll tell me tonight.'

Clifford said in an uneven voice, 'When I first saw Mrs Robson, she was dead. I never saw her before in my life.'

'What you saw, Clifford, was your opportunity. You and she were alone and you very much wanted her out of the way . . .'

He had to remind himself that this was a man, not a boy, not a teenager. And not simple-minded, not retarded. He was a teacher; he had a university degree. The blank, soft face looked even more spongy, but a spark showed in each dull eye. Clifford's voice squeaked. Fear or guilt or God-knows-what had done something to the vocal cords, leaving him with a eunuch's soprano.

'You don't mean you think I'd kill someone? Me? Is that what you mean?'

Not wanting to fall in with this play-acting, this vanity – for what else would explain it? – that made a man believe he could do as he pleased without fear of discovery, Burden said drily, 'He's cottoned on at last.'

Next moment he was on his feet and Diana too, stepping back from the table. Clifford had leapt up, face and lips white as if in genuine shock, his hands grasping the table edge and shaking it, vibrating it as his mother had shaken the wire gates.

'Me? Kill someone? You're mad! You're all crazy! Why've you picked on me? I never knew you meant that with all your questions, I never dreamed . . . I thought I was just a witness. Me kill someone? People like *me* don't kill people!'

'What kind do then, Clifford?' Burden spoke calmly as he lowered himself once more into his chair. 'Some say every-one's capable of murder.'

He met the other man's round staring eyes. A dew of sweat

had appeared all over the putty-like skin, the pudgy features, and a drop trickled down his upper lip between the two wings of the moustache. Burden felt for him an impatient contempt. He wasn't even a good actor. It would be interesting to hear how all that would play back, that stuff about killing people. He'd play it to Wexford, see what he thought.

'Sit down, Cliff,' he said, his growing contempt making him accord the man less than the dignity of his unabridged Christian name. 'We're going to have a long talk.'

Exhausted when the car dropped him at Sylvia's, Wexford would have liked a home of his own to recover in, the sole companionship of his own wife. He had to settle for a drink, the whisky Dr Crocker strictly forbade. Someone had brought in an evening paper; a story on the front page was about a man who had all day been 'helping the police with their enquiries into the Kingsmarkham bomb outrage'. There was no picture and of course no name or description, nothing to make even tentatively possible the identification of this man who had wanted Sheila dead, who had conceived for her that particular brand of cold, impersonal, political hatred.

The boys were watching television, Sylvia trying to write an essay on the psychological abuse of the elderly.

'I know all about that,' Wexford said. 'Would you like to interview me?'

'You're not elderly, Dad.'

'I feel it.'

Dora came and sat beside him. 'I've been to look at our house,' she said. 'The builders have been in and weather-proofed it. At least the rain can't get in. Oh, and the Chief Constable phoned, something about a house we can have if we like. We do like, don't we, Reg?'

A leap of the heart before he started feeling ungrateful to Sylvia. 'Did he say where it is?'

'Up at Highlands, I think. I'm almost sure he said Highlands.'

10

Remorse was perhaps too strong a word; it was distaste
tempered with a hint of shame that Burden felt throughout
that weekend. He said to himself, and he even said it to his
wife who was home again with their son, that this was what
the job was about, this was police work.

'The end justifies the means, Mike?' she said.

'It's the merest idealism to deny that. Every day in everything we do, it's implicit even if we don't come out and say
it. When we were going through that bad patch with Mark
and we decided the only way was to let him cry, that two
nights of that would cure him, we were saying the end justifies the means.'

He took the child on his lap and Jenny smiled.

'Don't teach it to him though, will you?'

He spared himself half an hour to play with Mark and eat
his lunch and then he was back at the police station in that
interview room, confronting Clifford Sanders once more. But
on the way the task behind him and the task ahead goaded
him, made him wrinkle up his nose at the nastiness of it.
How far removed from torture was it, after all? Clifford had
to sit there in that comfortless room, left alone for part of
the time for as much as an hour, food brought to him on
trays by an indifferent police constable. And it would not
have been quite so bad if Clifford had been tougher, less like
a child. He looked like a big child, a kind of fined-down
Billy Bunter. A stoicism had succeeded his bewilderment, an
air of being a brave boy and sticking it out a little longer.
But here Burden told himself he was being a fool. The man
was a man, educated, neurotic perhaps but sane, simply

lacking character and strength of mind. And look what he had done. The facts spoke for themselves. Clifford had been in the shopping centre, had been seen with Mrs Robson, had a garrote in his possession, had run away.

Was it likely that he had found the body, covered it up because it looked like his mother and then fled? Nobody behaved like that outside the pages of popular psychiatry. All that stuff which Serge Olson no doubt dispensed – about neurotics choosing girlfriends because they were looking for a mother, or employers as father-figures, or being put off sex because you'd seen your mother in her underwear – that was strictly for the books and the couch as far as Burden was concerned. And he was a fool to let himself feel a sneaking pity for Clifford Sanders. The man had meant to kill Mrs Robson and had succeeded. Hadn't he gone specifically to meet her armed with a garrote?

Probably his self-doubt was due solely to his failure so far to find the link between Clifford and Gwen Robson. He knew there must be a link and once he had found it, he would no longer be a prey to this unprofessional and certainly unfamiliar guilt. Facing Clifford again, with Archbold there to assist in this renewed interrogation and the tape recorder on, Burden reminded himself that the police had interviewed Sutcliffe the 'Yorkshire Ripper' nine times before he was arrested. And in the intervening time Sutcliffe had murdered his final victim. It would be a fine thing if Clifford Sanders were to kill again because he, Burden, had been squeamish.

He lowered himself slowly into the chair. Clifford, who had been gnawing at a fingernail, snatched his hand from his mouth as if he suddenly recalled nail-biting was something he must not do.

Burden began, 'Has your mother ever been ill, Clifford?'

An uncomprehending look. 'What do you mean?'

'Was she ever ill so that she had to stay in bed? When she needed someone to look after her?'

'She had what-do-you-call-it once. Like a kind of rash, but it aches.'

'He means shingles,' Archbold said.

'That's right, shingles. She had that once.'

'Did a home help come in to look after her, Clifford?'

But this approach led nowhere. Dodo Sanders had been confined to bed for no more than a few hours throughout the whole of Clifford's life. Burden abandoned this line of enquiry and carefully took Clifford through the sequence of events from the time he left Olson until he ran from the car park out of the pedestrian gates. Clifford got in a hopeless muddle with the times, saying he had got to the centre at five-thirty, later changing it to ten-past six. Burden knew he was lying. Everything was going according to his expectations and the only surprising thing which happened was when Clifford corrected him over the use of his name.

'Why have you stopped calling me Cliff? You can call me that if you like, I don't mind. I like it.'

Awaiting him in his office was a lab report on that spool of plastic-covered wire. There was a great deal of technical detail – Burden found himself back among the polymers – but the plain fact easily sorted out was that the shreds of substance found in Mrs Robson's neck wound were quite different from the stuff coating the wire in Clifford Sanders' tool-box. Well, he had been wrong. That might only mean, of course, that Clifford had disposed of the wire he used for his garrote – thrown it in the river or, more safely, stuck it in his own or someone else's dustbin. In the meantime Clifford could sweat for a day or two. Wexford was his immediate concern, Dr Crocker had strictly forbidden the Chief Inspector to return to work at the office and to see him Burden had to drive up to Sylvia's house.

'At any rate I shall be on the spot,' Wexford said. 'I'm going to be living up at Highlands. How about that?'

Burden grinned. 'That's right. There are two or three police houses. When are you moving in?'

'Don't know yet,' Wexford said, glancing through the paperwork Burden had brought him. 'I don't think the person – a useful genderless word – that the checkout girl saw talking to Mrs Robson was Clifford Sanders at all. I think maybe it was Lesley Arbel. But I'll tell you where I agree with you – when you say Mrs Robson was a blackmailer. I think so too.'

Burden nodded eagerly. He was always disproportionately pleased when Wexford approved some suggestion of his.

'She liked money,' he said. 'She was near enough prepared to do anything for money. Look at all that stuff you told me about the old man's will. She was running up and down the street searching for witnesses to a will under which she was to be the sole beneficiary. We may laugh about her bathing someone and cutting some other old man's toenails, but weren't those normally distasteful tasks undertaken for a very inflated payment? There's probably more of that sort of thing we haven't yet uncovered.'

'Mrs Jago says she did what she did all for her husband. There's an implication that this makes it all right, exonerates her. I imagine that was precisely the way Gwen Robson saw it herself.'

'Why did Ralph Robson specifically need money anyway?' Burden asked. 'Has anyone queried that one? I mean, if I said I needed money I'd really mean Jenny and Mark and me, my family. And you'd mean you and Dora, surely?'

Wexford shrugged. 'We've looked at her bank account at the TSB. She had rather a lot in it; I mean more than one would have expected. Robson has his own personal account and they've no joint savings. But Gwen Robson had something over sixteen hundred pounds and that could be the fruits of blackmail. Your idea is that Gwen Robson had evidence Clifford had done something reprehensible and was blackmailing him?'

Burden nodded. 'Something like that. And the worm finally turned. Clifford's pretty worm-like in most respects, I'd say, so why not in that one too?'

'What could Clifford have done? It would surely have to be an earlier murder. Nobody cares much about sexual irregularities these days.'

Burden's face indicated that he did. 'Gwen Robson cared about them.'

'Yes, but you can't imagine that the cramming school would – or Dodo Sanders, come to that. It would be hard to assign any sort of moral convictions to her. She strikes me as a person who has never heard of ethics, still less ever thought she needed views about them.'

Burden wasn't interested. 'I'll find out what it was,' he

said. 'I'm working on it.' He studied Wexford's face: the bruises that were fading, the cut that might or might not leave a permanent scar. 'They had to let that chap go, the one they thought was your bomber. It was on the news this morning.'

Wexford nodded. He had had a phone call about it and a long talk had ensued, culminating in a request to take part in a conference at Scotland Yard. Dr Crocker had sanctioned this with the utmost reluctance and there was no way he would have agreed had he known Wexford intended to drive there. When Burden had gone, Wexford wrapped himself up, adding a scarf of Robin's that was hanging in the hall in case Dora or Sylvia should come home early and see him. His car was on the garage drive and he noticed for the first time – no one had told him – how scarred the bodywork was by chips of flying glass. He got into the driving-seat, feeling that this was unfamiliar, a strange thing to be doing, an act he hadn't performed for a long time.

Closing the door, he thought he would just rest for a moment or two, sit there holding the ignition key. Now if this were a thriller, he thought, a television drama maybe, and he an unimportant character or even a villain, he would put the key in and turn it and the car would blow up. He tried to laugh at that but couldn't, which was absurd, because he had no memory of the explosion and the bangs he thought he heard were not memory but the invention of his imagination. Go on, jump, he said, pushing himself along the plank, easing to the edge of the springboard. He took a breath, pushed the key in, turned it. Nothing happened; the engine didn't even start. Well, why would it? Dora had left it in 'drive'. He moved the automatic shift before he realized what he was doing, the terrible step that was going to be his crossing point.

Because there was nothing now but to go on, he turned the ignition key.

Burden was walking down the High Street, occasionally looking into shop windows already decorated for Christmas, when he saw Serge Olson coming towards him. The psychotherapist wore a check tweed jacket, its collar of mock fur turned up against the sharp east wind.

He greeted Burden as if they were old friends. 'Hallo, Mike, good to see you. How are you?'

Taken aback, Burden said he was fine and Serge Olson asked if he was making much progress. This wasn't a question Burden was accustomed to being asked by those he thought of as the public and he couldn't help thinking it a shade impertinent. But he made a non-committal, vaguely optimistic reply and then Olson surprised him very much by announcing that it was too cold to stand about and why didn't they go into the Queen's Café for a cup of tea? Burden realized at once that Olson must have something he at least thought important to tell him. Why else would he make such a suggestion? For all his use of Burden's Christian name, the two men had met only once before and then strictly on a policeman-and-witness basis.

But when they were seated at a table, instead of imparting secrets of the consulting room, Olson began to talk only of the recent Arab bombers' trial, the huge sentences meted out to the three guilty men and the threat made by some allied terrorist organization to 'get' the prosecuting counsel. Burden was at last moved to ask what it was in particular that Olson had wanted to talk to him about.

The fierce bright animal eyes gleamed. There was an incongruity here, for Olson's voice was always calm and leisurely and his manner placid. 'Talk to you about, Mike?'

'Well, you know, asking me in here for a cup of tea, I thought there must be some specific thing . . .'

Olson shook his head gently. 'Perhaps I might say Clifford Sanders could be a killer in certain circumstances? Or that his manner was very odd when he left me that evening? Or that men of twenty-three who live at home with their mothers must be psychotic by definition? No, I wasn't going to say any of those things. I was cold and I fancied some good hot tea I didn't have to brew up myself.'

Unwilling to let it go at that, Burden said, 'You really mean you weren't going to say any of that?' Olson's head shook more rapidly. 'Surely it is odd a man living with his mother, even if she's a widow. Mrs Sanders isn't what one would call old.'

Olson said nearly incomprehensibly, 'Have you ever heard of the Fallacy of Enkekalymmenos?'

'The what?'

'It means "the veiled one" and it goes something like this. "Can you recognize your mother?" "Yes". "Can you recognize this veiled one?" "No". "This veiled one is your mother. Hence you can recognize your mother and not recognize her".'

There was something veiled about Mrs Sanders. Her own face was a kind of veil, thought Burden, surprised by his own imagination. But in a brusque policeman-like way he said, 'What's that got to do with Clifford?'

'It's got something to do with all of us and our parents, and with knowing and unknowing. Over the entrance to the oracle at Delphi were the words "Know thyself" and I'm talking about a very long time ago. In the two or three thousand years since then, have we heeded that advice?' Olson smiled and, leaving a moment for his words to sink in, added, 'She's not a widow either.'

'She's not?' This was firmer, better charted terrain. Burden checked his sigh of relief. 'Clifford's father's still living, then?'

'She and her husband were divorced years ago when Clifford was a child. Charles Sanders' people were farmers and that house had been in his family for generations. He was living there with his parents when he married. Putting it bluntly, his wife Dorothy was the family servant who came in daily to clean for them. It's not known what the parents thought about that. Obviously Clifford doesn't know. You needn't look like that, Mike, I'm not being a snob. It's not her menial status that set me wondering so much as – let's say her unattractive personality. I suppose she was good-looking and in my job I've learned that in nine cases out of ten that's enough. Five years later, he left them and he gave up the house to his wife and son.'

'What about the grandparents?' Burden asked.

Olson, who had eaten two elaborate iced cakes and a slice of fruit loaf, began brushing crumbs out of his beard with a green and yellow paper napkin. 'Clifford remembers them, but only just. He and his mother had his grandmother living with them when the father left. The grandfather had just died. There wasn't much money, and Charles Sanders doesn't seem to have supported them. It was a hard, lonely sort of life. I've never been to the house, but I imagine it's a bit grim and remote. She went out cleaning, did a bit of dressmaking and I'll give her credit where it's due; she insisted on Clifford's going to university – the University of the South, that is, at Myringham – though he had to live at home and take jobs in the holidays. I don't doubt she was lonely and fancied she needed him with her.'

Burden got up to pay. He felt curiously grateful that after his earlier incomprehensible remarks, Olson had managed to avoid jargon and Greek words and talk like anyone else. But something amongst what the psychotherapist had said touched a chord in his mind, set a vibration twanging.

'I invited you,' Olson said, 'but if you'll guarantee the ratepayers will foot the bill I'll give in gracefully.'

'What was that you said about Clifford taking holiday jobs?'

'The usual sort of thing, Mike, only even that kind of job is harder to come by these days. Unskilled labour, a bit of gardening, shop work.'

'Gardening?' Burden said.

'I believe he did have one job like that. He told me about it at some length – largely because he hated it, I suspect. He's not keen on an outdoor life and nor am I for that matter.'

There wasn't a chance, Burden thought. You didn't get your wishes coming true like that . . . 'You don't remember the name, I suppose?'

'No, I don't. But it was an old spinster woman in a big house in Forest Park.'

11

Waiting in reception, Wexford felt the guilt that comes from
disobeying a doctor's orders. It was really a fear of being
found out, of Dora or Crocker or Burden discovering that
he hadn't gone straight to Scotland Yard. In fact, he probably
wouldn't have phoned this woman, have come here, if he
hadn't been buoyed up by his own success at starting that
car, at driving that car, at eventually driving himself to the
station in it. Better to think of this as his reason than his
anxiety over the slow progress which was being made on the
case. Curious looks were no longer levelled at his face; the
discoloration had nearly gone. The cut was one he might
have made while shaving – if he had been drunk, for instance,
or all his life up to now had worn a beard. The Bomb Squad
people, when he presented himself, would hardly believe he
had been the victim of an explosion. But first there was
this alibi to check and some curiosity, perhaps pointlessly
aroused, to satisfy.

The brighter coloured of the two receptionists, the one
with orange curls, kept assuring him that Sandra Dale
wouldn't keep him a moment, then no more than one minute,
finally that she was on her way. Meanwhile Wexford contemplated *Kim* covers pinned up on the carpeted walls, photographs recording various *Kim* functions, a framed certificate
or diploma commemorating the award to *Kim* of something
or other. Someone touched him lightly on the shoulder.

'Mr Wexford?' He started easily but she didn't seem to
notice. She was a young girl, not in the least like the picture
in the magazine. 'I'm Rosie Unwin,' she said, 'Sandra Dale's

assistant. Would you like to come this way, please? I'm sorry to have kept you.'

They went down passages and up in a lift and then up a flight of stairs and along another passage. At least it wasn't open plan, one of those office complexes where it is impossible to shut oneself away. Rosie Unwin opened a door at the end of the corridor and Wexford saw a woman seated at a desk who was scarcely more like her own photograph than her assistant was. She got up and put out her hand.

'Sandra Dale.' She hesitated. 'It really is my name.'

'Good morning, Miss Dale.'

The photograph was purposely designed to make her look older, plumper, more motherly – or 'aunty'. Wexford didn't think this woman was much over thirty; to him she seemed a young girl, slender, long-legged, with a broad-browed round face and soft blonde hair. The picture made her into someone to be trusted, confided in, someone wise whose advice one could rely on. She asked him to sit down, herself retreating once more behind her desk. The other girl came into the room after him and stood looking not altogether confidently at a visual display unit where amber-coloured letters and geometric figures danced.

'Lesley's not here,' Sandra Dale said, 'but perhaps you knew that? She's away doing a course in working those things and I'm left to manage as best I can.'

'It's you I want to talk to,' Wexford said, 'and perhaps Miss Unwin too.'

The office was large and extremely untidy, though perhaps there was method underlying the apparent disorder. Letters lay all over Rosie Unwin's desk, face-upwards, and Wexford wondered if they could be of the kind he had read in Sylvia's copy of *Kim* but decided not. He wasn't able to read any of them and those he could see were nearly all handwritten. Another pile filled Sandra Dale's in-tray. She read his mind – or rather, misread it.

'We average about two hundred letters a week.'

He nodded. There was a little library of works of reference and two shelves of books: a medical dictionary and an encyclopaedia of alternative medicine, a dictionary of psychology, Eric Berne's *A Layman's Guide to Psychiatry and Psychoan-*

alysis. Rosie Unwin pressed a key and the screen emptied of its dancing figures.

'Would you like coffee?' Wexford had accepted before she added, 'It'll be instant and it comes in Styrofoam.'

He said to Sandra Dale. 'You'll have heard about the woman who was murdered in Kingsmarkham – you know she was Lesley Arbel's aunt?'

'I haven't seen Lesley since it happened. I know about it of course. Lesley's been very brave, I think – very gallant, carrying on with the course – considering Mrs Robson was more like a mother to her.'

'Didn't she have a mother of her own?'

She looked sideways at him, not slyly but perhaps rather mysteriously. 'You'll say she was only my secretary, but I know a lot about her. We all know a lot about each other in here. Sometimes I think the way we work is a bit like a kind of ongoing encounter group. It must be the effect of our . . . our clients.' There it was, that word again. 'Their problems – they bring things up in our own lives, I guess. Lesley wouldn't mind my telling you that her mother abandoned her when she was twelve and her aunt and uncle just took her over. She was already at boarding school so they didn't adopt her, but she was almost as much their daughter as if they had.' The phone on her desk whistled and she picked up the receiver, murmured into it, 'Yes, yes . . . right,' and said to Wexford, 'Excuse me just one moment. Rosie will be with you right away.'

But for a few minutes he was left alone. Curiosity that had nothing much to do with the case in hand impelled him to read the topmost letter on Rosie Unwin's desk. He didn't even have to get out of his chair, only lean to one side. Eyesight lengthens as age comes on and Wexford thought his had become about as long as anyone's could. Holding a book at arm's length was no longer any use to him. His arms were too short.

'Dear Sandra Dale,' he read, 'I know this is awful and horrible and I am disgusted with myself, but I can't pretend about it any longer. The fact is that I am experiencing very powerful sexual feelings towards my own teenage son. I think I am in love with him. All the time I struggle against these feelings of which I assure you I am deeply ashamed, but just the same . . .'

He had to stop and sit up straight again as Rosie Unwin came in with the coffee, but not before he had noticed that there was an address on the letter and it was signed. Strange. He had somehow assumed most letters would be anonymous.

'About point nought-nought-one per cent,' she said when he spoke these thoughts aloud. 'And most people send us a stamped addressed envelope too.'

'How do you make your selection? The ones you decide to print, I mean?'

'We don't pick the most bizarre,' she said. 'That one you were reading, that wasn't typical. You *were* reading it, weren't you? Everyone who comes in here reads the letters; they can't resist it.'

'Well, I admit I was. You wouldn't print that, though?'

'Probably not. That's for Sandra to decide, and then if there's any query it would be the editor's decision – I mean the editor of *Kim*.'

'Like going to higher court,' Wexford murmured.

'Sandra picks out those she thinks will have the widest appeal or impact – let's say common problems, the most human if you like. We'd only print the reply to that one from the woman who fancies her own son. We'd say, "To W. D., Wiltshire," and then write our reply. I mean we do draw the line. Can you believe it, we had a letter last week from someone asking us what the protein content of semen was . . . it's about somewhere.'

Wexford was saved from replying by the return of Sandra Dale. He waited until she was seated again, then asked her, 'So you last saw Lesley when? On Thursday November 19?'

'That's right. She didn't come in on the Friday, she phoned in and told me about her aunt, though I knew then, mind you: I recognized the name. And on the Monday – Monday the twenty-third, that is – she started the computer course. It was a bit of luck, if you can call it luck in the circumstances, that the course happened to be in the same town where her uncle lives.'

'She left here on Thursday afternoon, did she? What time would that have been – five? Five-thirty?'

Sandra Dale looked surprised. 'No, no, she took the afternoon off. I thought you knew.'

Wexford smiled neutrally.

'She finished at one. It was something about having to go down to Kingsmarkham to register for the course. She'd filled in one of the forms wrongly, something like that; she tried to phone the place, but their phone was out of order. Well, according to her it was. I'll be frank with you: I wasn't terribly pleased. I mean, I'd got to do without my secretary for a fortnight as it was, and all for the sake of doing our page on a word processor instead of a typewriter which had always suited us perfectly well.'

Wexford thanked her. This was not at all what he had expected to hear. He had hoped only to pick up from the agony aunt's department some useful pointers to Lesley Arbel's character. Instead he had been handed a smashed alibi.

Rosie Unwin said as he was leaving, 'I hope you won't mind my asking, but are you any relation to Sheila Wexford?'

He was always being asked that, so he ought not to have experienced that clutch at the heart. 'Why do you ask?' he responded rather too quickly.

She was taken aback. 'Only that I admire her very much. I mean, I think she's beautiful and a great actress.'

Not that she had heard something awful on the news, or been told of Sheila's fatal injuries . . . death . . . on breakfast television . . .

'She's my daughter,' he said.

They liked him now, they were all over him. He should have told them the minute he came in, he thought. He waited for one of them – the younger, surely – to tell him as most people sooner or later did that Sheila didn't look much like him, inferring really not so much lack of resemblance as the discrepancy between her beauty and his . . . well, lack of it. But they were tactful. They didn't say anything about wire-cutting either. He went off through the labyrinthine building with Rosie escorting him, talking of Sheila all the way, then they were taking his identification disc from him and signing him out. In half an hour's time he had an appointment at Scotland Yard for another session with the Bomb Squad, and he thought he might as well walk at least part of the distance.

So he made his way across Waterloo Bridge, beneath which the river lay sluggish as oil and above him not only the sun but the sky itself was invisible.

It was three days since he had last seen Clifford Sanders and in that time Burden's enquiries had confirmed most satisfactorily that he had indeed worked as a gardener for Miss Elizabeth McPhail at Forest House, Forest Park, Kingsmarkham. Her neighbours remembered him and one of them also remembered Gwen Robson's visits. What he would have liked was to have found someone who had seen them together, talking to each other. Perhaps this was a lot to expect. Beyond a doubt, Gwen Robson had received her offer of employment as Miss McPhail's full-time housekeeper four years ago. Clifford was twenty-three and four years previously would have been a year into his university course. Burden considered his strategy. Clifford would be at work now, at Munster's; he worked all day on Tuesdays until five. He would be tired when he got home and it would do no harm for him to find Burden there waiting for him, anxious for another talk either there in the back of beyond or down at the police station once more.

Davidson drove the two of them down the long lane that went past Sundays Park. At ten to five it was already dark and pockets of fog made very slow, cautious driving essential. The ivy-clad façade of the house loomed up out of the misty dark, looking alive, looking like a gigantic square bush or a surrealist nightmare of a tree. All the leaves hung limp and gleaming, dewed with water-drops. The car headlamps alone showed him the dark glistening mass, for not a light was showing amongst the coat of foliage. What did Dorothy Sanders do there all day – her son having taken the car and no bus stop nearer than Forby or Kingsmarkham, both at least two miles distant? Once a week Clifford took her to the Barringdean Shopping Centre, had his hour-long session with Olson, went to pick up his mother. What friends did she have, if any? How well did she really know Carroll the farmer? Each, it would seem, had been deserted by a partner; they were not far removed from each other in age . . .

549

The door opened and she was standing there. 'You back again? My son's not here.'

Burden remembered what Wexford had said about it being hard to associate her with ethics, with any moral sense. He was aware of something else, too, something he would never have thought of himself as sufficiently sensitive to feel – a coldness emanating from her. It was hard to think of her as having a normal body temperature, warm blood. And as he reflected these things, the whole passing rapidly through his mind as he stood on the doorstep, he felt also how very much he would hate to have to touch her, as if her living flesh would feel like rigor mortis.

She would think it was the icy air that made him shiver. He said, 'We'd like a few words with you, Mrs Sanders.'

'Shut the door, then, or the fog will get in.' She spoke of the fog as if it were some sort of elemental or ghost, always waiting outside for a chance unwise invitation.

Her face was thickly and whitely powdered, the lips painted a waxy red, her head tied up tightly in a brown-patterned scarf so that no hair showed. She was dressed in her favourite brown, jumper and skirt, ribbed tights, flat tan-coloured shoes. Following her into the living room, Burden noticed how thin and upright she was – her hips narrow, her back flat – so that it was something of a shock to see her frontal aspect reflected in the big mahogany-framed mirror, her stringy neck and the deep lines on her forehead. It was cold in there and, whatever she had said about keeping the fog out, it seemed already to have penetrated. A damp chill touched Burden's skin, the only heat in the room concentrated in the few feet around the coal fire. He glanced at the empty mantelpiece of dark grey flecked marble, the chest of drawers and cabinet in a rather dull dark wood, their surfaces equally bare.

'May we sit down?' She nodded. 'Your son worked as a gardener for a Miss McPhail of Forest Park, I believe. That would have been while he was at university?'

She detected criticism Burden had not meant to imply. 'He was a grown man. Men should work. I couldn't keep him; the grant he got didn't cover everything.'

Burden said simply, 'Mrs Robson worked as a home help for Miss McPhail.'

The words were hardly out of his mouth before he realized Dodo Sanders was going to do it again. Once more she was going to register incomprehension at the name of Robson. Robson? Who's Mrs Robson? Oh, that woman, that one who was murdered, the one whose body I found, that one. Oh yes, of course. She said none of these things but she looked them all, nodding when Burden reminded her is if recollection had come tardily.

'He didn't know her,' she said evenly in her robot's mechanical voice.

'If you didn't know her, or know she worked there, how can you know that?'

She showed no sign of awareness at having betrayed herself or her son. 'She was in the house and he was in the garden; you said that. She wouldn't go into the garden and he wouldn't go into the house. Why would he? It was a big garden.'

Burden left it and allowed a silence to fall before saying, 'Have you ever let the upstairs rooms in this house?' He asked because the idea of the furniture up there intrigued him in an awesome kind of way. He remembered Diana Pettit talking about all that furniture impeding them in their search.

'Why do you ask?' The robot was talking again, its microchip tone giving each word equal weight.

'Frankly, Mrs Sanders, the place is barely furnished down here and cluttered upstairs – or so I understand.'

'You're welcome to look at it if you want.' It was a cordial turn of phrase she used, but not uttered in a cordial way. So might the wolf in Red Riding Hood have said that its teeth were all the better to eat you with. The dome-like bluish eyelids half closed once more, the head went back and Dodo Sanders said, 'My son is coming now.'

Light from the Metro turning in at the gates trickled across the ceiling and down the walls. The woman didn't speak again; she seemed to be listening, to be straining in fact to hear something. There came the distant sound of a wooden door closing, a bolt being shot. Visibly she relaxed, sinking a little from the waist. Clifford's key in the lock was succeeded by the sound of Clifford's feet being vigorously wiped. He must have known by the presence of the car that Burden was here and he didn't hurry; he even pushed the door open very slowly. He entered the room, looked at Burden and Davidson without giving any sign of recognition, without speaking, and walked towards the single empty chair like someone under hypnosis.

But before he had sat down his mother did an astonishing thing. She spoke Clifford's name, just the bare Christian name, and when he turned to look slowly in her direction she leaned her head to one side and lifted her cheek. He moved towards her, bent down and planted an obedient kiss on the floury white skin.

'Can we have a talk, Cliff?' Burden found himself speaking with undue heartiness, as he might have done to a boy of ten or so who has had a fright, who requires jollying along. 'I'd like to talk to you about Miss McPhail. But first we're going upstairs to take a look round the attics.'

Clifford's head turned, his eyes rested momentarily on his mother and moved away. It wasn't exactly a glance requesting permission, more a look of incredulity that such a step might be allowed, had apparently already been sanctioned. Dodo Sanders got to her feet and they went upstairs – all four of them went. It had been a farmhouse once, so the first flight of stairs was handsome and wide, the second which led to the attics narrow and too steep to climb without grasping at banisters. At the top Burden saw closed doors all around him, smelt a cold mustiness, the smell of neglect, and an uncomfortable memory of past dreams came to him – of secrets and things hidden in lofts, of a hand coming out of a cupboard and a disembodied smiling face. But he wasn't imaginative as Wexford was. He put his hand up to a wall switch and a light of low wattage came on; then he opened the first door.

Mother and son stood behind him, Davidson behind them. The room was crammed with furniture and pictures and ornaments, but these were not arranged in any sort of order and the framed paintings were all stacked against walls. Pieces of china and books lay on the seats of chairs, cushions in a heap in the corner. None of it looked valuable, certainly not antique or even of curiosity value but dating from the twenties and thirties, a few pieces older and with turned legs and piecrust edges. Downstairs everything was clean and any

552

assessment of Dodo Sanders' character must have included her housewifely qualities, but up here there had been no sweeping and dusting. No vacuum cleaner had been lugged up the narrow stairs. Cobwebs hung from the ceilings and gathered in the corners in fly-filled traps. Because this was in the country, in a quiet place not much frequented by motor vehicles, the dust was not thick and flocculant, but dust there was: a thin, soft powdering on every surface.

The next room was the same, except that there were two bedsteads in there and two flock mattresses and feather-beds, bundles of pink satin eiderdowns and counterpanes tied up with string, sausage-shaped bolsters covered in ticking, rolled blankets, home-made wool rugs in geometric patterns and home-made rag rugs in concentric circles of faded colours. And there were more pictures, but this time they were photographs in gilt frames.

Burden took a few steps inside this room, picked up one of the photographs and looked at it. A tall man in tweed suit and trilby hat; a woman also wearing a hat, her dress shawl-collared and with a long flared skirt; a boy between them in a school cap, short trousers, knee socks, the group redolent of the mid-thirties. Man and boy closely resembled each other; it might have been Clifford's face he was looking at, the same pudginess, the same thick lips and even the same moustache, the same inexpressive eyes. But there was something in those people that Clifford lacked, an air in all of them of . . . what? Superiority was to put it too strongly. A consciousness of social position and social duties? Still carrying the framed picture, Burden looked into the other two attics while Davidson and Clifford and his mother silently followed him. Here was more furniture, more rolled-up rugs and watercolours mounted on gold paper framed in gilt, more books and china animals, but gilded pink Lloyd Loom chairs as well and a Susie Cooper teaset tumbled on a pile of cushions embroidered with flower gardens and country cottages. It was all rather dirty and shabby and practically valueless, but none of it was sinister or suggestive of the supernatural, none of it was the stuff nightmares are made of.

What had happened? Why was it all up here? He asked himself this as they descended. It wasn't as if the furnishings downstairs were superior to this or newer; nor that there was so much furniture downstairs that the surplus had found its way up here. Indeed, it was inadequate and Burden had come to the conclusion that mother and son must eat their meals from plates on their laps. He could imagine them with TV dinners or dehydrated messes, bought to save trouble. What he couldn't picture was this woman cooking the sort of food anyone would want to eat.

'Those are my grandparents and my father,' Clifford said, putting out his hand for the photograph.

Dorothy Sanders issued an order to him as if he were a schoolboy like the one in the picture. 'Take it upstairs, Clifford; put it back where it's kept.' Burden would have been more astonished to witness a protest on Clifford's part, a hesitation even, than to see what in fact happened – automatic obedience as he went immediately up to the attics.

'I'd like you to tell me a bit about your relationship with Mrs Robson, Cliff,' Burden said when they were all downstairs once more.

'His name's Clifford. It was my name . . . and he doesn't have relationships,' his mother said.

'I'll rephrase that. Tell me about when you first met her and what you talked about. It was at Miss McPhail's, wasn't it?'

Dorothy Sanders had withdrawn down the passage towards the kitchen regions. Clifford looked rather blankly at Burden and said he had once done gardening for Miss McPhail. He too seemed to have forgotten who Mrs Robson was; Burden reminded him and asked him if he ever went inside the Forest Park house – to have a cup of tea or coffee for instance, or to bring flowers in.

'There was a cleaning lady used to give me tea, yes.'

'That was Mrs Robson, wasn't it?'

'No, it wasn't. I don't remember her name; I never heard her name. It wasn't Mrs Robson.'

His mother came back and Clifford looked at her, childlike, as if for help. She had been washing her hands and reeked of disinfectant. To rid herself of contamination from all that furniture, or from that of the two policemen?

She said, 'I've already told you she was in the house and

he was in the garden. I've told you he didn't know her. You people don't seem to understand plain English.'

'All right, Mrs Sanders, you've made your point,' Burden said. He wasted no more time on her and looked away. 'I'd like you to come back to the police station with me, Clifford. We can get a clearer picture of things there.'

Clifford went with them in his docile way and they drove back to town. He sat at the table in the interview room and looked across it first at Burden and then at DC Marian Bayliss. His eyes went back to Burden, then were lowered towards the tiny geometric pattern on the tabletop. In a low voice, not much more than a mumble, he said, 'You're accusing me of murdering someone. It's incredible, I still can't accept what's happening to me.'

Much of the skill of a policeman in interrogation lies in knowing what to ignore as well as what to seize on. Burden said quietly, 'Tell me what happened when you first got to the shopping centre and met Mrs Robson.'

'I've already told you,' Clifford said. 'I didn't meet her, I saw her dead body. I've told you over and over. I drove down into the car park on to the second level and I was going to park the car when I saw this person lying there, this dead person.'

'How did you know she was dead?' Marian asked.

Clifford leaned forward on his elbows, holding on to his temples. 'Her face was blue, she wasn't breathing. You're beginning to make me feel what happened isn't true, that it wasn't that way. You're changing the truth with all this until I don't know any more what happened and what didn't. Maybe I did know her and I forgot. Maybe I'm mad and I killed her and forgot. Is that what you want me to say?'

'I want you to tell me the truth, Clifford.'

'I've told you the truth,' he said and then, looking away for a moment, twisting in his chair, he directed a curiously appealing gaze on Burden. His voice was the same, a fairly resonant adult male voice, but the tone was that of a child of seven. 'You used to call me Cliff. What stopped you? Was it Dodo stopped you?'

Afterwards, when he looked back, Burden thought it was at this point that he abandoned his theory of Clifford's being as sane as he and understood that he was mad.

12

Leaning over the garden gate, the new resident of Highlands surveyed the estate that would be his home for at least the next six months. It was one of those days that sometimes occur even in December, a clear sunny day of cloudless skies and a gradually falling temperature. The frost to come that night would silver all the little grass verges and turn everyone's miniature conifers into Christmas trees. On the hill behind Wexford's new home Barringdean Ring sat like a black velvet hat on a green cushion. The sky blazed silvery azure. At the bottom of Battle Lane he could see where Hastings Road turned off and make out the roof of Robson's house and the Whittons' and Dita Jago's. It was high up here, the highest point of Highlands, so that he could even see the cluster of latter-day almshouses that made up Berry Close.

The removal van, newly arrived with half the furniture from the bombed house, blocked any view he might have had of the town. Sylvia had taken the boys to school, then come with the van driver to help her mother move in. Wexford thought he would walk to work and then if he couldn't face walking home Donaldson could bring him. Dora would need their car. He went back in and said goodbye to her, looking round the bare, bleak little house, trying not to prejudice what living in these cramped quarters would be like, the neighbours and their noisy children separated from these rooms only by thin dividing walls, the strips of gardens partitioned by wire fences. More wire fences! Never mind, they were lucky to have somewhere, lucky not to have to go on living with Sylvia . . . and he reproached himself for the ungrateful thought as his kind busy daughter came in carrying a crate of his favourite books.

The air was nippy and the sunshine warm, but sun hung low on the horizon and the shadows were long. His route down into the town took him along Hastings Road and into Eastbourne Drive. There was no one about, the streets empty of people and nearly empty of cars. This was the last day of Lesley Arbel's word-processor course, but no doubt she would spend the weekend with her uncle. It was more than two weeks since Gwen Robson's death, nearly as long since someone had tried to kill Sheila. His cuts and bruises were nearly healed, his strength returning. He had several times driven his car, felt quite calm and assured at the wheel. The bomb experts kept on coming to him or getting him to go to them, pursuing their interminable questions. Try to remember. What exactly happened after you got into the car? Who are your enemies? Who are your daughter's enemies? Why did you jump out of the car? What warned you? He could recall none of it and believed those lost five minutes lost for ever. It was only in the night-time, in dreams, that he relived the explosion – or rather, instead of reliving what he couldn't remember, conjured up new versions for himself in some of which he died or Sheila died or the world itself disappeared and he hung suspended in a dark void. But last night, instead of the roar of the bomb he had heard thin reedy music and instead of Sheila's body, he had seen wheels spinning in the darkness, circles that shone and glittered and were filled with geometric patterns . . .

Striving to dispel these ideas and look at things rationally occupied his thoughts until he reached the police station. Once there, he somehow knew before he enquired that Burden had Clifford Sanders with him and Archbold in one of their interview rooms. Late in the morning Burden came out but kept Clifford there alone, sending in coffee and biscuits. Wexford couldn't tell what Clifford looked like after this continuous ordeal but Burden was haggard, his face pale and tense and his eyes exhausted.

'You were talking about the inquisition,' Wexford said. 'About executioners taking payment to garrote the condemned before they were burned at the stake.'

557

Burden nodded, slumped in his chair, his strained face rather ghastly in the pale, bright light from the sun.

'You said you'd read about it. Well, I've read of Inquisitors suffering as much as their victims, of the strain wearing them out and brainwashing them till they get like you. It's watching the torture that does it; you have to be a very special sort of person to be able to watch torture and not be affected by it.'

'Clifford Sanders isn't being tortured. I had doubts about that earlier on, but I don't any more. He's being put through a fairly heavy interrogation but not tortured.'

'Not physically perhaps, but I don't think you can separate mind and body like that.'

'He isn't kept awake artificially; he isn't under bright lights or kept on his feet or starved or denied a drink. He isn't even here all the time; he goes home to sleep. I'm going to send him home today, now; I've had enough for today.'

'You're wasting your time, Mike,' Wexford said mildly. 'You're wasting your time and his because he didn't do it.'

'Excuse me if I differ from you there. I differ from you most strongly.' Burden sat up revived, indignant. 'He had the motive and the means. He has strong psychopathic tendencies. Remember that book you lent me with that piece in it about psychopaths? The Stafford-Clark? "The outstanding feature is emotional instability in its broadest and most comprehensive sense . . ." Let me see, how does it go on? I haven't got your memory. ". . . prodigal of effort but utterly lacking in persistence, plausible but insincere, demanding but indifferent to appeals, dependent only in their constant unreliability . . ." '

'Mike,' Wexford interrupted him. 'You haven't got any evidence. You've trumped up what you've got to suit yourself. The single piece of evidence you do have is that he saw the body and instead of reporting it, ran away. That is absolutely all you've got. He didn't know Gwen Robson. He was a gardener in a place where she popped in sometimes in her home-help role, and he may once or twice have said hello to her. He wasn't seen talking to her in the shopping centre. He doesn't and didn't possess a garrote or anything that could be made into a garrote.'

'On the contrary, he has a hard and fast motive. I can't

yet prove it, but I'm convinced he committed a crime in the past which Gwen Robson discovered and started blackmailing him over. Blackmailers don't succeed for long with psychopaths.'

'What crime?'

'Murder, obviously,' Burden said on a note of triumph. 'You suggested that yourself. You said no one would care about some sex thing, it had to be murder.' His voice grew tired again as he suppressed a yawn. 'Who, I don't know, but I'm working on it. I'm probing into his past. A grandmother maybe? Even Miss McPhail herself. I'm having Clifford's past looked into for signs of any remotely possible unexplained deaths.'

'You're wasting your time. Well, not your time – ours, the public's.'

This was an accusation to which Burden was particularly sensitive. He was beginning to look angry as well as tired and his face grew pinched as it always did when he was cross. He spoke coldly. 'He met her by chance in the shopping centre, she asked for more money and after he had followed her down into the car park, he killed her by strangling her with a length of electric lead he was carrying in the boot of the car along with that curtain. This he took with him and threw away on his way home.'

'Why cover the body and run away?'

'You can't account for inconsistencies of that sort in a psychopath, though probably he thought that if he covered the body it might not be found for a rather longer time than if he left it exposed. Linda Naseem saw him talking to Mrs Robson. Archie Greaves saw him running away.'

'Mike, we know he ran away, he admits that himself. And it was a girl with a hat on that Linda Naseem saw.'

Burden got up and walked the length of the room, then came back to lean on the edge of Wexford's desk. He had the air of someone who is bracing himself to say something unpleasant in the nicest possible way. 'Look, you've had a bad shock and you're still not well. You saw what happened when you came back to work too soon. And for God's sake, I know you're worried about Sheila.'

Wexford said dryly but as pleasantly as he could, 'OK, but my mind's not affected.'

'Well, isn't it? It would be only natural to think it was – temporarily, that is. All the evidence in this case points to Clifford and, moreover, not a shred to anyone else. Only for some reason you refuse to see that, and in my opinion the reason is that you're not right yet, you're not over the shock of that bomb. Frankly, you should have stayed at home longer.'

And left it all to you, Wexford thought, saying nothing but aware of a cold anger spreading through him rather like a draught of icy water trickling down his gullet.

'I shall break Clifford on my own. It's only a matter of time. Leave it to me, I'm not asking for help – or advice, come to that. I know what I'm doing. And as for torture, that's a laugh. I haven't even approached anything the Judges' Rules would object to.'

'Maybe not,' Wexford said. 'Perhaps you should remember the last lines of that passage you like so much defining a psychopath, the bit about the ruthless and determined pursuit of gratification.'

Burden looked hard at him, looked in near-disbelief, then walked out, slamming the door resoundingly.

A quarrel with Mike was something that had never happened before. Disagreements, yes, and tough arguments. There had been the time, for instance, when Mike had lost his first wife and gone to pieces and later had that peculiar love affair – Wexford had been angry with him then and perhaps paternalistic. But they had never come to hurling abuse at each other. Of course he hadn't meant to infer that Mike was a psychopath, or had psychopathic tendencies or anything of that sort, but he had to admit it must have sounded like that. What had he meant then? As with most people in most quarrels, he had said the first hurtful, moderately clever thing that came into his head.

Some of the things Mike had said he was sure were right. In his assessment of the character of Gwen Robson he was right. She would do a great deal for money, almost anything, and what she had done had led to her death. He knew that and Burden knew it too. But he had chosen the wrong person from among her possible . . . what? Clients? Perhaps that

560

was the best word even in this context. Clifford Sanders was not Gwen Robson's murderer.

Wexford looked out of the window and saw him being shepherded out to one of the cars. Davidson was about to drive him home. Clifford neither trudged nor shuffled, he didn't walk with his head bowed or his shoulders hunched, yet there was something of desperation in his bearing. He was like one caught in a recurring dream from which to awaken is to escape, but which will inexorably return the next night. Fanciful nonsense, Wexford told himself, but his thoughts persisted in dwelling on Burden's chosen perpetrator as Davison drove out of the forecourt and on to the road, and all that could be seen of Clifford Sanders was his solid heavy-shouldered shape through the rear window, his round cropped skull. What would he go home to? That cold, dictatorial woman, that house which was big and bare and always chilly and where, according to Burden, everything that might have made it comfortable was stored away up in the attics. Useless to ask why he stayed. He was young and fit and educated; he could leave, make a life of his own. Wexford knew that so many people are their own prisoners, jailers of themselves, that the doors which to the outside world seem to stand open they have sealed with invisible bars. They have blocked off the tunnels to freedom, pulled down the blinds to keep out the light. Clifford, if asked, would no doubt say, 'I can't leave my mother, she's done everything for me, brought me up single-handed, devoted her life to me. I can't leave her, I must do my duty.' But perhaps it was something very different he said when alone with Serge Olson.

Wexford might not have gone to Sundays that day, might have sat on his office for a long time brooding over his quarrel with Burden, but a call came through from a man called Brook, Stephen Brook. The name meant nothing, then recall came with a recollection of the blue Lancia and a woman who had gone into labour while in the shopping centre. Brook said his wife had something to tell the police and Wexford's thoughts went at once to Clifford Sanders. Suppose this woman wanted to tell him something that would put Clifford entirely beyond suspicion? She might know him. It could, with some exaggeration, be said that in a place like Kingsmarkham everyone knew everyone else. It would bring him considerable satisfaction to have Clifford exonerated and might also heal the breach between himself and Burden – without if possible Burden's losing face.

The Brooks lived at the Forby Road end of town, their home a flat in the local authority housing area of the Sundays estate. From the window of their living room Sundays Park could be seen – its hornbeam avenue, its lawns and cedars, the cars of those taking the word-processor course parked at the side of the big white house. This small room was very warm and Mrs Brook's baby lay uncovered in a wicker cradle. The Brooks' furniture consisted of two battered chairs and a table and a great many small crates and boxes, all of them covered or draped with lengths of patterned material and shawls and coloured blankets. There were posters on the walls and dried grasses in stoneware mustard jars. It had all been done at the lowest possible cost and the effect was rather charming.

Mrs Brook was all in black. Dusty black knitted draperies was the way Wexford would have described her clothes if he had had to do so. She wore wrinkled black and white striped stockings and black trainers, and a very curious contemporary madonna she looked when she lifted the baby and, unbuttoning black cardigan and black shirt, presented one round white breast to its mouth. Her husband – in jeans, shirt and zipper-jacket uniform – would have appeared more conventional if he had not dyed his spiky hair to resemble the bird of paradise flower, a tropical blue and orange. Their modulated Myringham University accents came as a slight shock, though Wexford told himself he should have known better. Both of them were about the age of Clifford Sanders, but how different a life they had made for themselves!

'I didn't tell you before,' Helen Brook said, 'because I didn't know who she was. I mean, I was in hospital having Ashtoreth and I didn't really think much about all that.'

Ashtoreth. Well, it sounded pretty and was just another goddess like Diana.

'I mean, it was all a shock really. I meant to have her at home and I was all set to do that. Squatting, you know, not

562

lying down which is so unnatural, and three of my friends were coming to perform the proper rites. The people at the hospital had been really angry at me for wanting to have her the natural way, but I knew I could prove to them my way was right. And then of course they caught me. It was almost as if they set a trap to get me into hospital, though Steve says not – they couldn't have.'

'Yeah, that's paranoia, love,' said Stephen Brook.

'Yes, I just started these labour pains – how about that? I was in Demeter and these pains just started.'

'In what?' Wexford said before he remembered this was the Barringdean Centre's health food shop. Briefly, it had sounded like some obstetrical condition.

'In Demeter,' she said again, 'getting my calendula capsules. And I sort of looked up and through the window and I saw her outside talking to this girl. And I thought I'll go out and show myself to her and I wonder what she'll think – the way she used to go on saying she hoped I'd never have children, that was all.'

'He doesn't know what you're on about, love.'

Wexford nodded his assent to this as Helen Brook shifted the child to her other breast, cupping the soft downy head in her hand. 'Saw whom?' he asked.

'That woman who got killed. Only I didn't know; I mean, I didn't know what her name was. I just knew I knew her, then when we read in the paper that she'd been a home help and where she lived I said to Steve, that's the woman who used to look after the lady next door to Mum. I was in Demeter and I recognized her, I hadn't seen her for yonks. You see, she'd heard about the way Steve and I got married and she was all peculiar about it.'

'The way you got married?'

'Well, Steve and I didn't go to a register office or a church or anything on account of our beliefs. We had a very beautiful ceremony at Stonehenge at dawn, with all our friends there. I mean, they won't let you go up into the stones like Mummy said you used to, but it was very beautiful just being able to see Stonehenge. Steve had a ring made of bone and I had a ring made of yew wood and we exchanged them, and our friend who's a musician played the sitar and everyone sang. Anyway, the council let you have a flat even if you don't get married the official way. Mum told the lady – what was she called, Gwen? – Mummy told her that, but she was still really sniffy and when she saw me that's what she said. She said I hope you don't have children, that's all. Well, that was two years ago and I hadn't seen her since and then I did see her talking to this girl outside Demeter. They went off into Tesco's together and I was going to follow them and kind of say, look, how about that? And then I had this terrific pain . . .'

She sat there, smiling blandly, the baby Ashtoreth now recumbent in her lap and subsiding into sleep. Wexford asked her to describe the girl.

'I'm not very good at describing people. I mean it's the way they are inside that counts, isn't it? She was older than me but not all that much, and she had dark hair that was quite long and she was wearing the most amazing clothes; that's what stuck in my memory, her amazing clothes.'

'Are you saying she was smartly dressed?' Wexford understood at once that he was using very outdated terms and Helen Brook looked puzzled. She leaned forward as if she had misheard. 'Her clothes were particularly elegant?' he corrected himself, and added, 'New? Beautiful? Fashionable?'

'Well, not specially new. Elegant – that might be the word. You know what I mean.'

'Was she wearing a hat?'

'A hat? No, she wasn't wearing a hat. She had lovely hair; she looked lovely.'

A young woman ought to be able to judge the style of a contemporary. What she had told him had confirmed Linda Naseem's evidence – or had it? Hats, after all, can be temporarily taken off. If this were the same girl both she and Helen Brook had seen, it meant that Gwen Robson had met her in one of the aisles of the shopping centre and presumably walked through the Tesco supermarket with her, the two of them then leaving together for the underground car park. If it was the same girl . . .

It is rare to recognize someone at the wheel of a car. Generally, it is the car we recognize, then look quickly to identify the driver. Silver Escorts attracted Wexford's attention at present, as did red Metros, and a closer look at the one approaching showed him Ralph Robson in the driving-seat. So Lesley Arbel was without transport today . . .

'Turn round,' he said to Donaldson. 'Take me to Sundays.'

When they arrived, people were coming down the steps of the Regency mansion; the course had come to an end. There were as many men as women and most of them were young. Lesley Arbel, emerging from the open double entrance doors, stood out conspicuously from the rest by her looks and her clothes. Wexford, who when he first met her had been reminded by her sleek dressing of actresses in the early days of the talking cinema, now again recollected those thirties' films. Only in them was it possible to capture such a scene, where there was no room for doubting who were extras and who the star. But because this was not a film and Lesley Arbel no confident movie queen swanning on celluloid, her appearance was a little ridiculous by contrast with all those tweed coats and anoraks and jackets over tracksuits. She even came rather awkwardly down those steps, her heels so high as to throw her off-balance.

The Kingsmarkham bus passed along the Forby Road, stopping opposite the gates and Sundays Lodge, and it was no doubt this bus she meant to catch. But her heels and the long tight black skirt restricted her steps and she was making very slow progress towards the avenue when Wexford put his head out of the car window and asked if they might give her a lift home. It was more than a surprise, it seemed a shock, and she jumped. He had a feeling that if more comfortably shod, she would have made a run for it. However she came cautiously up to the car. Wexford got out, opened the rear door for her and she got awkwardly in ahead of him, ducking her head and holding on to her small black grosgrain hat.

'I thought we might have a talk in private,' he said. 'Without your uncle, I mean.'

She was too nervous to speak and sat with her hands in her lap, staring at Donaldson's broad back. Wexford noticed that her nails – which had protruded a good half-inch from her fingertips – had been filed down and were unpainted. Donaldson began to drive slowly down the avenue, between the lines of leafless hornbeams. The sun had just set and all the trees made a black tracery against a spectacular crimson sky.

Wexford said quietly, 'You didn't tell me you were in Kingsmarkham on the day your aunt was killed.'

She responded quite quickly and it was as if the question had been of no great significance. So might she have replied if a friend had reproached her for failing to make a promised phone call.

'No, I was upset and I forgot.'

'Come now, Miss Arbel. You told me you left Orangetree House early because you weren't feeling well.'

She muttered, 'I *wasn't* feeling well.'

'Your illness didn't prevent your coming to Kingsmarkham.'

'I mean I forgot it might be important where I was.'

She had been frightened, but she wasn't frightened now; this must mean he had not asked the question she feared to hear. 'It's very important where you were. I understand you came here to check that you were on this course that was to start the following Monday?' She nodded, relaxing a little, her body less rigid under the stiffly padded shoulders of her pink and black striped jacket. 'That can be verified, you know, Miss Arbel.'

'I did check up on the course.'

'You could have done that by phone, couldn't you?'

'I did try but their phones were out of order.'

'And then you went to meet your aunt in the Barringdean Centre.'

'No!' He couldn't tell if it was a cry of denial through fear of discovery or simple astonishment that such a meeting could have been suspected. 'I never saw her, I never did! Why would I go there?'

'You must tell me that. Suppose I told you that you were seen by at least one witness?'

'I'd say they were lying.'

'As you were lying when you told me you were ill on November 19 and went home early from work?'

'I wasn't lying. I thought it wasn't important just coming down here to look at a form and check up and then go back again. That's all I did. I never went near the Barringdean Centre.'

'You came and went by train?'

She gave an anxious nod, falling into his trap.

'You were very near the centre then, considering the pedestrian entrance is in the next street to Station Road. Wouldn't it be right to say you returned to the station from Sundays and, remembering your aunt would be in the Barringdean Centre at that time because she always was, you went in and met her in the central aisle?'

It was a vehement, tearful denial she made, but again Wexford had the feeling that whatever she was afraid of it was not this; it was not fear of having been seen with her aunt half an hour before her death that frightened her. And to his astonishment she suddenly exclaimed miserably, 'I'll lose my job!'

This seemed almost an irrelevancy, at least a minor matter compared with the enormity of Gwen Robson's death. He let her go, opening the door for her when the car stopped in Highlands outside her uncle's house. For a few moments he stood there, watching the house. Behind drawn curtains the lights were already on. She had gone up the path at a hobbling run and was fumbling with her key when Robson opened the door to let her in. It was closed very rapidly. Now for the long evening, Wexford thought; the making of tea and perhaps scrambled eggs, the chat about the day she had passed and he had passed, complaints about his arthritis and sympathy from her, the relief of television. What had people in that situation done before television? It was unthinkable.

Was it all out of the kindness of her heart? Was it that she had truly loved her aunt and now loved and pitied her uncle? A saint, an angel of mercy – that she must be to remain here for yet another weekend when London and her own home and friends were available to her, when there were three trains an hour to take her there. But Wexford didn't think she was an angel of mercy; she hadn't impressed him even as being particularly kind hearted. Vanity and self-absorption don't generally go with altruism – and what was the meaning of that final impassioned cry?

Dita Jago's daughter had called to collect her little girls

and Wexford said to Donaldson, 'You can take the car back and knock off if you like. I'll walk home from here.'

A momentary surprise crossed Donaldson's face, then he remembered where home now was. Wexford strolled across the road. The Highlands lights were not the gentle amber lamps of the street where his own house was but the harsh white kind, glass vases full of glare borne on concrete stilts. They stained the dark air with a livid fog and turned people and their clothes reptile colours, greenish and sour brown and sallow white. Melanie and Hannah – what was their name, Quincy? – looked tubercular, their lively dark eyes dulled and their red cheeks pallid. Their mother was wearing one of her own mother's brilliant knitted creations, a sweater that probably had as many colours as a Persian carpet, a skirt of thick gathered folds on which the intricate stripes, no doubt of rich and varied shades, undulated like shadows in the wind . . . only it all looked brown and grey in that light.

Nina was her name? As Wexford asked himself that, he heard Mrs Jago call her by it and Nina Quincy, having settled her children in the back of the car, went up to her mother, put her arms round her and kissed her. Strange, Wexford thought; they see each other every day . . . Mrs Jago waved as the car departed; a shawl wrapped her shoulders today, a tapestry-like square with a fringed border. It seemed to suit her monumental shape, the heavy-featured face with its load of bunched coils of hair, better than contemporary dress. She acknowledged Wexford calmly.

'You're living up here now, they tell me.'

He nodded. 'How are the memoirs?'

'I haven't been doing much writing.' She gave him that look peculiar to people who have something to confide but don't know if this is the right confidant. Should I? Shouldn't I? Will I regret it once the words are out? 'Come in a moment and have a drink.'

A chat with a neighbour on the way home. A sherry. Why not? But it wasn't sherry she gave him, far from it. A kind of schnapps probably, Wexford thought: icy-cold, sweetish and unbelievably strong. It made his eyebrows shoot up, it made him feel as if his hair stood on end.

568

'I needed that,' she said, though there had been no alteration in her pleasant friendly manner, no gasp of relief.

The pile of manuscript was precisely where it had been when he was last in this room, a hair lying across the top of the title page. He was sure that hair had been there last time. If Mrs Jago had not been writing she had been knitting, and the jungle landscape had grown several more inches from the long curled needle, palm trees now sprouting fronds and a sky appearing. The germ of an idea pushed a shoot into his mind.

'Did Gwen Robson know you were writing this book?'

'Mrs Robson?' It sounded like a measure, if not of her indifference to her dead neighbour, of the degree of acquaintance she had had with her in life. A remoteness was implied that Wexford found himself not quite believing in. 'She was only once in this house; I don't suppose she noticed.' Wexford thought for a moment that she was going to sneer, to add that Gwen Robson wasn't the kind to read books or be interested in them. But instead she said, in such sudden contrast as to be shocking, 'My daughter and her husband have parted. "Split up" is what they say, isn't it? I hadn't any idea of it, I hadn't any warning. Nina just came in this afternoon and said their marriage was over. My son-in-law left this morning.'

'My daughter's parted from her husband too,' Wexford said.

She said, rather sharply for her but with some justice perhaps, 'That's different, though. A famous actress, rich, with a wealthy husband, always in the public eye . . .'

'Only to be expected, do you mean?'

She was too old and experienced to blush; it was more a wince she gave. 'I'm sorry, I didn't mean that. It's only that Nina's got the two girls and it's terrible for the children. And women left on their own to bring up children, they lead a miserable existence. She earns so little from her job, it's only part-time. He's leaving her the house, he'll have to support them, but – if only I could see why! I thought they were so happy.'

'Who knows what goes on in other people's marriages?' said Wexford.

Leaving her, he set off to walk up the hill. Wexford's Third

Law, he thought, ought to be: always live at the foot of a hill, then you'll be fresh for climbing it in the morning. It was quite a steep haul up and all the way he could see his new home ahead of him, glowering uncompromisingly from the crown of the hill. There was no garage, so his car stood outside with Sylvia's behind it and behind that another unidentifiable one that might be a neighbour's. The removal van had gone. He wasn't out of breath as he opened the gate (wooden in the wire fence) and walked up to the front door. I must be quite fit, he was thinking as he turned his key in the lock, opened the door and had his ears at once assaulted by the voice of Sylvia – shrill, cross, loud, easily penetrating these thin walls: 'You ought to think of Dad! You ought to think how you're putting his life in danger with your heroics!'

13

The other car must have been Sheila's, rented or else a replacement for the Porsche. Both sisters were standing up, glaring at each other along the length of the room. It was a very small room and they seemed almost to be shouting into each other's faces. There was a door into the hall and another door into the kitchen and as Wexford came in through one Dora entered by the other, accompanied by the two little boys.

Dora said, 'Stop it, stop shouting!'

But the boys were indifferent. They had come in to secure a pocket calculator (Robin) and a drawing block (Ben), and they proceeded to forage for these items in diminutive school briefcases, undeterred by the slanging match going on between their mother and their aunt. Their reaction would have been different if this had been parents quarrelling, Wexford thought.

He looked from one young woman to the other. 'What's going on?'

Sylvia's reply was to throw up her hands and cast herself into an armchair. Sheila – her face flushed and her hair looking wild and tangled, though this might have been by design – said, 'My case comes up on Tuesday week, in the magistrates' court. They want me to plead guilty.'

'Who's "they"?'

'Mother and Sylvia.'

'Excuse me,' Dora said. 'I didn't say I wanted you to do anything. I said you ought to think about it very seriously.'

'I have thought about it. I hardly think of anything else and I've discussed it with Ned exhaustively. I've discussed it

571

with him because he's a lawyer as much as ... well, my boyfriend, or whatever you call it. And it isn't doing our relationship a lot of good, to tell you the truth.'

Robin and Ben gave up the search and carried their cases outside to the kitchen. Tactfully, Ben closed the door behind him.

It was as if this freed Sylvia to speak openly and she said in a hard, unsympathetic way, 'What she does is her own business. If she wants to stand up in court and say she's not guilty, that governments are guilty for breaking international law or whatever – well, she can do that. And when she gets fined and refuses to pay the fine, she can go to prison if that's what she likes.'

Wexford interrupted her. 'Is that what you're going to do, Sheila?'

'I have to,' she said shortly. 'There's no point otherwise.'

'But it's not just her,' Sylvia continued. 'It's all the rest of us she involves. Everyone knows who she is, everyone knows she's your daughter and my sister. What's that going to do for you as a police officer, having a daughter go to prison? This is a democracy and if we want to change things we've each got a vote to do it with. Why can't she use her vote and change the government like the rest of us have to?'

Sheila said tiredly, 'That's the biggest cop-out of all. If you had a hundred votes all to yourself down in this neck of the woods you couldn't change anything, not with a sitting Member with a sixteen-thousand majority.'

'And that's not the worst,' Sylvia went on, ignoring this. 'The worst is that when those people who tried to bomb her know what she thinks, when she gets up and says it in court, they're going to have another go, aren't they? They nearly got you by accident last time and maybe this time they really will. Or maybe they'll get you on purpose – or one of my children!'

Wexford sighed. 'I've been drinking schnapps with a lady of my acquaintance.' He glanced at Dora and gave her the ghost of a wink. 'I rather wish I'd got the bottle with me.' How wrong of me it is, he thought, that I love one of my children more than the other. 'I suppose you've got to do what you've got to do, as the current phrase has it,' he said to Sheila, but as he got up and made for the kitchen door –

572

made for the beer he trusted was in the fridge – it was Sylvia on whose shoulder he laid a caressing hand.

'Not all that current, Pop,' said Sheila.

Things calmed down. At any rate, Sylvia soon left to take her sons home and cook her husband's supper. Then Sheila and her parents went out to eat, no one yet feeling comfortable in what Dora called 'this horrid little house'. Sheila talked moodily about Ned not wanting it known that someone in his position was consorting with someone in hers, though she didn't explain what his position was and Wexford, true to his principles, wouldn't ask.

'When peace is so beautiful,' Sheila said, 'and what everyone wants, why do they treat workers for peace like criminals?'

Passing the police station on their way back from the restaurant in Pomfret, Wexford saw a light on in one of the interview rooms. Of course there was no real reason to suppose that Burden was in there with Clifford Sanders, yet he did suppose it with a chilling sense of unease. Forgetting Sheila and her troubles for a moment, he thought: I shall be embarrassed when I next see Mike, I shall feel awkward and therefore shall postpone that meeting. What am I going to do?

Burden had not meant to recall Clifford to the police station. His intention had been to call off his dogs for the duration of the weekend and let his baited creature make a partial recovery. The metaphor was his wife's, not his, and he reacted with some anger to it. He now regretted discussing the case with Jenny and wished he had stuck to the principle (never much honoured in the observance) of not taking his work home.

'I've had the same sentimental rubbish at work,' he said. He would normally have said 'from Reg', but he was too angry with Wexford even to want to think of him by his Christian name. Burden had a Victorian attitude in this area, rather in the manner of those fictional heroines who called a man William while they were engaged to him and Mr Jones after they had broken it off. 'I don't understand all this sympathy with cold-blooded killers. People should try thinking of their victims for a change.'

'So you've said on numerous previous occasions,' said Jenny, not very pleasantly.

That did it. That sent him back to the police station after his dinner and Archbold to the Forby Road to fetch Clifford again. He used the other ground floor interview room this time, the one at the front where the window gave on to the High Street, where the tiles were shabby black and tan (like an ageing spaniel, said Wexford) and the table had a brown-checked top with a metal rim.

For the first time Clifford didn't wait for Burden to begin. In a resigned but not unhappy voice, he said, 'I knew you'd fetch me back again today. I sensed it. That's why I didn't start watching TV; I knew I'd only be interrupted in the middle of a programme. My mother knew too; she's been watching me, waiting for the doorbell to ring.'

'Your mother's been asking you about this too, has she, Cliff?'

Again Burden reflected how much like an overgrown schoolboy he looked. The clothes were so much the conventional wear of a correct well-ordered teenager at a grammar school in, say, the fifties, as to seem either a mockery or a disguise. The grey flannel trousers had turn-ups and were well-pressed. He wore a grey shirt – so that it could be worn two or three days without washing? – striped tie, grey hand-knitted V-necked pullover. It was plainly hand-knitted, well but not expertly, the hand of the imperfectly skilled evident in the neck border and the sewing up. Somehow Burden knew it had to be Mrs Sanders' work. He already had an idea of her as a woman of many activities, but who did none of them well; she would not care enough to do things well.

Clifford's face was its usual blank, revealing no emotion even when he spoke those surely desperate sentences. He said, 'I may as well tell you. I tell you all the truth now, I don't hide anything, I hope you believe that. I may as well tell you that she says I wouldn't be questioned like this day after day, on and on, if there wasn't something in it. She says I must be that sort of person, or you wouldn't keep getting me down here.'

'What sort of person would that be, Cliff?'

574

'Someone who would kill a woman.'

'Your mother knows you're guilty then, does she?'

Clifford said with curious pedantry, 'You can't know something that isn't true; you can only believe it or suspect it. She says that's the sort of person I am, not that she thinks I killed anyone.' Pausing, he looked sideways at Burden in what the latter thought of as a mad way, an unbalanced way. It was a sly, crafty look. 'Perhaps I am. Perhaps I am that sort of person. How would you know till you did it?'

'You tell me, Cliff. Tell me about that sort of person.'

'He would be unhappy. He'd feel threatened by everyone. He'd want to escape from the life he had into something better, but that better would only be fantasy because he wouldn't be able to escape really. Like a rat in a cage. They do these psychological experiments; they put a piece of glass outside the open door of the cage and when the rat tries to get out it can't because it bumps into the glass. Then when they take the glass away it could really get out but it won't, because it knows it gets hurt bumping itself on the invisible thing outside.'

'Is that yourself you're describing?'

Clifford nodded. 'Talking to you has helped to show me what I am. It's done more for me than Serge can.' He looked into Burden's eyes. 'You ought to be a psychotherapist yourself.' To Burden's ears it was a slightly mad laugh that he gave. 'I thought you were stupid, but now I know you're not. You're not stupid; you've opened up places in my mind for me.'

Burden wasn't sure he knew what this meant. Like most people, he didn't like being called stupid even though the term was immediately revoked. But he had a feeling that Clifford would be even franker if they were alone and so he sent Archbold away, ostensibly to fetch coffee from the canteen. Clifford was smiling again, though there was nothing pleased in that smile, nothing happy.

'Are you taping all this?' he asked.

Burden nodded.

'Good. You've shown me what I'm capable of. It's frightening. I'm not a rat and I know I can't break the invisible wall, but I can force the person who put it there to break it.' He paused and smiled, or at any rate bared his teeth.

'Dodo,' he said, 'Dodo, the big bird. Only she's not, she's a little pecking bird with claws and a beak. I'll tell you something; I wake up in the night and think what I'm capable of, what I could do, and I want to sit up and scream and yell – only I can't because I'd wake her up.'

'Yes,' said Burden, 'yes.' He didn't much care for this sudden feeling he had of being in waters that were too deep for him. He had had enough too and would have liked to send Clifford home. Not very vigorously he asked, 'What are you capable of?'

But Clifford made no answer to this. Archbold came in with the coffee and at a nod from Burden left the room again. Clifford went on, 'At my age I oughtn't to need my mother. But I do. In a lot of ways, I rely on her.'

'Go on,' said Burden.

But Clifford sidetracked, saying, 'I'd like to tell you about myself. I'd like to talk about me. Is that all right?'

For the first time Burden felt . . . not fear, he would never have admitted this was fear – but apprehensiveness perhaps, a tautening of muscles, the cautionary chill of being alone with a mad person.

However, he only said, 'Go on.'

Clifford spoke dreamily. 'When I was young – I mean really young, a little boy – we lived with my father's parents. The Sanders family had lived in our house since the late seventeen-hundreds. My grandfather died and then my father's and mother's marriage came to an end. My father just walked out on us and they were divorced and we were left with my father's mother. Mother put her into an old people's home and then she moved everything out of the house that reminded her of my father and his people; she moved all the furniture and the bed linen and the china upstairs into the attics.

'We hadn't any furniture, only mattresses on the floor and two chairs and a table. All the carpets and the comfortable chairs were upstairs, locked away. We never saw anyone, we hadn't any friends. My mother didn't want to send me to school, she was going to teach me herself at home. Dodo! Imagine! She'd been a cleaner before she got married – Dodo, the maid. She hadn't any qualifications to teach me and they caught her and at last they made her send me to school.

576

She'd walk me into Kingsmarkham every morning and come and fetch me every afternoon. It's nearly three miles. When I grumbled about walking, do you know what she said? She said she'd push me in my old pushchair. I was six! Of course I walked after that; I didn't want the others to see me in a pushchair. There was a school bus, but I didn't know I could have gone on that: she didn't want me to, it was two years before I knew I could go on it and then I did. When she wanted to punish me she didn't hit me or anything; she shut me up in the attics with that furniture.'

'All right, Cliff,' said Burden, looking at his watch, 'that'll do for now.' He realized, when Clifford was silent and got up obediently, that he had spoken as a psychotherapist might: he had spoken in the manner of Serge Olson.

A confession was what he had expected from Clifford on the previous night. That confiding manner, that unprecedented free and open way of speaking, those discomfiting references to his mother's nickname had seemed to herald it. All the time they seemed on the brink of the final revelation, the ultimate admission, but it had not come and Clifford had digressed into that account of his early youth which was the last thing Burden wanted to hear. But one good thing had resulted; he no longer felt guilt or much unease. Jenny had been wrong and Wexford had been wrong. Clifford might be mad, might well be the psychopath Burden had designated him, but he was not being terrorized or pushed over some edge or driven to desperation. He had been almost cheerful, talkative, in command of himself, and he had seemed – odd though this was – actually to enjoy their talk and look forward to more.

It must only be a matter of time now, Burden would have liked to discuss all this with Wexford. Best of all he would have liked Wexford in on his next session with Clifford, sitting there at the table, listening and occasionally putting a question of his own Burden didn't feel like an inquisitor or torturer any more, but he did feel the responsibility, that it weighed heavily on his own shoulders.

In the morning Sheila made amends.

'Sylvia wanted me to apologize in court,' she said. 'Can

you imagine? I'm to stand there and make a public retraction and say I'm sorry to a bunch of terrorists, plead guilty and promise not to do it again.'

'She didn't mean that,' Dora put in.

'I think she did. Anyway, I'm not apologizing to anyone except you and Pop. I'm sorry I made a row in your . . . new home. Especially considering I'm kind of responsible for wrecking your old one.'

She kissed them goodbye and went off to Ned and Coram Fields. Half an hour after she had gone, Sylvia rang up to apologize for what she called 'that unnecessary scene'. Perhaps she could come over and explain what she really felt about the whole Sheila-wire-cutting situation?

'All right,' Wexford said, 'but only if you'll bring me every copy of *Kim* magazine you've got in the house.'

First of all she said she was sure she hadn't any copies; then when her father told her she was like her mother and never threw anything away, she said that she only kept them for the knitting patterns. In the afternoon she turned up with a stack too heavy to be fetched out of the car at one go and Wexford himself had to make two trips to carry them. There were more than two hundred, covering a period of something like four years. He knew that nothing except Sylvia's guilty feelings would have induced her to reveal to her father such a propensity for magazine-reading – and downmarket magazine reading at that. Dora said nothing when they were brought into the small living room, but her face registered a restrained dismay as Sylvia stacked them up into a kind of tower block between the bookcase and the television table.

Her explanation and a kind of manifesto of her views on the nuclear issue and the role of public figures in civil disobedience and non-violent direct action took a long while. Wexford listened sympathetically because he knew he would have listened to Sheila, and of course he bent over backwards to be fair to the daughter he loved less. Even thinking in those terms made him feel mean and rotten. And if she was really concerned that he might get blown up again, really worried about him and his life being in danger, he ought to go down on his knees to her in gratitude for caring that much for him. So he sat there hearing it all and nodding and agreeing or gently disagreeing, trying not to acknowledge the

578

enormous relief, the leap of the heart when the doorbell rang and, looking out of the window, he saw Burden's car at the kerb. The odd thing was that he forgot all about being embarrassed.

Burden had Jenny with him and the little boy, Mark. If Sylvia's children had been girls – a comparable pair for instance with Melanie and Hannah Quincy – they would have immediately taken the two-year-old under their wing, talked to him and played with him with a precocious maternity. But being male they merely looked at him with bored indifference and, when adjured by Sylvia to show Mark their Lego, responded with, 'Do we *have* to?'

'I was going to ask you to come out for a drink,' Burden said, 'but Jenny says she won't have any of that sexist stuff.'

Sylvia said enthusiastically, 'Absolutely not! I quite agree.'

At the old house Wexford would have taken Burden into the dining room but there was no such place here, only a corner behind a strip of counter called a 'meals area'. But the kitchen, though small, had a table in it and two chairs which there was just room to sit in if you weren't overweight and were prepared to keep your elbows close to your sides. The big fridge dominated the room. Wexford took out two half-pint cans of Abbot.

'I'm sorry, Mike . . .' he was beginning as Burden simultaneously started to say, 'Look, I do regret saying those things yesterday . . .'

Their joint laughter was shamefaced as embarrassment gripped them.

'Oh, for Christ's sake,' Wexford said, nearly groaned it. 'Let's get it over with. I never meant you had psychopathic tendencies – I mean, would I say anything so daft?'

'No more than I meant that the accident had made you – well, lose your grip . . . or whatever it was I said. Why do we say these things? They just seem to come out before you think.'

They looked at each other, each one holding his green can of beer, each rejecting the actual use of the glasses Wexford had fetched from the cupboard. Burden was the first to break the eye contact which anyway had been only momentary. He looked down, busied himself with the can fastener and said in an uneven, hearty voice, 'Look, I want to talk to you about Clifford Sanders. I want to tell you everything he's told me and hear what you think. And then I want something I don't think you'll consent to do.'

'Try me.'

'To interview him with me – sit in at one of our sessions.'

'Your what?' said Wexford.

'Sorry, I mean interrogations.'

'Tell me what he's told you.'

'I could play you the tapes.'

'Not now. Just tell me.'

'He's been going on about his childhood, about that weird mother of his. He keeps calling her Dodo and laughing. I don't want to have to think him unbalanced – that is, I don't care for the idea of him getting off on the grounds of diminished responsibility – but I reckon I have to.' And then Burden told him all that had taken place at the interview of the night before, detailing what Clifford had said.

'You don't want me there,' said Wexford. 'He'll clam up if I'm there.'

'You've changed your mind, though, haven't you? You agree with me he's guilty?'

'No, I don't, Mike. Not at all. I just see that your believing it is more reasonable than I thought it was. You've no weapon that you can trace to his hand. However you may be deceiving yourself, you've no motive, and frankly I don't think you've even got opportunity. You'll never prove it; you haven't a hope unless you get him to confess.'

'That's just what I do hope for. I'm going to have another go at him on Monday.'

When they had all gone peace descended on the little house on Battle Hill, a peace however that was not entirely silent for through the thin dividing walls could be heard neighbours' noise: light-switches clicking, inane cackles of televised laughter, children's running feet, unidentifiable crashes. Wexford sat down with the new A. N. Wilson and was absorbed in it when the phone rang.

Dora went to answer it, 'If that's anyone else wanting to come and apologize, tell them I'm quite at leisure.'

But it was Sheila. He heard Dora speak her name and

heard the deep concern and shock in her voice, then he was out of that chair at a bound.

She turned to him from the receiver. 'She's all right. She didn't want us to hear it on TV first. A letter-bomb . . .'

Wexford took the phone from her.

'It was there with the rest of my post. I don't know why, but I didn't like the look of it. The police came like a shot and they took it away and did I don't know what to it and it blew up . . . !'

She started sobbing, her words no longer comprehensible, and Wexford heard a man's voice murmuring comforting things.

14

'My grandmother Sanders had some money, but she left it all to my father,' said Clifford. 'I never saw my father again. He went away when I was five; he didn't even say goodbye to me. I can remember it all quite well. He was there when I went to bed and in the morning when I woke up he was gone. My mother just said to me that my father had left us, but that I should see him quite often – that he would come to see me and take me out. But he never did come and I never saw him again. It's no wonder my mother didn't want anything about the place to remind her of him; it's no wonder she put all his family things up there in the attics.'

Involuntarily, Burden followed his glance upwards to the cracked and rather discoloured dining-room ceiling. Beyond the french windows a thin mist hung over the wintry garden, and the hill that hid the prospect of Kingsmarkham was a grey, treeless hump. It was Sunday afternoon and at a quarter-past three already growing dark. Burden had not intended to come here – had meant, as he told Wexford, to postpone any further interrogation of Clifford until the following day. But as he was finishing his lunch Clifford had phoned.

There was no reason why he shouldn't have found Burden's home number, it was there in the telephone directory for anyone to see, but Burden was astonished to get the call, astonished and encouraged. A confession was surely imminent, an intuition he had which was very much substantiated by the low, wary tone in which Clifford spoke – as if he feared being overheard – and the sudden haste with which he rang off as soon as Burden said he would come. The suspicion was inescapable that Dodo Sanders had come into the room; another word and she would have guessed what Clifford was up to and surely tried to stop him.

It was Clifford who had admitted him to the house. His mother put her head round the door of what was perhaps some kind of washroom and stared, saying nothing. Her head was swathed in a towel, obviously because she had just washed her hair in spite of visiting the hairdresser three days before. But this brought to Burden's mind what Olson had said about the fallacy of 'the veiled one'. Of course he had not meant anything of this sort, that particular veiling surely referring to hidden aspects of personality or nature. The turbanned head ducked back and the door closed. Burden looked at Clifford, whose appearance was much as usual. He wore his school uniform clothes, no concession to the casual having been made for Sunday. Yet there was a subtle change in his manner, something indefinable that Burden couldn't put his finger on. Up until yesterday, he had come into Burden's presence grudgingly or with injured outrage or even straight fear. This afternoon Clifford had admitted him to the house not as one might a friend, not that, but at least as some visitor whose call was a necessary and inevitable evil, a tax inspector perhaps. Of course it must be remembered that he had come at Clifford's personal invitation.

A fire had been lit in the dining room and it was fairly warm. Burden was sure Clifford had done this himself. He had even drawn up two of the dining chairs to the fireplace – hard upright chairs, but the best he could offer. Burden sat down and Clifford launched at once into this resumed story of his life.

'Children don't question what they live on, where the money comes from, I mean. I was a lot older when my mother told me that my father had never paid her a penny. She tried to force him to pay her through the court, but he couldn't be found; he'd just deserted her and disappeared. And he had a private income, you know; I mean he had investments of his own, just enough to live on without working. She had to go out cleaning to keep us and then she made things, sort of cottage industry things – bits she knitted and sewed. I was nearly grown-up before I knew any of this. She never told me before. I was at school while she was working and of course I never guessed.'

Burden didn't know what questions to ask, so he said nothing. He just listened, thinking of his confession, pinning faith on that. The recorder was on the dining table; Clifford had placed it there himself.

'I owe her everything,' Clifford went on. 'She sacrificed her whole life to me, wore herself out to keep me in comfort. Serge says I needn't think of it like that, that basically we all do what we want and that was what she wanted. But I don't know. I mean I do know intellectually, I know he's right, but that doesn't do away with my guilt. I feel guilty about her all the time. For example, when I left school at eighteen I could have got a job; someone I knew at school, his father actually offered me an office job, but my mother insisted on my going to university. She always wanted the best for me. Of course I got the maximum grant, but I was still a drag on her; I wasn't earning money except for a bit I got from gardening for people like Miss McPhail. When I got to Myringham University I never lived in; I came back home every night.' Clifford shifted his eyes, looking quickly into Burden's and then away. 'She can't be left alone at night, you see. Not in this house, at any rate, and she always is in this house. She hasn't anywhere else to go, has she?' He made the astounding statement with low-key carelessness, 'She's afraid of ghosts.'

Another little shiver exacerbated Burden's discomfort and he found himself nodding, murmuring, 'Yes, yes, I see.'

It was quite dark outside now. Clifford drew the brown velvet curtains, remained standing, holding the border of one of them rather too tightly and clutching it in a fist. 'I feel guilty all the time,' he said again. 'I ought to be grateful, and I am in a sort of way. I ought to love her, but I don't.' He lowered his voice, glanced at the closed door, and then, bending towards Burden said in a near-whisper, 'I hate her!'

Burden just stared at him.

'My other grandmother died, the one called Clifford,' Clifford said, sitting down once more. He smiled in a slightly contemptuous way. 'My mother's mother, that was. My mother got her furniture and the money she had in the Post Office. It wasn't much, just enough to buy a secondhand car. We got that Metro and I learned to drive. I can learn things, I'm quite good at that. Not much good at earning my living though, and I feel guilty about that too, because there's a part of me knows that I ought to be able to pay my mother back for all she did for me. I ought to – well, buy her a flat to live in where she wouldn't be afraid of the ghosts and then I could stay on alone here, couldn't I? Actually, I think I'd like that. She'd take the glass wall with her and . . .'

The door was suddenly opened and Dodo Sanders stood there in her brown clothes, flat polished lace-up shoes, the white lined face on those trim shoulders always a shock, the scarlet mouth a clown's painted gash. A fresh turban concealed her hair which under the brown-patterned scarf was perhaps done up in curlers. She looked at her son, then slowly turned her head to fix her eyes on Burden. He tried to avoid meeting those eyes but he failed.

'You're wrong if you think he killed that woman.'

Burden thought of that machine voice on his tape, wondering if it would sound more or less metallic. 'Whatever I may think, Mrs Sanders,' he said mildly, 'I'm sure I'm not wrong.'

'It's impossible,' she said. 'I should know. My instincts would know. I know all about him.'

Clifford seemed about to bury his head in his hands, but instead he sighed and said to Burden, 'Could we talk some more tomorrow?'

Burden agreed, feeling confused and helpless.

Nothing had happened to her; she was all right. The letter had been sent to 'the occupier' and perhaps had not been meant for her or indeed anyone specific – was possibly a mere wanton arbitrary missive of destruction directed at whichever tenant of the flat might have the misfortune to open it. Wexford told himself all this as he descended Battle Hill, his umbrella up against the ferocious rain of Monday morning. But he didn't believe it. Coincidence had not that long an arm.

Next week she would appear in court to be charged, he supposed, under the Criminal Damage Act of 1971, and he repeated the charge over to himself: 'That you on Thursday, 19th November, at RAF Lossington in the County of Northamptonshire, had in your custody or under your control a pair of wire-cutters and did use them without lawful excuse to damage certain property, namely the perimeter fence belonging to the Ministry of Defence . . .' Something like that. Dora was right and Sylvia and Neil were right. She had only to make a statement in court to the effect that her action had been misguided – plead guilty, pay her fine, do no more. They would leave her alone then; they would let her live. He was tempted for a moment, seeing it briefly as such a small thing, such an easy thing to do in exchange for life and happiness, remarriage, children perhaps, a glorious career. But of course she couldn't do it. He almost laughed out loud at the idea, walking down there through the rain, and suddenly felt a lot better.

It wasn't Ralph Robson who admitted him to the house, but Dita Jago. Wexford furled his dripping umbrella and left it in the porch.

Mrs Jago said: 'We came in to see if we could get anything for him while we're out.'

Nina Quincy was sitting in that cheerful but somehow comfortless room, having taken her daughters to school, and Robson was in an armchair on the opposite side of the fireplace. He had taken up the hunched, lopsided attitude arthritic people adopt to minimize suffering, one leg stretched out, one shoulder raised. But even so his owl's face was sharp with pain. Dita Jago's daughter provided a cruel contrast to him, not only young and beautiful but blooming with beauty and health. Her face, innocent of make-up, was rosily flushed and her dark eyes bright; dark chestnut hair fell below her shoulders in a mass of waves. She had something of the appearance of a healthy Jane Morris, but Rossetti would have resisted painting anyone as fit and flourishing as she. Both women wore garments of unmistakable Jago manufacture, the younger a tunic of dark chenille patterned all over with stylized crimson and blue butterflies. In a stiff, rather formal way her mother introduced her to Wexford.

She held out her hand, said unexpectedly, 'I must tell you how I admire your daughter. We loved her in that serial. Not much like you, is she?'

It was a little meagre voice to emanate from so much rich, colourful beauty and momentarily he marvelled that someone could look so intelligent yet in a couple of sentences reveal she was not. He acknowledged her comment with a small, dry shake of the head and turned to Robson.

'Your niece has gone back to London, has she?'

'She went last evening,' Robson said. 'I shall miss her; I don't know what I'll do without her.'

Dita Jago said with unexpected briskness, 'Life must go on. She's got her living to earn, she can't stay here for ever.'

'She got down to it and spring-cleaned the whole blessed house for me while she was here.'

Spring-cleaning in December? It was an activity, anyway, which Wexford had imagined must be obsolete. Hard, too, to picture the exquisitely dressed and coiffed Lesley Arbel brushing ceilings and washing paint. His raised eyebrows elicited more information from Ralph Robson.

'She said she might as well give the place a complete turn-out while she was here. Not that it needed it; Gwen kept it like a new pin, as far as I could see. But Lesley insisted; she said she didn't know when I'd get it done again and she was right there. She had all the cupboards out, and the ward-robes, went through Gwen's clothes and took them off to Oxfam. Gwen has a good winter coat – only bought it last year and I thought Lesley might have liked to keep that for herself, but maybe it wasn't smart enough for her.'

Wexford saw Nina Quincy's lips twitch, her eyes shift if not quite cast up as Robson went on, 'She even went up in the roof, but I said to leave that; I said you can't take the blessed Hoover up there. There was no need to lift up fitted carpets either. But when Lesley does a thing she does it thoroughly and the place is like a new pin, spotless. I shall miss her, I can tell you; I'll be lost without her.'

Nina Quincy got up. Her attitude, her look showed her as a woman easily and quickly bored, needing new sensations. She yawned and said, 'Shall we go if you've got that list?'

Wexford parted from the two women when they reached the gate. Again he marvelled at Mrs Jago's light, springy tread as she made for the car under the yellow and black golfing umbrella her daughter held up over them. For no reason apparent to him at that moment, he found himself thinking of Defoe who had written his *Journal of the Plague*

Year as if it were autobiography, as if he had witnessed the plague's horrors instead of being an infant at the time.

Burden was in his office, awaiting the arrival of Clifford Sanders whom Davidson had gone to fetch. Clifford had asked on the previous day if they could talk again this morning and Burden was puzzled by the request, or had been for a while after it was made. But now his hopes had rallied and his expectation of a confession was restored.

When Wexford came in he said, 'I never thought I'd see the day when the hottest suspect in a murder case started asking to help us with our enquiries.'

It was delicate ground for Wexford and he put on a look of polite interest.

'He actually wants to come here this morning. I suppose it's one way of skiving off work.'

Wexford just looked at him. 'I'll tell you an interesting thing. Lesley Arbel's been spring-cleaning Robson's house, turning out all the cupboards, been up in the roof pretending to want to vacuum-clean it, had the carpets up. What was she looking for?'

'Maybe she was just cleaning.'

'Not she. Why would she? The house was clean enough for any normal person not a fanatic already. Young girls these days aren't mad about cleaning, Mike. They don't know how to do it, or else they don't care. It would have been a different matter if she'd come down to be with Robson and found the place in a mess. Then she might have cleaned up – if she was exceptionally kind and thoughtful for her age . . . which she's not. And then there's the matter of her fingernails. Her nails were long and varnished earlier last week, but when I saw her last Friday they'd been cut short. That means she either broke a nail cleaning or thought it wiser to cut her nails before the cleaning started. And I should think she was the kind of girl who would be as proud of her long red nails as any Chinese emperor's concubine.'

'Maybe she had to cut them for the computer.'

Wexford shrugged. 'No different from a typewriter keyboard, is it? She'd been typing with long nails for years probably. No, she sacrificed her nails in order to perform the supremely generous task of cleaning her uncle's house.'

'What is it you're trying to say?'

'That she wasn't cleaning, or that the cleaning was incidental or an excuse to make to Robson. She was looking for something; she was turning the house upside down, lifting up the carpets, going up in the loft in search of something. I don't know what it was, though I've got a few ideas. I don't know if she found it, but I think the search was what brought her here and kept her here so long, not devotion to Robson. And I don't think we'll see her here again very much, either because she found what she was looking for or because she realizes she isn't going to find it. And that means it isn't in the house or that it was very cleverly hidden indeed.'

Instead of asking the obvious question, Burden said, 'We haven't searched the place ourselves. Should we?'

Wexford was hesitating when the phone rang and Burden picked up the receiver. Apparently Clifford had arrived.

'I'll have to go. What was she looking for, anyway?'

'The documentary evidence on which Gwen Robson based her blackmailing activities, of course.'

'Oh, there wasn't any of that,' Burden said breezily. 'It was all hearsay, all just what she'd heard or suspected.' He didn't wait for Wexford's reply, but went off down to the interview room on the ground floor, the one done up in shades of ancient spaniel. Rain was streaming down the window, making the glass opaque. Clifford sat at the table with a styrofoam beaker of coffee in front of him, Diana Pettit on the opposite side reading the legal page of the *Independent*. She got up and Burden gave her the sideways nod that meant to leave them with the tape recorder running. Clifford half rose and put out his hand; Burden was so surprised that he had shaken it almost before he knew what he was doing.

'Can we start?' Clifford asked eagerly.

It was difficult for Burden to handle this. For the first time in his career as a policeman he had the feeling that he had been insufficiently trained or that a branch of his training had been neglected. 'What is it you want to tell me?' he asked in a voice he knew sounded tentative and unsure.

'I'm telling you about the sort of person I am. I'm talking about my feelings.' Clifford's eyes moved and to Burden's astonishment a mischievous gleam appeared in them; it was so incongruous as to be shocking. He laughed gleefully. 'I'm trying to tell you what made me do it.'

'Do it?' Burden leaned forward across the table.

'Do what I do,' Clifford said blandly. 'Lead the life I do.' He laughed again. 'That was a joke. It was meant to make you think I was going to say "murder Mrs Robson". Sorry, it wasn't very funny.' Drawing a long breath, he made a throat-clearing sound. 'I am a prisoner. Did you know that?'

Burden said nothing. What was there to say?

'I am my own jailer, Dodo has seen to that. Why does she want that, you ask? Some are born to be jailers. It's for power. I am the first person she has really had in her power, you see – the only one. The others resisted, they got away. Shall I tell you how she met my father? My father was quite an upper class sort of person, you know; he had an uncle who was the High Sheriff of the county. I don't know what that really means, but it's very important. My grandfather was a gentleman farmer, he owned three hundred acres of land. It was all sold when my father was young so that they could keep on living in the style they were accustomed to. A lot of Kingsmarkham is actually built on my grandfather's land.'

Looking at him with mounting exasperation, Burden felt resentful at the stupid trick which Clifford had tried to play on him, pretending he was about to make a confession. And Clifford said, annoying him still further, 'Your own house, wherever that is, is probably on a bit of land that was my family's.'

Clifford drank his coffee, clasping the small beaker in both hands and affording Burden a close-up of his cruelly bitten nails. 'Dodo came to work for my father's parents as a cleaner. That surprises you, doesn't it? Not a maid – oh, no – but a daily cleaner they had to do the rough work. They had had maids, and a chauffeur, but that was before the war. After the war they had to make do with my mother. I don't know how she got my father to marry her. She says "love" but she would. I wasn't born till they'd been married two years, so it wasn't that. Once she was married, she wanted to own the place, to be the boss and the jailer.'

'How can you know that?' Burden found himself saying uncomfortably, for he was beginning to understand that

Olson had meant with his fallacy of recognizing and not recognizing.

Clifford seemed to underline this when he went on, 'I know my mother. My grandfather died; he was very old and he'd been ill a long time. As soon as the funeral was over, my father left us – the very next day it was, I can remember all that. I was five, you see. I can remember going to the funeral with my mother and my father and my grandmother. I had to go; there wasn't anyone to leave me with, it was before I started school. My mother wore a bright red hat with a little veil and a bright red coat. It was new and she'd never had it on before and when I saw her in it I thought that was what women wore to funerals – bright red. I thought it must be the correct thing because I'd never seen her in that colour before. When my grandmother came down, she was in black and I said to her, "Why aren't you in red, Grandma?" and Dodo laughed.

'Now I'm grown-up, I've sometimes thought it was wrong of my father to abandon his mother. I mean, it was wrong of him to go anyway, but doubly wrong really to leave his mother with Dodo. Of course I didn't think about that when I was a child. I never thought much about my grandmother and what her feelings were. My mother put her into an old people's home; it wasn't long after my father left, only a few days. She didn't say goodbye either, just went out and never came back. I asked my mother how she managed it – I mean, I asked years later when I was in my teens. Somebody had said how hard it was to get old people into those council homes. My mother told me about it, she was proud of it. She had a hired car come round – it was when minicabs first started – and told my grandmother they were going for a drive. When they got to this home, she took her in and just said to the matron or whoever it was that she was leaving her there and they'd have to look after her. Dodo doesn't mind what she says to people, you see; that's one of the things that gives her power. People say to her, "I've never been spoken to like that in my life" or "How dare you?" but it doesn't bother her; she just looks at them and says something else awful. She's got through the inhibition barrier, you see, the inhibition on being rude.'

'My grandmother lived another ten years, all the time in

that home and then in a geriatric ward. The social services
tried to get my mother to take her back but they couldn't
force her to, could they? She just refused to let them in the
house. But before that, as soon as the minicab brought her
back in fact, she moved all the furniture upstairs. Mr Carroll,
the farmer – he and his wife were the only people I remember
we ever saw. They weren't friends but they were people we
knew, the only people. My mother got him to help her take
all that furniture up into the attics and then when – '

'What's all this leading up to, Clifford?' Burden put in.

Clifford ignored him, or appeared to ignore him. Perhaps
he responded only to what he wanted to hear. His eyes were
on the window. The rain had slackened and the streaming
water separated into trickling droplets between which a
green-grey blur could be seen and a lowering overcast. But
perhaps he saw nothing and the sense of sight was shut.
Burden felt uncomfortable and his discomfort increased with
every sentence Clifford spoke. All the time he was expecting
some sort of climax or explosion, expecting Clifford to jump
up and begin screaming. But for the present the man on the
other side of the table seemed locked in an unnatural calm.

He went on in a lighter, more conversational tone, 'When
I was disobedient or offended her in some way, she'd lock
me up in one of those attics. Sometimes it would be the one
with all the photos in and sometimes with the beds and
mattresses. But I got to know I'd always be let out before it
got dark. She wouldn't go up there in the dark because she's
afraid of ghosts. I think the supernatural is the only thing
my mother *is* afraid of. There are bits of our garden she
won't go near after dark – well, in the daytime, too, come
to that. I used to sit in the attic looking at all those faces.'

'Faces?' repeated Burden in a hollow tone.

'In the photos,' Clifford said patiently. He was silent for
a moment and the inspiration came to Burden to do as Serge
Olson did, to take off his watch and lay it on the table in
front of him. Clifford's eyes flickered as he observed the
movement. 'I used to study the faces of my ancestors and
think to myself, all those ladies in long skirts and big hats
and all those men with dogs and guns, all of them had just
ended up in me, that's all they'd come to in the end – me.
I'd watch the light fade till I couldn't see the faces clearly

any more and when that happened I knew she'd come. When she came it would be quite slowly, taking her time, and then the door would slide open and in a nice quiet pleasant sort of way, just as if nothing had happened, she'd tell me to come down and that my tea was ready.'

Burden said wearily, picking up the watch, 'Time's up, Clifford.'

He rose obediently. 'Shall I come back this afternoon?'

'You'll hear from us.' Burden almost said, 'Don't call us, we'll call you', and then, standing alone in the room after Clifford had been taken away, asked himself with near-disbelief what he thought he was doing. Didn't he expect an admission of guilt? Wasn't that what it was all about? He went up to his own office and began looking through the reports which were the result of seemingly fruitless efforts on the part of Archbold and Marian Bayliss to find evidence of unsolved murder in Clifford's past. Both grandmothers had died natural deaths, or so it seemed. Old Mrs Sanders had died after a heart attack in the council home where her daughter-in-law had dumped her; old Mrs Clifford had been found by a neighbour dead in her bed at home. Elizabeth McPhail had died in hospital after months of incapacity caused by a stroke.

Still, he must keep on questioning him – that afternoon if necessary, and next day and the day after, every day until Clifford reached the present and finally told him in that monotonous voice that he had killed Gwen Robson.

Wexford was in the Midland Bank in Queen Street. It was four-thirty and the bank had been closed to customers for the past hour. The manager had been cooperative and answered all his questions without protest. Yes, Mr Robson had an account at the branch but no, Mrs Robson – who hadn't banked there anyway – had nothing on safe deposit. Wexford hadn't really expected it. Whatever Lesley Arbel had been searching for was hidden elsewhere – or Lesley had already found it. The manager was plainly unwilling to tell him anything about Mrs Sanders' account, also at the branch, presumably because she wasn't dead.

He came out into grey drizzle, into early dusk. The greengrocer's display looked glistening wet even though the awning was up, a sheen like dew on green leaves and citrus rind. Behind the bow window of the boutique skimpy clothes in fruit-salad colours shimmered. Into the tawny-lit warmth of the wine market Serge Olson was disappearing, passing in the doorway a man who was also known to Wexford: John Whitton, Ralph Robson's neighbour. His baby nestled fast asleep against his chest in a carrying sling; the older child, muffled to the eyes in knitted wraps and quilted nylon, grasped with a gloved hand the hem of his Barber jacket, for Whitton's arms were fully occupied with his two carrier bags of wine. He looked at Wexford without recognizing him and made for the Peugeot estate car parked at the kerb. The meter had no more than a couple of minutes to run and a traffic warden was already bearing down.

Whitton put the baby into a cot on the back seat, the wine on to the floor, and had no sooner straightened up than the crying began. The three-year-old clambered in, viewing its brother or sister with that dispassionate mild interest children often show towards a younger sibling in distress. Wexford watched because he was wondering how poor Whitton was going to extricate the car without touching the one in front or the one behind, though 'touching' was hardly the word for what had recently been done to the Peugeot; its offside headlamp had been smashed and the metal surround buckled. Nevertheless he would have turned away, knowing the dreadful irritation of being watched while one is manoeuvring a car, had Whitton – now in the driving-seat – not called out to him.

'I say, would you mind awfully telling me how near I am?'

Those people who stand in front of drivers, beckoning and holding up a warning hand – Wexford had often been exasperated by them, had long ago resolved never to join their number. It was different, though, when one was invited. The car crawled forward and he signalled to Whitton to stop when within an inch of the rear mudguard of the Mercedes in front.

'You ought to make it on the next lock,' he said as Whitton reversed.

And then Whitton did recognize him, speaking above the baby's frenetic yells: 'You came to talk to me about Mrs

Robson.' The engine stalled and he swore, made an effort, smiled. 'I shouldn't lose my cool like that. That's what happens when you do.' A thumb cocked towards the left side of the car's bonnet indicated what he meant. 'My wife had a bit of a contretemps with a parking meter here three weeks ago.'

Wexford knew Whitton was telling him this because he was a policeman, because like so many of the public he thought all policemen, whatever branch of the force they belonged to and whatever their rank, were equally preoccupied by traffic offences. In a moment he would be defending his wife lest Wexford whipped out a notebook . . .

'Mind you, she didn't so much as scratch another vehicle, which was a miracle considering the way this young fellow in a Metro got at her.'

A polite, 'Really?' and a short preamble to saying goodbye were on the tip of Wexford's tongue. Instead he said rather quickly, though knowing it was a long shot, 'When exactly was this, Mr Whitton?'

Whitton liked talking. Without being exactly garrulous, he liked a chance to talk and naturally he would, having taken over the role long assigned exclusively to women where he was locked into a daily relationship with children too young for conversation. First, however, he reached into the back of the car and picked up the baby off the back seat, its cries at once fading to whimpers. Amused, Wexford saw that he was settling down for a long, companionable talk . . . and then he wasn't amused any more, but excited.

'Three weeks ago, as I said. Well, as a matter of fact, it must have been the day Mrs Robson was killed. Yes, it was. Rosemary had the car that day and she was picking up our fruit and veg on the way home. A quarter-to-six maybe, ten-to . . . ?'

15

It was Burden's idea to have him up in his office rather than in either of the interview rooms. He couldn't stand any more of those vinyl tiles and the blank walls and the metal rim round the table. It wasn't any less warm down there than up here, but there was a sense of chill, a feeling that draughts crept in between plaster and window frame and under the unpanelled door with its corroded metal handle. So Clifford was brought upstairs and he came in as if paying a social call – smiling, hand outstretched. Burden wouldn't have been surprised if he had asked him how he was, but Clifford didn't do that.

The blinds were down and the lights were on. They were soft lights though, coming from an angled lamp on the desk, and two spots on the ceiling. Burden sat down behind the desk and Clifford in front of it, in a chair with padded seat and wooden arms which Diana Pettit pulled out for him. She was still in the room, sitting near the door, but he seemed unaware of her presence. He was wearing a different grey shirt, this one with a button-down collar, and his pullover was of a darker grey with a cable pattern but errors had been made in the knitting of the cables. Burden found himself compulsively staring at one of these flaws up near the left shoulder, where the knitter in twisting the cable had passed the rib over instead of under the work.

'I'd like you to tell me about your relations with your other grandmother,' Burden began. 'Mrs Clifford, I mean, your mother's mother. Did you see much of her?'

Instead of answering, Clifford said, 'My mother's not all bad. I've given you a bad impression of her. She's really like everyone else, a mixture of bad and good, only her Shadow's very powerful. Can I tell you a story? It's a romantic story really; my grandmother Clifford told it me.'

'Go on,' encouraged Burden.

'When my mother was a little girl they lived in Forbydean, her and her mother and father. She used to go to school past Ash Farm on her bicycle and she got to know my father, who was a bit younger. Well, they played together; they got to play together whenever they could, which was mostly in the holidays because my father was away at his prep school. When she was thirteen and my father was twelve, his parents found out about the friendship and put a stop to it. You see, they thought their son was a lot too good for my mother even to play with: they said a farm labourer's daughter wasn't good enough for their son. And my father didn't put up any sort of resistance; he agreed with them, he hadn't understood before, and when my mother came round next time he wouldn't speak to her, wouldn't even look at her. And then my grandmother came out and told my mother she must go home and not come any more.'

Burden nodded abstractedly, wondering how long all this was going to take. It wasn't an unusual story for this part of the world at that period. Similar things had happened to his own contemporaries, forbidden for reasons of social snobbery to 'play in the street'.

Clifford went on, 'I'm really telling you this to show you the good side of my mother. I said it was romantic. Later on, you see, she went to work for them and they didn't recognize the little girl they'd prevented from playing with their Charles. And *he* didn't until she told him after he'd married her. I wonder what they all thought then?'

Burden was not sufficiently interested to hazard guesses. 'Did your grandmother Clifford come to see you when you were a child? Did you visit her with your mother?'

Clifford sighed. Perhaps he would have preferred to continue his speculations about the romantic story. 'I sometimes think I spent my childhood walking. I walked through my childhood, if you know what I mean. It was the only way to get anywhere. I must have walked hundreds of miles, thousands. My mother doesn't walk that fast but I was always breathless, trying to keep up with her.'

'You walked to your grandmother's, then?'

Clifford sighed again. 'When we went, we walked. There was the bus, but my mother wouldn't pay bus fares. We didn't go to my grandmother's very much. You have to understand that my mother doesn't like people and she didn't particularly like her mother. You see, my grandfather died very suddenly, then when my father walked out and my grandmother Sanders went into a home we were left alone with the house to ourselves. I think she liked that.' He hesitated, looked down at his bitten nails, said half-slyly, 'And she likes me, so long as I'm obedient. She moulded me into a slave and a protector. She made me like Frankenstein made the monster, to go wrong.' A small shrill laugh, which might have moderated those words, somehow made them the more terrible.

Burden looked at him with a kind of uneasy impatience. He was framing a question about Mrs Sanders' mother, a wild idea coming to him of Gwen Robson possibly having once been to her as a home help, when Clifford went on: 'Once when I wouldn't do what she wanted, she locked me in the attic with the photographs and she lost the key to the room. I don't know how she lost it – she never told me, she wouldn't – but I expect she dropped it down the plughole or it fell down a crack in the floor or something. She's accident-prone, you see, because she doesn't think about what she's doing; her mind's always on something else. So I expect that's how she lost the key. She's very strong even though she's small and she tried to break down the door by putting her shoulder to it, but she couldn't. I was inside, listening to her crashing at the door. It was winter and starting to get dark and she was frightened; I know she was frightened, I could feel her fear through the door. Maybe the ghosts were creeping up the stairs after her.'

He smiled, then laughed on a high shrill note, wrinkling up his nose as if in a mixture of pleasure and pain at the memory. 'She had to go and get help. I was scared when I heard her go away, because I thought I was going to be left there for ever. It was cold and I was only a little kid, in there in the half-dark with that old furniture and all those faces. She took the bulbs out of the sockets, you see, so that I couldn't put the light on. But that meant *she* couldn't put

598

the light on either . . .' Another smile and rueful shake of the head. 'She went to get Mr Carroll and he came back with her and put his shoulder to the door and burst it open. I never got put in there again, because the door wouldn't lock after that. Mrs Carroll came with him and I remember what she said; she turned on my mother and said she'd a good mind to tell the prevention of cruelty to children people, but if she did they never did anything.

'Mrs Carroll went away six months ago. She ran away from her husband – with another man, my mother said. It was Dodo who had to tell Mr Carroll. She sort of hinted to him that there was this other man and then she told him straight out. I thought he was going to attack her but people don't attack her, or they never have yet. He broke down and sobbed and cried. Do you know what I thought? What I hoped? I thought, my father left my mother and now Mrs Carroll's left her husband. Suppose Mr Carroll was to marry Dodo? That would be the best escape, wouldn'+ it, the cleanest way to get free? I wonder if I'd be jealous, though, I wonder if I'd mind . . . ?'

He was interrupted by a tap at the door, followed by the appearance of Archbold to tell Burden that Wexford would like to see him.

'Now, do you mean?'

'He said it was urgent.'

Burden left Clifford with Diana. Perhaps it was no bad thing to take a break here. He wasn't interested in Clifford's boyhood, but he valued the mood these reminiscences seemed to bring him to, a mood of open revelation and frankness. All these stories of his youth (which was precisely how Burden saw them) would lead Clifford, though by a crazy path, to the final incriminating outburst.

Instead of taking the lift, he walked upstairs. The door to Wexford's office stood a little ajar. Wexford was nearly always to be found either behind his desk or standing at the window thinking, while apparently contemplating the High Street. But this morning he stood abstractedly looking at the plan of greater Kingsmarkham which hung on the left-hand wall. He turned his eyes as Burden came in.

'Oh, Mike . . .'

'You wanted to see me?'

'Yes. I apologize for the interruption, but perhaps you'll see it wasn't exactly an interruption, more a breaking-off. Clifford Sanders – he didn't do it, he couldn't have done. You may as well let him go.'

Hard-faced, immediate anger starting, Burden said, 'We've been through all this before.'

'No, Mike, listen. He was seen sitting in his mother's car in Queen Street at five-forty-five on November the nineteenth. A woman called Rosemary Whitton saw him; she spoke to him and he spoke to her.'

'She was trying to move her car,' Wexford said, 'and she hadn't much room, only a few inches each end to play with – '

With the sexism of the stand-up comic, but straight-faced and deadly serious, Burden interrupted him: 'Women drivers!'

'Oh, Mike, come on! Clifford was sitting in the car behind her and he had a couple of yards behind him. She asked him if he'd move and he told her to go away. "Leave me alone, go away", was what he said.'

'How does she know it was Clifford?'

'She gave me a good description. It was a red Metro. She's no fool, Mike; she's something rather high-powered, a systems analyst, though I confess I'm not sure what that is.'

'And she says it was at a quarter to six?'

'She was late, she was in a hurry. Women like her are always in a hurry – inevitably. She says she wanted to get home before the kids were put to bed at six. When she first got back into the car she looked at the clock – I always do that myself, I know what she means – and it was exactly five-forty-five. Which means it was a good few minutes after that by the time she'd had her slanging match with Clifford and crunched the headlight on a meter.'

'Is that what she did?' asked Burden ruminatively, his frown threatening a further attack on women at the wheel. 'Why didn't he tell me that?'

'Didn't notice, I daresay. She says he moved as soon as it was too late to matter.'

The woman's statement would now have to be checked,

600

thoroughly investigated, and until that had been done Burden's interrogation of Clifford must be suspended. He didn't go back to the interview room. The anger and frustration which might more naturally have been vented on Wexford he wanted to splash furiously over the man downstairs. He could have put through a phone call to his own office but couldn't face explaining to Clifford, so he sent Archbold back with the message to let him go, to tell him he wouldn't be needed again.

'Where would you hide something, Mike, if you were Gwen Robson?'

Smarting from his defeat, not yet fully grasping what the result of exonerating Clifford would be, Burden said sullenly, 'What sort of something?'

'Papers. A few sheets of paper.'

'Letters, do you mean?'

'I don't know.' Wexford said. 'Lesley Arbel was looking for papers, but I don't think she found them. They're not in the bank and they're not with Kingsmarkham Safe Depository Limited – I've just tried there.'

'How do you know Lesley Arbel didn't find them?'

'When I spoke to her on Friday she was worried and unhappy. If she'd found what she turned the house out for, she'd have been over the moon.'

'I'm wondering if Clifford could have killed his other grandmother, his mother's mother. He's a very strange character altogether. He has all the salient features of the psychopath . . . What are you laughing at?'

'Leave it, Mike,' Wexford said. 'Just leave it. And leave the psychiatry to Serge Olson.'

Burden was to remember that last remark when Olson phoned him on the following morning. He had thought of very little apart from Clifford Sanders during the intervening time and everything he had done had been concerned with this new alibi. He had even interviewed Rosemary Whitton himself and, unable to shake her conviction of the relevant time, had questioned the Queen Street greengrocer. If no one in Queen Street remembered Clifford in the Metro, a good many shopkeepers recalled Mrs Whitton hitting the meter post. The manager of the wine market remembered the time: it was before he closed at six, but not much before. He had turned the door sign to 'Closed' immediately he returned from inspecting the damage. Unconvinced but obliged at any rate temporarily to yield, Burden turned his attention from Clifford Sanders to Clifford Sanders' father . . . As a temporary measure at any rate. He wouldn't speak to Clifford Sanders again for a week, and in the meantime he would root out Charles Sanders and begin a new line of enquiry there. But before he could begin, Serge Olson phoned him.

'Mike, I think you should know that I've just had a call from Clifford cancelling his Thursday appointment and, incidentally, all further appointments with me. I asked him why and he said he had no further need of my particular kind of treatment. So there you are.'

Burden said rather cautiously, 'Why are you telling me, Mr Olson – Serge?'

'Well, you're subjecting him to some fairly heavy interrogation, aren't you? Look, this is delicate ground – for me, at any rate. He's my client. I am anxious not to, let's say, betray his confidence. But it's a serious matter when someone like Clifford abandons his therapy. Mike, Clifford needs his therapy. I'm not saying he necessarily needs what I can give him, but he needs help from someone.'

'Maybe,' said Burden, 'he's found another psychiatrist. You needn't worry about the possible effects of what you call heavy interrogation anyway. That's over, at any rate for the time being.'

'I'm glad to hear it, Mike, I'm very glad.'

Putting it into words, that he had given up questioning Clifford, put things into perspective. Burden suddenly realized how much he hated being closeted with Clifford and hearing all these revelations. He would have no more of it – not until, that is, he had another positive lead. His mind made up, he looked out of the window to where they were putting lights in the branches of the tree that grew on the edge of the police station forecourt. It wasn't a Christmas tree or even a conifer, come to that, but an ash whose only distinction was in its size. Burden watched the two men at work. Putting coloured lights in tree was his idea, later backed up by the Chief Constable, in the interest of promoting jollier relations with the public. Wexford's comment had been a derisive laugh. But surely you couldn't go on feeling antagonistic towards or afraid of or suspicious about a friendly body that hung fairylights in a tree in its front garden? This morning he felt neither jolly nor friendly, in the mood rather to snap at anyone who made jokes about the tree. Diana Pettit had already had the rough side of his tongue for suggesting that all the little lamps should be blue. When the phone rang again he picked up the receiver and said, 'Yes?' testily.

It was Clifford Sanders. 'Can I come and see you?'

'What about?' asked Burden.

'To talk.' No time was mentioned and Burden knew what Clifford was like about time. 'You made me finish early yesterday and I'd a lot more to say. I just wondered when we could start again.'

In my own good time, my lad, Burden thought. Next week maybe, next month. But what he said was, 'No, that's it. That's all. You can get back to work, get on with your life – OK?' He didn't wait for an answer, but put the phone down.

It rang again ten minutes later. By that time the younger and more intrepid of the two men had climbed to the top of the ladder and threaded the lead with bulbs on it through some of the highest branches. Burden thought how disastrous it would be, and what the media would make of it, if the man fell and got hurt. He spoke a milder 'Yes?' into the phone and got Clifford's voice suggesting in an eager, urgent tone that previously they had been cut off. Burden said that as far as he knew they hadn't been cut off. All that needed to be said had been said, hadn't it?

'I'd like to come and see you this afternoon if that's all right.'

'It's not all right,' Burden said, aware that he was back into an earlier mode of addressing Clifford – talking as if he were a child, but unable to do otherwise. 'I'm busy this afternoon.'

'I can come tomorrow morning then.'

'Clifford, I'm going to ring off now. OK, is that understood? We're not being cut off, I've finished, I can't discuss this any more. Goodbye.'

603

For some reason this second call disturbed Burden. It gave him a curious feeling very much like the one experienced by those who, having had little to do with the handicapped, are brought into unexpected contact with someone who lolls and drools and paws at them with spastic hands. Their recoil and gasp are unforgivable, are outrageous, and Burden felt a little ashamed of himself as he put the phone down sharply, as he stepped back, looking at the phone as if Clifford or something of Clifford actually lived inside the brown plastic instrument. What a fool! What was the matter with him? He lifted the receiver once more and gave instructions to the switchboard to put no more calls from Clifford Sanders through to him; furthermore, to monitor all calls that came.

It would be useless to search the house. Lesley Arbel had had two weeks in which to do that and she might be less experienced at searching than Wexford's officers were, but she had had more time and presumably a personal interest in what she was seeking – whatever that was. A will? Gwen Robson had had nothing to leave. Something that would incriminate a guilty, frightened person? Wexford couldn't imagine her blackmailing her own, surely loved, niece. And yet Lesley had been desperate to find those papers, if it was papers.

'I'll lose my job!' she had cried out to him.

It seemed quite inconsequential. At one moment he had been asking her why she had not told him she was in Kingsmarkham that Thursday; the next, she was bewailing her threatened job. He walked up the path to Mrs Jago's house and rang the bell. She came quickly to the door – large, smiling, light-footed. The smile looked a little forced but not, he thought, because he as a policeman was unwelcome.

'All alone today?' he asked.

'Nina doesn't work on Tuesday or go shopping. I saw her yesterday.' They were in the living room now, in the jungle of knitted flowers and trees, but the manuscript was no longer on the table. Dita Jago followed the direction of his eyes. 'I didn't want to see her today. I'd had enough, I didn't feel I could take any more.'

The miseries of a deserted wife, did she mean? The plaints

604

of a young woman abandoned to bring up two children on her own? He didn't enquire. He asked her where she thought Gwen Robson would have hidden whatever it was she had to hide, but as he did so he remembered how she had disclaimed all but a bare acquaintance with the dead woman. She picked up the circular needle from which the great tropical landscape hung and he saw that she had reached the sky, a blue expanse with tiny clouds. But instead of resuming her work, she sat clasping the two reinforced points of the needle in her hands. She looked at him and away.

'I knew her so little. How can I say?'

'I don't know,' he said. 'The house is the same as this one. I was thinking there might be some peculiarity, some feature of the house well known to residents but absolutely unknown to outsiders?'

'A secret panel?'

'Not exactly that.'

'Perhaps the murderer took this mysterious thing away, whatever it was. Would you like a drink?'

He shook his head rather too quickly and her eyebrows rose.

'What's become of the book?' he asked for something to say. 'You've finished it and sent it to a publisher?'

'I haven't finished it and I never will. I nearly burned it last night and then I thought – who needs emotional gestures, dramas? Just put it away in a drawer – so I did. I had such a day yesterday, it upset me so. It's a funny thing, but I'd like to tell you about it. May I? There doesn't seem to be anyone else I could tell.'

'It makes a change,' he said, 'someone wanting to tell me things.'

'I like you,' she said, and it wasn't naïve or disingenuous; it sounded simply sincere. 'I like you, but I don't really know you and you don't know me, and I doubt if we shall ever know each other much better.' A glance levelled at him seemed to ask for confirmation and he nodded. 'Maybe that's an ideal set-up for confiding.' She was silent, but her hands were still and they no longer held the needle.

'My daughter told me that she had an affair with a man – no, not an affair, not so much as that, a one-night stand, I think it's called – and she was silly enough to tell her husband about it. Not at once; she waited a long while. She should have forgotten it, put it behind her. He confessed something of his own to her, some peccadillo, and she came out with a this thing of hers and instead of being as forgiving as she was, he said that changed everything – it changed all his feelings about her.'

'Like *Tess of the d'Urbervilles*,' Wexford murmured, 'and we think times have changed. She didn't say anything of all this to you till yesterday?'

'That's right. I'd asked her if there was any hope of a reconciliation. Well, I went so far as to ask her what was the basic trouble between them. You're a parent, so you know what I mean by "went so far". They don't like questioning even when it . . . well, springs from one's real concern.'

'No,' said Wexford, 'they don't.' He considered. 'May I . . . ?' He was unusually tentative. 'Would it be possible for me . . . to read your manuscript?'

She had picked up her knitting, but now she let it fall into her lap once more. 'Why on earth. . . . ?' A sudden eagerness in her voice nearly told him he was on the wrong tack, pursuing the wrong course altogether. 'You don't know any publishers, do you?'

He did, of course. Burden's brother-in-law Amyas Ireland had become a friend over the years, but he wasn't going to encourage false hopes there. Nor to tell the whole truth at this stage. 'I'm simply curious to read it.' He observed how her attitude towards the manuscript had changed since she had taken heart from confiding in him. 'Will you let me?'

Thus it was that he found himself making his way up a hill which seemed steeper than it had the evening before, carrying what felt like ten pounds' weight of paper in one of Tesco's red plastic bags. He had planned on finishing the A. N. Wilson that evening and longed to know how it ended – but this, this was important.

It was too early yet to switch on the Christmas lights in the tree, Burden thought, only December 8. However, no one showed any signs of wanting to switch them on and to passers-by they must be invisible. The evening was dark and misty. How long was it since they had seen the sun by day or, come to that, the moon by night?

There were the usual cars on the forecourt where the lamps made everything look like an out-of-focus sepia photograph. Someone had just driven up in a Metro which could have been of any colour. It meant nothing to Burden and he took his raincoat off the hook and went down in the lift. Home early for once! His little boy would still be up, bathed and powdered, running around in pyjamas; the radio on because Jenny preferred it to television; a smell of something exotic but not too exotic, one of the few examples of foreign cuisine he liked – pesto sauce, for instance, or five spices in a stir-fry being prepared for his dinner; Jenny harassed but happy in a blue tracksuit. Burden took a yearning, sensuous delight in these things. The clutter, the pretty paraphernalia of domestic life which are the aspects of marriage many married men dislike gave him intense pleasure. He never got enough of them.

He crossed the black and white checkerboard floor of the foyer and someone got up from a chair and came over to him. It was Clifford Sanders.

Clifford said, 'I've been trying to get hold of you all the afternoon. They kept saying you were busy.'

Burden's initial reaction was to turn on Sergeant Camb who stood behind the reception counter, but as he took a step towards him he remembered he had said nothing to the sergeant, or indeed to anyone, about not admitting Clifford to the police station. It hadn't occurred to him that Clifford would actually come here. Had he the right, come to that, to exclude him? He didn't know. He didn't know if he could legally keep innocent, law-abiding members of the public out. Anger against Clifford must be kept under control.

He said stiffly, 'I was busy. I'm busy now. You must excuse me, I'm in a hurry.'

The otherwise blank, childlike, pasty face seemed to have only one expression – puzzlement. A deep bewilderment left the eyes unclouded, puckered the skin of Clifford's forehead into a concentrated frown. 'But I've got a lot to say. I've only just started; I have to talk to you.'

Not for the first time, Burden thought that if he had seen this man in the street and not known who he was, he would have thought him retarded. These were deep waters, muddied and with strange things in their depths – but was it possible to be retarded not in the body or the brain but somewhere else? In the soul, the psyche? A horribly uncomfortable feeling took hold of Burden and he seemed to shrink away from the touch of his own clothes on his skin. He could no longer look into those infant's eyes, watch the working of thick, uncontrolled lips.

'I've told you, we've nothing more to say to one another.' God, he sounded like someone ending a love affair! 'You've helped us with our enquiries, thank you very much. I assure you we shan't want you again.'

With that he escaped. He would have liked to run, but dignity forbade it, that and self-respect. He was aware as he walked with deliberately measured tread towards the swing doors that Camb was watching him curiously, that Marian Bayliss who had just come in had paused to stare and that Clifford still stood in the centre of the floor, his lips moving silently and his hands held up in front of him.

Burden opened the door and, once outside, ran to his car. The red Metro he had seen come in but whose colour the yellow lamps had altered was parked beside it. Impossible to draw any conclusion but that Clifford had done this purposely.

And as Burden switched on the ignition, he saw Clifford come out. He ran up, calling 'Mike, Mike . . . !'

Burden didn't have to back. He drove straight out through the gates.

16

'He's made a transference,' Serge Olson said. 'It's a very clearly defined example of transference.'

'I don't know what that means,' Burden said.

They were in Wexford's office, the three of them. The psychotherapist's face amid surrounding and intervening bushes of hair was like that of an extremely intelligent vole peering out from a frondy sanctuary. And the bright beady eyes had their fierce animal look. Burden had expected to go to him, but Olson had said he would come to the police station as he had no clients on a Thursday morning. Throughout the previous day Clifford Sanders had pursued his course of trying to speak to Burden. None of his phone calls had been put through but Burden was told, to his considerable dismay, that fifteen had been made. And Clifford had returned to the police station in time to repeat his intercepting tactic as Burden left for home.

But it was his presence on the forecourt this morning – the red Metro parked just inside the gates and Clifford patiently seated at the wheel – which had really rattled Burden. He had had enough. No sooner was he inside than he was on the phone to Olson, and Olson had been there within fifteen minutes.

'I'll try to explain, Mike,' he said. 'Transference is the term employed by psychoanalysts to describe an emotional attitude the subject develops towards his or her analyst. It can be positive or negative, it can be love or hate. I've often experienced it with clients – though not really with Clifford.' Burden's puzzled face seemed to give him pause and he looked at Wexford. 'I think you know what I mean, don't you, Reg?'

Wexford nodded. 'It's not a difficult concept. It seems natural when you think about it.'

'You mean he's got to like me? He's kind of come to depend on me?'

'Absolutely, Mike.'

Burden said almost wildly, 'But what did I do? What in God's name did I do to set something like this up? I only put him through a routine interrogation; I only questioned him the way I must have questioned thousands of suspects. No one ever did this before, they were only too glad to get shut of me and this place.'

Wexford was at the window. The red Metro was still down there, its bonnet a few inches from the trunk of the tree decorated with the lights. Clifford sat in the driving seat, not reading, not looking out of the window, just sitting with bent head.

'People are different,' Olson was saying. 'People are individuals, Mike. You can't say that because no one ever made the transference before, no one ever would. Were you particularly gentle with him? Paternal? I don't mean paternalistic. Sensitive in your approach?' The expression in those gleaming dark eyes rather indicated Olson's doubts of such a possibility.

'I don't think so. I don't know. I just listened, I let him talk; I thought I'd be more likely to get somewhere that way.'

'Ah.' Olson gave a reflective smile. 'Listening, letting the client talk – you did what the Freudians do. Maybe he prefers a Freudian therapist.'

Suddenly it began to rain. In straight glistening rods the rain bore down on the tarmac, the roofs of the parked cars, the roof of the Metro, hard enough to create immediate puddles. Wexford turned from the streaming glass with a quick, repudiating shake of the head.

'What's to be done then?' he asked.

'It's a good rule, Reg, not to yield to the subject's wishes. Part of his problem, you see, is the way in which he wants to fashion his world. But the world he makes isn't conducive to his happiness, to his adjustment. It doesn't tally with reality; it just looks easier to him. Do you understand that, Mike? If you see Clifford now, you'll be allowing him to make his world in the shape he wants and people it with the people he wants. For instance, because he's lost his own father he wants to put you in his world as his father. I'd say sure, do that, if it would be best for him, but I don't think it would be. It would deepen the transference and create even greater divergencies from reality.'

'Are you suggesting I simply have someone go out there and send him home?' asked Wexford. 'I don't know why but it seems . . . irresponsible.'

Olson got up. Taking no risks with the weather, he had arrived wrapped in yellow oilskins and these be fastened and zipped round himself once more, his sharp nose sticking out from under the canary-coloured hood.

'He's a very badly disturbed human being, Reg,' he said. 'You're right there. But you and Mike, you have to understand I'm a professional. You, Mike, were kind enough to call me "doctor" when we first met and though I'm not that, I have to have professional ethics. I can't go up to Clifford and tell him to come back to me. I can't go and tell him he's got his usual appointments at five today and mind not to be late. All I can do is go and get in that car beside him, sit there as his friend and try to persuade him to confront what he sees as his relationship with you and maybe get it into a more . . . reasonable perspective.'

They both watched from the window. The increasing torrent of rain made it difficult to see. Olson's figure looked like a bright yellow bird hopping and flapping its way to a dry nest. The Metro's door shut on him and once more the rain enclosed the car in walls of water like reeded glass.

'I suppose it's sound,' Wexford said, 'that stuff about not letting him create his own world, about not giving away to him. I must confess to feeling a bit apprehensive.'

'Of what?' Burden asked almost rudely.

A car driven recklessly, a fatal accident that was only partly accident, a handful of pills washed down with brandy, a rope slung over the beam of an outhouse . . . Wexford put none of this into words. He saw the Metro begin to back, sliding slowly through sheets of water and sending up jets

611

of spray. It turned and headed for the gates, Olson still inside.

'That's fixed him for a bit,' and Burden. 'Thank God for it! Now perhaps we can get on with some work.'

He shut the door rather too hard behind him. Wexford turned his back on the window and the rain and thought about the dreams he kept having of wheels spinning in space, of circles with squares inside them. Had they anything to do with the fact that the evening before and the evening before that he had been reading the manuscript of Dita Jago's concentration camp experiences? It was with him in the office today, Donaldson having come for him that morning in the car.

'Is it any good?' Dora had asked.

'I don't think I'd answer that question if anyone else had asked it. But "as an offering to conjugal unreserve", frankly, not much. As a writer, she makes a fine knitter.'

'Reg, that's unkind.'

'Not when it isn't heard outside these four flimsy walls. Who am I to judge, anyway? What do I know? I'm a policeman, not a publisher's reader. It's not for its style or atmosphere that I'm reading the thing.'

In her discreet way she hadn't asked why he was reading it, any more than she had asked why he always had his nose in *Kim* magazine. She knew better than that. He turned to where he had placed a marker between the sheets. It was at a point about half-way through and the young Dita Kowiak had begun work in the Auschwitz Krankenbau – the hospital – as an orderly. Wexford should have been moved by the description of emaciated patients, the administering of intracardiac injections of toxic substances, the hurling of naked corpses into trucks. Dita had survived because for a time at any rate the hospital workers were regularly fed, even if the diet of turnip soup and mouldy bread was inadequate. She told of Russian prisoners-of-war poisoned with Cyclon-B gas, the burning of five hundred corpses in the space of one hour. But instead of being affected, he felt only that he had heard all this before. She had no gift for delineating place or bringing a character to life. Her prose was wooden and repetitious and there was no impression of her own sufferings permeating the text. She might never have been there; she might have copied all this piecemeal from the concentration camp autobiographies which, after all, were legion. And perhaps she had . . .

Several times he had come to points in the narrative where pages were missing, but up till now those pages had always turned up later on. The lack of numbering made things difficult. Here, however, the narrative stopped abruptly in mid-sentence, in the middle of an anecdote about a doctor at the hospital called Dehring. Wexford carefully scrutinized all the remaining pages of the manuscript, but could find no further mention of Dehring's name. There was at least one page missing, perhaps two.

But would Dita Jago have let him take the manuscript if it contained – or conspiciously did not contain – something incriminating? It would have been easy to refuse. 'I couldn't bear to have anyone read it,' would have done the trick. Or when he asked where the manuscript was, she need only have said that she had sent it away to be typed or had even, as she threatened, burned it.

Whatever efforts Serge Olson had made, they failed to have any effect on Clifford Sanders. He made five phone calls to Kingsmarkham police station in the course of the afternoon, though none of these was actually put through to Burden. Next morning there was a letter for him, sent to his home. At the police station someone else might very likely have opened any missive that came, but here Burden naturally opened his own post. This brown envelope he had at first supposed to contain the bill for fitting a new carpet in the dining room.

Clifford addressed him as Mike. This was probably Olson's doing, Burden thought. The letter began 'Dear Mike'. The writing was a child's – or a teacher's – a round, neat, admirably legible hand, upright but with the slightest tendency to a backward slope. 'Dear Mike, I have a lot I want to say to you and I think you would be interested to hear it. I know you want me to think of you as my friend, and that is how I do think of you. In fact, I don't find it easy to confide in people, but you are an exception to this rule. We really get on well together, as I am sure you will agree.'

Here Burden laid down the letter for a moment and sighed. 'I do understand that other people, those in authority over you I mean, are doing everything in their power to stop our meeting, and I expect you feel threatened with the loss of your job. Therefore I suggest we arrange to met outside your working hours. Even employers like the police surely cannot object to their officers having their own personal friends. I will phone you tomorrow . . .' Burden noticed that he mentioned no precise hour and recalled what Olson had said about Clifford's attitude towards time. 'Please tell them you expect a call from me so that if you are out they can take a message. My idea is to call on you at your house this evening perhaps or during the weekend. With best wishes. Yours ever, Cliff.'

Burden's little boy had climbed on to his lap and he stroked his hair, held him close for a moment. Suppose his Mark should grow up into such a one? How could you tell? Clifford had looked like this once, been as endearing, inspired perhaps the same breath-catching love. Only I shan't walk out on him when he's five, thought Burden. But when he tried to summon up pity for Clifford, he failed and felt only exasperation.

'I'm taking no calls from this man,' he said when he got to the police station, 'and I'd like him to be told that no message he leaves will reach me. Right?'

After that he concentrated on the quest of the moment, finding the whereabouts of Charles Sanders. If Sanders had never paid maintenance to the wife he had deserted and she, presumably, had been too proud to ask for it, he could not be traced through the courts or social services. It wasn't an uncommon combination of names. Telephone directories and electrol registers yielded a number for Archbold, Davidson, Marian Bayliss and Diana Pettit to call on, and Archbold had run to earth a likely-sounding Charles Sanders in Manchester. Burden had plans to go up there and see him, though he wanted to get the man on the phone first, and as yet he hadn't even managed to hear the sound of his voice. Engaged signals alternated with ringing tones as if Sanders unplugged his phone between answering calls. However, he never answered Burden's.

Later in the morning when he saw the red Metro come on to the forecourt, Burden had to suppress a feeling that was not too far from panic. He was being hounded, persecuted. The anxious fears which had been building up inside him had the effect which such an accumulation sometimes does, that of heightening the powers of his imagination. He found himself envisaging a future in which Clifford Sanders dogged his footsteps, in which every time he lifted a phone receiver he heard Clifford's voice at the other end of the line, in which – worst of all – when he looked in a mirror he saw Clifford's face over his shoulder. You are a hardened, tough police officer, he told himself fiercely. Why do you let this boy shake you? Why are you rattled by it? You can keep him off, others will keep him off. Calm yourself. Ignorant as he acknowledged himself to be of the workings of the psyche, he nevertheless recognized the evidences of paranoia in Clifford's letter and now he saw them in himself. And then he recalled the precise moment when he had first recognized Clifford's madness.

A memory came to him of something he had been told by his historian wife: how going to look at the mad people in Bedlam was as popular a pastime in the late eighteenth century as safari park visiting was today. How could they? His instinct was to put himself as far from the mad as he could, to pretend they didn't exist, to build walls between them and him. Yet Clifford wasn't mad in a padded cell, straitjacket way; he was only disturbed, deprived, lonely, his thought processes somehow askew. Burden picked up the phone, arranged for Sergeant Martin to go out there and tell Clifford to leave, to tell him he was trespassing or something.

He wondered if Wexford had seen him and felt a sudden need to talk to Wexford about it, to be franker on the subject of his feelings in respect of Clifford than he had been up to now. But as he was going down, had got so far as entering the lift, he remembered that Wexford – for some mysterious reason of his own – had gone to the Barringdean Shopping Centre. Burden thought he would like a drink or even a Valium, though he hated the things and feared them. Instead he sat at his desk and briefly put his head in his hands.

The sandwich, according to the claims of Grub 'n' Grains, was 'American style', pastrami and cream cheese on rye. If he hadn't been told that it was pastrami, which he had never tasted before, Wexford would have sworn he was eating corned beef of the well-known Fray Bentos type. He had been doing a bit of crime reconstruction, mostly in his head, but the true scene of the crime seemed the right place in which to do it.

The fountain played in the left-hand concourse, its jets of spray concealing the ascending and descending escalators and the entrance to British Home Stores. But opposite him Wexford could see the several clothes shops and between them and Boots the Chemist the wools and crafts shop called Knits 'n' Kits. Next door to the café was December with its bakery adjacent, then a travel agent, then W. H. Smith. Wexford drank his tropical fruit cocktail, paid for his lunch and made his way up to Demeter.

The health foods store kept its herbal remedies on shelves immediately to the left of the window and Wexford soon found the calendula capsules. It was these which Helen Brook had been looking for when she saw Gwen Robson outside in the aisle between the shops in conversation with a very well-dressed girl. And here she had been taken with the first of those early labour pains which prevented her from going up to Mrs Robson and speaking to her. Wexford bent down, took a jar of capsules from the shelf and dropped it into his wire basket. Then he straightened up and looked out of the window. Boots the Chemist could be seen and, this side of it, the wools and crafts shop, with the Mandala – circles of chrysanthemums and cherry-fruited solanum today – cutting off sight of the entrances to Tesco. Gwen Robson had shopped in Boots, bought her toothpaste and talcum powder, paused to look at the Mandala flowers perhaps, and there encountered the girl Helen Brook had seen her speaking to. It must have been Lesley Arbel, Wexford thought, who – perhaps having time to spare before the departure of the London train – had come in here specifically to meet her aunt. He imagined a conversation, surprise expressed by Mrs Robson, a brief explanation from Lesley about the word-processing course, a promise perhaps that she would see her aunt on the following night. Or had it all been more sinister?

It must have been on this side of the Mandala that they had stood, for Helen Brook to have seen them. And somehow Wexford knew that if the girl were Lesley she would not have been looking at flowers but, even while talking to her aunt, would have had her eyes fixed on those shop windows to the left of her with their window displays of clothes and shoes. He looked at them himself, at the space Dora's sweater had occupied which was now filled by an extraordinary red and black frilled corselette; on to the next window which was a medley of red and black and green and white shoes and boots, to the window of Knits 'n' Kits. Here a loom with a half-completed piece of work on it — a wall-hanging or rug — predominated. He thought inescapably of Dita Jago. Did she use this shop? Making his way to the door with the basket over his arm, his thoughts miles away from herbal remedies and packets of nuts, he was jolted to attention by an indignant voice.

'Excuse me, but you haven't paid for your tablets!'

Wexford grinned. That would be a fine thing, a turn-up for the book, a detective chief inspector getting done for shoplifting. As bad as, or worse than, his daughter going to prison. But he didn't want to think about that, he wouldn't think of it. Under the resentful gaze of the shop assistant, he replaced the calendula capsules on the shelf, leaving the wire basket on the floor.

It had been there in his mind, lying under a level of consciousness, for days now . . . well weeks. Gwen Robson had been dead three weeks. It drew him to that window. Of course he had already dimly glimpsed it, half-noticing it as he came into Demeter. The pairs of knitting needles were hung in a sort of zig-zag pattern all down the right-hand side of the window, hanks of wool on the left and the loom with its half-completed achievement in between. But they weren't, strictly speaking, all pairs. Wexford went in. Better not attack the window display, he thought, not yet.

Men didn't come in here much. There were two women at the counter, one leafing through a book of patterns. Wexford found a metal stand, the kind of thing that used to be called a 'tree', with packets of needles hung all over it. He unhooked the one he wanted. Lesley Arbel might have come in here before she met her aunt. Why not? She would have known the shop was here and known what she wanted. Dita Jago too, seeking only a replacement perhaps and later finding another use . . .

With a sharp tug he pulled the circular knitting needle out of its plastic pack and held it up as one might hold a divining rod, each hand clasping the thick metal pins at each end, the long wire hanging slack between and then pulled taut. Wire and pins were coated in a pale grey plastic substance. His eye caught sight of the obvious victim to experiment on – a torso in styrofoam wearing a lilac lacy jumper, with an extravagantly elongated neck on which the head was poised at an unnatural angle. Approaching it with the garrote at the ready, he was aware of a hush in the shop, then of the three pairs of eyes fixed on him and following his moves.

Hastily, he replaced the circular needle in its packet. He had found his weapon.

17

Clifford Sanders came to Burden's house at nine in the evening. It was no surprise to Burden; he had been expecting this from the moment he got home and thinking of various ways to handle it so as to avoid a confrontation. He considered getting his wife to answer the door or asking his elder son John, who had come to eat supper with them, to answer it; he thought of taking the whole family, including little Mark, out to eat. In a wild moment he even had an idea of going away for the night, booking a room in an hotel. But when the time came, he answered the door himself.

It was the first time for days that he had actually faced Clifford and spoken to him. Clifford wore a raincoat, navy blue, very like a policeman's. His face was pale, but that might have been due to the light from over head in the porch. Behind him hung a thin greenish fog. He put out his hand.

Burden didn't take it but said, 'I'm sorry you've come all this way for nothing, but I have explained I've no more questions to ask you at present.'

'Please let me talk to you.'

The foot in the door – Clifford had taken a step forward, but Burden planted himself firmly between door and architrave. 'I have to insist you understand you can give us no more help with our enquiries. It's over. Thank you for your help, but there's nothing more you can do.' Every parent knows the expression on a child's face just before it cries: the swelling of tissues, the seeming collapse of muscles, the trembling. Burden couldn't bear it, but he couldn't cope with it either. 'I'll say good night, then,' he said absurdly. 'Good night.' And stepping back, he closed the door hard.

Retreating across the hall, standing and listening, he waited for Clifford to ring the bell. He was bound to do that – or try the knocker. Nothing happened. Burden was sweating; he felt a trickle of sweat run down his forehead and one side of his nose. Mark was in bed, Jenny and John still in the dining room at the back of the house. Burden went into the living room which was in darkness, made his way stealthily to the window and looked out. The red Metro was parked at the kerb and Clifford was sitting in the driving-seat in that accustomed pose of his, the way he perhaps passed several hours of each day. Burden was still standing there watching when the phone rang. He answered it in the dark, still looking out of the window.

It was Dorothy Sanders.

Burden was obliged to recognize the voice, for she did not identify herself or ask if she were speaking to Inspector Burden. 'Are you going to arrest my son?'

In other circumstances Burden would have made some discreet and non-committal reply. Now he was beyond that. 'No, Mrs Sanders, I'm not. There's no question of that.' A mean, despicable kind of hope took hold of him that he could get this woman on his side, enlist her aid even. But he only said, 'I don't want to see him, I've no more enquiries to make of him.'

'Then why do you keep getting him down there? Why don't you leave him alone? He's never here, I never see him. His place is at home with me.'

'I quite agree,' said Burden. 'I couldn't agree more.' As he spoke the car door opened, Clifford got out and once more came up the path towards the house. The bell ringing made a searing sound in Burden's ears, almost pain. He found himself gripping the phone receiver in a wet palm as the doorbell rang again. 'He'll be back home with you in ten minutes,' he said, screwing up his nerve, feeling anger bring a fresh flood of sweat.

'I can complain to the proper authorities, you know. I can complain to the Chief Constable – and I will.' Her tone changed and she said in a slow deliberate way, pausing between the words, 'He didn't do anything to that woman. He didn't know her and he hasn't anything to tell you.'

'Then you'd better lock him up, Mrs Sanders,' Burden said

indiscreetly. He put the receiver back, heard John go to the door, a murmured exchange and then John, who had been primed, said firmly, 'Good night.'

In the dark there, Burden thought wildly of an injunction to restrain Clifford from persecuting him, of seeking out a judge in chambers, of arresting and imprisoning Clifford when he broke the order. He heard the Metro door close and listened, holding his breath, for the engine to start up. The silence seemed to endure a long time and the eventual sound of the motor turning and firing was a glorious relief. Burden didn't watch the departure of the Metro but when next he looked out of the window it was gone, the street empty, the fog thick and still and opaque as muddy water.

Returning the manuscript, he asked about the missing pages, but there were no guilty reactions and no evasions.

'I realized as soon as you'd gone,' Dita Jago said. 'I took two pages out to check something on them at the public library.' She looked at him steadily – too steadily? 'You remember I told you I was at the library on the day Mrs Robson was killed? I was checking up something about a man called Dehring.' She didn't ask if he had enjoyed reading the manuscript or what his impression was, commenting only, 'You read that far!'

While she was out of the room fetching the pages, he examined quickly the circular needle from which the great wall hanging depended. The pins at each end of the wire were of a much finer gauge than the one he had handled in the Barringdean Centre and would not have stood up to excessive pressure. But that meant nothing. Mrs Jago would have other circular needles, probably in every available size. He glanced at the sheets of paper she showed him, noting corrections made in red ballpoint. She made no comment on his interest, but as he walked down the path and glanced back he saw her watching him from the window, her expression one of benign mystification.

Ralph Robson was cleaning his car, a popular Saturday afternoon pastime at Highlands. Out here he managed without his stick, holding on to the bodywork of the car for support. Wexford said good afternoon to him and suggested that the task on which he was engaged was not perhaps the wisest activity for someone in his condition.

'Who's going to do it if I don't?' Robson said belligerently. 'Who's going to give me a helping hand? Oh, it's one thing when anything like that first happens. They're all coming round. Can I do this and can I do that? That soon cools off. Even Lesley. You wouldn't credit it, would you, but I haven't seen Lesley for a whole blessed week. She hasn't so much as phoned.'

Nor will she, Wexford thought. You've seen the last of her. She either got what she wanted or knows there's nothing in it for her.

'There's one bright spot though.' Robson winced as he straightened up from rinsing out his cloth in the bucket of water. 'I'm getting my hip done. Doctor's transferring me to another what they call health area the week after next. Sunderland. I'll be getting my replacement up in Sunderland.'

The Saab passed Wexford as he began the climb up the hill, passed him and drew into the kerb ahead. His thoughts had shifted, as they mostly did these days, from the Robson case to Sheila. She was coming to stay the night; it was years since they had seen so much of her as they had in these past few weeks, and inevitably he speculated as to why this was. Because she understood and sympathized with his anxieties for her safety? Or because she was sorry for her parents having to live in this poky, uncomfortable little house? A bit of both, maybe. She got out of the passenger side of the Saab and his heart leapt with the usual old relief.

'Pop, this is Ned.'

The man in the driving-seat was young, dark, distinguished-looking. Wexford knew at once that he had seen him somewhere before. They shook hands over the seats and Wexford got into the back of the car.

'Ned's not staying, he's on his way to Brighton. He's just going to drop me off.'

'That sounds like an early warning in case we start evincing our well-known lack of hospitality.'

Ned laughed, and there was a bit of an edge to the sound. Because Wexford had said 'early warning' which had another, quite separate, significance?

'Oh, Pop,' said Sheila, 'I didn't mean that.'

622

'At least I hope he'll stay for a cup of tea,' Dora said when they reached the house.

'Of course I will. I'd like to.'

They had rather taken it for granted that with both daughters married all this sort of thing would be over. There would be no more suitors brought home, the sight of whom aroused dismay or resignation or hope. Sylvia indeed had married so young that before Neil there had been no more than a couple of casual boyfriends. But Sheila's men had come in a constantly changing series until at last the chosen one, Andrew Thorverton, had surely put an end to this parade. Or so it had seemed to those naïve parents who, because of their age, inevitably regarded marriage – at any rate in their own family – as an institution of permanence. Was this Ned a prospective second husband? Sheila seemed to treat him in a rather cavalier fashion.

He was gone on his way to Brighton before Wexford found out his surname. She could go back on the train; he wasn't to trouble himself about her – that was Sheila's airy parting shot as she and her father stood in the flowerbed sized front garden watching him go.

'Nice car,' Wexford said tactfully.

'Well, I suppose. It's always having to have things done to it. I mean, that last weekend you were in the old house and I came down, it was in being seen to. I offered to lend him mine as a matter of fact, but considering what happened it was just as well he hired a car instead.'

They went back into the house. With the coming of early dusk the fog was returning. Wexford closed the front door on the dank chill outside. 'I've seen him somewhere, him or his picture.'

'Of course you have, Pop. His photograph was all over the papers when he was prosecuting those Arab terrorists.'

'Do you mean to say he's Edmund Hope? You're "Ned" is Edmund Hope the barrister?'

'Of course he is. I thought you knew.'

'I don't quite know how you could have thought we knew,' said Dora, 'considering you never introduced him. "This is Ned" doesn't convey much information.'

Sheila shrugged her shoulders. Her hair was tied back in a ponytail with a length of red ribbon. 'He's not "my" Ned.

We're not together any more – just friends, as they say. We actually lived together for four whole days.' Her laugh had a hint of bitterness in it. 'It's all very well these brave statements: "I don't agree with what you say, but I'd die for your right to say it". That sort of thing doesn't amount to much when it comes to the crunch. He's like the rest of you – well, not Dad – who don't want to know me if I go to jail.'

'That's not fair, Sheila. That's very unkind and unjust. I'll never not want to know you.'

'I'm sorry, Mother – not you either, then. But Ned didn't even want other people to know he knew me. And I went along with it – can you imagine?' She came up to Wexford, who had been silent and staring. 'Pop . . . ?' Her arms were on his shoulders, her face lifted up to his. She had always been uninhibited, demonstrative, a 'touching' person. 'Is this nasty house haunted? Have you seen a ghost?'

'You actually offered to lend Edmund Hope your car for the weekend while he was in the middle of prosecuting those terrorists?'

'Don't be cross, Pop. Why not?' She made a face at him, lips protruding, nose wrinkled up.

'I'm not cross. Tell me the circumstances. Tell me exactly when and how you offered to lend him the Porsche.'

Extreme surprise made her step back and hold out actressy hands in a wide sweep. 'Goodness, I'm glad I'm not one of your criminals! Well, he'd stayed the night and when he tried to start his car in the morning it wouldn't start, so I drove him to court – the Old Bailey it was. And before I dropped him I said he could borrow my car if he wanted.'

'Could anyone have heard you say it?'

'Oh, yes, I expect so. He was standing on the pavement and I called it out after him; it was a sort of afterthought. I said something like, "You can have this car for the weekend if you like", because I knew he was supposed to be staying with some friends in Wales, and he called back thanks and he'd take me up on that. Only after that I remembered I'd said I'd come down here, and I was quite glad when he rang up in the evening and said his own car would be ready in the morning.' Realization came to her quite suddenly and drained the colour from her face. The white stood out round the blue irises of her eyes. 'Oh, Pop, why did I never think of that? Oh God, how awful!'

'The bomb was meant for him,' Wexford said.

'And the letter bomb too? That was during our – er, four-day honeymoon.'

'I think we'd better tell someone, don't you?' He picked up the phone, feeling an unlooked-for, absurd happiness.

The night had passed without disturbance or dreams. Burden lay awake for a long time thinking about Charles Sanders One – the Manchester one, who had eventually answered his phone and turned out to be twenty-seven years old – and Charles Sanders Two, from Portsmouth, with children of Clifford's age, a young wife and an Australian accent. But his mind was not fraught with anxieties and soon he slept heavily and uninterruptedly. The dense fog which enveloped town and countryside brought its own kind of silence, the muffled sensation less of there being no sound to hear than of deafness. Jenny was up and Mark was up on Sunday morning before he awoke to see the bedroom curtains drawn back and a fluffy whiteness pressing against the window-panes. It was the phone ringing which had awakened him and in spite of his peaceful night, the first possible caller that occurred to him was Clifford.

Jenny must have answered it on the other phone, for the ringing stopped. Burden picked up the receiver at his bedside and to his enormous relief heard Wexford's voice. It was Wexford wanting to tell him the solution to the bomb puzzle; wanting also to come round later in the day with another solution, the answer to the mystery of the weapon Gwen Robson's killer had used. Burden said nothing about Clifford or Clifford's mother's phone call. That could wait till later, till he saw Wexford – or perhaps might never need to be told.

The morning passed with no more phone calls and no more visits. There was usually considerable traffic in Tabard Road, which was a through road, but today it was quiet, the fog keeping people at home. Was it also keeping Clifford at home, or was there another reason for his absence? Burden wondered how much his mother's power and influence over him would enable her, at her level of necessarily far less physical strength, to be his jailer.

The fog did not dissipate as it had on the preceding days, but seemed to thicken as afternoon came on. His sister-in-law Grace and her husband came to lunch, also Jenny's brother. Burden thought how awkward it would have been if the red Metro had arrived and Clifford presented himself once more at the front door, but nothing like that happened. His guests went at about four, when the fog darkened and the yellow gleams of streetlights faintly penetrated it. None of them lived far away and they had all come on foot. Watching the departure from the front window, he saw Amyas encounter Wexford just outside the gate. This was about as far as it was possible to see, and even so the figures of the two men seemed as if swathed in lightly swaying pennants of gauze.

'It was a huge relief,' Wexford said, taking off his coat in the hall. 'Yet when you come to think of it, what does that amount to? Aren't I really saying I'm glad it's someone else's child and not mine that's threatened? There but for the grace of God, in fact – which is only another way of saying, "I'm all right, Jack". '

'Edmund Hope may be all right too. It's likely they've found another target by this time. After all, it's more than three weeks ago.'

'Yes, and more than three weeks since Gwen Robson's death. How's this for a garrote, Mike?' Wexford drew from his pocket the circular needle he had bought at the Barringdean Centre; the pins at each end were a quarter of an inch in diameter, forming tough, strong handles to hold on to. 'You're the plastics expert,' he said. 'Would this be the right sort of stuff?'

'It's the right colour. I should say it's pretty obvious a thing like this was used. Does that necessarily make it a woman who used it?'

They went into Burden's living room, where a fire had been lighted; the blaze from it lit the room with flickering yellow. Burden put up the fireguard in case Mark came in.

'This was a premeditated crime,' Wexford said, 'only in the sense, I believe, that the perpetrator had had an idea of killing for some time and was waiting only for opportunity.

626

But I don't think he or she went into that car park with the weapon at the ready. It's more likely it had just been brought in the shop where I got this one, and that means the prospective user might have bought it or someone else purchased it *for* the prospective user. In other words, it was on a shopping list, so the purchaser could have been a man or a woman.'

'And he or she,' Burden went on, 'came up into the car park looking at it perhaps? I mean, perhaps it came loose from its packaging and the purchaser was curling it up and replacing it?'

'Or the purchaser, who wasn't the prospective user and maybe had never seen such a thing before, was fascinated by such a peculiar thing. It *is* a peculiar-looking thing, Mike. The purchaser might have just been standing there unwinding it and looking at it when Mrs Robson came along.'

A car drew up outside. Its progress sounded slow, as it would necessarily have had to be in the dense fog. Burden jumped up a bit too quickly and went to the window – not Clifford, but Burden's next-door neighbour whom he could see getting out to open his garage drive gates.

'It's not too early to draw the curtains, is it?'

'I didn't know there was any prescribed time for it,' Wexford said, eyeing him speculatively.

'It seems a pity to lose the last of the light.'

The impenetrable greyness outside made nonsense of this remark. It was now impossible to see across the street, in fact to see much beyond the pavement and kerb on this side. Burden pulled the curtains across the window and was switching on a table lamp when the phone rang. He gave a nervous start which he knew Wexford had seen.

'Hallo?'

His mother-in-law's voice and his wife's intermingled as Jenny picked up the bedroom extension. He couldn't control the little gasp of relief. Wexford said with quick intuition, 'Has Clifford Sanders been hounding you?'

Burden nodded. 'I think it's stopped though. He hasn't phoned or been here all day.'

'Been here?'

'Oh, yes. He was here last night, came to the door twice, but I do think it's over now. Anyway,' Burden lied, 'it's not important, it's not a problem. Your Mrs Jago – do you see her as . . . ?'

Instead of answering directly, Wexford said, 'Dita Jago might very well have been one of Gwen Robson's blackmailees. She had the means to kill her. Of everyone in this case, she was the most likely to have been buying a circular knitting needle in the shopping centre that afternoon. On the other hand, she says she was in the public library, the central branch in the High Street, with her grand-daughters. I jib a bit at asking those two little girls to alibi or not alibi the grandmother they're obviously fond of; I won't do it if I can avoid it, but . . .

'Anyway, the papers Lesley Arbel was looking for – and ransacked or spring-cleaned her uncle's house in the process of so doing – weren't sheets from Dita Jago's manuscript. They were photocopies of letters.'

Burden said, 'Do you mean letters Gwen Robson took or borrowed from the homes of her clients? Incriminating letters she then had copied?'

'Not quite, her niece got these letters for her. It was Lesley Arbel who made the copies to show to her aunt. Not because she thought they could be used for any criminal purpose, certainly not that, but to amuse her, I think – to entertain someone who loved gossip and took the same kind of pleasure in sexual irregularities as some of our Sunday newspapers do – gloating over matters that ostensibly they deplore.'

'Are you talking about letters to the agony aunt?'

'Of course. Lesley Arbel had easy access to them and a photocopier in the office where she worked. Some of the letters would appear in *Kim* – my God, Mike, the amount of *Kim* I've grubbed through in the past week – but most wouldn't and some, even in these days of licence, would be considered unfit for publication. And even though there's an unwritten law in the agony aunt's department that staff preserve discretion – lip service to a kind of poor woman's Official Secrets Act – it must have seemed harmless enough, what she was doing. None of it would go beyond the four walls of the house in Hastings Road . . . What is it, Mike? What's wrong?'

Burden had jumped up and stood with head lifted. 'Did you hear a car?'

Drily Wexford said, 'I hear a car every minute of my life when I'm not asleep. How do you escape it in this world?'

The door opened and Mark came in, followed by his mother. But Burden continued to stand transfixed, only holding out an absent hand to the child. Mark wasn't shy; he went up to Wexford, wanting the pencil he held in his hand, then the pad on which notes had been made, finally climbing on to Wexford's knees. Burden went to the window and parted the curtains with both hands. His knuckles had whitened and his shoulders drooped a little.

'Oh, not again?' Jenny said. 'He's not back again?'

'I'm afraid he is.' Burden turned back into the room and faced Wexford. 'Am I overreacting when I say I'm seriously thinking of applying for an injunction?'

Instead of answering directly, Wexford said, 'Let me go.' He lifted the little boy on to the floor, sacrificed pad and pencil to him. 'Don't get it on the carpet, or your Mum'll be after me.'

As he came out into the hall, the bell rang. Wexford let it ring again. Burden had joined him, was standing just behind him. The letter-box lid started flapping as fingers pushed at it and then the other hand pounded on the knocker. The fingers appeared under the opened letter-box lid and there was something about them and the smear marks they left on pale paintwork that made Burden draw in his breath with a rough hiss. Wexford crossed the hall and opened the door.

Clifford took a step back when he saw him. He was looking beyond Wexford's bulk and when he saw Burden he smiled. Wexford eyed him in a kind of stricken silence, for Clifford was covered with blood. His grey shirt and knitted pullover and the zipper-jacket he wore, his grey flannel trousers, his striped tie and grey socks and lace-up shoes – all were thick with blood, matted and plastered with it, and in places the blood was damp still, glistening still. And Clifford, smiling, stepped over the threshold into the hall with no one to impede him until the little boy came out of the living room, and Burden, sweeping him up in his arms, shouted, 'Don't let him see. For God's sake, don't let him see!'

18

The driving-seat of his mother's car which had always been
a curious place of refuge for Clifford, a sanctuary and scene
of unimaginable cogitations, was bloodied from his clothes.
Easy to make an analogy here with wombs, but Wexford
shied away from that one. Though it was dark and foggy,
he had the seat of the car and the blood-encrusted steering
wheel covered up before it was towed away. Now they sat
in the first of a convoy of police vehicles, Clifford between
him and Burden, crawling through the fog. Donaldson's
headlights made two green bars of radiance that petered out
into the wool-like greyness after a few feet. Behind them
another driver clung to Donaldson's rear lights and a third
followed, all moving at about fifteen miles an hour.

Clifford had Burden to himself now, a captive therapist,
and his face wore an expression that was at the same time
serene and insane. At appalling cost he had got what he
wanted. He talked. He spoke uninterruptedly, sometimes
lifting up his bloody hands which had smeared Burden's door
with stains, the bitten nails blackened with blood, turning
them over and looking at them with wondering pleasure.
Already he had told Burden what he had done and – insofar
as his conscious mind understood this – why he had done
it. But he repeated himself as if he enjoyed the sound of his
own monotonous, now measured and almost complacent
voice.

'She sent me up into the attic, Mike. She thought she could
shut me in like she did when I was little. I was to go up there
and fetch her down a lamp. The one in the dining room had
got broken, there was a fault in the connection, and she said

to fetch her one of the lamps that had belonged to my grandparents. But I'm cunning, Mike, I'm cleverer than she is basically, I've got a better brain. I knew she would rather sit in the dark than use anything from up there. She wouldn't use a lamp my father's mother had used.'

Burden was returning his gaze with what looked like blankness unless you knew Burden as Wexford did and then you understood it was controlled desperation.

'The truth was she wanted to keep me from seeing you. When she told me she'd phoned you to complain about our seeing each other – when she told me that, I saw red. But I didn't show my feelings, I kept everything suppressed, I didn't even answer her. I went upstairs like an obedient little boy. Of course I couldn't be sure what she was up to then; I wondered what she was at. I knew she was following me up, though, and I said to myself, why is she following me when she's asked me to fetch her something? If she's going to come up too, why couldn't she have fetched it herself?'

Forcing the words out in a voice that sounded unlike his own, Burden said, 'So what . . . what did you do, Clifford?' He had already cautioned him. It had been a bizarre ritual taking place in the hall of Burden's own house, Clifford pleasurably pointing out individual blood-stains on his jacket, his shirt, his trousers, beginning on a confession whose utterance held a childlike innocence, while Burden mouthed in that same strangled tone the words of the caution: 'You are not obliged to say anything in answer to the charge but anything you do say . . .'

Now Clifford continued in the same blithe, confiding way, 'It wasn't the attic where Mr Carroll had to break the door down. We'd never had that door mended. The photographs were in there. It was the one with the bedroom furniture.' He brought his face closer to Burden's – said in an intimate way, as to one familiar with the secrets of all hearts, 'You know what I mean.'

Donaldson braked hard as they came suddenly up against the headlights of a huge truck. It was carrying earth-moving equipment, cranes and scoops that loomed dinosaur-like out of the rolling mist. Slowly the convoy edged past it, they were beyond Sundays now, in the narrow lane that led nowhere but to the Sanders' house and the farmer's bungalow. Fog filled the channel between high hedges, hung overhead like dark fallen cloud. They weren't far from the entrance now. Donaldson crept along, stopped the car once or twice – like a dog sniffing, scenting its way to the familiar ground. And it seemed that down here in the least likely place, a low place still in the river valley, the fog had lifted a little, for a high wall of hedge was visible and a tree like a great figure with arms upraised.

Clifford hadn't once looked out of the window; Burden's face seemed the only view he required. He said conversationally, 'All those mattresses were in there, and blankets and things. I expect you remember that time I showed you. And there was a lamp there too, like she said there was. She's clever, she knows about getting her details right. But there was something she forgot. It was the wrong sort of plug, the old-fashioned sort with no earth, an old ten-amp plug with no earth. It was so absurd I could have laughed out loud, only I didn't feel like laughing then, Mike . . .'

The gap in the hedge was found and Donaldson turned in carefully. Tyres crunched on the gravel. The leafy wall of the house, a great square of dark, still, hanging foliage, reared before them. Clifford turned his head at last, gave his home an indifferent look.

'She came up behind me. She was quiet enough, but I was prepared for her. Strange, isn't it, Mike? She's a mystery, she's hidden behind a mask, and she's slow and gliding like all mysterious people. But I know her and I knew what she was going to do; it was so obvious. Her hand went down to the door handle to pull out the key and I was standing there with that old lamp in my hands – '

'Come on, Clifford,' Burden said, 'we're here.'

The air felt wet; it was just as if a cold, wet hand wiped their faces as Wexford walked up to the front door. Dr Crocker was getting our of the car behind with Prentiss, the Scene-of-Crimes man, and there was a new photographer he didn't recognize. Clifford wouldn't separate himself from Burden but stayed close to him, nearly but not quite touching him. If he had actually touched him, Burden thought he might have cried out in horror, though he would have exerted all the control he was capable of to avoid this. It was bad enough knowing some of the blood adhered to his own clothes after that nightmare car journey. He knew he would have to burn everything it had touched.

Wexford asked Clifford for the front-door key and Clifford's answer was to pull out his pockets, the pockets of his jacket and trousers. They were all quite empty. He had left his ignition key in the Metro. As to the others . . .

'I must have dropped them somewhere. I've lost them. They must be somewhere in the garden here.'

Under the wet grass, among the blackened weeds beaded with waterdrops, or on the road in the gutter outside Burden's house. Wexford made the decision quickly.

'We'll force the door. Not this one, it's too heavy. A door at the back.'

It was a slow, grim procession that made its way round the side of the house to the back regions where the rear wall and shed were just visible in the light of Archbold's and Davidson's torches, but nothing beyond. The beam of light played on a back door that looked solid enough, but was less weighty than the massive studded oak barrier whose key Clifford had lost. Davidson was the biggest of them after Wexford and he was also the youngest, but it was Burden who pushed forward and put his shoulder to the door. He had energy which must be released, some act of violence he needed to perform.

Two hard runs at it and the door went down. The crash it made set Clifford laughing; he laughed merrily as they stepped over the shattered boards, the broken glass. Olson would have said, Wexford thought, that it was more than a citadel of bricks and mortar they had broken into and laid open. The flooding of the place with light brought a kind of relief, not that a really bright illumination was possible for Mrs Sanders had been mean with the electricity. It was colder here even than outside. A little of the fog seemed to have got in as Burden recalled the woman had once warned him it would, waiting ghost-like on the threshold to slip in. The damp chill seemed to penetrate clothes and prick skin with icicles.

'Stop that laughing,' he said roughly.

His voice wiped Clifford's face clean of all amusement. It was at once grave and rueful. 'Sorry, Mike . . .'

They went upstairs, Wexford leading the way. Through

633

some lunatic quirk of meanness or indifference, it was impossible to turn upstairs lights on from downstairs, so that one walked out of light into a yawning darkness before a hand could reach out for a switch. The comparatively elegant staircase gave way to the steep attic flight. Wexford could see nothing at the top, only deep blackness. He put out his hand for Archbold's torch and the thin beam of light showed him a half-open door at the head of the stairs.

The light switch wasn't even on the staircase wall but up in the passage. He deliberately averted his eyes from the open door and the room until the light was on. Then he entered the room with Burden and Clifford at his heels, the others close behind. Wexford put the attic light on and then he looked.

Dorothy Sanders lay half on her back, half-sideways on one of the mattresses. A small, thin woman, composed of wire only in metaphor and fancy, she had had as much blood in her as anyone else and most of it seemed to have spilled from that fragile frame. Face and head were a mass of blood and tissue, cerebral matter and even bone chips. Her hair was lost in it, drowned in it. She lay in her own blood, dark as wine and clotted to a paste, on a mattress dyed crimson-black.

Beside the body, not flung down but set up precisely on a small round-topped beside table, was a lamp in the art nouveau style, a sculptured lily growing from its heavy metal base, its shade composed of frayed and split pleated silk. It was a forensic scientist's ideal, this lamp, from the clots of blood and bloody hair which encrusted its base to the stain which transformed its now bent silk shade from green to an almost total dark brown.

Of them all only Clifford was unused to sights such as this, but he alone among them was smiling.

It was very late. They had done everything – what Sergeant Martin insisted on calling 'the formalities'. But the idea of going to their respective homes had scarcely entered Wexford's head, still less Burden's. Burden's face had that look of a man who has seen indelible horrors. They are stamped there, those sights, but showing themselves in the staring

634

eyes and taut skin as the skull inside the flesh reveals itself, a symbol of what has been seen and a foreshadowing of a future.

Burden couldn't rest. He stood in Wexford's office. He just stood, keeping his eyes averted from Wexford's, then bending his head and pressing his fingers to his temples.

'You had better sit down, Mike.'

'You'll be saying it wasn't my fault in a minute.'

'I'm not a psychiatrist or a philosopher. How would I know?'

Burden moved. He held his hands behind his back, came over to a chair and stood in front of it. 'If I had left him alone . . .' He didn't finish the sentence.

'Strictly speaking, it was he who wouldn't leave you alone. You had to question him in the first place; you couldn't be expected to foresee the turn things would take.'

'Well, if I hadn't . . . rejected him then, when he wanted to talk to me. It's ironical, isn't it? First he didn't want me and then I didn't want him. Reg, could I have averted this by letting him come and talk to me?'

'I wish you'd sit down. I don't know what it is you want, Mike. Do you want the hard truth or something to comfort you?'

'Of course I want the truth.'

'Then the truth probably is – and I realize it's hard to take – that when you in your own words rejected Clifford, he felt he had to do something to draw your attention to him. And the best way to draw a policeman's attention to someone is to become a murderer. Clifford, after all, isn't sane; he doesn't have sane reactions. Of course he attacked his mother to prevent her locking him in that room, but he could have achieved that without killing her. He could have overpowered her and locked her in there himself. He killed her to attract your attention.'

'I know, I see that. I realized it when we were there . . . in that room. But he was a murderer already. Why couldn't he have admitted killing Mrs Robson? That would have attracted my attention all right. Do you think – ' Burden drew in his breath, expelled it with a sigh. He was sitting down now, leaning forward and holding on to the edge of Wexford's desk with both hands. 'Do you think that's what he wanted to talk to me about when he kept on trying to see me? Do you think he wanted to confess?'

'No,' Wexford said shortly. 'No, I don't.'

He was anxious now to bring this conversation to a close. The question he was sure Burden was going to ask would be far better postponed till the morning. Burden was in a bad enough state as it was without this further addition to his guilty feelings. For this would be the ultimate guilt. Of course he would have to know tomorrow, he would have to know as soon as possible in the morning . . . before the special court sat. 'Mike, would you like a drink? I've got some whisky in the cupboard. Don't look like that, I don't tipple the stuff secretly – or even un-secretly, come to that. One of our . . . clients offered it to me as a bribe and because I thought it would be handy to have, I took it and gave him the current Tesco price for it. Six pounds forty-eight, I think it was.' He was talking for the sake of talking as, burbling on. 'I won't have one, though. Let me have the Clifford tapes, will you, and then I'm going to drive you home. I'll give you a stiff one and then take you home.'

'I don't want anything to drink. I shall feel like hell in the morning. If I could justify what I did, I'd feel better. If I could tell myself the only possible way we could have nailed this man was by waiting for him to commit another murder – giving him enough rope, so to speak. You say you don't think he wanted to confess?'

'I don't think he wanted to confess, Mike. Let's go home.'

'What time is it?'

'Nearly two.'

They closed the office door and walked down the corridor under the pale, steady, bleaching lights. Clifford was downstairs, at the back, in one of the cells. Kingsmarkham police station cells were more comfortable than most prisons, with a bit of rug on the floor, two blankets on the bunk and a blue slip on the pillow, a cubicle with loo and basin opening off the tiny room. Burden cast a backward glance in that direction as they came out of the lift. Sergeant Bray was on duty behind the desk with PC Savitt beside him, looking at something in a file. Wexford said good night but Burden said nothing.

For the first time, the Christmas lights were on in the tree.

636

Burden had noticed them as something unreal in the fog, a kind of mockery, as they returned from Ash Farm bringing Clifford with them. Either they were on a time clock which had failed to work, or someone had forgotten to switch them off. The reds and blues and whites came on for fifteen seconds, then the yellows and greens and pinks, then the lot, winking hard before the reds and blues and whites returned alone. By now the fog had almost lifted and the colours glimmered in a thin mist.

'Wicked waste of the taxpayers' money,' Burden growled.

'I haven't got my car,' Wexford said. 'It seems so long ago that I'd forgotten. I suppose I meant to drive you in your car.'

'I'll drive you.'

A town that slept, a town that might have been emptied of its folk that silent night – inhabitants who had fled, leaving a light on here and there.

Burden said, climbing up to Highlands, turning into Eastbourne Road, 'I still can't see how he did it – killed Gwen Robson, I mean. He must have been in that car park by a quarter to six, met her as she came in to get her car and killed her. He would have been getting out of his mother's car and she walking up to hers. That must have been the way of it – unpremeditated, a frenzied act on the spur of the moment. He'll tell us now, no doubt.'

Wexford began to say something about the grotesqueness, the incongruity, of a young man stepping out of a car and happening by chance to be holding a circular knitting needle. They passed Robson's house – dark, all the curtains drawn – and Dita Jago's where a light was on, a red glow behind drawn crimson curtains. A cat came out of the Whittons', streaked across the road. Burden braked hard as it leapt clear, on to a wall, up a tree.

'Damned things,' said Burden. 'One shouldn't brake, one shouldn't give way to one's reflexes like that. Suppose there'd been someone behind me? It was only a cat. Look, Reg, that woman Rosemary Whitton has to be wrong. I mean, it's pretty hard for me to have to face that, because it means I was irresponsible in not consenting to talk to Clifford when he wanted me to. I took her word, of course I did. But we never really confirmed it.'

Wexford sighed. 'I did.'

'What? Took her word? I know. But she was wrong. And the wine-market manager was wrong too. Rosemary Whitton must have seen Clifford ten minutes earlier and he'd gone before she hit the meter. It was a genuine mistake, but it was a mistake.'

Up Battle Hill to stop outside his gate. The house was dark; Dora had gone to bed long ago.

Wexford unclipped the seat belt. 'Wait till the morning, shall we?'

He said good night, dragged himself upstairs and fell exhausted into bed – then awoke immediately, energetically, into a prospect of sleepless hours. When they were past and he was back down there, preparing for Clifford's appearance before the magistrates, he was going to have to tell Burden the facts: that he had checked and double-checked Rosemary Whitton's statement; that he had not only checked with the wine-market manager and three occupants of flats above the wine market, but had also found the traffic warden who, arriving on the scene to examine the damaged meter, had – while talking to Rosemary Whitton – seen Clifford drive away. It had been five to six.

19

Dorothy Sanders had never been divorced; Davidson's investigation of records had established that. Nor had she needed to keep herself by the humble sewing and knitting – traditional occupations of the poor virtuous woman she had once read about in some historical romance? – which she told her son had supported them in his childhood. For during those years she had been regularly drawing on the joint bank account that was in her name and her husband's. Now that she was dead, access to that account was no longer denied to the police.

It had been fed by the interest on Charles Sanders' investments, mostly unit trusts. Over a period of eighteen years since their separation, only she had drawn on it. From the bank manager's slightly defensive manner, Wexford gathered that this perhaps curious fact had never been noticed. He was a man opposed to new technology and blamed the fault, if fault it was, on the fact that in recent years the administration of the account had been by computer. Wexford marvelled at Mrs Sanders' capacity for lying and sustained secretiveness. It made him wonder if she had ever been married to Sanders, even if Clifford was her own child, but these facts were soon established. Dorothy Clifford and Charles Sanders had been married at St Peter's, Kingsmarkham in October 1963 and Clifford born to her in February 1966.

Wexford had himself driven back to Ash Farm and he took Burden with him, insisted on it. Burden had accepted Clifford's innocence of the first crime at first with reservations and arguments, then with a deep and bitter self-reproach. It was clear to him, and this Wexford was unable to deny, that the death of Dorothy Sanders had come about as the direct result of his refusal to continue the sessions with Clifford.

Burden was silent for a while. Then he said, 'I think I shall have to resign.'

'For God's sake, why?'

'If it's true that I could drive a man to murder – and it is, I did do that – I'm not fit to be a police officer. It's part of my duty to prevent crime, not provoke it.'

'So, logically, you should never have questioned Clifford in the first place. Suspecting him of the murder of Gwen Robson, you should nevertheless have ignored him because he appeared to be an unbalanced person with abnormal reactions.'

'I'm not saying that. I'm saying that having once questioned him I shouldn't have . . . well, abandoned him to his fate.'

'You should have gone on talking to him day after day, for hours on end, session after session? For how long? Weeks? Months? What about your work? Your own sanity, come to that? Am I my brother's keeper?'

Burden took that question which Wexford had meant rhetorically – which perhaps Cain had meant rhetorically – in a literal way. 'Well, yes, maybe I am. What was the answer to it, anyway? What did whoever it was – God, was it? – say?'

'Nothing,' said Wexford. 'Absolutely nothing. Come on, forget about resigning. You're not resigning, you're coming with me to the scene of the crime.'

In gloomy silence Burden sat beside him in the car. It was a passive sort of winter's day, neither cold nor mild, the sky pale grey and clotted like porridge. Sometimes the sun appeared low on the horizon, a shiny disc of plate showing through where the gruel thinned. The shop windows in the High Street were full of pre-Christmas glitter and a huge imported Christmas tree, gift from some town in Germany no one had previously heard of but which was twinned with Kingsmarkham, had been set up outside the Barringdean Centre. Burden remarked in a sour way about the amount it must cost to run that electronic digital arrangement at the Tesco end which announced alternately that here were gifts

640

for all the family and that nine shopping days remained until Christmas.

'What are we coming here for, anyway?'

He meant to Ash Farm, down long winding Ash Lane, where the grass verges were grey with splashed mud and dead elms with peeling trunks awaited the axe. But the air was clear today and in the distance the outline of the hummocky hill that hid the town could be seen. Ivy-clad Ash Farm slid into view, its many eyes peeping from amongst the evergreen growth. Two police cars were parked in front of it and a policeman in uniform was on duty at the foot of the flight of steps.

'I hadn't thought of going inside,' Wexford said.

'You said we were visiting the scene of the crime.'

Wexford made no reply but nodded to PC Leonard who saluted him and said, 'Good afternoon, sir.' In spite of what he had seen on the previous evening he found it hard to realize that Dorothy Sanders, so strong and upright and confident, was dead, the metallic voice silenced for ever. And when he looked through the dark gleaming glass into the thinly furnished room where the ashes of a fire lay in the grate, he half-expected to see her there, moving across the uncarpeted floor, issuing her orders with a pointing finger. A ghost, that would have to be, and she had been afraid of ghosts, afraid of the dark and of letting fog enter the house . . .

With Burden following him and Donaldson, he walked round the house into the back garden. It was new to him, but Burden had been out there before on the day of the search, triumphantly discovering garrotes in the shed attached to the rear wall. A curious place to put a shed, wasn't it? In order to reach it, a considerable area of damp grass had to be crossed. Earth, whether turfed or not, is always wet in winter, even during dry spells. He felt his shoes sink into the squelchy softness.

Dorothy Sanders had paid less attention to her garden than to her house, but had nevertheless achieved out here a similar kind of barren neatness. There were few plants that looked cultivated, though it was hard to tell at this time of the year, and even fewer weeds. It looked as if Mrs Sanders – or Clifford, on her instructions – had watered the flowerbed areas with the kind of toxic stuff that destroys broad-leaved plants. It looked as if at some point during her life in this house she had set about destroying the garden as it must once have existed. The few trees had been savagely lopped, so that from the stumps of amputated branches new twigs grew out at strange angles. A faint pinkness had appeared in the sky, sign of sunset. It would be dusk very soon, then deeply dark. Nine shopping days to Christmas, seven long nights and seven short days to the Solstice. One day to Sheila's court appearance . . .

These short days, cut off in mid-afternoon, hindered his progress. Nature still had the upper hand . . . just. Or, rather, he couldn't be absolutely sure the expense of using powerful lights was warranted. He padded through the wet grass to the furthermost corner of the garden and there, up against the back fence, he could just make out in the distance the low roof of what must be Ash Farm Lodge, rising above screens of Leyland cypress.

'Would you like to introduce me to Mr Carroll?'

They drove down the lane in the sunset light, the last of the light. With a rattling cry, a cock pheasant rose out of the hedge on seldom-used cumbersome wings. There was the sound of a shot and then another.

'It's only Carroll,' said Burden. 'The way Kingsmarkham's become urbanized, we forget we live in the country sometimes.'

Carroll's dog came timidly to meet them. Perhaps, though, it wasn't timid – perhaps it was shyly creeping up preparatory to an attack. Wexford put out his hand to the dog and a harsh voice shouted, 'Don't touch him!'

The farmer appeared with a dead hare slung round his neck, in his left hand a pair of redleg partridges he was holding by their tail feathers.

Wexford said mildly, 'Mr Carroll? Chief Inspector Wexford, Kingsmarkham CID. I believe you've met my colleague, Inspector Burden.'

'He was this way before, yes.'

'Can we go inside?'

'What for?' Carroll asked.

'I want to talk to you. If you'd rather we didn't go into your house, you can come back to the police station with us. That will suit us just as well. It's up to you, one or the other.'

'You can come in if you want,' Carroll said.

The dog preceded them in, head down and tail between its legs. Carroll made a growling noise at it, a remarkable animal noise which might have been expected to come from the dog, not it master. This was apparently the signal for it to go into its basket which it did like a hypnotic subject, curling itself into a circle and putting its head on its paws. Carroll hung up the twelve-bore, took off his boots and put them on the now stained and corrugated magazine on the oven top which was still just recognizable as a copy of *Kim*. The hare and the birds trailed bloody heads into the sink. The table was a mass of papers, chequebook and paying-in book from the Midland Bank, a VAT ledger, crumpled invoices. Wexford knew the chances of his being asked to sit down were around a hundred to one, so he had seated himself and motioned to Burden to do the same before Carroll had got his slippers on.

'Where's your wife, Mr Carroll?' Wexford began.

'What's that to you?' He didn't sit down, he stood over them. 'It's her up the road that's dead, and her boy that's potty did it. You stick to that, you see he's put away for life; that'll keep you lot busy, not coming poking into my business.'

'Rumour has it that your wife has left you,' Wexford observed.

For a moment he thought the farmer was going to strike him. Unpleasant as that would be, it would at least provide a reason for arresting him. But Carroll, having clenched his fists and put them up, stepped back, setting his teeth. Wexford decided just the same that he might feel more at an advantage on his feet. He was a bigger man than Carroll, though older.

The kitchen was rapidly growing dark. He reached for the only switch in the room and unexpectedly bright light poured from the central blumb in its incongruous shade: pink frilled cotton in the shape of a mob-cap. There were other such touches in that grim place: a battery-operated wall clock, its face a sunflower, a calendar that pictured a kitten in a basket, the day May of this year. In the bright light Carroll blinked.

643

'It was about six months ago that she left, wasn't it? End of June?' If Carroll wouldn't answer, there wasn't much he could do. He changed tack a little. 'Tell me about your neighbour, Charles Sanders? Did you know him? Were you here when he was living here?'

Carroll growled. It was the same language he used when issuing commands to his dog, but succeeded by reasonably comprehensible English. 'His dad died. Day after the funeral he upped and left. What do you want to know that for?'

'You don't ask the police questions, Carroll,' said Burden. 'We ask you. Right?'

Another growl. It was almost funny.

Wexford said, 'He never came back. He never came back to see his son, he never contributed to his wife's support or his son's. He left his old mother in his wife's care and she dumped her in an old people's home. I'm being very frank with you, Mr Carroll, and I'd like you to do the same by us. It's eighteen years since Sanders left. You were newly married, newly arrived here. I don't think he left, I think he's dead. What do you think?'

'How should I know? It's no business of mine.'

'What did your wife think, Mr Carroll? She knew, didn't she? Somehow or other she found out about Sanders. Did she tell you what she knew, or did she keep it to herself? Maybe she told only one person?'

'What person?'

By that remark Wexford had meant to infer nothing that could in fact be of momentous significance to Carroll, but the farmer read into it more than was implied and his face grew red and seemed to swell. Although he made no immediate move, a change had come over him – a kind of concentration, a gathering and intensifying of power, enough to make Burden spring to his feet and push back the chair. It was that which did it. Carroll reached behind him for the gun on the wall, unhooked it and, stepping back, levelled it at them from a distance of about four feet.

'Put that down,' Wexford said. 'Don't be a fool.'

'I'm giving you one minute to get out of here.'

At least now they would be able to arrest him, Wexford thought. The farmer could look at them and keep his eye on the sunflower clock at the same time. One eye open, the dog

644

watched from his basket. This was something it understood – a gun aimed, a helpless quarry. When I double up full of shot, Wexford thought ridiculously, maybe it will come and retrieve me.

Burden said, his head cocked towards the door, 'There's Donaldson coming now,' as if he heard footsteps.

It was a trick and it worked. Carroll turned his head and Wexford's fist shot out to catch him on the jaw. The gun went off as he fell, and in that low-ceilinged bungalow room it made an enormous noise, a noise like a bomb, a noise like the bomb in his front garden which Wexford couldn't remember hearing. The farmer rolled over and the gun dropped from his hands to clatter away across the tiles. Bits of plaster dropped from the ceiling where shot had peppered it. Smoke and a stench of gunpowder and the bewildered dog looking from side to side, beginning a helpless, forbidden barking. And then Donaldson did come, pounding up the path and throwing open the back door.

'Are you OK, sir? What happened?'

'I don't know my own strength,' said Wexford. He considered poking at Carroll with his toe, but thought better of it and heaved the man up by the shoulders. Carroll groaned, his head sagging. 'I don't suppose we've got any handcuffs in the car, have we?'

'I don't think so, sir.'

'Then we must do without, but I don't think he'll give much trouble.'

Carroll was a big man and it took the three of them to get him into the car. They shut up the dog in the kitchen and Donaldson, who was fond of dogs, gave him a bowl of water and the hare.

'That's the way to undo years of training in half an hour,' he said cheerfully.

The artifacts that lay all over the surfaces in Wexford's office – in court they would have been called 'exhibits' – included Carroll's twelve-bore, a muddied copy of *Kim* magazine, a circular knitting needle, size six, and some of the contents of the dead woman's coat pockets. There was something distressing, though scarcely pathetic, about that lipstick in its shiny gilt case, the red of a fire engine. The almost white face powder with its faint iridescence had been marketed for someone young and fair, someone like Lesley Arbel. The chequebook for the joint account was in the names of C. L. Sanders and D. K. Sanders and – at least during the lifetime of this particular book it had been used only to draw sums of cash. A hundred pounds a month was what Dorothy Sanders had drawn during the past two years. It wasn't much, it was modest, but for the past two years her income had been supplemented by Clifford's earnings.

That morning Kingsmarkham magistrates had committed him for trial on a charge of murder and remanded him in custody until the trial was due. Even Burden could see now that there could be no other murder charge for him to face, that it was impossible for him to have been guilty of the death of Gwen Robson. He had seen Clifford driven away to the remand prison at Myringham before he and Wexford left for Ash Farm and had not mentioned him since. But now he came into Wexford's office and spoke abruptly.

'I felt I should have stood up before the magistrates and said I wanted to make a statement. I should have admitted my responsibility – well, my share in what that poor little guy did.'

' "Poor little guy", is it now? What's become of your much-vaunted principle of reserving pity for the victim?' Wexford was reading a letter, nodding from time to time as if what he read brought him a long-awaited satisfaction. He winced at the sounds that were coming from the depths of the building, a steady crash-crash-crash, and looked up at Burden irritably.

'I've let him down all along the line. I should have publicly admitted my part in what he did.'

'You'd make yourself a laughing-stock. Imagine what used to be called the press, and are now for some daft reason called the media, would make of that. Excuse me.' Wexford's phone was ringing and he picked up the receiver. 'Yes, yes, thank,' he said. 'You've a record of that on your computer, have you? Is it possible for me to have some sort of print-out? Yes . . . yes. Someone will come down for it before the library closes. When do you close? Six-thirty tonight? That's just about an hour. All right. Thanks for your help.'

'What's that noise?' Burden opened the door a crack the better to hear the banging. When Wexford shrugged, he asked in a tone of minimal interest, 'What was all that about?'

'A woman's alibi. And another one has just fallen neatly into place. Just a matter of clearing things up really, eliminating remote possibilities. Do you remember that gale we had in the middle of last month? It blew down the phone lines at Sundays and Ash Lane.'

'You think I'm a maundering idiot, don't you? It's all hot air and bullying with me, but underneath I'm weak and water. I was scared of Clifford, do you know that? When he came to my house, I was afraid to answer the door.'

'You did answer it though.'

'Why was I so set on it? Why did I make up my mind it had to be him when all the evidence was against it?'

'At any rate you admit that now.' Wexford sounded bored, languid. 'What can I say? Anything I say sounds like saying I told you so. Well, no, I might tell you to let it be a lesson to you. You'd like that, wouldn't you?' He got up and looked out of the window at the tree with its winking lights, the red, blue and white sequence, the yellow, green and pink sequence. The sky was dark but clear, a dome of deepening blue with stars. 'Mike, I truly think that if he hadn't killed her then, he would have killed her one day. Tomorrow or next week or next year. Murder's infectious too. Have you ever thought of that?' Clifford killed his mother because she was there and because she was restraining him and . . . to draw your attention to him. But perhaps he also killed her because the idea had been put into his head, because he knew, if you like, that it was possible to kill people. He had seen a murdered woman he thought at first was his mother. Hoped it was his mother? Maybe. But the idea was planted, wasn't it? Others could do it, so he could do it. It infected him.'

'Do you really think so?' Burden's face was desperately hopeful, the face of a man who may drown if the flung hand can find nothing stronger than a straw. 'Do you honestly think that?'

'Ask Olson, he'll tell you. Let's go home, Mike, and make a few enquiries about our prisoner on the way.'

The phone rang again as they reached the door and Wexford went back and picked it up. The voice at the other end was so clear that even Burden heard from three yards away, 'I have Sandra Dale on the line.'

Wexford said into the phone, 'It doesn't matter, I don't need it any longer,' and after listening for a moment, 'that doesn't surprise me. You won't find it now.'

He thanked her and said goodbye and they went downstairs. PC Savitt told them that Carroll, who had been put in the cell previously occupied by Clifford, was quiet now. Dr Crocker had seen him and offered him a sedative, which Carroll had surprisingly accepted. Before that he had threatened to break the place up, though had got no further than a regular lifting up of two of the legs of the iron bedstead prior to letting them crash on to the floor.

'Could you hear him, sir?'

'I should think they could hear him in the Barringdean Centre.'

Burden stood on the steps outside the swing doors. 'It's a funny thing the way you can do something, take a determined course of action over a length of time and be absolutely sure you're right, not have a shadow of doubt. And a week later you can look back amazed at what you did, hardly able to realize it was you who did it, and wonder if anyone like that can actually be sane. I mean, I wonder if anyone like *me* can be.'

'I'm cold,' said Wexford. 'I don't want to stand about here.'

'Yes, all right, sorry. What was that you were reading?'

Wexford got into his car. 'It was the letter Lesley Arbel was searching for and Sandra Dale has been searching for, which I have been searching for and have at last found.'

'Aren't you going to tell me what was in it?'

'No,' said Wexford and he shut the car door. Rolling down the window half-way, he said, 'I would have done but you're too late, you've missed the boat. I'll tell you in the morning.' He grinned. 'I'll tell you everything in the morning.'

And he drove away, leaving Burden standing there watching the car depart, not sure if he understood quite what 'everything' implied.

Burden drove the car down to the second level and parked as near as he could to where Gwen Robson's body had lain nearly a month before. Every space on the level was now full and would be all day, every day, up until Christmas and beyond during the end-of-the-year sales.

Serge Olson was the first to get out of the car. He had come into the police station just as they were leaving to enquire when and how he would be permitted to visit Clifford Sanders in the remand prison, and Wexford had invited him to go with them. An Opel Kadett and a Ford Granada were now parked where Gwen Robson's Escort and the Brooks' blue Lancia had been. A Vauxhall came nosing round looking for a space and proceeded down the ramp towards the third level. But apart from themselves there were no people. It was car world, an area of car life where bodies were cars and people their brains or moving spirits. Oil and water lay in pools, car excrement and the place smelt of car sweat.

Wexford shook himself out of fanciful imaginings and said, 'Lately we seem to have lost sight somewhat of our victim, of Gwen Robson. But if she wasn't the first to be murdered, she was at any rate the first we knew of – the first to draw our attention to this case.' Burden looked enquiringly at him, but he only shook his head.

'She brought her death on herself; she was a blackmailer. But like a lot of blackmailers she was – I won't say innocent, she was naïve. She tangled with the wrong person. And I think she justified what she was doing by the reason for which she wanted the money, which was to pay for her husband's hip replacement. If he was to have this operation on the National Health service, it was possible he would have had to wait up to three years, by which time she feared he might be totally crippled. Three or four thousand pounds would pay for the replacement to be done privately and for hospitalization. At the time of her death, she had accumulated about sixteen hundred.' Wexford's glance took in Olson and his driver. 'Let's go into the centre, shall we?'

It was one of those freak December days that are like April; all that was missing were the leaf buds on the trees. The flags on the turrets of the Barringdean building fluttered in a light breeze and the sky was milky-blue with clouds like shreds of foam. They came out of the metal lift with its graffiti into mild sunshine.

' "This castle hath a pleasant seat", ' Wexford said dryly. And if you half-closed your eyes the centre's medieval fortress look was compounded by the trolleys tumbled about the car-park entrance and across the roadway like siege-engines abandoned by their users. 'I've already discussed this with you, Mike. We know that Lesley Arbel brought her aunt photocopies of letters received by the agony aunt at *Kim*, the magazine she worked for, in disregard of the undertaking she had given when she got the job not to divulge or discuss the contents of such letters. Nevertheless, she did make photocopies of certain letters and she did show them to Gwen Robson. Now Gwen Robson, being a salacious woman, was interested in a general way in what she was shown, but she was far more deeply interested in letters coming from people who lived in this neighbourhood.'

Walking along the covered way that would bring them to the doors in the middle of the central gallery, Wexford went on, 'I don't know what gave her the idea of blackmail, but it was an idea both obvious and clever. True, she might have picked up information of a damaging kind about her clients while she was working, but it was unlikely she would have been able to acquire documentary evidence. She had tried other ways of raising money, but these ways had either ceased – the old people who paid for special indulgences had died, for example – or failed, as in the case of Eric Swallow whom she was unable to induce to make a will in her favour. Blackmail remained, the blackmail of women whose secrets they dared only divulge to a more or less anonymous oracle, an agony aunt.

'Two letters particularly interested Gwen Robson both because of their sensational content and the addresses of the women who had written them. One was from a Mrs Margaret Carroll of Ash Farm Lodge, Ash Lane, Forbydean, and the other . . . well, here we are halfway between Tesco and British Home Stores. Shall we go into the café for coffee, or a healthful veggie juice in Demeter?'

The dissenting voice was Olson's, who would have preferred the vegetable juice. But he gave away gracefully, only stipulating decaffeinated coffee.

'I believe,' Wexford went on, 'that Gwen Robson's blackmailing efforts had been successful up to a point, that is, her two women victims had been paying her for her silence over a period of weeks or months. No doubt because, poor things, they couldn't raise a lump sum. Let us come to the day in question, November 19, a Thursday and four-thirty in the afternoon, the time when more of the residents of Kingsmarkham seem to be in here than at any other. Gwen Robson arrived at four-forty, parked her car in the second level and came in most probably by the way we did, under the covered way and through the central door. Now we know what shopping she did, though not the order in which she did it, and we have no way of knowing how much window-shopping she indulged in. But we can make an intelligent guess that she started at British Home Stores where she bought her light bulbs and went on to Boots for her toothpaste and talcum powder. Let us say that brings us to five o'clock.

'Helen Brook is in Demeter next door here, buying calendula capsules. She sees Mrs Robson out of the window and at once recognizes her as the busybody home help who criticized her lifestyle and said she hoped she would never have children – this presumably because she feared they would be illegitimate. Helen Brook intends to show herself to Mrs Robson as ample proof that she is indeed about to have a child, but before she can do this she actually goes into labour, or has her first labour pain. However, she has already noticed that Mrs Robson is in conversation with a very well-dressed girl. Whom do we know that we should describe like that?

Lesley Arbel. The Robsons' niece Lesley Arbel, whom we know to have been in Kingsmarkham that afternoon.'

The coffee came and with it a slice of Black Forest cake for Burden. He must be eating for comfort. Not for the first time Wexford marvelled at the manifest untruth expressed by healthy eating experts: that if you give up sweet things, you soon lose your sweet tooth. He turned his eyes from the chocolate cake, the cream and the cherries, and looked at the concourse where in time for Christmas a sub-aqueous arrangement of coloured lights turned the fountain jets to red and blue and rose.

'The killer had in his or her possession, or so we have supposed,' he went on, 'a circular knitting needle of some high-numbered gauge – that is with thicker pins at each end of the wire. But suppose it was Mrs Robson herself who had it, and her killer took it from her? This is possible if in her innocence she showed it to her killer. She might have been into the wool and crafts shop immediately prior to her meeting with the well-dressed girl. Why did Lesley Arbel come in here when she knew she would see her aunt on the following day anyway? She wanted the photocopies of those letters back; she was starting to regret ever leaving them in Gwen Robson's possession.

'Lesley Arbel is a narcissist, entirely self-absorbed, interested only in her appearance and the impression she makes on others. You'll have to tell me if this is a sound description, Serge?'

'Near enough,' said Olson. 'Narcissism is extreme self-love. The soul-image is not projected and a relatively unadapted state develops. A narcissist would be suspended in an early phase of psychosexual development where the sexual object is the self. This girl, does she have friends? Boyfriends?'

'We never heard of any. The only person she seems really to have liked was her aunt. How do you account for that if they don't care for others?'

'The aunt might simply be a mirror. I mean – it's Gwen Robson you're talking about, isn't it? – if Gwen Robson was much older than she and nothing much to look at, but really admired Lesley and flattered her and showed her off, that would be the only kind of "friend" Lesley could tolerate.

Her function would be to reflect the most flattering kind of Lesley-image. A lot of girls have that kind of relationship with their mothers – and we call those good relationships!'

'I think that was it,' said Wexford. 'I think she also liked and valued her job and was very much afraid of losing it. Not only are jobs hard to come by anyway, but she feared that if she lost her job on *Kim* for this particular reason, a flagrant breach of confidence, she would in some way be blacklisted among magazines – and for all I know she was right. She wanted those letter copies back and she wanted to be sure they had not been copied in their turn.'

'Why would she kill Gwen Robson for that?' Olson asked, his frown deepening, his eyes very bright.

'She wouldn't. She didn't. It was only after she knew her aunt was dead that she became afraid about the photocopies and took the place apart trying to find them. As far as we know Gwen Robson didn't knit: there was no evidence of her knitting in the house. And I am sure Lesley Arbel didn't. Neither of them bought a circular knitting needle on the afternoon in question. Lesley, anyway, wasn't even there. It is true, as she said, that she came to Kingsmarkham, but she came for the purpose she said she did – to make certain she was properly registered for her word-processor course. According to British Telecom the phones at Sundays were out of order all that day, the cables having been damaged by wind on the previous night. Lesley was unable to get through on the phone, so down she came. All quite clear and reasonable. Far from entering the Barringdean Centre, she went straight to the station and was on a train before her aunt left home.'

Burden objected. 'But Helen What's-her-name saw her.'

'She saw a well-dressed girl, Mike. The well-dressed girl was talking to Gwen Robson out in the Mandala concourse and the time was about five. Clifford Sanders was half-way through his session with you, Serge. Where was Dita Jago? Now from the first, I was very interested in Dita Jago. She of all possible suspects possessed the weapon – or versions and repeats of the weapon: she had in her house probably half a dozen circular knitting needles in various sizes, of small and large gauge. She is a heavily-built woman, but strong and light on her feet. Suppose she was another of

653

Gwen Robson's blackmailees – the hold which her neighbour had over her being the fact that far from being on the receiving end, so to speak, in Auschwitz, she had in fact assisted the authorities? That afternoon we know that her daughter took her own two daughters and Dita Jago shopping, dropping her mother off at the public library and presumably leaving the two children with her. But perhaps that is only an alibi concocted by the two women. Perhaps Dita went with her daughter but instead of going into the centre, preferred to sit and wait for her inside the car in the car park.'

'Would anyone prefer sitting in that car park?'

'Someone like Dita Jago might, Mike, if she had something to knit or to read – both quite likely occupations in her case. Let us say that Gwen Robson parted from the very well-dressed girl, whoever she may be, and entered the Tesco supermarket on her own where she helped herself to a trolley and began her shopping. Now your Linda Naseem, Mike, says she saw her at about five-twenty but it might have been a bit after that. Most probably it was a little before five-thirty. Again she was observed talking to a girl, but this time only the girl's back was seen. It may have been the same girl and it may not. All we know of her was that she was a girl, was slim and wearing some kind of hat. By now, Serge, Clifford is just about taking his leave of you prior to beginning his meditations in the car in Queen Street.'

'If you've finished, shall we pay the bill and take a walk? You've got chocolate icing on your chin, Mike.'

'Ratepayers?' queried Olson, eyeing the chit.

'I don't see why not.' Wexford led them out into the I-shaped gallery, crossed the wide area between the line of seats and moved towards the concentric circles of flowers: poinsettias again today, fleshy-leaved kalinchoe and the Christmas cactus with spiky vermilion blossoms.

'The Mandala,' said Olson. 'Schizophrenics and people in states of conflict dream of these things. In Sanskrit, the word means a circle. In Tibetan Buddhism, it has the significance of a ritual instrument or mantra.'

Looking at the flowers but taking in Olson's words, Wexford couldn't help seeing the instrument, also circular when so manipulated, that had killed Gwen Robson. And then he remembered his own dreams after the bomb – the circular images full of patterns, kaleidoscopic designs of extreme and severe symmetry. And there was comfort in what Olson was saying: 'Its order compensates for the disorder and confusion of the psychic state. It can be an attempt at self-healing.'

They paused outside the window and the wool and crafts shop. Today the display was of canvases for tapestry work; the hanks of wool and needles had disappeared.

'Go on, Reg,' said Olson.

'Gwen Robson talks to the girl in the hat, packs her shopping in two carrier bags and leaves the centre by the Tesco supermarket exit which brings her out some two hundred yards or so to the left of the covered way. She follows the path through the car park, probably pushing her two bags in a trolley which she abandons in the trolley park at the lift-head, then goes down in the lift to the second level. It is still full of cars, the time being no more than five-forty.

'Dita Jago, sitting in her daughter's car knitting, sees her come in and also sees her opportunity. She pulls the circular needle out from her work, leaves the car, goes up behind Gwen Robson on her light feet, and, as Gwen Robson is unlocking the door of the Escort, strangles her with this highly efficient garrote.'

'Is that really what you think happened?' asked Burden as they entered Tesco. He took a wire basket, having always in such places a uneasy feeling that to walk through without one might not be illegal but was suspect and reprehensible behaviour, likely to lead store detectives to the belief that you were up to no good. He even helped himself to a can of aerosol shoe polish. 'You really think she is our perpetrator?'

'You'll destroy the ozone layer,' Wexford said. 'You'll coat the earth in black froth – and all for the sake of shiny shoes, you narcissist. No, I don't think Dita's our perpetrator; I know she isn't. The librarian at the High Street branch of the library remembers her being there with the two little girls from somewhere around four-fifty until about five-thirty, when her daughter came back to collect her. She was checking up on facts for this book she's writing, we now know. The librarian remembers because the little girls kept asking the time; they were supposed to be reading, but they kept asking their grandmother if it was half-past five yet and then they asked other people and had to be hushed. Dita Jago took out three books and the date is on the library's computer.'

Burden took his aerosol to Linda Naseem's checkout. If she recognized him she gave no sign of it, but as they passed on he looked back and saw her chattering in whispers to the girl next to her. The main exit doors slid open to let them pass through into the sunshine. There was a seat out there, just outside, with a strip of turf dividing the centre from the biggest above-ground car park. Wexford sat down in the middle of it with Olson on his left and Burden – after examining his purchase, scrutinizing the label to see if what Wexford had said of it might be true – on his right.

Wexford said, 'We'll return to those letters. Now I knew that these particular letters would have to be out of the common run, not quite of the my-boyfriend-keeps-pressurizing-me-to-go-all-the-way genre. They were going to be the kind that even in these days *Kim* wouldn't care to print. The agony aunt's assistant gave me an example of this type when she said someone had enquired about the protein content of semen.'

'You don't mean it?' said Burden, horrified. 'You're joking.'

'I only wish I had that much imagination, Mike.' Wexford grinned. 'One thing I did understand – where the letter copies had gone. The killer took them out of Gwen Robson's handbag after the deed was done, that much seemed obvious. The killer's own letter and the other. One of the writers was Mrs Margaret Carroll, but Gwen Robson never blackmailed her; she had nothing to blackmail her about. So we come to the other.

'My daughter Sylvia brought me copies of *Kim* magazine covering four years, about two hundred copies therefore. When I read through the agony aunt's pages I wasn't looking for a letter. I was looking for an answer, only because I was hoping against hope that this would be one of those appeals considered too . . . well, what? Obscene, indecent – hardly. Too open and revealing perhaps to print. But the agony aunt's reply would be printed under a heading with enough information to give me more than a clue as to who the writer was.

'There are common initials to have and highly unusual

ones. I'd say mine, RW are pretty ordinary – and yours too, Mike, MB. And your wife and your elder son both with JB even more so. "JB, Kingsmarkham" wouldn't convey much, would it? But your initials, Serge, are something else; SO isn't a usual combination at all. And the combination I was looking for must be even rarer.

'Well, I found it. Take a look at this.'

He had made a copy of the relevant back page of *Kim* and he passed the original to Burden and the copy to Olson.

Burden read his aloud: ' "NQ, Sussex: I understand and sympathize with you in your dilemma. Yours is certainly a difficult and potentially tragic situation. But if there is the slightest possibility that the man you mention could be an AIDS carrier, you must see your doctor at once. Tests can be easily and quickly carried out and your mind set at rest once and for all. Feeling guilty and ashamed is pointless. Better realize that by delaying you are putting your husband, your marriage and your family life in danger. Sandra Dale." '

'Nina Quincy?' said Burden when he had finished. 'Mrs Jago's daughter?'

'The letter that was never printed was photocopied by Lesley Arbel and shown to Gwen Robson. The full name and address were on that, of course. And Gwen Robson knew at once who it was; she had met Nina Quincy in Mrs Jago's house when she was hunting for two people to witness Eric Swallow's will. She was introduced to her and noted the unusual name. Nina Quincy lives in a big house in Down Road, she had her own car. To someone like Gwen, she would appear rich and a fine potential for blackmail.

'And for a time, I believe, she paid up. She has a part-time job of her own, and the likelihood is that for some weeks she was giving a considerable part of her salary to Gwen. You must understand that she was worried sick. Picture what it must have been like. Her husband had been away abroad on business and she had gone to a party, drunk too much, spent the night with a man she afterwards discovered to be bisexual and actually living with someone dying of Aids. She was afraid to go to a doctor, especially as by the time she made her discovery her husband had been home for some-time and they had been leading a normal sex life. Or so I suppose. I haven't seen this letter because the copy of it no longer exists and *Kim*, who claim to keep all letters sent to them for a three-year-period, are unable to find either this or the Carroll letter.

'On November the nineteenth, Nina Quincy – who still had not consulted her doctor or said anything of this to her husband, though the reply to the letter appeared in *Kim* last May – went as usual to the Barringdean Centre, having dropped off her mother and the two children at the library, entering here at about five to five. The first shop she went to was the wool and crafts place where she bought the first item on her mother's shopping list, a circular knitting needle gauge number eight – that is, a length of plastic-covered wire with a stout peg at each end measuring perhaps a quarter of an inch in diameter. This, or something similar, would be a purchase she had often made in the past for her mother.

'Coming out of the shop, she encountered Gwen Robson by the Mandala. It wasn't very imaginative to us to conclude that someone Helen Brook thought well-dressed would also appear well-dressed to us – at least to Mike and me, a couple of conventional coppers. Helen Brook would have turned her nose up at Lesley Arbel's pencil skirts and high heels. But Nina Quincy was dressed in just the way Helen admired: elaborate tapestry knits, a patterned beret and her hair down her back, a fringed shawl no doubt, a peasant-style skirt, jacquard socks. You see how I've worked on getting my terms right. Anyway, that's well-dressed in Ashtoreth's mother's book. What did she have to say to Gwen Robson? I think she pleaded with her to ask for no more. I think she told her that it was impossible to go on paying her at this rate – fifty pounds a week or perhaps more? And we must conclude that Gwen Robson did not relent, but said something to the effect of her need being greater than Nina's and perhaps that Nina shouldn't have done what she did if she didn't expect to pay for it. She was that sort of woman, was Gwen.

'If you've sunned yourselves enough we may as well take a look at their Christmas tree, see if it's as good as ours, then we'll go underground once more.'

'Are you going to tell us,' said Olson, 'that Nina followed her while she was shopping? That sounds grotesque.'

'Not necessarily; they may have encountered each other

658

again at the checkout. After all, whatever trouble she was in Nina did continue to lead the life of a housewife and mother; she did do her own shopping and her mother's. She had to do it and then she had her mother and her daughters to pick up at five-thirty. So, yes, we'll say the met again at the checkout and more words passed between them, only a back view of Nina and her beret being visible to Linda Naseem. But they left the Tesco separately, meeting for the third time that afternoon only when they were both in the car park.

'Those white lights look a bit stark, don't you think? I prefer our rainbow effect.'

The three of them stood underneath the Norway spruce which towered to a height of thirty feet. A notice at its foot announced that Father Christmas would be in the centre to meet children every day from Tuesday December 22. The date reminded Wexford of what today's was, one week before that, and raised into the forefront of his mind Sheila's court appearance. She would have left the court some hours ago and the waiting photographers and television cameras would have departed. By now it would be in the papers. Not for her the angry hand pushed against the lens, the averted head or coat held up like a yashmak, the veil to inhibit recognition. She would want to be seen, want the whole nation to know... He made one of those shifts that are much a remarkable feature of man's mental processes, as if a lever were lifted and a new picture dropped into place, or a kaleidoscope shaken. With the others following, he stepped into the shade and cold of the covered way.

'We can't tell exactly what happened next,' he said, 'but Nina Quincy – having settled matters at last, having taken action and perhaps feeling relief – had gone into her car and driven away. She picked up her mother and her children and took them home. The blackmail was over; Gwen Robson would never menace her again. She, however, had something left to do. Now that this particular threat was past, she had to go to her doctor and arrange to have that test.

'Well, eventually she did and the test was negative. She had nothing to fear and she knew her husband was an unforgiving man. Yet when he confessed to her some indiscretion of his own which he'd committed while he was in America, she was silly enough to tell him the whole story . . . and he left her.'

Beyond the open gates, across Pomeroy Road in his window sat Archie Greaves. Wexford put up his hand in a salute, though sure the old man wouldn't be able to see him, certainly wouldn't recognize him. But there was an answering wave from beyond the glass, the wave Archie would give to any friendly customer in the Barringdean Centre. They went down in the lift and stepped out at the second level. A car went round rather too fast, splashing oil from a puddle – a red car, of course.

'You didn't say anything about her taking the letter copies from Mrs Robson's bag,' said Burden.

'She didn't take them.'

'But someone – '

'Once she had made her decision, she had nothing to fear from that letter. She had already told Gwen Robson while they were in the centre that blackmail was pointless as she intended to go to her doctor and confess to her husband.'

There was a space now where the Robson Escort had been parked, and the space where the blue Lancia had been was empty too. Burden stood in the middle holding out his arms in rather a dramatic way, a foot on either side of the dividing white line. And in a voice made shrill by exasperated bewilderment, he demanded to know why it was then that Nina Quincy had done murder.

21

They stood for a while on the spot where Gwen Robson had died.

'You know, Mike,' Wexford said, 'I don't think we've considered sufficiently what a horrible crime this was. We've accepted it, not put it into perspective. Only a very few people would be capable of committing such a crime. What – approach a woman either from behind or face-to-face and garrote her with a wire? Imagine the horror of it, the helpless thrashings of the victim, her struggles . . . who but one of those psychopaths you're so keen on could stand it?'

'I must say,' Olson put in, 'I wouldn't have thought a . . . well, fairly sheltered ordinary middle-class sort of girl like Nina Quincy with a conventional lifestyle capable of it. But I'm not a policeman, I don't know. The affectivity might be there, but it's just that a young mother – that's the last category you'd pick on for this kind of crime. In my game, that is.'

'And in mine,' said Wexford. 'When I said that Nina Quincy felt satisfied because she had taken action, I meant only that the action she had taken was her defiance of Gwen Robson, her decision to get medical help at last. Of course she didn't kill her, though I daresay she sometimes would have liked to, which is what I think you mean. But she didn't kill her. In order to be back in the High Street and at the library by five-thirty, she must have left the Barringdean Centre by five-twenty at the latest, and we know the earliest time at which Gwen Robson could have died was five-thirty-five.'

The acrid stench of petrol made Wexford wrinkle up his nose. 'If we want to save our lungs, we'd better get back in the car,' he said. 'Before we go into the next sequence of events, perhaps we should take a look at the couple called Roy and Margaret Carroll. We already know that the writer of the other letter was Margaret Carroll – a woman with something of a social conscience, a woman who was upset when she discovered that her neighbour was in the habit of punishing her little boy by shutting him up in cold, dark attics.'

'Do you know who they are?' Burden said to Olson. 'Neighbours of Clifford and the late Dodo Sanders? Does it mean anything to you?'

'Clifford mentioned her,' Olson said carefully. 'He said she once threatened his mother with the cruelty-to-children's people.'

'That's right. She was also concerned about another aspect of the Sanders' life, though this was something she didn't begin to suspect until last summer. Strange, isn't it, how all these things erupted last summer around May and June? Her own life was none too easy, I suspect, with a husband of a kind usually called a brute – a Cold Comfort Farm kind of character, only grimly for real. He was going to have a go at us last night with a twelve-bore. Did Mike tell you?'

Olson raised his brown tufty eyebrows. 'Where is he now?'

'In custody, where I hope he'll remain for quite a while.'

'And the wife? what's happened to her?'

'She left him last summer – something else that happened then, about June, I think. The wonder was that she didn't go years ago. Well, no, I'm deceiving you and I don't want to do that. Let's say only that she seems to have left him; at any rate she disappeared. Clifford believes there was a man friend and Carroll gives the impression of believing that too. I don't. I think Margaret Carroll is dead, just as Charles Sanders is dead. A year after Roy Carroll and his wife came to live at Ash Farm Lodge, Charles Sanders died. That was why he never came back to see his little boy, why he seemed to abandon his old mother, why he contributed nothing to his son's support, why his wife was obliged to live on what she drew from their joint account – an account steadily

though meagrely fed from Charles Sanders' investments –
and incidentally why Mike hasn't been able to find him.

'Let's go back, shall we? We've renewed our acquaintance
with the place; we can hold what we need to in our mind's
eye.'

Burden reversed the car and circled slowly towards the
upward ramp. 'Is that what they're doing up there at Ash
Lane, searching for Charles Sanders' body?'

'Well, the remains of it, Mike. It's eighteen years past and
there won't be much left. Frankly, I don't know where to
begin the search for Mrs Carroll, but there are ways of help
open to us.

'You see, Mrs Carroll suspected Sanders was dead when
she was in her branch of the Midland Bank and saw Dorothy
Sanders drawing a cheque on a joint account. She happened
to stand next to her and quite innocently saw this over her
shoulder. At any rate I think so; it's an intelligent enough
guess. Did other others then begin to fall into place? The
sudden and quite unexpected death of Charles Sanders'
father? This death immediately followed by the departure of
Charles? The memory soon after of secret digging? Not
enough for her to come to us – or perhaps she couldn't bring
herself to the enormity of such a step. It was a pity she
didn't; she might be alive today if she had.'

When the car turned into the High Street something
recalled Wexford's mind to Sheila and the tribulations of her
day. She or someone representing her would have phoned
Dora by now. What had happened to her – an account of
what had happened with pictures – would be in the evening
paper. It would be on the streets by now; the London evening
papers were always on Kingsmarkham streets by three and
it was nearly four. The sun was setting, dyeing the sky a
gold that would fade to pink and darken to dusky purple.
He caught sight of a newsboard with something on it about
missile treaty talks and felt a ridiculous relief because Sheila's
name wasn't there. As if Sheila's court appearance, Sheila's
fate must as a matter of course be the lead story.

'Mike,' he said, 'put the car on one of those meters in
Queen Street, will you? I have to buy a paper.'

Her face looked at him, framed in newsprint, not smiling
nor laughing, no raised hand waving at cameras. She looked

663

frightened; her expression was grave and big-eyed. She was leaving the court and even without reading the caption it didn't take a policeman's knowledge to recognize where she was going and with whom. The headline he couldn't help reading, though he forced himself to postpone further elucidation until he was at home: 'Sheila Goes to Jail', the picture caption said. '*Lady Audley's Secret* star gets a week inside.'

The man behind the counter, an obliging, nothing-is-too-much-trouble Indian, smiled patiently at this apparently stupefied customer who didn't know you had to pay for an evening paper. He coughed discreetly. Wexford put two tenpence pieces on the counter and crushed the paper clumsily into his pocket.

Olson and Burden were out of the car, standing outside Pelage.

'Come up to my place,' Olson said. 'I'll make you a cup of tea.'

The steep narrow staircase was a bit like the attic stairs at Ash Farm, Burden thought. But there was something cosy, something sane for all its bizarreness, about what awaited them at the top. He remembered how it had once felt threatening and now he wondered why. What had he meant? He had become a therapist himself since then – with disastrous results. His own, sometimes timid, psyche suddenly seemed less important. Wexford, who had never been up here before, saw the poster with the globe and its ruined continents, with Einstein's ominous words, and it brought home to him Sheila's fate so that he flinched. He wondered if the others had seen, decided they hadn't and anyway, so what? Olson was using spoonfuls of powdered stuff called instant tea. Inwardly Wexford laughed at himself for minding, for caring about trivia in the midst of . . . all this. He said:

'Thanks to your tapes, Mike, I know exactly what Clifford told you. Whether those tapes could be admitted now, whether you were strictly correct to make them, doesn't matter. Clifford told you he hoped his mother and Roy Carroll might get together – might even possibly marry – and he told you how all the information about Margaret Carroll having a lover, another man in her life, came to Carroll from Dorothy Sanders. It was Dorothy Sanders, the neighbour, who was in a position to see who visited Ash

Farm Lodge while Carroll was out in the fields and perhaps also to see whom he went out to meet. Or so Carroll could be made to believe.

'Carroll is a jealous, possessive man. She inflamed his jealousy and terribly damaged his pride, but for her own sake she had to do it. Clifford was wrong when he guessed Carroll might be attracted by his mother or enjoyed her company; all he got from her was information about his wife's infidelity. When his wife disappeared he thought he knew why and who with, but the last thing he wanted was for the rest of the world to know. That was why he never reported her as missing when she disappeared last June. He preferred to keep her disappearance dark but if anyone suggested to him, as we did, that his wife might be somewhere living with another man, he went out of his mind with rage.'

Burden drank his tea as if it were the real stuff brewed from leaves in a hot, dry pot, as if the milk in it had come yesterday from a cow. 'So Carroll didn't kill her?'

'There was only one person in this case capable of committing these crimes, and that person is beyond our reach now. Retribution, if you like, or chance or misfortune has caught up with her. Only Dorothy Sanders could have killed a husband, depriving a child of its father and a mother of her son. Only Dorothy Sanders could have gone up to her victim and garroted her with a length of wire.

'Here's the letter Margaret Carroll wrote to *Kim* last spring,' Wexford went on, holding out the photocopy to Burden. 'I went back to Ash Farm last night and found it slipped into the back of a photograph frame in one of those attic rooms. The picture, incidentally, was of a family group I take to be Charles and his parents. I wonder why she didn't burn the letter? Because something she had done murder for must be precious? Or one day to have it to show to Clifford or Carroll if a defence was needed? We shall never know. The original would have been kept by *Kim* for two years, except that Lesley Arbel saw to that when she couldn't find the copy. She destroyed both those letters as soon as she got back after her Sundays course.'

Burden read it aloud: ' "Dear Sandra Dale, I am in a terrible dilemma and cannot decide what to do. I am so worried it is stopping me from sleeping. I have good reason to believe that a neighbour of mine killed a person close to her nearly twenty years ago. The person was her husband. I won't go into what made me think this after so long, but the new evidence I got made me remember certain suspicious things happening all that time ago. Her father-in-law died too and he was a healthy strong man, not old. My husband does not like the police and would be very upset I think if I had to explain all this to them, if we had police here questioning me etc. I cannot mention names here. It has taken months to screw myself up to write this. I would appreciate your advice . . ." ' He looked at Wexford. 'Did this Sandra Dale reply?'

'Oh, yes. She didn't print the letter, of course, or the reply. She wrote back very properly advising Margaret Carroll to come to us and lose no time in doing so. But Margaret Carroll didn't – too frightened of the husband, no doubt. And by then Gwen Robson had got hold of the letter through Lesley.'

Olson put in, 'But how did she know who Margaret Carroll meant by her "neighbour"?'

'She was a Kingsmarkham woman: she knew the area and knew Mrs Carroll only had one neighbour. I daresay she remembered Clifford from the Miss McPhail days. Anyway, she took herself down to Ash Farm and asked Dorothy Sanders for money – weekly payments if she liked, she didn't mind instalments – not to tell the police about the contents of the letter. By that time she was already successfully extracting payment from Nina Quincy, stashing it away for her husband's expensive op.

'She wasn't concerned with Margaret Carroll. It wouldn't have excited her interest if she had known that Margaret Carroll had disappeared soon after Dorothy Sanders made the first payment. Besides, it was in her interest to steer clear of Mrs Carroll who, had she dreamed of what was going on, probably would have been stirred into coming to us, would have saved her own life and killed one of the geese that laid golden eggs. Dorothy Sanders made no second payment. A second payment was asked for when Gwen Robson encountered her by chance in the Barringdean Centre that

Thursday afternoon, but Dodo saw to it that it was never paid.'

Burden objected. 'But look, didn't you say you saw her come into the car park as you were leaving it at ten-past six? Gwen Robson was dead by five-to.'

'I saw her come back a second time, Mike. She had been there before.'

'She went back?' Olson said. 'When she'd committed murder? Why didn't she just leave, go home, anything?'

'She's not like other people, is she? We've already agreed on that. She didn't have their responses, their reactions, their emotions. This is what I think happened, all we'll ever know now of what did happen. First of all, it was she that Linda Naseem saw from the back talking to Gwen Robson. She had a girl's figure, we've commented on that: she looked like a girl from the back, or when you couldn't see her face and hair. Either she went with Gwen Robson into the car park – arguing perhaps, threatening even, trying to make her change her mind – or else she followed her. I lean rather towards the alternative and think she followed. You see, by then – it wasn't yet five-thirty – she hadn't finished her shopping.

'So they entered the car park more or less together. While Gwen Robson was unlocking her car Dodo went up to her and garroted her with the circular knitting needle she had bought in the centre after she had had her hair done. Remember, we know she had been in there because she had bought the grey knitting wool she placed in the boot of her car. The job done, she returned to the centre.'

'But why? If she was going to report the death to us, why not do it then? Why not pretend, as she later did, that she'd discovered the body?'

'She had her shopping to finish, Mike. She only came to the centre once a week and she wasn't going to upset her routine. There was still her fish to buy and her groceries to get. Didn't I say we aren't dealing with an ordinary normal woman here? Dodo was special, Dodo was different. She had probably killed her father-in-law, she had already killed a husband, very likely with a knitting needle garrote, and a neighbour also by the same means. Maybe she even used the garrote afterwards to knit Clifford's sweaters. Waste not, want not! She went back to get the rest of her shopping done. It was not yet a quarter to six. Possibly she thought some other car driver would see the body, for the car park at that time would still have been half-full. However, no one did. Only Clifford did, coming in at six o'clock. He thought it was his mother, he thought the body was Mother Dodo. And he did a mad thing, a typically Clifford thing. He covered it up with a curtain from the boot of the car and then he ran away, pounding down the stairs as I was coming up in the lift, bursting out through the pedestrian gates for Archie Greaves to see.

'Dodo came back at ten-past-six, so that I was permitted a sight of her emerging from the covered way, and she entered the car park as she truthfully told us at precisely twelve minutes past. One useful thing only came out of my being here, my seeing her. She was carrying two bags of shopping but not the grey knitting wool, which is how I know she had been in the car park earlier. Did she expect to find a crowd there, even the police there? By the time I saw her, she must have realized that wasn't happening. Only one thing had happened – someone had covered it up. Who? A policeman? A car driver who had gone off to get help? What? One thing was clear; it wouldn't do for her just to do nothing. Her car was there but no Clifford. If he had been there perhaps they could just have driven off, taking no action. But he wasn't and she couldn't drive. Margaret Carroll wrote about her particular dilemma. Dodo's was worse. What was she to do?

'Wait. Think. What if the driver of the only other car on the second level turned up, the blue Lancia? Where was Clifford? Where was the man or woman who had covered up the body? At least she didn't realize at that time that it was her curtain which had been used – or rather a curtain from up in her attics. She went down by the stairs or in the lift, looking for Clifford, and that was the first time Archie Greaves saw her. The second time she was screaming and raving and shaking those gates. Her nerve had broken; it was all too much, the waiting and the knowing and . . . the silence.'

Olson nodded. He offered more tea, not seeming to notice the haste with which it was refused, then pushed his hands through the dense bush of curly hair. 'I suppose there was no real motive for those early murders? She was a true psychopath? Because if we're looking for self-interest, it was surely in her interest to keep her husband alive?'

'Oh, there was a motive,' said Wexford. 'Revenge.'

'Revenge for what?'

'Mike can tell you the story. He knows it, Clifford told him. Clifford thought it romantic; he couldn't see through the veil his mother wore. Her life had been dedicated to an act of revenge against the people who said she she wasn't good enough for their son, and against the son who agreed with them.

'She was a multi-murderer who killed dispassionately but who was afraid of her victims after they were dead. She disinfected herself to be rid of their contamination and was frightened of their ghosts.'

Burden and Olson had begun a discussion on paranoia, on infantilism and transference, and Wexford listened to them for a moment or two, smiling to himself as Burden said, 'We live and learn.'

'We live at any rate,' said Wexford and he left them, walking the few hundred yards back to the police station when he got into his own car under the Christmas lights which were already winking away on the ash tree. There he sat and read about Sheila, read the statement she had made, her refusal to pay the fine demanded on conviction – her brave, foolhardy, defiant declaration that she would do it all again as soon as she came out.

'The Chief Constable rang,' Dora said as he came into the house. 'Darling, he wants to see you as soon as possible; he couldn't get you at the office. I suppose it's about this place.'

I don't suppose so for a moment, said Wexford but to himself, not aloud. He knew exactly what it would be about and felt the crackle of the evening paper in his raincoat pocket. For some reason, for no reason, he gave Dora a kiss and she looked a little surprised.

'I don't suppose I'll be long,' he said, knowing he would be.

Dusk, nearly dark, a little before five. His route to Middleton where the Chief Constable lived took him along his old road. It would be the first time he had been there since the

669

bomb and he knew he had consciously avoided it, but he didn't now. The sky was jewel-blue and windows along the street were full of Christmas lights. Bracing himself for the shock of devastation, he slowed as he came to the strip of open ground, the empty site. He braked, pulled in and looked.

Three men were coming out of the gate, up to a van with ladders on its roof. He saw the contractors' board, the stack of bricks, the concrete-mixer covered up against the frost. He got out and stood looking, smiled to himself.

They had begun to rebuild his house.